Pride & Prejudice:

The Scenes Jane Austen Never Wrote

Edited by
Susan Mason-Milks
and Abigail Reynolds

Introduction

Imagine the scene: The summer of 2011. A small gathering of Austen Authors having tea and scones together in Bath, England. They are enjoying a rare warm, sunny afternoon, when someone mentions the fact that just two years hence will be the 200th anniversary of the publication of *Pride and Prejudice*.

"Austen's own 'beloved child'!" someone proclaims.

More tea is sipped and luscious Devonshire cream slathered on scones.

"So you know what that means, don't you?" someone asks with an impish grin.

Blank stares around the table.

"Based on that timetable, September of *this* year is the 200th anniversary of Charles Bingley leasing Netherfield Park!"

"Hey, I wonder what Netherfield Park's steward thought of Bingley when he came to look around?"

This thought brings speculative chuckles, and then a brief silence as each writer's imagination takes flight.

"Wouldn't it be amazing if we could retell *Pride and Prejudice* in 'real time' - just 200 years after the fact?"

And so the idea for the Austen Authors' *Pride and Prejudice 200 Project* (P&P200) was born. A timeline was created and the writing began. First, we decided to re-imagine existing scenes from different points of view. For example, what were Mr. and Mrs. Hurst's impressions of the Meryton Assembly or the ball at

Netherfield? What was Mrs. Bennet thinking on the morning Mr. Collins tried to propose to Elizabeth?

Even more fun, there are all those delicious scenes Austen herself left out! Envision the chaos in the Bennet household as the sisters dressed for the Meryton Assembly? Or Darcy's thoughts after the Bennet sisters left Netherfield following Jane's recovery? Wouldn't this be a great opportunity to fill in more of the back stories of other characters such as Charlotte Lucas? The possibilities were endless. So many tempting and tantalizing scenes to create!

P&P200 started on the Austen Authors blog in September 2011 and finished with a flourish in November 2012 with the big double wedding - and oh, of course, those wedding nights for Elizabeth and Darcy and Jane and Bingley!

What you will read in these pages is not a novel. It is a collection of scenes imagined and created as compliments to the original story. You can read it from start to finish or just dip in to the scenes that sound interesting to you. Along the way, you may notice a few inconsistencies in the timeline or find slightly different versions of events. This is not a mistake or careless editing. We made a conscious decision to let the scenes stand as each author was inspired to write them.

Did P&P200 really happen this way? Were some of the Austen Authors gathered over tea in England? Oh, how we wish it were true, but it doesn't really matter now, does it? Regardless of how it all began, the result is our loving tribute to the genius of Jane Austen.

About Austen Authors

Austen Authors...because there's never enough Jane Austen!

Who are the Austen Authors?

Austen Authors is a collective of published novelists in the Jane Austen sub-genre of literary fiction whose focus is on sharing our unique visions of Austen's world through our blog posts and fun events as well as promoting the awareness of our genre and blog to the broader reading audience.

Founded in 2010 by Abigail Reynolds and Sharon Lathan, the goal of Austen Authors is to shine a light on the varied visions that exist since every Austen writer is inspired differently. There are modern spins, sequels, retellings from a particular character's point of view, secondary character novels, variations and what ifs, zombies, vampires, werewolves, and much more.

Over the three years of its existence, membership has changed. Some authors have moved on to write other kinds of stories while other authors have joined to take their places. The number of members varies but is usually between twenty and twenty-five.

Authors take turns blogging about subjects related to Jane Austen, post excerpts from upcoming books, promote each other's books, sponsor monthly giveaways, and post unpublished fiction on the site's "The Writer's Block."

Pride and Prejudice: The Scenes Jane Austen Never Wrote (or *P&P200* for short) is the first group project we've undertaken. It was followed in 2013 by a Reader's Choice serial story in which fans voted at the end of each chapter as to the plot direction for the next chapter. This means each week one of our authors wrote a brand new chapter in a matter of just days. The first Reader's Choice story was called *The Bennet Brother* and ran from January to September 2013. The second Reader's Choice story, called *The Darcy Brothers* began in October 2013 and is still in progress as of the publication of this book. Future plans include a modern Reader's Choice story and *Persuasion 200* (a retelling of *Persuasion* in real time beginning spring 2014). All of these will eventually be published in ebook format.

If you'd like to more about how Austen Authors was founded, please visit our web site at **www.austenauthors.net**.

The Table of Contents begins on page 767.

From the Journal of the Netherfield Housekeeper by Heather Lynn Rigaud

Household Ledger of Netherfield Estate
Mrs. Robert Johnson, Housekeeper

September 17, 1811

The apple harvest continues, 3 bu collected today.

2 dz eggs, 4.5 gal milk.

Mr. Anderson, Sir Frederick's solicitor, sent word today to expect him tomorrow. He is bringing a possible tenant for the house. I have set Mary & Roseanne to preparing the rooms for inspection.

September 18, 1811

5 bu apples, 2 bu pears gathered

2 ½ dz eggs, 4.5 gal milk

Groom reports one of the greys has gone lame. Ferrier has been hired to poultice.

Met a Mr. Bingley today as a possible tenant for Netherfield. He seems a good, well-mannered young gentleman, despite having a slight whiff of trade. If he and Mr. Anderson can come to terms, he'll be occupying the house immediately. While I doubt Lady Pryce Wellington, may she rest in peace, would have ever wanted to see Netherfield let out, I believe it will be good to have some persons here to care for and to provide needful work. Mr. Bingley mentioned his sisters, so we can expect he will bring guests, if he does decide to take the house.

I caught Roseanne being all together too friendly with the footman Wilkenson and had to have words with her. Hopefully she will heed my advice, although she is a foolish girl.

Netherfield Park is Let at Last!
by Abigail Reynolds

September 18, 1811

Mr. Anderson reined in his horse at the top of a hill. "And there you have it, Mr. Bingley," the solicitor said. "Netherfield Park!"

"So this is Netherfield!" Bingley shaded his eyes for a better view. "It looks delightful."

"The proportions are indeed excellent, as you will see as we approach the house. Come, the drive is just ahead."

Bingley had rarely seen such pleasant countryside. He turned his head from one side to another as they rode, trying to take in every detail to report later to Darcy.

They trotted past an orchard where a gnarled old man clung precariously to a ladder as he plucked apples from an equally gnarled old tree. Mr. Anderson said, "As you can see, the land here is rich and productive. And the hunting! You have surely heard of Lord Pryce-Wellington's famous hunting parties, Mr. Bingley."

Bingley could not recall anything of the sort, but he nodded obligingly. "My sister will love this house. She has always wished for a country estate." He doubted Caroline would wish to have hunting parties in any case; she would be more concerned with hosting house parties for her well-bred friends. Darcy would enjoy the hunting, though, and if Darcy liked it, Caroline would adore it.

"Will Miss Bingley wish to view it as well?"

Bingley smiled broadly. "No, it is to be a surprise for her." Just a few weeks past, Caroline had praised Darcy's habit of purchasing surprise gifts for his sister. Bingley had immediately decided to take a page from Darcy's book, and there was nothing Caroline wished for more than a fashionable country estate. She would be delighted!

Mr. Anderson cleared his throat. "Perhaps your sister might prefer to see the house before you sign the contract," he said delicately. "There is no accounting for a lady's taste in these matters."

Bingley waved away the suggestion. "Unless the interior disappoints, I see no cause for concern." He paused with a frown. "It does not have a parterre, does it? Caroline despises parterres. She says they are ridiculously old-fashioned."

"I do not recall any mention of parterre gardens, but we shall see for ourselves. Come, the housekeeper is expecting us and will give us a tour of the house."

Lady Catherine Interviews
Mr. Collins
by Diana Birchall

September 19, 1811

Mr. Whitaker, the clergyman of Hunsford, was dead. Lady Catherine, however, could not bring herself to regret it. "Certainly," she said, "I shall mourn as much as is proper; that is, I shall wish him every mercy at the seat of Judgement, but that, of course, is no more than what is due to us all. In my own judgement however, his life on earth was peculiarly dissatisfying."

"He was a good clergyman, was he not, ma'am?" Mrs. Jenkinson ventured timidly.

Lady Catherine made a contemptuous tut-tutting sound. "Speak only of what you are qualified to assess, Mrs. Jenkinson," she said. "You know I have often told you that your opinions are all too weak-minded. I would not wish the person who is companion to my daughter to be otherwise; to hold strong, decided opinions would be a drawback in your position. Biddibility, and gentility, are what I ask, and I make no complaint of you. But you are unable to discern a good sermon from a bad, and therefore I must inform you that Mr. Whitaker was very wanting in his abilities in that capacity."

Her visitor, Lady Metcalfe, a lady of a similar time of life and equal dignity as Lady Catherine, put down her teacup. "Is that so, Lady Catherine? I never heard Mr. Whitaker, but if he was such an inferior practitioner of his duties, it is most fortunate that you now have the opportunity to replace him."

Lady Catherine nodded vigorously, and the lace on her headdress shook. "To be sure. I confess, however, Lady Metcalfe, that in this instance I am quite at a loss. Mr. Whitaker died suddenly, having been so foolish as to catch a cold, and most unjustifiably leaving me unprepared with a suitable successor."

"A cold? did he?" commented Lady Metcalfe. "He cannot have been of very stout constitution. We have had dry weather this summer, and it is only the first of September."

"Mr. Whitaker was so kind as to visit me every day," spoke up Miss de Bourgh, "in my most recent illness."

"But I question if his fatal cold was caught by visiting you, Anne. Hers was only a very slight catarrh," she turned to Lady Metcalfe, "always a matter for the very greatest care, with delicacy like Anne's, and she was confined in bed for some weeks, but it ought not to have been anything a man like Mr. Whitaker could not counter."

"Do you not think it may have been our summoning him four and five times each day?" asked Mrs. Jenkinson hesitatingly. "He could not have had a full night's sleep for at least a month, because of his extreme exertions."

"Bah! That was no more than his duty, and it was the dirty Hambly family in the village, all down with scarlet fever, that did the mischief, I am sure. I told them to keep their farm animals out of the cottage and to wash themselves with lye soap, but did they? They did not. I have no patience with such people."

"And so now you are in the position of finding a new clergyman," said Lady Metcalfe meditatively. "I should think you the very last person to be without resources. You have always supplied your circle with suitable governesses, and servants."

"And my own four nieces," said Mrs. Jenkinson, "are so happily settled, and all because of Lady Catherine's wonderful cleverness and benevolence."

Lady Catherine looked graciously. "Those are the qualities for what I am famed," she admitted simply.

"Mama, is it not the usual thing, in such cases, to inquire at the universities?" asked Anne languidly.

"You are right, my dear, and I have written to the Master of Balliol. He is my cousin," she told Lady Metcalfe, "but I do not like the tone of the letters I have received in return. Young men of the present day show no suitable deference. Do you know, one young man has written to demand a curate, not paid for out of the living, but presumably from my own pocket! As if the stipend were not of almost unheard-of liberality! And another candidate, a Mr. Blaylock, who seemed a more modest kind of young man, refused to submit his sermons to me for approval, or confine himself to less than half-an-hour."

"Shocking!" said Lady Metcalfe.

"Is not it? And a third, a very respectable young man or so I thought, wishes the family's cottage-visiting, and other charitable works, to be entirely under his own direction. Heaven and earth! I do not know what will become of the Church at this rate, if its servitors are all to be of this stamp."

"There is a young man I have heard of," Lady Metcalfe said thoughtfully, "our new governess, Miss Harrison, was telling us of a friend of her brother's, who was lately ordained with him. I believe he was at Oxford with Mr. Pope. I will make inquiries if you like."

"I would be most obliged, Lady Metcalfe. Do write. Find out how old the gentleman is – he must be under thirty, so that he is ductile enough to get used to my ways. He need not be a remarkable genius; I should prefer obedience, and a young man who would be sensible that to hold the living of Hunsford is a great privilege. Only think! he will be able to see Rosings from his very doorway."

"To be sure," replied Lady Metcalfe, "not many young clergymen in the kingdom could expect to be as fortunate as your new rector."

"And he must not be bred too high. I do not require a high-and-mighty gentleman, but naturally he must be a gentleman. Find out what his family are and be sure he is of a docile, agreeable temper, but without inconvenient prejudices, or set in his ways. We will want him to make up a card table and not be overly censorious about such practices as Sunday visiting."

"I will inquire of Miss Pope at once and have her write to her brother. I believe the young man's name is Mr. Collins."

* * *

Since his ordination, Mr. Collins had kept his lodgings at Oxford, in hopes of maintaining himself by tutoring while waiting for more remunerative preferment; but there had been no pupils so desperate as to seek out the ministrations of a man who had little reputation for cleverness or learning, and no valuable appointments had offered. On receiving Lady Catherine's letter, which followed Miss Pope's inquiry, Mr. Collins did not hesitate. With such speed and dispatch as his slowness to form long sentences required, he wrote a return letter full of obsequious professions of gratitude and eagerness to demean himself. Lady Catherine thought his alacrity to perform any duty she might wish, most promising, and wrote a condescending answer; and so it was fixed that he would wait upon her at Rosings, only a sennight after his receiving the first communication.

Mr. Collins arrived promptly as expected, and Lady Catherine was disposed from the first to be pleased with him.

"So you are Mr. Collins. What is your age?"

"Five and twenty, your ladyship."

"And what was your father?"

"He was a farmer, your ladyship."

"A farrrmer!" Lady Catherine trilled, and lifted her heavily marked eyebrows. "Then you are not the son of a gentleman. How did you come to be a clergyman? There is some mystery here. I do not like mysteries."

"Madam, my father was certainly not a very great gentleman by your standards; he was not rich, and did not frequent the court or move in genteel society, as you and your noble daughter are entitled to do." Mr. Collins made a clumsy bow and a scrape, simultaneously. "Yet he was of good blood, of the Hertfordshire Collinses; and my mother was own sister to the late Mr. Bennet of Longbourn of whom you may, perhaps, have heard. Mr. Bennet disapproved of her marriage, and after my mother's death, quarrelled with my father, so that there was a breach; but I have reason to believe that Mr. Bennet's son is of a more amiable disposition. And by a fortunate circumstance, whenever the present

8

Mr. Bennet, my cousin, dies, I am the heir by entail to the valuable property of Longbourn."

"Are you indeed? Well! And is it a large property, Mr. Collins? What do you suppose Mr. Bennet's income to be?"

"Longbourn is nothing compared to the unrivalled magnificence and beauty of Rosings, of course, your Ladyship. You would think nothing of it. It is, however, a good sized, modern-built house, in the village of Meryton, and Mr. Bennet is said to have a thousand pounds a year. He is not an economical man, I have heard, but has so far managed to keep the property together, so that I can expect to inherit a respectable estate."

"You do not take possession until his death," pursued Lady Catherine, "and how old a man do you suppose him to be?"

"Mr. Bennet is between forty and fifty and has five daughters."

"Indeed! And no son. That is well for you, but I must be assured that if you come to Hunsford, we will not be in danger of your abandoning us in the space of a twelvemonth for Meryton."

"I do not think there is the remotest danger of that. Mr. Bennet is in good health, and I would rank my duties at Hunsford as far above any other earthly ones, should I be so unspeakably fortunate as to be granted your Ladyship's patronage."

"That is well. And you are versed in all the duties that will attach to your station?"

"Indeed, I have made good use of my time at Oxford, and have learnt about tythes, and sermon-writing, and visiting the poor."

"About writing sermons," Lady Catherine fixed him with a suspicious eye, "how long do you consider the proper Sunday sermon to be?"

"Not more than five and twenty minutes, my lady, and I assure you I would always submit to direction from my benefactress with the most extreme obligingness."

Lady Catherine seemed pleased. "Hm. Very good. And you will not object to being at Rosings often, to fill in at the dinner table, and make a fourth at cards, whenever it is desired? You will be available day and night at a moment's notice?"

Mr. Collins took a deep breath. "Lady Catherine," he said feelingly, "I should consider my being admitted to visit Rosings as the very greatest honour I have ever had in my life."

She nodded. "A most appropriate sentiment. And you will not interfere with my decisions as magistrate of the village?"

"I should never presume to do such a thing, madam!"

"The living is five hundred a year, but it is capable of improvement and has a very good house attached to it. I will take you to see it – it is time for Anne's walk, and we will take it together. The house is in need of some repairs, and I will undertake these for you before you take possession, on one condition."

"Anything you desire, Lady Catherine!"

"You must marry and bring a wife hither." She made an emphatic rap on the floor with her silver walking-stick.

Mr. Collins looked all acquiescence. "I would be only too happy to gratify you in such a way," he bleated. "I think it right that a clergyman like myself should have a wife, to serve as a very praiseworthy example to the parish; and I assure you that to marry is my object."

"That is well. We are too retired a society here and require a neighbor. Someone who is not too proud, and will be very attentive to Miss de Bourgh and me, yet always know her station."

"That is exactly what I should look for in a wife. I confess I had thought – "He stopped.

"Well? What is it?"

"The five Miss Bennets have all a reputation for great gentility, economy, amiability, and – and beauty, ma'am."

"Have they now? But you are not on terms with your cousin, their father."

"No, but if I should be so unspeakably fortunate, beyond all men, as to accede to Hunsford living, I would, by your Ladyship's leave, take a journey into Hertfordshire, to offer an olive branch to the family and to see for myself if the Miss Bennets are as respectable and fair as reputed."

"That's well thought of." She looked at Mr. Collins with condescension and approval. "Only be sure that the Miss Bennet you chuse is the right sort of girl, mind."

"I would by no means wish to marry anyone who would be in any degree offensive to my patroness."

"You show a most suitable spirit. Yes, Mr. Collins, I believe, on mature consideration, that we are of like mind, and that you are the very man to whom I wish to give my patronage and raise to all the privileges of the Rector of Hunsford."

"Oh, Lady Catherine, I cannot speak my infinite gratitude," he said, with the very lowest bow of which he was capable, and a tremble in his voice. "I can only promise you that I will fulfill every one of the duties I owe to your gracious Ladyship, and of course to the Church of England."

"Then it is settled," said Lady Catherine, satisfied. "You will preach your first sermon the last week in September or the first of October – whichever you prefer."

"The sooner the better, dear Madam. You may expect me on the earliest date."

Bingley Seeks Darcy's Opinion
of Netherfield Park
by Regina Jeffers

September 20, 1811

Darcy closed his eyes and pictured Georgiana. For a fleeting moment, he could vividly imagine the sweetness of her smile. He slowly refolded the letter, savoring the moment as if it were a magical interlude, and then placed it in the inside pocket of his morning jacket. The sound of Caroline Bingley and Louisa Hurst in the morning room interrupted his reflections. He would be required to join them for breakfast, but he would sorely prefer to dwell awhile longer on his thoughts of his sister's recovery. Georgiana had made great progress. Reluctantly, he unfolded his frame, stood, adjusted his clothing, and strode purposely from the library to join his hosts.

"Ah, Mr. Darcy, I see you have risen before the remainder of our party," Caroline said as he entered the room.

Darcy made a quick bow to both Caroline and her sister before crossing to the breakfast repast to refill his cup one last time. He politely replied, "It is true, Miss Bingley, I prefer to rise early. It is a habit my late father instilled in me many years prior. This morning, in addition to your family's hospitality, I have read a letter from my sister."

"How is dear Georgiana?" she replied without any true concern evident in her voice.

Typical for Caroline Bingley, thought Darcy; *she knows the right words to say in each situation, but Miss Bingley possesses no real emotion—no real thoughts of her own. The lady mimics those about her.* "My sister enjoys her time in London with her favorite pastime—music." He had hoped this simple explanation would end Caroline's attentions, but unfortunately, the lady strolled over to where Darcy examined the choices under the covered dishes. Supposedly, she wished to refill the chocolate in her cup, but they both knew she sought a closer proximity to him. She would display her "wares" for his pleasure: a glance at her long, elegant neck, her creamy complexion, and her décolleté. As a man of wealth, a man often targeted by women in pursuit of a husband, Darcy recognized her game. He had gracefully learned to avoid such claims on his time by employing a haughty, prideful manner; his esteemed father had pointed out long ago that a man of fortune could offer indifference to such ambitions. Now, as Caroline sashayed across the room playing up her feminine qualities, Darcy took on a familiar somber attitude.

"I do wish Georgiana could have joined us at Netherfield," she said, refilling the cup and taking a step closer to him. "Surely, you could send for her, Mr. Darcy. I so long to renew our acquaintance."

Again, the lady says what is polite, Darcy reminded himself, *but not what is sincere.* If Caroline knew the real Georgiana, the lady would understand keeping company is one of my sister's least favorite activities.

"She has her studies to which to attend," Darcy responded as he purposely walked away, lengthening the distance between them, and taking up a position by the window. Turning to observe the grounds, he continued, "Will your brother be down soon? I had hoped we could survey the estate today."

As if on cue, Charles Bingley sauntered into the room. "Come, Darcy, tell me I am not tardy? You speak, Sir, as sternly as my former tutors regarding my punctuality," he said good-naturedly as he bent to kiss his eldest sister's upturned cheek. "We will have plenty of time to explore my lands." He winked at Darcy. "Of course, they will never compare to your Pemberley, but it will be a fit beginning, do you not think?"

Making a slight nodding bow to his friend, Darcy could not help but become caught up in Charles's enthusiasm. Darcy's smile came easy when he was with Bingley. Although their acquaintance had been a short one, he and the young man had formed a fast friendship. "In my opinion, nothing can compare with Pemberley except possibly Inveraray in Argyll or that property I observed in Rambouillet, outside of Paris. Of course, it had an English style park," he said genially, as he permitted the servant to refill the dark tea in his cup. "I suppose St. James might measure up." He laughed at his own attempt at humor. In a more serious vein, he suggested, "We should survey the fields, the fence line, and observe the homesteads on the estate. Then we may assess what to address immediately and what to delay until the new growing season. We should do so before the obligatory calls from your neighbors begin and before you decide to stay in Hertfordshire."

"I am most agreeably considering my new neighbors," Bingley replied as he prepared a plate of eggs and ham and sliced fruit.

"I fear," said Darcy, assuming his superior attitude once again, "you will find little true society in Hertfordshire. It is a country setting and is likely lacking in manners and refinement."

"Darcy, you should open yourself to new adventures," Bingley teased.

"I concur with Mr. Darcy," Caroline intoned haughtily. "I cannot imagine what would lead anyone to think Society existed outside of London. Surely, Hertfordshire lacks any idea of fashion or fine manners."

Bingley's countenance took on its usual teasing attitude. "If that be so, Caroline, you will be credited with changing my neighbors' lives forever. Every woman will want to copy your style, and men will be eating from your hand."

Caroline dropped her eyes in a coy manner after darting a glance at Darcy. The lady, obviously, hoped Darcy found her "style" to his liking. *Not today, Caroline,* he thought. *Your feminine wiles are wasted on me. When I choose a mate, she will be refined and a credit to the Darcy name. She will possess an innate intelligence and a temper remarkably easy. She will, of course, be everything that is generous and considerate, especially to my sister, and the lady in question will be sensible of her uncommon good fortune of marrying into the Darcy family.*

Thirty minutes later, Darcy had changed into his riding coat and boots and had rushed toward the stables; since he was in leading straps, he had loved being in the saddle. Cerberus waited for him at the mounting block. Normally, a man of property would conduct such an inspection of his land in the springtime, but Charles Bingley had made an impetuous decision. He had only of late decided he should take possession of Netherfield Park–without the usual inquiries of the soundness of the structures or the condition of the land. Then Bingley had "begged" Darcy to lend his expertise in what items to address in the estate's upkeep. Bingley was quickly learning that in Society land ownership determined acceptance. Darcy had inherited Pemberley through a system of primogeniture. As Bingley's father had made his wealth in trade, he held neither ancestral ties to the land nor any real knowledge of the accountability involved in owning an estate.

As they prepared to ride out, Darcy, perfectly in his element, noted, "I have observed several points of interest over the past few days of which you should be aware." He watched while Bingley climbed into the saddle aboard a gray gelding. "Netherfield Park holds areas where drainage should be addressed in a timely manner, but it also possesses immediate grounds offering paths and parkways for its owner's pleasure. You may have stumbled across a slightly tarnished gem. The question to be determined is how tarnished?" Darcy smiled largely as he kicked Cerberus's sides.

"A treasure hunt!" Bingley declared as he followed Darcy into the forested area behind the main house. For the next hour they rode together, stopping periodically for Darcy to point out what Bingley's untrained eyes could not see. Finally, Bingley led them to a small hill where they might hold a better view of the prospect leading to Netherfield's main drive. Smugly, Bingley queried, "Well, Darcy, do I have your blessing in this matter?"

"Perhaps we should wait a bit longer, my friend," Darcy began, "until you have spent a winter at Netherfield. A fine home in the late summer or early autumn may be a drafty pit in the winter."

"Darcy, you are the voice of gloom," Bingley laughed. "Why can you not be happy for me?"

Darcy flushed with his friend's taunt. Despite Bingley's sometimes-impulsive nature, he truly enjoyed the man's company. He had missed having a close male companion with whom he could share moments such as these. With his duties to Pemberley and to Georgiana, Darcy sometimes saw life with a stern resentment. Bingley's spirit of activity brought a new aspect to Darcy's life. "Gloom appears sound reason from my perspective," he reasoned, but thought once again of his consciousness of misery. Of late, he could not quell the loneliness, which had invaded his soul.

Bingley turned his mount toward his new home. Shaken from his thoughts, Darcy circled Cerberus to follow, but a glint of color moving along the road below them and to the right caught his attention. He pulled up on the reins to keep the horse in place, and upon closer inspection, he realized a young woman strode along at a robust pace. *How unladylike*, he thought. Yet, her obvious joy at ignoring propriety had momentarily intrigued him, and he had found himself smiling at the sight of such unbridled freedom. *She is delightfully happy*. He watched the lady until she was out of sight, and while he looked on, he could not help but wonder if he had ever been so delightfully happy. Had he ever known pure abandonment in something as simple as walking along a country road?

Upon their return to Netherfield, both men washed the dust of their rides away and retired to the study to recapture their thoughts on Bingley's investment. "The lodge is stately and will serve you well, especially for shooting parties."

"The stream is adequately stocked, although the wooded area was a bit over grown," Bingley observed.

"Being able to harvest some of the wooded area for heating purposes will serve the estate, Bingley, and you may choose to sell off some of the lumber for profit. Yet, be certain seedlings are available to replenish the area."

"I never considered those possibilities, Darcy. Your counsel is invaluable to me."

Darcy again felt the comfort of friendship: Something missing from his life of late. "As for the house itself, the lighting in the dining room, morning room, and study is pleasantly suited, taking advantage of the early light. Of course, for my taste, I hope, Bingley, you will address the library's need for comfortable furniture and adequate evening lighting."

"Sometimes, I forget, Darcy, how much you pride yourself on the reputation of Pemberley's library. Although I am not the reader you are, I will certainly address my home's shortcomings," Bingley mocked.

Their conversations continued along this vein until supper when the gentlemen dressed for the meal and escorted the ladies into the formal dining room. Congenial conversation followed the meal of several courses. "We received," confided Miss Bingley, "several cards and invitations from our neighbors. I expect some gentlemen to call tomorrow to pay their respects."

"I am anticipating becoming acquainted with the locals," Bingley beamed.

"Do not imagine the local gentry has much to offer in the way of polite society." Darcy had returned to his earlier disparagements. As he said the words, he thought of the girl on the road again. She had certainly abandoned all propriety. "Country manners, I find, are greatly lacking in a sense of decorum. One might note the preponderance of gross ignorance, some meanness of opinions, and very distressing vulgarity of manners. No doubt many of your neighbors will be intolerable."

Caroline added, "I expect Mr. Darcy to have the right of it, Charles. In the country, the peoples' very rank, fortune, rights, and expectations will always be different from what we know in Town."

From the Journal of the Netherfield Housekeeper
by Heather Lynn Rigaud

Household Ledger
Mrs. Robert Johnson, Housekeeper.

September 25, 1811

Apples 2 bu, pears

3 bu

Eggs 2.5 dz.

Today started as an excellent day as we welcomed the new Master of Netherfield. Mr. Bingley came accompanied by his sister and his man. He graciously condescended to meet the house staff and was very friendly with all. Indeed, I don't believe I've ever met such an open and easy-going master. He spoke to me at some length to explain his plans and expectations for the house. He's planning a large party of guests to come down in a fortnight, including his other sister, Mrs. Hurst. He was anxious that all be made ready for his company, and I assured him that Netherfield would be in perfect order. He also spoke of possible shooting parties and a ball. His sister, Miss Bingley, condescended to say that we have a great deal that must be done to make the house presentable.

I have determined to hire another girl for the duration of Mr. Bingley's guests' stay. Miss Bingley's maid arrives tomorrow, but there will be an increase in laundry and tidying that will require more staff. I will also engage a few girls and a man for to be on call for the master's future balls and larger entertainments.

Despite Miss Bingley's comments, I am satisfied with the condition of the house and feel we have served Netherfield well. I had a moment of concern when I caught Roseanna introducing herself to St. James, Mr. Bingley's man, but he made it immediately clear that her attentions were unwelcome. I have set Roseanna to work on polishing all the plate, in hopes that will give time to reflect on her behavior.

Bingley Takes Possession
of Netherfield
by Abigail Reynolds

September 25, 1811

Caroline Bingley glared at her brother as their carriage rattled over the cobblestones of a little country town. "Charles," she said in a deceptively honeyed voice, "You know I do not like surprises."

Bingley rubbed his hands together gleefully. "You will like this one." She had been trying to wheedle the information out of him since they had left London, but he was determined not to tell her until the last minute. He could not wait to see the look on her face when she realized that Netherfield was theirs! "We are almost there, in any case."

"Good. I have had more than enough of being gawked at by the locals. One would think they had never seen people of fashion before. That woman – her dress must be at least five seasons old, and she has the audacity to actually point at us!"

Bingley glanced out the window and smiled at a particularly pretty girl. "I am given to understand that there are a number of excellent families in the area, but strangers must be something of a novelty."

Caroline's lips twisted, but she did not trouble herself to reply.

Ten minutes later the carriage pulled up in front of Netherfield. Caroline barely glanced at the house. "What is this place?" she asked scornfully.

"It is called Netherfield Park." Bingley tried to suppress a grin of anticipation.

"My surprise is here? Charles, don't tell me you have purchased another horse!" She curled her lip as the footman opened the carriage door for her.

Bingley hurried around the carriage to hand her out. "No, my dear. It is not that your surprise is here, but rather that here is your surprise!"

"What on earth do you mean, Charles? I see nothing but the house."

"How many times have you said we must find a country estate? Well, here it is. I have signed the lease, and it is ours."

She turned an ominous stare on him. "You leased an estate without discussing it with me first? Charles, what in God's name were you thinking? This is in the middle of nowhere, and heaven alone knows what condition it is in!"

Bingley's shoulders sagged. This was not at all how Georgiana Darcy reacted to surprises from her brother. Perhaps it was just the shock of the moment. "I showed the drawings and the estate books to Darcy, and he said it was a good idea."

"One can hardly trust the word of two men in the matter of a household!" she snapped.

"Come, let me show you the interior before you say anything further," he said, then played his trump card. "Darcy says he will come for a long visit once we are settled in."

"Hmmph," she snorted, but with a thoughtful look. "A long visit, you say?"

"Yes. Look, there is the housekeeper waiting for us." He bounded up the steps, leaving her to trail behind him. "Mrs. Johnson, it is a pleasure to see you again! Allow me to introduce my sister, Miss Bingley, who will be acting as my hostess here."

The housekeeper curtsied deeply, but Caroline barely spared her a glance. Instead, she looked around slowly, examining the hall. "I suppose this will do, although it could be larger, and the furnishings are hardly to the latest fashion."

Bingley's spirits brightened. From Caroline, that was practically praise. "The library is to our left, and a ladies' sitting room on the right. But come through here – you must see the grand staircase and the drawing room. It is in the shape of an octagon, and I immediately thought of you when I saw it."

Caroline rolled her eyes, but proceeded through the gilded doorway with him. He had hoped for a better response to the grand staircase, which was indeed of the caliber of anything seen at Pemberley, but she said nothing until they reached the drawing room. There she stopped in the center of the room and pivoted around, slowly nodding her head. "I suppose you could have done worse," she said grudgingly, then turned to the housekeeper. "It will take a great deal of work to make this presentable."

Mr. Bingley Returns
Mr. Bennet's Call
by Susan Adriani

October 5, 1811

Longbourn's master turned the page of the thick tome in his hand—a rare first edition his brother-in-law happened to procure for him in London—and chuckled at the passage he was reading. With a smile, he leaned forward to grasp his tea cup, raising the painted china to his lips and taking a slow sip as wisps and curls of steam unfurled from its shallow depths. A flash of vibrant colour drew his eyes to the window, and Mr. Bennet shook his head with amusement.

The weather was unseasonably crisp that morning, but apparently not so much as to prevent his second daughter from escaping the confines of the house for her early morning constitutional. Elizabeth had never been one to sit idly inside with her squeamish mother and sisters when the pull of wooded paths, lush meadows, and bubbling streams beckoned her so emphatically toward adventure. Though her mother never approved of Elizabeth's vigorous habit, Mr. Bennet had not the heart to dissuade her from something she clearly loved, or the temporary freedom it afforded her, and so turned a blind eye to Elizabeth's forays and a deaf ear to Mrs. Bennet's complaints.

It was but a moment later that he heard the front door open and the distinct click of the lock as it closed, followed by muffled footsteps in the hall. A soft knock sounded upon the door to his library, and the gentleman laid aside his book. "Come in, Lizzy," he called, linking his fingers upon his stomach as he reclined in his chair.

The door opened to reveal his second daughter, whose dark tresses, and even darker eyes, belied the natural lightness of her disposition. Her lively intelligence and sharp wit had long since earned her the title of his favourite, though he was willing to concede that Jane had perhaps a bit more sense than his three youngest daughters. With Elizabeth, though, Mr. Bennet could always count on being entertained with keen observations and sensible conversation, two attributes he had ignored when choosing his wife, but, in hindsight, heartily wished he had not.

"Good morning, Papa."

Mr. Bennet's astute eyes noticed his daughter's flushed countenance and the mud-stained hem of her skirts. "Good morning, my dear," he said with a wry turn of his mouth. "I see you have already been out this morning, scampering through the countryside in the chilled air while your sisters, though far from sensible, stayed at home to indulge in more respectable pursuits. Tell me, were you perhaps hoping to catch a glimpse of the infamous Mr. Bingley on your rambles, for you know your two youngest sisters would never forgive you if you were to meet with him first?"

Elizabeth grinned. "No, sir. Unlike Kitty and Lydia, I believe I can wait until the assembly to see him. No doubt, making my acquaintance in the middle of a muddy field would leave Mr. Bingley with a very poor impression of me, indeed!"

"I would say so," her father replied, "and I daresay your affectionate mother would never find it within her heart to forgive you."

"True," Elizabeth laughed. "True."

A loud bang was heard above stairs, and then a clatter, closely followed by shrill voices raised in argument, his wife's amongst them. Mr. Bennet repressed a weary oath and rolled his eyes heavenward.

"Is there nothing I can do for you, sir?" Elizabeth asked, one brow arched impudently.

"Nothing at all, I am afraid, that does not involve engaging your mother's attention so that I might read my book in peace," he replied, his tone equally light.

Another bang echoed through the house, and the master of Longbourn straightened in his chair, leaning forward to pat his daughter's hand affectionately. "As much as I enjoy our chats, Lizzy, I am certain your less sagacious sisters are anxious to plague you with questions for which you will have no answers they truly wish to hear. Off with you now," he sighed, "before they all come below stairs and disrupt the quietude of my sanctuary."

Elizabeth did as she was bid and left him, but Mr. Bennet had no sooner resumed his reading than he was interrupted a second time. "Enter," he cried, his patience fraying.

Longbourn's butler, Mr. Hill, entered the room and presented his master with an elegant calling card. Mr. Bennet accepted it with a frown, but upon reading it his countenance brightened. Motioning for Mr. Hill to usher his guest into the library, he cast his book aside and stood, straightening his coats in anticipation.

A moment later the door was thrown open, and his guest announced.

"Mr. Bingley," Mr. Bennet said politely as the door closed behind Netherfield's new master, "to what do I owe such an honour this morning?"

Mr. Bingley was all smiles as he returned his host's greeting, bowing cordially in turn. "I have been meaning to re-pay your visit far earlier than this date, Mr. Bennet, but regret that certain matters at Netherfield have taken up much of my time over the last several days. I suppose such demands come with the territory of owning an estate, and I will grow used to them in time, but confess I am much more inclined at the moment to acquaint myself with all of my new neighbours. How do you do?"

Mr. Bennet inclined his head with a chuckle. "You find me well this morning, Mr. Bingley. Have a seat." He motioned to one of two chairs situated in front of his desk, and then reclaimed his own. "I understand from my steward that there are some issues with drainage on the far side of the Netherfield estate. I hope they will not prove too troublesome for you come spring."

Mr. Bingley smiled pleasantly. "With any hope we will have it all in check before year's end. I have ridden out with my steward, Mr. Middlebrook, every day this week and, before I took possession of the place, consulted a very great friend of mine who owns a vast estate in the north. He is excessively clever in his management of his own affairs, and so I begged his assistance with mine. Between them, Darcy and Mr. Middlebrook have come up with some very interesting solutions to the problem at hand; of course, at the moment I cannot seem to recall much of their complicated proposals or their detailed instructions regarding which parcels need to be cleared and which need to be filled, with any degree of clarity. I am afraid it is all Greek to me."

Mr. Bennet chuckled. The young man before him might do nicely for one of his younger daughters, or even Jane, but he could tell by Mr. Bingley's simple, nonchalant attitude that he was likely to have little luck holding Lizzy's interest for long. For a woman, his second daughter was far too intelligent and discerning for her own good. Like Lizzy, Mr. Bingley had a cheerful disposition, to be sure, but apparently possessed little in the way of substance regarding more serious matters, and Mr. Bennet doubted any man, even one as agreeable as Mr. Bingley, would appreciate the merit of having a wife who proved more clever than he was.

"Fear not, sir," Longbourn's master said. "I have enough on my plate with my own fields, and so will leave my inquiries until another time. If you are ever in need of assistance, though, I hope you will not hesitate to ask for it. With a wife and five daughters, I assure you I shall welcome any intelligent thoughts you have to communicate."

Mr. Bingley's eyes lit up at the mention of Mr. Bennet's daughters. "And how is your family, Mr. Bennet?" he asked, his expression eager as he leaned forward in his chair. "The weather has been very fine—perfect for walking out in the afternoon. I trust they are all in good health?"

And here we arrive at the heart of the matter, Mr. Bennet thought, his lips quirking with amusement. God help the man if my wife was right in assuming he wants a wife! Deciding to have a bit of fun with his neighbour, the elder man steepled his fingers beneath his chin and said evenly, "I assume they are all as well as ever. When I last saw them at breakfast they appeared to have arms and legs enough between them."

Mr. Bingley's mouth fell open before he quickly snapped it shut, a look of half-laughing alarm on his face. He shifted in his chair and cleared his throat. "Ah. Yes. Well, that is excellent news, indeed. I had the pleasure of receiving a visit from Sir William Lucas yesterday, and he was quite generous in his praise. He assured me that all of your daughters are very lovely, especially the two eldest."

Mr. Bennet lowered his head and smirked. "Yes, well, it is Jane, my eldest, who is the most handsome of the bunch, but as for the three youngest, I suppose you will have to judge for yourself as to whether their beauty is consolation enough for being several of the silliest girls in England; though, I must put in a good word for my Lizzy. I find she has a fair bit more sense than the rest."

It was clear by the return of the shocked expression upon his face that Mr. Bingley hardly knew how to react, and so remained silent, his mouth opening and closing several times before smartly abandoning any attempt at a reply. Mr. Bennet took pity on him, however, and engaged him with talk of the surrounding area for several more minutes until Mr. Bingley finally rose to take his leave. They parted with the assurance that Netherfield's master would return to dine with the Bennets on the morrow; a prospect that Mr. Bennet knew would please his anxious wife and curious daughters exceedingly.

Mr. Bingley Goes to London
by C. Allyn Pierson

October 9, 1811

By the time he reached London, his horse was lathered and faltering, but his enthusiasm was unimpaired. He could hardly wait to reach the Hurst's townhouse to tell his sisters about the wonderful opportunity to meet the people of Meryton. The Hurst's butler bowed deeply when he opened the door to the scion of the Bingley family and allowed himself a dignified smile while he greeted him.

"Come in, sir! Mrs. Hurst and Miss Bingley are in the drawing-room, and I am sure they will be happy to see you!"

"Thanks, Bledsoe, I will show myself up." Charles ran up the stairs three at a time and entered the drawing-room. "Caroline! Louisa! I have the best news!"

Both ladies dropped their needlework onto their laps and stared at their brother. Finally, Caroline spoke. "What *can* you be talking about, Charles?"

"I have just returned from Hertfordshire to gather you all up and take you to Meryton. They have an assembly tomorrow night! It will be a wonderful opportunity to meet the local gentry!"

Caroline glanced at her sister and back to Charles. "I cannot imagine why you are so in alt about this, Charles. Or why you leased this manor in such a backwards place in the first place."

"Oh come, Caroline! Netherfield is a very comfortable manor and the people are friendly. The hunting season is starting soon and it looks like the coverts are well stocked." He turned to his friend Darcy, who was leaning silently against the mantel, his face a mask.

28

Charles tried again. "Darcy, don't you think a few weeks in the country doing some hunting and some visiting sounds pleasant?"

Darcy's lip lifted in a brief sneer, which was quickly suppressed. "You will find the society something savage, Charles. If you want some country air we should go to Pemberley."

Caroline sat up straighter in her chair. "Oh yes, Mr. Darcy! Pemberley must be lovely at this time of year! I long to visit!"

Charles' pleasant face hardened slightly. "Caroline, you have been to Pemberley, and now that I have a manor of my own to visit, I was under the impression you were to take charge of the house for me."

"Of course Charles, of course, but I am not particularly thrilled about the wilds of Hertfordshire. I cannot imagine that there is society of any kind there. I think you should drop this lease and we can stay in London until Mr. Darcy leaves for Christmas at Pemberley. We might even see Miss Darcy. Did you not say that she was to spend a few days in London soon, Mr. Darcy?"

Darcy had been watching this family squabble and suddenly felt a pang for his friend and his enthusiasm for his new home. He stood up suddenly. "Well, I think I must go home and pack my things, Charles. What time do you want me to be ready in the morning?"

Miss Bingley and Mrs. Hurst both pursed their lips and glared at Darcy as he traitorously gave in to Charles' ridiculous whim. When Darcy caught and held her eyes, his lips compressed, Caroline squirmed in her chair. When she could not tolerate it any longer, she broke out, "Well, all right Charles. I suppose we must go if it means that much to you."

Bingley grinned at the two of them, knowing Louisa would give in if the two dominant personalities had ceded.

They spent the rest of the evening packing and preparing for their sojourn in Hertfordshire, while Mr. Hurst had his postprandial nap on the drawing-room settee.

The Bennet Sisters Prepare
by Karen Doornebos

October 15, 1811

"Oh my!" Jane let out a gasp at her dressing table, and when she stood, her stool fell over, while the bun she had been arranging atop her head fell down.

Lizzy ran to the dressing table, half undressed herself, broom in her hand. "Is it that mouse again, Jane?" She raised the broom, readying it. "Wherever did it go, Jane?"

"I cannot say," Jane said as she uprighted the stool. "It gave me quite a fright. He seems to be growing bolder. He nearly ran across my dancing slippers this time. But Lizzy, please, I implore you to put that broom down. It is nothing Mr. Dimples can't take care of."

Lizzy propped the broom up against the wall, and even though she was just in her stays and chemise, with one stocking on and one off, she folded her arms and gave their cat, sitting on his haunches, a glare. "Really, Mr. Dimples, you do test me. You are quite the haughtiest cat I know. Too proud to catch a mouse?"

The black cat simply closed his eyes and turned away. It wasn't the first time he had been admonished by Elizabeth.

Jane repinned her hair in the mirror while Lizzy pulled on her other stocking when, all aflutter, and with a great noise, Lydia and Kitty burst into Jane and Lizzy's bedchamber.

"Lordy! Have we had a laugh! I daresay we're ready for the assembly, aren't we now, Kitty?" It was Lydia, in an overpowering cloud of lavender water.

Kitty giggled.

"Lydia!" Elizabeth with her gown on, but not yet buttoned, put her hands on her hips. "What can you be thinking putting on so much lavender water? What will father say?"

Lydia laughed. "He'll say nothing, of course! He scarcely notices these things! Regardless, he's sure to be in his library when we leave. He hasn't a care in the world! Why can't you be more like him, Lizzy?"

Elizabeth frowned, noticing that Lydia's white gown had been dampened to a most revealing effect. "Lydia. You must change that gown, and change it now."

Jane turned around from her dressing table, and upon seeing Lydia, she blushed.

Lydia stamped her foot, to ill effect, in her dancing slippers. "Why?"

Lizzy paced the floor. "Because it is not respectable, Lydia, and you know that well enough. Shall I ring for Hill or will you take care of the matter yourself?"

"I shall do nothing of the kind! You are not my mother. Even though you do not approve of my attire, at least I'm dressed. Mary's in her bedchamber with her nose in a book, and she'll make us all miss the assembly. I say we just leave her here! She won't even notice we have ditched her!"

Jane sighed and stood while Lizzy made her way to Mary's chamber. Upon passing the stairway she heard Mrs. Bennet, who had been dressed and ready for a full six hours, raising her voice at Mr. Bennet, and Lizzy resolved she'd have to have another discussion with her father about Lydia, but now wasn't the time. It never seemed to be the right time, really.

"Mr. Bennet," Mrs. Bennet said. "Sir William will be at the assembly, why not you? Oh! My poor nerves! Surely, I am the only lady in all of Meryton who attends such functions without her husband!"

"Exactly, my dear," Mr. Bennet said. "If I were to suddenly attend this gathering, the entire town might believe something is amiss. Better that I stay home. There. It is resolved."

Mrs. Bennet fanned herself furiously. Lizzy could hear it all the way up the stairs. "It is no use then?"

"None. I shall be in my library until your return. The carriage is being readied."

The library door shut.

"Oh, Hill," Mrs. Bennet sighed. "Who knew that I was marrying a hermit? He does torture me so! My nerves are sorely tested. I shall need a good sit-down, now."

Lizzy came away from the stairs, opened Mary's door, and there she was, in her chemise and bare feet, with her hair still in curling papers, propped up on her bed with a book. It was all Lizzy could do to keep herself from shaking the girl. They were due to leave in half an hour or they'd be late. Lizzy leaned up against the door, conjuring the proper words to motivate Mary.

"Mary, you should like to play the pianoforte at the assembly, tonight, I believe, would you not?"

Mary looked up from her book and took off her glasses. "I should like that very much, Lizzy. I know exactly what to play."

"Then there is only one minor detail yet to arrange, Mary."

Mary looked dumfounded.

"In order to play at a public assembly, one must be dressed for– the public. You have exactly fifteen minutes to get ready. And, please, Mary, do not forget your stockings this time."

Down the hall, Jane screamed, and nothing ever caused Jane to scream, so Lizzy dashed back to their bedchamber, where Jane giggled and Kitty, and Lydia, dressed in a dry gown, laughed hysterically.

It was Mr. Dimples. He had caught the mouse and held it by its tail in his mouth.

"And you thought he was too proud, Lizzy!" Jane said.

Louisa and Edward Hurst
at the Meryton Assembly
by Mary Simonsen

October 15, 1811

"Edward, you look so handsome tonight," Louisa Hurst said to her husband of six years. Although short, portly, and balding, Mr. Hurst was the apple of Louisa's eye. Others might criticize his appearance or misinterpret his silence as a lack of wit or vocabulary or intelligence, but that was because his company misunderstood him. Unlike Darcy, who rarely spoke without saying something that would amaze the whole room, or Charles, who hated pregnant pauses and would rattle on endlessly, Edward engaged others in conversation only when he had something substantive to contribute. His darling wife knew there were few who appreciated Edward's sardonic wit or who guessed at the fun they had behind closed doors. After a half dozen years of marriage, there were few married couples who could make such a claim for contentment.

"Do you really think so, my dear? The buttons on my waistcoat are popping," Edward said while looking at his bulging vest.

"That is true, my love. But do you not think a flat stomach is a sign of poverty? Besides, it takes effort and fine dining for one to burst one's buttons," his wife said while tickling his middle.

"I am so glad you think so. I know your sister does not approve of my expanding girth."

"Please give me one example of anyone, other than Mr. Darcy and Miss Darcy, who my sister *does* approve of?" Louisa asked, her mood immediately souring.

"No one comes to mind, except, as you say, the Darcys Will you allow Caroline to lead you around by the nose tonight?"

"Of course I shall. If I do not, she will whine and pout and stamp her foot, and if that does not work, she will say something unkind about you and that is something I cannot bear."

"Your sister is in need of a set down. I wonder if anyone is up to the task."

"If such a thing does happen, it will have to come from Mr. Darcy as Caroline does not give a brass farthing about anyone else's opinion."

"I wish it would happen sooner rather than later. Even though I do enjoy annoying your sister with my snoring, I am tired of pretending to fall asleep on the sofa every night."

"Well, you shan't have to pretend tonight as we have an assembly to attend, and while I am dancing, you will visit the card room and win lots of money for us as you always do."

"That certainly is my intention." Edward gave his wife a quick kiss.

* * *

"Oh my, Louisa!" Caroline said, covering her mouth with her fan. "This assembly is worse than anything I could have imagined. There is not one person here whom I would consider to be fashionable. And the smells! The finest perfume from Paris could not conceal them."

"I couldn't agree more," Louisa answered. *But considering we are in the country, not Grosvenor Square, really, what did you expect?*

"Other than Miss Jane Bennet, who is presently dancing with our brother, there is not a pretty face in the room. I am sure Mr. Darcy agrees. Did you see how he walked away from Miss Bennet's sister?"

"Yes, he did turn up his nose at her," *before turning around and staring at her for fifteen minutes.*

"He refused to even consider dancing with her."

"Yes, I noticed that as well." *I am sure it had nothing to do with the fact that she had walked away from him because she had found* him *to be rude and above his company.*

"I think Mr. Darcy has decided that Miss Elizabeth Bennet is beneath his notice. Even at a country assembly, he will not lower his standards by dancing with her."

"Yes, Caroline," *which is why he keeps staring at her. He absolutely, positively wants to make sure he has no interest in her whatsoever.*

"Here comes Mr. Hurst. As he is smiling, I shall assume he won at cards," Caroline said. "Your husband is incredibly lucky."

"Yes, he is." *His "luck" paid for all the finely-carved French furniture in the townhouse you share with us.*

"Edward, your pants are bulging. Are they laden with newly-won coins, or are you just happy to see me?" Louisa whispered.

"Behave yourself, Louisa, that is, until I do not want you to," Edward whispered in her ear.

"Will the two of you please stop that?" Caroline protested.

Although Caroline had been a proponent of Louisa marrying Edward Hurst, it had never occurred to her that Louisa would actually fall in the love with her husband. How gauche! In order to get away from the cooing lovers, Caroline moved toward Mr. Darcy.

"I can hardly believe Caroline is still in hot pursuit of Mr. Darcy," Edward said as soon as his sister-in-law was out of earshot. "Doesn't she realize Mr. Darcy is a snob and would never marry the daughter of a merchant?"

"What about a farmer's daughter?"

"Whatever do you mean, Louisa?"

"See that dark-haired lady in the yellow frock," Louisa said, pointing her fan at Elizabeth Bennet who was talking to Miss Lucas. "Mr. Darcy has been stealing glances at her ever since our arrival. She is the daughter of Mr. Bennet, a gentleman farmer, and because her father is a gentleman, she and Mr. Darcy are equals."

"But some people are more equal than others," he said with a laugh. "I can't imagine the grandson of an earl being interested in a farmer's daughter."

"Shall we test my theory?" Edward eagerly agreed. "Mr. Darcy has asked me to dance the next with him. While I am dancing, you will watch Mr. Darcy and then tell me what you think."

Louisa, who found Mr. Darcy to be of a taciturn nature on the best of occasions, made little attempt to engage him in conversation, and he was perfectly content to have it so. After the conclusion of the dance, Mr. Darcy offered to get Louisa a glass of punch. During his absence, she hurried to Edward's side.

"Well, what do you think now, my love?"

"By Jove, Louisa, you have got it right. The man is smitten. While dancing, it was as if he had an owl's head. No matter which way you turned, he was looking at Miss Elizabeth. I declare him to be a lost cause."

"I agree. While you were in the card room, I was busy eavesdropping on Miss Elizabeth's conversations, and I can tell you that she will humble him."

"Mr. Darcy, humbled?"

"Yes, Mr. Darcy of Pemberley will have to climb off his pedestal if he wishes to engage that particular lady."

"Well, Louisa, I thought it was going to be rather dull in the country," Edward said, chuckling, "but it looks as if will be anything but. Who would have guessed that the staid Mr. Darcy would provide the entertainment!"

Charlotte Lucas at the Meryton Assembly
by Abigail Reynolds

October 15, 1811

Not so many years ago, Charlotte had hated attending assemblies. Now they were among her chief pleasures, as she enjoyed the music and the opportunity to visit with her friends, but when she had been younger, she had been agonizingly aware that she might as well have been invisible to the young gentlemen in attendance. Their eyes would always slide past her to the prettier girls, and while any of them would have described her as a good sort, she had rarely been sought out as a partner.

As her pretty friends became wives one after another, Charlotte grew somewhat resigned to her lot. She had always wished to marry and have her own establishment, but spinsterhood was not so bad, after all, not when she had three brothers who would support her after her father passed away. She was grateful not to be in the precarious position of her particular friend Elizabeth Bennet; without any brothers, Elizabeth would eventually face a life of genteel poverty if she did not marry, and although Elizabeth possessed the beauty Charlotte herself lacked, her liveliness tended to frighten off potential suitors.

This particular assembly had begun auspiciously. Mr. Bingley, their charming and wealthy new neighbor, had asked her for the first set of dances, and proved to be an excellent dancer. Charlotte was sensible enough to take pleasure in the act of dancing rather than to waste her time dreaming of anything more, knowing that a gentleman of Mr. Bingley's caliber would have no real interest in her. True to form, early in the first dance Mr. Bingley spotted the lovely Jane Bennet. He was apparently quite struck by her, immediately asking Charlotte who she was and angling transparently for an introduction. It would make a fine story for her to tell Lizzy later on.

It was no surprise when Mr. Bingley asked Jane Bennet to dance the next set with him, while Charlotte, as usual, was without a partner. Her father took the opportunity to introduce her to Mr. Robinson, a gentleman of about her own years who was paying an extended visit to their nearest neighbor, Mr. Willoughby. She had seen him on several previous occasions, but he had never paid her the slightest bit of attention. Now Sir William's maneuverings practically obliged Mr. Robinson to ask her for the next set. The poor man; she was sure he wanted to do nothing of the sort. Her father's well-meaning but pointless attempts to find her a husband had put many an innocent young man in an embarrassing position, but Mr. Robinson proved to be not only amiable, but seemed to find her company diverting, asking her about her interests. If she had been anyone else, she would have thought he was actually flirting with her, but no one ever flirted with Charlotte, so that was impossible. Still, it was a delightful half hour.

Afterwards Mr. Robinson returned her to Sir William who was in conversation with Mr. Bingley. Although reluctant to lose Mr. Robinson's company, Charlotte decided to slip away before her father tried to embarrass Mr. Bingley into dancing with her again. She was only a few paces away when she heard Mr. Robinson ask, "So, Mr. Bingley, how do you like the assembly?"

"I like it very well indeed!" said Mr. Bingley stoutly.

"Are we not fortunate to have so many pretty women in the room? Which do you think to be the prettiest?"

"Oh! the eldest Miss Bennet beyond a doubt, there cannot be two opinions on that point," replied Mr. Bingley immediately and with great enthusiasm.

This intelligence gave Charlotte an excellent reason to seek out Lizzy Bennet, to whom she repeated the story.

Elizabeth agreed heartily. "Mr. Bingley must be half in love with her already. I heard him tell that dreadful Mr. Darcy that she was the most beautiful creature he had ever beheld. Then he encouraged Mr. Darcy to ask me to dance, even though he had been refusing to acknowledge the existence of any ladies besides those of his own party. Fortunately for me, Mr. Darcy announced that I was tolerable, but not handsome enough to tempt him." She laughed. "As if I would ever want to tempt such a proud and unpleasant man! It would be a punishment to have to dance with him."

"It is fortunate Mr. Bingley did not try to make him dance with me, then, since if you are only tolerable, I hate to think of how Mr. Darcy would describe me!" said Charlotte.

Elizabeth said, "I think you may have made a different conquest. Mr. Robinson seems unable to take his eyes off of you."

Charlotte laughed at Elizabeth's foolishness. "If he is looking this way, it is you he must be looking at." She glanced over her shoulder only to discover her friend had been correct. As Mr. Robinson's eyes met hers, he gave a slow smile that made her feel a little odd inside.

She smiled back, which he seemed to take to be enough an invitation to join them. As he spoke to her warmly, Charlotte found herself blushing, something she had thought to have left behind her years ago. Then, instead of asking Elizabeth to dance as Charlotte had expected, Mr. Robinson said, "Miss Lucas, would you permit me – or do I ask too much – to request the honor of the next set with you?"

Charlotte could not remember ever having been asked to dance twice by the same man at an assembly, but she managed to keep a calm demeanor as she accepted, ignoring Elizabeth's amused glance.

After another enjoyable set, Mr. Robinson, noting that she was slightly out of breath, offered to bring her some lemonade. Charlotte acquiesced, enjoying the novelty of having a gentleman fetch her refreshments. Jane Bennet always had a cluster of admirers eager to serve her, but Charlotte, like Elizabeth, was usually left to her own devices.

Mr. Robinson returned carrying two glasses of lemonade. Charlotte revised her opinion of him upward; the men of Meryton were all drinking something much stronger. She made room for him to sit on the bench beside her. He sat closer to her than she expected, enough so that she once again found herself blushing under his scrutiny. She was grateful that the crowd around them hid her from general view; she did not wish to be subject to the inevitable teasing merely because a man had danced with her twice.

She struggled to find a subject of conversation to distract herself from improper thoughts. "How did you come to meet Mr. Willoughby?" she asked.

"Willoughby? Oh, we were acquainted at Cambridge, but then I lost track of him until last year when we met again in London. A capital fellow, Willoughby."

"Indeed," Charlotte said non-committally. She wondered how well Mr. Robinson actually knew Mr. Willoughby, who was considered to be quite a rake. He had cut a swath through the local female population, even turning his eye on Charlotte at one point. Fortunately, she had been too sensible to fall for Willoughby's wiles; she knew he only wanted one thing from her. It surprised her that such a respectable man as Mr. Robinson would be his friend, but perhaps there was more to the story than she knew.

"I cannot tell you how grateful I am for your company, Miss Lucas. I feel quite a stranger here," Mr. Robinson said. "I had not hoped to discover a lady who was so easy to talk to and an excellent dancer as well."

Had he made the usual compliments about her beauty, Charlotte would have dismissed him completely as a flatterer who wanted something from her, but it was a novelty to discover a gentleman who cared about something besides a lady's appearance. Nothing would ever come of it, but she told herself there could be no harm in enjoying a man's company for a few minutes.

Post Assembly Discussion
at Longbourn
by Susan Adriani

October 15, 1811

"Enough," cried Mr. Bennet. "I beg you, Mrs. Bennet, not another word about lace!"

Lydia twirled a lock of hair around her finger and yawned as her mother regaled her father with details of Mr. Darcy's slight against her sister Elizabeth. *Lord,* she thought, *Who cares about that?*

Kitty leaned to whisper in her ear, "I thought the lace on Mrs. Hurst's gown beautiful, did not you think so, too?"

"Of course," she agreed in a hushed voice, "but I daresay Mrs. Hurst pays dearly for it. Her husband was half in his cups before he even got through the door of the hall. Can you imagine being saddled with such a dull, useless man? Why, he did not dance one dance with his own wife the entire night. I wonder how she does not divorce him. If I were her I would not care one bit about causing a scandal. I would get rid of him quick as a rabbit and find another rich man (a handsome one) to take his place."

Kitty shook her head. "It was awful, was it not? I would be furious if I had a husband who ignored me all evening long like Mr. Hurst ignored his wife, but I do not know that I would have the nerve to divorce him! One has to wonder how she could have married him to begin with. I found him incredibly unremarkable in figure and in looks, though he does dress the part of a fashionable gentleman. You would think, would you not, that he might do more to make himself attractive, but I suppose when one has money one may do as one pleases. Mr. Hurst obviously does." Her countenance deepened to a rosy hue as she said in a hushed voice, "Mr. Bingley and Mr. Darcy were certainly attractive, though. They had lovely calves. Did you notice how muscular they were, Lyddy? Why, I thought I would die!"

Lydia snorted and rolled her eyes. "Kitty," she laughed, "do not tell me that you believe you have a chance with either of them?"

"Why wouldn't I?" Kitty asked indignantly. "Perhaps Mr. Darcy is a bit too dour, but Mr. Bingley is very agreeable, and he danced with me in the beginning of the evening, you know."

"Of course, he danced with you," Lydia said with exasperation. "Mr. Bingley danced with half the ladies in Hertfordshire this evening, but you must see that he was half in love with Jane before the end of their first dance. She is the only lady who he danced with twice, and you ought to know that once a man notices Jane, we may as well be chopped liver. There is nothing for you in that quarter, I daresay, or any of us, so you best just forget about it and go back to pining over Robert Goulding."

Lydia could not help the resentfulness of her tone any more than she could help wishing that she had been the object of Mr. Bingley's admiration, and not her beautiful eldest sister. What a good joke it would have been if she had caught his eye instead! Lydia would have been gratified, indeed, to have been able to crow to her four sisters that it was she, and none of them, who the handsome and rich Mr. Bingley had chosen to fall in love with.

After laying eyes upon the attractive Mr. Darcy, she had entertained hopes of him taking an interest in her as well, but as soon as she saw how disagreeable and dour he was, Lydia had quickly lost interest in pursuing him. Despite the fact that he was ridiculously rich and tall beyond a doubt, there were just some things that were not worth putting up with. With ten-thousand-a-year and a masculine figure she could not help but admire, Lydia could not imagine why the man did not dance with anyone except that snooty Miss Bingley and Mrs. Hurst, and even then it was only two dances! *Not only was Mr. Darcy brooding and dull*, Lydia decided, *but a simpleton as well. Lord, what idiotic man did not dance at an assembly?*

As Kitty giggled at their mother's remarks about Mr. Bingley and his attentiveness to Jane, Lydia huffed petulantly. Though the youngest, she was determined to one day meet a handsome, engaging man of her own. He would take one look at her and fall madly in love, and barely even notice Jane or Lizzy. *Yes,* she thought with a quiet giggle, *I will show them all that I am just as beautiful and desirable as they are. The entire village will talk of nothing but my romance and my good fortune, and every lady in Hertfordshire will be jealous of me.* It was a thought that gave her much pleasure, and Lydia Bennet, then but fifteen, took heart in the idea that someday, and sooner rather than later, she would surely make her wish a reality.

Darcy Realizes He is Susceptible to Elizabeth Bennet's Charms
by Regina Jeffers

October 16, 1811

> "…It is often only carelessness of opinion."

As was his custom, Darcy had risen before the remainder of the Bingley household. Sitting alone in the breakfast room at Netherfield was becoming a habit. The bitter taste of coffee reminded him of his "distaste" for the previous evening's entertainment. He had never seen such gaucheness gathered in one place and at one time—from the supercilious Sir William to the many women of little intelligence, few true manners, and disagreeable temperaments. "Their ranks, fortunes, rights and expectations will always be different," he reminded himself. A shudder of disgust briefly racked his body before an enigmatic smile and an arched eyebrow played fleetingly across his memory. Placing the cup down hard on the table, Darcy purposely shook his head attempting to rid himself of the image. Disturbed by the vision but not knowing why, he rose quickly and strode through the hallways of Netherfield heading toward the stables. He should wait on Bingley, but it would be several hours before his friend came down. At the moment, Darcy needed to be free of the form and free of this feeling of uncertainty. Cerberus, thankfully, stood ready at the mounting block; and without realizing what he did, he turned the horse toward the same hill from which he had seen the flash of color along the road several days prior.

***

Having ridden hard, Darcy returned to Netherfield to find the Bingleys relaxing in the morning room. Their foray into Hertfordshire society had, evidently, exhausted them in so many ways. Bingley acknowledged Darcy's entrance before remarking, "I see our friendship did not impact your decision to ride out without me. I had hoped we could continue our survey of the estate."

"If you are honest with your reproofs, I beg your pardon most profusely, Bingley. Your hospitality is an honor I cherish." Darcy gazed steadily at his friend. Fitzwilliam Darcy gauged Charles Bingley's friendship as more than favorable. After having lost Mr. Wickham's acquaintance as a result of the man's perfidy, Darcy had waited a long while before accepting the intimacy of a close male friend. Other than his cousin, Colonel Fitzwilliam, he trusted few people with the details of his life.

"Really, Darcy," blustered Bingley, unaccustomed to such self-reproach from his friend, "I value your opinions and your company. Although my tone reflects my weariness, my words were meant in jest." They presented each other a quick bow indicating mutual respect. Bingley emitted a soft laugh to relieve the unanticipated tension while both men moved to the serving tray to partake of the items there. "Did you enjoy your ride, Darcy?" Bingley asked cautiously.

Darcy confessed in perfect truth, "It was an excellent way to clear away last evening's vestiges." Turning to Charles's sister, he said, "Miss Bingley, your refinement and charity were never so appreciated as they were yesterday evening." He suspected the lady would denigrate her brother's successes last evening in order to earn Darcy's approval; Darcy meant to circumvent Miss Bingley's manipulations.

Bingley responded cheerfully, "Yes, my Dear, you and Louisa were much admired. I received so many compliments on your behalf last evening. I am indebted to you for establishing our family's standing in the community. Your successes are our family's triumphant."

Darcy knew Miss Bingley had despised last evening; she had confided as much to him several times during the assembly; yet, she said, "Your attention honors me. We shall endeavor to do our duty, and I pray my contribution to the evening solidified your presence in the neighborhood, Charles."

"I say, Darcy, would you mind if we took our meal in my study?" Bingley asked anxiously. "I foolishly agreed to meet with Mr. Ashe this afternoon. I would appreciate your further insights regarding Netherfield's soundness prior to that time."

"Of course, Bingley. I would be happy to be of service."

* * *

Leaving the ladies to their own devices, the gentlemen retired to the study to continue their review of the Netherfield books and accounts. Ashe was Bingley's man of business, and the solicitor would bring with him the final papers for Bingley's assuming the property at Netherfield Park. Darcy thoroughly enjoyed these hours of withdrawal from the niceties society placed on gentlemen; what transpired behind the study door remained within his control. It held no double-edged expressions to dance around—no prejudices—and no enigmatic smile hauntingly resurfacing in his memory.

However, those hours passed too quickly, and he and Bingley were forced by good manners to join the ladies for the evening meal. Unfortunately for Darcy and Bingley, Caroline could control her opinions no longer, and they were required to listen to Charles's sister decrying his neighbors' manners; the tirade started at supper and increased in its vehemence. Darcy watched aghast with contempt. Miss Bingley possessed no empathy for her brother's feelings. Miserable, Bingley suffered greatly, but Darcy felt far from being agreeable; he sat with a pronounced grimace.

Bingley insisted, "I never met with more pleasant people. Everyone offered their attentions and their kind regards; there was no one putting on airs or posing with false countenances; I was pleased to make the acquaintance of many of my new neighbors."

"Charles, you lack judiciousness," Miss Bingley intoned her contempt. "The women may be pretty by your judgment; yet, they lacked conversation and fashion. Were you not aware of their conceit?"

Bingley argued, "Your censure surely cannot be laid at Miss Bennet's feet. Would you not agree, Darcy?"

Darcy's honest nature allowed him only to concede that Miss Jane Bennet was attractive, but "she smiles too much." He authorized the smallest degree of arrogance as acceptable.

"Smiles too much!" Bingley nearly came out of his chair in disbelief. "I can think of no one of my acquaintance more beautiful."

Darcy spoke from principle, as well as pride. "I observed a collection of people who move in circles so distinct from my own. I find no manners and little beauty. I take no interest or pleasure at the prospect of renewing their acquaintances." Yet, as soon as the words escaped his mouth, Darcy felt a twinge of betrayal. He wondered, for a moment, if a man could afford to cherish his pride so dearly.

Taking pity on their brother, Mrs. Hurst and her sister finally allowed Jane Bennet to be a sweet girl and declared their desire to know her better. They, therefore, established Miss Bennet as someone they admired and liked; Bingley accepted their praise of Miss Bennet, and Darcy watched as his friend, obviously, permitted the pleasure of thinking of the lady as someone he too would like to know better.

* * *

Over a fortnight Bingley continued to prefer the company of Jane Bennet to all others in Hertfordshire. Darcy had observed his young friend fall in and out of romantic relationships before, but he had never recalled Bingley to be more besotted. Bingley had danced with Miss Bennet four times at Meryton, had seen her one morning at his house, and had dined in company with her four times.

Unfortunately, as Bingley appeared to give his heart to a woman clearly below him, Darcy discovered to his horror his own tendencies in that vein becoming more distinct. Every time Bingley sought Miss Bennet's company, he placed Darcy, as Bingley's companion, in Elizabeth Bennet's presence. And each time as he swore he would ignore Miss Elizabeth, Darcy found himself more enticed by her. Unconsciously, he placed himself where he could observe her, where he could listen to her conversations, and where he could interact with her. Although he rarely spoke to strangers, Darcy began to plan ways to afford verbal exchanges with Miss Elizabeth.

When they did converse, however briefly, a verbal swordplay occurred between them; he understood she desired an apology for his behavior at the assembly; Darcy also assumed Elizabeth Bennet recognized he had a right to such behavior. His distinct station in life afforded him an air of superiority. Darcy had determined she purposely flirted with him through these "verbal assaults," and belatedly, he discovered they had worked remarkably well.

Only last evening, Miss Elizabeth had made inroads into Darcy's tranquility. In the fullness of his belief, he had accused, "I hope to force you to do justice to your natural powers, Miss Elizabeth."

With a raised eyebrow, a gesture, which he would never admit to anyone but himself had great power over him, the lady had retorted, "How delightful to feel myself of consequence to you, Mr. Darcy."

As usual, she had stormed away in a huff, but Darcy had taken prodigious delight in the flush upon the lady's cheeks and the natural sway of Miss Elizabeth's hips. He would acknowledge to no one it was an enticing sight—one that had inspired several of his dreams of late. As the days passed, he ascertained he could offer no culpability to Bingley; he felt in nearly as bad of a position.

As Bingley and Darcy discovered themselves distracted by the Bennet ladies, Miss Bingley's acute awareness of the changes in her brother and of his esteemed friend increased her fervent rebukes, especially those directed toward the second Bennet daughter. He knew Miss Bingley had congratulated herself when Darcy openly expurgated Elizabeth Bennet's failings. He had made observations regarding Miss Elizabeth's not having an appealing countenance; he had said with a critical eye that her figure lacked any point of symmetry; and he had asserted that the lady's manners showed no knowledge of fashionable acceptance. Yet, as he publicly castigated Miss Elizabeth's virtues, in private thoughts, he found her face possessed a soul of its own, as her dark green eyes often danced with life; he recognized her figure to be light and pleasing; and he had determined that her manners demonstrated a relaxed playfulness. "Not necessarily lovely, but certainly enchanting," he told his empty chamber.

Charlotte Lucas
on Guy Fawkes Day
by Abigail Reynolds

November 5, 1811

Elizabeth said, "It is evident whenever they meet, that he does admire her; and to me it is equally evident that Jane is yielding to the preference which she began to entertain for him from the first, and is in a way to be very much in love. I am pleased, however, that her feelings are not likely to be discovered by the world in general, since Jane unites with great strength of feeling a composure of temper and a uniform cheerfulness of manner, which should guard her from the suspicions of the impertinent."

"It may perhaps be pleasant," replied Charlotte, "to be able to impose on the public in such a case; but it is sometimes a disadvantage to be so very guarded. If a woman conceals her affection with the same skill from the object of it, she may lose the opportunity of fixing him; and it will then be but poor consolation to believe the world equally in the dark." Besides, there were other ways a lady could guard the privacy of her affections. She and Mr. Robinson had silently conspired not to be overly attentive to each other; when they conversed, it was often in a dark alcove or in the shadows poorly lit by candles. Even Elizabeth had not guessed at her interest, but Mr. Robinson understood her well enough.

Charlotte could see Elizabeth was not convinced, so she continued, "There is so much of gratitude or vanity in almost every attachment, that it is not safe to leave any to itself. We can all begin freely—a slight preference is natural enough; but there are very few of us who have heart enough to be really in love without

50

encouragement. In nine cases out of ten, a woman had better show more affection than she feels. Bingley likes your sister undoubtedly; but he may never do more than like her, if she does not help him on."

"But she does help him on, as much as her nature will allow. If I can perceive her regard for him, he must be a simpleton indeed not to discover it too."

"Remember, Eliza, that he does not know Jane's disposition as you do."

"But if a woman is partial to a man, and does not endeavour to conceal it, he must find it out."

"Perhaps he must, if he sees enough of her. But though Bingley and Jane meet tolerably often, it is never for many hours together; and as they always see each other in large mixed parties, it is impossible that every moment should be employed in conversing together. Jane should therefore make the most of every half hour in which she can command his attention. When she is secure of him, there will be leisure for falling in love as much as she chooses." Charlotte had been following her own advice in this matter. She had seen Mr. Robinson on three occasions since the assembly, and each time she made sure to single him out. He was responding beautifully, and she herself was happier than she had ever been.

"Your plan is a good one," replied Elizabeth, "where nothing is in question but the desire of being well married; and if I were determined to get a rich husband, or any husband, I daresay I should adopt it. But these are not Jane's feelings; she is not acting by design. As yet, she cannot even be certain of the degree of her own regard, nor of its reasonableness. She has known him only a fortnight. She danced four dances with him at Meryton; she saw him one morning at his own house, and has since dined in company with him four times. This is not quite enough to make her understand his character."

"Not as you represent it. Had she merely dined with him, she might only have discovered whether he had a good appetite; but you must remember that four evenings have been also spent together—

and four evenings may do a great deal." It had sufficed for her to reach the point where she could communicate with Mr. Robinson by a mere look across a crowded room.

"Yes; these four evenings have enabled them to ascertain that they both like Vingt-un better than Commerce; but with respect to any other leading characteristic, I do not imagine that much has been unfolded."

"Well," said Charlotte, shaking her head over Elizabeth's romantic nonsense, "I wish Jane success with all my heart; and if she were married to him to-morrow, I should think she had as good a chance of happiness as if she were to be studying his character for a twelvemonth. Happiness in marriage is entirely a matter of chance. If the dispositions of the parties are ever so well known to each other, or ever so similar before-hand, it does not advance their felicity in the least. They always contrive to grow sufficiently unlike afterwards to have their share of vexation; and it is better to know as little as possible of the defects of the person with whom you are to pass your life."

"You make me laugh, Charlotte; but it is not sound. You know it is not sound, and that you would never act in this way yourself."

Charlotte knew better than to argue with her strong-minded friend, but she was already acting on her opinion. Mr. Robinson was amiable, presentable in company, and he admired her; and she felt a sharp tug of attraction when he looked at her in that certain way. Only last week he had found the opportunity to surreptitiously rest his hand on her lower back after they had danced together, making shivers run through her. He had leaned his head close to her when speaking to her alone so that the warmth of his breath tingled her ear, and the first time his lips had brushed against her ear she had thought it an accident, but by the second time she knew better. She did not think it would be a hardship to share his bed, and she saw no reason to examine any other flaws he might have. She would discover them soon enough if he made the offer she was hoping for. What a surprise it would be to everyone, include Elizabeth who was so certain of her own perspicacity!

Sir William Lucas prided himself on his status as the sponsor of various civic activities in Meryton, including hosting the celebration of Gunpowder Treason Day. All traces of hay had been removed from the field behind Lucas Lodge. Sir William had donated the traditional two cartloads of coal, which, when added to sticks of wood collected by the local youngsters, created a bonfire impressive enough that Sir William was noted to say on more than one occasion that it was as fine as any he had seen near St. James' Court. A few of the local gentry saw fit to attend, though they mostly remained inside Lucas Lodge except during the fireworks.

Charlotte had her own plans for the evening based on an earlier whispered communication from Mr. Robinson. She made a point of supervising the outdoor activities, wrapped in a dark, heavy shawl for warmth. Once darkness had fallen, Sir William with all due pomp thrust a lighted torch into the pile of combustibles. Cheers rang out as flames rose into the air, sending out a welcome pulse of heat. Children jostled to be as close as they dared, shouting to be heard over the crackling of the fire.

Charlotte allowed herself to drift toward the back of the crowd furthest from Lucas Lodge. She had not seen Mr. Robinson that evening. Perhaps he had been unable to come after all. Disappointed by his absence, she was disinclined to join the conversation inside and so remained on the periphery of the festivities. As the first fireworks shot into the sky created a cloud of sparkling lights, she felt hands descend on her hips and a familiar voice whispering her name in her ear, this time accompanied not by a brush of the lips but by a shocking nibble on her earlobe. "Will you walk with me?"

She understood now why he had not shown himself earlier. She would not have been allowed to walk out with him in the darkness, but this way she was free to go with him. All eyes were on the bonfire, though she knew other couples would be stealing away. There were always several hurried marriages after Bonfire Night.

He did not offer her his arm but rather laced his fingers through hers, which had the effect of making them look like the more ordinary peasant couples. He had also dressed in dark colors and simple clothes. Charlotte smiled to herself at the success of her plan. Finally, after all these years, she would have her own moment with an admirer.

As they ambled toward the small woods bordering the field, Mr. Robinson said, "I was hoping to speak to you privately tonight. Miss Lucas… Charlotte, we have not been acquainted long, but I feel as if I have known you for years. I will be going to visit my parents tomorrow, and I would like to seek my father's approval on asking a certain question, but I would not wish to make free with your name when addressing him without your permission. Would you, or do I ask too much, allow me to name you when speaking to my father?"

It was not precisely what she wished to hear, but she had to admire his delicacy in discussing the matter with his family prior to making an offer, and it was thrilling simply to know that he wished to. "I would have no objection," she said demurely. "Will you be away long?"

"I will return within a fortnight," he said with certainty, "and then I will speak to your father."

They reached the edge of the woods and he was still urging her on. Charlotte hesitated a moment, then followed him. After all, a few stolen kisses would only bind him to her more.

A Party at Lucas Lodge
by C. Allyn Pierson

November 10, 1811

Charlotte tapped her foot impatiently as she stared into the mirror and tried different looks for her hair. Tonight was her family's first party since Mr. Bingley and the militia had come to Meryton and her budding friendship with Mr. Robinson, as well as fresh infusion of gentlemen into the neighborhood, gave her a feeling of youth, even though she was twenty-seven years old and long on the shelf. After twenty minutes of struggling, she sighed. No matter how she swept her hair up she was still plain, old Charlotte, a woman of no fortune from a family who was barely hanging onto the appearance of gentility.

Finally, she gave in and had the maid put up her hair as she usually did for parties: smooth bands in front fastened up into a knot at the back of her head. No curls in her stubbornly straight, brown hair, just a small comb with paste jewels on the top for decoration. The maid finished her hair and helped her into her dress, the same she had worn last year, but which fitted her well and was suited to her plain, discreet appearance.

Once the guests began arriving, Charlotte helped her parents greet their guests and did her part as eldest daughter in making sure the servants kept the refreshment table filled. In between these duties, she talked to her friend Lizzy Bennet and observed the other guests. As a woman who was almost an ape leader, and knowing the Mr. Robinson was not known to her parents and therefore not expected tonight, her main enjoyment with this party would be to watch the young men and women in the dance of love, and tonight she had a particularly large number of potential couples to spy upon.

As was usual, the eldest Bennet sisters, her best friends and the beauties of the neighborhood, had a great deal of attention. Elizabeth was besieged by the officers, but, although she was pleasant and friendly to all, none of them seemed to make a particular impression upon her.

Charlotte herself was more interested in the colonel of the regiment, although she laughed at herself for suddenly feeling an interest in single men. How Mr. Robinson's attention caused her to feel more young and attractive she did not know, but so it was. Colonel Forster looked to be about thirty-eight and had a high enough rank to have a decent income to support a wife in comfort, if not in elegance. And, according to report, he was unmarried. She took an opportunity, while the younger officers were dancing attendance around the Bennet girls, to approach Colonel Forster and remind him to enjoy the refreshments available in the dining-room.

"I thank you, Miss Lucas, I am well taken care of and am fully occupied watching my younger officers to make sure they know how to behave in public." He smiled at her, his face with its ginger side-whiskers really quite pleasant. She returned his smile and tried to find something interesting to say, but was only able to come up with, "And how do you like Meryton, Colonel?"

"Very well, I thank you, Miss Lucas. More than half of my men are new to the militia and much in need of training, and it is excellent that they have so many opportunities to go into society here. We are most grateful for the welcome we have received in the community."

As she was steeling herself to respond in a somewhat flirtatious tone, Lizzy Bennet joined them, and the colonel became much more lively in his conversation, forgetting Charlotte immediately. Charlotte sighed to herself, once again resigning herself to be the invisible woman at the party. She did not blame either the colonel or Lizzy for dousing her hopes of gaining the colonel's interest. There was just no denying that the eldest Bennets were lovely, and she could not fault any man for preferring their company to hers.

After excusing herself to again check the refreshments, Charlotte poured herself a glass of punch and found a seat out of the way of the party-goers. Some of the older guests moved into the small parlour, where there was a pair of card tables, to escape the din, but Charlotte stayed where she was.

Across the room, well within her view, Miss Bennet stood talking to Mr. Bingley, she calm and smiling, and he eager, leaning toward her. Charlotte was reminded of a conversation she had had with Lizzy not long before. Her friend had agreed that Jane was well on her way to being in love with Mr. Bingley, but they had not agreed on how Jane should behave. Lizzy had been happy that her sister's demeanour was such that she would be spared the gossip of the vulgar over her friendship with Mr. Bingley, but Charlotte had differed. She had pointed out that to be so very guarded might cause the object of Jane's affections to not realize how deep her feelings were towards him. Lizzy had been rather shocked and pointed out that Jane did not yet know Mr. Bingley well enough to know if she truly liked him, or if he had some fatal flaw which would lead to disgust of him during a marriage.

She saw nothing this night to change her mind. If she had been a stranger to Jane, she would have had difficulty telling whether she was merely being her usual courteous self, or if she had a serious tendre for him. Charlotte sighed. If she had had the felicity to draw the attention of a handsome, wealthy man such as Mr. Bingley she would have made sure—in a lady-like way, of course—that he was in no doubt of her feelings.

As she scanned the crowded drawing-room, she noticed that Mr. Darcy, who had placed himself out of the crowd as she had, was watching Lizzy closely as she talked to the colonel. When Lizzy curtseyed and moved towards Charlotte, Mr. Darcy's eyes continued to follow her. Lizzy's first comment to Charlotte was, "What does Mr. Darcy mean by listening to my conversation with Colonel Forster?"

Charlotte smiled and answered, "That is a question which Mr. Darcy only can answer."

"But if he does it anymore, I shall certainly let him know that I see what he is about. He has a very satirical eye, and if I do not begin by being impertinent myself, I shall soon grow afraid of him."

When Mr. Darcy approached soon afterwards, Charlotte could not resist the temptation of challenging her friend to speak to him. Lizzy took up the challenge and spoke to him teasingly about her conversation with Colonel Forster. As the conversation became a bit more pert than Charlotte felt was to her friend's advantage, she opened the piano and urged Elizabeth to play. After a protest against playing for those who had heard the first performers play, Lizzy finally agreed, and Mr. Darcy settled into a corner to listen. While Darcy watched Elizabeth, Charlotte watched him, and was surprised to see the softness of his looks towards her friend.

After finishing a couple of ballads, which were very pleasant to listen to, Lizzy arose from the piano bench and Mary Bennet pushed her way onto it. Charlotte groaned. Mary's only interests were in acquiring accomplishments, but she had little talent and no taste, just an endless desire to exhibit to others.

It was not long before several of the officers were dragged over to an open space by Lydia and Kitty, the carpet rolled up, and an impromptu dance begun. Tsk. Those younger Bennet girls were brazen in their flirtations and quite hoydenish. As usual, Mrs. Bennet just looked on as her girls danced, not seeming to see any defects in their behavior. Perhaps she thought such boldness would improve their chances of capturing husbands. Charlotte could not deny the girls were very popular with the officers, but could Mrs. Bennet think that all these penurious younger sons would truly make good husbands? After watching Jane Bennet and her younger sisters, she sighed, longing for the girls to achieve a happy medium in their behavior between boldness and perfect serenity.

During the dancing, Charlotte noticed her father approaching Mr. Darcy and winced inwardly. She dared to hope he would not embarrass his family with his obsequiousness. Mr. Darcy seemed to take her father's comments very coldly, but he at least answered Sir William's sallies instead of merely walking away. Soon Charlotte saw

Lizzy passing the two men, her attention on her sisters, who were becoming rather boisterous. Sir William stopped her and spoke with her and she seemed rather nonplussed as Mr. Darcy bowed and reached out to take her hand. Elizabeth's cheeks reddened and she shook her head and smiled, but Charlotte could see that her friend was quite embarrassed. Finally, Lizzy gave Mr. Darcy an arch look and walked off to control her sisters, while he continued to stare after her with a complacent look on his face.

Charlotte saw Miss Bingley making her way towards Mr. Darcy with a sardonic look on her face, and longed to hear their conversation. She swept towards them, looking away as if she was merely heading towards the door, but stopped just behind them to adjust her bracelet, which had, fortuitously, become entangled in the fringe of her shawl. She heard Miss Bingley say, "…which lady has the credit of inspiring such reflections?"

Darcy, his eyes still on Elizabeth, said, "Miss Elizabeth Bennet."

Charlotte glanced up in surprise. The speakers seemed to feel her presence and lowered their voices, but Miss Bingley appeared to be teasing Mr. Darcy while he listened with perfect indifference. Charlotte was perplexed. Did Mr. Darcy actually have a compliment to pay Lizzy, or had she misunderstood their words?

Caroline Invites Jane to Netherfield
by Kara Louise

November 12, 1811

Caroline Bingley marched with strident steps back and forth, her arms folded tightly in front of her. She was quite perturbed that Charles had accepted an invitation to dine with some officers in Meryton. She was perturbed not so much that he was going, but that Mr. Darcy agreed to accompany him, commenting that he hoped to find intelligent conversation amongst them. She shook her head and let out a huff. What would it take for the man to realize he could readily find that with her? And so much more?

When it was settled that the two gentlemen and Mr. Hurst would go, Charles approached his sister with a suggestion.

"Caroline, since we will be away, this would be a perfect opportunity to invite Miss Bennet to tea so you and Louisa can further your acquaintance with her." He smiled eagerly, waiting for her to respond in hearty agreement.

Her mouth opened, but she could not formulate words to express what she truly thought of his suggestion. She could have readily explained to him how little she wished to do this, that she thought Miss Bennet a sweet girl, but certainly not the right one for him. However, Caroline determined to display nothing but polite acquiescence to him, especially with Mr. Darcy seated nearby. She returned a smile and told him she thought that was a splendid idea. She reluctantly sent an invitation to Miss Bennet to join her and Louisa at Netherfield.

On the morning of the concurrent visits, a dreary chill invaded the county, very much like what Caroline felt, despite the warmth inside Netherfield. Thick clouds settled over Meryton, and Caroline was fairly certain a storm was imminent. She wondered whether Miss Bennet might be forced to abandon the plan if it began to rain. In truth, she ardently hoped she would!

Caroline was determined to make some good out of this situation, and when Mr. Darcy joined her in the sitting room as he waited for the other two men, she summoned the housekeeper.

In a rather loud voice she said, "Mrs. Lewis, I want to make sure everything is ready for our guest later today. She is to be received with the utmost hospitality, and I will spare nothing for her comfort."

The housekeeper nodded. "Yes, Miss Bingley. We have everything prepared for her visit as you requested."

"Good! I am so glad to hear that!" She stole a glance at Mr. Darcy, hoping he had overheard and would be impressed with how well she performed her duties as Mistress of Netherfield. For her greatest wish was to be Mistress of Pemberley!

As the men prepared to leave, Caroline watched Mr. Darcy don his heavy overcoat. Such a fine specimen of a man! She let out a soft sigh as she considered that not many of Charles' friends were much of a benefit to him, let alone to her. Mr. Darcy certainly had changed all that.

When the men took their leave, Louisa and Caroline sat in front of the blazing fire in the sitting room. As they waited for Miss Bennet, each silently hoped that the time spent with her would pass quickly. Caroline gazed out the window, noticing how dark it had become, and soon after, they heard the sound of rain pelting the windows.

"Oh, Louisa! It is a torrent out there. I daresay Miss Bennet will most likely not venture out in this! I would imagine we will spend our afternoon by ourselves!" She settled back comfortably into her chair and let out a long, drawn-out sigh, followed by a satisfied smile.

"Such a pity!" laughed Louisa.

"Yes," Caroline said softly. Then turning to Louisa, she added, "For Charles!"

At the sound of the bell a short while later, the two ladies looked at each other in surprise. Neither said a word, but it was apparent they were both thinking the same thing. Certainly it could not be Miss Bennet!

When Mrs. Lewis appeared at the door and announced Miss Bennet, Caroline could do little to conceal a gasp. Their guest was soaking wet, water was dripping onto the floor, and her appearance was completely deplorable.

"My dear Miss Bennet!" Caroline exclaimed, forcing herself to rise to her feet. "Whatever has happened? You are positively drenched from head to toe!"

Louisa and Caroline quickly attended to Miss Bennet as she explained that she had ridden over on a horse in the hopes of escaping the storm, but it had begun to rain much earlier than she had anticipated. Dry clothes were ordered for her and they had their ladies' maid escort her upstairs to assist her in changing into them.

When she left the room, they could not hold their tongues about the foolishness she had exhibited in riding from Longbourn to Netherfield on horseback instead of taking a carriage. In a rain storm! She should not have ventured out at all!

"Upon my word, Louisa! I can hardly believe it! Such reckless actions!"

"I quite agree, Caroline. What could she have been thinking?"

"It shows an ill-bred thoughtlessness, if you ask me."

The two ladies agreed that someone established in good society would never have exhibited such behaviour.

While Miss Bennet was still upstairs, Caroline tugged at her sister's sleeve. "Louisa, I am becoming more and more convinced of Miss Bennet's unsuitability. While she is here today, we shall have the perfect opportunity to determine exactly what her family connections are."

Louisa gave her a quizzical look. "Do you have any doubt they shall prove to be deficient, Caroline?"

Caroline let out a cackle. "Of course not, but it shall be fun prying the information out of her!" The two ladies laughed in conspiratorial accord.

When Miss Bennet returned, she expressed her gratitude to the ladies, and they repaired to the dining room.

Caroline and Louisa questioned Miss Bennet politely about her family, her accomplishments, and a variety of other carefully picked subjects. She was most forthright in her answers, but it was her admission that she had an uncle in trade in Cheapside that prompted Louisa and Caroline to exchange pointed glances with each other. This was abominable!

At first, Miss Bennet acquitted herself reasonably well to the interrogation. However, Caroline soon began to notice that her face was ashen and she did not have the usual serene countenance that she normally displayed. At length it became apparent that she was feeling quite ill, and they thought it best to adjourn to the sitting room where she could be settled in front of the warm fire.

As the rain continued to pour down in torrents throughout the rest of the afternoon, Caroline and Louisa became resigned to the fact that Miss Bennet would be forced to remain with them at Netherfield. It would be uncivil to send her home in this tempest when she was feeling so poorly.

As Caroline attempted to make Miss Bennet comfortable, she inwardly hoped the gentlemen would return directly or that the rain would let up. Unfortunately, her hopes were in vain; Miss Bennet continued to exhibit increasing distress, the men were absent the whole of the afternoon, and the rain continued without intermission.

Caroline and Louisa saw to it that Miss Bennet was taken to a room and settled comfortably in bed, and then Caroline sent a missive to Longbourn informing her parents of her illness.

The two ladies returned to the sitting room and Caroline heaved a sigh as she sat down in a plush chair. "This has certainly been an interesting day, Louisa. I did not think anything could surpass Miss Bennet's grand arrival, but then to hear her talk about her uncle in trade…"

"In Cheapside, no less!" added Louisa with an air of disgust. "And she volunteered that information so readily! It appears she feels no shame in admitting it!"

"I daresay she does not." Caroline slowly clasped her hands together.

"We would never mention our…"

"No, we would not!" Caroline cut her off directly.

Louisa cast a side glance at her sister. "Will Charles feel the same repugnance we feel in this matter?"

"Oh, Louisa, I fear our brother may not." Caroline's voice trailed off.

A sly smile appeared as she thought of something – Mr. Darcy! He would have influence over her brother and would certainly show him how inferior Miss Bennet is… if he does not realize it on his own.

And having Miss Bennet here for her to care for would allow Mr. Darcy to see just how compassionate she could be toward someone in ill health. She nodded her head slowly and a devious gleam appeared in her eyes. Yes, she would go out of her way to ensure Miss Bennet's comfort and see to her every need. Mr. Darcy would have every reason to be impressed!

She settled back into her chair and began to hum.

"You seem quite content, Caroline," Louisa said. "Whatever are you plotting?"

"Plotting? Me?" She waved a hand at her sister. "I am merely thinking that things may work out much better than what I ever expected."

Darcy's Interest Piques as Miss Elizabeth and Miss Bingley Take a Turn about the Room by Regina Jeffers

November 15, 1811

(Scene: Earlier in the day, Elizabeth has defended Charles Bingley against Darcy's criticism of the man's poor penmanship. She also has praised Bingley's amiability.)

As the evening progressed, Darcy, having finished his letter to his sister, wished to relieve the earlier tension. "Might I apply to you to entertain us on the pianoforte?" He directed his request to both Miss Elizabeth and Miss Bingley.

Jumping, literally, at the opportunity to do something to secure Darcy's favor, he watched in bemusement as Miss Bingley was beside the pianoforte before she realized her duties as the manor's hostess. "Miss Elizabeth," she had said through gritted teeth, "would you favor us by going first?"

"Please continue, Miss Bingley," Miss Elizabeth responded sweetly. "Your skill should take precedence to my pleasure." Feeling her superiority, Miss Bingley had entertained their party with several Italian love songs.

Enthralled with her performance, at Lucas Lodge Miss Elizabeth's deferment to Miss Bingley initially had disappointed Darcy. Still, being given the comparable pleasure of watching her figure as she posed before the pianoforte was nearly as intoxicating. Over the weeks he had observed her, he had mentally created a list of Miss Elizabeth's mannerisms—the biting of her lower lip when concentrating on her needlework, the creased forehead when she challenged him, and the unruly curl, which often fell, along her chin line in a caress of her neck and with which she fought a constant battle. Fitzwilliam Darcy had seen little about Elizabeth Bennet, which had not fascinated him.

Before he realized what he had done, Darcy moved up to stand beside Miss Elizabeth at the instrument. The moment he found himself in her close proximity, the air intensified around him, and a sudden thud stunned his heart. He shifted his shoulders to appear relaxed, but his body screamed to know more of her. Feigning disinterest, he, too, thumbed through the sheet music scattered about the instrument's polished surface.

He recognized the instant Miss Bingley became aware of his nearness to the second Bennet sister. The lady ceased her rendering of the love sonatas and offered instead the charm a lively Scottish air. Yet, even that manipulation of the room's atmosphere did not change the hypnotic trance Elizabeth Bennet held over him. He quite suspected it would be so, even if he found himself across from her on the most crowded dance floor that Almack's could offer. Unexplainably, he was drawn to the lady, and he had surrendered to the allure. Unable not to engage her in witty repartee, Darcy turned to Elizabeth and said, "Do you not feel a great inclination, Miss Bennet, to seize such an opportunity of dancing a reel?"

As soon as he said the words, annoyance filled him. He wanted desperately to say something, which would engage Elizabeth and would make her see him in as a charming conversationalist. Instead, she could easily think Darcy meant to bam her country manners. Those of refined and exacting taste did, after all, not prefer reels. Miss Elizabeth could easily interpret his words as a poorly hidden cut.

She smiled, but made no answer. Her silence surprised him. Instantaneously, Darcy wished to know why she kept her tongue; he could not alter the original question, so he repeated it

"Never fear, Mr. Darcy, I heard you before, but I could not

immediately determine how to reply. You wanted me, I know, to say 'Yes,' that you might have the pleasure of despising my taste; but I always delight in overthrowing those kinds of schemes and in cheating a person of their premeditated contempt. I have, therefore, made up my mind to tell you I do not want to dance a reel at all— and now despise me if you dare."

Darcy could not disengage his mind from thoughts of Elizabeth soft lips. She was resplendent! That was all he could think. "Despise you? Indeed I do not dare. No, Madam, I could never have such an opinion of you, Miss Elizabeth," he said, before bowing to her as he took his leave of the room, feeling her eyes piercing his back. He sought refuge in Bingley's study. Pouring an abundant serving of brandy, Darcy collapsed into a nearby chair. As he ran his fingers through his hair, he realized no woman had ever affected him in such a manner—he felt bewitched by Elizabeth Bennet. And were it not for the inferiority of her connections, Darcy could easily imagine himself in some danger of falling in love with the lady.

* * *

Suppertime found changes in the spherical makeup of the Netherfield party; Miss Jane Bennet made an appearance in the drawing room upon the meal's completion. With the woman's entrance, Darcy offered his congratulations regarding her recovery before amusedly watching his close friend stoking the fire to warm the room and to attend to Miss Bennet's every need. Bingley was quite besotted of the lady.

Meanwhile, Darcy found a chair where he could observe Miss Elizabeth, who obviously delighted in the attention being given to her sister by the master of the house. Having no wish to play cards, Darcy had chosen a book to cover his interest in the lady. It was not surprising then to him when Miss Bingley also chose a book. Of course, Caroline held no real interest in improving her mind; her pretense was for Darcy's sake, and his was to disguise his obsession with Miss Elizabeth. It was all quite ironic. Caroline, obviously, had recalled his previous remarks to Miss Elizabeth regarding the qualities of a refined lady. "All this she must possess, and to all this she must yet add something more substantial in the improvement of her mind by extensive reading."

He recognized Miss Bingley's plan to interfere if he showed attention to Miss Elizabeth. It was a clever trick many women of the *ton* practiced when a fit of jealousy plagued them. Therefore, her predictable questions on what he read and what it meant had not taken Darcy unawares. As far as good manners would permit, he ignored Caroline Bingley. He steadfastly continued to read his book choice.

A deep sigh of exasperation accompanied Miss Bingley's tossing aside her chosen book, but still Darcy refused a response. With a renewed resolve brought on by the warm brandy, he had made it plain that he would ignore both Miss Bingley and Miss Elizabeth, but he had not anticipated Caroline's next maneuver. The lady called upon the one area in which she, evidently, felt she excelled over Elizabeth Bennet—physical beauty, and she took it upon herself of being noticed by walking about the room. Darcy, upon whom she directed her attention, remained content to read, never raising an eyebrow or looking her way.

He had thought himself quite clever until desperation overcame Caroline's jealous tendencies. She sweetly said, "Miss Eliza Bennet, let me persuade you to follow my example, and take a turn about the room. I assure you it is very refreshing after sitting so long in one attitude."

Miss Bingley had succeeded in one area: she had received Darcy's attention; he looked up, surprised to see Miss Elizabeth reluctant consent to such a devious plan. Why Caroline chose to invite Elizabeth to join her had piqued his curiosity. Elizabeth, too, appeared wary of the invitation. After all, the two women had "fenced" their way through multiple conversations over the previous month. No one with any degree of intelligence would think them intimates. Without knowledge of his actions, Darcy unconsciously closed his book.

"Will you not join us, Mr. Darcy?" Miss Bingley nearly purred.

"I will decline your kind offer, Madam. I assume you have but two motives for choosing to walk up and down the room together, and I would interfere with either of them."

"What could he mean, Miss Eliza?" Miss Bingley queried. The woman could never decipher his double-meaning barbs, but he quickly noted the delight dancing in Miss Elizabeth's eyes. She would be an excellent match for his propensity to play with words.

Miss Elizabeth would recognize his playful tone; she would meet his double *entendre* with one of her own—matching him wit for wit. Darcy recognized the resolve of her shoulders, the half stifled grin playing about her lips, and the arching of an amused eyebrow. All these things sent sensations down his body; every nerve pulsed. Pausing briefly to make her point, Miss Elizabeth turned slightly toward Darcy. It was all he could do not to walk over and take her in his embrace She taunted, "Depend upon it, he means to be severe on us, and our surest way of disappointing him will be to ask nothing about it."

Very good. It was exactly the type of banter he had come to expect from Elizabeth Bennet.

Predictably, Caroline, who would not risk his poor favor, said, "Nonsense. We must know the gentleman's meaning. Mr. Darcy, whatever can you mean by such a remark? You must explain, as we are very anxious to know its meaning."

Darcy had considered his response for its impact on Elizabeth Bennet. It was with her he flirted. "I have not the smallest objection to explaining them. You either choose this method of passing the evening because you are in each other's confidence and have secret affairs to discuss, or because you are conscious your figures appear to the greatest advantage in walking." At this point he left a purposeful pregnant pause to increase the drama of the situation. "If the first, I would be completely in your way, and if the second, I can admire you much better as I sit by the fire."

Take that, Elizabeth Bennet; the triumph crept across his countenance. His eyes met Elizabeth's, burrowing deep into the green pools and locking in a secret desire. Maintaining his gaze with her companion, Darcy heard Miss Bingley's stunned response, "Oh! Shocking! I never heard anything so abominable. How shall we punish him for such a speech?"

Darcy waited with anticipation for Elizabeth's response. "Tease him—laugh at him. Intimate as you are, you must know how it is to be done." He had never expected the lady would dare to laugh at him. As much as he had hoped to maintain her gaze, Darcy experienced a momentary glint of uncertainty and dropped his eyes, breaking the bond.

Naturally, Miss Bingley would never speak ill of Darcy; she desired his good opinion too much to defy him on any subject. "Mr. Darcy is the superior companion," the lady declared. "He has no faults."

Having bested him in their battle for dominance, Miss Elizabeth, carried away with the mirth of the situation, would not permit her love of nonsense to wane. She professed, "Mr. Darcy does nothing which might amuse his acquaintances? I would not require many such friends for I dearly love a laugh."

Not able to abandon the serious armor, which had served him well in the past, Darcy assumed an air of superiority. He had required Miss Elizabeth's respect and the lady's understanding. He had thought her a good match for his sister Georgiana, but her willingness to attack him with intent caused Darcy to reconsider. "Miss Bingley has given me more credit than can be. The wisest and best of men—nay, the wisest and best of their actions—may be rendered ridiculous by a person whose first object in life is a joke."

He had thought his words might provide her pause, but without considering the effect, Miss Elizabeth replied, "Certainly, there are such people, but I hope I am not one of them. I hope I never ridicule what is wise or good. Follies and nonsense, whims and inconsistencies, do divert me, I own, and I laugh at them whenever I can. But these, I suppose, are precisely what you are without."

Having spent his life hating any form of weakness, Darcy's former affectionate gaze took on a steeled impalement; nearly biting the words, he said, "Perhaps that is not possible for anyone. But it has been the study of my life to avoid such weaknesses which often expose a strong understanding to ridicule."

"What sort of weaknesses, Mr. Darcy? Would, say, vanity or possibly pride be such a weakness?" she retorted.

Swallowing hard, Darcy steadied his response. "Yes, vanity is a weakness indeed. But pride—where there is a real superiority of mind, pride will be always under good regulation."

Miss Elizabeth's suppression of a smile had surprised Darcy. He had found nothing amusing in what he had said; he had meant his response to be a serious, diplomatic answer. He considered her reaction beyond the pale. Amusing repartee was one thing, but he would not be her target, no matter what attraction he had felt for this insipid miss. He glared at her with an intensity he did not think possible.

"I beg you," Miss Bingley spoke into the room's silence. "Let us forget this foolish talk. We must find some other means to amuse ourselves."

He watched in disgust as Elizabeth feigned innocence and coquettishly played down her affront. "I agree with you, Miss Bingley, Mr. Darcy has no faults; perfection is within his reach."

Her sideways compliment had infuriated him. "No!" he growled. "I have made no such pretension." Miss Elizabeth, obviously, knew nothing of superior society. "I have faults enough," he continued, "but they are not, I hope, of understanding. My temper I dare not vouch for. It is, I believe, too little yielding—certainly too little for the convenience of the world. I cannot forget the follies and vices of others so soon as I ought, nor their offenses against myself. My feelings are not puffed about with every attempt to move them. My temper would perhaps be called resentful. My good opinion once lost, is lost forever."

Earlier in the day, Miss Elizabeth had defended Bingley's appearance of humility, but she now attacked him! Darcy had come to the speedy conclusion she knew nothing about him and cared not to recognize his worth. He had misjudged Elizabeth Bennet's excellence! His full being retreated from the woman to whom he had given his exclusive attention of late.

"Your faults, as you define them, Mr. Darcy, are not open to scorn; possibly they are a bit too dark in nature, but they are not failings. I will not laugh at you, Mr. Darcy; you have nothing to fear from me."

She had given him a slight curtsy and had turned away. He thought, *Wait this is not finished!* Before Elizabeth could exit, he froze her step by coldly saying, "There is, I believe, in every disposition a tendency to some particular evil—a natural defect, which not even the best education can overcome."

"And your defect is to hate everybody."

"And yours, Miss Elizabeth," he replied with a smile, "is willfully to misunderstand them." For a moment they held each other's application; then, Darcy nodded his head to permit Elizabeth to return to her sister. His emotional turmoil became difficult for him to conceal from the others so he made his excuses and retired for the evening. Yet, he carried the heat of their confrontation between his shoulders as he climbed Netherfield's main staircase. Tonight, he had discovered that paying so much attention to Elizabeth Bennet was not as delightful as he had imagined it to be.

Darcy Adheres to His Book
by Abigail Reynolds

November 16, 1811

To Mr. Darcy it was welcome intelligence—Elizabeth had been at Netherfield long enough. She attracted him more than he liked—and Miss Bingley was uncivil to her, and more teasing than usual to himself. He wisely resolved to be particularly careful that no sign of admiration should now escape him, nothing that could elevate her with the hope of influencing his felicity; sensible that if such an idea had been suggested, his behaviour during the last day must have material weight in confirming or crushing it. Steady to his purpose, he scarcely spoke ten words to her through the whole of Saturday, and though they were at one time left by themselves for half an hour, he adhered most conscientiously to his book, and would not even look at her. – Pride & Prejudice

"I will leave you to your book, then." With those words, Bingley departed the room, leaving Darcy and Elizabeth in sole possession of it.

Good God! Had it not been struggle enough to avoid engaging Elizabeth in conversation all morning, saying nothing beyond the very least required for civility? How could Bingley have actually left him alone with Elizabeth? Darcy was not prepared for such an eventuality, having been certain that Miss Bingley would not permit such a tête-à-tête, but she was off somewhere, no doubt haranguing the housekeeper for some imagined fault. And here he was, at last alone with the woman who had so bewitched him, with nothing but his own determination to stand between them.

He had to forcibly remind himself of the importance of demonstrating to Elizabeth that she should have no expectations of him; it was bad enough that Bingley was constantly dangling after her sister. Beautiful and well mannered as Miss Jane Bennet might be, she would not do as a wife for him. Bingley needed a bride of higher breeding to improve his status in the *ton*; Georgiana, when she came of age, would be a far better choice for him, and it would solve Darcy's own dilemma of finding a husband for her who would not intimidate her or take advantage of her gentle nature. And Elizabeth Bennet would be an even less suitable bride for the Master of Pemberley.

No! He could not afford to even consider such a thing; it brought visions of Elizabeth more suitable for his private nocturnal imaginings of her. He needed to focus on his book and on appearing completely indifferent to her presence. How much easier that was said than done! He had already quite forgotten what he had been reading about, although the page was still open in front of him.

The sound of turning pages alerted him that Elizabeth must have picked up a book as well, and he mentally breathed a sigh of relief. He could not look at her; that would defeat his entire purpose, but surely it would not hurt to steal one brief glance in her direction when she was engaged in reading.

He immediately regretted his decision. Another woman might appear uninteresting when reading, but not Elizabeth. Her lips were half-parted in a smile at whatever she was reading, and with her free hand, she was unconsciously toying with one of the dark curls that lay against the soft skin of her face. That was the damnable thing about Elizabeth; her hands were so often in motion, seeming enamoured of exploring every tactile sensation in her vicinity, so that a man could think of nothing but how she might touch him with the same sensual curiosity. It was a subtle betrayal of the passionate nature so clearly within her. She might be unaware of it now, but the right man would be able to awaken it, and all that suppressed passion would pour forth onto that fortunate soul. God, but he hated to think of her with any man but himself! That she could turn those fine eyes on anyone else or that such incredible fire might burn for another man! But she was not for him. She could not be for him. He had duties and responsibilities, and he must remember that at all cost.

It was better to think that she would never marry and that she would pass her lifetime in the enchanting unawakened state he witnessed now. Or perhaps her husband might be one of those with little interest in his wife, and never see the sensual possibilities in Elizabeth's bearing and even the way she breathed. What sort of man was he to be wishing an indifferent husband on this bewitching woman? He knew the answer to that too well: he was the sort who would do almost anything to possess her himself. *Almost* anything. His family honor and duty must take precedence even over his near-desperate physical need.

Perhaps he should speak to her after all – her sparkling repartee could be no more dangerous to his self-control than his private thoughts, and at least in those moments of conversation, he could imagine he was the only man in her world. But no, he must protect *her* as well from expectations of him; it was the only honorable thing to do. Damn honor! Why must it stand in the way of him taking for his own the one woman in all of creation that he wanted above all others?

He heard another page turning, and realized with a shock that he himself had been staring blindly at the same page for a quarter hour now. Quickly he flipped to the next page and forced his eyes to scan the lines, though for the life of him he could not take in a word of it. It might as well have been in Chinese for all the sense it made to him. How could he think of anything else when Elizabeth was but a few feet from him? Good God, how her mere *breathing* light up the entire room on this cloudy, dismal day?

Elizabeth's soft, musical laugh filled the air, and he risked another glance in her direction, just to reassure himself that it was her book and not himself that gave her amusement. At least that was his excuse; the truth was that he could not resist. The ladies of the *ton* would never lower themselves so far as to laugh; it would not fit the bored, languid persona demanded by high style. Elizabeth showed her amusement frequently, as suited so lively a woman, and it did not matter how much he knew she would be scorned in the London ballrooms for it. His body reacted viscerally every time she laughed, wanting to hear that lovely sound again at the same time as he longed to stop it with his own lips. Not for the first time during her stay at Netherfield, he thanked merciful heaven for the fashion in trousers. If gentlemen were still required to wear tight breeches, he would have had to spend half his time hiding behind furniture.

He was starting to lose the battle with himself. He was too desperate for her, too desperate for her to turn those laughing fine eyes on him, to awaken that part of his soul that had remained dormant these many years during which he had been unmoved by the most beautiful ladies of the *ton*. He needed to gaze his fill of her – as if that could ever happen! – and to cross verbal swords with her once more before she left Netherfield. What if he never saw her again, or only across a crowded room, never close enough to share a conversation with her? It was untenable, just as untenable as the idea that he, Fitzwilliam Darcy, Master of Pemberley, would lose his vaunted self-control to any woman, much less one as unsuitable and hauntingly tempting as Elizabeth Bennet.

Just then Miss Bingley entered the room, saving him from himself. If only he could manage to be grateful for the interruption, and not feel like he had lost something precious because he could no longer sit in silence alone in a room with his own Elizabeth!

Elizabeth and Jane
Leave Netherfield
by Susan Adriani

November 17, 1811

Darcy watched from his bedchamber window, solemn and serious, as Elizabeth Bennet shook hands with Caroline Bingley on Netherfield's front steps, a polite smile upon her lips as she took a step backward toward the carriage, where a solicitous Bingley waited with her sister Jane. The master of Pemberley did not have to see the expression on Miss Bingley's face to know that she was likely nothing short of ecstatic to bid farewell to her guests.

Though Darcy did not quite share the same level of enthusiasm for the ladies' departure as his hostess, he could not deny he was relieved by their going. Four days in the same house with Elizabeth Bennet had been long enough; long enough to acquaint him with her arch looks and the melodic sound of her laughter, the depth of her dark eyes and the intelligent turn of her mind, the sway of her hips as she moved about a room, the lone, glossy curl that rebelled against its constraints in order to brazenly, constantly, lovingly caress her cheek. It was the exact manner in which Darcy had dreamed of touching her himself every single night since he had noticed her—truly noticed her—in Sir William Lucas' drawing room not so long ago.

At last Miss Bingley turned and entered the house, her steps quick and purposeful, no doubt eager to put an end to any discourse and hasten the Bennets' departure. Darcy could not help but notice the smile Elizabeth wore grow considerably warmer for Bingley as he handed her into the carriage and shut the door, rapping upon the side to signal the driver while waving to the ladies within. Elizabeth continued to smile from the curtained window, her fair sister settled serenely by her side. She raised her gloved hand in adieu, and a moment later the conveyance lurched forward, commencing the three mile journey to Longbourn.

Darcy expelled a slow, measured breath as the carriage turned onto the main road and disappeared entirely from his sight. Surely, three miles should be safe enough, he thought pensively. After all, three miles was a far greater distance than the three meager place settings laid between himself and Elizabeth at Bingley's dining table, or the three paltry meters between their chairs when they sat reading together in the library the day before. Darcy closed his eyes and swallowed thickly as his thoughts wandered, as they often did, into far more unsettling territory: namely, the three imposing, but penetrable doors between their respective bedchambers that had driven him to indulge in more brandy than usual the evening before.

Several torturous hours had followed, where Darcy paced his apartment like a caged tiger; wild, lust-induced declarations on the tip of his tongue as a slightly drunken haze encouraged him to contemplate a most improper rendezvous. It was nearly dawn before the rational portion of his head had prevailed over the deepest desires of his heart and he was finally able to sleep. But sleep had come at a price, and that price was the last vestiges of his sanity as Elizabeth Bennet once again invaded his dreams with alluring eyes and a sultry smile. Pink lips and pale skin, lush curves, and a tangle of limbs—both hers and his own—were Darcy's sweetest torture until his man Jennings cruelly threw open the curtains, chasing the enchanting nymph from his bed, leaving Darcy alone, squinting in the harsh sunlight; cursing his own existence while his head throbbed painfully.

Frowning at the memory, Pemberley's master walked into the adjoining sitting room, his fingers massaging stiff muscles at the back of his neck. Good Lord, he was tired! He doubted he had slept more than a handful of hours in the last four days, and none of them restful. Whether awake or asleep, his head—and even more disturbing, his heart—was forever full of Elizabeth Bennet. Constantly did he torment himself by imagining the ecstasy to be found buried in her warmth; the succulence of her taste, or the incredible intimacy of knowing her most tantalizing, forbidden scent. Darcy inhaled raggedly, closing his eyes as his breaths quickened and his entire body pulsed with desire at the thought. He clenched his fists and his jaw as he attempted to find some modicum of calm amidst this maelstrom of emotions in which he found himself, forcing himself to recall her unsuitability, her lack of fortune, and the lowness of her connections; reciting each out loud, with the fervent hope that his words and the direness of his situation would finally register sense.

He sank heavily onto an upholstered chair by the hearth and cursed himself for his complete lack of control where Elizabeth was concerned. Obviously, three miles was not going to be nearly adequate enough to effectively distance himself from this impertinent enchantress. Darcy forced a bitter, sardonic laugh at the irony of it all and covered his eyes with slightly shaking hands. Considering the all-encompassing power this slip of a woman managed to wield over him in so short a time, he suspected that not even three days distance would be enough to inure him to her charms, and he was damned if he knew what to do about it.

Mr. Collins at Longbourn
by Susan Adriani

November 18, 1811

Mr. Collins was not a sensible man. – Pride & Prejudice

"My dear Mr. Collins," Mrs. Bennet gushed, "I always knew you would be a sensible man!"

Her husband rolled his eyes as the clergyman smiled complacently at Longbourn's mistress, inclining his head in a show of practiced deference while Mrs. Bennet stirred the fire. Mr. Bennet had found the man anything but sensible since his arrival the day before, and was now greatly disappointed that the novelty attached to his ridiculous cousin had lost its luster and rubbed his patience raw so early on in the visit. He shook out his newspaper and reached for his tea, attempting to ignore the other two occupants of the room and their indolent chatter.

"Being in possession of such a generous living as Hunsford must be a most agreeable situation," his wife continued. "Luck has certainly smiled upon you, sir, firstly with that odious business of the entail, and secondly with the bestowal of such an attentive benefactress. To be the recipient of such astounding good fortune must be something, indeed!"

"I cannot complain," Mr. Collins grinned, "especially after seeing Longbourn and all of its bounty; and by bounty, I must, of course, include your daughters, madam, for, outside of the incomparable beauty of Rosings Park—which, as you already know, is very grand—I have never met with lovelier creatures. God has certainly been good to you! To be blessed with such comely daughters is surely amongst the highest accomplishments any parent can hope to achieve. If you would permit me to be so bold, their beauty is solely a credit to you as their mother."

Mrs. Bennet tittered satisfactorily.

"But," he entreated, "allow me to thank you, my dear lady, for so efficiently and conscientiously bringing to my attention the news of the eldest Miss Bennet's prior attachment and pending engagement, for I would never wish to come between the connubial felicity of any two persons, even if it means risking the displeasure of my noble patroness, Lady Catherine de Bourgh, whose generosity and condescension deserves every courtesy and consideration, I assure you."

"But surely," Mrs. Bennet observed with much energy and feeling, "Her Ladyship will be equally pleased, if not more so with your second choice, sir, for my Lizzy is as dear, sweet, compliant a girl as ever there was! I daresay she will make you an excellent wife, Mr. Collins. I feel I must give you a word of advice, though. My second daughter, you see, is somewhat…shy when it comes to the business of courting, and may require a bit of encouragement on your part—nothing out of the ordinary, mind you. I have confidence in you, Mr. Collins! A gentleman such as yourself—so charming, so well-mannered—can do the job handsomely."

Upon hearing Elizabeth's name mentioned in such a disturbing context, Mr. Bennet choked on his tea. What the devil can that silly woman be thinking now, pairing Elizabeth with this fool of a man! From what he had seen of his cousin in the last twenty-four hours alone, he was fairly certain that his cleverest daughter, with her rapier wit and even sharper tongue, could never make such a man as Mr. Collins happy; and Mr. Bennet was further convinced that the sycophantic, weak-minded Mr. Collins was probably the last man in the world whom his impertinent Lizzy could ever be prevailed upon to marry.

As he was not privy to Mr. Bennet's thoughts on the subject, Mr. Collins merely giggled. "You are too kind, madam, and I daresay very astute in your observations, for I happen to pride myself on having quite a talent for flattery. Being a clergyman, you see, I feel it is part of my humble duty to pay to those of the fairer sex such elegant little compliments as will serve to gratify their vanity without offending their delicate sensibilities. Be it an observation about a young lady's beauty and dress, or a few well-chosen words in reference to her taste and feminine accomplishments, I am always happy to provide such a service as the occasion at hand requires; of course, I do try to give my little speeches as unstudied an air as possible."

Mr. Bennet snorted. He was under no illusion that his second daughter would not have a very different opinion on the subject, and though he felt in his heart that he ought to warn her of the impending doom that awaited her at her mother's hands, for the time-being he decided to hold his tongue. Perhaps, he chuckled to himself, Mr. Collins is still good for a bit of entertainment after all.

As the clergyman chattered on to his wife in much the same manner as he had been, Mr. Bennet rose from the table, folding his paper and tucking it neatly beneath his arm. He had had enough amusement for one morning, and was determined to preserve what was left of his good humour for later, when Elizabeth would no doubt learn of her supposed fate. His Lizzy was anything but predictable, though, and Mr. Bennet could hardly wait for the spectacle to commence.

Wickham and Denny in Meryton
by Jack Caldwell

November 19, 1811

Lydia's intention of walking to Meryton was not forgotten; every sister except Mary agreed to go with her; and Mr. Collins was to attend them (...) In pompous nothings on his side, and civil assents on that of his cousins, their time passed till they entered Meryton. The attention of the younger ones was then no longer to be gained by him. Their eyes were immediately wandering up in the street in quest of the officers, and nothing less than a very smart bonnet indeed, or a really new muslin in a shop window, could recall them. - Pride & Prejudice

The return from London by post was not unpleasant for Archibald Denny, lieutenant of militia, but his good humor was not only due to his traveling companion. George Wickham was an engaging sort of rascal much like himself, always ready to enjoy a drink or a barmaid. Their lively conversation made the hours in the crowded coach fly by, and before he knew it, Denny was back in Meryton.

No, Denny's happy mood was due to two different reasons. First, his contacts in Town had finally borne fruit, and there was at last the opportunity to acquire the funds he needed to buy a lieutenancy in the Regulars. Second, with his return to Hertfordshire, Denny hoped to further his acquaintance with Miss Lydia Bennet, the pretty and lively daughter of a local gentleman.

"To what sort of place have you brought me, Denny?" said Wickham, looking out the window as the carriage came to a stop.

"A most delightful country town," Denny assured him. "The fellows in the regiment are a jolly bunch, and the local girls are comely and friendly."

Wickham grinned. "Jolly and comely—my favorite sort of people! Lead on, my friend!"

Upon exiting the post carriage, Denny arranged for their trunks to be delivered to the militia's camp, but instead of reporting directly to Colonel Forster and finalizing Wickham's commission in the regiment, Denny agreed to Wickham's request to see more of Meryton first. They had not walked five minutes before Denny was glad he agreed to Wickham's suggestion. There, on the other side of the street, was Miss Lydia with three of her sisters and a tall, stocky man dressed in the clothes of a clergyman.

Denny bowed at Miss Lydia's wave, and he heard Wickham's light whistle of approval. "Well, you were right about the comely ladies, Denny," his friend said in a low voice.

Denny smiled. "Come, I will introduce you."

They crossed the street, Denny unconsciously straightening his uniform jacket. He addressed the company directly and entreated permission to introduce his companion, Mr. Wickham. Wickham began conversing with Miss Bennet and Miss Elizabeth, which gave Denny the opportunity to talk with Miss Kitty and Miss Lydia. Both officers ignored the ladies' cousin, a Mr. Collins of Kent, as blustery a fool as Denny had ever met.

Miss Kitty was nervous and coughing as usual, but to Denny's disappointment, Miss Lydia was more interested in Wickham than himself.

"And where did you meet the gentleman?" she asked for the second time. Denny was about to answer her when two gentlemen rode up. At a glance, Denny recognized Mr. Bingley and his guest, Mr. Darcy.

The gentlemen began the usual civilities; Mr. Bingley was the principal spokesman and Miss Bennet the principal object. He had been, he said, on his way to Longbourn on purpose to inquire after her, a statement Mr. Darcy corroborated with a bow.

At that moment, Wickham, who was facing Miss Elizabeth, his back to the newcomers, turned, and something extraordinary happened. Wickham locked eyes with Mr. Darcy and both changed color; Wickham paled, while the gentleman on horseback grew red. Wickham, after a few moments, touched his hat—a salutation which Mr. Darcy barely deigned to return.

Denny was shocked. *Why was George afraid of Mr. Darcy?*

Mr. Bingley continued to speak with Miss Bennet for another minute, without noticing what had passed between the two men. Then seeming to sense his friend's unease, he took leave and rode on with Mr. Darcy.

There was no opportunity for Denney to inquire about the incident for the ladies announced their intention of walking to Mrs. Philips' house, and the two men accompanied them.

"Will you not come in with us?" cried Miss Lydia at the door of the house, her eyes more on Wickham than Denny.

"Lydia," Miss Bennet gently admonished the girl.

"We would not want to intrude," said Wickham.

"Oh, you will not!" returned the girl. "Our aunt loves company, especially that of handsome officers!"

"Lydia!" It was now Miss Elizabeth's turn to correct her sister.

At that moment, the window was thrown open and a matronly lady stuck her head out. "Oh, there you are, girls! I have been waiting an age, I am sure!" Mrs. Philips took in the gentlemen with a glance. "Oh, sirs, you are well met! Please come in! You must come in!"

Denny was tempted, but duty came first. "I thank you, madam, but we must report to headquarters. Pray forgive us." The entreaties were pressed and refused one last time before the officers took their leave of the party, but only after promising Miss Lydia more firmly that they should all meet again soon.

After Denny and Wickham were a distance away from the house, Wickham glanced at him. "Do you know that tall, dark-haired man we met just now?"

"On horseback? That was Mr. Bingley's guest, Mr. Darcy, a gentleman from the north. Do you know him?"

Wickham smiled tightly. "I do. Tell me, what do the people hereabouts think of him?"

"Not very much—only that he is grave and quiet—and many say his pride sets him above the common folk in the country."

"Pride!" cried Wickham. "Yes, I should say that man is very proud indeed!"

"You sound as though you know him."

"I do, very well. I daresay there is no one who knows him better." Wickham grinned. "We grew up together at his family's estate in Derbyshire. His father was my godfather."

"I am surprised at that, for it looked to me that he all but gave you the cut direct in the middle of the street!"

"That is no surprise, for he hates me."

"His father's godson? You cannot be serious!"

"I am." Wickham looked around. "Too many ears about. Let us find a tavern, and I will tell you my tale of woe."

Denny was tempted, but he knew this was not the time. "Later, George. We must hurry to Colonel Forster. We have to get you sworn in and fitted out with your kit. You are in the king's service now, and your time is not your own."

Wickham rolled his eyes. "You are right, I suppose. Damn that Darcy! I was meant for better things, but that is all behind me now. I am a soldier, as you said. Let us to the colonel's tent!"

Supper with the Philipses
by J. Marie Croft

November 20, 1811

No objection was made to the young people's engagement with their Aunt Philips for a nice, comfortable, noisy game of lottery tickets and a little bit of hot supper afterwards. All Mr. Collins's scruples of leaving Mr. and Mrs. Bennet for a single evening during his visit were most steadily resisted. At a suitable hour, the Bennet carriage conveyed the parson and his five cousins to Meryton through a light but relentless rain.

Combined with Kitty's giddy excitement, Lydia's steady chatter sorely tried the forbearance of the coach's other passengers; but such disturbances could hardly be avoided. Red-coated officers of the _____shire militia were invited to supper, and the appearance of a certain dashing new arrival in Meryton was especially anticipated by the two youngest girls. Despite an assortment of reproofs, any expectation of composure was altogether hopeless.

The horses were halted in front of the Philips's home, and an attendant opened the carriage door. Collins clumsily clambered out first, wrested an umbrella from the servant's hand, and shooed away the discomfited fellow. Nothing would do but that Collins himself would gallantly assist each of his fair cousins as they stepped out, into an ill-timed downpour.

Beneath a wide-brimmed hat, Collins's hair was plastered to his head. Slickness due to inclement weather might be pardonable; but Lydia suspected his was due to an application of some oily, foul-smelling pomade. *Ugh! Must everything about that greasy creature be repellent and odious?* Unwilling to suffer even her cousin's gloved touch, Lydia ignored his proffered hand and bounded from the coach unassisted. Her foot plunked squarely into a puddle.

"Oh, blast and bother!"

"Lydia!" Elizabeth turned and gave her sister the gimlet eye as best she could through the raindrops.

Lydia pouted and ran to catch up with her older sisters. "Well, how would you like to spend the evening with a wet foot? 'Tis bad enough we shall have to spend it with a wet blanket."

Mary, accustomed to such abuse, was forestalled from speaking in her own defense.

"The Netherfield party will not be attending," said Elizabeth. "I am happy to report we shall all be spared his censure tonight."

"Ha, ha, ha, Lizzy! I didn't mean Mr. Darcy. I meant the other wet blanket." Lydia twitched her head in the parson's direction.

Elizabeth leaned toward Jane and muttered, "I wonder at the lesser of tonight's two evils – our wet-blanket cousin or our wet-behind-the-ears sister."

"I heard that! La! My ears aren't even wet yet. If we don't get out of this rain, though, my pelisse will be soaked through and my muslin dampened beyond propriety."

"You, worried about propriety? This is already an evening of wonders."

Lydia paused and resisted the urge to stick out her tongue. She did roll her eyes, albeit behind Elizabeth's back. She grabbed Kitty's hand and said, "Come, make haste inside. I declare my whistle is the only part of me that needs wetting. Ha, ha, ha! Oh, I do hope our Aunt Philips will set out negus and a good spread for supper. Lord, I am famished already! To think we dined only hours ago, and I gorged myself on ham and cake. Though I am the youngest, I'm the stoutest and, I swear, the hungriest. Mama says it is because I am well-grown and have such high animal spirits. Well, I daresay I am wild for some game tonight. Do you suppose we shall have sliced hunter's beef or boiled fish? I rather fancy our aunt's custards and sippets. Or pickled oysters. I dearly love pickled oysters and soused herring. I suspect our Uncle Philips is pickled and soused already. Ha, ha, ha, what a good joke! Oh, do stop coughing so, for heaven's sake! I can scarcely hear myself speak with you hacking up a lung like that. If you insist on coughing all night, I shall go distracted; and the officers will think you horrid unpleasant. I hope Mr. Wickham has come and is wearing regimentals. Mmm, would that not be a swoon-worthy sight? Oh, look, here's our aunt to meet us at the door."

The Longbourn party entered, and the girls had the pleasure of hearing that Mr. Wickham had accepted their uncle's invitation and was already in attendance. They filed into the drawing room, and Lydia flung herself onto the settee facing the fireplace. She slouched, slipped off her sodden shoe, and stretched her soggy-stockinged toes toward the welcome warmth of the crackling blaze … until Elizabeth put her foot down.

"Remember where you are, and do not behave in the indulged manner you are suffered to do at home."

"Lord, Lizzy, isn't that what Mama said last week to you? Don't be such a wet blanket. Mama would never put a damper on any pleasure of mine. She encouraged me to have a jolly good time tonight, so you needn't get all high and mighty."

Lydia opened her reticule and pulled out a dainty handkerchief, three hair pins, two ribbons, a comb, a brass button that suspiciously looked like it belonged on a military uniform, an empty scent bottle, a fan, and a serviette. Baffled by the last item, she unfolded it to reveal a squashed bun and a piece of cheese. "Oh! I quite forgot about this. Ha, ha. It's from breakfast yesterday. I thought I might get peckish and like to have a roll while visiting the officers. But look here! Mama lent me her favourite ivory fan. Isn't it pretty? Fans were once used for flirting, you know. Mama showed me her book about the art of coquetry and its secret signals. I declare, flirting with a fan is such a breeze! Oh, Lord, was that a pun? Ha, ha (snort). Anyway, I learnt the rudiments in no time at all and could have flicked a fan with great proficiency. See?" Lydia smiled sweetly and twirled the fan in her left hand. "That means I wish to be rid of you."

Elizabeth stood and said, "Very well, Lydia, I will leave you to your own folly. But, first, for what it's worth, here is my advice about flirting. Everyone, even Mr. Collins, deserves to be heard. Instead of the art of coquetry, you would do well to learn the art of listening. There is a good reason you have two ears but only one mouth. Listen twice as much as you speak, do not behave like a loose fish, and please do not embarrass your family too much tonight." Elizabeth glanced down. "And put your shoe back on."

"If you're so worried about embarrassment, instead of lecturing me, you ought to be speaking to our cousin." Lydia began to cram all the items back into her reticule. "What do you suppose that smarmy clod is prattling on about now?"

Kitty answered indifferently, "Last I heard, he was speaking to our aunt about china on the mantle and something about an eight hundred pound chimney-piece at Rosings."

"Ha! What a laugh! If the chimney-piece weighed that much, how did they carry it into Lady Catherine's drawing-room? Eight hundred pounds... of all things! Ha, ha, ha! Lord, our cousin is a bacon-brain. I cannot listen to him. I would much rather listen to some music. Oh, I wish our Aunt Phillips had an instrument. I would dearly love to dance tonight, even if it meant we'd have to listen to Mary's ghastly playing." Lydia ignored her middle sister's wounded expression, stood, and looked around. "Oh, my stars and garters!" She clutched at Kitty's arm. "The redcoats are coming in!"

As the men walked into the drawing room, all dullness was overthrown by a dazzle of gold-trimmed scarlet coats. Only the day before, Lydia and Kitty had considered a few of the officers to be stupid, disagreeable fellows in comparison to Wickham. But the young blades of the _____shire militia were, in general, a very creditable, gentlemanlike set; and the best of the corps was of the present party.

Wide-eyed and fairly bouncing with enthusiasm, Kitty pointed and said, "There's Chamberlayne, Denny, Captain Carter, and

Colonel Forster. Are they not magnificent? I daresay it's weeks since I've received pleasure from the society of a man in any other colour than red … well, except for our brief encounter with Mr. Wickham. Ah! Here he comes now … and, oh! In a red coat!"

Lydia heaved a lusty sigh. "Oh, Lord! I declare, Wickham in regimentals is a sight for sore eyes. He is as far beyond them all in person, countenance, air, and walk, as they are superior to our broad-faced, stuffy, old uncle." She giggled and said, "Dear Uncle Philips may breathe port wine; but as a country attorney, he will never achieve grapeness."

"Lydia!" said Elizabeth for the second time that evening.

"What? Lud, Lizzy, it's not as if it's my fault our uncle is a lowly attorney… and portly."

Elizabeth said, "I'll have you know that, in bygone days, portly meant something else entirely. It described a stately or dignified appearance and manner."

"Oh, Lizzy," said Jane, "it would be unseemly to describe Mr. Wickham and his fellow officers as portly."

"True, and I would never be so rotten to the corps. I must admit, the militia uniform certainly does Mr. Wickham no disservice. No disservice, indeed!"

Wickham was the happy man towards whom almost every female eye was turned. Even the demure, eldest Bennet sister, besotted as she was with another, turned to admire the jaunty fellow.

"Well, Jane," said Lydia, "I daresay even your Mr. Bingley has neither such strong calves nor such a swagger as that." Silently she prayed. *Oh, Lord, please let him sit by me, please let him sit by me, please let him sit by me!* When Elizabeth was the happy woman by whom Wickham finally seated himself, Lydia stomped her foot. She had not heeded her sister's earlier advice; and, still unshod, she left a distinct print on the Philips's velvety Wilton carpet.

The youngest Bennet sister absently twirled a lock of hair while she covetously watched Wickham chat with Elizabeth. Their trifling discussion of the wet night and probability of a rainy season filled

Lydia with both despair and ennui. *Lord, I cannot abide dreary weather and dull conversation!* She slipped her dampish foot back into her begrimed shoe, petulantly accepted the hand she had been dealt, and shuffled off toward the card tables. Her four sisters soon followed suit.

Mr. Collins, who could not compete for the notice of fair ladies with such rivals as Wickham and the other dashing young blades, sunk into insignificance until Mrs. Philips plied him with coffee and muffins and asked him to join her for whist.

Mr. Wickham, on the other hand, did not play at whist but was received, with ready delight, at the table between Elizabeth and Lydia. The latter nearly squealed with glee when she realized she would be seated betwixt the red-coated shoulders of Denny and Wickham for the duration of the lottery tickets game. Cards were dealt to the large company crowded around the table; and fish-shaped gaming counters made of bone, ivory, and mother-of-pearl were distributed. Lydia's first bet was that she would, indeed, have a jolly good time that night.

At first there seemed danger of her engrossing Wickham entirely, for Lydia was a most determined talker. "How snugly we are all crammed together! Are you quite comfortable, Mr. Wickham? You may move your chair closer this way, if need be. What a merry party we shall have at this table! I don't care three straws about whist. La! If I had to play at that other table, I would wistfully wish to be here. Ha, ha! Do you like it here, Mr. Wickham? Here in Meryton, I mean. Denny, Captain Carter, and the others are already nicely entrenched, and I hope you are settling into our local society as well. Are you satisfied with your quarters?" Lydia was startled when a muscled thigh briefly pressed against her own. *Oh, Lud! Talk about tight quarters!* She had the decency to blush until the pressure was removed. She then turned to admire Wickham's fine countenance and awaited receipt of his pleasing address. "Where are you billeted, sir?"

"I am lodging at the Wry & Ginger. I must say, for a man who sells ale, the publican has a rather dry sense of humour; and his wife is a fiery wen... pardon, a lively woman. I am quite enjoying her... ah, their warm hospitality."

"Well," said Lydia, "I am sure you will find us all very warm and welcoming in this neighbourhood. Why, even the gentleman who recently let Netherfield Park is well-disposed. Just last Thursday I reminded Mr. Bingley that he had promised to give a ball. And what do you suppose? He asked me to name the very day of the ball, which shall be on the 26th. What a jolly good time we will have then! I dearly love to dance and am never without a partner at an assembly." Lydia gave Wickham an opening to ask for the honour of a set and was momentarily crestfallen when he did not jump at the chance. She shrugged and said, "Now that Captain Carter and Mr. Denny are returned from London and you have joined the regiment, I shall insist Colonel Forster give a ball as well. La! Having the militia headquartered here for the whole winter is quite a diversion in itself. Is it not, Kitty?"

Across the table, Kitty coughed, nodded, and said, "I think ..."

"See! Kitty agrees with me. She and I often encounter your fellow officers while walking to our aunt's or to the milliner. Why, we are practically encamped in Meryton ourselves! Ha, ha, ha. Now, Mr. Wickham, you must tell us if Colonel Forster is truly to be married, which private was lately flogged, and ..."

"Lydia!" said Elizabeth for the third time that night.

Wickham was grateful for the interruption. Extremely fond of lottery, Lydia soon grew too much interested in the game, too eager in making bets and exclaiming after prizes, to have attention for any one in particular. Allowing for the common demands of the game, Mr. Wickham was then at leisure to quietly talk to Elizabeth.

Lydia impatiently waited to be dealt her ticket card. *Lord, Lizzy is terribly dull tonight! Poor Mr. Wickham. I wonder what they are discussing so grimly. Mr. Darcy? Lord, could there be a duller subject than...* "Ha, ha, ha! I win again! Why, Kitty, I believe I shall name one of my fish after you. A gudgeon! They are easily caught, and you are easily taken in." She waited for recognition of her quick-wittedness in vain. Taking matters into her own hands, she clapped and said, "What a laugh! Ha, ha, (snort), ha!"

Elizabeth frowned and said, "What a laugh, indeed, Lydia. Most unladylike. If I were Kitty, I would name one of my fish after you – a carp. Pray, continue, Mr. Wickham."

Lydia huffed. *I'm unladylike? Well, Mama says you're a hoyden because of the way you scamper around the countryside. So there! I would not walk three miles for anyone … unless there was an agreeable young officer or two at the other end.* "Hurrah, another win for me! I daresay you must all envy my good luck. What a pity, Captain Carter, you are losing all your fish. You must be deuced unlucky. Ha, ha, ha."

While the dealer delivered a facedown card to each player, Lydia eavesdropped on Wickham's conversation with Elizabeth. She nearly gasped when she heard of Mr. Darcy's infamy. *First he insults Lizzy, and now we learn of further vileness. Well, he may be a tall fellow, but Darcy is not a man of high standing. Poor, poor Wickham! To be so ill treated! Dastardly Darcy is obviously rotten to the core; but I am determined one bad apple shall not spoil my barrel of fun. And neither shall my sister spoil my evening, even though she is being a horrid wet blanket.*

"What sort of a girl is Miss Darcy?" Elizabeth asked Wickham.

Lydia drummed her fingers on the table and hummed a tune while she waited for others to place their bets. She could scarcely hear Wickham's answer and could scarcely care. She was, however, a tad curious about the schooling Mr. Darcy's very, very proud sister was receiving. "Lord, I'm glad I don't have to suffer through a lady's intensive education. It sounds horrid dull."

"Lydia!" cried Elizabeth for the fourth time that night.

"It is quite all right, Miss Elizabeth," said Wickham. "What I mentioned, Miss Lydia, is that a lady superintends her education. However, knowing her fastidious brother, Miss Darcy is, no doubt, receiving superb and intense tutoring."

Elizabeth smiled at him but turned serious as she addressed her sister. "It is not polite to intrude upon the conversation of others, Lydia, as you are very well aware."

Lydia placed a wager without audibly acknowledging her sister. *Lord! Make up your mind, Lizzy. Earlier this evening you told me to listen better. Now you're telling me not to listen. I swear Mary, Jane, and Lizzy lecture me more than our parents do. It hardly signifies, though. I bet I could stand on my head with my skirts about my ears, and Mama would approve. She says I am the apple of her eye. Then Papa always replies, 'The nut does not fall far from the tree.' I think he's got it wrong. Isn't it supposed to be 'The chip doesn't fall far from the block'? Oh, well. As if I give three straws! Papa certainly wouldn't give two figs if I stood on, or fell on, my head. Lord, I must stop thinking so much. Fish, apples, nuts, and figs remind me how hungry I am. When do we eat? I shall soon faint if I don't...* "Oh, I've won again! Ha, ha! Mr. Chamberlayne, look at all my counters. I've won the most, have I not? Am I not the best player? See here, Lizzy? You have not won any at all. La! You called me a loose fish, but tonight it seems I can scarcely lose fish at all."

The whist party soon afterwards broke up, and those players then gathered round the lottery tickets table. Although Lydia's raucous laughter prevailed over the hubbub, Wickham and Elizabeth continued talking together until supper put an end to cards, to their private conversation, and to Lydia's hunger.

During supper and on the carriage ride to Longbourn, neither Lydia nor Mr. Collins were once silent. Lydia talked incessantly of lottery tickets, of the fish she had lost, and the fish she had won. Collins, in describing the civility of Mr. and Mrs. Philips, protested that he did not in the least regard his losses at whist, enumerated all the dishes at supper, and repeatedly feared crowding his cousins.

While he spoke, Lydia sighed and rolled her eyes. *Lord, I can scarcely get a word in edgewise! That sorry man is an insufferable flap-gill! Does his pompous prattle never cease? Our cousin would do well to take Lizzy's advice and listen twice as much as he speaks. Lud, he blathers nothing but tripe. Oh. Tripe. La, I'm hungry again!*

Both Collins and Lydia had more to say than they could well manage before the carriage stopped at Longbourn House.

Nestled beneath her goose-down counterpane for the night, Lydia looked back on the past evening; and its remembrance gave her pleasure. She fondly recalled her lottery game triumphs and the thrill of being positioned between two handsome officers. She smugly recollected the muscular leg firmly, albeit briefly, pressed against her own below her aunt's table.

Appetite insatiable, Lydia lit a candle and rummaged through a pile of discarded clothing until she found her reticule. She removed and unfolded the linen serviette. As she sat upon her four-poster, she bit into the stale, crumbly biscuit and shrugged. *At least my foot is finally warm and dry, and there shall be no more wet blankets to endure. La! So what if I might share my bed with a crumb or two?*

Darcy's Resolution
by Susan Mason-Milks

November 23, 1811

Darcy cleared an opening on the desk in the study at Netherfield, marveling at how Bingley could find anything, let alone get work done with papers and correspondence stacked everywhere in such a careless manner. Clutter and disorder always inhibited Darcy's ability to think clearly. His hope in retreating to the study was to find a few minutes of peace in which to write a letter to Georgiana. Taking quill in hand, he paused, uncertain what he wanted to say. What was foremost in his mind was probably not something his sister should read. Pouring himself some of Bingley's excellent brandy, he moved to look out the window hoping it would clear his head. As he watched the dark clouds making their way across the sky, his thoughts returned to how nothing had been the same since Miss Elizabeth and her sister had left Netherfield. All conversation bored him, and even the usual pleasures of reading did little to fill the space she left when she departed.

Worst of all, Miss Bingley had sensed something, awakening a primal reaction in her. Like a predator following the scent of its prey, she had begun tracking him around the house. If he went to the library to quietly read, she found that she, too, was in need of a new book. Since she was never sure what to read, she always asked for his suggestions. By the time he helped her chose a book and returned to his own, he had usually forgotten what he had been reading. It made no difference anyway, because she continually interrupted asking a question every few minutes. When her ceaseless chatter became too much to tolerate, he would get up and move to another room. Inevitably, she followed after a few minutes, and thus the cycle repeated. What a contrast to Elizabeth who had once sat in the library with him for more than half an hour without saying a single word!

After a week of her relentless pursuit, Darcy, fortunately, remembered Miss Bingley did not like horses. Since that time, riding had become his favorite occupation. As his friend Bingley was not an early riser, Darcy often went out in the morning alone. The exercise seemed to renew his spirit and help him think more clearly. Usually after an energetic ride, he walked his horse Hector slowly along the lanes in the neighborhood. At first, he told himself he was just exploring, when in truth, he had to admit he was secretly hoping to discover where Miss Elizabeth went on her morning walks. Once as he ambled along, he almost crossed paths with her. A noise nearby alerted him just in time to see her coming out of a small wooded area. Quickly turning Hector down a path to his right, he was able to disappear before she saw him.

Darcy generally used the pleasant silence on his rides to recall and analyze every word that had passed between them during Elizabeth's stay at Netherfield. As he reviewed their interactions, he frequently thought of something he should have said that was far cleverer than his actual response. Other times, he found himself caught up with imagining entirely new conversations. In these scenarios, instead of being tongue-tied, he knew exactly the right thing to say to amuse her. It was all so clear in his mind that it was almost as if he could hear her voice as they engaged in verbal sparring. When Darcy imagined making such a witty comment as to amuse her, he was certain he could hear her laughter. As he closed his eyes to listen to that sweet music, just the thought of her brought warmth to his core, and when that heat began moving downward in his body, he bent over in the saddle and groaned aloud. Cursing, he quickly looked around to see if anyone had heard him, but fortunately no one was nearby. To keep himself from thinking about her, he took an extra long ride that day so that he and Hector were both exhausted by the time they returned to the stables.

At first, Darcy considered these daily imaginary conversations with Elizabeth as harmless amusement. He could talk to her as much as he wished as long as no one knew. He was not harming her reputation or putting himself in danger, but as he became more and more preoccupied with thoughts of her, he began to realize he was playing with fire. It was not right to let this continue, and one day out on a solitary ride, he vowed to banish Elizabeth from his mind forever.

Once back at the house after his ride that morning, Darcy found he was out of sorts and irritated with the world. He was short with Jennings, his valet, over the way his cravat was tied. He complained that the temperature of the water for his bath was too cold and then found something wanting with the polish on his boots. Later, he felt guilty for being so abrupt. Since an outright apology would only embarrass them both, he tried to let Jennings know he was sorry by sending him to Meryton for the afternoon on an errand they both knew to be invented. Darcy thought the man might enjoy getting outside in the lovely fall weather for a change and even gave him some extra coin so he could stop for hot cider along the way.

When he realized trying to banish Elizabeth completely from his mind had only resulted in making him uncivil, he decided he would allow himself the pleasure of thinking about her, but only when he was out riding alone. This strategy worked at first, but soon Darcy found his preoccupation spilling over into other parts of his day. There was no escape. The rooms at Netherfield were alive with memories of her. The drawing room made him recall the mischievous look on her face as they discussed the accomplishments of a lady. In the dining room, he thought about the grace of her slender hand as she reached for her wine glass. Whenever they repaired to the music room, he remembered how his eyes had followed the curve of her shoulder to the hollow at the base of her neck and how he longed to touch that place with his lips. And how could he forget the swell of her…Oh, Lord, what was it about this woman that seemed to drive all rational thought from his head!

Once when he was thus occupied, Miss Bingley had asked him a question. To avoid having to admit he was not attending, he mumbled agreement and much to his displeasure found she had been asking if he would like to join them at cards. He was forced to spend a miserable hour at the table until he could politely extract himself from the game and retreat to his rooms.

When Darcy realized that for some time he had been calling Elizabeth by her first name in his thoughts, he knew he could not let this continue. What if he slipped and actually said it aloud? Leaving Netherfield as soon as possible was his only choice. Unfortunately, there was the upcoming ball to consider. It was a major event for Bingley and would firmly establish his friend's place in the neighborhood. As Darcy knew he must lend his support, he was forced to stay until after the ball. Upon forming this plan, he rationalized that since he was leaving soon, there was nothing wrong with letting himself continue to think about Elizabeth for just a few more days. After that, he would be safely in London where their paths would most certainly never cross.

As his thoughts returned to the present, the rain slowed, and off in the distance he could see a small patch of blue that promised better weather to come. Just at that moment, he resolved to ask Elizabeth to dance at the ball. He had no idea where this impulse came from, and although he knew he should resist, something inside him cried out for one more opportunity to look into her fine eyes and touch her hand, even if it was only through her glove. Darcy decided he would allow himself to admire her, to drink in her sweet charms just one more time, and then he would be gone. He only hoped that indulging himself in this way would allow him to exorcise her from his mind once and for all.

Brandy finished and his thoughts arranged in a more orderly fashion, he returned to the desk. Picking up the quill, he dashed off a short note to Georgiana informing her of his plans to return to London within the week.

Waiting for the Netherfield Ball
by Caitlin Rubino-Bradway

November 25, 1811

The worst part about the rain was the sound it made. The incessant rat-tat-tattling against the windowpanes. The thrumming, drumming of water against the roof. The unceasing noise. The complete lack of escape.

Kitty was thinking of attempting it, though. Jane had ridden to Netherfield in a storm almost as bad as this, and then Lizzy walked the three miles there simply to check on Jane, and everybody had gone on and on about how brave Lizzy was and what a good sister. Kitty could at least make it the one mile to her Aunt Philips. Nobody had been out of the house for three whole days now—three days of no Meryton, no officers, no news, and no relief. There were only so many times she and Lyddie could look over their gowns to decide what to wear to the ball.

Only today was different, because today Lyddie started digging through Kitty's things, only to emerge triumphantly waving the pink embroidered silk. They were in the bedroom they shared, with Mama in the window seat exclaiming over everything. The wardrobes were pulled open, dresses left in puddles on the floor or dripping down the backs of chairs. "What about this one, Kitty? I think it will look very well on me."

"I was going to wear that one," Kitty protested, but Mama was already gushing how lovely Lydia would look. "It's mine," Kitty said, louder.

"Oh, but you have dozens of dresses, and I don't have anything to wear. Not for a private ball," Lyddie said blithely. "Besides, you know you can't wear pink, it makes you look like a tomato."

Lyddie was just saying that to make her give up the dress. Kitty looked better in pink than any other color, and if she let Lyddie have the dress, then she would have to wear the white with the blue plaque on the front, which had been Mary's years ago. Most of Kitty's dresses had first been Mary's, who had an unerring eye for the unflattering, while Lydia had to suffer having new things made up whenever she wished. But what Lyddie always wished was what anybody else had.

"Mama?" Kitty appealed, rushing to get it out all at once before The Answer came. "Mama, tell her it is mine, and she shall not wear it!"

"Oh, for heaven's sake, Kitty, let her have it," Mama snapped. "My nerves cannot bear to see one of my daughters being so selfish to her own sister."

"But it is mine! I shall tell Papa," Kitty insisted.

But Lydia only laughed. "Tell Papa what you like. We all know he doesn't listen to a word you say."

All the air rushed out of Kitty's lungs, and Lyddie was laughing, and Mama was still tutting about how pretty Lyddie would look in Kitty's dress. Kitty turned and rushed out, slamming the door behind her only to realize, when she was in the hallway, there was nowhere to rush to. That never happened in novels.

It wouldn't have hurt if there was somewhere to go, something to do, if the hateful rain hadn't imprisoned them here like Emily in Udolpho, with only each other for company. Kitty hated the rain. She hated being trapped here, in this small, airless house, hated the way her chest went tight and she couldn't breathe.

Stupid Lydia. Stupid, selfish, spoiled Lydia. She got everything and Kitty got nothing, and nobody even cared. They didn't even remember her half the time. Only last week she overheard Lieutenant Denny referring to her as the one who wasn't Lydia. And Kitty was so sick of being introduced to gentleman, only to have them immediately ask if she was Jane's sister, and wasn't Miss

Bennet the most beautiful thing anyone ever beheld? And Lizzy—everybody remembered Lizzy. Everybody said she was the smartest, cleverest, prettiest girl in the county; she even had stuffy Mr. Darcy staring at her all the time, which men always did in books when they liked you, or in reality when you accidentally spilled something on your dress, which Kitty had done at an assembly last summer, and Papa had only just stopped teasing her about.

Papa would be in the library. Papa was always in the library because he liked books better than people, and because the only way the Bennet family could survive being trapped together on rainy days was to shut themselves up in separate parts of the house so that they could avoid each other as much as possible. Kitty was tempted to march down there and speak to Papa anyway, just to show Lyddie. Except talking to Papa would be useless. He didn't care about anything they did as long as they left him alone, and, besides, at the moment he was suffering from a severe case of Mr. Collins.

Mary was in the drawing room. Kitty could hear her pounding away at some concerto. With the way she attacked the piano, Kitty wondered if Mary even liked playing. Still, she might do as an escape. Mary would ignore her as long as Kitty sat still and didn't cough too much. Her playing was almost loud enough to drown out the rain. Almost. Three days now and Kitty could feel the way it rattled off the windows, like a hundred little pinpricks on her skin.

There was always Jane and Lizzy. But Jane and Lizzy were all that Jane and Lizzy seemed to need. At the moment they were shut up in Lizzy's room. If Kitty knocked, they might open the door. What were they doing in there? The two of them had been hiding away all of Friday and Saturday and Sunday and looked to be there for the rest of forever, but Kitty didn't care about that anyway. Besides, she wasn't feeling very charitable towards either of them today. In the first place, it was hard enough listening to raptures about her eldest sister's beauty all the time. But it was harder still when that sister was just as sweet and nice to everyone in the entire world as to you. Sisters weren't supposed to like everyone equally. They were supposed to like you best.

Kitty loved her family, because you were supposed to— you had to— but she didn't like them very much. She knew they didn't like her. But Papa and Lizzy were the worst. They were clever. And Kitty wasn't, not like them, but you didn't have to be clever to know when someone was being mean. Papa and Lizzy were mean all the time. Did they think nobody could hear them? Or did they just think everyone else in the world was too stupid to know when they were being made fun of?

They had had fun last night at dinner. Kitty spent the meal imagining pitching the table over, just to hear the sound it made when everything smashed to pieces.

She heard Lyddie's voice in the room behind her, and realized she hadn't moved. Realized there wasn't anywhere to go.

When Kitty went back into the room, Lydia was in front of the mirror, twirling. Pink silk skirts swirled around her. She smiled at Kitty in the mirror. "Well then?"

Kitty wondered what would happen if she just started screaming. Wondered if the sound would bounce off the walls.

"You were right, Lyddie. It looks very well on you."

Darcy Prepares for the Ball
at Netherfield
by C. Allyn Pierson

November 26, 1811

Darcy awoke early on the 26th and immediately realized that the day of the ball had arrived. He tried to ignore his excitement over another chance to see Miss Elizabeth Bennet. And… to ask her to dance. Yes, he was still determined to dance with the lovely Miss Elizabeth and what could be more natural? Of course he would dance all night, helping to entertain his friend's company at this, Bingley's first ball. No one would even notice when he asked *her* to dance.

His resolute calm was dented as soon as he entered the breakfast parlour and found the entire Bingley clan at table.

"My! Aren't we all early risers today?" Bingley quizzed his friend.

Darcy kept his face unmoved, and answered, "I would not know, Bingley. I am usually back from my morning ride before your face appears in the breakfast parlour."

Bingley laughed, and Darcy could tell that his friend was excited about his ball and would be twitting him mercilessly all day. He took a place at the far end of the table, which unfortunately put him next to Miss Bingley and across from Mr. Hurst.

"So, Mr. Darcy," Miss Bingley purred, "are you prepared to gallop around the ballroom with the Meryton maids tonight?" She turned to her brother. "Charles! You are going to order the orchestra to play a few waltzes, aren't you?"

Charles considered. "I had thought not. The waltz is not yet accepted in polite society in Hertfordshire, and I would not like to offend anyone. Also, I don't know if the local ladies and gentlemen have yet learned the steps."

"Don't be absurd, Charles, of course they have. Just because some old tabbies won't allow it at the local dances does not mean others might not like it! and, I shudder to hear you describe the gentry of Hertfordshire as 'polite society'. What a joke that is!"

Darcy tuned out the bickering and concentrated on his eggs and gammon. What would Elizabeth wear to the ball? The gown she wore to the assembly at Meryton was simple and not particularly notable…except for the way if fit her form and emphasized her graceful movement. And the way it clung to her shape!

His daydreaming was suddenly severed by Miss Bingley's voice, sounding a bit impatient, as if she had spoken his name more than once. He turned to her.

"Yes, Miss Bingley? I am sorry, I did not hear you as I was wondering if the last book I ordered would come in today's post." (Whew. Lame, but at least a comprehensible sentence!)

"I was asking, Mr. Darcy, what your opinion was of the waltz. Do you think Charles should ask the orchestra to play 2 or 3 during the course of the evening? I despise letting narrow-minded provincials determine what music we should play."

Darcy swallowed convulsively as he thought of waltzing with Elizabeth, her right hand held in his left for the entire dance, while his right hand touched her waist, feeling the warmth of her body as they whirled through the ballroom, the others blending into a swirl of color that left the two of them alone in their own private space. He swallowed again, trying to pretend a bit of gammon needed to go down, then spoke, "I do not think it would be a good idea to shock the locals at Charles' first ball. I would wait until the next before trying to set fashion forward. But, it is entirely up to Charles, after all."

Miss Bingley turned petulantly from him to harangue her brother.

Darcy escaped from the table as soon as he decently could and went up to his room to make sure his valet was prepared for tonight. His black coat and black satin knee-breeches were already hanging up, fresh from the iron, and it was clear he could not hide in his room while his valet spun from task to task like a dervish. He sighed and decided to go for a walk… No, he would be obliged to ask his hosts if they would like to join him, and he was in no mood for idle chatter or petulant complaining. A sudden thought caused him to smile. Billiards! He would ask Hurst for a couple of games, effectively banishing Miss Bingley from that bastion of masculine entertainment!

Eventually, the long day drew towards evening and the Netherfield gentry gathered for a substantial tea to fortify them for the ball. When he finished his second cup, Darcy firmly put it away from him and marched up the stairs to his dressing room. He felt like a knight girding his loins for battle…for such was his usual intercourse with Miss Elizabeth Bennet.

As Jennings primped and polished him for the evening he tried to put himself into a trance…thinking about how beautiful the fall leaves were at Pemberley, and how soon he would see Georgiana. Finally, he heard, "There you are, sir. All finished."

He looked into the mirror and carefully examined his hair, his cravat, and his clothes. His face looked a bit pale, but the heat of the ballroom would soon remedy that. He heard the first carriage draw up to the door and swallowed the lump in his throat, pulling the cravat just a fraction looser in hopes he could breathe. Even now she might be here, in a silk gown and pearls…simple adornments to emphasize, but never overshadow her loveliness. He heard a throat clear.

"Is everything all right, sir?"

Darcy turned to the anxious valet. "Yes, everything is quite all right." And he turned to the door.

Mr. Darcy's Valet Has his Doubts
by C. Allyn Pierson

November 26, 1811

"Mr. Jennings, is there something amiss with your dinner?"

Jennings came to an awareness of his setting with an almost audible thump.

"Ah…not at all Mrs. Nicholls, quite to the contrary, the dinner is delicious. I was merely contemplating which waistcoats I should lay out for my master. With all the work you have done for the ball, I would want the master to be an ornament to honour your efforts, but I am not sure of my choice…I don't know why I should worry, for the master will make his own choices, and very elegant they will be, but, as you know, I may be able to influence him by my selection of several from which he can choose." He gave her a simpering smile and was relieved when she smiled graciously upon his compliments.

What he had, in truth, been contemplating was the very odd behaviour of his master. He had never known Mr. Darcy to fuss over his toilette…to the contrary (as he had commented to Mrs. Nicholls). Darcy's clothes were all of the first style of elegance, tailored by Weston to fit his form like a second skin. The master insisted on quality, made sure his cravat was perfectly tied…then he forgot about his clothes. He did not check his appearance in every mirror he passed like the Bond Street Beaux, nor did he try to skimp by with flashy but inferior goods. But never—not in his entire eight years of service—had Jennings ever seen Mr. Darcy in such a state as he now was.

Naturally, he had not said anything to the master, since he did not seem to want to discuss it, but he had been as resty the past two days as a three-legged dog in a butcher shop. Pacing, unable to sit down for more than a few moments, and trying very hard to avoid the Bingleys…not that he could blame him for that since Miss Bingley had been excoriating the staff mercilessly all week to make sure the ball was up to her standards. He was sure Hertfordshire had never seen such an entertainment before, but she had been a sore trial to her servants and, undoubtedly, to her family and friends.

Still, he did not think Miss Bingley's ill-humour was to blame for his master's mood. He seemed to be thinking about something which absorbed all his attention and made it impossible for him to concentrate long enough to even choose a waistcoat in the morning, veering from intense particularity over his choice to sudden insensibility within seconds.

Now that he thought about it, the master had been a bit out of sorts since Miss Bennet went home after her unfortunate illness. Wait a minute…surely his master could not be falling for Miss Bennet himself? He would never perform such a turn on his friend…would not even look at Miss Bennet after Mr. Bingley had chosen her as his favourite in Hertfordshire. No…no, it was not possible…but it would certainly explain Mr. Darcy's mood if he had developed a tendre for Miss Bennet.

Miss Elizabeth Bennet he set aside. She, while a lively and attractive young lady, was in no way up to the master's standards for female pulchritude. The servants, every one, felt both Misses Bennet were Quality, in spite of their appalling mother and sisters, all of whom had invaded Netherfield while Miss Bennet was ill, giving the servants a great deal to talk about belowstairs. The local servants had much to say about the Bennet family, but the plain truth was they were bad *ton*, barely scraping by as gentry and in the unfortunate position of being too poor to overcome their low connections when it came to the Marriage Mart.

Still and yet, the two eldest Bennets were the beauties of the county and the heart did not always listen to the head. He was stricken with a sudden chill as he thought of the possibility of Mr. Darcy developing a tendre for a country miss. How could he hold up his head in the servants' hall if his master was taken in by a pretty face attached to vastly inferior birth. It was not to be thought of.

He must try to observe the guests during the ball. Once this accursed meal was over he would find a discreet position from where he could spy on…well perhaps he would stick with the word "observe"…his master and see if he could determine his thoughts.

Caroline Bingley's Generous Appraisal of the Evening
by Marilyn Brant

November 26, 1811

Insupportable. Really, there was no other word for it.

Caroline Bingley had done her level best to point out to her brother how unnecessary and ridiculous it would be to have such an event in their home —*and for what? to appease some silly Bennet girls?*— but it was futile. Charles, the fool, would not be dissuaded. "I made a promise," he argued back. "I am a gentleman of my word."

So, here she was, not only in the midst of an evening that would have been beneath her to attend, and sheer punishment at that, but indeed, she was now one of the hosts of it. She took a steadying breath, adjusted the trim on her sleeve and caught sight of Mr. Darcy. He, at least, had the decency to look appropriately displeased by the goings on.

And what was going on? Good heavens, what was *not* going on! Those younger Bennet girls were racing around the ballroom and giggling like peasant children who'd just seen their first Red Coat. Their mother was gossiping to that Lucas woman in tones that could drown out the voice of a commanding officer. And that middle Bennet girl — that horribly unmusical one — was fingering her piano music, just biding her time until she could unleash her immorally bad taste on the party. Caroline sniffed. If desperation had an odor, this would be it.

But, as annoying as they all were, these people were of little consequence to Caroline. No, she had far larger issues to contemplate. Her very own brother was staring at the eldest Bennet daughter as if he'd just seen Aphrodite personified. It was revolting. And Jane Bennet herself could hardly keep from smiling in her sweet but, clearly, simpleminded little way at everybody. Nobody was that good all the time, unless they were lacking in sense and sophistication.

Nothing, however, inspired the nausea deep in Caroline's belly quite like having to look at Miss Elizabeth Bennet for any sustainable length of time. She watched her on numerous occasions throughout the course of the evening: Dancing with that odd, uncoordinated man at the start of the night (something-or-other Collins, she'd overheard the Bennet mother say). Laughing with Miss Charlotte Lucas, though over what topic Caroline would hardly chance a guess. In the company of her mother or one of her many sisters, always eyeing the world with her particular brand of impertinent regard. But it was her dance with Mr. Darcy that distressed Caroline most of all. She was positively mystified as to why he would have committed himself to Miss Elizabeth for so many precious minutes while she — *Caroline herself!* — was available for both dancing and conversation.

She was quite sure it must have been an act of pure graciousness on his part. He, too, must be doing his best to be the type of generous host that she knew herself to be, making sure each guest had at least one bright moment in their otherwise dreary little lives. That was why she'd insisted to the head cook that the punch be sufficiently spiked with rum. The locals might not have appreciated the more delicate flavors in the drink, but they would be aware of the absence of their favorite element. See how she was thinking of others? How anxious she was to please the common people? Mr. Darcy must be doing the same although, in Caroline's opinion, he was, perhaps, taking his kindness to an extreme in this case.

Fortunately, during the course of that particular dance, Louisa came bustling up to her with news of Jane Bennet, who'd been asking questions about Mr. George Wickham, an officer Caroline knew was most repugnant to Mr. Darcy. Caroline soon gathered that Miss Bennet's interest was, without a doubt, inspired by Miss Elizabeth's personal curiosity. She smiled to herself. At last, she had something helpful to impart to that obnoxious second Bennet daughter. Knowledge that *she* had — that Miss Elizabeth *did not* — which would prove just how much higher in esteem Mr. Darcy held Caroline's company over hers…despite the other's supposedly "fine eyes." What utter nonsense that was.

Caroline needed only to wait until the dance was over, and then she would seek out Miss Elizabeth and kindly —*so very kindly*— enlighten the silly girl on how things really stood. That would knock down a few of Elizabeth Bennet's undeserved airs! And she would be doing a great service to Mr. Darcy in the process, as well as to everyone who had the misfortune of being socially connected with the Bennet family.

The very thought of her own generosity made Caroline almost blush with a rare sense of delight. And this made the insupportability of the evening just a bit more tolerable. For a brief moment, the Netherfield Ball was almost…enjoyable.

White Soup
by Nina Benneton

November 26, 1811

"Cook, more of the militia regimen has joined us this evening." Mrs. Nicholls entered through the kitchen in a harried manner. "Have we enough white soup?"

With some displeasure, Cook noted the housekeeper's entrance had distracted little Tilly from her duty at the fire. She barked at the little kitchen maid. "Pay close attention, girl. Don't burn the almonds."

"Have we enough white soup?" Mrs. Nicholls repeated.

"Who wants to know?" Cook snapped, not pausing in her stirring. She and her poor overworked staff had been blanching, beating, and boiling almonds for what seemed like an eternity now. She was sick of the blasted white soup.

"Miss Bingley," Mrs. Nicholls said, a note of wariness in her voice, which did little to pacify Cook's ire at the housekeeper's intrusion into her kitchen.

"La! Soup la reine for the queen." Cook gave a mock curtsy. "Tell Her Highness eating white soup won't make her any more palatable to the gentleman from Derbyshire."

Tilly and the other kitchen servants giggled. Mrs. Nicholls flicked them a warning glance. Abruptly, the giggling stopped.

Though she knew she shouldn't encourage the lower servants, Cook said, "Let them have a little laugh at their betters."

Mrs. Nicholls eyes remained fixed on the other servants. "Then laughter's the only thing that will fill their bellies when they're dismissed after tonight."

The servants gasped.

Cook banged her ladle on the side of the pot then pointed the ladle at the housekeeper. "That better be an empty threat, Mrs. Nicholls."

The housekeeper's eyes met Cook's. "It won't be an empty threat if they continue their impertinent revelry at their mistress's expense."

Cook lowered the ladle to the soup and resumed stirring. She'd just added the almond paste, beaten eggs, and cream to the veal stock, and she didn't want this batch to be ruined." No need to carry the point, Mrs. Nicholls. I'm just in a temper, 'tis all."

In a weary voice now, Mrs. Nicholls said, "We've all been working very hard preparing for the ball. It was Mr. Bingley, actually, not Miss Bingley, who wanted white soup served tonight."

The appeasing words soothed Cook a little. It wasn't the housekeeper's fault the Bingleys were ignorant upstarts. No one served soup for a ball supper unless they were trying too hard to impress others with their grandness and generosity. Still, she would rather work for wealthy tradesmen's children who paid a decent wage rather than parsimonious, impoverished, titled tightfists.

"I'm certain Mr. Bingley will tell you all tomorrow how much he appreciates all your hard work," Mrs. Nicholls added.

Cook noticed the housekeeper didn't say anything about Miss Bingley's giving them praise. The smell of roasted almonds was becoming stronger. Cook hoped Tilly paid close attention and wouldn't burn the almonds they would be using to garnish the soup. After a small taste of the soup, Cook lifted the ladle to the housekeeper. "Tell me if it needs a little more salt."

Mrs. Nicholls leaned forward and tasted. Straightening, she pronounced, "Simply perfect."

Cook hid a pleased smile. The housekeeper was a smart woman; she didn't miss the conciliatory offering, and she was wise enough not to admit it needed more salt. "Be gone with you upstairs and let us finish making the soup. Yes, we have more than enough for a whole regiment. Don't you worry."

Denny at the Netherfield Ball
by Jack Caldwell

November 26, 1811

Lieutenant Denny, immaculate in his Number One uniform, paid his respects to his hosts, Mr. and Miss Bingley, before following Captain Carter into the main room of Netherfield. At his shoulder were his comrades, Pratt and Chamberlayne. His friends were looking for diversion, something that Denny sought as well, but he had a task to perform.

"Ah," said Pratt, "Carter is making for the card room."

"All the better to avoid Miss Watson," drawled Chamberlayne. "You know she has set her cap for him."

"At her age? I do not believe it."

"Stranger things have happened. I say, who is that? The young lady with the freckles?"

"Her?" Pratt looked over. "That is Miss Mary King. The word is that she has expectations of an ill grandfather and ten thousand pounds."

"Ten thousand? That might make up for her *atrocious* fashion sense," Chamberlayne sniffed.

For not the first time, Denny wondered about Chamberlayne. At that moment, the Bennet family arrived and Denny smiled. Miss Lydia was particularly fetching tonight, and Wickham was not there to get into his way. As his two companions made their way to the punch table, Denny slowly approached the Bennet ladies, wishing to accomplish his mission as soon as possible.

"Ah, Mr. Denny!" cried Miss Lydia. "Is he not handsome, Kitty? So fine in his uniform and sword! I believe I shall swoon!"

"I shall swoon as well," parroted Miss Kitty.

"Girls, that is enough," Miss Elizabeth said quietly. "Good evening, Mr. Denny. I hope I find you well." As she spoke, her eyes were scanning the room, obviously looking for someone.

As was Miss Lydia. "But where is Mr. Wickham?"

"I bear unfortunate news," said Denny. "My friend is not in attendance. Wickham was obliged to go to Town on business yesterday and will not return until tomorrow. He sends his regrets."

Lydia and Kitty were vociferous in their displeasure at this pronouncement, and Miss Elizabeth was clearly disappointed, particularly when Denny, with a significant smile, added in a low voice meant only for Miss Elizabeth's ears, "I do not imagine his business would have called him away just now if he had not wished to avoid a certain gentleman here." He gestured with his head at Mr. Darcy, who was standing in a corner across the room.

Wickham had told Denny of the shameful treatment he had received from his godfather's son, and a shocked Denny felt sympathy for his friend. The rich had their own rules, he had reflected, and a poor man could do nothing but make his own way in the world. Opportunity was scarce in the militia, which was why Denny was determined to join the Regulars and rise in his chosen profession.

Lydia, who had heard nothing of Denny's last comment, stamped her little foot. "Well, pooh! If Mr. Wickham thinks that business is more important that dancing with ladies, then I say he is a dull fellow! As for me, I shall dance the night away!"

Denny extended his arm. "If you are not otherwise obligated, may I request the first set? And Miss Kitty, the second?"

Lydia took his right arm and flashed her eyes coquettishly. "Why, Mr. Denny, that would be very agreeable."

Kitty took his left. "I should dance first! (*cough*) I am almost two years older!"

Denny knew he had to defuse this potentially explosive situation. "Ah, but Pratt would never forgive me, Miss Kitty, as he has spoken of claiming your first."

"Oh!" Kitty was exceptionally pleased.

Denny turned to make his excuses to Miss Elizabeth, only to see she was in conversation with Sir William Lucas's plain daughter. He walked away towards his comrades as Miss Lydia asked whether the rumors were true that Colonel Forster would marry soon.

The ball was like any other ball as far as Denny was concerned. After the first sets with Miss Lydia and Miss Kitty, he danced with several of the other ladies of the district. Denny was amused that Captain Carter stood up with Miss King. Not that there was anything wrong with Mary King—if one's tastes ran towards the uninformed and insipid. But a potential ten thousand pounds was an attractive inducement for attention in some men. Men not like Archibald Denny. He liked lively people.

There were interesting moments during the ball. Denny was surprised at first that Miss Elizabeth danced with Mr. Darcy, knowing that Miss Elizabeth was distressed over the man's treatment of Wickham. Amazement turned to amusement when he noticed two things. First, Miss Elizabeth was clearly scolding Mr. Darcy during the set. Second, Mr. Darcy seemed to be unaware of it, and Denny thought he caught flashes of admiration in the rich man's eye.

The proud and unpleasant Mr. Darcy is attracted to a lady who hates him! he thought. I know a man of his stature would never offer for her, but I wonder what would happen if he did? Would Miss Elizabeth flatly refuse him, puncturing his pride, or would she do the prudent thing and accept him and make the rest of his life miserable?

* * *

Denny was enjoying Miss Lydia's company at dinner when Miss Mary Bennet began her concert at the pianoforte. Her playing was truly appalling, but he was embarrassed at the way Lydia and Kitty openly laughed at her. It was not his place to correct her, but he suspected that for all her loveliness and high spirits, Miss Lydia needed a firm hand to guide her to better behavior. He had not the right to do that, but he could stop those who were abetting her conduct.

"Pratt," he hissed, "pray stop providing punch to Miss Lydia and Miss Kitty. Can you not see they have had enough?"

"And very good punch it is" laughed Chamberlayne, "especially with all the whisky *someone* added to it!" He winked at Pratt.

"*What?*" Denny was outraged. Officers were meant to act as gentlemen, and this was not the action of a gentleman! "Pratt, this is insupportable!"

"Aw, shut your gob, Denny," drawled Pratt, half-way into his cups. "Just having a bit of fun. Besides, I don't have to listen to you. You're not my commanding officer."

"True, but I am your brother officer, and I tell you this is wrong."

Pratt, bleary-eyed, leaned over and belched. "You ain't in the Regulars yet, Denny, so hold your bloody tongue. Or are you going to be a damnable scrub and report me to Carter?"

Denny pulled his lips tight. There was a code in the ranks— *stand by your comrades*—and Denny was not going to break it. At least, not over this. But it went against the grain. "I think it best that the ladies receive no more punch. Can I depend on you?"

Pratt raised his hand in defeat. "As you wish. Besides, it leaves more for me and Chamberlayne."

Chamberlayne laughed again. "I thank you for my share, Pratt!"

"Denny?" asked an inebriated Lydia. "Are you arguing with Pratt?"

"Not at all, Miss Lydia. May I get you some punch?" He glanced at his chuckling comrades. "There is a different batch that I highly recommend."

Lydia grinned. "Lord, you are so sweet! Is not Denny sweet, Kitty?"

"Yes." Kitty blinked happily.

Denny moved over to a different punch table, one that was halfway across the room, bemoaning the fact that it would still take almost nine months before his uncle's shipment arrived from India and provide the last of the promised funds he needed to purchase his commission in the Regulars. Ah, to leave this collection of militia misfits behind! September of '12 could not come fast enough!

Charlotte Lucas
at the Netherfield Ball
by Abigail Reynolds

November 26, 1811

Charlotte had dressed with unusual care for the Netherfield Ball. Her dress was one she had worn only once before. The deep blue of the bodice brought out the color of her eyes, which were perhaps her best feature. At the last minute, she had torn out the lace along the neckline, making it more revealing than anything she had worn before. She wanted to see admiration in Mr. Robinson's eyes.

More than anything, though, she wanted to see *him*. He had promised to return in a fortnight, and he was already a week past his time. The delay had caused her more anxiety than she cared to admit. If his father refused to give his blessing to the match, would that be enough to change his mind? She could not believe it, not after he had been so touchingly tender to her during their encounter in the woods. But thinking of that made her even more uncommonly anxious when she considered his tardy arrival.

She was counting on the Netherfield ball to reunite them. All the neighborhood would be there, and even if Mr. Robinson had found it difficult to separate himself from his host, Mr. Willoughby, neither of them would miss this occasion. She had played through the possibilities for their meeting in her head. She would not chide him; nothing would make a man flee faster than the possibility of a shrewish wife. She would greet him warmly and welcome him back, making no mention of the delay.

A quick glance around the ballroom revealed that he had not yet arrived. To distract herself, she sought out Eliza Bennet, whom she had not seen in a week. She hardly needed to say anything, since Lizzy was quite ready to pour out the tale of her own woes over the absence of her Lieutenant Wickham. It made Charlotte grateful that she had not said anything to Lizzy about her interest in Mr. Robinson; she did not want anyone watching her reunion with him. She listened with half an ear as Lizzy, her good humor finally restored, told her of the odd cousin who was visiting the family at Longbourn. When she pointed him out, Charlotte could not see anything so odd about him, but Lizzy's standards were always impossibly high. A woman of little beauty could not afford to be so choosy.

No one asked her for the first dance, the one she had hoped to dance with Mr. Robinson, so she retired to the side of the room where she could observe without interruption while she tried to control her own anxiety. Lizzy was dancing with her cousin, and apparently an inability to dance must be added to any deficiencies of that gentleman, for he showed no grace. Charlotte winced in sympathy when she saw him step on Lizzy's toes for the third time. Still, even a poor dance partner was better than none.

Charlotte had some relief when one of the officers asked her for the next set. He was a homely fellow with spots, but he danced well enough and laughed easily, and more importantly he took her mind off Mr. Robinson's absence for a few minutes. Whenever they reached the end of the line, though, she could not stop herself from scanning the room. She bade her partner adieu at the end of the second dance with no regrets. Almost immediately Lizzy appeared beside her, asking about her new beau, which gave Charlotte quite a jolt until she realized her friend was referring to the officer who had partnered her.

Mr. Darcy came over to them then and asked Elizabeth to dance – quite a surprise since he had once found Lizzy not handsome enough to tempt him, but then again Lizzy did tempt most gentlemen. After accepting him, Lizzy began to bemoan her fate anew. Charlotte had no patience for her, though, for she had just spotted Mr. Willoughby across the room, and his friend Mr.

Robinson was still nowhere to be seen. For the first time, she admitted to herself the possibility he might not come to the ball at all. With a sick feeling at the pit of her stomach, Charlotte could muster no sympathy for Lizzy for having to dance with a handsome and rich gentleman, and so she said only, "I daresay you will find Mr. Darcy very agreeable."

That was enough to set Lizzy off again. Shaking her head, Charlotte told her impractical friend in a whisper, "Do not allow your fancy for Wickham to make you appear unpleasant in the eyes of a man of ten times his consequence!" She doubted her words would make any difference, given Lizzy's impulsive ways.

As her friend went off with Mr. Darcy, Mr. Willoughby approached Charlotte and requested that she honor him in the next set. Normally she would refuse, knowing that a dance to him was but an excuse for an attempt at seduction, but tonight she was too eager for news of Mr. Robinson to avoid his friend. She had fended Willoughby off often enough in the past. It was odd, though, that he should ask her to dance, when in general he wanted nothing to do with her since the time she had exposed his behavior to her family and friends. Perhaps he had a message from Mr. Robinson to deliver.

Mr. Willoughby's stare was as insolent as ever when they lined up for the first dance of the set. Charlotte calmly chatted about the weather, getting very little reply from him. The music started and they began to dance their way down the set. Charlotte said, "I do not see your friend Mr. Robinson here tonight. Is he still visiting you?"

"He left a fortnight ago after settling a certain wager with me." Willoughby bared his teeth in the approximation of a smile. "I had wagered him, you see, that he could not succeed at enjoying the favors of a certain oh-so-proper lady without the benefit of marriage. Under normal circumstances, I do hate to lose a wager, but in this case, it was well worth two hundred pounds just to know how the mighty are fallen." He slowly raked his eyes down her body as if stripping her naked. Then he released her hand as they

124

separated to walk down the outside of the dance set.

It was marvelous, Charlotte thought, how she could continue to dance and smile as if nothing had happened when there was a knife twisting in her gut. Worse than that; there was no knife spilling her life-blood, and therefore no hope of a merciful death. She did not waste her time wondering if it was true; experience had taught her that the cruelest interpretation of a man's behavior was most likely the correct one. It had been too good to be true, that a man would care for plain, long on the shelf Charlotte Lucas. At that moment, she hated every man in the world, even her own brothers and father.

She had no intention of giving this particular man the satisfaction of thinking her hurt. When they came back together at the head of the line, she raised her chin and said, "Is that what Mr. Robinson told you? Even I know better than to believe a man's boast about a woman, especially when there is money at stake."

"But I have my proof," he said softly in her ear. "I watched you go into the woods with him, and again when you walked out over an hour later, with twigs in your hair and your skirt wrinkled."

Charlotte resorted to an old game of pretending she was somewhere else as he continued to take advantage of the dance to whisper ever more vulgar insinuations. She focused on keeping her head up and smiling as if her world were not crumbling. She ignored Willoughby when the dance ended, instead chatting with another dancer for a few minutes before making her way to the safety of Lizzy, whose sharp tongue would keep even Willoughby at bay. Fortunately, Lizzy's preoccupation with Mr. Bingley's fascination with Jane seemed to keep her from noticing anything was amiss with Charlotte, and soon they were interrupted by Lizzy's cousin, Mr. Collins, who had the remarkable ability to carry a conversation without very little input from anyone else.

The ball seemed to last an eternity as Charlotte labored to keep her composure. She could hardly eat a bite of supper. All the gossip around her about the presumed future happiness of Jane Bennet with Mr. Bingley only rubbed salt in her wounds.

Oh, how could she have been foolish enough to get into this predicament? Usually she was so sensible, but this time her feelings had led her further astray than she would have believed possible. And what if there were consequences of that night in the woods? She would have no defense, and she would disgrace her entire family. As it was, she could be the target of humiliating gossip if Willoughby chose to spread his poison. He seemed to be taking great pleasure in smirking at her whenever she looked his way.

In self-defense, she began to talk more to Mr. Collins and to distract his attention from Lizzy. His conversation might be silly, but he was presentable enough, and the world would only see a tall fellow with grave and stately manners talking intently to her. At least this way Willoughby would see that she could still engage a man's interest without the incentive of a large sum of money. It was little enough consolation when she considered her now-blighted future, the degradation of having believed like a fool that Mr. Robinson actually cared for her, and the strong possibility that Willoughby was not yet done humiliating her. If she proved to be with child, or if Willoughby went to her father with his claims, it could be even worse. If only she could somehow escape from Meryton… but there was nowhere for her to go.

The Hursts Discuss
the Netherfield Ball
by Mary Simonsen

November 26, 1811

"Louisa, you absolutely outdid yourself tonight. The musicians played brilliantly, our guests stepped lively, and most of the young ladies who exhibited were truly talented. The wine selection was excellent and the food superb. However did you manage it?"

Louisa had to chuckle at her husband's compliments as the musicians had been recommended by Edward's sister-in-law, Lady Banfield. As for the refreshments, the Bingleys' butler and cook had seen to everything, and it was Edward who had selected the wines. But she understood the reason for his excessive praise: She was feeling sad, and he knew it.

"Thank you, my darling. Everything was exactly as it should have been—at least on our end," Louisa said, thinking of Mary Bennet's unfortunate exhibition on the pianoforte and Mrs. Bennet spilling sherry on one of the officer's trousers. There was also some excessive drinking among the younger officers, but that was to be expected. On the other hand, no one got sick—or none who she knew about. Louisa admitted, all in all, the ball had been a great success.

"Then why are you sailing in the doldrums?"

Louisa, who had been sitting at her dressing table brushing her hair, put down the brush. "Did you see how happy Charles looked tonight?"

"Yes, I did. It was as if his smile was painted on his face. And how could he not be happy? He is in love with Jane Bennet, and every moment he could spare from his duties as host was spent with her. I expect we shall have news of an engagement very shortly."

After completing her toilette and dismissing her maid, Louisa told her husband that there would be no such news of a betrothal. To the contrary, she believed they would be leaving Netherfield Park within the week.

"Because you were in the card room, you did not see Mr. Darcy and Miss Elizabeth Bennet dancing," Louisa explained. "It was obvious to me Miss Elizabeth did not want to dance with Mr. Darcy. Her jaw was clenched so tightly, I could practically hear her teeth cracking. But Mr. Darcy, being so enamored of the lady, did not notice and attempted to engage her in conversation. Miss Elizabeth responded with those tired platitudes one always hears in a ballroom until broaching the subject of Mr. Wickham, and Mr. Darcy's whole demeanor changed. Barely a civil word passed between them from that point on. When the dance was over, they could not get away from each other fast enough."

"Yes, I understand Wickham is a sore spot with Darcy, but Miss Elizabeth could hardly be expected to know of their mutual dislike. Surely Darcy must know that."

"Although we do not know the particulars of their estrangement, Caroline and I are convinced Mr. Darcy's sister was somehow involved. If that is the case, then anyone who is a friend of Mr. Wickham's is not a friend of Mr. Darcy's."

"But we were speaking of your brother. What do Charles and Miss Bennet have to do with Darcy and Miss Elizabeth?"

"Caroline is well aware of Mr. Darcy's interest in Miss Elizabeth, and from the time she saw the first spark ignite, she has been looking for a way to get Charles to leave the country. Up to this point, she was alone in her efforts, but now she will have an ally in Mr. Darcy. He, too, will want to leave Hertfordshire."

"But that does not change the fact that Charles is in love with Miss Bennet. You cannot convince a man who is so in love that he is not."

"Oh, that is not how they will pursue the matter," Louisa tsked at her husband's naiveté. "Caroline and Mr. Darcy will try to convince my brother that Miss Bennet does not love *him*."

"But how?"

"Miss Bennet is a placid creature and gives nothing away with her looks. Although I personally believe she is in love with my brother, only the most acute observer would be able to discern any particular regard on her part. Because of that, I believe Mr. Darcy and my sister will succeed in convincing Charles that Miss Bennet is not in love with him. If they are successful, then there is no reason for us to remain in the country, and we shall all return to London."

Edward shook his head. "Your predictions are so dark because you are tired from your exertions this evening. You look perfectly done in."

"This is not merely guesswork on my part, Edward," Louisa said, patting her husband's hand. "Caroline told me that it is her intention to speak to Mr. Darcy tomorrow about Charles and Miss Bennet. She is quite determined to separate them."

"It is possible you may be wrong, my dear."

"Knowing my sister as I do, I know that I am right."

Mr. Collins Proposes
by Susan Mason-Milks

November 27, 1811

After the ball, Mrs. Bennet lay awake delighting in thoughts of Jane's wedding to Mr. Bingley. He had not yet proposed, but after making his preference for Jane so clear at the ball tonight, it was surely only a matter of time before he declared himself. What fun it would be to shop for new wedding clothes in London, and of course, her eldest daughter must have the very best! Although Netherfield was a grand house, the furniture and draperies were quite another story. They would definitely have to be replaced, and Jane would need her advice on the colors, the fabrics, and style. The prospect excited her more and more. It was all she could do to keep from clapping her hands together with joy. The idea of having a daughter settled so close by was delightful. She would be able to visit nearly every day!

When Mrs. Bennet awoke late the next morning, her head throbbed from lack of sleep and possibly that final glass of punch at the ball last night. As she lay abed absently pondering her plans for Jane's wedding, she noticed some enticing smells coming from downstairs, and following her nose, made her way to the breakfast room. Yes, a little coffee was just the thing she needed to clear her head this morning.

As she sipped, she did a mental inventory of the family. Mr. Bennet had already retreated to his library and would probably not emerge for the rest of the day. Jane and Lydia were still in bed, while Elizabeth and Kitty lingered in the breakfast room talking softly—thank goodness—about the ball. And Mary? Oh, no one cared where she was as long as she refrained from practicing the pianoforte today. The noise would simply be intolerable.

Having finished her first cup of coffee, Mrs. Bennet was just spreading butter and jam on a thick piece of bread when Mr. Collins appeared and addressed her, asking for a private interview with Miss Elizabeth. Suddenly, all her senses were alert! She had been hoping for this for the past several days but had not expected Mr. Collins to approach her this morning!

"Oh, dear! Yes, certainly. I am sure Lizzy will be very happy–I am sure she can have no objection. Come, Kitty, I want you upstairs."

As surprised as Mrs. Bennet was at his application, she was even more surprised by her second daughter's reaction. Lizzy, looking startled and confused, begged her mother and Kitty not to leave her. To Mrs. Bennet, this seemed like a strange response. Surely, after Mr. Collins' attentions the last few days, her daughter must have been expecting his proposal. She should be happy to hear he had requested a "private interview." When Lizzy's eyes narrowed in one of her defiant looks, and she appeared ready to bolt from the room, Mrs. Bennet glared at her and firmly insisted she stay and listen to what Mr. Collins had to say. Taking Kitty by the arm, she pulled her toward the door.

"Mama, please," Kitty whined. "You are hurting my arm!"

Mrs. Bennet silenced Kitty with a withering look, and then quickly directed her best reassuring smile at Mr. Collins. Exiting the room, daughter in tow, she was careful to leave the door slightly ajar. After shooing Kitty off to rouse her other sisters, she moved back to the breakfast room doorway. At first, all she could hear was the throbbing of her head.

Then she heard Mr. Collins nervously clear his throat several times and begin his speech. His proposal started off with promise. He generously complimented Elizabeth on her modesty and enumerated her other admirable traits. *Thank goodness, he does not yet know what a trial the girl can be,* Mrs. Bennet thought to herself. Then he went on for some time explaining how he had singled her out as the companion of his life almost from the first moment he entered the house. Mrs. Bennet frowned. She knew this was not exactly true.

His first interest had been in Jane, but after a few hints about Jane's anticipated engagement, he had quickly redirected his attentions to Lizzy.

As Mr. Collins began a rather long-winded recitation of his reasons for marrying, Mrs. Bennet nearly stomped her foot in irritation. She could not understand why he did not just get on with it! No one cared why he wanted to marry. It was only important that he did. But the self-absorbed parson was not to be hurried. Droning on, he complimented himself on his generosity in choosing his bride from among his cousins, as this would ensure the security of the rest of the family once he inherited Longbourn. The comfort of knowing that if Mr. Bennet died they would not be put out into the hedgerows made the pounding in Mrs. Bennet's head begin to subside.

As Lizzy started to speak, her voice was so soft her mother had to strain to hear. What was she saying? Why was she disagreeing with him? It took all of Mrs. Bennet's self-control not to push the door open and rush into the room so she could shake some sense into her foolish daughter. How could she do this to her family? Although Mrs. Bennet tried to calm herself, the pounding intensified in her head again. It began to feel as if it might explode. Of course, Lizzy would come to her senses and accept him. She simply must! The conversation went back and forth for several minutes with Lizzy remaining firm in her refusal, and Mr. Collins refusing to accept her protestations. She had to give Mr. Collins credit–he might not be a very exciting man, but he was persistent.

Feeling secure that Lizzy would see reason and do the right thing, Mrs. Bennet retreated into the vestibule, took a few deep breaths, and waited for the appropriate time to rush in and express her surprise and happiness at their engagement. After a few minutes, her daughter emerged, and without even a glance in her mother's direction, retreated up the stairs towards her bedchamber. "Lizzy, dear, where are you going?" Mrs. Bennet waved her hands wildly and called after her, "You must come back. Lizzy! Lizzy?"

Mrs. Bennet pressed a hand to her throbbing head. Then shrugging her shoulders, she sighed and rushed into the breakfast room to congratulate Mr. Collins in the warmest terms and express her joy that they would soon be more closely related. He happily received her felicitations.

"Her modest refusals of my proposal only show what a bashful, delicate creature she truly is. Certainly, her purpose is to increase my love by suspense, and that she most assuredly has accomplished. I am now more eager than ever to call her my wife," he said, brushing back an oily lock of hair that was stuck to his forehead.

Although Mr. Collins did not seem disturbed by his ladylove's reluctance, Mrs. Bennet quickly became concerned. Something was not right. "Depend upon it, Mr. Collins!" she assured him. "Lizzy shall be brought to reason. I will speak to her about it directly. She is a very headstrong, foolish girl and does not know her own interests, but I will make her see reason."

At this, the smile on Mr. Collins' face faded a bit. "Pardon me for interrupting you, madam, but if she is really headstrong and foolish, I wonder if she would be a very desirable wife for a man in my situation. I am one who naturally looks for happiness in the marital state. If she persists in rejecting my suit, perhaps it would be better not to force her into accepting me. Such defects of temper would not be conducive to marital felicity."

Suddenly, Mrs. Bennet felt faint and wavered on her feet. Oh, no, he could not be allowed to change his mind! To keep from toppling over, she grabbed the back of a chair for support and began reassuring him that Lizzy was only headstrong in matters such as this—whatever that meant. She told him again of her daughter's gentle nature even though she knew in her heart Lizzy could be just like her father—very stubborn indeed! Mr. Collins would find that out for himself once they were married, but by then, it would be too late, and Lizzy would be securely established at Hunsford.

"I will go directly to Mr. Bennet, and I am sure we shall have it all settled very soon," she said. Without giving Mr. Collins a chance to reply, Mrs. Bennet left and flew directly to the library where she knew she would find Mr. Bennet ensconced among his books. Although she was certain the sound of her excited breathing should have alerted him to her arrival, he did not seem to notice her standing there for at least a minute. When her husband finally did look up, he appeared disinterested.

"Yes, what is it, Mrs. Bennet?"

While trying to keep her voice from becoming too shrill, she begged for his help in making Lizzy accept Mr. Collins. As sweat popped out on her forehead from the exertion, she began dabbing at it with her hankie. In spite of the urgency she tried to convey, Mr. Bennet continued to look at her blankly as if she were a fly buzzing around the room. Why did he not offer to help? After all, he was not doing anything important—only reading a book. Mrs. Bennet's agitation rose in direct proportion to his refusal to understand her. How could he not support her in this? Certainly, he understood the importance of finding suitable husbands for their five daughters? She had discussed this with him repeatedly although she often suspected he was only pretending to listen.

Finally, much to her relief, Mr. Bennet seemed to grasp the situation and agreed to speak with Lizzy. Confident her husband would take her side, she waited for him to take charge.

After asking Lizzy a few questions, Mr. Bennet cleared his throat. "Very well. We now come to the point. Your mother insists upon your accepting Mr. Collins. Is it not so, Mrs. Bennet?"

"Yes, or I will never see her again," she declared firmly crossing her arms across her chest. Certain he was about to tell Lizzy she must comply, Mrs. Bennet stopped listening for a moment and began congratulating herself on her success. Then, suddenly, Lizzy was smiling. Mrs. Bennet looked at them both in confusion. Something had gone horribly wrong! What had she missed? Surely, he would never allow his daughter to refuse a perfectly good proposal? The pounding in her ears increased until it sounded like an entire drum corps marching through her head.

"What do you mean, Mr. Bennet, in talking this way? You promised to insist upon her marrying him."

"Mrs. Bennet, I promised no such thing. I said I would speak with her about it, and that I have done. The matter is settled." When she did not move, he added, "I would appreciate having my library to myself again—as soon as possible." And with that, he returned to his book.

At first Mrs. Bennet was not certain she had heard him correctly, but as she watched her daughter leaving the room looking happy, she fully realized what had just happened. He had taken Lizzy's side, and she was being thrown out of his library—in her own house! This was not to be tolerated! "Oh, Mr. Bennet!" she cried and ran from the room.

Since her husband had once again proved to be of no help, she knew it was entirely up to her to salvage the situation. With that in mind, Mrs. Bennet burst into Lizzy's room and began trying to wear her down, urging her again and again to accept Mr. Collins before he changed his mind and would not have her. She coaxed, cajoled, pleaded, and tearfully called for Lizzy to have mercy on her poor nerves. Finally, she resorted to threats in a desperate effort to convince her disobedient daughter.

When she was exhausted and her head began to pound, Mrs. Bennet gave up and returned to the breakfast room, sitting down with a loud sigh. Just as she was pouring another cup of coffee and wondering if she should add a bit of Mr. Bennet's brandy—medicinally, of course—she was startled by the appearance of Charlotte Lucas. Without considering that news of Lizzy's refusal might become fodder for neighborhood gossip, she took up her case with Charlotte. As Mrs. Bennet continued to fan herself with her handkerchief, she bemoaned to her new audience that no one seemed to be taking her part in the dispute.

"I have only the best interests of my daughters at heart. Surely, you understand that, Charlotte. Perhaps you could explain it to Lizzy for me," she said, directing a scowl in the direction of her second daughter who had just entered. Waving a handkerchief in front of her face, she moaned, "No one is concerned for me! Oh, the flutterings, the spasms of my poor nerves! What did I do to deserve such a disobedient daughter?"

"I am certain everything will work out for the best," Charlotte said giving her a reassuring look. As Mrs. Bennet felt Charlotte put a comforting hand on her arm, she wondered why her Lizzy could not be more like her sweet friend.

Glancing up, Mrs. Bennet saw Lizzy looking unconcerned and very satisfied with herself. At times like this, Mrs. Bennet could see her daughter's resemblance–both in temperament and in expression–to her father, and it was infuriating!

When Mr. Collins arrived and basically withdrew his offer, Mrs. Bennet completely lost heart. Unable to think of another strategy, she succumbed to her headache and retreated to her bedchamber. Jane, her good, kind daughter, who would never betray her the way Lizzy had, came and laid a cool compress on her mother's head. "You must not worry, Mama. All will be well," Jane said softly.

Mrs. Bennet took her eldest daughter's hand in hers, "Oh, Jane, I was so certain today when Mr. Collins asked for a private interview that I would have at least one of my daughters engaged before the morning was over. I do not understand what went wrong! Now it is all up to you to secure Mr. Bingley, my dear."

Mr. Darcy and Miss Bingley Conspire
by Kara Louise

November 27, 1811

Mr. Darcy walked into the breakfast room eager for a cup of coffee and some solitude to allow him to think more about the events at the Netherfield Ball. Particularly regarding Miss Elizabeth. Despite his less than amicable dance with her, he could not dismiss her from his mind. But he knew he must.

He was surprised and more than a little disappointed to discover Miss Bingley already there. He greeted her politely and asked the servant for a cup of coffee, seating himself at the table.

He took a sip of the freshly poured drink, thanking the servant with a nod of his head. Turning to Miss Bingley, he asked, "Do you know what time Bingley is departing today for London?"

"I believe as early as possible," she answered with a smile, which quickly faded. "You are still planning to go with him?"

"I am not inclined to remain here any longer." His fingers gripped the cup tightly.

Miss Bingley waited until the servant left the room and closed the door behind him. She looked back at Darcy and quite unexpectedly uttered a commanding, "Mr. Darcy, you cannot leave!"

He turned toward her, astonished at her exacting demand. "I beg your pardon, Miss Bingley?"

"Mr. Darcy," she said, as a smooth smile replaced her previously disturbed countenance. "Please accept my apologies for my outburst. I see we are both of like minds; neither am I inclined to remain here even one day more! The society here is intolerable!" She leaned forward and in a conspiratorial whisper said, "However,

I have something of the utmost import to discuss with you and it can only be done whilst Charles is away. I see no other alternative but to request that you remain at Netherfield!"

Darcy's brows pinched in curiosity. "What is so urgent that I remain behind, Miss Bingley?"

"We must discuss this Miss Bennet disaster directly!" Her voice rose to a fevered pitch. "You must agree with me after what we witnessed at the ball last night that Charles should be made to see the imprudence of this affection. Naturally, we cannot discuss it whilst he is in our midst, and I am relying on your counsel, for I know he will listen to you. I fear it may prove to be too late if we delay discussion of this until you both return!" She shook her head vehemently. "We must formulate a plan to separate him from her!"

Darcy slowly lifted his coffee cup and gazed into the swirling liquid as if it might hold the answers to all his unanswered questions. He pondered Miss Bingley's words silently and then took another sip.

Miss Bingley continued, "Mr. Darcy, you beheld her family. Have you ever witnessed such undignified behaviour? Each member of that family is objectionable!"

Darcy glanced up to see Miss Bingley eyeing him. He wondered if his tightening jaw betrayed to her any sign that he was still drawn to Miss Elizabeth's fine eyes, sparkling wit, uncommon intelligence. He shook his head to remove her from his thoughts.

"Certainly you were appalled at the lack of breeding displayed. It would be insupportable for Charles to marry into that family!" She continued in a softer, yet more determined manner, "Please, I beg you to consider remaining at Netherfield so that we may discuss what we shall do without fear of Charles overhearing!"

Mr. Darcy lifted his eyes to her and was about to reply when Miss Bingley added, "You heard her mother, did you not? Miss Bennet is a dear, sweet girl, but her mother! Is it not quite clear that her sole purpose in promoting a marriage between her eldest and my brother is to elevate their family in society?"

Miss Bingley's pleading was halted by the entrance of Bingley himself, and they both turned in surprise towards him, fearful he may have heard her last comment. It was apparent he had not, for he entered the room in a buoyant manner and with a most jovial greeting.

"Good morning, Caroline! Good morning, Darcy! Beautiful day, is it not?"

Miss Bingley's eyes darted to Mr. Darcy as she answered, "I suppose it is."

Bingley looked to his friend, who merely took a sip from his cup of coffee. "I simply hate to quit Netherfield today," he continued. "I have had such a pleasant time here… especially at the ball. I do believe everyone enjoyed themselves. I know I did."

A smile beamed from his face as Miss Bingley looked down and rolled her eyes. "Yes, Brother, but I believe *some* enjoyed themselves more than *others!*"

"Tell me, Darcy, do you still wish to accompany me to town? I should thoroughly enjoy your company on that tedious journey thither!"

Miss Bingley looked at Mr. Darcy, biting her lip as she awaited his answer.

Darcy paused, rubbing his chin as he contemplated what to say. "I know I told you I was considering it, Bingley, but I fear I cannot. I regret that I have news from my steward of pressing business at Pemberley, and I do not think I have the time for a London visit. If you anticipate being in town any length of time, I shall endeavour to join you at a later date."

Bingley accepted his friend's words good-naturedly and without question. Miss Bingley, upon hearing his comment, looked well-pleased.

* * *

Later that day after Bingley took his leave, Mr. Darcy sat with Miss Bingley and Mr. and Mrs. Hurst in the sitting room. The two sisters were of like mind in their plotting and scheming as they attributed a most disheartening account of the Bennet family's behaviour at the ball.

Miss Bingley's eyes pleaded with Mr. Darcy as did her argument. "Certainly you agree with me that Mrs. Bennet is a most presumptuous woman! How dare she speak so openly and freely about her expectations for Charles and Miss Bennet to become engaged directly? I am quite sure she has the whole of Meryton prepared to offer felicitations."

"Quite imprudent," agreed her sister.

"Now exactly how did Mrs. Bennet phrase it as she was enumerating the many advantages of the match?" Miss Bingley pointedly asked. "I believe it was something to the effect, 'Their marriage will be such a promising thing for my younger daughters, as Jane's marrying so greatly must throw them in the way of other rich men!'"

Upon hearing those words, Mr. Darcy grimaced and took a final gulp from the cup of coffee he gripped in his hand. He had to admit he had been appalled when he overheard Mrs. Bennet speaking so loudly and in such a tasteless manner.

"And the youngest sister; you observed her, I am sure, displaying such unrestrained manners! Is there a redcoat in Hertfordshire unworthy of her flirtations? I could barely keep my countenance!"

Her eyes locked onto those of Mr. Darcy. "We cannot allow any sort of attachment between Charles and Jane Bennet. He is far too guileless to withstand the arts of a family looking to elevate their status. And if they succeed in their scheme, what will become of Charles then? Left to care for an ambitious mother-in-law, obliged to entertain soldiers for the sake of flirtatious, ill-bred sisters? It is not sound!"

Darcy took in a deep breath as he deliberated on her words carefully. But before he could reply, Miss Bingley offered up one more observation from the night of the ball.

"It must have come as quite a shock to you, Mr. Darcy, to learn of Miss Elizabeth Bennet's admiration for Mr. Wickham. I could not understand myself how she had come to be so enamoured of him." She cast a glance at Mr. Darcy and appeared pleased at the effect of her words.

Darcy took in a breath to steel himself for what he was about to say. He stood up and walked to the sideboard, setting down his empty cup. "You are correct, Miss Bingley. What you have said about separating Bingley and Miss Bennet is something upon which I wholeheartedly agree."

Darcy turned to his co-conspirator. "I will concede that Miss Bennet is pleasing of countenance and manner, but it is more than that. In all the times I have had the opportunity to observe her, she displayed no outward regard for Bingley. I believe you may be correct in that she is receiving his attentions to secure a husband of fortune so as to benefit her family, and that is solely due to her mother's encouragement. I would be doing a disservice to Bingley to allow him to ask for Miss Bennet's hand in marriage."

"Yes, you are so correct, Mr. Darcy," Miss Bingley agreed. "She shows no affection toward him. None at all. It is as though she cares nothing for him! What can be done about this?"

Very slowly and deliberately Darcy replied, "We must keep him from returning to Netherfield."

Miss Bingley looked to her sister and then back to Mr. Darcy. "Yes! We shall all depart on the morrow for London and I shall instruct the servants to close up Netherfield for the remainder of the winter. We shall inform them that it is very unlikely that any from our party will return any time soon." A smile came to her face. "And once we are on our way, I shall have a polite little missive sent to Miss Bennet to inform her of our plans and not to expect us back."

"This will hardly please Bingley," Darcy countered.

"He will be displeased for but a short while. You know how easily he falls in and out of love. Once he has been away from Miss Bennet, she will soon be forgotten, as will any attachment for Netherfield. He listens to *you*, Mr. Darcy. He regards *your* opinion most highly." She let out a breath and a smile appeared. "And perhaps there is a pleasant, young lady in town, someone of excellent breeding and disposition, who will soon come to take Miss Bennet's place in his heart."

"Perhaps," Darcy said, not really hearing her words. "I believe it *would* be prudent for *him* to be separated from Miss Bennet to discourage any sort of admiration to continue." Darcy let out a raspy breath. "I heartily concur. We must leave on the morrow! This unsound attachment must be obliterated in its entirety!" Darcy spoke with such force and command that Miss Bingley appeared surprised.

Once these words were out, Darcy felt an odd sense of hopelessness and regret, as he struggled with the fact that Miss Elizabeth's family was completely unsuitable–for Bingley perhaps– and for himself unquestionably. With pinched brows, Darcy slowly sat back down, realizing that the weight of his argument was directed chiefly towards himself. He needed to distance himself from Miss Elizabeth and he was going to destroy his good friend's prospect for love and marital felicity, as well as his own, by doing so.

Georgiana Receives Darcy's Letter
by Sharon Lathan

November 28, 1811

"Miss Darcy, the post was delivered and contains a letter from Mr. Darcy."

Georgiana leapt from the piano bench sending two sheets of music flying off the rest to flutter to the carpet. They would lay unnoticed for over an hour, the young lady's focus entirely upon the folded parchment pieces she snatched from the hand of her companion.

"Thank you, Mrs. Annesley. My, this makes four letters in two weeks!" Her fingers were already slipping under the edge to break the wax seal with the scrolled FD imprinted. "My brother has ever been attentive to his correspondence with me, but this is proving to exceed his previous efforts by a far margin."

"Perhaps he is bored in Hertfordshire."

Georgiana's eyes scanned the first lines, her head shaking negative. "I would consider that highly unlikely, even if not for the lengthy reports of his activities." She glanced upward and noted the puzzled expression crossing Mrs. Annesley's face. Smiling, she explained, "I know your association with Mr. Darcy has been brief, Mrs. Annesley, so naturally you would assume that he, as most gentlemen of his class, must prefer the busyness of London Society. Yet this is far from the truth. Oh, if only I was awarded a sovereign for every time William complained when business or social demands required him to quit Pemberley for Town! My dowry would be tripled by now, I daresay."

A frown settled between her brows at the unbidden mention of her dowry. The dark cloud of remembrance for her recent near elopement with Mr. Wickham was still painful even after several months. That episode, as she now knew, was only the result of Mr. Wickham conspiring to access her dowry and harm her brother, but the awareness of his evil nature did not ease the heartache.

She shook her head and forced the smile to return. "You shall discover in due course that my brother vastly prefers the open countryside to the closed spaces and crowds of the city. No place compares to Pemberley, of course. However, his descriptions of Hertfordshire have been incredibly comprehensive. Far more than when he wrote of his visit with Mr. Sommerston in Berkshire or Lady Catherine in Kent. In fact..."

Georgiana absently sat onto the chair, unfolding the letter she had just received and resuming her reading while simultaneously pulling open a small drawer in the end table and retrieving a tied bundle of letters. She remained silent for a long span of time as she read through the newly delivered missive, and then the previous ones written while he had been in Hertfordshire with Mr. Bingley. Altogether she had received eight letters, the frequency and length increasing as the weeks passed.

Mrs. Annesley called for tea and cakes before sitting across from her charge to wait patiently. Miss Darcy had read portions of the letters to Mrs. Annesley – those portions not personal – and a sense of the man who wrote them had formulated in Mrs. Annesley's mind. Added to her prior impressions of the Master of Pemberley, she was beginning to piece together a sketch of his character. Mr. Darcy had severely questioned her ere accepting her application for employment and then thoroughly investigated her background before consenting to hire her on a conditional basis. Constant scrutiny by fierce eyes amid a face fixed into a permanent scowl had unnerved her during her first weeks as Miss Darcy's companion, but gradually his suspicion and vigilance had ebbed. It had pained him to leave for London in October, although she knew his distress was primarily a result of not wishing to separate from his sister rather than distrust of her. Mrs. Annesley had yet to decipher the cryptic references well enough to uncover what the "incident at Ramsgate" was (although she had her theories), but there was no doubt that Mr. Darcy felt deep guilt over the situation and worried for his sister's emotional state. Mrs. Annesley saw the numerous letters as an expression of his concern and remorse (and indeed they were), but in the most recent correspondences she sensed something else. Something of a more personal nature that had little or nothing to do with Miss Darcy.

Apparently Miss Darcy was beginning to suspect the same.

"A page and a half in this letter all about the hunt he and Mr. Bingley went on." She waved the pages in the air. "Half a page in this one lists the paintings hanging on the walls of Netherfield and a section on the gardens. Today's letter recounts with a poet's clarity the incessant rain falling in Meryton which is, to my brother's chagrin, displacing his ability to ride his horse. Then he embarks on three paragraphs describing the landscape enjoyed while riding, including two long sentences about the horse!" She shrugged one delicate shoulder and looked up at Mrs. Annesley. "The last I can understand due to our shared love of riding and horses. The details of rain and trees and grass? Now that is strange indeed."

"Perhaps he is simply assuring you that, while missing Pemberley, he is surrounded by terrain and activities that please him and allay his homesickness," Mrs. Annesley suggested, not for a moment believing that the reason.

Georgiana nodded slowly, but did not seem convinced. "Perhaps. He has never done so in the past to such depth of descriptiveness, but this time…" She clamped her lips to stop another spontaneous reference to unpleasant matters, inhaled, and resumed in a rush, "What is oddest is that usually his letters are filled with droll commentary on the antics of the people he interacts with. This will undoubtedly surprise you, Mrs. Annesley, and must remain our secret, but Mr. Darcy is quite witty and possesses a keen sense of humor. Only those dear to him ever see this side of his personality, however. His letters to me are replete with his witticisms and I see some of this in his comments about Mrs. Hurst and Miss Bingley, who are ridiculous and annoy…"

She stopped abruptly, one hand flying to cover her mouth and her eyes widening. "Oh! Please forgive me for speaking unkindly about another! I should be more tolerant and accepting. My brother would reprimand me harshly if he heard me speaking so!"

"Be still, child," Mrs. Annesley calmed, her laughter ringing. "It is the duty of an older brother to impress proper manners upon his sister, but I am certain Mr. Darcy would not expect you to not have opinions of your own. Clearly he has opinions about those he meets, hence his 'droll commentary' that you so enjoy. Being polite is one thing. Liking everyone you meet is entirely different. The former maintains peace and is birthed from mature restraint, whereas the latter brands you a fool!"

"Oh, but I do like Mr. Bingley. He is kind and funny and warm. I cannot imagine a person alive not adoring him."

"Yet not his sisters?"

Georgiana flushed and hid her face behind her teacup, taking several gulps before answering. "To be frank… I… well, I cannot abide them. Mrs. Hurst isn't as horrid as Miss Bingley, and it isn't easy to place my finger upon the precise reasons why Miss Bingley troubles me. She is beautiful, fashionable, properly conducting herself with excellent manners, yet," – again that one shoulder shrug – "I only know I wish she would not accompany Mr. Bingley when he visits Pemberley and I pray daily that William will not choose her to be his wife."

Mrs. Annesley's brows rose. "Is that a possibility?"

"Miss Bingley wishes for it, I do know that."

"But if he wanted to marry her, he probably would have already. Fret not, Miss Darcy. Pray instead that he fall in love, perhaps with a lady in Hertfordshire."

Mrs. Annesley's subtle nod at the letters piled in Georgiana's lap served as a reminder of where her thoughts had been heading. Georgiana picked up the topmost letter – the one delivered less than an hour ago and dispatched three days ago – and scanned through it again.

I cannot recall with certainty if I wrote in my previous letter of Bingley and I chancing upon Miss Bennet and her sister some two days after Miss Bennet's restoration of health and departure from Netherfield. I feared you may be concerned, dearest, since I had written to you of Miss Bennet's illness and her sister's close attendance as nursemaid. Miss Bennet appeared hale enough when we met with no obvious lingering deficiency. Miss Elizabeth looked quite well indeed....

The rain is not constantly falling in torrents, yet the respites are brief and do not accord time to venture beyond the stout walls of the house. I confess to being overwhelmed with restlessness and frustration at the forced imprisonment, and did succumb to my need for exercise earlier today. I, and my horse, ended soaked as a result, but it was worth the discomfort. I can only imagine how the Bennet sisters are enduring, most especially Miss Elizabeth, who is a fine walker and appreciates the beauties of a picturesque countryside.

It is odd how empty Netherfield has seemed this past week. Conversation has been sorely lacking anything remotely intriguing. Miss Bingley and Mrs. Hurst apparently know nothing besides gossip and fashion. I find myself longing for one of Miss Elizabeth's challenges or lecturing discourses. She is altogether far too opinionated and argumentative for a proper lady. Nevertheless, I admit that her verbal liveliness did inject the air with a dose of welcomed animation and intelligence.

The ball Bingley was impressed upon to host is scheduled for tomorrow night. Again I must suffer through an interminable evening of engaging those unfamiliar to me in idle chatter. My displeasure aside, I have promised to behave and play the part of interested guest. Yes indeed, dear sister, I shall condescend to dance. I pray the idea does not shock you into a swoon! I assure you I will be selective, and no rules of etiquette will induce me to ask the pleasure of any Bennet sister other than Miss Elizabeth and Miss Bennet. Miss Elizabeth, especially, is a fine dancer so I might enjoy myself to

a degree, albeit using the word "enjoy" in as loose a manner as
possible.

Georgiana lifted her eyes to her companion. "Miss Elizabeth. In all of his letters he writes of her. Oh, he mentions other people as well, but none with this frequency or positive remarks. And note the pattern." She handed the entire missive to Mrs. Annesley. "Each time he writes her name he then launches into a long dissertation about the weather or landscape or the decorations for the ball. Decorations for the ball!" She shook her head and laughed. "I can swear on the Holy Word that William has never, not once in my years of knowing him, ever talked about how a place is decorated!"

The two women stared at each other. Mrs. Annesley's wiser face was set in a knowing expression. Georgiana's face was set in one of stunned amazement. Then a slow smile spread and her blue eyes began to glitter.

Charlotte Waits at Lucas Lodge
by Abigail Reynolds

November 29, 1811

Charlotte wrapped herself in a second shawl and returned to the window seat in upstairs sitting room. The windowpanes were still edged with early morning frost. It was too cold for sitting so far from the fire, but it served the purpose of keeping her family at a distance. Her younger sisters were sitting as close to the hearth as possible, and it was too much trouble for them to call over to her every time they wanted to include her in the conversation.

After spending three days listening to Mr. Collins' excess verbiage, she was not in a mood to converse with anyone. She prayed that all her attentiveness had not been for naught. After dinner last night, she had thought him on the verge of making her an offer when he rambled on about his hopes for the companion of his life. At the last moment he had changed the subject, despite all the encouragement she had given him, telling him how fortunate he was in his position, how anyone would envy his proximity to Rosings Park, and even expressing a desire to hear one of his sermons some day. She could understand how the set-downs Lizzy had given him would give him pause, but he was due to leave Hertfordshire the following day, which meant she had only one more chance to bring him to the point of proposing. As soon as the hour was late enough, she would pay a visit to Longbourn for a final effort.

She did not know what she would do if she failed, despite all the sleepless hours she had spent trying to resolve the issue. Her courses should have begun last week, and while it was not unusual for the time to differ for her from month to month, she feared the worst. Mr. Collins' arrival in search of a wife was providential. She could not like or respect him, but she could tolerate him, and he would take her away from Meryton and Willoughby's mocking eyes. He did not seem to care much that she was plain-featured as long as she flattered him. And he was safe – he was not clever enough to pull the wool over her eyes the way Mr. Robinson had. He was also dull enough that she could most likely fool him into believing her a virgin if she was careful to make sure he drank a few glasses of wedding brandy first. She could cry out as if in pain at the appropriate moment, and a pin secreted in the bed would serve to help her produce a few drops of blood for the sheets. But first he had to be brought to propose.

Just then she spotted a dim figure coming down the lane. A moment of blowing on the windowpane to clear the frost revealed it to be Mr. Collins himself, despite the early hour. An overwhelming wave of relief surged through her. She would not be disgraced; her family would not cast her off, leaving her to a life on the streets. Instead, she would be respectably married to a man of good prospects, and when she returned to Meryton someday, her position as mistress of Longbourn would put her above worries about what Willoughby might say or do. It was the perfect solution to her dilemma.

She would make it as easy for him as possible. Snatching up her bonnet, she hurried out the door, and set out to meet him accidentally in the lane.

Charlotte Confesses Her Engagement to Elizabeth by Abigail Reynolds

November 30, 1811

One dreaded task remained for Charlotte, and that was telling Lizzy about her engagement. Her dearest friend could not have made it clearer that she thought Mr. Collins barely worthy of acknowledgment, and this news would come as a blow to her. Charlotte's anxiety over the event was mixed with annoyance; after all, marrying Mr. Collins would be prudential even if she had no other incentive than a desire for independence, but Lizzy would not see it that way, and she had no intention of humiliating herself by telling her friend the whole truth.

Indeed, Lizzy's reaction was all that Charlotte had feared. "Engaged to Mr. Collins! My dear Charlotte—impossible!"

This reproach was so strong that for a moment Charlotte could not help biting her lip, wondering if she should tell her friend everything. She only regained her composure as she contemplated the unfairness of Lizzy's reaction. After all their years of friendship, apparently Lizzy still had no faith in her judgment.

Charlotte raised her chin slightly. "Why should you be surprised, my dear Eliza? Do you think it incredible that Mr. Collins should be able to procure any woman's good opinion, because he was not so happy as to succeed with you?"

Apparently Lizzy heard the reproach in her voice, for she sat quietly and took a deep breath before saying, "Of course not, my dear it was merely that you took me by surprise. Of course I am pleased for you, and I wish you all imaginable happiness."

"I see what you are feeling," replied Charlotte. "You must be surprised, very much surprised, so lately as Mr. Collins was wishing to marry you. But when you have had time to think it all over, I hope you will be satisfied with what I have done. I am not romantic you know. I never was, I ask only a comfortable home; and considering Mr. Collins's character, connections, and situation in life, I am convinced that my chance of happiness with him is as fair as most people can boast on entering the marriage state." Lizzy was too young and innocent to realize that, compared to men like Mr. Willoughby and Mr. Robinson, Mr. Collins was a candidate for sainthood – or perhaps Lizzy was just fortunate enough never to have been mistreated by a man.

Elizabeth quietly answered, "Undoubtedly."

In the awkward silence that followed, Charlotte knew that Lizzy would never understand, and most likely would hold this decision against her forever. Would she lose her dearest friend as one more consequence of a night's indiscretion? But a still voice inside her reminded her that her intimate friend truly ought to have more faith that she knew what she was doing.

Mr. Collins and
His Successful Love
by Diana Birchall

December 3, 1811

Mr. Collins was not left long to the silent contemplation of his successful love.
— Pride & Prejudice

Mrs. Bennet, on learning the result of the interview between Mr. Collins and her daughter, hurried to her husband's library, to remonstrate with him, and to insist on his making Lizzy marry Mr. Collins. While the three were talking over the matter, Mr. Collins, left alone in the breakfast room, had some time to consider his suit. It was true, he thought, that if Elizabeth continued to refuse, the question being put to her a second, and perhaps even a third time, he would be obliged to concede that she was, indeed, a headstrong, obstinate girl, who did not know her own good fortune in being selected by him from so many other young ladies, including her own sisters. He could not, however, admit the possibility of her being so foolish, for more than a moment. In the first place, his observation, by no means very acute, was at least tolerable enough to collect that Elizabeth was by far the wittiest and the brightest of the sisters. He had some doubt if her cleverness was quite necessary, or would please Lady Catherine; but surely, once married, she would submit, as a good wife ought, to her husband's will, and become quiet and obedient. Then, her mother had assured him that she was only foolish and headstrong in such matters as these, and he was perfectly willing to attribute her reluctance to maiden modesty and to take her real good-nature on faith.

Mr. Collins had studied Logic at Oxford, and by such like reasonings and deducings, he came, as quickly as the slow workings of his mind would permit, to the logical conclusion: Elizabeth would not persist in refusing him. At this very moment, her respected father must be having the word with her that would bring her to reason and compliance. Assured of a happy ending and a pretty and vivacious bride, Mr. Collins called for the servant to bring him writing-materials, and there, in the breakfast room, he happily composed a letter to his Patroness, Lady Catherine de Bourgh. Signing with a flourish and sealing it, he handed it to the servant with instructions to carry it to the post at once, and gave him, in the overflowing pride of his heart, an extra sixpence to speed it along.

This important letter was written, and sent, on the morning of Wednesday, the twenty-seventh of November; and as the servant put it into the morning post, the letter was received at Rosings, no later than Friday, and placed into Lady Catherine's hands. In the parson's absence, that lady had considered it highly praiseworthy and sensible to spend the morning looking into cottages, to make sure that everything inside them was going rightly. Her daughter was not strong enough for such an expedition, and Mrs. Jenkinson remained with her, but Lady Catherine sallied out in a party that included her great friend Lady Metcalfe, her two daughters, Annabella and Isabella, and their governess, Miss Pope.

Word had spread in the village that the ladies were abroad and on the prowl, and the people were in a panic. Some shut the doors tightly and pretended not to be home. Some housewives had the thought of jumping back into bed, pulling the covers up over their heads, and pretending to be sick. Others collected their children and fled to the market in haste. Lady Catherine and Lady Metcalfe, therefore, were quite shocked to find one cottage abandoned, with the fire still blazing merrily in the hearth; another with overturned footstools, children playing, and no housewife in sight; and in a third cottage, a woman apparently expiring of a chest complaint, for she could hardly breathe.

Lady Catherine flung open the door. "My good woman! Lady Metcalfe, have you ever heard such sterterous gasps? She must surely be dying. Fling water upon her, Annabella, will you?"

"Who can she be?" asked Lady Metcalfe, who was very short-sighted. "Poor woman! This is very dreadful."

"It is the Swansons' cottage, is not it, Harrison?" Lady Catherine addressed the governess. "Yes, I believe it is; Swanson is the carpenter, and will be in his shop, or out on some job of work. My good woman, are you able to speak? Where is your husband?"

"He has gone," came the faint whisper. "He has left me – and all my babies."

"Left you; has he? He had no business to do that. I will have a word with him, and he will behave better in future, if he ever wishes to be employed at Rosings again. But why, in his absence, have you kept this cottage so untidy? That floor has not been swept in a week." Lady Catherine ran a silken-gloved finger along the rough wooden mantelpiece. "Pah! I thought so. Soot, as black as night. A disgrace! No wonder you are having trouble breathing. Illness is no excuse for slovenliness. You must get up and dress immediately, Mrs. Swanson, upon my orders, and set about your tasks at once."

"She already is dressed, Lady Catherine," pointed out Isabella laconically.

"Bless me, so she is! What can be the meaning of this? Is the wretched creature shamming?" Lady Catherine moved close to the bed and peered into the heap of blankets. With a swift movement, she pulled them away, revealing a fully clad countrywoman, apron, boots, and all. Leaping out of bed, the woman fell to her knees before her.

"Begging your pardon ma'am," she pleaded, "I was only a-lying down because – because I was took so bad. Jem – that is my husband – left before first light saying as he had a job over three miles past Hunsford, and I have a terrible suspicion he is taken with a woman over there."

"He has, has he," said Lady Catherine grimly. "I will settle that, quickly enough. Harrison, when we get back to Rosings, you will send a man after this recalcitrant workman. Mrs. Swanson, this is no time to be malingering. Your children are hungry, and I see here some potatoes. You ought to boil them, but don't serve them plain; the infants require some more nourishing food. Have you some meat handy?"

"No ma'am, nothing, my man hasn't left me with any money this last ten days you see," she protested sullenly.

"Never mind. Send your oldest boy – you there, run to the butcher's, at once, and tell him to bring your mother a pound of beef, with Lady Catherine's compliments." She turned swiftly to the lamenting woman. "You can pay for it by sewing for me later. Now, come along, Lady Metcalfe, I want to get to the bottom of the strange appearance of some of these other cottages."

Scarcely were they three feet from Mrs. Swanson's door, when a servant from Rosings came running up, a letter in his hand.

"What is that, Morton? What is the matter?"

"A letter come express, ma'am, from the minister, it is, and housekeeper said I was to run and find you," he panted.

"A letter? From Mr. Collins?" She turned it over, frowning. "Surely that might have waited. What can Mr. Collins have to say? He is expected back here tomorrow. I hope he has not written to put off his return."

"Open it and see," pursued Lady Metcalfe. "I confess myself to be curious."

"Very well." Lady Catherine opened the fine seal, and after perusing the letter for a moment, exclaimed. "Gracious Heaven! He has found a wife already."

"Mr. Collins, married?" Lady Metcalfe exclaimed.

"No, no. I will read it to you."

Longbourn House, near Meryton.

To the Right Honourable Lady Catherine de Bourgh,

156

Your Ladyship will forgive me for addressing you in so unexpected and forward a manner, as may not entirely become one of my station, but that it seems to me the office of clergyman in the Church of England is equal to the highest in the land, always supposing his duties are carried out in the spirit of humble self-effacement that I am always wont to practice. I believe I do not presume too highly, in supposing that you will evince all the gracious kindness I have already met with from you, in receiving the news which I am about to relate. I have found the young woman whom I have nominated to be my wife; and when I return into Kent on Saturday, I expect to be in the happy profession of an affianced man. The young lady has not quite accepted my overtures as yet, which is natural, in her modesty and timidity; but she is with her father at this moment, and I have no doubt that she will emerge from his sanctum carrying the orders that will make her consent to be my wife.

This young lady, who is to be united with me as soon as may be, is the second daughter of my cousin Mr. Bennet, whose heir by entail you know I have the honour to be; and although her fortune is negligible, yet it is a highly estimable connection. And Miss Elizabeth makes up for her lack of wealth, by all the qualities that make a true lady and worthy helpmeet. She has wit, and vivacity, to charm me and to brighten our fireside circle at Rosings if I may presume so far; but she also possesses the virtues of economy, prudence, and obedience, as well as youth, good health, and a capacity for hard work that will perfectly suit the situation of a clergyman's wife. I therefore apply for your approval for my seeking her hand, and hope for a speedy acquiescence from the young lady, on which you may depend I shall bring you the happy tidings on Saturday.

I remain, your devoted, honored, and obedient servant, William Collins.

"Well! That is remarkable," finished Lady Catherine dryly.

"Hm! Very suitable, I suppose," said Lady Metcalfe, with some indifference, as it was beginning to rain.

Lady Catherine noticed the same, and putting the letter into her reticule, she climbed into the carriage and directed the coachman to take them home forthwith. They talked of the remarkable letter all the rest of the wet afternoon.

Mr. Collins returned to Hunsford late on Saturday, and the ladies did not see him until church on Sunday morning. There was no opportunity to speak to him, therefore, until they shook his hand after the service, which might not have seemed the best moment to speak of secular matters, but Lady Catherine thought marriage a sacrament, and therefore a subject perfectly suitable for Sunday. As he bowed low over her hand, she condescended to allow a sly smile to linger on her strong features.

"I believe," she said in a lowered tone, "if I am not mistaken, that we may have occasion, to-day, to congratulate you, Mr. Collins?"

He looked up, turned violently red, and stammered as he nodded. "Oh! Yes, yes. That is true. I am indeed the happiest of men, in securing to myself the hand and heart of my most beloved Charlotte."

Lady Catherine looked puzzled. "Charlotte? Excuse me, but – I thought your affianced was called Elizabeth. Miss Bennet, is not she?"

"No, no, she is Miss Charlotte Lucas, of Lucas Lodge. The daughter of Sir William Lucas, the neighbor of – of my cousin, Mr. Bennet."

"Here is some mistake. You wrote to me that you were engaged to Mr. Bennet's daughter. I am sure of it. I have the letter here." She lifted her heavily marked eyebrows in some surprise, and indicated her reticule.

"Yes, yes I know I did, but – I must explain – confidentially, that is - Miss Bennet did not accept – and Miss Lucas was – "

He stopped, in confusion, as a hearty man of fifty came up with his wife and train of children, extending his hand.

"A fine sermon, Collins, 'pon my word! My compliments, Lady Catherine," with a bow.

"Good morning, Sir Basil," said Lady Catherine distractedly. "Mr. Collins, we will speak of this later. Come to tea this afternoon, if you will," she nodded at him with firm finality, gathered her skirts, her daughter and her companion, and moved toward her carriage.

"Yes – certainly, Lady Catherine," he called after her forlornly. For Mr. Collins yet dreaded making known to her the circumstances of his engagement, undoubtedly happy though he was in his successful love.

Swaying Bingley's Opinion of Jane
by Kara Louise

December 8, 1811

Darcy paced back and forth in the sitting room awaiting his guests. He knew this meeting was not going to be easy, but it must be done. Promptly at two o'clock, the Bingley party was announced. Charles Bingley walked in jubilantly ahead of the others and greeted Darcy with a firm handshake and a broad smile upon his face.

"Goodness, Darcy! I can understand my sisters following me into town, but your arrival has certainly taken me by surprise! But do not take me wrong, I am pleased to see you!"

"Thank you, Bingley. It was unfortunate you had already left when I received word from my steward that the issue at Pemberley had been resolved and there was no need for me to make the trip there."

Darcy greeted the others, and Miss Bingley swept into the room. "Good afternoon, Mr. Darcy. It is so good to see you again! Is your sister here? How we would so enjoy seeing her!"

"No, I regret she is not."

Miss Bingley looked to her brother. "Oh, is that not a shame, Charles? She is such a sweet girl. We must make plans to see her soon!" She turned back to Darcy with an enthusiastic smile.

Darcy simply gave a nod of his head and extended his hand toward the chairs and sofa. "Please, come in and sit down."

Bingley settled himself into a chair, sitting on the edge and leaning forward. "So how did you decide to come to town?"

"We began talking about how envious we were of you, Charles, in such superior society and…" Miss Bingley looked over to Darcy for confirmation, "…the next thing we knew, it was decided that we would all quit Netherfield the following day and set out for London."

Bingley gave his sister and friend a brief smile. "But Netherfield… I had hoped to return in a day or two."

"There is no need to rush back, Charles," Miss Bingley began. "We all concurred how much we missed the excellent society here that was so lacking in Hertfordshire. It has been far too long."

"When do you think we might return to Netherfield?" Bingley asked, turning from his sister to Mr. Darcy.

"I see no reason to hurry back at all." Darcy took in a deep breath. "Bingley, in all honesty, Netherfield was a decent house in the country, but I fear it would not prove to be a wise purchase. I must agree with Miss Bingley that the neighbourhood lacked any sort of good society."

"Just what are you saying, Darcy? I found everyone to be most friendly!" Bingley looked squarely at his friend.

"Perhaps that is true, but unfortunately I found them to be simple country folk. No one of any great esteem lived in the vicinity. You must begin to think about those with whom you associate; mere amiability cannot be your only standard."

A flicker of concern crossed Bingley's face. "They were all good people," he protested.

"They were, Charles," added Miss Bingley. "But therein lies the problem. They were merely good. They lacked the connections, the breeding, the status to which we are accustomed… to which we are entitled."

Bingley turned back to Darcy. "Are you of the opinion, then, that I should not make an offer to purchase Netherfield?"

"I do not believe you should."

Bingley suddenly stood up and shook his head violently." But what of Miss Bennet? I must go back so I can further our acquaintance!"

Darcy walked over to him. He normally stood a few inches taller than his friend, but the distance seemed greater now, as Bingley's posture was slightly slumped and Darcy's very erect.

"For what purpose, man?" Darcy asked, his mouth suddenly dry.

"What purpose? She is an angel! She is everything I have longed for! I intend to offer her…"

"Bingley." Darcy subdued him by placing both hands firmly on his shoulders and looked him squarely in the eye. "Certainly you viewed Miss Bennet as nothing more than a delightful distraction."

"Delightful distraction! Good Lord, Darcy! She was much more to me than that! Could you not see how taken I was by her?"

"But was she as taken with you?"

Bingley's eyes narrowed as he looked from his friend to his sister and then back to his friend. "Yes, I believe she was."

Miss Bingley stepped forward and with a cunning, condescending smile said, "Indeed, she is a very sweet, amiable girl, Charles, the most delightful person in all of Hertfordshire, but…" She looked beseechingly at Darcy for assistance.

"But what?" Bingley demanded.

Darcy spoke softly, but forcefully, to his friend. "Bingley, it pains me to say this, but she exhibited no outward regard for you. She received your attentions very politely…"

"Politely?" Bingley interrupted, his countenance reddening and his whole demeanour shaking. "You are all quite mistaken!"

"Bingley, consider this. You came to Hertfordshire and singled her out. Without taking into consideration her family connections, you deemed her worthy of your undivided esteem. With the pressure from her mother to secure a husband of at least moderate fortune as their home is entailed away, she had no choice but to accept your attentions."

"No! It is much more than that!" Bingley directed his attention to Louisa and her husband, who had been sitting quietly, observing the machinations of Darcy and Miss Bingley. "Certainly you beheld her admiration for me!"

Louisa raised her eyebrow and shook her head. "No, my dear brother, I honestly cannot say I did."

In a fit of frustration, Bingley pounded his fist against the wall. "You did not make her acquaintance as deeply as I, nor did you apprehend the admiration in her eyes as she spoke, the tenderness of her voice, or the warmth in her smile. She loves me! I am convinced of it! And I love her!"

"Bingley, I am willing to allow that she has a most serene nature, but there is more to consider than merely that and her angelic beauty." Darcy fortified himself with a deep breath and continued. "She is continually pressured by her mother to marry a man of fortune, her family connections are nothing, their behaviour time and again points toward their ill-breeding, and she challenges every word you say!" His eyes flashed with anger.

Every eye turned in astonishment to Darcy, who closed his own as he realized his blunder.

"Challenges my every word?" gasped Bingley. "How could you accuse her of such a thing?" He sat down, completely spent. Shaking his head, he softly uttered, "You just do not know her. None of you. You do not know her!"

Miss Bingley interjected while Darcy made an attempt to gain back his composure. "Charles, Miss Bennet may have appeared to be everything you have ever wished for in a woman, but is it worth taking the risk of going into a marriage where love is not returned?"

Bingley's face lost all expression, paled, and he looked down at the ground. "I... I..." He shook his head and raked his fingers through his hair. "I really thought she returned my affection. How could I have been so mistaken?"

Miss Bingley threw a triumphant smile at Darcy and then drew near to her brother, placing a hand lightly upon his shoulder. "Love can sometimes blind us, Charles, and we need those who love and care for us to point these things out when we cannot see them ourselves."

Darcy stepped back and leaned against the wall for support. The fire in his eyes was suddenly displaced by a searing pain and anguish. Despite the apparent victory, a sense of defeat and resignation swept over him as he realized he felt as much grief in losing Miss Elizabeth as his friend felt in losing Miss Bennet.

Caroline's Letter to Jane
by Monica Fairview

December 18, 1811

Caroline was in the parlor instructing her housekeeper on household matters when the front doorbell rang.

The time for morning calls was over. Who could this be?

The unmistakable voice of Mr. Darcy reached her. She dismissed the housekeeper and looked to the doorway in anticipation.

"Mr. Darcy," announced the butler.

"Mr. Darcy?" said Caroline with a tinge of concern as he entered, for he looked pale and slightly disheveled. His cravat was askew and his perfectly combed hair was ruffled.

"Nothing has happened to Charles?" she said in alarm.

"No," said Mr. Darcy. "Charles was well when I last saw him."

She searched in her mind for a reason for his perturbance, but could find none.

"And dear Miss Darcy?"

"Georgiana is well."

"Won't you sit down, Mr. Darcy? I will ring for some tea."

Mr. Darcy sat down, but scarcely had she time to tug at the bell-pull when he was up again. He began to pace the room.

A sudden glimmer of hope rose up in Miss Bingley's heart. Her pulse quickened. She could only account for his strange behavior with one thing. Surely not? Could it be? Did he intend to—?

"Miss Bingley," he said.

Caroline pressed trembling hands together. This was it, the moment she had been aspiring to for so long.

"Miss Bingley," he said again.

Say it, willed Caroline. Say it.

"I have determined that you must write them a letter."

"A letter?" she gawked at him, though she never gawked, trying to make sense of his words. Her heart plummeted. She controlled her sense of disappointment with difficulty. Foolish, foolish girl, she told herself.

"Write a letter to whom, sir?" she asked. "You mock me surely? It is you who are the more experienced correspondent. You write such charming letters."

She was beginning to have an inkling what this was about. Bitter disappointment rose up in her.

"I cannot write to them with any propriety," said Mr. Darcy. "It would be unseemly."

She schooled herself to show no expression, but inside her heart was like lead.

"I am afraid you have lost me, Mr. Darcy. I do not understand you."

He put a hand to his brow and approached the armchair.

"You must write Miss Bennet a letter," he said urgently. "She will surely be expecting your brother to return to Netherfield. You must make matters entirely clear. You must remove from her mind any expectancy or desire for such a possibility."

Surely such a letter did not call for such turmoil. Was that the way of it, then? A woman's instinct does not fail her and she knew then that the message was not for Miss Jane Bennet at all but for Elizabeth Bennet.

Even as pain lanced through her, she felt a kind of fierce joy. He was denying himself then. He was bidding Elizabeth Bennet farewell.

"I shall write the letter, Mr. Darcy," she said. "You are perfectly correct, as always. We cannot give Miss Bennet false hope regarding my brother. It will not do at all. Tell me what I must say, and I will be happy to do so. I am always at your service, as you know, Mr. Darcy."

Darcy Suffers on Christmas Eve
by Sharon Lathan

December 24, 1811

The snowflakes drifted slowly downward. They were enormous flakes and floating so delicately on the air that, even in the inky darkness behind the thick glass with only the faint glow of lamplight reflecting, Fitzwilliam Darcy could visualize the minute crystals and unique geometry of each flake. It was mesmerizing and oddly calming to his tumultuous thoughts. He sipped the cocoa that was now lukewarm, watched the snow fall and gather into piles on the panes, and struggled to stir up the Christmas cheer one was supposed to enjoy on Christmas Eve.

It was not working.

He couldn't readily recall the last Christmas that was truly joyous. Surely it was before his mother died, but the memories were faded and supplanted by so many years of forced gaiety. Oh, they exchanged presents and decorated the house and went to church and delighted in a lavish feast. Often they visited Rivallain for the day, the estate of his uncle and aunt, the Earl and Countess of Matlock, and once or twice they had dwelt at Darcy House in London for the holiday activities there. But like all festivities since his mother's passing, and now his father's, the celebratory atmosphere was muted.

Of course he strived to celebrate the day for his sister Georgiana's sake, understanding that a child needed the merrymaking. And lauding the birth of their Savior was indeed a commemoration he took very seriously. Yet personally, he often felt that the entire season could easily pass by without him noticing or caring.

Darcy had grown so accustomed to the attitude that it hardly registered any longer. Even while plotting and planning for Georgiana and purchasing gifts—that a delight he truly did enjoy—his internal zeal for Christmas was dim. He did not dread the holiday nor was he particularly gloomy over it; he just did not care all that much.

So why was this year so different? Why did he feel a melancholy blanketing his soul? And why did the dreams continue to invade his sleep? Why was she persistent in burrowing into his mind and head...? No! He refused to even think it! This Christmas was no different than the previous twenty-seven.

He sighed unconsciously and continued with his rapt contemplation of the falling snow and abstracted sipping of the cooling cocoa.

Georgiana Darcy sat on the sofa near the fire. She had been reading aloud but halted several minutes ago when it became clear that her brother was not listening to her. Now she studied him in perplexity. Georgiana was well aware that Christmas was not exactly a period of crazed jubilation for her brother, but he usually showed some enthusiasm. He never failed to create a special atmosphere for her and showered her with expensive gifts. Since she knew no different, it honestly never occurred to her to yearn for more. Georgiana was a girl quite complacent and content in her life. Her only desire was to please her family, that being primarily her adored older brother. Thus, she was disturbed by his current distraction and somberness.

None would refer to Fitzwilliam Darcy as gregarious or buoyant, but the private man was one of tender humor and affection. That he was overwhelmingly devoted to his sister could be denied by no one, especially Georgiana. She held him in tremendous awe and respect, but also took his love and playful teasing for granted. Yet ever since his return from Town and the sojourn in Hertfordshire with Mr. Bingley, he had been... odd.

She shook her head. It made no sense whatsoever. Naturally it distressed her. Not for her sake but because she loved him too much to think of him as being in pain. Yet, with the overconfidence of youth and the towering admiration of a worshipful younger sister, she shrugged it off. In her mind, her brother was fearless and capable of solving any dilemma.

So she smiled and rose to bid him goodnight. He smiled genuinely in return and held her close for several minutes, wished her sweet dreams and gave a teasing reminder not to wake him at the crack of dawn, and after a tender kiss to her cheek, she retired to her room no longer fretting over her complicated sibling but losing herself in dreams of presents.

Darcy watched her gracefully exit the parlor, his heart surging with happiness as it always did when considering his sister. But as soon as she left, seemingly taking the light and music and laughter with her, the pensiveness drenched him once again. It was late and he felt simultaneously weary and jittery. He stared at the faint light beyond the doorway, imagined the shadowy corridors between this chamber and his suite of cold and empty rooms—*Where did that thought come from?*—and actually shuddered.

Then, just as abruptly as the sadness, he was jolted by a flare of anger. He muttered a harsh curse, strode briskly to the low table where the tea and snacks sat, and placed the drained mug onto the silver tray with a plunk. He squared his shoulders, straightening to his full and considerable height, and marched purposefully from the room.

His thoughts were darker than the illuminated hallways. What was it about Elizabeth Bennet that had bewitched him so? He truly felt as if under a spell that consumed him and made no sense whatsoever. She was so completely unsuitable! She was infatuated by George Wickham, for goodness sake. That spoke volumes. And her family? He shuddered anew.

Oh, but she was beautiful. Indeed, so very beautiful.

He paused outside his dressing room door, one hand on the knob as his throat constricted and heart lurched with longing. He cursed again, a habit that was quite unlike him normally but lately seemed to be occurring frequently, and reached to loosen the cravat that was strangely now choking off his air supply. He pivoted and entered his bedchamber. For tonight, he would manage to undress himself. Facing the calmly professional presence of his valet while he was in what could only be termed "a mood" was intolerable!

Yet as he resisted slamming the door violently behind him with tremendous restraint, he discovered his steps slowing. He halted in the middle of his room. He gazed at the comforting surroundings, savored the warmth of the crackling fire as it seeped into his chilled skin, and awaited the peaceful relaxation that inevitably washed over him when alone in his sanctuary.

It did not come.

Rather he recalled the dreams that had, in one shape or another, been haunting him nearly from the moment he encountered a vivid pair of brown eyes within the crowd at an obscure dance assembly in Meryton.

He wanted to be angry.

He wanted to be disgusted with himself.

And he wanted to forget her.

At least that is what he told himself. But even now, as he remembered his dreams and remembered their conversations in Hertfordshire, he knew a smile was spreading over his face and heat was flushing through his body.

Some of that, he knew, was due to the nature of many of his dreams. It annoyed him to a degree, and he was embarrassed to a degree. But he logically deduced that it had nothing to do with Miss Elizabeth personally. No, indeed not! It was simply that he had reached the point where needing a woman, a wife, was a physical necessity. Surely that was the primary reason why increasingly erotic musings were causing him to bolt awake in a sweat of unfulfilled desire.

If it was always Elizabeth Darcy—*Bennet!*—who brought him to such a state, well that could be logically explained as well. Right?

Of course! It was because she had enchanted him in some way that he could not comprehend. Her passionate personality, her fire as she argued with him, her intelligence as she countered every last one of his held beliefs, her teasing smile and sparkling eyes as she laughed at him—*At him! Mr. Fitzwilliam Darcy of Pemberley!*—drove him virtually insane until he no longer controlled his faculties. Until his dreams, both day and night, were invaded by her.

Yes, that was it.

And if he was beginning to dream of her as the mother to his children?

Well, that was more troubling.

He again scanned the room, only now he was seeing it as in the recent dreams. Elizabeth curled up in his chair, wearing a soft gown of blue with a baby at her breast. He and Elizabeth reclining on the bed with several children jumping on the mattress as they all laughed. The door to the unused dressing room, once belonging to his mother, ajar with Elizabeth brushing her incredible hair and smiling at him via the mirror while he held a child in his arms. Elizabeth pregnant and standing before him while he caressed the swell of her belly with his hands. Elizabeth...

He shook his head to clear the strange and disturbing visions that had started in earnest these past two weeks.

Since returning to Pemberley.

Since preparing for Christmas.

He passed a hand over his face.

You are lonely, Darcy, he thought. *Admit it. You want a wife and a family.*

Of course this was not a huge revelation. He had longed for a family of his own for most of his adult life. He had envisioned the silent halls of Pemberley echoing with the noise of childish laughter and running feet. He had desired a relationship as his parents possessed. He had searched endlessly for a woman to love.

Did he love Elizabeth Bennet?

172

He crawled under the counterpane, the cold linen upon his flesh a sharp contrast to the imaginary fever he felt flowing over his skin while dreaming of her. The flames of passion and tranquil warmth of affection were so incredibly real. Yet, he did not know the answer to his question. Did he love Elizabeth Bennet? Or did he merely desperately crave a connection that presently eluded him? Was he simply weary of searching and being alone?

He no longer knew. But as the tendrils of sleep claimed him, he recognized that his anger and disgust were a sham. The edges of his unconscious mind accepted the love he refused to acknowledge in broad daylight. He reached for the dreams, however they would come to him on this night, Christmas Eve, as an intoxicant that he wanted and required.

"Elizabeth," he whispered as sleep overtook him, not even aware that he had done so.

And eventually the dream came.

This one was different, as they all were, although the essence was the same.

He walked down the main floor corridor toward the parlor with a spring in his step that was utterly inconceivable in his real world but completely normal in this imaginary world. Happy voices, laughter, and singing reverberated down the hall, growing in volume as he neared the gaping portal. He distinguished each one of them, placing names to the individual tones with warm, deep emotion attached. Many of the names would escape him when he woke—this he knew on some level—but in his dream they were dear and intimate.

There was Richard and Georgiana, his Aunt Madeline and Uncle Malcolm, even Jonathan and Priscilla. These were not a surprise. But as he turned the corner and crossed the threshold, his eyes instantly scanned the room and alit upon the one voice dearest of all.

Elizabeth.

He always knew she would be there, somewhere in the midst of those he loved most in the world, belonging there as surely as he did.

She stood next to Richard laughing at some joke his cousin had made. Her ringing laugh, the one he insisted annoyed him while in Hertfordshire but he knew never had, was now the sweetest music. It filled him to bursting with a joy unlike anything he had ever experienced. Even not directed at him, her happiness was a profound balm to his soul, and the smile that had been forming before entering the room grew wider.

Then she noted his presence and turned in his direction, her glorious eyes engaging his. And there quite simply were no words in the English language to describe what passed between or to relate how he felt. Yes indeed, it was magical, and the enchantment feared in his waking moments was wholly understood in this visionary place as the purest form of bonded love.

He accepted it. He relished it. He claimed it. And he returned it wholeheartedly.

He took a step toward her, intending to enfold her into his arms and press her against his heart, but his legs were abruptly engulfed.

"Papa! Papa!"

Dreaming-Darcy was not the slightest bit surprised by the chaotic assault of several tiny arms and piping voices. In fact, his spirit soared higher, the missing pieces of his puzzled real life snapping together instantly, into a masterpiece depicting earthly paradise. A booming laugh launched from his mouth and he knelt to administer hugs and kisses to the surging mass of children clamoring to accept his love.

Then Elizabeth was there. His wife. He stood, gazing at her with his entire soul visible in his eyes. She smiled simply, raising one hand to lightly touch his cheek, and said, "Happy Christmas, William."

On some level his rational mind knew it was fantastical, as the number of offspring defied what was physically possible unless Elizabeth had birthed triplets once a year! But of course, dreams have a way of melding reality and allegory. Besides, it was the emotions attached to the fabricating dream that counted. The power of hearing her utter his name, the shortened name only those dear to him used, was so strong. Add to that the intensity of affection from a multitude of quarters and his sleeping mind was soothed as it never was in his waking life.

The dream proceeded as all dreams do. It flipped incoherently from scene to scene, some bizarre in their content and hazy while others were crystalline. The strange mingling of credible specifics—such as Georgiana a grown woman and the heirloom Christmas decorations adorning the Manor—with points impossible—like his parents conversing with Elizabeth—seemed normal within the boundaries of the dream.

It wasn't the details that resonated but the themes of family and love. And as happened every night, he jerked awake before the final consummation of expressing his love to his wife. The ache of need with heart pounding and perspiration rapidly chilling his skin brought on tremors and groans.

He lurched to his feet, crossing the room to stir the smoldering logs. He stared into the flames, his body warming as he tried to make sense of it. The questions flashed through his brain as they did every night. Why her? Was it possible to love in such a way? Was it fated for him as he hoped? Had he childishly imagined his parents possessing such a love? Would he ever have a family of his own? Was he a romantic fool destined to be disappointed?

Did he love Elizabeth Bennet?

And then it dissolved, as it inevitably did. The cold air restored his clarity, the fuzzy sentiments dissipated, his rational intellect reinstated, and logic took over. It was only because he was lonely. It was due to the nature of the Christmas holiday focusing on love and felicity leading to nonsensical musings.

He could not be in love with the lowborn, argumentative, fiery Elizabeth Bennet!

The dreams were nice, pleasant, and passionate, but harmless. *Just enjoy them while they last,* he thought to himself. Why not? They will pass. You will never see Miss Bennet again. God will bring a suitable mate to you. The years will unfold sensibly and composedly. Indeed, serenity will prevail, as it should.

So with that comforting thought conquering the turmoil, his mind calmed and his heart beat a regular rhythm. He returned to his bed, his slumber, and his dreams.

Lady Catherine's Christmas
by Diana Birchall

December 25, 1811

Christmas makes the strongest demands of any sacred day upon a clergyman, but one might particularly feel for Mr. Collins, whose maiden Christmas sermon he must preach before his formidable patroness, Lady Catherine de Bourgh. All went off well, however, and he was gratified to be invited, after his efforts, to take his Christmas dinner at Rosings. To him this was the crown of his ambitions, and he took his seat at the foot of the table, and followed Lady Catherine's minute directions for carving the roast of beef, with such alacrity and compliance that her ladyship actually smiled upon him.

"I must say, Mr. Collins, you make a better job of carving than our previous clergyman, Mr. Horner, ever did. I never could persuade him attend to my instructions properly. He would always carve the meat against the grain, and it ended, as it must, in strings. Strings, Mr. Collins!" Her Ladyship told him.

"Strings! Very sad, upon my word," he answered, looking complacently at the platefuls he was filling rapidly with nice thick rosy slabs.

"Yes; and he never would listen to my directions about his sermons, either. Quite indecent, they were. Why, once he preached a sermon about how the sin of pride would keep one out of Heaven, and he looked most meaningly at me for its entire length. Insufferable man!"

"And I do believe," put in Mrs. Jenkinson, Miss de Bourgh's companion, "that he had designs in matrimony – above his station."

She nodded and winked vigorously, so the lace on her specially fashioned Christmas headdress swung, as she cast her eyes on Miss de Bourgh, who blushed and simpered.

"That is never to be spoken of, Miss Jenkinson," said Lady Catherine severely. "Never. What the man's presumptions might be is no concern of ours."

"Shocking, shocking," chimed in Mr. Collins, starting to attack his beef and parsnips with a good will. "A clergyman, of all people, ought to know the meaning of the hymn, 'The rich man in his castle, the poor man at his gate, God made them high and lowly, and ordered their estate.'"

"That might be the subject of your next sermon," ventured Miss de Bourgh with the air of saying something very daring.

"Indeed it might," nodded Lady Catherine, "those fine sentiments cannot be too widely promulgated."

"I hope," asserted Mr. Collins, "that I know my place. A clergyman such as myself, should be very certain to know it. A man of the cloth, educated at Oxford as I was, is of course a gentleman, equal in some ways to any in the land; yet in his calling, he must ever show a proper humility. That is exactly what I did when I cogitated upon the important matter of selecting a companion for my future life."

"And you seem to have done it very well," said Lady Catherine approvingly. "Mrs. Collins, that is to be, has no ideas or airs above her station, I collect, but is a modest country woman, who knows how to mend and make do."

"Indeed, that she is; my Charlotte is a very model for prudence and economy. I will warrant, Lady Catherine, that you will find nothing at all in her to disapprove."

"I am sure of that. I know, in fact, that you have chosen where you should, and as you should. It will be well to have a clergyman who is wisely married, and not subject to any preposterous ideas."

"Oh, I hope I never have any ideas at all, Lady Catherine," he assured her earnestly. "That would be most inappropriate – most unfit. To think of your daughter, who might marry anyone!"

Lady Catherine drank a glass of French wine reflectively, and swirled it in its crystal. "Yes – that is the question. Now that you are so soon to be married yourself, Mr. Collins, and as you are a man of the cloth, after all, I believe I may confide in you."

"Confide – in me?" he almost stammered, and lay down his knife lest he drop it in his excitement. "It would be the greatest honour of my life, and be very sure that you may count upon me, in my sacred office, to keep anything you say, perfectly confidential."

"I am sure you would," she nodded, and fixing him with her penetrating dark eye, she proceeded. "You are an uncommonly intelligent young man, Mr. Collins, with more than ordinary perception, and I suppose it has occurred to you to wonder about my daughter's marriage, has not it?"

"It is not my place, madam," he began, but she continued.

"What you may not be aware is that my late sister, Lady Anne Darcy, and myself, destined her to be the bride of her son and my nephew, Mr. Darcy. You have met that gentleman, I believe?""Why yes, I have indeed – I told you he was at Netherfield, the home of some neighbors of my cousins at Longbourn. They – the Bingleys, I mean – perhaps had hopes that he would become attached to Mr. Bingley's sister, but I never saw any sign of it."

"Naturally not. His hand and heart are both intentioned to be the property of my daughter."

"Oh!" Mr. Collins clasped his hands together with an ecstatic smack. "That will be a marriage such as has never been seen before between Kent and Derbyshire. What an alliance of family and fortune, to say nothing of the abundant personal qualities of gentleman and lady!"

"They will be a most handsome couple," added Mrs. Jenkinson, tipping her head affectedly.

"When is the wedding to be?" asked Mr. Collins. "You know I am engaged to bring my Charlotte into Kent only a scant few days after these Christmas festivities. I hope we will be in our little nest at Hunsford before the middle of January. As I will be traveling to bring her to her new home, I probably ought not to offer to be available for the ceremony before the fifteenth, or perhaps the twentieth, of that month. But I need hardly tell you how honoured, how gratified, I would be, to perform these distinguished nuptials. Unless," a thought distracted him, "you mean her to be married in Derbyshire?"

"No, no, Mr. Collins, you mistake me." Lady Catherine's dark brows beetled together and she looked thunderous, so that Mr. Collins quailed.

"Have I said anything – "he said with compunction, trembling a little.

"Certainly not. It is only that I have not made myself clear. There is no engagement as yet."

"No engagement? But I thought the match was planned, between you and Mrs. Anne Darcy.

"So it was, and Anne is docile and obedient in this matter, just as she ought to be. The difficulty is the gentleman himself. He is more than of age, and yet he has never come forward to fulfill the pledge made by his mother."

"That is bad – very bad," commented Mr. Collins. "What do you suppose is the reason for this hesitation?"

"I am afraid," said Lady Catherine grimly, "that he has a spark of self-will, my nephew. It is difficult for us to conceive, but he may consider that a promise made by his mother, and not by himself, is not a necessary one to keep."

"Oh, surely that could never be!" Mr. Collins drew back in horror. "That would hardly be possible. Mr. Darcy is a byword for proper thinking and behavior, he is a very fine gentleman, from all I have ever heard, and seen with my own eyes. I have had quite a bit of conversation with him, too. You know I consider myself a judge of gentlemanly behavior, as is only proper and becoming to my position."

"Have you conversed with him, indeed? Then you may have seen something of his pride and self-will."

"He was all graciousness and condescension to me, I assure you, Lady Catherine. My cousin Elizabeth – " he pronounced her name with a little embarrassment that his patroness did not miss, "she wanted to check me from speaking to him; but I told her I must know better than a young lady like herself, and I was right."

"Miss Elizabeth," said Lady Catherine suspiciously. "Is she one of your cousin's daughters?"

"Yes, she is. The second," he said shortly.

"Is she a pretty girl?"

"Some might say so. I prefer, I confess, the looks of my own dear Charlotte."

"As is very proper. But this Miss Elizabeth – she is acquainted with Mr. Darcy?"

"She is indeed. They danced together at Netherfield, and it was the talk of the neighborhood."

Lady Catherine was silent for a moment. "So!" she exclaimed, in a tone of extreme anger. "This is where the mischief lies!" She pondered a little longer. "Wait – that letter you wrote to me, announcing your engagement to one of your cousin's daughters. This girl is the one?"

Mr. Collins was beet red in his confusion. "Yes – no – it was all a mistake. I never had any serious thought but for anyone but my Charlotte," he stammered.

"So, this girl is a minx and a vixen, and she is causing trouble." Lady Catherine nodded emphatically to herself. "I knew there was something amiss somewhere. It is well. I thought things were awry when we were not invited to Pemberley this Christmas."

She drummed her thick fingers on the lace-covered mahogany table. Everyone was silent as she considered. "I know what I must do," she said at last.

"Wh – what?" asked Mr. Collins, awed.

"I will go to Pemberley this minute. Yes, and take Anne, and you may accompany us, Mrs. Jenkinson. Summon the maids to pack, and tell Harris to inform the coachman to make ready for a long trip with the best horses. If we leave immediately after breakfast tomorrow, we will be only one night on the road, and be at Pemberley by this time tomorrow night."

"What will you do there, madam, if I may ask? Am I to remain here?" asked Mr. Collins nervously.

"Certainly you are to remain here," she said impatiently. "You are not going into Hertfordshire yet, and we will return well before it is time for your own wedding-journey. No, I am going to see Mr. Darcy," she stood and rapped her mahogany stick sharply on the shining floor, "and make him see what is his duty."

Charlotte Lucas at Year's End
by Abigail Reynolds

December 31, 1811

Charlotte had managed to avoid making any appearance in public since her ill-fated dance with Mr. Willoughby at the Netherfield Ball. No one doubted her when she made the excuse that she was too busy preparing for her wedding to attend this party or that dinner. After all, why should they doubt practical, dependable Charlotte? She would never let them know the truth – that she stayed at home to avoid a possible encounter with Willoughby. Her sole excursion each week was church services. Willoughby belonged to a different parish, so it was a safe haven for her.

She counted down each week as it went by. This would be the penultimate Sunday service she would attend in Meryton – just one more Sunday, then a few days until she was free. That it would be her wedding as well did not signify much to her compared to that it would be the day she would leave Hertfordshire behind, along with her terror of discovery and the possibility of any contact with Willoughby. Twelve days and she would no longer need to fear the consequences of her rash actions.

After the service, she stepped outside for some fresh air, knowing that her gregarious father would spend the next half hour or more chatting with his friends and neighbors. Afterwards he would exclaim, as he did every week, that he had no idea where the time had gone. Next week would be the last time she would hear that as well.

She jumped when a voice that had haunted her dreams came from behind her. She turned to see the face she had done her utmost to avoid remembering, but it had done no good. "Charlotte, I must speak to you," Mr. Robinson said urgently.

If only she could run from him – but no, she was practical, dependable Charlotte. Instead, she inclined her head and said coolly, "It is *indeed* a surprise to see you here once again. Beyond that, I have nothing whatsoever to say to you." Clutching her shawl tightly around her, she started to walk away.

Her effort to escape was stymied as his hand firmly grasped her elbow. "Please, Charlotte. I just want a few minutes of your time."

Her lips tightened. There were too many people nearby. She could ill afford to draw their attention – it could ruin everything. "You have precisely three minutes, then. What is it you are so eager to say, then?"

He had the audacity to look injured. "Who is he?"

"Who are you talking about?" She saw no reason to make this easy for him.

"That man – the one you plan to marry." His face twisted as if the words tasted sour in his mouth.

"I can't see that it is any of your business."

"Of *course* it is my business! I thought we had an understanding."

She laughed incredulously. "The only understanding was the one you had with your friend Willoughby. Tell me, was it worth it?

"Was *what* worth it?"

"All that *distasteful* effort of suffering through my company. Was it worth two hundred pounds, or do you think you deserve more?"

He paled. "What are you saying?"

"Did he not tell you? Mr. Willoughby was *kind* enough to explain your wager to me when you did not return as you promised. You played your little game, you won your money *fairly*, and I am the one who paid for it all – and am likely to keep paying for it if I were to stay within Mr. Willoughby's reach. Now leave me alone and find some other poor woman who has never done you any harm to torment."

"That is not what happened! You must believe me. That may have been how it started, but I cared for you, Charlotte, or I would not be here."

She snorted. "You said you would return within a fortnight. You are over a month late, and I am not a fool."

He made a helpless gesture. "When I went home, I discovered my father was gravely ill. I could not leave until he was out of danger, and then it was almost Christmas. It never occurred to me that you would not wait for me. How could you agree to marry someone else so quickly?"

"How *could* I? How could I do anything *else*, under the circumstances?"

His eyes widened. He was a fine actor, she would have to give him credit for that. "Charlotte…"

Suddenly her father stood between them, for once lacking his jovial smile. "Mr. Robinson, did I not make myself clear in my letter?"

Mr. Robinson bowed. "Sir William."

Her father tucked her hand in his arm and escorted her away. "I hope he was not annoying you too much, my dear. I told him in no uncertain terms that he was not to trouble you again."

Charlotte's chest felt tight. Did her father know what had happened? Had Willoughby *told* him? "How did you come to be corresponding with him?" she asked suspiciously.

Sir William patted her hand. "Oh, he sent me a letter asking my permission to make you an offer. I took care of it."

Her free hand stole to her neck. "How did you take *care* of it?"

"I told him you were already engaged to a fine gentleman. I thought that would be the end of it. But he wrote again, saying there must have been some kind of mistake because you and he had an understanding, so then I had to be firm. You have certainly had your share of admirers lately, my dear!"

"*When* did he write you?"

"Oh, I do not recall precisely. A few days after you wisely accepted Mr. Collins' offer, I believe. You made the right choice there, my dear; he has a fine living now and will inherit Longbourn someday, whereas Mr. Robinson's prospects are more limited. All's well that ends well, as they say!"

They had reached the carriage where the rest of the family waited for them. There could be no further conversation on the topic, but Charlotte could not stop her thoughts so easily. She no longer knew what to believe. Had Mr. Robinson been serious after all? Had Willoughby been lying to her? But no, Mr. Robinson had not denied the wager, and that should be enough of an answer. But why then would he write to her father?

It did not matter. In the end, she would be married to Mr. Collins in less than a fortnight, and she would never know the truth of the matter.

Charlotte Lucas - New Year's Day
by Abigail Reynolds

January 1, 1812

Lady Lucas was all aflutter at their first visitor in the year of Our Lord 1812. "A happy new year to you, Judge Braxton! This is an unexpected pleasure. I cannot recall the last time our home was honored with your presence. Please sit down and allow me to order some refreshments."

Charlotte was paralyzed for a moment until she realized the judge was alone. Even then, after a polite greeting, she attended to her work with more than her usual diligence. She had no reason to suspect this was anything more than a social call, but it seemed odd that Willoughby's uncle would make a rare appearance just at this moment.

The judge was slightly more stooped than she recalled, but his pride of bearing was still evident. "The pleasure is mine, and please accept my good wishes for the new year. I spend most of my time in London these days, but even I can wish to see my own home at Christmas, and if it affords an opportunity to renew my acquaintance with my neighbors, so much the better. I am hoping to persuade you to attend a Twelfth Night dinner at Ixton Place. Not a ball, just a friendly gathering."

Lady Lucas clasped her hands together as if this were the most delightful news she had ever heard. "We would be honored to attend. Would we not, Charlotte?"

Charlotte forced a smile. "It would be a pleasure." She would run away from home before she would go willingly to Willoughby's home.

"Splendid!" He nodded at Charlotte. "And I hear there is to be a wedding soon. I hope you will forgive me if I still half expect you to be a young girl rather than a lady on the brink of matrimony."

After a visit of perhaps half an hour, the judge announced that he must be going. When Lady Lucas, all attentiveness, would have seen him out, he instead requested the company of the bride-to-be.

Charlotte, her stomach clenched in knots, walked beside him until he stopped just short of his carriage.

"Miss Lucas, as much as I respect your parents, the main purpose of my visit was to speak to you."

"To me, sir?" said Charlotte faintly.

"Yes. A rather disturbing report regarding my nephew has come to my attention, and I hope you can assist me in determining whether it is true." His keen eyes drilled into her.

"I do not know him well." How had he learned of the wager? Had Willoughby bragged about it so freely?

"Still, perhaps you have heard of this business. Apparently he made a wager that required another young buck to seduce and abandon a certain young woman of his acquaintance, a young lady against whom he held some past grudge. Do you know anything of this?"

"Your nephew mentioned as much to me when we met last," Charlotte said tightly.

"Are you aware of the nature of the grudge?" His tone demanded a response.

She hesitated, feeling sympathy for barristers forced to plead their cases before him. "I can only surmise that it may have related to a time years ago when he approached the lady without any intentions which could be called honorable. The lady reported it to her brothers, who took some sort of action against him, but I cannot say what it was." It was the truth. They had taken great pleasure in refusing to tell her what they had done.

"I see." The judge nodded. "Is it your impression that his intention was to injure the lady in question?"

188

"To injure and humiliate her, and perhaps to blackmail her," she said bitterly. "He made that much clear."

He frowned. "I am very sorry to hear it. However, I will make certain that he does not trouble you again."

"I would appreciate that." Charlotte heard her voice trembling.

"I would also be particularly grateful if you would attend my Twelfth Night gathering rather than indulging in a headache or whatever else it is that young ladies do these days. I can promise you that my nephew will *not* be in attendance."

"In that case, I will do my best."

"Nor will he escape unscathed from this sordid affair. My apologies, Miss Lucas, that you were affected by it." He inclined his head in what was obviously a farewell.

"Judge Braxton?" She spoke to his retreating back.

"Yes?"

"May I ask how this matter came to your attention?"

He gave her a long, thoughtful look. "I received a visit from the man – I cannot call him a gentleman – who had accepted the wager. To his credit, he apparently now regrets it, and was concerned that you might come to further harm from my nephew. Under the circumstances, I did not consider his word to be reliable, hence my visit today."

"I understand. Thank you."

"Please accept my best wishes for your marriage, and my sincere hope that your husband will be more worthy of your faith than these men who are best forgotten."

"I hope so as well." She curtsied as he stepped into the carriage.

"I will look forward to seeing you on Twelfth Night, Miss Lucas," he called through the window as the carriage began to move.

Charlotte bit her lip as she waved with a smile that belied her feelings of humiliation.

Her mother was waiting for her just inside Lucas Lodge. "What did the judge say to you, Charlotte? He sounded very serious."

"Nothing of great import," said Charlotte, practical and calm as ever. "He wanted to be sure I would be able to attend Twelfth Night with my wedding so soon."

"What condescension!" Lady Lucas said admiringly. "Then again, he did seem particularly fond of you when you were a child. Mr. Collins will be delighted!"

Charlotte Lucas at Twelfth Night
by Abigail Reynolds

January 6, 1812

Charlotte was relieved to find Judge Braxton was as good as his word. There was no sign of Willoughby at his Twelfth Night dinner. Her relief did not last long, though, when she discovered that his guest list included Mr. Robinson. Of course, the judge had never promised her he would not be there, but she had assumed there would be no reason for Mr. Robinson to attend a dinner consisting of six or seven families from the neighborhood. Was this why the judge was so insistent that she attend? And why?

She felt horribly exposed whenever she caught Mr. Robinson looking her way. Was he thinking of that night in the woods? Her body remembered both the pleasure and the pain of it, as well as the humiliation that had come afterward.

She still did not know what to make of his letter to her father asking for her hand. Had it been only guilt speaking? Despite what he had said outside the church, she refused to allow herself to believe that he actually cared for her. That would be asking for heartbreak, and she refused to start down that road.

She managed to avoid him for the early part of the evening. At dinner, he was seated across from her, which meant she would not converse with him, but she had to look at him each time she turned her head to speak to one or the other of the men sitting beside her. She did not need to work at emulating a fashionable lack of appetite; she felt her food would choke her.

At the end of the long meal, the judge called for their attention. After the usual expressions of pleasure in seeing his neighbors, he said, "I have something more today to celebrate than the final day of the Christmas season, and I am particularly glad you could all be here tonight, since it also has bearing on the future of the neighborhood." He paused, allowing the interest to build.

"Since my late wife and I never had the good fortune to have children of our own, it has always been my intent to leave my property to one of my sisters' sons. You have all met my eldest nephew, Willoughby, who made his home here since he left school. Today I would like to introduce you to my youngest sister's son, Henry Briggs. Henry has just finished his first year at Oxford, and his reputation as a sober and industrious scholar is already established. He hopes to follow me into the legal profession someday."

He held his hand out to a young man whose spots showed he had not left boyhood behind yet. "I have decided that he will follow me as the master of Ixton Place as well, and I have rewritten my will to that effect. Henceforth Henry will spend whatever time he can spare from his studies here, learning about the estate and hopefully becoming better acquainted with all of you. His cousin Willoughby has already relocated to London." The judge looked directly at Charlotte and gave her a slight nod.

There were exclamations of surprise and pleasure all around, but Charlotte was silent. For the first time in her life, she felt faint. This must be why he wanted her to be present today, so that she would know of his decision to disinherit Willoughby – and that it was, at least in part, because of what he had done to her. It had always been a given that Willoughby would inherit Ixton Place and his uncle's fortune, and now he had lost all his prospects.

She could not stop herself from looking across the table at Mr. Robinson, the only other person present who might guess at the true reason for this unexpected change. He was watching her steadily. She could tell this news was not a surprise to him. But what did he think of it? If the judge was to be believed, Mr. Robinson had come to him with the story of the wager in an attempt to protect her, and his action had resulted in his friend being disinherited. She would have expected him to be horrified, yet here he was, sitting at the judge's table while Willoughby was exiled to London. He had chosen his side in the battle. Willoughby would never forgive him, and no one knew better than Charlotte what it meant to be the victim of Willoughby's anger. It had changed her entire life.

Charlotte was in a daze as the cake was eaten and the King and Queen of Misrule crowned. The conversation around her buzzed with speculation about why Willoughby being disinherited, and at least one gentleman made a derogatory reference to rakehells. It made her less vigilant, so she did not notice Mr. Robinson approaching her until it was too late. The best she could manage was to arrange her features into a semblance of disinterest.

"Miss Lucas," he said with a bow, "Would you do me the honor of sparing me a few minutes of your time? There is a quiet alcove over yonder where we could speak in private – and the judge is watching us, so you are perfectly safe." His brief smile reminded her of the good times they had shared.

She glanced automatically at the judge who immediately gave her a benign wave. He was in conversation with none other than her father. Charlotte felt her cheeks grow hot.

She gave Mr. Robinson a social smile in return, knowing instinctively that he would know the difference between that and a true smile. "It would be my pleasure. I would not wish to interfere with such a carefully planned maneuver."

He hesitated, as if uncertain whether to offer her his arm, then apparently decided against it, inviting her instead to walk with him. "Sometimes planning is necessary to achieve a goal."

"And precisely what is your goal?" She did not intend to allow him to take control of the conversation.

He drew a breath. "Since you ask so directly, I will answer as directly. I am hoping to convince you to break off your engagement and to marry me instead."

Her stomach gave a lurch as a treacherous rush of pleasure went through her. So he did care… or he wanted her to believe he did. "Why would I want to marry a man who took on the wager you did?"

His smile faded and died. "You deserve an explanation for that. I wish I could exculpate myself from it, but it would be untrue. I accepted the wager out of a combination of desperation, cynicism, and too much brandy."

She raised an eyebrow. "The brandy and the cynicism I can believe, but desperation seems a bit extreme."

"I owed money to Willoughby, and he threatened to call in my debt. It is a long story as to why my financial straits were so dire, but at that point I had the choice of fleeing the country, debtor's prison, going to my ill father for money he could not afford to give me, or accepting the wager. I was foxed and angry with women in general, so I took the wager. Once accepted, I could not refuse to follow through."

"Ah, yes. It would be dishonorable to back down on a bet, so you did the honorable thing and chose to dishonor an innocent woman instead."

He paled. "Yes, that is exactly what I did, but then you were an unknown, faceless woman who had, by Willoughby's report, treated him badly. It was not until after I came to know you that I began to think there might be another side to the story. I realized you were different from the woman who had angered me so much – different in a wonderful way – and I began to look forward to seeing you for myself, not because of the bet."

"But you made certain to win the bet anyway."

"After I told you I wished to marry you, which is something completely different from the bet. But yes, I did take advantage of it to redeem my IOUs from Willoughby so that I could go home and face my father. He was depending on me to marry an heiress. I could not tell him that not only was I choosing to marry a woman without a dowry, but that I was also in debt. I thought I would be able to return soon and that we would be formally engaged before Willoughby ever knew the difference, and it never even crossed my mind that even he would sink so low as to tell you about it. Please, Charlotte, give me another chance."

"You seem to have an answer for everything, but your father is a barrister, not a penniless gentleman who could be bankrupted by two hundred pounds."

"That would have been true a year ago, before we discovered the extent of my elder brother's gambling debts, a shock which caused my father's health to fail."

"You led me to believe you were the eldest son. I have heard enough lies."

"I said I was my father's heir. My brother fled to America to avoid his creditors, and my father disinherited him in favor of me, just like Willoughby. Not that there is much to inherit – just the country estate and the townhouse, and barely enough rents to cover the expenses for them. We will be selling the townhouse now since I am not marrying an heiress. I cannot offer you riches, only my affection."

She wanted to believe him, but how could she after all he had hidden from her? "How am I to know that you are not lying now, and that Willoughby is not paying you to convince me to break my engagement and then to disappear yourself, leaving me abandoned and shamed?"

He fell silent, then finally said quietly, "I suppose I deserve that, though it is not true. I could try to convince you of it, but it would make no difference, would it? It is too late." He gazed searchingly at her for a minute, then added, "I should not have opportuned you tonight. Your Mr. Collins can provide for you well, and he has never betrayed you as I did, so I cannot blame you for choosing him. I am sorry, Charlotte, to have caused you so much pain. Please accept my wishes for your future health and happiness."

He turned away, but not before she saw a suspicious sheen in his eyes. She dug her fingernails into her hands, hard, until it hurt. Was he such a good actor as that? Or was she the one being unfair? She knew the true reason of her doubts.

"Mr. Robinson, *why* would you want to marry me? You could easily find a younger, prettier girl, and as you say, I have no dowry to speak of. Why *should* I believe you?"

He turned to look at her in surprise. "Because you actually listen to me when I have something to say, and when you say something, it is worth hearing, not merely to fill empty air. Because you are good and honest – I have told you things tonight that my closest friends do not know, and I can trust you with them. Because you give affection and respect as a matter of course, not because you hope to get a gift out of me. Because I know you will never lie to me or try to trick me."

That was not what she had expected to hear. Flattery, blandishments, and avowals, yes, but not this. "You must have encountered some particularly unpleasant ladies if you find those things so remarkable," she said, her voice just barely unsteady.

"You do not know how remarkable you are," he countered. "And I neglected to mention that it is also because of what we have shared."

She did not want to recall that night in the woods and the intimacies they had shared, not here, not now. She needed to keep her strength.

He apparently sensed her weakening. "If you are convinced that I will not leave you at the altar, will you reconsider?"

Her hands were bunched in her skirts. "How can you possibly convince me?"

His smile of relief convinced her more than anything else. "I will not convince you, but the judge will."

* * *

The judge took the high-backed leather chair by the fire and gestured to an upholstered chair for Charlotte. "Forgive me, but my old bones require a warm hearth after a long day such as this. Now, what is this matter of great importance?"

Mr. Robinson leaned his elbow against the mantel. "Miss Lucas is concerned that I might be misleading her in suggesting marriage and that I would abandon her at the altar. She understandably has some doubts as to my motives, but she will believe *you* if you tell her I will not fail her."

The judge studied him closely, one finger tapping on the arm of his chair. "Do you give me your word you will marry her as promised, if she agrees? And that I may take any action I chose if you fail?"

Mr. Robinson nodded fervently. "Yes, sir, I do."

The judge turned to Charlotte. "He is telling the truth."

"May I ask how you can be so certain of it?" Charlotte said coolly.

"An excellent question. His father is a well-respected barrister, and he hopes to follow in his father's footsteps. I could make that impossible for him with just a word, and his father would agree with me when I told him why."

Charlotte considered. "So you believe him?"

"Yes, but whether he will go through with the marriage may not be the only factor to consider. You have a decision before you, Miss Lucas, and I recommend that you weigh every aspect. Your current intended – what is his name?"

"Mr. Collins."

"I understand that he is considered to be a good match, a man with excellent prospects."

"He will inherit Longbourn one day."

The judge steepled his fingers. "Have you considered what Mr. Robinson can offer you in terms of material comfort? He is not a gentleman of means but must work for his living as his father did. You would not be poor if you married him, but neither would you be wealthy. You would likely have only a maid or two in the early years of your marriage, leaving some of the household work to you."

Charlotte cocked her head. "I am not afraid of work."

"Good for you, my dear. Does your Mr. Collins have any vices? Is he prone to gambling beyond his means? Does he drink to excess?"

"I cannot say for certain, but he is rather straight-laced. He was reluctant to play cards with the ladies for very small stakes."

"Robinson has a history of both, and of accepting a wager that was immoral at best. He appears to have learned a lesson, but if he were to return to those habits, it could make your life quite difficult."

Mr. Robinson interrupted, his face pale. "You may be certain I would do nothing of the sort!"

The judge turned a shrewd look on him. "As you know, I make my decisions based on evidence, not on promises. I would note, Miss Lucas, that when Robinson first came to me with his concern, he properly refused to name you as the lady involved, but when I pressed him hard, he did so. Would your Mr. Collins give in to pressure?"

Charlotte laughed. "It would not be needed. He would have told you the first time you asked, and thanked you for condescending to interest yourself in his affairs."

"A point to Robinson, then, for at least making the effort to resist. You seem to have doubts of Robinson's honesty – quite understandable under the circumstances. Do you have concerns over Mr. Collins' honesty?"

Charlotte considered this. "Only to the extent that he offers flattery to an almost embarrassing degree. He does not have a talent for dissembling."

"Is he a responsible man? Will he treat your children well?"

"He takes his responsibilities very seriously, and I believe he would be reliable, if easily swayed on occasion."

"Can you say the same of Robinson?"

Mr. Robinson opened his mouth to protest, but the judge waved him to silence.

It was a much harder question. Mr. Robinson had deceived her, had admitted to gambling debts and to seeking a bride for purely mercenary reasons, and had been a friend of Willoughby's. On the other hand, he seemed truly devoted to his father and to care greatly for his good opinion. "I do not know."

"Fair enough. Marriage is also for companionship. You are an intelligent young woman and no doubt would like to be able to discuss matters with your husband. Who would be the better companion for you?"

"Mr. Collins is not a particularly sensible man," she admitted.

"Another point to Mr. Robinson, then, since you seem to have enjoyed his company in the past. Do you have any doubt that Mr. Collins will follow through on his promise to marry you?"

Finally an easy question! "None at all, sir."

The judge leaned back in his chair. "You have a difficult decision before you, Miss Lucas. You can marry Mr. Collins, who is responsible, reliable and honest but dull and obsequious, and you would need have no fears for your future or whether he will be able to provide for your children. Or you can choose Robinson whose company you prefer, but with the risk that he may prove unreliable as he has in the past, gambling away the money needed to run your household, leading you and your children into poverty. Do be quiet, Robinson, and allow the lady to think."

"You seem to take a great interest in this matter, sir," Charlotte said.

"My wife, God rest her soul, was a lady of great intelligence who could reason an argument as well as any man. She would have made a fine judge herself if we allowed women such opportunities. She was never *Missish* and always answered questions directly. You remind me of her, Miss Lucas. If my nephew Henry were ten years older, I would be trying to marry you off to him."

"I am honored," Charlotte said, and meant it. She had never heard such words of praise from a man she could respect so highly.

He raised himself stiffly to his feet. "I am going back to my guests now. I believe you may be forgiven a few minutes of private conversation, but please have mercy on me and keep it brief. Sir William is not precisely pleased with me at the moment. I gather I am overruling his parental authority." He gave Charlotte a conspiratorial look as he left the room.

Charlotte looked down at her hands to give herself a moment to think, then raised her eyes to meet Mr. Robinson's. "I will give you an answer before I depart tonight."

He smiled ruefully and took her hands in his. "The judge has already ruled against me, and there is no fairer or more honest judge in all of England. That was why I dared approach him regarding Willoughby. I knew he would weigh the merits of my argument without regard to his own wishes. He is kind-hearted, though, so he gave me this time to say goodbye."

"I have not refused you," Charlotte said sharply, conscious of the warm comfort of his hands and her physical response to his body so near his own. "But perhaps *you* have changed your mind in light of the judge's power to punish you."

He shook his head. "My wishes and desires are unchanged, and if you choose in my favor, you will make me the happiest of men. But my father has told me too many times that he has learned that if he is on the opposing side of an argument from Judge Ixton, it is a sign that he should rethink his own opinion since it inevitably meant there was something he had not considered. I saw tonight how little time it took him to determine the sort of woman you are, and to be able to explain it more succinctly than I can after knowing you since October." He shook his head dismissively. "At least he cannot fault my taste in women. That was a very high compliment he paid you. He adored his wife."

"I am still trying to take that in," Charlotte said. It was true. She had always believed that her plain face and lack of dowry meant that she had little to offer to a man, and even now she doubted Mr. Robinson in large part because she could not believe that he would truly care about *her*, about practical, dependable Charlotte Lucas. How she had grown to hate those words over the years!

At the moment, though, she was anything but practical and dependable. He had raised one hand to cup her cheek, looking down at her tenderly, and all she wanted was for him to kiss her.

"I wish I had could prove to you that I am not an irresponsible cad, but the only way to do that would be to demonstrate it over time, and time is the one thing I do not have, not with your wedding in three days." Then he did kiss her.

It was sweet and it was tender. Charlotte longed to be in his arms, but the pain of the last month was still fresh enough to hold her back. Still, her lips clung to his until the awareness of time passing made her pull away. "We should return to the others," she said.

The corner of his mouth quirked up, but he did not move. "So we should."

It was then that she knew her answer. She crossed to the door, and he had to hurry to open it for her. She stopped halfway through the open door and turned to him. It was respectable enough; plenty of people could see them, yet no one would overhear soft conversation.

She took a deep breath, conscious of a stabbing pain deep inside. That was another factor to consider; he had the power to hurt her badly with his words and actions, something Mr. Collins did not. She would never face heartbreak at Mr. Collins' hand, because he did not possess her heart. "You tempt me, Mr. Robinson. You truly do. But I am someone who values certainty and dependability. I can tolerate adversity when I must, but I am not one to seek it out. I would be making a gamble by choosing you, and I am not by nature a gambler."

He took it stoically. She had to give him credit for that. "So the judge was right again?" he asked.

She nodded, closer to tears than she wished to admit. Who would have thought it of practical, dependable Charlotte? Her father was approaching them, and she must be calm.

He must have seen Sir William as well, because he said quickly, "May I see you one last time? I will not try to change your mind, I promise; but there are things I have not had the chance to tell you."

And go through this pain of separation again? But she already knew she would find some way to grant his request. "I will consider it," she said just as her father reached them. Her perfect social smile, the pride of practical, dependable Charlotte, was already in place.

Jane Calls on Caroline and Louisa
by Susan Mason-Milks

January 7, 1812

Jane found herself sitting in the parlor at the Hurst's home on Grosvenor Street waiting for Caroline Bingley and Louisa Hurst to appear. Perched on a velvet covered chair, she felt a little uncomfortable and out of place. The house was not large, but almost everything about it was pretentious, as if designed to impress visitors with the financial standing of its owner. Jane deemed the decoration of this particular room much too formal and stuffy for her taste. The only personal touch was a small grouping of miniatures on a nearby table.

Examining the tiny portraits more closely, Jane recognized Caroline and Louisa. Both appeared to have been painted when they were about fifteen or sixteen years of age. The artist had generously rounded out some of the sharp angles of Caroline's features making her appearance softer than it was in person. Jane smiled to herself noting how he had also considerably reduced the size of her nose.

The miniature that interested Jane the most, however, was of Charles Bingley. As she picked up the tiny portrait to examine it more closely, she involuntarily took a quick deep breath, exhaling it slowly with a quiet sigh. She had spent many weeks denying how much she felt for this man, but seeing his likeness brought it all back in full force causing that now familiar empty feeling to return. Jane lightly touched her finger to the painting as if she could actually stroke his face. All the pain of loss she had been holding inside now threatened to rush out. She would not allow herself to cry. It would not do to let anyone, especially his sisters, see how much she was hurt.

Mr. Bingley was everything she had ever hoped for in a suitor, and that made his loss all the more difficult to bear. It was not his fault his friendliness and charm had caused her to misinterpret his attentions. He was, after all, known for his good manners and friendly mien. Jane had been so certain he was developing an attachment to her and that his affection equaled hers. When he did not return to Netherfield, she had been forced to awaken from the delightful dream of becoming his wife that she had created for herself. She knew in the future any man who sought her attentions would be compared with him—her first love. The sad truth was Charles would marry someone like Georgiana Darcy and forget he had ever known Jane Bennet of Longbourn. She had just been an amusing diversion during his stay in the country. Jane thought she had no one to blame but herself for thinking it was more than just a flirtation. If his heart had been truly engaged, he would never have left without a word. In spite of what happened, Jane still hoped she would be able to continue her friendship with his sisters that had begun so promisingly in Hertfordshire.

Before Jane left for London, she had written to Caroline and Louisa informing them of her arrival in town, and also giving her Aunt and Uncle Gardiner's direction so they could write in return or come to call. More than a week had passed, but she had heard nothing from her friends. Jane was certain if Caroline had received her most recent message, she would have replied. The silence could only mean the letter had somehow been lost. That thought was what had prompted Jane to take the initiative of calling on them first.

"I cannot believe she has actually called upon us!" moaned Caroline. She and Louisa were still in her dressing room freshening up to meet their guest. "I thought my letter made it clear she should not hope for more from Charles." Caroline was very unhappy she would be forced to be pleasant to Jane Bennet. Whatever would she say to that country bumpkin? Caroline intentionally had not answered Jane's last letter with the hope of avoiding just this very situation, but she had come to call on them rather than taking the hint. Caroline was certain she had done everything she could to imply that Charles's affections were otherwise engaged.

"Should I send word I am indisposed with a headache?" Caroline asked her sister.

"Do not be silly. We cannot both claim a headache, and I am not meeting with her alone," Louisa replied. "Caroline, she is a sweet girl. I believe we must see her."

Caroline let out a snort of disgust.

"You know it would be unforgivably rude not to at least spend a few minutes with her," Louisa counseled.

"Then we must have a plan for cutting her visit short. What should we say?"

"I have no idea. You are the one who excels at making up excuses," said Louisa absently as she checked her hair once more in the mirror.

"I shall instruct Graves if we have not emerged in ten minutes, he should come to the door to remind us we must leave almost immediately for our appointment." Caroline frowned as she smoothed imaginary wrinkles from her dress.

"Oh, stop fussing," said Louisa slapping at her sister's hand.

Caroline jumped back and threw Louisa a nasty look. "Do not do that! You are not Mama!"

Louisa rolled her eyes, and then focused her attention on their problem again. "You could also inform her Miss Darcy is dining with us this evening," she said slyly.

"Perhaps that will provide sufficient discouragement," Caroline replied.

Just as they were ready to exit the dressing room, Caroline put a hand on her sister's arm. "Oh, dear! Louisa," she said with a look of horror on her face. "Courtesy will require us to make a return call. I am not sure I can bear the thought of going to…to…"

"Cheapside!" they moaned simultaneously as if the very word was disgusting to pronounce.

"If you recall, I warned you this might happen! Next time Charles gets an idea in his head to pay attention to someone as unsuitable as she is, we must put a stop to it much sooner," said Caroline as she linked arms with her sister.

Just before they entered the room where Jane waited, Caroline took a deep breath and set bright smile on her face.

"Oh, Jane, dear! How very lovely to see you!" she cooed in her sweetest voice as she floated into the parlor. "Why did you not let us know you were coming to town?"

"I sent a letter a few weeks ago just before leaving Hertfordshire. Perhaps it was lost," Jane offered.

Caroline thought it was so very like Jane to conveniently offer her own explanation. It saved Caroline the trouble of making something up on the spot.

"And is your family all in health?" Louisa inquired politely settling into a nearby chair.

"Oh, yes, thank you. Everyone is very well. And your family?"

"Yes, they are all well," Louisa responded.

Jane looked down at her hands. "Is your brother also in health?" she asked tentatively.

Louisa and Caroline exchanged looks. "Oh, yes, of course, but we rarely see him these days. He has been spending so much time at the Darcys' we are beginning to think he lives there," Caroline responded with a forced laugh.

"And how are the Darcys?" Jane asked more out of politeness than actual interest.

"Mr. Darcy was somewhat out of sorts upon his return from Hertfordshire, but I believe he is feeling well enough by now," said Caroline. After all, it was perfectly understandable. Being forced to endure the company of so many unpleasant people in Hertfordshire had made her feel ill, too.

"Miss Darcy is also in excellent health," Louisa added. "She is such a lovely young lady. Who would not be taken with her beauty and accomplishments?"

Caroline brightened. Louisa had created the perfect opening. "Yes, we are looking forward to Miss Darcy dining with us this evening!" She did not add that Charles would be out with Mr. Darcy at the home of an old school friend. It would not hurt if Jane assumed the gentlemen would be joining them as it would further the idea there might possibly be more than one union between the two families. Caroline still seethed with hatred for Eliza Bennet because of Darcy's marked preference for her. She thought it would not hurt a bit if Jane wrote to that impertinent sister of hers that two of the Bingleys were on very intimate terms with the Darcys. Fine eyes, indeed! Let her be the one who was jealous!

An uncomfortable silence fell in the room. They really had so little in common other than their brief acquaintance in Hertfordshire.

"Have you been to any assemblies or balls since we left?" asked Caroline, stifling a smirk behind her hand.

Jane looked confused for a moment. "Oh, yes, we attended a wonderful ball on New Year's Eve, and during December there were many parties and dinners in the neighborhood."

"How lovely for you," said Caroline. Louisa launched into a lengthy discourse about all the balls and dinners they had attended since returning to London. By describing in great detail some of the fabulous gowns and jewels they had seen at these events, she hoped to impress Jane and further emphasize the gap between the Bingleys and the Bennets.

As Louisa rambled on, Caroline frantically tried to think of another topic. Since nothing came to mind, it seemed as good a time as any to mention they must be leaving soon. A sudden inspiration hit, and she jumped into the conversation interrupting her sister.

"Mr. Darcy has been gracious enough to send his carriage for us so we may call on Miss Darcy this afternoon. I am afraid we only have a few minutes before it will arrive to whisk us away," Caroline said with an artful swish of her hand. She thought it was especially clever of her to invent this little tale, as it was yet another example of the close relationship between the two families.

Just at that moment, Graves appeared in the doorway. Caroline rose immediately from her chair indicating the call was over, and Jane followed her lead.

"It is so unfortunate we will not return to Netherfield and will be robbed of the pleasure of seeing your dear family again. You must send them our regards," said Caroline sweetly as they ushered Jane to the front door.

Even though she had already given her card to the butler when she arrived, Jane reached into her reticule and pulled out another card with the Gardiners' direction. "I would love to have you call at my aunt and uncle's home while I am in town. Please come any time."

Both Caroline and Louisa assured their guest that she would see them very soon. Once the door closed behind Jane, the Bingley sisters looked at each other and fell into fits of laughter right there in the hallway.

When Jane reached the sidewalk, she turned to look back at the house. Something did not seem quite right, but she just could not put her finger on what it was. Their promise of a return call sounded hollow and forced. They had not even offered her the courtesy of refreshments. Suddenly, it hit her. Why were the Bingley sisters going to call on Miss Darcy this afternoon if she was coming to their house for dinner that very evening? It did not make sense.

Although Jane puzzled over this all the way back to Cheapside and debated about seeking her aunt's opinion, in the end she decided she must have misunderstood. Caroline and Louisa were her friends. Assuring herself that they would return her call very soon, just as they promised, she began to arrange her schedule so she would be at home to receive them when they came.

Charlotte's Final Day
as a Single Woman
by Abigail Reynolds

January 8, 1812

Charlotte's farewell visit to the Bennet ladies was not one she would remember with pleasure. Mrs. Bennet, who had always been kind to her until she became engaged, was ungracious throughout it. Lizzy had the courtesy to walk her downstairs afterwards, which Charlotte particularly appreciated since she wanted to invite her to visit in Kent. She had not forgotten the judge's words about finding her companionship elsewhere than her husband, and Lizzy had been her closest friend for years.

Lizzy at first tried to dodge the invitation – hardly surprising given her dislike of Mr. Collins – but finally agreed, to Charlotte's great relief. It meant a great deal to know that she would have a friend still, even if Lizzy still couldn't hide her disapproval of Charlotte's marriage. Sometimes she forgot just how young Lizzy was, and the difference between the ages of twenty and eight-and-twenty. Lizzy's world was so simple; she lived in the present and did not think of the future. People had few shades of grey in her mind. Charlotte wondered what Lizzy would think if she knew the truth of her situation.

Apparently feeling some guilt over her reluctance to visit, Lizzy offered to walk back to Lucas Lodge with her, but Charlotte declined graciously. "I need a little time alone to think. Once I am home, I will be inundated with wedding preparations."

Lizzy, who loved solitary walks, apparently saw nothing odd in this, and waved to Charlotte as she set off down the drive. But

Charlotte had no intention of taking the usual road back to Lucas Lodge, and soon veered off on a narrow path into the woods. Her pulse raced, but not from the exercise, and anxiety gnawed away at her insides. Would he be there, or had he already left Hertfordshire?

She hitched up her skirts for the final climb to the ruined chapel on the hilltop. Overgrown by trees, no one ever visited it, but it had been a favorite childhood retreat of hers. Now it was something else entirely. Still, to be safe, she circled the ruins to make certain there were no other visitors, and then she walked past the chapel to the old hermitage.

He was standing in the doorway waiting for her. She hurried into his arms, turning her face up for his kiss. There was no point in denying what was to happen; he would have realized her intent as soon as he received her note specifying this location. This was where they had gone on Guy Fawkes Night.

He was already unbuttoning her spencer as he kissed her.

They were better prepared today than they had been on Guy Fawkes Night. Mr. Robinson had somehow managed to bring a blanket with him, and his greatcoat served as their bed, but still on this chilly January day, they wore most of their clothes. Most, but not all, which was enough to make Charlotte happy. Then again, she was in the habit of finding contentment where she could, but she had never thought it would be in the arms of her lover on the day before her wedding to another man. How shocked all her friends and family would be at practical, dependable Charlotte right now! The thought made her even happier.

Mr. Robinson – Edward – ran his forefinger down the valley between her breasts. "Thank you for today. You cannot imagine what it means to me that, even if we have no future together, that we part with happier memories. And I will do my best to wish you happy in your future."

Charlotte did not want to think about that future, or the man she was to marry who was waiting for her at Lucas Lodge. She wanted to treasure this moment and the sensation of being held by the man she cared for. She did not question her decision to marry

Mr. Collins, at least not seriously. She was happy to be with her Edward, happy to feel his touch and hear his words of love, but she also recognized that fundamentally he was a weak man who was too easily swayed by what he desired at any given moment. If they married, that trait would eventually kill her affection for him. She would rather have the memories of today to carry with her through the years ahead.

She could not think of the future now, though. "You said before that there were things you still wanted to tell me."

"And you expect me to remember them when you are with me like this?" He kissed her lingeringly, his hand sculpting the curves of her body, coming to rest on her stomach. "Some of it is not important now, such as the story of why I was so angry with women, which had to do with an heiress who first led me on and then humiliated me with a public refusal. It does not signify now, because all I want to think about is you. But there is one thing I would ask."

"Yes?"

He kissed her again before speaking, as if he were fearful that she would not wish to kiss him afterwards. "Were there any consequences of that night in November?"

She did not pretend to misunderstand him. "I cannot say. I have had no proof that I am not in that condition, but it is not unusual for me not to have proof on a regular basis."

The pressure of his hand on her stomach increased slightly, as if he were trying to discover what lay within. "I do not know whether I wish for it or not, but it will be hard never to know."

"If you wish, I can try to send a message through Judge Braxton, although it might be some time before I have the opportunity to do so. I do not know how often I will return here, and he is often in London."

"I would appreciate some word, and it will be... good to know I will hear from you again, at least that once." His voice was melancholy.

Charlotte did not want this moment clouded with grief, She distracted him with kisses and roving touches until she was sure his interest lay in a distinctly different direction.

"My delightfully passionate Charlotte! No one would know to look at you what is hidden inside." A shadow crossed his face, and she knew he was thinking the same thing she was, that tomorrow night she would be doing this with another man. "Where does he live, your Mr. Collins?" he said with an edge to his voice.

She closed her eyes in anticipation. "In the village of Hunsford in Kent, not far from Tunbridge Wells.

"I know where it is. It is just over ten miles from my father's house. I visit there frequently and it someday will be mine."

Her eyes widened. She slid her hand behind his head and pulled him down until she could kiss him. "And?"

"Tell me that you will allow me to see you again, at least from time to time. I will find a way to make it work. Please, Charlotte."

Her smile this time came from a special place deep within her. "We will have to be discreet, but I would be very sorry if you did not."

His face was full of a heartfelt delight, which almost immediately transmuted into a more physical expression of his feelings. Charlotte was content to allow herself to become lost in his lovemaking.

Afterwards, she had little time to spare. She had already been gone from Lucas Lodge too long, and would have to think of a good excuse for why she had lingered at her farewell call to the Bennets, but she did not care. This was not a final goodbye, and that made all the difference.

He sat watching her as she restored order to her clothing and smoothed her hair with the comb and extra hairpins she had secreted in her reticule for this very purpose. Then he pulled her to him for a final kiss. "To tide me over until we are together again."

Charlotte tied her bonnet strings. "And until then, it is back to practical, dependable Charlotte Lucas."

He caught her hand once more. "You are practical and dependable – but there is much more to you than *that*. Remember that when you remember me."

She looked into his eyes and nodded slowly. "I will remember."

Lady Lucas Receives Mr. Collins
by Nina Benneton

January 8, 1812

"Lady Lucas, it is an honor." Bowing, Mr. Collins's lips scraped over Lady Lucas's gloved hand.

"Welcome, Mr. Collins." Lady Lucas smiled, reminding herself that burnt bone powder mixed with crumbs of toasted bread could easily remove oily spots. *Happiness in a marriage is a matter of chance.* How many times had she advised her daughter of that?

"It is not Longbourn, but you will find no better welcome for your particular company now than at Lucas Lodge, sir." Sir William smiled affably. "We have been waiting anxiously for your arrival."

"I was afraid you might have changed your mind and not come," Lady Lucas's young son William piped.

At her brother's words, Charlotte's cheeks reddened.

Mr. Collins smiled at Lady Lucas's eldest daughter. "I assure you, there is no heart more constant than mine once I have requested a lady's hand in marriage."

Charlotte's returning smile was forced. "Your travel from Kent was uneventful, sir?"

"The jolts and jounces of the coach through fifty miles of bad roads are nothing when the heart anticipates such a reward at the destination, Miss Lucas." Mr. Collins eyes blinked in the manner of a deformed mooncalf.

Lady Lucas decided to save her daughter from this unseemly public display of lovemaking. "Charlotte, Mr. Collins must be famished after his travel. Please go and see if cook's ready with dinner."

After casting a grateful glance toward Lady Lucas, Charlotte quitted the drawing room with alacrity. Lady Lucas invited their guest to sit while she busied herself with pouring out a cup of tea.

"Charlotte made the pies for dinner, sir," young William said.

Mr. Collins beamed. "Lady Catherine will be most pleased to hear the future Mrs. Collins is capable of managing in the kitchen when the need arises. Though, I assure you, Hunsford Parsonage has a very competent maid-of-all-work to aid your daughter."

As she was about to hand her future son-in-law a cup of tea, Lady Lucas paused. It was not prudent to scald the young man before he married Charlotte. She gave him a smile she usually reserved for the witless Mrs. Bennet. "How lovely."

"An honor for Charlotte to be under the attention of such a lady," Sir Williams said.

Lady Lucas suppressed an impatient sigh. "It would not do, Sir William, for the daughter of a man who has been presented at St. James to only have one competent maid-of-all-work to aid her in her new household. Is it not fortuitous we were discoursing this morning about gifting the young couple with the service of one or two additional servants?"

"Eh? What's that?" Sir William gave her a puzzled look, to which she returned with a significant glance toward their young son. Charlotte being safely married would mean less strain on young William in the future, as he would be relieved of his care for a spinster sister. Surely a mere five or ten pounds a year now to ensure Charlotte's domestic comfort was worth it?

Lady Lucas's husband hesitated for a moment longer before he gave her a reluctant nod before turning back to their future son and discussing Lady Catherine.

Happiness in a marriage is a matter of chance, Lady Lucas silently repeated. Was that not what her own mother had said when she pressed her to accept the penny-pinching Sir William's hand in marriage?

Smiling, she handed Mr. Collins his tea. She was confident she had prepared her Charlotte well to deal with a fatuous, parsimonious spouse.

Charlotte's Wedding
by Abigail Reynolds

January 9, 1812

Charlotte had never been one to have romantic dreams about a
perfect wedding. She knew she would never be a beautiful bride
that women would cry over, and there was not even to be a wedding
breakfast, since she and Mr. Collins were to leave for Kent from the
church door. Lady Catherine apparently felt he had been absent
from his post a bit too often in these last months, so naturally Mr.
Collins was determined to return at the earliest possible moment. It
was going to be a very long day, especially with a wedding night at
the end where she would need to have all of her acting skills at their
best.

The ceremony went smoothly, which was all Charlotte had
hoped for. The only shock came when she walked back down the
aisle with her new husband and saw some unexpected faces in the
pews. Judge Braxton sat between his young nephew and Mr.
Robinson.

She allowed her eyes to rest on Mr. Robinson for just a
moment. He gave her a slight smile – not a happy one, but neither
was it completely false – and then she was past his pew. She
wondered at his presence, but he could not be planning to cause
difficulties if he was with the judge.

The newlyweds were surrounded by well-wishers at the church
door. Charlotte could hear Mr. Collins droning on to someone or
other in his usual manner with frequent references to Lady
Catherine de Bourgh and Rosings Park while she was bidding her
final farewells to her family and friends. She could not keep herself

from glancing around every few minutes in search of Mr. Robinson, oddly embarrassed at what he would think of her new husband.

When she saw him, it was a worse shock. He was actually being introduced to Mr. Collins. Her social smile firmly plastered in place, she hurried to Mr. Collins' side, hoping that her interest looked like nothing more than the eagerness of a devoted bride to be with her new husband.

"Yes, of course, near Rosings Park," said Mr. Robinson smoothly. "I remember it well. My father was a great friend of Sir Lewis de Bourgh, and during that gentleman's lifetime, we often called at Rosings. He and my father were both devotees of chess and whiled away many an afternoon with one match after another."

"If you have met the family, then you comprehend the great honor I feel in having the opportunity to be Lady Catherine's most humble servant." Mr. Collins showed the same eagerness to impress that he had when meeting Mr. Darcy at the Netherfield Ball.

"Indeed I do. I recall standing quite in awe of Lady Catherine. Rosings Park is, of course, among the finest houses in the county. I am sure there are many who are envious of your position." His eyes momentarily slid toward Charlotte with a very different message about his envy.

As Mr. Collins thanked him at length for his great condescension, Charlotte wondered what on earth he was about. It certainly had not taken him long to take the measure of Mr. Collins' nature, and he was playing to it beautifully.

"I was delighted to hear that Miss Lucas – Mrs. Collins – would be taking up residence in Hunsford. She is just the sort of practical, dependable lady to be a perfect clergyman's wife. In fact, I was hoping you would not object if I introduced my younger sister to her acquaintance. This was to have been Mary's first Season until my father became ill, and she is disappointed to be spending it in the country instead. I believe Mrs. Collins would be an excellent steadying influence on her, with your permission, of course."

Mr. Collins turned to Charlotte, rubbing his hands together with every evidence of pleasure. "We would be delighted, would we not, Mrs. Collins?"

Charlotte curtsied slightly. "I would be very happy to meet a new friend in Kent." She was not certain whether she was more amused or horrified at his initiative in asking her husband for permission to call on her.

He bowed. "In that case, I will look forward to seeing you again very soon, Mrs. Collins, but I will not keep you from your other guests any longer."

She offered him her hand, and he bowed over it deeply, giving her fingers a little squeeze as he did so. It was as if a little spark passed from him to her, but she felt no urge for anything more. Today was not the day to be thinking of him.

She was relieved when the hired carriage pulled away from the church and she was alone with Mr. Collins. She listened absently as he talked on at length about what a success the day had been and how pleased Lady Catherine would be that Judge Braxton himself had condescended to attend the ceremony. "She will be glad to hear that you are already acquainted with one of our neighbors, but I must admit I did not quite catch his name – was it Rogers, my dear?"

"You refer to Mr. Robinson?"

"Ah, yes, Robinson, that was it. And to think his father had the honor of knowing Sir Lewis de Bourgh! I will have to tell Lady Catherine about him. How did you come to meet him?"

"Judge Braxton is a friend of Mr. Robinson's father, and is acting as a mentor of sorts to the son. Mr. Robinson attended many of the social occasions in Meryton during his visit to the judge." She was pleased by the apparent detachment in her voice. "But I hope you will tell me more about what I should expect to find in Hunsford and at Rosings Park. One can never be too prepared, after all."

As she hoped, that sent him off into a long monologue of praise, waxing eloquent about every detail of Rosings. It was rather soothing, actually, since he required so little from her apart from the appearance of attention. She was used to this sort of effusive behavior from her father, so it did not trouble her greatly.

She folded her hands in her lap and made herself as comfortable as one could be in a coach with fewer springs that might be wished for. She had no complaints, though. Today was evidence enough for her that she had made the correct decision. She might feel an attraction to Mr. Robinson that she did not for Mr. Collins, and she would certainly enjoy his company more, but her pleasure in their time together did not prevent her from noticing that today he had shown himself once again to be a skilled liar with a talent for manipulation. His willingness to involve his sister in the situation did not speak well for him, either. If she were married to him, she would always have doubts about his motives and his veracity, and if he could lie so easily and disguise what must be serious dislike for his rival, it was quite possible he could fool her about other things.

No, Mr. Robinson would not have made the kind of husband she could depend on. She remembered him with pleasure, and looked forward more than she might like to admit to their next meeting, but she knew where she stood with Mr. Collins. If his effusiveness bordered on embarrassing, she could learn to ignore it. She would finally have an establishment of her own, a comfortable income, and hopefully children to raise. She could visit Hertfordshire without worries about Willoughby, though.

"Is something the matter, my dearest Charlotte? Is the motion of the carriage too much for you?"

"I am a little tired, perhaps, but quite well," she said, patting his hand. "I do hope Lady Catherine will approve of me."

That was enough to distract him, and he was off again on his monologue, leaving her with the quite satisfactory thought that Mr. Willoughby would be most distressed if he knew how much she had benefited from his attempt at revenge. Without him she would not have made the desperate attempt to attract Mr. Collins' attention when he hoped to marry one of the Bennet sisters, and she would still be an aging spinster destined to be dependent on her brothers forever. Instead, thanks to Willoughby, she had a new home, the prospect of someday being mistress of Longbourn, a husband to provide for her, and a lover to remind her that there was more to her than the practical, dependable Charlotte everyone else knew. Yes, she had a great deal for which to be thankful.

In Which Charlotte Collins
Faces the Inquisition
by Diana Birchall

January 20, 1812

Charlotte had now been married a month, and was quite as satisfied with her situation as she had ever dared hope to be. If her husband was not the pleasantest of companions, there was only one of him, and any man, not vicious, might easily be managed by a clever woman. In the case of Mr. Collins, it was only needful for Charlotte to be willing to adapt her expressions to the flattering sort he plainly needed for his contentment. This was but a small sacrifice, for Charlotte, though ordinarily a plain spoken woman, felt it a gratifying improvement to have only him to please, by such simple and expedient means. At Lucas Lodge, she had been required all through her young womanhood to assist her mother with the care of her many younger brothers and sisters, a slavery that had reduced her to little more than a bonne or nursemaid. How much, therefore, she now delighted in having her own house, may be imagined; and with her intelligence and tact she was quite equal to the business of keeping Mr. Collins happy, occupied, and not too much in her own way. In the intervals when Mr. Collins was silent, or away from the house, as did happen for several hours of each day, she could enjoy her own peaceful occupations, to her heart's content.

February was too early a month for gardening, but Charlotte discerned that Mr. Collins was all eagerness to be planning and planting, and she encouraged him to draw up handsome schemes for laying out the vegetable and flower gardens, and set him to pore over seed catalogues. Then he must spend a good deal of time surveying his parish, and visiting those parishioners who were in difficulties. In this he was frequently joined by his patroness Lady Catherine de Bourgh, who had the greatest delight in cottage visiting, and considered Mr. Collins to be her adjunct, rather than the other way round, as might have been supposed. They were often busy for several hours together, in the happy occupation of looking into their villagers' affairs, and no one would disturb Charlotte, although on her husband's return she must pay the tax of listening to the whole story of what Lady Catherine had done, and said, and decreed, to every person in and around Hunsford. Charlotte generally took out her sewing then, and while Mr. Collins talked, need not give more than half an ear to him, with an occasional interjection of, "That was very well done, my dear, upon my word."

Fortunately, he was as a man about the house not unamiable, nor difficult to please for one who was such an efficient housekeeper and judicious manager as Charlotte, and she had only to accept his compliments on her contrivances, which was no severe hardship. From the start, he violently approved of her disposition of cupboards and cabinets, and of her pleasant but firm manner with their domestics. And as the cooking in the establishment improved immeasurably, under Charlotte's direction, from the bachelor meals he had ordered, he really did not know how to be grateful enough, or more pleased with his own acuity and genius for selecting such a paragon of a wife. In moments, he shuddered at the narrow escape he had from his cousin Elizabeth, whom he was now certain would never have suited him at all.

As for more intimate matters between husband and wife, Charlotte had always known she must accept them as a matter of course, and there was nothing about the person of her young and healthy husband to disgust; especially after she had given him a little tactful and delicate instruction. Mr. Collins often rewarded her with expressions of assurance that she pleased him, more than any other woman in the world could have done; and in being very conscious of his blessings, he did much to reconcile Charlotte to hers.

So the marriage prospered from its earliest days; but Charlotte was also fully aware that that there was a second person, not in her household, whom she must conciliate. This was Lady Catherine de Bourgh. Charlotte had come to Hunsford prepared to endure much interference in her business, and she resolved ahead of time to meet every attack with patience. That Lady Catherine should approve of Mr. Collins's wife, was of the most extreme importance. Charlotte could scarcely be more cognizant of this than Mr. Collins himself. Lady Catherine had nothing less than the power to make or to ruin her happiness; and so she deliberately set out to please, and to promote the most harmonious intercourse possible between Hunsford and Rosings. Charlotte well knew that the benefit of Lady Catherine's patronage was inestimable; she might help her brothers find places, her sisters husbands. Elizabeth might have found it disagreeable to dance attendance upon a Lady Catherine, but Charlotte sensibly accepted it as part of the price of her happiness, and she welcomed the most outrageous impositions willingly, or at least quietly. This was greatly, be it noted, to the relief of her husband, who had been anxious that nothing like conflict should arise between the two women most important to him.

Lady Catherine allowed one week to elapse, from the arrival of Mrs. Collins in Hunsford, until she set about making an inspection of her methods. There had been one dinner already, and her Ladyship declared herself perfectly pleased by the quiet, neat appearance of the parson's new wife, and of the deference with which she addressed her superiors. She seemed a modest, proper, sensible sort of young woman – not too young, but all the better for that. A sennight was enough to allow for Mrs. Collins to put herself in order. Lady Catherine was impatient, but at last the seven days were passed, and she sallied forth, curious to see with what economy the new broom managed her household.

Lady Catherine came therefore when least expected, resolved to give Mrs. Collins no warning, no chance to clear up any disorder or to give her house a better appearance than it might have in the ordinary way. At eleven o'clock on the Tuesday forenoon, as soon as she knew that Mr. Collins had gone out in his gig, to make his regular circuit of the parish, Lady Catherine ordered one of her own carriages, and presented herself at Charlotte's door.

Charlotte, discerning her from the window, came out to welcome and invite her into the house.

"I came," announced Lady Catherine, "to satisfy myself as to the state of your arrangements."

"I hope you will be pleased," Charlotte answered calmly, "will your Ladyship have some tea?"

"Tea! I am not one of those ladies who require tea at this hour. But stay – what sort of tea do you purchase, Mrs. Collins?" she asked suspiciously. "Fine India tea is a luxury that does not become a clergyman's household, you must know. Where do you order yours, say?"

"It is some I have brought from home," replied Charlotte. "I mean to keep it only for company, indeed, for distinguished guests; and as we expect to have few visitors, my supply will last for some years."

"Is that so? That is well thought of. Well, now, let me penetrate into your kitchen quarters."

"Certainly," said Charlotte. "If your ladyship will step this way. I have had the maids hard at work scrubbing the cook-stove, which I am sorry to say was quite black with crocks and smuts; Mr. Collins as a single man seldom ventured himself into these quarters, and the cooking regions have had to be thoroughly cleaned from top to bottom."

Lady Catherine nodded approvingly, at two kitchen maids deedily down on their knees, and the sparkling stove. "That is satisfactory, most. And here is the pantry, I declare. Let me look inside."

"Dry goods are here, you see, and I am using this little room for a creamery for it is quite cool, and we can use it as an ice-house in summer."

"Cleverly thought of, upon my word. And I see you have used these canisters for – what? Flour?"

"Yes; and barley is here – and nuts – and cream of tartar…"

"I have no fault to find," Lady Catherine said, in a tone of mild surprise. "But tell me now – what did you and Mr. Collins eat last night, pray?"

"Why, the Sunday joint of beef, we had warmed over yesterday; and today we shall have hash."

"Most economical," nodded her Ladyship. "Well: let us go down the corridor, and look into this room – and this – "she ran her finger along a mantelpiece, and looked out window to judge of its cleanliness and clarity. "But what is this? Why are your writing-things and books in this dark little back drawing room? Surely the lady of the house ought to use the handsomer apartment in the front? Would that not be more proper?"

For the first time Charlotte blushed. "I thought it best," she said, "for Mr. Collins to retain his own book room – he is happy in it, and that way, I can have my own privacy, that is," she floundered, lost for words, "a room of my own…"

"Hum! I should have thought it inconvenient, but you know your own interest, Mrs. Collins, I see," said Lady Catherine shrewdly.

"I hope I am putting my husband's interests first, as is my duty," she hastened to answer, with modesty.

"It was not thought necessary in Sir Lewis de Bourgh's family. But then as a bride I had a fortune of my own, which you are unhappily without."

"I hope to be a useful helpmate to Mr. Collins, and by economy ensure that he makes the most of his money," Charlotte said earnestly.

"Aye, no doubt; and I begin to suspect you will succeed, Mrs. Collins," said Lady Catherine with a small and grudging smile of approval. "Now. Show me your bed-chamber. It this where you keep your under garments?"

Jane's Dreams
by Susan Mason-Milks

January 22, 1812

Jane moved slowly back and forth in the rocking chair in an attempt to soothe herself as she might an unhappy child. Four weeks in town had passed, and she had neither seen nor heard from Mr. Bingley. Jane was persuaded by something Caroline had let slip that her brother knew she was in town, but still he did not come. Even as sanguine as she usually was about such things, she finally knew she had to accept he was gone forever from her life.

Her call at Grosvenor Street earlier in the month to see Caroline Bingley and Louisa Hurst had been awkward and uncomfortable, but it was nothing compared to what had transpired when Caroline finally called on her here at Gracechurch Street. From the moment she arrived, Caroline had looked bored and indifferent. Although Aunt Gardiner tried to be helpful, attempting to smooth over the awkward pauses, the conversation lagged as Jane had no heart to try and Caroline no interest. Mercifully, the call was short.

Jane never liked to think ill of people, but at last, she knew she must. Miss Bingley had been wrong, very wrong to be so duplicitous in pretending to be her friend. In the beginning, Jane was certain Miss Bingley's efforts to form a friendship had been sincere, but now she even doubted that. Had Caroline's attentions been just a way to pass the time while in the country? Or had she only wanted to know Jane better because her brother had taken an interest in her? If that were true, then it made sense Miss Bingley's interest had faded just as her brother's had.

In spite of the hurt she felt, Jane did not regret having known Charles Bingley for those wonderful weeks. They were some of the happiest of her life. If only she could let go of the vision she had created of Mr. Bingley as her gentle and attentive husband, their comfortable home, and most importantly, the children they would have together. She had been so certain he was forming an attachment to her, but then he had just disappeared.

In her darkest moments, she despaired of ever again meeting someone as amiable as Mr. Bingley. What would happen to her now? As the eldest of five girls, Jane felt a responsibility to marry well in order to provide for her mother and sisters in the event of her father's death. Several gentlemen in the neighborhood had shown an interest in her recently including Mr. Wyatt, a very nice widower with two small children. Jane did not mind the idea of becoming mother to his children. Caring for and nurturing children came naturally to her. Mr. Wyatt had a small estate about the size of Longbourn, but he was a much more attentive landlord than her father. As a result, the estate prospered, and she knew her life would be a pleasant and easy one. Surely, it would not be such a terrible thing to be married to a man like that. At least she respected him and knew he would treat her respectfully as well. Maybe love would even grow between them. Perhaps, when she returned to Longbourn in the spring, if he were still unattached, she would make more of an effort to talk with him.

Jane continued to rock to soothe herself. Several times, she cried silently, salty tears rolling down her cheeks. She would allow herself this moment of self-pity, and then she would go on with her life and not look back. At least that was what she told herself. In truth, she knew she would never forget Charles Bingley who had been so perfectly suited to her. How she had loved it when his eyes came alive and sparkled when he saw her. She had felt as if it made her come to life, too. Her mother always told her how beautiful she was, but Jane did not believe it until she saw herself reflected in his eyes. He had called her his angel.

Jane dreaded writing to Lizzy about recent events because she would have to acknowledge how wrong she had been about Caroline. It would be difficult to admit to Lizzy that she had been right all along, but Jane knew if circumstances repeated themselves, she would most likely be deceived again. She had nothing to reproach herself for. Her behavior had been sincere and true. Caroline Bingley would have to live with the unkind way she had acted. In her heart, she felt pity for Caroline whose happiness seemed to depend so much on things outside herself – her social connections, her clothes, her money. Jane knew that she herself was rich in the things that really mattered.

So, Jane rocked. First, she began to feel calmer and finally, she grew sleepy. Abandoning the rocking chair, she crawled into the bed she shared with her eldest niece who was her namesake. Sensing her aunt's presence in the bed, Janie moved to cuddle up against her. In turn, Jane was comforted by the little girl's warmth. Kissing her niece, Jane smoothed her tangled curls on the pillow and soon fell into a deep sleep.

A Surprise Visit
from Lady Catherine
by C. Allyn Pierson

January 24, 1812

Charlotte sat down at the little table in her parlour with just a hint of a sigh. For the first time since her marriage she had no ready task at hand to occupy her. Her correspondence was all up to date and another letter would merely imply that she was bored with her new life...which was really not true. Not true at all.

Her house and her domestic concerns kept her quite busy, but yet she had enough time to rest for a few minutes, as she was doing now. Perhaps a cup of tea would refresh her.

She rang the bell and ordered the tea from the housemaid who answered; a country girl of little polish herself, but who did an excellent job of polishing the brasses. Perhaps a few minutes reading would occupy her.

She searched the small bookcase by her chair for the book she had been reading, a novel by Mrs. Radcliffe. As she flipped the pages, trying to find her place, lost in her move to Hunsford, her mind wandered unchecked. Life with Mr. Collins had been very much as she expected, and she had no complaints of her husband's character or amiability. The worst moments, undoubtedly, were during their wedding night.

She could feel herself flushing at the memory. They spent the night in this very house after a long drive from Hertfordshire. Mr. Collins spent the drive holding her hand with his damp fingers and talking about Hunsford. When they finally arrived, it was just after dark, and Charlotte was weary from the sound of his voice, but very impressed at his ability to talk for hours without drawing breath.

The housekeeper had put a small, cold supper in front of them and then discreetly disappeared into the kitchen. Charlotte examined the dining-room while she ate and commented favourably on its decor to her husband, when he paused to take a bite.

"Oh yes, my dear, Lady Catherine made all the decisions on paper and carpet to ready the house for you."

"Indeed! Her ladyship is most kind to offer her opinion."

"Indeed she is...she could not be more condescending when it came to offering advice which will make you comfortable!"

Charlotte subsided into silence as he meandered through a story illustrating Lady Catherine's manifold kindnesses, and Charlotte found her mind wandering, as it had often before the wedding. She imagined Mr. Collins replaced by Mr. Robinson. What would he have done with a new bride? She pictured him finishing his wine and drawing her up from the table and into a kiss.

"Mrs. Robinson, shall we go upstairs?" would be whispered in her ear, and she would smile at him and take his hand as they left the dining-room. Perhaps they would stop at the landing and he would crush her to him for another kiss, and lightly run his tongue over her lips before picking her up and carrying her to the bedroom...their bedroom, where they could, for the first time, abandon themselves without fear of discovery and hold each other all the night long.

Her fantasy had been jerked back to reality by Mr. Collins that night. She thanked God that she had enough experience to guide the process, or their wedding night would have been an exquisite embarrassment. As it was, she sent him off to ready himself for bed and let the maid undo all the tiny buttons of her dress and help her into her nightgown.

When her husband returned, she was waiting for him, reading her Bible verse for the night. He sidled into the room with a nervous smirk on his face and she quickly doused the candle for both their sakes. Yes, the darkness would help them both, giving him the courage to fumble with the ties of her nightgown, and allowing her to gaze up into the darkness and picture Mr. Robinson in her arms.

Suddenly, the housemaid came into the parlour, followed closely by Lady Catherine. Charlotte felt her face flush as she jerked her thoughts back to the present and offered their patroness a chair.

"Please, my lady, have a chair. Molly, another cup and more hot water, please."

Lady Catherine's eye fell upon the novel Charlotte was holding in her lap.

"I certainly hope that you are not making a habit of reading novels, Mrs. Collins!"

"Oh, no, Lady Catherine! I was just beginning to take the books out of this shelf to see what was there. I would like to give away many of these so that I can fit my books on the shelf. I believe that most of these belonged to the previous family who had the living. Is there, perhaps, a lending library in Hunsford which might appreciate some novels?"

"Give it to me and I will send it down the next time my maid goes to change my books."

"How very kind of you, my lady." Charlotte handed her the book, hoping that the slip of paper she had used for a marker did not have any identifying marks on it.

"And what have you been doing with yourself, Mrs. Collins? I know your husband is out visiting the sick. Did you not attend him?"

"No. No, my lady. I—I had some chores to finish and he wished to leave early." She paused for a moment, desperate to change the course of Lady Catherine's interrogation. "Actually, my lady, I have been most perplexed over what to do with the closet in the guest bedroom. I wish to have it be comfortable when my father and sister visit in the Spring, but it is most inconvenient. There are several hooks to hang clothes, but it is very small and tucked into a tiny corner. Surely there is some way to make it more useful!"

Lady Catherine's eye's brightened. "Let us go up and look at it. I am sure I can suggest something, Mrs. Collins. Perhaps more hooks or even shelves would make that corner more useful."

Charlotte smiled and led Lady Catherine up the perfectly proportioned and sized front stairs to the guest bedroom.

The Impressions of Anne de Bourgh
by Diana Birchall

January 26, 1812

"My dear Anne," Lady Catherine de Bourgh said to her daughter, "I do hope you will be taking your drive today. You need an airing."

"Is is so cold," Anne replied fretfully, "I do not see how a constitutional drive can be expected to do any one good in the month of January."

"You know what Dr. Shaw said," Lady Catherine put down her eggshell-thin teacup deliberately. "Your health requires a great deal of fresh air, and today it is sunny."

"A pale sunshine, and I do not believe it is going to last. There are several black clouds. And it is so dreary sitting up in the pony phaeton alone."

"Take Mrs. Jenkinson," urged Lady Catherine, "Upon my word, I would go with you myself, only I have an immense deal of correspondence. There are important matters occurring in the nation, and I, as a magistrate, must inform the Prime Minister of my views. And then I must do some sick-visiting. There is a laborer in the village who is refusing to labour, and I am certain he is just shamming."

"I could come with you there," said Anne, brightening up a little.

"No; if he is ill, we could not run the risk. You are not strong, Anne, and would be liable to catch cold, in those chilly cottages. Besides, I wish that you would call at the parsonage."

"The parsonage?" Anne frowned. "Oh, Mama, have we not paid sufficient attentions – and more – to those odious people?"

"My dear! Mr. Collins is our clergyman, and a very good sort of young man, I think. Certainly he has shown himself properly deferential to me, as is very right, and treats me as he ought, considering that I am his patroness, squiress, and superior, in every way. Besides, it is to Mrs. Collins that I wish you to speak."

"Me!" Anne drew back with horror. "What have I done that you must inflict her upon me?"

"Why Anne! She is a harmless creature enough. Where is your objection?" Lady Catherine poured some more tea, and urged it upon her.

"No, I won't have more tea, Mama. I am too upset. The whole trouble with that Mrs. Collins is that she is common. And you know it."

Lady Catherine's heavily marked black brows drew together. "I cannot say that you are not right – but then, I myself urged Mr. Collins not to marry any one high born, or with pretensions. Mrs. Collins appears to me to be a very good sort of housekeeping body."

"She is not a lady. And her husband is a clown."

Seldom, very seldom, had Lady Catherine been so at a loss for a reply. After a moment's consideration she said, "So, this is why you never speak to them at dinner, and are so silent. I had observed that."

"You are correct. And if I may dare to say so, Mama, it is my opinion that you have been inviting them here to Rosings far too often. I know precisely what sort of pushing, presuming people they are, and if you give them an inch they will take an ell! They have been here seven times in their month of married life, and will soon begin to believe twice weekly visits to Rosings are theirs by right. You are altogether too soft hearted and susceptible to inferiors, Mama."

"I have ever been celebrated for my kindness of heart, it is true," Lady Catherine agreed complacently, "but if I may contradict you, my dear, I do believe them to be quite harmless, and agreeable enough. And you know how little company we can have here in these dark winter nights. It is well that a tame clergyman and his wife can be called over at any time for a game of cassino or quadrille."

"Pah! I would much rather sit with a book, than listen to the pratings of Mr. Collins, or the flatteries of his wife."

"So that is why you never open your lips from one end of a card game to another, either," her mother mused. "I see."

"Exactly so. And may I remind you, Mama, that we need not be so desperately craven for society, as that. When I am married to Darcy, the society at Pemberley will be quite another thing. And you shall spend the whole of every winter with us, I am determined on that."

"Ah, Anne, your sweetness is fabled. I know Darcy will never be able to resist it, when he sees you. He must be quite ready to settle down by now, and I do hope that another season will see you the happy mistress of Pemberley, as your dear aunt and I always planned. Surely this will be the year."

"Of course it will," murmured Anne, who had always seen this fate before her, and in her pride and self-satisfaction, it had never occurred to her to doubt it. "When I am Mrs. Darcy, you know, I will never have converse with such common women as that Mrs. Collins. Did you see her at dinner the other night? Her gown so very drab and plain, and she could not even eat her soup delicately. That shows her to be so very ill bred."

"Her father, Sir William Lucas, is a knight," Lady Catherine pointed out doubtfully. "A recent creation, it is true, but they say he was presented at court."

"Well, it did nothing for his daughter's manners," said Anne tartly. "You know she was nothing but a baby nurse to that dreadful brood of brothers and sisters she talks about, and she has no elegance, no refinement, no air about her at all. And is that the sort of person you want me to associate with, so soon before my elevation to be Darcy's wife, and chatelaine of Pemberley?"

236

"I only wanted you to give her the receipt for beef tea that old Nanny wrote out for me," said Lady Catherine, in a tone of unwonted meekness. "Mrs. Collins believes her husband's voice is strained, owing to the rigors of his last sermon, and a chill upon his throat. It would be a kindness, my dear."

"Oh, very well," said Anne crossly. "I'll call for the phaeton." She pulled irritably at the bell-rope, and Mrs. Jenkinson came hastily into the room.

"I am sorry, my dear Anne," she said breathlessly, "but I was only talking to Nanny about that receipt your mother wanted, at her request. Shall you drive over to the parsonage now?"

"Apparently so," Anne replied ungraciously. "I must be a ministering angel to the lowly. Pretty preferment, upon my word, is it not?"

"May I come and keep you company?" asked Mrs. Jenkinson humbly. "I could carry your cashmere shawl, so you will not catch a chill when you get out of the carriage."

"No; to be sure not. If I am alone, I will say that it is not a regular call, and then I need not get out of the carriage at all. They can come to the gate. I will not give them even one quarter of an hour." And she swept out of the room, her small, thin figure upright, to put on her driving costume.

Lady Catherine and Mrs. Jenkinson, left alone, met each other's eyes.

"It is true that the Collinses are common, very common," said Lady Catherine, "but I do wish Anne could try to be a little more engaging. She thinks she will have nobody to do with at Pemberley but the high born, but managing a great house like that, makes many demands."

"Oh, but she was born to the task," said Mrs. Jenkinson, rolling up her eyes and looking at the heavens earnestly. "Was it not Mr. Collins who said that she would be an ornament to the rank of duchess? He never spoke more truly."

"To be sure," said Lady Catherine, pleased. "Her grace and condescension are such as are not often seen. Oh, I know Darcy will be very taken with her, when he comes. This must and shall be the year."

Mr. Bingley Regrets
by Susan Mason-Milks

February 9, 1812

Charles Bingley lingered at the breakfast table over a cup of coffee that had grown cold long ago. Although the newspaper from London was open in front of him, he had not read a word. His heart and mind were engaged elsewhere. Closing his eyes, he could see Jane Bennet's face looking up at him serenely as they danced. Just one glance from her was enough to leave him completely speechless. Charles Bingley, speechless? That was something new! Her eyes were so bright and completely without pretense; her gloved hand in his, light as a feather. She had no idea how alluringly beautiful she was. Jane truly was an angel.

He knew he had a tendency to be too impetuous, to speak before thinking, and her sweet, gentle nature was the perfect counterbalance. Once when she was sitting beside him, he had started to open his mouth to make some rash pronouncement, but she had placed her hand ever so gently on his arm for just a second. Although her touch had been so light, as if a small bird had perched there briefly and then flown away, it was still enough to slow him down, to make him think before he spoke. In all the time they had spent together, he had never heard her say a derogatory word about anyone or pass on gossip, an activity his sisters seemed to delight in. His Jane always believed the best of everyone. His Jane. He liked the sound of that. Taking a deep breath, he let it out slowly. She *could* have been his Jane, but he had thrown away all away.

Bingley had been so certain Jane returned his affections that it had come as a complete shock when Caroline and Darcy told him they believed she was indifferent and just paying attention to him to please her mother. How could he have read the signs so incorrectly? At first he listened only to his heart, which told him they must be wrong. Jane was not a coy, sophisticated woman like so many he had met. There was no artifice about her. The Jane he knew had more true sweetness than any other woman of his acquaintance. Although Caroline had insisted the Bennets had no connections, no status in society, and had implied Jane was not good enough for him, Bingley felt exactly the opposite – he was not good enough for her.

But what if it were true she did not care for him? Perhaps, she had already begun to favor some other gentleman as soon as he had departed. Bingley did not know what to trust – the pull of his own heart or the warnings from his sister and Darcy. His friend had never steered him wrong before, but then Darcy did not know Jane the way he did. No, he had not been wrong. She did care for him just as he cared for her.

Jane Bennet was a treasure, but he had given her up. He knew there was a distinct possibility he would regret her forever. Why did I listen to them instead of my heart? Perhaps, he should defy them all, return to Netherfield, and pay court to his angel again. He shook his head. No, he could never return. If he was right and Jane had harbored true feelings for him, she must hate him by now for abandoning her with no word. Caroline had said she would write to Jane and break it to her that they would not be returning. If his sister believed Jane did not care for him, then why had she told him she would try to let her friend down gently? Then it occurred to him – Caroline's reasons for not wanting him to return to Netherfield could be more in her own self interest than out of concern for him.

After a few minutes of contemplation, Bingley's head began to hurt. Putting his fingers to his temples, he closed his eyes and rubbed in a circular motion hoping to relieve the pain.

Just then, he heard a rustling of silk and detected the scent of Caroline's perfume as she crossed the room. Bingley knew it was rude of him not to acknowledge her or stand as she entered, but he was too irritated with her to be polite. Instead, he pretended he was studying the paper so intently that he had not heard her approach.

"Louisa and I are going shopping this afternoon. You did not have other plans for the carriage, did you?" Caroline asked, as if daring him to deny her request. As her fingers drummed on the table, each tap felt like a blow to his already sensitive head.

Bingley remained silent. He was not sure with whom he was more angry – Caroline for trying to influence him or himself for believing her. *Why do I still put up with her antics?* In the past when he had tried to rein her in, she always pouted or did something else to make his life miserable.

"Charles, are you listening to me?" Her voice had that sharp edge to it he always took as a warning not to cross her, but this time, he ignored it.

"Caroline, have you had a letter from Miss Bennet recently?" he asked suddenly. As he waited for her answer, Bingley noticed that the only sound in the room was the ticking of the mantle clock.

"I believe I received a letter in December," she responded slowly, examining her perfectly manicured hands.

"I remember she mentioned the possibility of visiting her aunt and uncle in town during the winter. Did she say she was coming to London?"

Caroline looked off and to the left as if searching for an answer. "Let me see now. Hmm… No, I do not believe she mentioned any visits to town." She followed this with a smile that stopped short of her eyes.

When he did not respond, she continued, "Then you have no objection to our taking the carriage for the afternoon? And one of the footmen to carry our parcels." He noticed how smoothly she had changed the subject.

Bingley was about to protest as he had planned to meet Darcy at the fencing club for a little sparring. They had both been engaging in that vigorous activity with some frequency of late. It would be inconvenient, but he could make other arrangements. Perhaps that would be easier than telling Caroline "no." Denying her would only result in much unpleasantness. He knew at some point he would have to begin standing up to Caroline, but this was a relatively small matter. He thought it wiser to pick his battles carefully.

Caroline took his silence as assent. She nodded and stood to leave. Looking down at her dress as she smoothed out the tiny wrinkles, she said distractedly, "You must go with us to the Chadwicks' dinner party on Tuesday. We cannot have you at home moping about."

From the doorway, she added, "I understand their eldest daughter is very accomplished."

"Mmm… accomplished," he replied, but his thoughts were already back in Hertfordshire.

Darcy Comes to a Decision
by Sharon Lathan

February 14, 1812

Darcy closed the door behind him and did something he rarely did: He collapsed against it and released a loud moan of relief.

"What a horrendous afternoon," he muttered. He ran a hand through his hair before grasping the knot of his cravat and tugging. Futilely, as it turned out. "Damn! He would choose today to bind me with some new fangled tying technique."

As if my cravat is the deciding factor in whether a woman will find me appealing. Stupidity!

He pushed away from the door with a grunt and crossed directly to the sidebar. Something strong was needed to scorch the taste of tea and repugnance from the back of his throat.

"What a horrendous afternoon," he repeated, this time with a growl. "What was I thinking?"

The question was rhetorical, so he felt no need to answer himself. Thankfully. *Have I so unraveled that I have now resorted to talking aloud?* He clamped his lips shut before the answer slipped out audibly.

Yes.

He finished the glass, finally feeling a measure of calm, even though his neckcloth was still choking him. He had tried. At least he could say he had given the matter considerable thought and explored all reasonable options.

After the hell that had been Christmas with Elizabeth Bennet invading his every waking moment and creeping into his dreams,

Darcy had been so desperate for anything to divert his attention that he had agreed to accompany his aunt and uncle to Sir Cole's annual Twelfth Night Masque. Normally an agony of socializing that he avoided like the plague, this year he had practically leapt across the room to pen his acceptance to the invitation. Furthering his surprise, he had enjoyed the evening more than typical and largely that was due to Amy Griffin.

He had not seen the youngest daughter of Sir Griffin of Alveston Hall in Derby for four years or more. She had grown, as young ladies are wont to do, and he had felt an instant interest. Attraction, to be honest. Immediately he recognized why she appealed to him: She bore similarities of temperament and physique to Elizabeth Bennet. Yet rather than annoying or discomfiting him, it was a thrilling prospect.

Perhaps, he had wondered with an inner voice that hinted of a prayer, *my infatuation with Miss Elizabeth was merely to prepare me for finding Miss Amy.* The latter woman, after all, was utterly more acceptable than the first. With relief he figuratively girded his loins, and for a month waged an internal war he was determined to win decisively as it should be. Logic and rational facts engaged the enemy that was emotion and wild impulse. The intelligent, cultured, beautiful daughter of a wealthy landowner with an impeccable pedigree had the battle advantage, so the victory was assured. Right?

Apparently practical tactics were no good when it came to matters of the heart. Today had cinched it. Sitting in the parlor of Alveston Hall sipping tea and nibbling on sweet cakes while struggling to keep up his end of the conversation, halt the infernal comparisons to Elizabeth, and not bolt from his chair to run for the nearest exit when Miss Amy batted her lashes and casually commented about it being Valentine's Day – *How could I have forgotten that?!* –Darcy had finally admitted defeat. It defied everything he knew to be sensible, but at the end of a handful of social encounters Miss Amy had lost the battle to the woman who continued to brutally ram into his head.

A knock on the door interrupted his thoughts, and since they had already started to veer into areas he wasn't quite prepared to embrace in the light of day, he answered it gladly. It was a servant of the inn in Derby delivering the day's post. Darcy lifted a brow in surprise, having not anticipated receiving any mail since he only planned to be here for a week, maybe two tops (although after today that was unlikely), when he left Town six days ago. There were only three letters and as soon as he saw his Aunt Catherine's familiar scrawl it made sense. Mrs. Smyth, his housekeeper at Darcy House in London, would automatically assume that any correspondence from the great Lady Catherine de Bourgh of the utmost, critical importance! Darcy hardly agreed, but considering the timeliness of preventing him from dwelling on the memory of Elizabeth Bennet's fine eyes, superb figure, lush hair especially as it fell in a tousled cascade down her back, flushed cheeks, warm hands, intoxicating scent....

He shook his head violently, inhaled deeply, and ripped open the letter. *God! Please be a long letter droning on about the boring activities of your corgis or how your tenants fawned over you when you last condescended to visit them!* He started reading while still standing in the middle of the room. *Ah! Excellent! Mr. Collins! Yes, talk of him will do!*

How wrong could a man be?

It started off well enough. Several sentences about the horrible substitute reverend she had endured while Mr. Collins was away – *Could he truly be worse than the sniveling Collins must be as a preacher?*– followed by a whole paragraph detailing the report she had written to the archbishop – *I'm sure he loved that*!

Then she turned to the subject of Mr. Collins recent marriage, beginning with claiming responsibility for his matrimonial state. She went on to write that it was she who encouraged him to seek a wife and listed all the various reasons – *Terrific, just what I need to be reminded of now* – one of which was the logic in picking from one of the five Bennet daughters.

All the blood drained from his face and he threw the parchment pieces onto the floor. He couldn't breathe, and the pain slamming through his chest was excruciating. He had been there, at the Netherfield Ball, his eyes following Elizabeth Bennet everywhere she went no matter how hard he had tried to stop himself. Anger, born from jealousy he had refused to acknowledge, had noted every one of the men who danced with or even talked to her. He had wanted to strangle every last damn one of them! So of course he had noticed how the pathetic Mr. Collins had dogged her steps and danced too close to her. Although somewhat amusing at the time, only a fool would not have seen that he was paying special attention to her. Darcy was not a fool – *Well, maybe a little* – and although not as irritated at Collins as he had been some of the other, slightly handsomer gentlemen who occupied Elizabeth at the ball, now it was all too clear.

Suddenly it wasn't himself he was envisioning in loving, passionate moments with Elizabeth. He felt truly ill and stumbled to the nearest chair. Would she have married Collins? He shuddered and again tore at the constricting neckcloth, managing to loosen it a bit, not that it helped. A tiny part of his brain not throbbing with pain admitted that his aunt's logic was sound. *And aren't you the King of Logic?* The thought was laced with bitter irony. Look where logic had gotten him. The woman he loved – *Fine! I said it! I love Elizabeth Bennet!* – was probably married to that man and beyond his reach.

He snatched the papers off the floor. He had to know. It may well kill him, but he had to know. Rapidly he scanned the sentences. His aunt's words had never in his life elicited such a welter of emotions. In a matter of minutes he ran the gamut from despair to giddy relief, finally emitting a whoop of joy.

It was Charlotte Lucas who married the imbecile! Elizabeth had refused him! The day after the Netherfield Ball, in fact.

Why?

The question hit him square in the chest. Dare he hope that she had refused Collins for more than just that the man was ridiculous? *Might she have been thinking of me?* Granted their interactions didn't precisely fall under what anyone would consider courtship-like, but he knew she enjoyed debating with him. Surely that meant something. Besides, he had far more to offer her than Collins! Refusing that man's proposal only increased her worth in his eyes.

As quickly as it came the pain eased. *I love her.* Strangely, it was remarkably easy to say. The fight was gone. The search was over. The debates were done.

"I love Elizabeth Bennet," he said aloud, and did not feel silly in doing so.

He jumped up from the chair invigorated. Plans would be made once back in London. For now he just wanted to leave Derby and get closer to Hertfordshire. *Closer to her.* He smiled brightly and started gathering his belongings. And, yes, he was whistling.

Caroline Bingley Schemes
to Catch Darcy
by C. Allyn Pierson

February 17, 1812

Caroline tapped her quill against her tightly pursed lips as she contemplated the dilemma before her. So far, her plans to dazzle Mr. Darcy with her wit and elegance had not yielded the matrimonial fruit which she had hoped to cultivate. But...all was not yet lost. Now that their party had retreated to London and the abominable Bennets were no longer flaunting their milkmaid prettiness in front of Bingley and Darcy, perhaps she could divert Darcy's mind enough from her brother's stupid infatuation to focus on her availability (and eligibility).

Perhaps Georgiana could help her...oh, not knowingly, of course. The dear girl would not say boo to a goose, let alone try to manipulate her revered elder brother. But...Charles was spending most of his free hours with Darcy, hanging around at their stupid club, shooting at Mantons, or riding in Hyde Park. Certainly, she could shake out her riding habit and start showing her face in the park, but it would probably be more effective to arrange some outings with Georgiana.

She turned to her daybook and perused the next two weeks. They were already engaged to dine with the Darcys in two days. Perhaps Georgiana would enjoy a visit to the British Museum. It would be devastatingly boring, but would likely impress Darcy with her affection for his sister and show him what a good sister-in-law she would be. Of course, any time spent with Georgiana would also allow her a closer relationship with Charles…surely he would forget Miss Bennet with such a superior young lady in his company!

She felt an urge to write down a list of her plans, but knew that would give too much appearance of planning if it fell into the wrong hands, so she just wrote a quick invitation to Georgiana and sent it off with a footman.

He soon came back with an acceptance, and the next day she stopped at the Darcy townhouse and picked up Georgiana.

"How delightful you look this morning, Miss Darcy! Are you ready for our outing?"

"Yes Miss Bingley. I am looking forward to visiting the museum. Do you suppose there is any chance Lord Elgin's marbles will be purchased by the museum so we can see them whenever we want?"

"We can only hope, my dear Miss Darcy"

They spent two hours in the museum, most of it in the Egyptian Hall. Georgiana showed a quite gruesome interest in the disgusting mummies.

"Ugh! How *can* you bear to look at those hideous things, my dear Miss Darcy? They are nasty!"

"Oh, Miss Bingley! How can you say that! Just think…these are the mortal remains of real people from one of the greatest ancient civilizations! Does it not give you the chills to think about what grandeur and history these people saw?"

Miss Bingley shuddered. "All I can think about is their disgusting current appearance, which does, indeed, give me chills."

"Oh."

Miss Darcy's shoulders slumped a little and she moved on to the next room, giving a glance back at the mummies before she did so. Miss Bingley thought she should put this outing on a more interesting level.

"My dear Miss Darcy, shall we find a cup of tea to refresh us before we go home? My brother tells me we will be seeing you tomorrow evening for the theatre."

"Yes, my brother told me about it. I am looking forward to it."

Later, when Caroline reached home, she gave a sigh of relief. What an exhausting day! Hopefully, the opera would be more stimulating. Perhaps she should go to the lending library and find out more about the opera and the composer. She had no interest in such things, but Darcy certainly had an ear for music and she must convince him she was worthy of his interest.

Her hopes were destined to be dashed. Darcy and Georgiana both kept their eyes on the stage for the entire performance and had their heads together talking about it during the interval. Miss Bingley tried to enter their discussion, but found herself overwhelmed by their talk of the staging, the sets and the costumes, as well as the story and music. Who in the world cared about such things! Their late supper was no better. Caroline managed to seat herself next to Georgiana, but Darcy, whom she thought was directly behind her, somehow ended up across the table between Charles and Louisa. Damn his over developed courtesy! Georgiana was still taken up with the opera, which she talked about *ad nauseum*, and Caroline was stymied.

Later that night, she sat up in bed, contemplating her hunt for Darcy, but she was too exhausted to come up with another plan of attack. Tomorrow she would begin anew, she resolved as she blew out the candle.

Miss de Bourgh's Expectations
by Diana Birchall

February 19, 1812

Lady Catherine prided herself on her deportment, which consisted in a magnificently upright carriage, and a way of moving that might be called an arrogant glide. To display a need for haste, would be deserving of contempt; a lady did not hurry-skurry like a schoolgirl. Yet on this morning, Lady Catherine did enter the small summer breakfast-parlour at Rosings with such unwonted rapidity that Miss de Bourgh and Mrs. Jenkinson looked up startled from their work.

It was only March, yet the ladies liked to sit in this room of a morning because it had good light for stitching, and was in its way more comfortable than many of the grander rooms. Anne, who hated to walk before noon, liked to sit and sew, and look out of window. She was engaged in making yet another garment for her trousseau, which had been her self-assigned daily task for many years. Almost since she was a little girl sewing her sampler, had she worked on the embroidered linens and night-dresses for her marriage to Mr. Darcy. She seldom accomplished more than one or perhaps two stitches a minute, but fortunately Mrs. Jenkinson had worked more steadily and great piles of fine Irish cloth and delicate laced muslins were put up in lavender in the massive cedar-lined chests, waiting in the great store-rooms of Rosings for the happy day.

"My dear!" trumpeted Lady Catherine. "Here is news, tremendous news."

"Oh!" Mrs. Jenkinson exclaimed, "is it something that must be broke to her in stages, Lady Catherine? Anne is delicate. You know we are always saying that she is not at all strong. Shall I fetch some water?"

"No, no," impatiently returned Lady Catherine, "it is good news – the very best."

Anne's eyes grew wide and a pink colour mounted in her sallow face as she sat forward in her seat. In no other way did she betray her expectations, but they were no less than that the letter her mother so excitedly flapped, should contain a proposal from Mr. Darcy.

"Only think!" Lady Catherine cried. "Darcy is coming! He will soon be here!"

Anne made an impatient gesture with her needle and a satin flounce. "Why, yes, Mama. We know that. He always said he would come in the spring – perhaps with Fitzwilliam, to make their yearly tour of inspection. But is that all the news?"

"No, it is not all. Stay and you shall hear. Darcy will be here as early as next week. Yes! He will be at Rosings for Easter. And you know what that means, Anne!"

Anne rose to her feet, her face scarlet. "Has it come? So soon!"

"Soon, you call it!" Lady Catherine made a "tsk" noise of impatience. "My dear girl, you are eight and twenty years old. Darcy has not been at all forward in settling your marriage, indeed I have at times been almost cross with him for being so – not reluctant precisely, but – Naturally I could never be truly cross with dear Darcy, but you will allow that he has not been expeditious."

"Oh, but Lady Catherine," protested Mrs. Jenkinson. "So much as Mr. Darcy has to do! With running the Pemberley estate, and the house in town, and overseeing Miss Georgiana's education – he never meant to marry until his sister was a young lady in society herself, I am sure. Now she is out, and will be a perfect companion for Miss Anne, when Mr. Darcy brings her home to Pemberley."

"Does he – does he say anything about that, Mama?" Anne ventured.

"Well, no, not directly. He would hardly do so in a letter. Darcy was always the very soul of delicacy and discretion. But, depend upon it, he will make his declaration in form when he is here. A springtime engagement! Only think! That is what he has been waiting for, I know."

"So romantic!" simpered Mrs. Jenkinson. "All the little sheep and lambs, and the primroses too."

"But we are hardly prepared," Lady Catherine bethought herself, drawing her heavy eyebrows together.

Mrs. Jenkinson lifted her hands with a wordless sigh. "Oh, Lady Catherine! Not prepared! Why, we have been sewing Miss Anne's trousseau for these twenty years at least! The bed-sheets alone – the Mechlin lace – oh! She will be the envy of many a Duchess."

"That is not what I mean," said Lady Catherine, frowning. "I am talking of Anne's own person, her own tout ensemble."

"Why, she has as many pretty gowns as any young lady in the kingdom, surely, Madam. Any one would be sufficient to invite the proposal."

"Her clothes are well enough," returned Lady Catherine shortly.

"Mama, you don't mean – do you not think Mr. Darcy will be pleased with me? Will he not think me handsome enough? Perhaps there are other young women of his acquaintance who are – showier."

"Certainly not, Anne," snapped Lady Catherine, in a manner that betrayed it was exactly what she meant. "You are handsomer than the very handsomest girls, because you have so decidedly the aristocrat in your lineage. No, no, the lines of your nose, the bearing of your head..."

Anne felt comfortable again. "That is true," she said complacently, "I don't suppose Darcy can have been associating with any girls of such antecedents as mine. Our own family is the noblest of all, even more than those of higher rank. And what sort of people can he have met in traveling lately, in Hertfordshire, with his friend Bingley?"

"Yes, very common people there," Lady Catherine sniffed agreement. "Assembly balls and things of that sort, where you might meet anyone. And Darcy has not lost his sense of what he owes the family. He has the proper Darcy pride, and would never forget himself."

"Oh, Lady Catherine!" sighed Mrs. Jenkinson. "I am sure he would be the very last young man to do that."

"Very true. Still, he has been seeing a great deal of the world, and so I think it expedient – that is, it cannot do any harm, for Anne to look her very best for the meeting."

"Why, what more can I do?" asked Anne perplexed. "I did think I would wear my green sarsanet – it is my best gown this season, and cost seventeen pounds, you know. And Helene is well schooled in all the best Parisian ways of curling my hair. Ringlets, you know, are all the style, and you see they become me so well." She shook her curls so they bounced, like a dozen brown mice.

"Green!" Lady Catherine fell back in her chair, momentarily lost for words. "My child, no woman ever received a proposal in that unfortunate colour. And your figure – "She looked her daughter up and down, and her expression grew grave.

Anne regarded her parent with astonishment. "Why, mother, you have always said my figure was the perfect size for true elegance! It is not fleshy, but rather more aerial."

"The truth is, I am afraid you may be too thin," muttered Lady Catherine. "What if Darcy's taste is for a fleshpot, a tall, full-figured woman."

"Not in a wife, surely!" ejaculated Mrs. Jenkinson with horror.

Anne had regained her poise. "Really, Mama, where did you get such an extraordinary notion? Mr. Darcy could not wish his wife to look like a milkmaid. He will want her to be a person of refinement, and ton, and of course, related to him in an advantageous way."

"And the promise was made when the children were still in their cradles, do not forget that," reminded Mrs. Jenkinson.

"Yes. Why, you have always promised me that I would marry Mr. Darcy. Mama, how can you forget?"

"It ought to be so," said Lady Catherine, troubled.

"And I will take your advice in one thing, and wear my pink India muslin. That will give my complexion a rosy hue."

"You will look like an angel on a cloud," enthused Mrs. Jenkinson breathlessly, "a pink cloud."

"Perhaps you are right," said Lady Catherine, still with some air of doubt.

"Of course I am right, Mama. Never fear." Anne got up and went to the beveled mirror above the sideboard, and regarded herself with her head on one side, again shaking her new-fangled ringlets, a style which in truth did little for her mouse-coloured hair and pallid skin. "I think I am most uncommon looking, with all the tints of real refinement."

"She is like a painting, an oil painting," nodded Mrs. Jenkinson in ecstasy. "I have always said so. Or perhaps a really elegant water-colour."

"And Mr. Darcy will assuredly honour his obligations in the course of this visit. He has the reputation of being the very pattern of honour. And it is high time! He must know that I do not want to be a bride at thirty."

"I only hope he has not been forming any new attachments, that is all," said Lady Catherine thoughtfully. "It would explain his dilatoriness. But no, no, I know that to be impossible. Darcy is far too proud to lower himself to such nonsense."

"Proud! Of course he is. And I have a very good pride of my own," cried Anne. "We are so alike, it is quite ridiculous. I laugh about it to myself all the time."

"And," Mrs. Jenkinson reminded them, turning back to her stitchery, "remember, no matter how many girls he has known, he has remained single-minded, and pure. He has been saving his heart for no one but Anne."

"So sweet a notion," Anne sighed. "But you will say, Mama, that we are being too romantic. Even in a prudential sense, then, remember all that Darcy gains in marrying me."

"True," Lady Catherine agreed. "Not many girls have such a fortune." Then she remembered something. "Girls – yes. I had forgot that the Collinses are here almost every night. We must put a stop to that."

"Why ever bother?" asked Anne. "Darcy surely will not pay any attentions to Mr. and Mrs. Collins, so common and dull as they are. He will converse with us, and on the first night I will say – "She swirled the satin material about her and did a little dance in her thin slippers. "Shall we not take a turn, I will ask him? That young lady friend of Mrs. Collins can play the pianoforte well enough for an accompaniment, and we shall dance."

Lady Catherine and Mrs. Jenkinson's eyes met and there was apprehension in each. They were both thinking about the contrast the pretty Miss Bennet might make with Anne, and they acknowledged their mutual thought, without any words.

"Oh, no," said Lady Catherine decidedly, "we won't want them here."

"Certainly not. Do you wish me to write a note, Lady Catherine?"

"That won't be necessary. The invitations shall simply cease, until, of course, everything is settled – or not."

"It will be settled," Anne assured her complacently, fluffing up her ringlets. "Don't worry, Mama. Have not you always said that Darcy and I are the perfect match?"

Caroline Bingley Schemes
to Catch Darcy, Reprise
by C. Allyn Pierson

February 27, 1812

Drat that man! All her efforts had not, thus far, made the slightest dent in his reserve, in spite of their removal to London! Miss Bingley had been positive that their little conspiracy to separate Charles from that Bennet chit would bring her together with Darcy in a more intimate way. She had certainly had opportunities to ingratiate herself with Miss Darcy, but one could only do so much with praise for her musical talents and crawling at a snail's pace around dusty old museums. It was becoming intolerable!

Before she had resolved all her annoyance over these issues, the Hurst's butler entered and announced, of all people, Miss Bennet! Louisa, who had been plying her embroidery needle in a desultory fashion and pouting over her boredom while Caroline mumbled angrily to herself, brightened up at the thought of a visitor…any visitor. Her sister, however, was on her feet immediately, greeting Miss Bennet coolly and apologizing for the fact that they were on their way out.

"I am so sorry, Jane, since it is so lovely to see you again, that we have an engagement we must go to very soon. Won't you please sit down, though, for just a moment and tell us what brings you to London? I was certain you would not be able to get away from Hertfordshire."

"My aunt and uncle most kindly invited me to stay with them for a few weeks and enjoy some of the pleasures of the city. Did you not receive my letters?"

"How...lovely, but no I have not received any letters from you in...oh, quite some time. Are any of your other sisters with you?"

"No. Lizzy will be visiting Mrs. Collins in the Spring, however, and we will travel back to Longbourn together."

"Oh, so you will be here some months, I take it."

"Yes, I very likely will."

"How delightful! I must pop by for a visit. Your aunt and uncle live in Cheapside, do they not?" Caroline could hardly bear to say the name of such a low neighborhood.

"They do. Here is my direction, should you be able to visit."

Caroline suddenly remembered Charles would be home soon, and abruptly stood. "Well, it is lovely seeing you, dearest Jane, and I hope we meet often. Do you go to the theatre much?"

"Occasionally, when my uncle has time away from his business to escort us."

"Wonderful, perhaps we will see you there as well...oh, dear! We must be going, Louisa. Ring for the footman please."

Louisa complied and Miss Bennet was hustled out with kind expressions of happiness.

Afterwards, Caroline thought over the risks of having Miss Bennet in London and an idea occurred to her. Perhaps she could use this event to her advantage. She immediately sat down at her writing desk and wrote a note to Darcy requesting that he come see her (when Charles was not at home) to discuss a disastrous difficulty regarding the previously considered unfortunate friendship of her brother's. Fortunately, Charles was engaged to dine with some friends from Cambridge and would be out all evening. After reading through the letter to make sure there were no errors of spelling or penmanship, she sent it off with Louisa's second footman. Within an hour the messenger returned with Mr. Darcy's response: "I will come at nine of the clock."

Caroline smiled delightedly. Now she must get rid of the Hursts, which should be not at all difficult since they were to attend a concert and late supper with friends.

When it was but a half hour to their departure for the evening, Louisa was summoned to Caroline's room by her abigail and came bustling in. "I really must hurry if I am not to be too late, Caroline. What do you want?"

Miss Bingley was lying on her bed with a cloth saturated with lavender water on her forehead. She weakly lifted her hand to her sister. "I am so sorry, Louisa. I came up to dress for dinner but I suddenly developed the most ghastly headache."

"Headache! You are never ill Caroline!"

"I know, I know. Perhaps that is why it is so bad. It has taken a severe illness to bring me down."

Louisa looked alarmed. "Do you wish me to summon the doctor, my dear? Perhaps I should cancel our engagement and stay home with you."

"NO!" Caroline gasped. "No, no, my dear, I am sure it will go away if I lie quietly here with my vinaigrette for the evening. Even the healthiest must occasionally be brought low and I am sure it is nothing serious and I will feel much restored in the morning."

"Well...if you are sure. We will go to the Clarkes' concert, then, and your abigail can immediately send for us if you should feel worse."

Caroline relaxed back on her pillow. "Yes. Enjoy yourself, Louisa. Quiet is all I need."

As soon as her maid confirmed that the Hursts had departed, Caroline jumped up from her bed and instructed the maid to bring her a dinner tray and to make sure her pomona silk gown was in order...no, perhaps not the pomona...green might not be the most flattering colour in the dim light she had planned. "The claret silk. That will be the best. Elegant, and it will give color to my cheeks. Also, it looks sufficiently serious for the cause...I do not want to look like I am on my way to a ball!"

At five minutes before nine Caroline was waiting in the best drawing-room after dismissing all the unnecessary servants with orders to go to bed early as (she told them sternly) she was planning

259

to retire immediately and did not want to be disturbed by their talking and stomping around when she was not feeling well. They looked surprised and uneasy at these odd instructions, but, except for a few inquisitive glances, they had too much respect for Miss Bingley's temper to question her orders.

She heard the bell ring and the footman, an elderly servant who was almost blind and deaf, came slowly up the stairs and announced Darcy. She had arranged for the drawing-room to have a lovely warm fire and several branches of candles to make it bright and inviting, and she immediately rose and held out her hands, nodding to the footman to go. "I'm sorry to make such a to do over this, Mr. Darcy, but I do not want Charles to find out that Miss Bennet is in London. She will be visiting her aunt and uncle in Cheapside for, probably, several months! We must do something to insure he does not see her or all is lost!" While saying this she had guided him in front of the sofa, where it would be virtually impossible to avoid sitting next to her, and waited for his answer with every appearance of concern.

He managed to not see her hands reaching for him and awkwardly nodded at her greeting, his eyes showing white like a nervous horse. To Caroline's annoyance he turned and began pacing the room, his hands clasped behind his back as he showed a face deep in thought. Finally, after a few laps around the room, he cleared his throat and opened his lips to attempt responding to her questions, when the drawing-room door opened and Louisa plunged into the room, saying petulantly, "Mr. Darcy! Withern said you had just arrived... how delightful it is to see you, especially as our evening has been a complete disaster! So annoying! Lisette Clarke decided to develop the measles, of all things! It is too bad of her!"

Caroline blew out her bedside candle and tried to compose herself for sleep. How stupid Louisa was! All that planning gone to waste and now Mr. Darcy would be suspicious if she tried compromising him again. She had had everything arranged to perfection... her maid was going to give her fifteen minutes to settle Darcy on the couch with her and lure him close with her frantic whispers, then 'accidentally' burst in on them and discover them unchaperoned in the virtually empty house. Even if Darcy was suspicious of the circumstances, he could not know if he had been set up and his sense of honor would force him to marry her to protect her good name. But no...Louisa had come blundering in like the cow she was and ruined everything! All her hopes turned to dust...

But then...he was not married yet, so perhaps her chance would yet come. Miss Bingley smiled to herself and closed her eyes.

Maria Lucas's First Impressions of Hunsford and Rosings Park
by C. Allyn Pierson

March 4, 1812

Maria gave up and pulled off her mittens so she could nibble on her fingernails. The excitement was just more than she could bear as the coach trundled up the road past the palings of Rosings Park. Charlotte's home must be very near. This was the first time she had traveled away from home. She had tried so hard to be a young lady instead of a girl just released from the schoolroom, but her nerves had finally overcome her.

It was so strange to think of Charlotte married after all these years...and her husband, worthy though he was, just did not fit into any sort of romantic context...at least not any romance Maria had read. The thought of...sleeping next to Mr. Collins...it did not bear thinking about. She shuddered.

At last! The coach pulled onto a trim graveled entry and pulled to a stop. When Mr. Collins pulled down the steps of the coach, Maria helped her father hoist himself up, groaning all the while about how stiff he was from the travel. As he straightened himself out and greeted Mr. Collins and Charlotte, Maria looked up at the house.

Really, it was very pleasant! A moderate-sized house, very trim and neat, with beautiful flower borders and a picket fence. The house was not as big as Lucas Lodge, but then there was not a quiver full of children living in it either!

Charlotte escorted Maria and Miss Elizabeth Bennet upstairs

while Mr. Collins went on and on about how serviceable the staircase was. The inside of the house was not large, but there were several parlours and the colours were pleasant; the furniture, while not elegant, was attractive and comfortable. Maria decided her long stay in Hunsford would be very pleasant, but it was not until Charlotte took the two ladies upstairs that she realized she was to have her own room! This was a luxury of great import to a girl who came from a large family of limited income, and as soon as Charlotte left her to change out of her travel clothes Maria threw herself on the bed to enjoy being able to stretch out as far as she wanted.

Maria remained in this happy state during the unpacking and settling in and it only faded when Mr. Collins brought back an invitation to dine at Rosings Park. All she had heard of Lady Catherine had given her a healthy fear of her ladyship and the idea of eating in such a rich setting make her stomach fill with butterflies. She caught Lizzy going upstairs and whispered to her, "What shall I wear to dinner at Rosings? I don't have anything suitable, Lizzy, and I am afraid I will look like Charlotte's poor relation."

Lizzy smiled at her kindly and answered, "Mr. Collins assures me Lady Catherine likes to maintain the distinction of rank and so would be insulted if you wore gowns as rich as hers and Miss de Bourgh's. Just choose the best gown you have, my dear, and it will be suitable."

"I will wear my pink muslin then, shall I?"

"Perfect! You will look charming, Maria."

In spite of the resolution of the gown question, Maria was very apprehensive during the walk to Rosings Park while Mr. Collins informed them of how much it cost to build the manor and how many windows it had. Her apprehensions were nothing, however, compared to the reality. Lady Catherine sat them down in the drawing-room while she sat on what could only be called a throne set in front of a ten foot high painting of a hunting scene showing a pack of dogs ripping apart an embattled boar while the humans sat on their horses in the background and watched. It was not something that enhanced her appetite, and Lady Catherine's catechism of each of her visitors, and her forthright statements of her opinion really almost terrified Maria to the point of being physically ill.

The dinner table was set with eight pieces of silver flatware at each place and Maria was kept on her toes (metaphorically) watching the others so she would not use the wrong utensil for each dish. By the time dinner was over and Lady Catherine had forced them to play whist (or cassino, in the case of the younger ladies) Maria was exhausted and ready to tumble into bed.

While she shivered in her bed, in spite of the nice warming the housemaid had given the sheets, Maria reviewed the two days since her arrival. Perhaps, she decided, her sister's comfortable future was earned at a rather high price.

Mr. Collins's Cucumber
by Mary Simonsen

March 5, 1812

Engaged to Mr. Collins? Impossible!

Lizzy winced at the memory of her reaction to Charlotte's engagement to her cousin. Without thinking highly either of men or matrimony, for Charlotte, marriage had always been her object. Once Lizzy accepted the fact of the engagement, she understood the reason: It was the only honorable option for a young woman of small fortune, and now here she was in Kent to observe in close quarters the union of these two dissimilar souls.

Weary from a day of traveling, Lizzy was eager for her bed, but before saying good night, the parson had extracted a promise that his cousin tour the gardens the next morning. After a hearty breakfast, Lizzy followed Charlotte and Mr. Collins into a large plot, handsomely fenced, adjacent to the parsonage. To Lizzy's mind, it looked very much like the vegetable garden at Longbourn and Lucas Lodge and every other house in the Meryton neighborhood, but that was before Mr. Collins mentioned his cucumber.

"Have you ever seen a cucumber of such size, Cousin Elizabeth?" he asked, pointing to the lengthy gourd at her feet, and Lizzy admitted she had not.

"Her Ladyship has encouraged Mr. Collins to tend to his garden so that we might have sufficient vegetables for our table," Charlotte explained.

Mr. Collins had happily accepted Her Ladyship's decree. "Lady Catherine visits regularly. She has been as captivated by this plant as I have, watching it grow, inch by inch by inch, until reaching its current length. If stood erect, I am sure it would reach a length of nine inches."

"Mr. Collins, I am speechless!" Lizzy said, trying to suppress the urge to laugh. She very nearly lost the fight when Charlotte mentioned the enormous oblong vegetable was planted next to her husband's radishes, also of a goodly size.

After Mr. Collins retreated to his study, Lizzy asked her friend how she had kept a straight face throughout the exchange.

"Because he shows me his cucumber at least twice a week, usually on Wednesdays and Saturdays."

And, finally, with Mr. Collins out of earshot, the two ladies had their laugh.

At Hunsford Garden Gate
by Nina Benneton

March 6, 1812

"Jenkinson, tell me what you noticed about the Mudsworth baby."
Anne de Bourgh braced her right slipper against the footboard of
her phaeton and leaned forward. She flicked the whip at the ponies'
rumps. No response. Lazy beasts! She half-stood and whipped
harder. Still no response. Their tails swung side to side with the
same maddeningly unhurried pace. Her strenuous effort merited no
more than a blink from them.

Beside her, Mrs. Jenkinson answered. "Would you allow me to
take the reins, Miss de Bourgh?"

"No," Anne said, crossed that the woman had dared to ask. *No
one takes the reins from a de Bourgh!*

"I do not want you to become too fatigued, trying to get the
ponies to go faster."

Anne glared at her servant. "I was simply trying to swat at some
flies."

Mrs. Jenkinson coughed. "I see."

"I asked you about the Mudsworth baby." Anne settled back
against the seat.

Mrs. Jenkinson stared straight ahead. "I did not see anything
wrong with the baby's foot."

"Foot? What was wrong with his foot?" Anne had only seen
that the baby's face was full of spots. The mother claimed it was
normal baby spots, but what if the babe was infected with the pox?

Though she knew she was not a great beauty, she took great pride in her unblemished complexion.

"Mr. Mudsworth's father was the younger brother of Mrs. Mudsworth's father."

A gust of wind blew and a chill sliced through Anne. She shivered. "What has that anything to do with the baby's foot?"

"We are near Hunsford Parsonage." Mrs. Jenkinson pointed at a distance ahead. "Shall we stop there for a rest and some warmth?"

"No." Anne resisted the urge to take her whip to her companion. "What was your point about the Mudsworth baby?"

With some show of reluctance, Mrs. Jenkins answered, "Baby Mudsworth has six toes on his left foot."

"Is that all?" Anne almost laughed aloud, relieved. Jenkinson was not that obtuse. The woman would have noticed something unusual with the baby's spots. "You make such a fuss about a baby with six toes? All the great families have children with an extra digit or two."

"As a poor curate's daughter, Miss de Bourgh," Mrs. Jenkinson said. "I am not acquainted with great families, except yours. If what you say is true, then I'm certain…"

"Certain, what?" Anne tightened her hand around her whip. It would not do to swat at Jenkinson's head in public. "Pray, continue."

"When you and Mr. Darcy get married, I hope your children will be blessed with many, many extra digits."

Anne glanced at her companion's face, trying to detect any note of impertinence, but the old lady's expression was unreadable. Anne turned her attention back to the road. Cousin Darcy had convinced her mother to purchase this open carriage for Anne. Lightweight yet stable, a low phaeton with four wheels using ponies instead of high-spirited horses was easy enough for a gentle, delicate lady to handle, that was Darcy's opinion. Anne wished he had restrained himself and not taken the trouble. Mother had taken it to mean he was hinting the future mistress of Pemberley should begin to visit tenants. And that was why Anne was now out with Mrs. Jenkinson making calls on spotted babies with six toes on their left feet.

Jenkinson said, "I wonder if Mr. Collins has had any success with getting his cucumbers to grow bigger. They are rather stunted and deformed, a failed attempt at cross-breeding, I am of the opinion. The seeds he used came from too familiar, too close a source—"

"Fine," Anne interrupted, exasperated. "We will stop at Hunsford so you could have you discourse with Mr. Collins about his cucumbers."

Once they reached Hunsford, Anne stopped the phaeton at the garden gate. She declined the Collins' repeated invitation to alight from the phaeton and be introduced to their visitors. She was not in the mood that day to bestow any great favour. Besides, it gave her no small pleasure to keep Mrs. Collins out of doors in the wind and to watch Mrs. Collins' father–a knighted nobody–stand at his station by the doorway.

After ten minutes of watching Sir William Lucas bowing and scraping each time she looked his way, greatly diverted and feeling generous, Anne issued an invitation to the whole Hunsford Party to dine at Rosings the next day. In the event she'd caught the pox from the Mudsworth baby, she wished for company at Rosings' graveyard.

Lady Catherine's Easter
by Diana Birchall

March 7, 1812

The wished-for proposal did not come. The green sarsanet, the primrose silk, the floral printed gown with the fichu, were all cunningly constructed so to give Miss de Bourgh's figure consequence, and accordingly worn with her best French ringlets and hair decorations. None of these things, nor all of them, brought Mr. Darcy to a declaration. To Lady Catherine's mortification, Darcy was invariably polite, and listened to her deliver strictures and dictates with commendable patience, but he seldom seemed to even notice that Miss de Bourgh was in the room at all.

Darcy and Fitzwilliam had arrived with promptitude, just when they were expected, in the week before Easter; and they were welcomed with all the festivity that was at the command of Lady Catherine in doing the honours of her own house. She had hoped that Anne might be equal to charming and entertaining at least one of her cousins, but Anne said very little, and whether from embarrassment or from pique, remained a silent stick in the corner each evening, despite Lady Catherine's grossest and most urgent attempts to bring her forward.

"I do wish Anne could play to you. She has such taste! Mr. Collins the other day said that never did he see a young lady with more real musical ability, who did not know how to play, and that her preference for Mozart over Haydn showed her taste to be very nearly divine."

There was nothing to say to that. Mr. Darcy and Colonel Fitzwilliam looked at each other, and Fitzwilliam consulted his pocket-watch. It still lacked an hour to supper.

"We do miss hearing some good music," Fitzwilliam finally offered. "Do you know, Lady Catherine, to-day we walked over to the Parsonage, and the young lady guest there, Miss Bennet, is said to play rather well. Perhaps," he hinted, "the family there might make up an evening party."

That was not to Lady Catherine's purpose. She could not wish the tame vicar and his female entourage to be the prime entertainment offered to the young men, or for the prettyish Miss Bennet to perhaps be a distraction to prevent Darcy from making the proposal so ardently desired by mother and daughter. Yet to her chagrin, she had to confess to herself that the visit was not going altogether as she would wish. Both Darcy and Fitzwilliam loved Rosings immensely, she knew, and had nothing but the greatest respect for herself and her daughter; but still, they were young men, and in this bleak, not-quite-spring weather, there was not much for them to be doing outdoors, no hunting, no field sports. They liked their walks, and she had already observed that nearly every day one or both walked through the park of Rosings and past the palings to the Vicarage, and generally spent all the afternoon there, not returning until nearly time for the evening meal. Dull, plain Mrs. Collins could not be the attraction, nor yet her insipid sister who was as silent as Lady Catherine's own daughter. No, it was with some displeasure that she suspected it was that Miss Bennet they crossed the park to see; and as this must be discouraged, she took the step of planning a very fine supper and inviting some of her grander neighbors of the county.

On the whole this was the worst failure of all. Lady Metcalfe and her red-nosed old husband, who fell asleep over the fire with his port, and the Lassiters of Saddlefield Place, who liked to quarrel as soon as they picked up a set of cards, and the Munnings, with their three spinster daughters in their forties, giantesses who liked to talk about their ailments, were not the most enlivening society. The talk and the food were heavy alike, and both Darcy and Fitzwilliam, though their manners were perfectly proper, were anything but animated. Fitzwilliam found less to say than usual, and Darcy never opened his lips except to eat the oysters and the ragout.

After the guests rolled away in their carriages, and the two young men went to their rooms, Darcy pleading a headache and Fitzwilliam fatigue, Lady Catherine hopefully tried to assure Anne and Miss Jenkinson that all had gone well.

"Well! I must say that was a delightful occasion. One of our successful soirees. Rosings is a house made for hospitality. That is what Mr. Collins always says, and it is true."

"Mr. Collins was not here," Anne pointed out dryly.

"No, I thought that he and the ladies of his household would have felt rather out of their element, in such a noble society as this. Sir George Metcalfe a baronet, and the Munnings related to the Duke of Beaufort."

"Mrs. Collins's father is a knight," said Anne.

"Pah! A creation within memory, and only as a reward for civic duties, at that. He is quite vulgar, Anne, quite, though there is no real harm in the man. No; they were not to be made uncomfortable. Our guests to-night were more in Darcy's rank of life."

"He did not seem to enjoy their company so very much, Mama. He barely spoke."

"That was the head-ache, to be sure, nothing more. I sent him to bed with a posset. He was most grateful for the attention. 'Lady Catherine,' he said, 'thank you.'"

"I thought he did not eat his dinner very well, either," put in Mrs. Jenkinson. "He only ate three oysters, and did not touch the salad."

"He asked to be helped to the ragout twice," began Lady Catherine repressively.

"Oh, Mama! You make the best of it, but the evening was not a success. Such company as the Lassiters and the Munnings are no pleasure for two such young men. They are all so old."

Lady Catherine was thoughtful for a moment, and adjusted her purple satin bandeau over her forehead in an absent way. "They do go to the vicarage daily," she admitted. "I cannot presume to conjecture what merit they find in the society there, but perhaps we ought not to avoid giving the invitation to the Collinses any longer, after all. I did hope…"

"That I would get a proposal?" demanded Anne, tears beginning to show themselves.

"My dear!" cried Mrs. Jenkinson, going over to the sofa where she sat and enfolding her in her arms.

"Now, Anne, there is no call to be blaming yourself," said Lady Catherine with some distaste. "Heaven knows, I am sure, we did everything. The lace round your neck tonight, and that locket…well, well. If only you could be a bit more animated…"

"I cannot be forward, Mama!" cried Anne, putting her fists to her eyes. "Some girls can but I cannot. Have you not taught me that forwardness was common, unladylike behavior? And common is just what I can never, never be."

"No, certainly not," answered her mother uncomfortably. "Well, there's nothing for it then. After church, on Easter Sunday, we shall ask Mr. Collins and the ladies to come to Rosings. They can come in the evening, you know, when Darcy and Fitzwilliam seem most to have the wish for company."

"We would have to invite them anyway, would we not?" asked Mrs. Jenkinson practically. "Mr. Collins is the clergyman and will have just given his Easter sermon that morning."

"Exactly so," nodded Lady Catherine. "It is a very proper attention indeed."

On the Easter Sunday evening, then, Mr. Collins, rather tired after his exertions, was pleased to spend his time looking over an album of horse engravings in Lady Catherine's best sitting-room. Mrs. Collins, showing herself to be truly well bred, sat between Miss de Bourgh and Mrs. Jenkinson, trying to converse, and admiring their bead-work.

Mr. Darcy and Col. Fitzwilliam were leaning over the pianoforte as Elizabeth played to them, so that their lively conversation was not audible, over the music, to the ladies seated across the room. Lady Catherine made one or two attempts to call out and ask what they were speaking of. She gave her opinions on her and her daughter's taste in music, with many instructions on how necessary practicing was to Darcy's sister. With each attempt, however, the conversation quickly moved away from her, to her displeasure, and nothing was heard in the intervals between songs but the intimate, congenial murmur of Elizabeth talking with the two young men.

There was something Lady Catherine did not like at all, in the intent way Darcy was looking down at Elizabeth, and when she heard Darcy's words "You have employed your time much better," she took alarm and called out once more to require them to tell the subject of their conversation. Elizabeth immediately began playing again. Lady Catherine tried some further remarks on Anne's taste, with expressive gesturings toward her daughter, but Darcy barely turned his head in their direction. Elizabeth, still playing, thought to herself that she saw no symptom of love in Mr. Darcy toward his cousin, nor any likelihood of their supposed marriage.

In a still more open attempt to remove her nephew from his absorption in Elizabeth, Lady Catherine rose to her feet, approached the piano, where she stood in state, and proceeded to take apart her performance.

"Do you not see, Miss Bennet, that your fingering is too heavy in that arpeggio? Cramer is meant to be played adagietto there. I fear you have not the light touch requisite for the classical form."

"I think Miss Bennet plays very well," said Fitzwilliam warmly. "The Scotch airs particularly. Won't you play us some more of those?"

"Yes, I think you are right, Fitzwilliam – simple, peasant music is best for such a beginner," said Lady Catherine condescendingly.

Mr. Darcy looked angry and shot a look at Fitzwilliam that would urge him to speak for both of them. "On the contrary,"

Fitzwilliam countered, "the lovely simplicity of the best Scottish songs takes confident playing, and great taste. Miss Bennet has them both. What would you like her to play, Darcy?"

"I liked those airs by Burns," he said reluctantly, and would say no more.

"Burns! Dreadful man," exclaimed Lady Catherine. "I wonder you can tolerate him, Darcy."

Col. Fitzwilliam's eyes twinkled. "I think my cousin would like you to play and sing 'My Love is like a Red, Red Rose,' Miss Bennet," he said. "Isn't that right, Darcy? Why, man, you are blushing as red as a rose yourself."

"Blush? Darcy? Surely not. I see nothing of it. What do you mean, Fitzwilliam?" rapped out Lady Catherine.

To forestall further comment, Elizabeth began to sing.

> *0, my love is like a red, red rose,*
>
> *that's newly sprung in June.*
>
> *0, my love is like a melody,*
>
> *that's sweetly play'd in tune.*
>
> *As fair thou art, my bonnie lass,*
>
> *so deep in love am I,*
>
> *And I will love thee still, my dear,*
>
> *till a' the seas gang dry.*

Her eyes caught and held Darcy's, in spite of herself. He was fathoms deep in love by this time, and moved forward, holding out his hand, with what gesture in mind no one could tell, for Lady Catherine at once intervened and said with asperity, "Well! We will have no more of that immoral ploughboy! Some instrumental music, Miss Bennet, if you please, and no more of that coarse singing. It is not at all the thing among the gentry, though you might be forgiven for not knowing that."

Mr. Darcy was moved to speak. "Aunt Catherine," he objected with some heat, "Miss Bennet, in my opinion, marries good breeding and good taste to perfection. You will oblige me to not speak of her in such a way."

Lady Catherine lost her temper. "I do not know what you mean in the least, Darcy. Miss Bennet has not a trace of the breeding and taste of Anne."

Mr. Collins heard the strident tones and hurried across the room, anxious to forestall trouble. "Perhaps my cousin has sung long enough, Lady Catherine," he said anxiously, "we do not wish to tire you, of all things. Shall I place the card tables? Would Miss Anne care for a game of Cassino?"

"Yes," came her faint voice from the sofa. "I should like that. Will you not play with me, Mr. Darcy?"

"Another time," he replied shortly, not turning around to look at her. "Now we are having the pleasure of listening to Miss Bennet. Will you play 'Ae fond kiss,' Miss Bennet? That is another favourite of mine."

She played the first few notes. "Who would have thought, Mr. Darcy," she said with an arch look, "that you would be a person of such romantic sensibility? You would think that Burns had a heart, after all. It is such a sad song."

> *Ae fond kiss, and then we sever;*
> *Ae fareweel, and then for ever!*
> *Deep in heart-wrung tears I'll pledge thee,*
> *Warring sighs and groans I'll wage thee.*

"Yes, a sad song, yet it makes me happy," he observed at its conclusion, low.

No one heard his words but Fitzwilliam, standing next to him, who looked surprised, but Lady Catherine saw or thought she saw enough to say tartly, "I consider that it is surely time for this evening to draw to an end. If you must have Robert Burns, Darcy, then let Miss Bennet sing Auld Lang Syne."

Charlotte and Elizabeth Discuss Marriage
by Susan Adriani

March 8, 1812

It was with a sigh of relief that Elizabeth watched Charlotte close the door to her own private parlour, effectively silencing Mr. Collin's frantic rambling as he made his way with haste through the narrow hall and out of the front door to pay his daily call upon the occupants of Rosings Park.

The room was small, but inviting in appearance, with a plush carpet and delicate floral wallpaper. A comfortable looking sofa sat before the fire, flanked by two end tables, and positioned before the lone window, several cushioned chairs. Sunlight streamed through the sheer curtains, lending the room an air of cheerfulness and flooding it with natural light, making it an ideal location for reading, letter writing, or needlework. Elizabeth smiled to herself. Though Lady Catherine had apparently done much with the rest of the house, Elizabeth could see no sign of Her Ladyship's condescension here, only her friend's simple, yet refined taste.

Elizabeth made her way to the window and pushed the curtains aside. She had a bird's eye view of Mr. Collins's garden and, when she looked toward the far side of it, could easily make out his prized cucumber along the fence. She immediately let the sheer fabric fall back into place, momentarily grateful that she would not have to hear him regale her with another story of his noble patroness's praise for its large size and impressive girth. She feared she had heard quite enough talk of Mr. Collins's cucumber to last her a lifetime. Shaking her head, Elizabeth moved to stand beside her friend. "It is a lovely room, Charlotte. I can see why you chose it for your own."

Charlotte smiled warmly. "The light at this time of day does make it a very inviting place to pass the time, not to mention practical. Mr. Collins's study is in the front of the house and has three windows, all of which afford him a perfect view the road. If he cannot be found in his garden, he is usually there, where he is well able to spot the residents of Rosings Park, should they happen to drive by." She held her hand out to her friend, and both ladies settled upon the sofa. "An entire day can pass," Charlotte mused, "when we have not spent more than a few hours in each other's company."

Elizabeth raised her brow. That was a happy situation, indeed. "You must enjoy being mistress of your own home."

Charlotte folded her hands upon her lap and said cryptically, "There are advantages, to be sure, though some might come at a higher price than others."

Elizabeth did not doubt it one bit, for one only had to look upon Mr. Collins to imagine what Charlotte had to endure daily. It was difficult enough to watch him eat, but to imagine passing any deal of time in his company beyond a few days was something she dared not think about. "You have a very attentive neighbour in Lady Catherine," she said, recalling her cousin's reverence whenever he had spoken of his patroness. He had spoken of her often.

"Yes," Charlotte agreed. "Lady Catherine is a very attentive neighbour, and she condescends to visit us often. My husband could not be more delighted."

The corners of Elizabeth's mouth quirked. "And you? Are you delighted with her as well?"

Charlotte gave her friend a knowing look. "As you may have observed, nothing is too trifling for Her Ladyship's notice, and Lady Catherine kindly takes it upon herself to instruct me on many issues from the management of my household accounts, to the acceptable number of chickens to keep."

"How lucky for you that she has an opinion on every subject!"

Charlotte smiled. "She also encourages Mr. Collins in his duties, so her solicitation, I have found, on occasion can be very beneficial."

"So you are truly happy, then?" Elizabeth asked, studying her friend.

Charlotte inclined her head. "I have very little to repine, Lizzy. I always believed that happiness in marriage is entirely by chance, and I confess I find myself as content with my situation as I always expected to be. Mr. Collins is not unkind, and treats me with much consideration." She gave her friend a sly look and lowered her voice. "Of course, it does not hurt that he is often from home attending to matters of the church, or waiting upon Lady Catherine, or, like I said, tending to his garden."

"So," Elizabeth said, coyly, tilting her head to the side, "you do not mind Mr. Collins showing you his cucumber twice a week?"

Charlotte shook her head. "In the grand scheme of things, being subjected to such a thing is a small price to pay for marital felicity, and as long as I offer several well timed compliments it is over quickly enough, and I can go about my business as though I had never been inconvenienced in the slightest."

Elizabeth giggled and shook her head with an unladylike snort. *Well placed compliments, indeed!*

Mr. Collins's Cucumber
Goes Missing
by Mary Simonsen

March 12, 1812

Charlotte and Elizabeth were returning from the village when they saw Mr. Collins coming down the lane. As he was frantically waving his black parson's hat as if hailing a London cab, it was apparent the man was in distress.

"Charlotte, you must come! Come quickly!"

"What is the matter, dear," Charlotte said, quickening her pace.

"My cucumber has gone missing."

After a quick glance at his breeches, Mrs. Collins informed her husband that his cucumber was still there. Lizzy, stifling a giggle, hinted that Mr. Collins was referring to the cucumber in his garden.

"Oh, of course," Charlotte said, blushing."

The two ladies hurriedly made their way to the garden where the theft of the ten-inch gourd, pinched off at its root, was confirmed. After Mr. Collins informed Charlotte and Lizzy that he had already interrogated the staff to make sure they had not pilfered his plant, he asked if they knew of its whereabouts. Both shook their heads in unison. But then Lizzy pointed to footprints embedded in the path, revealing the culprit to be female. After following in the bandit's path, they arrived at the gate that fronted the road to the village. It was there that they discovered tracks made by a carriage, the get-away conveyance of the thief.

After careful study, it became apparent the carriage was of a goodly size and drawn by four horses. Obviously, the person who had nicked the gourd was someone of considerable means and not some hungry passerby.

"Dare I say it, Mr. Collins," Charlotte said in a gentle voice, "the only person in the neighborhood who owns such a conveyance is Lady Catherine."

"Lady Catherine!" the parson croaked. "Impossible! She has her own garden. Why would she want to take hold of my cucumber?"

"I suspect it is cucumber envy," Elizabeth said. "Did you not say just a few evenings ago you imagined no one could look upon your cucumber with anything less than admiration? I suspect Lady Catherine was one of those who were envious of your accomplishment in growing such a lengthy vegetable."

"But, but…"

"My dear, I must agree with Elizabeth," Charlotte added. "I think when Lady Catherine was on her way into the village, a vision of your cucumber appeared, and being a wee bit jealous of its size, stopped her carriage and grabbed the gourd."

"But that would be stealing!" a shocked Mr. Collins answered.

Charlotte shook her head and explained that because Lady Catherine actually owned the parsonage and the acres surrounding it, including the garden, she probably saw it merely as taking possession of something that already belonged to her. "I am sure, by this time, your cucumber has been sliced, diced, and served up on a platter for supper."

In an attempt to comfort her grieving husband, who compared the loss of his cucumber to losing a vital organ, Charlotte mentioned his huge radishes. Unfortunately, it was then discovered that those, too, had gone missing. But wasn't it to be expected? In order to have a satisfying salad, the one was as necessary as the other in achieving the desired result.

Darcy Discovers Elizabeth
Is at Rosings
by Regina Jeffers

March 13, 1812

One evening just Darcy and his sister dined at his London townhouse. Mrs. Annesley had been given the evening off to visit a beloved nephew. They took a light repast together and casually enjoyed each other's company in the drawing room. Uncharacteristically, Darcy partook of more brandy than he should; he was not inebriated, but the warmth of the liquid had lowered his defenses.

"Will you travel to Kent to see our aunt at Easter?" Georgiana asked as she casually flipped the pages of the book she held.

"I will; our cousin arranged a leave from his military duties so we will be available to tackle our aunt's many business issues together. It is not a trip to which I look forward. Our aunt can be so…"

"Demanding," Georgiana added, perhaps a bit too quickly.

Darcy arched an eyebrow at his sister's response; although she never expressed those opinions beyond his hearing, he was well aware Georgiana had become more opinionated of late. "Our aunt can be very solicitous. Has she said something to you, my dearest?"

"It is just her usual reproofs to practice my music and to maintain the proper manners. Sometimes I resent her constant remarks. I know I should not feel these things about a beloved relative, but, honestly, Fitzwilliam, her rebukes are very upsetting."

"I am well aware our aunt can irritate even the most devout, but I would be remiss in my duties as your guardian if I encouraged you to be rude to our mother's only sister. However, I would say it was permissible in private to overpass many of Lady Catherine's sentiments."

He noted how his sister bit her bottom lip in anticipation. "Fitzwilliam," Georgiana began tentatively, "was not Mr. Bingley satisfied with his estate in Hertfordshire?"

Darcy felt the caution shoot through him. "Why do you ask, my Dear?"

"Mr. Bingley quit the estate on impulse it seems. Did something amiss occur?"

Darcy felt a bit uncomfortable knowing his part in removing Bingley from Netherfield. He shifted his weight, gulped down the last of the brandy, and poured himself another."Bingley is such an impetuous young man," he extended an explanation.

"I am confused," Georgiana began shyly. "He speaks well of his short time there and expresses a fondness for the company of Miss Jane Bennet."

Darcy said prudently, "Does he now?"

Georgiana continued, "He appears so downcast. Is Jane Bennet not the sister of Elizabeth Bennet? Your letters from Netherfield mentioned her several times. I had hoped when I read your letters that if Mr. Bingley remained at Netherfield I could visit also. I thought I might like to meet Miss Elizabeth. It would be nice to have a friend such as you described. Do you think Miss Elizabeth could have seen me as an acquaintance she might like to make?"

"I am certain of it," Darcy began slowly. "I often considered the possibilities."

Georgiana's interest perked up. Leaning forward and giving him her full attention, she asked, "Would you tell me about Miss Elizabeth?"

Darcy held his glass of brandy to his lips, but he did not drink. Impressions of Elizabeth Bennet came so easily to him, as if he had seen her but five minutes earlier, rather than it having been nearly eleven weeks. He began slowly, guarding his words, fearing to betray his susceptibility to the woman. "I believe I described Miss Elizabeth physically previously. Miss Elizabeth's features are not as refined as her sister's, but they tend to be more classical. Her eyes are the key to her soul, a quick note of what she really thinks. She says she loves to laugh, and I find her humor to be teasing in nature at times. I have not discovered many women with a more agreeable character. Everything is united in Elizabeth Bennet: she possesses a superior intelligence and good understanding; generally correct opinions, which she often expresses without regard to the time or the situation; and a warm heart. She demonstrates strong feelings of family attachment, without calculating pride or insufferable weaknesses. Miss Elizabeth judges for herself in everything essential." Darcy stopped himself at this point, fearing he had said too much.

Georgiana sighed heavily when he paused. "Miss Elizabeth Bennet appears the perfect mixture of sense and judgment. I hope someday I hold the opportunity to make her acquaintance. I always wished for an intimacy such as you describe."

Leaving his reason behind, Darcy said wistfully, "It would be pleasant to have Miss Elizabeth's company again."

Images of Elizabeth Bennet and Georgiana together at Pemberley invaded his dreams that evening. The images instantly created happiness without the misery, but when awake, Darcy could only dwell on the misery of such happiness: the lady was not for him.

Late February brought signs of spring, and Darcy, Georgiana, and Mrs. Annesley returned to Pemberley. He had buried himself in his estate work, explaining his plans to increase the production of crops to his tenants. His steward, Mr. Howard, was a respected overseer, and they spent many hours planning a four-crop rotation among the farmers. The system, developed by the Second Viscount Charles Townsend, had been successful in the Americas since the early 1700s. Pemberley used a three-crop rotation for many years, usually wheat, barley, and the third field left to fallow. Yet, the land was being used up too quickly, and production decreased, leaving many of Pemberley's tenants unable to maintain their farms.

Darcy had hoped the four-crop rotation plan would save his estate and the livelihood of his tenants. Nitrogen-rich legumes would be used to put back into the soil the nutrients the grain crops drained, and the grain crops put back the minerals the legumes used. They fed each other; it was a simple plan; now, he had to convince his tenants of the necessity of the changes. Mr. Howard would examine each farmer's soil makeup and decide who would plant which crops.

The excitement of getting back to the land had relieved Darcy of the agitations of his mind. He had not thought about Elizabeth Bennet more than a couple of times over the past few weeks. Then he received a letter from his aunt.

18 March

My dear Nephew,

I am anticipating your upcoming visit; your cousin Anne is most anxious to renew your relationship. Her health appears much improved; I am certain you will notice the difference. With your visit, I had hoped to introduce you to my new curate Mr. Collins and his wife, but much to my chagrin, I find you met them both while you were in Hertfordshire with Mr. Bingley.

Darcy's heart stopped. The supercilious Mr. Collins married someone from Hertfordshire. Pictures of Collins's attentive behavior to Elizabeth flashed across his mind. The man had danced with Elizabeth at the Netherfield Ball, and after supper, Collins had adamantly refused to leave Elizabeth's side, drowning her in misery and unable to dance with other gentlemen. *Please, God, do not allow Elizabeth to be married to Mr. Collins!* he prayed. Mrs. Bennet would marry Elizabeth off to Collins just to be rid of one of her daughters. Collins kissing Elizabeth—the thought brought a murderous rage to Darcy's heart. With shaky hands, he returned to the letter.

Charlotte Lucas has made Mr. Collins a reasonable match.
Her temperament is most pleasing, and I assured Mr. Collins
of my approval in his choice.

Darcy's breath came in ragged bursts. *Charlotte Lucas! It was not Elizabeth!* He nearly cried with relief. Although Collins would provide Miss Lucas with a steady income and a protective home, he hated to see any woman's attentions wasted on such a pompous arse, as was Mr. Collins. Even without her being Elizabeth's special friend, Darcy actually liked Charlotte Lucas. He would not wish Collins upon anyone.

Mrs. Collins's father and sister have come to stay at Hunsford.
Sir William spoke highly of you, as was natural, and of
making your acquaintance in Hertfordshire; the younger Miss
Lucas is quite pretty, in a plain sort of fashion, and I find her
very attentive to my advice. I am certain she receives no such
direction at home, and I plan to spend some time with her.

Good! His aunt's reproofs could be directed toward someone besides Georgiana. He made a mental note to speak to his cousin about Lady Catherine's censure of Georgina; Darcy did not like anyone interfering in his sister's life.

There is another member of the Collins's party at the
Parsonage. Mrs. Collins's friend Miss Elizabeth Bennet has
also come for a visit.

Darcy reread that line several times to be certain his eyes did not play tricks on him. Elizabeth? His Elizabeth? Could she really be at Rosings Park residing within an easy walk of his aunt's house? Reading on, Darcy realized his eyes did not deceive him. His aunt actually spoke of Elizabeth. The irony of it all! Elizabeth Bennet stayed upon his aunt's estate.

I understand you have also made the acquaintance of Miss
Bennet. My pleasure in introducing you has been lost. I will
forego that pleasure with you, but, at least, it will still be my
honor to introduce the Collins's party to your cousin, the colonel.

Miss Bennet, I find, is a very outspoken young lady. She has been permitted to run free with little reproach from her parents. She offers her opinions without regard to her station in life; this is most unusual for one so young. I cannot say I approve of her manners or her upbringing. She is one of five daughters, as you know. Her parents saw no benefit in exposing any of them to the masters. None of them draw; Miss Bennet's talents on the pianoforte are limited. I told her she could only improve with more practice. Besides having no governess to supervise her upbringing, the worst offense I find in her parenting is all five daughters are out in Society at the same time. The youngest are out before the eldest has married. When I expressed my disdain, you would not believe what Miss Bennet said.

Darcy laughed out loud for the first time in months. Without being told her response, he could just imagine Elizabeth's retort, which was likely accompanied by the "flash" in her eyes, a shift of her shoulders, and the hint of a mischievous smile. His sister could learn much from Elizabeth Bennet; he realized quickly that Lady Catherine did not intimidate Elizabeth.

Her reply was very disrespectful. She seems to exist under the ill-abused conception that having all five daughters Out at the same time is perfectly acceptable. Miss Bennet believes her younger sisters deserve their share of Society and amusement as much as does she and her elder sister. She indicated it was not equitable for her younger sisters to be denied their share of fun and courtship just because neither she nor her elder sister has had the means or the inclination to marry. Miss Elizabeth does not feel it would be "very likely to promote sisterly affection nor delicacy of the mind." I was astonished by this response. I hope to temper her rough spirits before she leaves Hunsford.

His aunt may wish to temper the lady's spirits, but he knew Lady Catherine was no match for Elizabeth Bennet.

Miss Bennet simply needs an example of proper society to complement her undeveloped genteel attributes. Sir William, I am afraid, will depart before your arrival, but the ladies will remain another month. We will invite them to Rosings if you so wish to renew their acquaintances. Your cousin Anne and I look forward to your and Edward's stay at Rosings.

Your Aunt, Catherine

Elizabeth Bennet, possibly the first person to do so, obviously, had dared to challenge the dignified impertinence of Lady Catherine. So, Elizabeth stayed at Rosings; he was glad to know prior to his arrival. It would be a good test of how well he had recovered from her charms. In thinking such, Darcy did not acknowledge the swirl of his emotions when he feared Collins married Elizabeth as being anything more than a true concern for her happiness. He would be able to meet Elizabeth again as indifferent acquaintances; Darcy was certain of that fact.

His cousin Edward Fitzwilliam had come to Pemberley on the twentieth. He would spend a few days with Georgiana before he and his cousin departed for Rosings. Along with Darcy, the good colonel served as Georgiana's guardian, and he adored her nearly as much as did Darcy.

"Darcy, Georgiana has spoken to me of Miss Elizabeth Bennet," Edward teased. "Now, I am most anxious to meet our aunt's visitors. At first, I was not looking forward to meeting a 'country miss with poor manners,' but Georgiana seems to feel you hold Miss Elizabeth in some esteem. If she impresses Fitzwilliam Darcy, she must be something extraordinary, I daresay."

"Pull in your tendrils, Edward," Darcy cautioned. "Miss Elizabeth is not for you. As the younger son of an earl, you must find a woman of wealth to keep you in style. I am afraid although Miss Elizabeth is a gentleman's daughter, she has no wealth of which to make her a person of interest for a man in your position." Darcy did not believe he could tolerate the idea of Elizabeth with his cousin. She would be family, but not his to touch.

"I see," Edward began. "That is my bad luck. Someday I will find a wealthy woman with whom I might also find affection. I do not want to just marry for money; some level of affection is not too much to ask is it, Fitz?"

"I never knew you felt that way." Edward's words had stunned Darcy.

"Oh, well, at least," Edward said with resignation, "Miss Elizabeth may help brighten our time at Rosings, can she not?"

"Miss Elizabeth, I found, can brighten most any room," Darcy whispered to himself.

A Fortnight at Hunsford
by C. Allyn Pierson

March 19, 1812

Elizabeth sighed and folded away her embroidery. Charlotte and Maria had gone to town to visit an ailing parishioner and take her soup and tea, and Elizabeth had decided to stay at the parsonage and enjoy the peace and quiet for a short while. Mr. Collins was at Rosings Park visiting Lady Catherine and the morning chores were done, so the house was silent except for the faint buzzing of the bees coming through the open window at her elbow. Early as it was in the spring, Mr. Collins' efforts in the garden gave her a fragrant and soothing background to her stitching.

Two weeks she had been at Hunsford. Sir William Lucas was already home, and Elizabeth and Maria had settled into a quiet routine of walks and domestic concerns between long talks with Charlotte. Her friend, unlikely though it might be, seemed to be happy in her marriage, and Mr. Collins was proving to be a conformable husband. The park at Rosings was lovely and had many pleasant walks, and she went out and enjoyed them daily when the weather allowed her.

Still, life was a bit dull in Hunsford. Lady Catherine had informed them that Mr. Darcy and his cousin would be coming for Easter, and Elizabeth was not quite sure how she felt about that. The gentlemen would certainly add interest to their evenings at Rosings, but she could not think of anyone she would not prefer to Mr. Darcy as company. Well…perhaps Mr. Collins would be of less interest. She hoped Darcy's cousin, who was called Colonel Fitzwilliam, would have better manners and more interesting conversation than Mr. Darcy.

What was wrong with the man, anyway? She had never met a man so difficult to understand as Mr. Darcy, or so severe in countenance. Still, she would be in Hunsford for a number of weeks and even a reserved and rude man was an improvement on Lady Catherine's "conversations," which bore a great resemblance to lectures. Only last evening she had criticized Maria's gown as dowdy and poorly tailored, reducing her nearly to tears when she had to admit her sewing skills were not adequate to correct the flaws. Unfortunately, she had also acquired just a bit of mud on her hem on the walk from the parsonage and this, too, was cause for criticism. Poor Maria was trembling with fear and completely inarticulate by the time Lady Catherine had finished. Fortunately, Mr. Collins asked Lady Catherine about a problem with one of his parishioners and deflected her "helpful" lecture away from his sister-in-law. Bless the man. Stupid Mr. Collins might be, but he was not an evil man.

Ah well. Perhaps the early rain had dried enough for her to take a walk now. She gathered her pelisse and bonnet and pulled on her gloves, then set out towards Rosings Park.

Fitzwilliam and Darcy
on the Road to Rosings
by Jack Caldwell

March 23, 1812

Colonel the Honorable Richard Fitzwilliam of the ___rd Light Dragoons was trying to make himself as comfortable as possible in the rocking carriage—a mighty task, for the fineness of the Darcy coach could not make up for the ruts in the road through Kent. The other gentleman in the carriage had more success.

The colonel was just thirty years of age. Other than that, he was most unlike his companion. Fitzwilliam was of moderate height with a ruddy complexion and sandy-reddish hair. His lean body sported broad shoulders due to his profession. He was not particularly handsome, but his character was friendly and open. He liked people very much. Usually easy-going, his patience was stretched to its limits that day.

"Blast!" Colonel Fitzwilliam cried as he cracked his head against the side of the carriage. "I knew I should have ridden my horse! I knew it!"

His cousin and great friend, Fitzwilliam Darcy, rapped on the roof with his walking stick. "A more moderate speed, if you please, Edwards," he said. He did not shout, but his forceful tone carried over the noise of the road. There was a muffled affirmative answer and the vehicle slowed. Now it simply rolled alarmingly from side to side.

"Oh, that is so much better! Thank you, Cuz."

"No need to be sarcastic, Fitz. The winter was beastly. It is no wonder the roads are in such a condition."

"The weather was just as bad in Derby, but you will not find the roads to be like this; my father would not stand for it."

"My uncle takes a prodigious interest in his roads."

Colonel Fitzwilliam laughed. "All because the old man likes his feet warm and bum comfortable!"

Darcy glanced at him, trying to hide a smile. "I have missed you, Fitz. I am happy you are back from Spain."

The colonel stretched. "For a time. Wellington does not need much in the way of cavalry to lay siege. After our *coup de main* at Ciudad Rodrigo in January*, I am allowed a few months leave in the loving bosom of my family." Darcy frowned, and Fitzwilliam noticed. "Do not glare at me, Darcy! You know of what I speak!"

Darcy's chin rose. "It is our duty to visit Lady Catherine at Easter."

"It is *your* duty to review Lady Catherine's accounts and meet with the steward at Easter," Fitzwilliam returned. "It falls to me to play court jester for the amusement of my aunt and cousin. By the way, could you condescend to spend some time with Anne this year? The way you ignore her is disgraceful."

Darcy looked away, his face flushed. "You know why I cannot."

Fitzwilliam grew a little angry. "You choose not! That poor girl suffers and not just from her ailments. Cooped up at that overdone mausoleum of a house with only Aunt Catherine and her companion to keep her company, no wonder she is ill! I know well our aunt's wishes. Lord, the whole family does! No one supports her in this. If you and Anne choose not to marry, the family would stand by you."

Darcy was unfazed. "I must act as I see best, Fitz. Anne understands."

Fitzwilliam grimaced at his friend. *Oh, Cuz—one day that famous Darcy pride will get you in trouble!* He changed the subject. "How is Georgiana getting on? Truly?"

Pain flashed over Darcy's features. "Not as well as I had hoped. She has not yet recovered from Ramsgate."

Fitzwilliam cursed. "If only I had been there instead of in Spain! There would be one less rascal in the world, I can assure you!"

"Then it is well you were not, for there would then be one less reckless colonel serving the king," Darcy shot back. "You would do Georgiana no good being hung for the murder of George Wickham."

Fitzwilliam crossed his arms. "It is better to pay him off?"

"I only covered his debts—he got nothing more from me."

"*This* time."

Darcy shook his head. "There will not be a next time. Wickham has shot his bolt. He cannot talk of Georgiana, for he still thinks to make his way in the world by marrying into society. Should word of Ramsgate get abroad, he would be shunned."

"It would not do Georgiana any good, either."

"Do you not think I know that?" Darcy shouted.

Fitzwilliam grew alarmed. Darcy never lost his temper. "Of course, of course. Easy, old man—"

Darcy's face fell into his hands. "You have no idea, Fitz! No idea at all how this whole affair haunts me! I failed her—I failed the person I love best in the world."

Fitzwilliam placed a hand on his cousin's shoulder. "Come now, none of that. You did nothing wrong. The blame must be borne by those responsible: Wickham and that Younge woman—"

"I should have investigated her references more thoroughly."

You are crying over spilled milk, old friend, Fitzwilliam thought. Aloud he said, "You did the best you could. I am sure her references were of the highest quality. They usually are. Deceitful people are expert at obtaining such things."

"I should have done better."

Fitzwilliam shook his head. *What will bring you low first, Darcy— your pride or your habit of taking too much upon yourself? You cannot yet deal with the whole truth—that Georgiana bears some of the responsibility for this near-debacle.* He had to change the subject again.

"Tell me of Town. I understand our friend, Bingley, is moving up in the world."

Darcy looked up. "Yes. I spent the bulk of last summer with him, after... well, after that. He leased a place in Herefordshire and wanted my opinion of the place. I think he will give it up when the lease runs out."

"Something wrong with it?"

"No. Netherfield is a fair prospect, and with improvement should prove to be profitable."

"Then, why? Gentleman farming not up to snuff for Bingley? Or should I say Miss Bingley?"

"It is Hertfordshire and the folk who reside there that Miss Bingley finds lacking." Darcy paused. "I was relieved to return to London before December." He looked out the window.

"Missed Georgiana, I daresay. Did you enjoy the Season?"

Darcy turned and gave his cousin a look. "Have I ever enjoyed the Season?"

Fitzwilliam laughed at Darcy's incredulous expression. "I see— just the same! Still fighting off mercenary mamas and their insipid daughters."

"Not me this time, but I had to help an acquaintance of ours."

"Really? Who was it? Knightley? I have never understood why he has not married by now."

"Fitz—"

"Or maybe Bingley? He falls in love at the drop of a hat."

Darcy held up his hands. "I shall not reveal names. But I must congratulate myself for saving a friend from a most imprudent marriage."

"When was this? You said you have not been in Town long this year."

"Oh, it was last year. There were very strong objections to the lady, particularly her family."

"It must have been bad."

"Bad enough. But pray keep this to yourself. It would be unpleasant indeed if this became known to the family involved."

Fitzwilliam raised his hands in protest. "I shall be discretion itself."

"That would be the first time."

"Darcy, you wound me! Am I likely to meet with this unnamed family in any case?"

An unreadable look came over Darcy's face. "No—it is not likely at all."

Fitzwilliam had no time to contemplate Darcy's countenance. "Ah! Rosings! We are here!"

Darcy and Colonel Fitzwilliam Call at Hunsford's Parsonage by Regina Jeffers

March 24, 1812

On the morning after their arrival at Rosings, Mr. Collins presented himself to the gentlemen, and as Lady Catherine was making calls on some of her tenants, Collins fawned and preened before Darcy and the colonel. With Edward affable personality, Darcy's cousin found the man's obvious insincerity amusing.

"Do you return to the Parsonage?" Darcy asked, attempting to sound nonchalant, when, in reality, his heart raced with anticipation.

"Indeed, Sir, I do."

"Then may my cousin and I join you? I would like to offer my congratulations to Mrs. Collins, and the colonel has not had the pleasure of your wife or your cousin's acquaintance.

Collins was beside himself with self-importance. "You do my household a great honor, Sir. We would deem it our pleasure to share our humble abode with two gentlemen of such consequence."

"Then it is settled," Darcy retrieved his gloves from a nearby table. "Come, Edward, we are to Hunsford to pay our respects."

Without turning his head, Darcy felt the total disbelief that colored his cousin's countenance. Never had Darcy considered it necessary to pay his respects to anyone of such asinine tastes before—he might have shown disdain, but respect—that was out of the question. He felt it too. What in the world was he thinking to place himself within Miss Elizabeth's presence again? He should come up with an excuse to extricate himself from this impetuous act, but when his cousin said, "Yes, I am looking forward to the pleasure of the acquaintance," Darcy knew he must see it through. With both anticipation and dread, Darcy followed Collins to Hunsford Cottage–to the dubious pleasure of being in the same room as Elizabeth Bennet again.

The doorbell announced the three gentlemen. Collins led the way into the room, followed closely by Colonel Fitzwilliam; Darcy came last. He schooled his gaze not to look directly at Elizabeth as soon as he entered the room, but it was not easy; steadying his nerves, he took on his usual reserve and first offered compliments to Mrs. Collins, and then with an appearance of composure, which belied his actual thoughts; he likewise did the same to Elizabeth. It had been so long since he had beheld beauty of her imperfect features that for a moment all he could do was stare. Their eyes locked, and he noted the usual flash of curiosity, but Elizabeth merely curtsied to him without offering a word of greeting.

Edward stepped forward. "Mrs. Collins and Miss Bennet, it is with great pleasure we finally meet. My cousin has spoken most fondly of his time in Hertfordshire. It is pleasant to put faces to some of his stories."

"Did he now?" Elizabeth began, and Darcy anticipated more, but her friend's grasp on Elizabeth's arm stifled what Darcy had hoped would be her first words directed to him.

Edward permitted the tone of her brief remark to pass. "Yes, indeed," he added quickly. "Mrs. Collins, your improvements to the Parsonage are duly noted. I have never seen it look so well. Do you not agree, Darcy?" Edward prompted.

"Yes, Mrs. Collins, the place has taken on a new life," he stammered. "It is as if I am seeing it for the first time." Darcy could not recall ever having called upon the Parsonage prior. He felt so foolish; could he not hold a conversation in the woman's presence without guarding his every word and thought?

Darcy noted the humorous smirk gracing his cousin's lips. Likely, he would question Darcy extensively when they returned to Rosings. It was not a conversation to which he looked forward, but for now, he would simply enjoy the smell of Miss Elizabeth's perfume, a fragrance he had sorely missed. And he would watch the way her lips twitched with delight when she thought no one took note of her double *entendres* and the glint in her eyes when her cousin did something horrendously gauche. He wished he could think of something clever to engage her in conversation, but Darcy would simply have to be satisfied with feeling her energy coursing through him.

Eventually, Elizabeth interrupted his thoughts. She said sweetly, "Come, Colonel, tell us more of you. I fear Mr. Darcy shared little of your service to King and Country or of your obviously close relationship."

Without realizing how it happened, Darcy's agitation increased. He did not like the situation; Elizabeth gave her attentions to someone else. Again. Her attention to Mr. Wickham was one thing, but not to his cousin. For years, he had played second to Edward's affability, but he would not lose Elizabeth Bennet to his cousin. He held the longer acquaintance.

He allowed himself to appear in control as he watched his cousin engage Elizabeth with his usual readiness while Darcy made small talk with Mr. and Mrs. Collins, but, try as he may, Darcy spoke very little to anyone. He could not stop staring at his cousin and Elizabeth; his response dwelled on anger, but he really had nothing of which to be angry. Elizabeth did not belong to him; she was free to choose whomever she pleased, but he did not think he could tolerate her choosing his cousin. She would then be a part of his family, but he would never know her sweet intimacy. In fact, the thought of her choosing anyone else repulsed him. If Elizabeth could not be his... he started, but he could not finish the thought.

The sound of soft laughter emanated from the corner in which Darcy watched his cousin entertain Elizabeth. It was that delightful gurgle of hers, which he so enjoyed. Wanting to be a part of what they were saying, he found himself moving toward them. Not certain how to begin, he offered up the required pleasantries. "May I inquire, Miss Elizabeth, as to the health of your family?"

"My family was well, Sir, when I left Hertfordshire," she answered in the usual manner. "Thank you for asking." Then he watched as a thought flashed through her eyes. "My eldest sister has been in Town these three months. Have you never happened to see her there?"

Panic filled Darcy's chest. Did she know his involvement in separating Bingley and her sister, or was she just making conversation? Either way, her words chilled Darcy to the bone. His attempt at engaging her in conversation diverted to his prejudice toward her connections.

He faltered, "Regrettably, Miss Elizabeth, I did not have the good fortune as to meet Miss Bennet while in London." And as quickly as he moved to speak to her, Darcy withdrew. He could not betray Caroline Bingley, nor could he truly explain his objection to Charles Bingley's aligning himself with the Bennet family. Obviously, Charles had less to lose than did Darcy, and here he was drooling over a woman far below his station in life.

Soon enough, his cousin indicated it was time to return to the great house. Feeling the elation of his hopes draining into the hard Kent soil, Darcy set his feet in action. They made their farewells and were well away from the cottage before Edward said, "Would you like to explain to me what all that was about?"

"Nothing," Darcy grumbled. "I simply called upon former acquaintances." As they walked the well-worn path in silence, Darcy cursed himself for getting caught up in the unknown that was Elizabeth Bennet. Being near her made him feel he was on trial. Did she take such great joy in tormenting him? He nearly showed himself; he had flirted with his own destiny. He had vowed to be rid of Elizabeth Bennet, and this was to be his test. First Elizabeth and then his cousin had waited for his response. Could they read his countenance? Had he shown them how he had foolishly succumbed to the idea of making Elizabeth Bennet his? Decidedly brutal honesty needed to prevail: He could never make Miss Elizabeth his wife, and the sooner he accepted that particular fact, the better.

Darcy could not soften the truth: The lady was too far below his family's expectations for the future Mrs. Darcy.

Darcy Is Seen at Church
on Good Friday
by Susan Adriani

March 27, 1812

Though Colonel Fitzwilliam had been a regular visitor at the parsonage since his arrival in Kent several days prior, Mr. Darcy was not seen again until Good Friday, when the family from Rosings entered Hunsford Church. He was difficult to miss, elegantly attired in a rich blue dress coat, dark breeches, and gleaming black top-boots. Handsomely dressed, handsomely mannered, and handsome in general seemed to be the consensus of the women assembled throughout the small congregation. Their whispered words and admiring glances made Elizabeth's lips quirk indulgently. Though she could not deny that Mr. Darcy was, indeed, physically attractive, she had become too much acquainted with his manners during his stay in Hertfordshire to share any other sentiments uttered in her midst. To Elizabeth Bennet, the master of Pemberley, even in his regal blue coat, looked every bit as proud and disagreeable as ever.

Sitting composedly in one of the pews in the back, Elizabeth bowed her head and clasped her hands upon her lap as Mr. Darcy strode swiftly into the church from the vestibule, his head held high as he removed his hat and tucked it and his cane neatly beneath his arm. She observed him through lowered lashes; the way his body stiffened as he approached her; the way his eyes scrutinized her before he trained them forward once more, quickening his pace.

His response to Mr. Collins' simpering welcome had been everything Elizabeth had expected of the master of Pemberley. She could hardly blame him, she supposed, for her cousin's overt gestures of subservience had reached new heights since the arrival of Lady Catherine's distinguished nephews. After Mr. Darcy's abrupt dismissal of Mr. Collins' attentions, however, Elizabeth was pleased to see that he at least possessed manners enough to exchange the distasteful expression on his face for one of civility as he greeted Charlotte, who wore a polite smile despite any mortification she must have felt at the moment for having such a husband.

Colonel Fitzwilliam's manners were infinitely superior. While Elizabeth suspected the smile he wore—especially as he addressed Mr. Collins—was indeed well practiced, it did not come across as forced or unnatural. What a far cry from the dour expressions and general rudeness of his aunt and two cousins! Not for the first time was she left wondering how such an entirely agreeable gentleman as the colonel could possibly be related to Mr. Darcy, Lady Catherine, and her droll, sickly daughter.

The illustrious party reached the front of the church, and Elizabeth continued to watch Mr. Darcy with keen eyes. According to Mr. Wickham, Mr. Darcy was destined to marry Miss de Bourgh, so it came as quite a surprise to her when the master of Pemberley did not, in fact, take a seat beside his intended, but gestured instead for Colonel Fitzwilliam to do so. While his good-natured cousin rolled his eyes in an exaggerated fashion, the expression on Lady Catherine's face showed anything but amusement. She leveled both men with a look of immense dissatisfaction, and even went so far as to swat the colonel's shoulder with her cane, commanding him to make way for Mr. Darcy. Before the colonel could comply with his aunt's demand, however, Mr. Darcy's hand was upon his other shoulder. Colonel Fitzwilliam sat down heavily. Mr. Darcy released him and claimed the seat at his side, at the very end of the family pew.

Lady Catherine appeared furious, and Elizabeth suspected, had they not been in church, that Her Ladyship would not have hesitated to give her nephews quite a tongue lashing for their defiance; but neither man so much as glanced in her direction. Lady Catherine pursed her lips and faced forward, striking her cane sharply upon the floor for emphasis, causing more than her daughter to jump in alarm. For better or worse, both Mr. Darcy and Colonel Fitzwilliam continued to ignore her. They had produced their prayer books and appeared to be studying them with devoted interest.

Lady Catherine narrowed her eyes at them and struck her cane upon the ground once more, making Miss de Bourgh jump a second time. Mr. Collins hurried to his pulpit, nearly tripping over his own feet in his haste. Colonel Fitzwilliam, who had looked up from his prayerbook just in time to witness the parson's gracelessness, snorted. With a grin, he leaned toward Mr. Darcy and whispered in his ear. Mr. Darcy turned his head a fraction of an inch and elbowed him in the ribs. Colonel Fitzwilliam, an affronted look upon his face, elbowed him back. Lady Catherine cracked her cane upon the floor thrice more in succession, her countenance positively dangerous. Miss de Bourgh startled a third time, emitting a small squeak.

Elizabeth saw the spectacle unfold before her with incredulous eyes. At the moment, the two impeccably attired gentlemen seated with their pensive cousin and angry aunt bore far more of a resemblance to ill-behaved little boys than they did respectable, grown men. She found herself biting her lip in an effort to keep from laughing, lest Lady Catherine turn her disapproving glare upon her, instead of her wayward nephews.

Easter Sunday at Rosings
by Abigail Reynolds

March 29, 1812

It had started at church, which had been the usual affair of attempting to disguise the fact that he could not stop stealing glances at Elizabeth combined with utter disdain for Mr. Collins' foolish sermon. Easter and rebirth – he had that much right, but the ridiculous ramblings that followed would have been laughable had they not been so dreadfully dull. Darcy had already steeled himself to the knowledge that he would not have the acute, painful delight of seeing Elizabeth again until the next week's service when he heard Lady Catherine invite Mr. Collins and his party to join them at Rosings that evening.

He wanted to be dismayed by the news. It was better to limit his exposure to Elizabeth to once a week at church, where he could remember why he could not have her as his own, but no matter how well he knew he should stay away from her, he could not find the least trace of regret in his heart that he would have another hour in her company, another hour of feeling alive, that evening.

Anticipation of her visit haunted him throughout the day, making him unusually restless. Colonel Fitzwilliam even commented on his preoccupation, which brought Darcy back to the present for a few minutes, but the colonel could not compete with the bewitching Elizabeth who filled his thoughts.

After all his agitation, her arrival was anticlimactic. Since Lady Catherine insisted upon monopolizing his attention with her incessant demands, he could only watch her from across the room while his cousin was fortunate enough to seat himself by Elizabeth and enjoy her lively smiles. Darcy could only make out fragments of their conversation, but they conversed with such spirit and flow that he could not deny to himself that she seemed to be enjoying Colonel Fitzwilliam's company more than she ever had his. It did not matter, though. Neither of them could ever have her, so there was no point thinking about it – and certainly no call for obsessing constantly about it.

It would be beneath him to feel jealous of his landless, often fundless cousin. He tore his gaze away from them and tried to focus on his conversation with his aunt, monotonous as it was, until out of the corner of his eye, the noticed his cousin leading Elizabeth into the next room, presumably to the pianoforte. The sound of their laughter floated through the opening between the rooms.

He was certainly not jealous, but he did not choose to be deprived of the opportunity to rest his eyes on Elizabeth's loveliness, so he excused himself and stationed himself where even the colonel would realize that he commanded a full view of them.

Elizabeth must have noticed as well, since at the first convenient pause, she turned to him with an arch smile, and said, "You mean to frighten me, Mr. Darcy, by coming in all this state to hear me? But I will not be alarmed though your sister does play so well. There is a stubbornness about me that never can bear to be frightened at the will of others. My courage always rises with every attempt to intimidate me."

What was it about her teasing that intoxicated him so and sent the blood racing through his body? He smiled slowly before offering his rejoinder. "I shall not say that you are mistaken because you could not really believe me to entertain any design of alarming you; and I have had the pleasure of your acquaintance long enough to know, that you find great enjoyment in occasionally professing opinions which in fact are not your own."

Elizabeth laughed heartily at this picture of herself, and said to Colonel Fitzwilliam, "Your cousin will give you a very pretty notion of me, and teach you not to believe a word I say. I am particularly unlucky in meeting with a person so well able to expose my real character, in a part of the world where I had hoped to pass myself off with some degree of credit. Indeed, Mr. Darcy, it is very ungenerous in you to mention all that you knew to my disadvantage in Hertfordshire—and, give me leave to say, very impolitic too—for it is provoking me to retaliate, and such things may come out, as will shock your relations to hear."

He smiled, confident that her teasing could have no malice. "I am not afraid of you."

"Pray let me hear what you have to accuse him of," cried Colonel Fitzwilliam. "I should like to know how he behaves among strangers."

"You shall hear then—but prepare yourself for something very dreadful. The first time of my ever seeing him in Hertfordshire, you must know, was at a ball—and at this ball, what do you think he did? He danced only four dances! I am sorry to pain you—but so it was. He danced only four dances, though gentlemen were scarce; and, to my certain knowledge, more than one young lady was sitting down in want of a partner. Mr. Darcy, you cannot deny the fact."

Why should he deny it? "I had not at that time the honour of knowing any lady in the assembly beyond my own party."

"True; and nobody can ever be introduced in a ball room." This time her tone had some bite. "Well, Colonel Fitzwilliam, what do I play next? My fingers wait your orders."

His mind whirled. Why was Elizabeth taking aim at him? Perhaps she had misunderstood what he meant. "Perhaps I should have judged better, had I sought an introduction, but I am ill qualified to recommend myself to strangers."

"Shall we ask your cousin the reason of this?" said Elizabeth to Colonel Fitzwilliam. "Shall we ask him why a man of sense and education, and who has lived in the world, is ill qualified to recommend himself to strangers?"

"I can answer your question," said Fitzwilliam, "without applying to him. It is because he will not give himself the trouble."

They had both turned on him, and in the most painful way.

His cousin knew how he had failed to achieve acceptance in certain circles, that same success that came so easily to the colonel. "I certainly have not the talent which some people possess, of conversing easily with those I have never seen before. I cannot catch their tone of conversation, or appear interested in their concerns, as I often see done," he said stiffly.

"My fingers," said Elizabeth, "do not move over this instrument in the masterly manner which I see so many women's do. They have not the same force or rapidity, and do not produce the same expression. But then I have always supposed it to be my own fault—because I would not take the trouble of practicing. It is not that I do not believe my fingers as capable as any other woman's of superior execution."

Relief flooded him. She understood, more than he had ever imagined she would understand, how he struggled to avoid giving offense, yet failed again and again – and she was showing him in the best possible way that it was not necessary to be perfect to be appreciated. He smiled and said, "You are perfectly right. You have employed your time much better. No one admitted to the privilege of hearing you, can think anything wanting. We neither of us perform to strangers."

Here they were interrupted by Lady Catherine, who called out to know what they were talking of. Elizabeth immediately began playing again. Darcy watched her in a daze, his world shifting under his feet. He had seen Elizabeth as witty, amusing, attractive – oh, so attractive! – and temptation personified, but this was a side he had never known existed. How had she known so perfectly what he needed to hear when just at that moment?

He had forced himself to ignore his desire for her, but this new realization showed him she was more than just a bewitching woman. She was vital to him.

Family and duty be damned. He was going to marry Elizabeth Bennet.

Darcy Begins His Campaign
to Win Elizabeth's Affections
by Regina Jeffers

March 30, 1812

Darcy lay under the counterpane, stretching his limbs to relieve the tension the evening's entertainment had brought. He had spent the last few months declaring his freedom from Elizabeth Bennet, but the evening had persuaded him to reevaluate his feelings. It seemed since Elizabeth Bennet had entered his life, Darcy had spent numerous hours debating about whether he could legitimately succumb to her charms. He realized he was forever lost to her; Elizabeth Bennet would be the mark by which he would judge all other women. Yet, he still could not justify his pursuing Elizabeth and the aligning of his family name with her poor connections; however, Darcy could also not release her. Unless he did something soon, the quandary in which he found himself would further rob him of his sleep, as well as his waking sanity.

If he could not rid himself of his obsession, then Darcy had rationally to plan how he could achieve Elizabeth's regard and limit his association with her family. Of course, that may not be achievable. If so, he would have to determine how best to soften Elizabeth's liabilities. He thought he could tolerate the company of Miss Bennet and probably their father. Would regularly seeing those two be enough for Elizabeth? Pemberley was a good distance from Hertfordshire, and it would not be easy for Elizabeth's family to visit. He could arrange business in Town when Mrs. Bennet and the younger sisters descended upon his estate. In addition, he would have to be diligent in overseeing those connections' having too much influence on Georgiana.

It would not be ideal, but the Bennets could be brought to Pemberley when others were not expected. It could be achieved, and the trouble involved would be worthwhile if Darcy could earn Elizabeth's love. A few moments of intolerable disdain would be pale indeed to all the pleasures of Elizabeth's company. The gift of Miss Elizabeth's love and devotion had been a prayer he had recited more than once over these last few months. "The prayer the Devil answers," he chuckled out loud as the darkness enveloped him. With a renewed resolve, he fell asleep. Images of Elizabeth at the pianoforte frequented his dreams, and her smile was all for his pleasure.

Dawn came early for Fitzwilliam Darcy; he found himself wrapped in the bedclothes and turned askew; his battle with himself and sleep had taken its toll, but he had made a decision during the night's long hours. Pushing himself from the mattress, Darcy swung his legs over the bed's side and reached for the bell cord to call his man. Today, he would seek out Elizabeth's company; today, he would begin to win her heart; although she probably held no knowledge of its depth, he knew Elizabeth to be, at least, aware of his interests. Now, Darcy would demonstrate to the lady that despite his concerns with her family, he would apply himself to winning her love.

Today would be the first day of the rest of his life. Following his morning ablutions, Darcy carefully created, in his dress, the appearance of a gentleman open to new possibilities. He set out through the parklands surrounding Rosings, but his destination was not to be the park itself; he planned to call on the Parsonage. The little over a quarter mile path was short lived, and before he knew it, he stood outside Hunsford. For a few painful seconds, he thought to turn around and return to the manor house. Yet, his heart said he must see this through; he could not alter his course. His entrance into the gate at the Parsonage would be well known. So noted, Darcy rang the bell, and a servant soon admitted him to the inner room. He had expected the Collinses to be at home, but he found only Elizabeth in attendance. Having planned to engage the household's occupants in conversation, his apprehension increased. He had rehearsed what he would say to each of the cottage's occupants. And although it was a pleasant surprise, it was necessary for him to shift his emotional being to face Elizabeth one-on-one.

"Mr. Darcy, what a surprise!" she began, sounding a bit uncertain.

"Miss Elizabeth, I apologize for invading your privacy," he stumbled along trying to sound uneventful, but feeling aroused by her closeness. "I understood the Collinses were within. I pray I have not interrupted your solitary pleasures."

"An interruption does not necessarily have to be unwelcome, Sir," she curtsied. "I am afraid Mrs. Collins and her sister have gone into the village. I hope your appearance here does not mean your family at Rosings has taken ill. Are Lady Catherine, Miss de Bourgh, and your cousin, the colonel, all in health?"

"Do not know distress, Madam; their health is well," he returned her bow, while all the time thinking, She welcomes my company!

"Then, please be seated, Mr. Darcy," she offered politely, while gesturing to a nearby chair. "Would you care for tea, Sir?"

"No, thank you, Miss Elizabeth. I am quite content." For several minutes, Darcy stared at her; he was so fascinated by her beauty that he nearly forgot the need for conversation. He looked up to observe Elizabeth's questioning gaze. He cleared his throat. "May I ask of your journey from Hertfordshire."

"Quite pleasant, Sir. Miss Lucas and Sir William thought the scenery delightful," she said with her usual sardonic attitude.

Darcy's breathing relaxed. They would hold another of their stimulating conversations. "And you did not, Miss Elizabeth?"

"On the contrary, Mr. Darcy, I enjoyed the beautiful landscapes, but I fear I do not possess Sir William's way with words.

His descriptions of Kent and of Rosings are likely to be legendary in Meryton by the time of my return."

"And the weather?" he said with enthusiasm.

Elizabeth chuckled, "As we both know, England is famous for its weather. Even Sir William Lucas would be at a loss for words in describing God's grace in Kent. But please be assured I found it very comfortable."

"And Mr. Bennet? Is your father in health?" He thought it best to speak of those within her family of whom he held some respect.

"My father is well. He lives to read and to make sport for our neighbors." Darcy was not certain what Elizabeth saw as an endearing quality in her father was one he would admire, but before he could inquire further, she said, "And what of Mr. Bingley? Is your friend likely to return to Netherfield?"

He had not expected Elizabeth to bring up the subject of Bingley and Netherfield so quickly, but Darcy had anticipated her comment, especially after her mentioning Miss Bennet's presence in London. As casually as possible, he assured Elizabeth of the unlikelihood of that situation. "I have never heard Mr. Bingley say so; but it is probable he may spend very little of his time at Netherfield in the future. He has many friends, and he is at a time of life when friends and engagements are continually increasing."

He noticed her frown, but he hoped this explanation would temper her curiosity. Darcy changed the text of their conversation. "This appears a very comfortable house. Lady Catherine, I believe, did a great deal to it when Mr. Collins first came to Hunsford."

"I believe she did—and I am certain she could not have bestowed her kindness on a more grateful object," Elizabeth said with a smirk.

He cautioned, "My aunt is an excellent benefactor for Mr. Collins; such improvements are the exception rather than the rule." Elizabeth simply nodded. Yet, it was not of the house he wished to speak; he wished to know of her thoughts on marriage. He began, "Mr. Collins appears to be very fortunate in his choice of a wife."

"Yes, indeed, his friends may well rejoice in his having met with one of the very few sensible women who would accept him, but in a prudential light, it is certainly a good match for her."

Elizabeth did not appear to favor the match despite her friend's sensibility of marrying for monetary advantage. Darcy took her words to mean wealth was important, but Elizabeth wanted a loving relationship for herself. That was acceptable situation to him; he wanted to replicate his parents' partnership; he had the necessary wealth, and he would wholeheartedly love Elizabeth if she would accept him.

Darcy added, "It must be very agreeable to Mrs. Collins to be settled within so easy a distance of her own family and friends."

A bit shocked, Elizabeth replied, "An easy distance, do you call it? It is nearly fifty miles."

A challenge was before him; they would engage in their usual verbal swordplay. "And what is fifty miles of good road? Little more than half a day's journey. Yes, I call it a very easy distance," he remarked as he leaned forward, as if offering a challenge.

Elizabeth shifted her weight, straightened her shoulders, and leaned in, as she countered, "I should never have considered the distance as one of the advantages of the match. I should never have said Mrs. Collins was settled near her family."

Darcy could detect the lavender scent that was her favorite; it was all he could do not to caress her cheek. "It is a proof of your own attachment to Hertfordshire. Anything beyond the very neighborhood of Longbourn, I suppose, would appear far." He smiled while thinking of her at Pemberley and realizing the additional distance between his home and her home and how it would give them relief from her connections.

Elizabeth argued, "One would need more fortune than the Collinses possess in order for the distance to be an easy one. It is comfortable for you to consider distance from a different perspective, Mr. Darcy. Where there is fortune to make the expense of traveling unimportant, distance becomes no evil. But that is not the case here. Mr. and Mrs. Collins have a comfortable income, but not such a one as will allow frequent journeys."

Darcy had the financial stability to make Elizabeth's travel wishes a matter of choosing in which carriage she wished to traverse the distance. He could offer her so much; obviously, Elizabeth would learn to love him. Darcy drew his chair a little toward her and said, "You cannot have a right to such very strong local attachments. You cannot have been always at Longbourn." His feelings for Elizabeth caused Darcy's breath to be ragged and shallow; they locked eyes momentarily, and he saw an image of her uncertainty. He quickly realized he must check himself; he had moved too quickly. Despite wanting to scoop her into his arms and to carry her off to Pemberley, he reluctantly moved his chair back. There was a newspaper lying on the table, and as he picked it up, he said nonchalantly, "Are you pleased with Kent?"

Elizabeth leaned back casually in her chair. The intensity between them subsided, and small talk remained. When Mrs. Collins and Miss Lucas returned, Darcy explained he had thought all the ladies of the house were at home when he had called upon the cottage. After a series of civilities, he begged their leave and returned to Rosings Park.

It was a beginning, he thought as he made his way along the well-worn path. Elizabeth must, obviously, recognize my intentions; now he must determine if she will willingly accept him as her husband. The possibility thrilled him while, at the same time, it sent a shot of pure panic through him.

Over the next several days, Darcy continued to call at the Parsonage; sometimes he came with his cousin; other times he came alone. To his chagrin, his former reluctance to speak easily reappeared when others were about. He realized he must find a means to engage Elizabeth privately again. Therefore, having eavesdropped on her conversations with his cousin, Darcy had lighted on an idea. Miss Bennet chose a particular path at Rosings to be her favorite; he would arrange a *rencontre*. They would walk together and become more thoroughly acquainted; tomorrow Darcy would embark upon the second stage of his pursuit of Elizabeth Bennet.

Fitzwilliam and Darcy Visit the Parsonage Again
by Jack Caldwell

March 31, 1812

"Mr. Darcy and Colonel Fitzwilliam," the servant announced.

The party ensconced at the Hunsford Parsonage stood about the small parlor. Colonel Fitzwilliam quickly took in the scene: Mr. Collins, tall and stocky, was literally bowing from the waist.

Steady man, the colonel thought. I am not my father, the earl.

Mrs. Collins, plain and pleasant, stood next to her husband, her slight curtsey all that was correct for a woman of her station and that of her guests. Closest to the fireplace was Mrs. Collins' young and awestruck sister, Miss Lucas. By the table was her pretty friend, Miss Bennet.

"Mr. Darcy! Colonel Fitzwilliam! You honor us most acutely by your presence! That you would lower yourselves to once again enter this humble abode! Not that this house is so very humble, for what parsonage in all of England could boast of the careful attentions, generosity, and taste of Lady Catherine de Bourgh! Such approbation! Such compassion to my relations! But who could expect less from the nephews of my most generous patroness?"

In this manner, Mr. Collins continued, and Fitzwilliam was hard pressed to hide his smile completely at the man's foolishness. He managed it by smiling as he greeted the ladies. In short order, he found himself seated at a small table with Miss Bennet, while the others attempted to attend to Darcy.

Darcy was behaving as he usually did, his cousin noted. Uncomfortable in any social situation away from his close friends and family, the man fell back into cold politeness and taciturn statements. Fitzwilliam was accustomed to it and hardly noticed, but the same could not be said for his fair companion.

"I am sorry all sport is done, Colonel," she said.

"I did not know that ladies paid any great attention to gentlemen's pursuits, Miss Bennet."

"Oh! You are severe on us!" Her smile took away any bite to her words. "We ladies do talk of things beside lace and finery. Gentlemen's activities are always of great interest to us, for it is said that a man grows ridiculous without an occupation, and the follies of our fellows are the very heart of gossip."

The colonel laughed heartily. "How well you know us! Indeed, sloth is abhorrent to me and my friend, too."

Miss Bennet's eyes darted to Darcy. "I have heard it said of your cousin that he dislikes quiet Sunday afternoons."

"I cannot say that is an accurate description of Darcy."

"I must bow to your superior knowledge, sir. But to defend myself, I was told by a very good source that there is no more awful object than that gentleman at his own house on a Sunday evening, when he has nothing to do."

Fitzwilliam laughed again. "Now that is true! Darcy always wants to do something useful, particularly for someone else. He has not accepted the idea that he must rest like us mere mortals!"

"Are people always dependent on his advice and efforts, then? He sounds very much like his aunt."

Fitzwilliam glanced about the room. It was a small, modest house, but Lady Catherine had seen to improvements. The furniture might be sparse, but it was of good quality, castoffs from the last redecoration of Rosings. The paint and wall coverings were relatively new and fresh, and Fitzwilliam could see his aunt's hand in the sensible arrangement of the furnishings.

Knowing my aunt's attention to detail, the Collinses are probably frightened out of their wits to move any of this more than an inch without prior approval!

"I would say that both my aunt and my cousin take a prodigious interest in the concerns of those under their care." *Although for dramatically different reasons! Darcy truly cares for his servants and tenants, like his father and mine, while Lady Catherine only desires to exercise control over the lower classes.*

Miss Bennet nodded to herself as if the colonel's words had reinforced a previously held opinion. She glanced again at Darcy, and Fitzwilliam could see that he was staring at her.

Darcy is showing unusual attention to my pretty companion. I believe there is some admiration in it. Is the lady's teasing a sign that she is aware of it and approves? I cannot tell. Her wit is so sharp I wonder if she means to tickle or wound.

Tea was then served, which gave Miss Lucas an excuse to join the pair. Mr. Darcy remained on the sofa, an unwilling recipient of Mr. Collins' insipid conversation.

Twenty minutes later the cousins were walking back to Rosings.

"Darcy," cried Fitzwilliam, "I know you can be reserved to a distressing degree, but if you insist on continuing to call on the Collinses, at least you could actually carry on a conversation with them."

Darcy shook his head. "I believe I talked as much as ever."

"You hardly talked at all!"

Darcy looked over at his friend. "Compared to you, anyone would seem struck dumb—" he paused dramatically, "save Mr. Collins!"

"Too true. There, you see! You do have a wit! You should show it if you mean…"

"Mean what?"

Fitzwilliam held his tongue. If Darcy was attracted to Miss Bennet, he would never admit it anyone until he was ready. Besides, the colonel reminded himself that he might be mistaken.

"If you mean to show yourself to good advantage," Fitzwilliam finished lamely.

"Show myself to good advantage? To whom, Fitz? A foolish country parson, one who is suitable to no one save my overbearing aunt?"

"Darcy, that is harsh!" At Darcy's raised eyebrow, he added, "But true!"

They walked on for a little while. Upon beholding the front door of Rosings, Darcy blurted out, "We should visit the parsonage again tomorrow if the weather holds."

Fitzwilliam grinned. *Well, I say! Darcy is lost to the charms of Miss Bennet!*

Darcy Hints Elizabeth Would Find Rosings Park More Welcoming If She Returned There as His Wife
by Regina Jeffers

April 3, 1812

He awoke early and left Rosings's warmth behind to brave a chilly morning and to wait for Elizabeth's company. Darcy had thought he knew which path she had described to Edward, but after a half hour's stay, he questioned the information. Reasoning that Elizabeth likely assisted Mrs. Collins with the lady's household duties, he gave himself permission to wait another quarter hour before he would return to the manor house. To his relief, he finally spotted Miss Elizabeth as she approached the roughly hewed clearing where he awaited her. By design, wishing the appearance of an accidental meeting, Darcy stepped into the shadows.

Not expecting to encounter anyone along the pathway, Elizabeth started when Darcy appeared before her. "Mr. Darcy," she gasped and clutched at her chest, "You surprised me, Sir."

"Miss Elizabeth," he feigned surprise, "as you did me." He bowed properly, but he searched her countenance for Elizabeth's true feelings at encountering him. "I did not realize you too preferred solitary walks. They are most pleasant, are they not?"

"You know me to be a person who is not afraid of a healthy walking distance," she appeared a bit unnerved by the mischance of their meeting., but she spoke with welcome.

Darcy brushed away the reluctance she displayed. Instead, he said, "Are you nearing the end of your preamble?"

"Yes…yes, Sir," she stammered. "I believe I will turn back."

"Then allow me, Madam," he said, doffing his hat, "to escort you to the Parsonage. I would be remiss in my duty if I permitted you to return alone." He liked the way this scenario had fallen into place. Everything was as he had imagined.

Elizabeth flashed a questioning look in his direction, but she accepted his extended arm as her support. Darcy resisted placing his free hand over hers; the warmth of her fingers tantalized his senses. They walked for a few minutes in what he considered to be companionable silence; yet, he did not want to waste the precious time he would spend with her so he forced himself to offer up observations about the beauty of Kent. "It has been many years since the shire has sported early blooms and greenery. The temperate weather has been kind to the parklands."

"Yes, it is quite beautiful," she said softly. "I have thoroughly enjoyed my walks."

Elizabeth's response he barely heard, being so consumed by the moment, but he caught enough of the words to realize she found Kent to be very pleasant.

"Would you consider returning for another visit?" he ventured.

"Such would be a pleasurable sojourn," she turned to look unexpectedly up at him. He prayed she would know his affections soon. Darcy glowed with the hopes that Elizabeth would think it more pleasurable if he were in Kent, as well.

"How do you find Rosings Park?" he questioned, engrossed in her closeness.

"It has a pleasant prospect when one first takes in its beauty," Elizabeth began. "Its many wings confuse me, however. Lady Catherine has offered use of her library, but I must admit I found the billiard room instead. It is a bit amusing upon recollection."

Darcy caught the glint of a smile, and he joined in her ease. "I am certain if you were to return as a Rosings's guest, the likelihood of making such a mistake would be greatly reduced."

The ambiguity of his words was not lost on Elizabeth, and that pleased Darcy. He wanted her to think of him in a different role. To realize he was much more than she imagined. She glanced at him briefly and shook her head. The movement of her bonnet caught his attention, and Darcy partook of the flush of her cheeks and of her thick eyelashes.

The walk was coming to an end, and they drifted into silence once more. Approaching the gate, he loosened the latch with his free hand. In reality, he truly disliked parting from her company, and he walked with her to the door of the Parsonage. "Thank you, Mr. Darcy," her eyes rose to meet his.

"It was my pleasure, Miss Elizabeth. Your presence made the walk more agreeable." Before she could respond, he offered her a quick bow and strode away. Waiting until he was certain no one at the Parsonage could observe his reactions, Darcy finally gave himself permission to stop, lean against a tree, and replay the reflections of the last half hour.

It was another beginning. Darcy would like to think this was another step in his winning Elizabeth's regard when, in reality, most of his previous beginnings had been faltering attempts. Accustomed to being the prey, not the pursuer, he knew what to do to sustain an interest once it began, but Darcy had never met a woman such as Elizabeth Bennet and had never initiated a relationship. Yet, he felt more hopeful; Bingley, and especially the gentleman's sisters, had thwarted Darcy's attempts at Netherfield; here at Rosings, his cousin had frustrated his designs. Darcy realized he needed privacy to secure Elizabeth's affections; the solitary paths of Rosings would permit him the means and the mode to win the lady's heart.

Darcy Is Determined to Make Elizabeth His Wife
by Regina Jeffers

April 7, 1812

On the third day that Darcy had met Elizabeth along her favorite path, he encountered some resistance on her part, but he had prepared himself for her reluctance. "Miss Elizabeth," he began upon meeting her accidentally for the third time in as many days, "I have purposely sought you out." His words registered a mild shock upon Elizabeth's face. "After leaving you yesterday at the Parsonage, I recalled a particularly pleasant prospect I believe you would enjoy. I came today in hopes of having the pleasure of showing it to you."

"Thank you, Mr. Darcy," she countered, "that shall not be necessary."

He said apologetically, "I understand if you are too tired. I should have thought better than to intrude upon your time." He retrieved his gloves from where they lay upon a bench. "I had only thought of how much you have enjoyed the park while we have kept each other company. The walk I had thought to share was one of my late mother's favorites. I had forgotten about it until Lady Catherine reminded me." He prayed that such a small prevarication would not come back to haunt him. "I simply thought you might find it a pleasant choice for a solitary walk.

Elizabeth hesitated briefly before saying, "If it is not too far, I would take delight in seeing it, Sir. Thank you for considering my pleasure." She rested her gloved hand on his proffered arm.

Walking along the narrow, winding path, Elizabeth often

moved closer for support, as the footing was a bit rough with tree roots. Lost to her closeness, Darcy considered the pleasure he would know by lifting Elizabeth into his arms and carrying her along the path. To feel her clinging to his chest would be pure bliss, but he resisted any rash impropriety.

In less than ten minutes, they emerged from the thick-trunk, tree-lined path into a clearing painted by the sun. Darcy pushed aside some branches and permitted Elizabeth to step into a field of vibrantly colored wildflowers—primroses, bluebells, wild hyacinths, and anemones. He enjoyed the gasp she emitted upon seeing what the clearing had to offer.

"Mr. Darcy," she exclaimed, "this is magnificent!"

He could not stop the smile erupting upon his lips. As Elizabeth stepped away from him and scampered toward the field, Darcy reluctantly released her. He watched as she stopped suddenly, spread her arms wide, and turned around and around, looking skyward with joy. He did not expect such unencumbered pleasure, but he could not turn his head. She was the most exquisite creature he had ever seen.

She walked through the field at several angles, stopping to enjoy the various flowers; then she strode purposely toward him. "Mr. Darcy, you have honored me by sharing this clearing. I cannot understand why you chose to do so, but it will be a treasured memory of my journey to Rosings."

"My mother loved nature, Miss Elizabeth. I believe she would have been pleased to know you approved of her favorite refuge," he offered. Realizing he could not press her too quickly, he said evenly, "Are you prepared to return to the Parsonage?"

"Yes, Sir, I believe I am." He extended his arm, and anticipating the pathway's unevenness, she took a firmer grip than previously. Her rich, mellow hazel eyes sparkling as she turned around and around in the field had filled Darcy with happiness. He loved Elizabeth Bennet; the realization of admitting his feelings flashed through his being; no more would he say he loved her eyes or loved how she spoke her mind; no longer would he think of his feelings being only a strong attraction; Darcy loved Elizabeth. It was as simple as that: he loved Elizabeth Bennet. Finally openly acknowledging his devotion for her to himself, Darcy wanted to scream it to the world. Instead, he forced himself to swallow hard and say, "I am pleased my intrusion was not unpleasant, Miss Elizabeth."

"I believe I told you earlier not all intrusions are unwelcome, Sir."

"Our acquaintance has been long enough for us to know something of the other's preferences." She looked at him with questions hidden behind her eyes; Darcy realized Elizabeth would now expect him to make known his intentions: He shared his mother's favorite refuge with her, and he had told her of his wishing to share precious parts of his life with her. The lady could no longer doubt his purpose.

Broken only by occasional civilities regarding the weather and of books recently read, the companionable silence returned between them. As customary, he left her at the Parsonage's door, but this time as he strode away he allowed himself the pleasure of turning for a final look at her; Elizabeth stood transfixed and looking toward where he brought up; he touched the brim of his hat to bid her farewell and strolled away. After he turned toward Rosings the second time, he did not observe her perplexed stare.

Tomorrow—he thought as he made his way along the path; tomorrow he would offer his hand to Elizabeth. He would depart from Rosings in two days; therefore, tomorrow would be the day. The prayer the Devil answers, he reminded himself. Let the Devil beware, Darcy thought. He would declare his love for Elizabeth Bennet; she would accept; and then Darcy would deal with those whose censure would surely come. Tonight he would prepare a proper proposal; he would tell Elizabeth how despite their differences, his regard for her had grown. He imagined her happiness at his declaration. That evening Darcy slept well with the knowledge that on the morrow Elizabeth Bennet would be his.

Fitzwilliam and Elizabeth
Walk in the Woods
by Jack Caldwell

April 9, 1812

Colonel Fitzwilliam was not in the best of spirits as he left the main house. He loved Darcy like a brother, but there were times when his cousin's high-handedness drove the colonel to distraction. The reason for today's irritation? Darcy had hinted that he might extend his visit to Rosings. Again.

Blast and damnation! cursed the colonel. *I have little more than a month left to my leave, and then I must return to Spain. I had hoped to spend some of this time with my family and Georgiana. As fond as I am of Anne, I do not want to spend what little time I have in England trapped in Kent!*

Fitzwilliam brooded, trying to determine Darcy's real reasons for staying at Rosings, when he spied a likely motive. Miss Elizabeth Bennet was walking towards the house, perusing a letter in her hand. Fitzwilliam's countenance lightened as he began to contemplate the mystery of the level of acquaintance between Darcy and the lovely young lady from Hertfordshire.

Miss Elizabeth looked surprised when she glanced up and saw him. Putting away the letter immediately and a smile gracing her face, the lady shared the usual greetings with the gentleman.

She added, "I did not know before that you ever walked this way."

"I have been making the tour of the park," the colonel replied, "as I generally do every year, and intend to close it with a call at the parsonage. Are you going much farther?"

"No, I should have turned in a moment."

And accordingly she did turn, and they walked towards the parsonage together. "Do you certainly leave Kent on Saturday?" said Miss Elizabeth.

"Yes, if Darcy does not put it off again. But I am at his disposal. He arranges the business just as he pleases." Fitz tried to hide any irritation he felt.

"And if not able to please himself in the arrangement, he has at least great pleasure in the power of choice. I do not know anybody who seems more to enjoy the power of doing what he likes than Mr. Darcy."

"He likes to have his own way very well," replied Fitzwilliam. "But so we all do. It is only that he has better means of having it than many others because he is rich and many others are poor. I speak feelingly. A younger son, you know, must be inured to self-denial and dependence."

Miss Elizabeth's fine, mocking eyes flashed. "In my opinion, the younger son of an earl can know very little of either. Now, seriously, what have you ever known of self-denial and dependence? When have you been prevented by want of money from going wherever you chose or procuring anything you had a fancy for?"

Fitz was forced to grin. "These are home questions—and perhaps I cannot say that I have experienced many hardships of that nature. But in matters of greater weight, I may suffer from the want of money. Younger sons cannot marry where they like."

"Unless where they like women of fortune, which I think they very often do," the lady teased.

Fitzwilliam shrugged. "Our habits of expense make us too dependent, and there are not many in my rank of life who can afford to marry without some attention to money."

His companion colored at the idea, but recovering herself, said in a lively tone, "And pray, what is the usual price of an earl's younger son? Unless the elder brother is very sickly, I suppose you would not ask above fifty thousand pounds."

Fitzwilliam was surprised that she had mentioned the exact amount of Anne's fortune. *How could she have heard of it? Her cousin, the parson, perhaps? He knows all too much of my aunt's business.* He hid his disquiet well, however, answered her in the same style, and the subject was dropped.

After a period of quiet, Miss Bennet ventured, "I imagine your cousin brought you down with him chiefly for the sake of having somebody at his disposal. I wonder he does not marry to secure a lasting convenience of that kind. But perhaps his sister does as well for the present, and as she is under his sole care, he may do what he likes with her."

"No," said Colonel Fitzwilliam, "that is an advantage which he must divide with me. I am joined with him in the guardianship of Miss Darcy."

"Are you, indeed? And pray what sort of guardians do you make? Does your charge give you much trouble? Young ladies of her age are sometimes a little difficult to manage, and if she has the true Darcy spirit, she may like to have her own way."

The lady's playful speech alarmed Fitzwilliam. For an instant he wanted to shake her—make her tell him of what she had heard of Georgiana. *Had Wickham talked of Georgie? I will KILL him!*

He controlled his temper, however, but only barely. "I am curious as to why you suppose my cousin likely to give uneasiness to anyone."

"You need not be frightened," she directly replied. "I never heard any harm of her, and I daresay she is one of the most tractable creatures in the world."

Fitzwilliam relaxed as the lady continued. "She is a very great favorite with some ladies of my acquaintance—Mrs. Hurst and Miss Bingley. I think I have heard you say that you know them."

So relieved was Fitzwilliam that he did not mind his next words well. "I know them a little. Their brother is a pleasant, gentlemanlike man. He is a great friend of Darcy's."

"Oh, yes!" said Miss Elizabeth drily. "Mr. Darcy is uncommonly kind to Mr. Bingley and takes a prodigious deal of care of him."

"Care of him!" Fitz laughed. "Yes, I really believe Darcy *does* take care of him in those points where he most wants care. From something that he told me in our journey hither, I have reason to think Bingley very much indebted to him."

Suddenly, the colonel realized that he might have said too much. "But I ought to beg his pardon, for I have no right to suppose that Bingley was the person meant. It was all conjecture."

"What is it you mean?"

Fitz saw no harm in continuing. "It is a circumstance which Darcy, of course, would not wish to be generally known, because if it were to get round to the lady's family, it would be an unpleasant thing."

"You may depend upon my not mentioning it."

"And remember that I have not much reason for supposing it to be Bingley! What he told me was merely this: That he congratulated himself on having lately saved a friend from the inconveniences of a most imprudent marriage but without mentioning names or any other particulars, and I only suspected it to be Bingley from believing him the kind of young man to get into a scrape of that sort and from knowing them to have been together the whole of last summer."

"Did Mr. Darcy give you his reasons for this interference?"

In a gossipy tone, he said, "I understood that there were some very strong objections against the lady."

"And what arts did he use to separate them?"

"He did not talk to me of his own arts," said Fitzwilliam, smiling. "He only told me what I have now told you."

Miss Elizabeth made no answer and walked on. After watching her a little, Fitzwilliam asked her why she was so thoughtful.

"I am thinking of what you have been telling me. Your cousin's conduct does not suit my feelings. Why was he to be the judge?"

Fitzwilliam heard displeasure in her voice. "You are rather disposed to call his interference officious?"

"I do not see what right Mr. Darcy had to decide on the propriety of his friend's inclination, or why, upon his own judgment alone, he was to determine and direct in what manner that friend was to be happy!

"But," she continued, recollecting herself, "as we know none of the particulars, it is not fair to condemn him. It is not to be supposed that there was much affection in the case."

"That is not an unnatural surmise," said Fitzwilliam after a self-conscious chuckle, "but it is lessening the honor of my cousin's triumph very sadly!"

The lady did not seem to enjoy Fitzwilliam's jest, and therefore, abruptly changed the conversation. The two talked on indifferent matters till they reached the Parsonage, where the colonel took his leave.

As he returned to Rosings, he was uneasy. *Miss Elizabeth was decidedly unhappy. Could I have offended her?*

A ridiculous question! Of course not.

Darcy Plans His Proposal
by Susan Mason-Milks

April 9, 1812

Fitzwilliam Darcy was a man whose entire life was about responsibility and duty. Since boyhood, he had always done what people expected of him. His parents, his relations, and his friends all knew he would eventually marry a young lady from the highest circles. In addition to her beauty, she would have impeccable manners and breeding and would have been training all her life to fulfill the role of mistress of a great house like Pemberley. They would be the perfect couple in the eyes of the *ton*.

The longer he waited to select a wife, the more intensely society mothers competed to gain his attention for their daughters. His friends, acquaintances, and even strangers began to enter their bets in the book at White's as to when Fitzwilliam Darcy would finally decide to marry and who the fortunate young lady might be.

Darcy always believed he would follow the path set out for him since birth – then he met Miss Elizabeth Bennet. Last fall, she had taken him completely by surprise, upsetting his regulated, well-ordered world in ways he could never have imagined. She was unlike anyone he had ever met before. Though only the daughter of a country gentleman, she was enchanting, enticing… yes, even bewitching. Almost from the moment he met her, he began to comprehend he was in serious danger. The more time he had spent in her company, the deeper he fell under her spell. In order to keep his feelings under strict control, he had endeavored to limit his interactions with her, but the pull to be near her had sometimes proven more powerful than his resolve.

Unlike other women of his acquaintance, she never tried to gain his attention. Even more unusual, she appeared unimpressed by his wealth and social standing. At first, he thought her apparent lack of interest might be part of a game to attract him, but very quickly, he realized she was completely lacking in pretense. The more time he spent in her presence, the more difficult it became to resist her.

In spite of the ache he felt for her, he knew it was impossible to consider making her an offer of marriage. Because of her family's lack of connections, she would never be considered an appropriate wife for a man of his standing. A lifetime of training in duty and responsibility to his family name told him he must forget her. And so last fall, he had left Hertfordshire, certain he would never see her again.

During the winter months, she had haunted his dreams in spite of his diligent efforts to blot her from his memory and remove her from his heart. When he arrived at Rosings to spend Easter with his aunt, Lady Catherine de Bourgh, he was not prepared for the shock of finding Miss Elizabeth also in the neighborhood visiting with her friend Mrs. Collins. Was it chance or a cruel joke of the gods to put her in his path once again? Wrestling with his feelings every night, he found sleep elusive. Each morning he arose with dark smudges beneath his eyes and his patience in short supply.

A few nights ago over the pianoforte, his beautiful Elizabeth taken him to task, and at the same time, artfully let him know she understood his struggles to overcome his shyness in conversing with people. When she suggested he should practice the art of conversation, he hoped she was hinting she would be his tutor in this endeavor. He could see clearly how her natural charms would help him through those socially difficult situations in which he usually floundered. To this marriage, he would bring his social standing, old family name, and wealth, while she would bring her sincere and caring nature, her talent for witty conversation, and her innate understanding of people. Together, they would be a formidable couple. Logic was nothing compared to the desire he felt for her — he must have her as his wife.

After that encounter, Darcy knew he must act. Late at night, sitting alone in the library with only the tick of the mantle clock for company, he considered what to say in his marriage proposal to her. The problem was he was not practiced at expressing his admiration to young ladies. In fact, thus far, all of his efforts had involved finding ways to fend them off. As a result, he knew he must plan and rehearse his speech in advance because when he looked into her dark, expressive eyes, he invariably lost the ability to form a coherent sentence.

First, he would declare how ardently he admired and loved her. That seemed a good start. Then, he would add emphasis to the strength and depth of his feelings by describing his struggle to overcome the many objections and obstacles to their union. He would say, that in offering for her, he was going against the wishes of his family and friends, and in truth, against his own better judgment, but emphasize that where she was concerned logic had no place. The inferiority of her family's connections, which should be of concern to him, was unimportant when compared to the joy of having her as his wife.

Yes, this was the correct approach. His lovely Elizabeth had an intelligent mind and would appreciate knowing how he had struggled with this decision. She would understand that, in the end, reason and logic had given way to love.

Feeling satisfied with his plan, he retired for the evening. In a dream that night, he walked with her in the grove. He saw himself taking her hands in his and reciting his proposal. As he spoke, her eyes grew warmer, and she smiled up into his face. "Yes," she said, "I would be honored to marry you." Raising her hand to his lips, he kissed it softly. More kisses followed until they were suddenly at Pemberley in his room, in his bed.

Darcy awoke with a start in a tangle of linens, confused and disappointed to find he was still at Rosings. The delight of holding her soft form in his arms lingered, creating an aching need inside him. At least, he could take comfort that after today it would not be much longer until she was with him in reality, not just in a dream.

After dressing with great care, he left the house praying she had kept to her usual morning routine of walking in the grove. As he approached the area, he saw her, but she was not alone. She was walking with his cousin. Blast that Fitzwilliam for getting in his way again! His irritation grew as he thought about how often his charming cousin had monopolized Elizabeth's attentions in the past few weeks. Now he would have to find a way to speak to her later in the day. Frustrated, he turned on his heel and stalked back to the house feeling very put out that his plan had been thwarted.

Later that morning at the breakfast table, Darcy learned from his cousin Anne that the Hunsford party was coming early that evening to drink tea at Rosings. He hoped that at some point during their visit, he would be able to quietly ask Elizabeth for a private audience, either later that evening or the following day, but when the parson and his family arrived, Elizabeth was not with them. Darcy could barely refrain from rolling his eyes as the ridiculous Mr. Collins bowed and bobbed and begged Lady Catherine to accept the apologies of his cousin Elizabeth, who had stayed behind with a headache.

Frustrated, Darcy excused himself from the group and went into the library to rethink his plan. Was she truly suffering or could it be possible she had invented the headache in order to stay behind and create the opportunity for him to be alone with her? In either case, he must go to her immediately.

All the way to the parsonage, he went over and over his speech. Upon arrival, he was pleased to discover she was in the parlor and could receive him. Entering the room, he was so distracted by the scent of lavender that he almost forgot to inquire after her health. When he did, her answer was polite but cool, and she seemed slightly uneasy. He brushed it off, confident he had been correct in his assumption she had invented a reason to stay behind in the hopes he would visit her.

When he looked into her lovely, expectant face, his resolve nearly failed. Sitting down, he took a moment to gather his thoughts and review what he planned to say. Then he rose, and taking a deep breath, he began, "In vain I have struggled. It will not do. My feelings will not be repressed. You must allow me to tell you how ardently I admire and love you."

Fitzwilliam Takes His Leave of the Parsonage
by Jack Caldwell

April 10, 1812

"Are you comfortable, Colonel?" asked Mrs. Collins.

"Perfectly, madam," he replied.

"Of course Colonel Fitzwilliam is comfortable, Mrs. Collins!" cried Mr. Collins. "Did not Lady Catherine de Bourgh herself pick out these very chairs? I assure you, my dear colonel, that your most excellent aunt arranged this room just in this manner, and we have taken pains so see that nothing is out of place, even by an inch! Surely, Lady Catherine's condescension knows no bounds!"

"Certainly you are right, Mr. Collins."

"Such a fine, fine lady. Always thoughtful and punctual. Unlike others— but I should hold my tongue..."

"Yes. Mr. Collins," said his wife. "Do you see Eliza yet?"

Colonel Fitzwilliam relaxed in his chair in the parlor of the Hunsford parsonage. He was seated next to a window, and the morning sun felt good on his shoulders as he visited Mrs. Collins and Miss Lucas, all the time wondering where Miss Bennet could be. Mr. Collins apparently felt the same—he was staring out the window for the misplaced young lady, muttering apologies.

The colonel's calm demeanor and pleasant conversation gave the lie to the excitement at Rosings over the last eighteen hours. When Fitzwilliam walked out the day before and met Miss Bennet in the park, he had just come to terms of spending another week as a guest at Rosings. But a little while later at tea, an agitated Darcy stormed in late and announced that he was to quit Kent the next morning.

What an uproar that announcement caused! Lady Catherine raged and cajoled, and even Anne begged Darcy to stay, but it was to no avail. The man would not be moved. He was very sorry, but he was determined to return to Town.

"I hope you have enjoyed your stay, Colonel," said Mrs. Collins. "I am sorry that Mr. Darcy is unwell."

"I thank you for your concern, but do not distress yourself. A trifling headache will not lay my cousin low for long," Fitzwilliam assured her.

Later in Darcy's rooms, Fitzwilliam tried to learn the reason for Darcy's extraordinary demand. There were times his friend and cousin could be high-handed, but this behavior was well beyond anything Darcy had ever done before. By then his cousin had calmed down, but he refused to speak of it. Darcy apologized for the inconvenience, which took a bit of the sting out of Fitzwilliam's ill-treatment, but would say no more. He requested, politely but firmly, that he have some privacy for the rest of the evening.

Fitzwilliam had no recourse but to agree. He knew Darcy could be as stubborn as a mule when he put his mind to it.

"Colonel," said Miss Lucas timidly, "I have been meaning to ask you… but—oh, it is silly."

Fitzwilliam smiled kindly. "What do you wish to know, Miss Lucas?"

The girl was nervous and blushing. Finally she declared, "Why do you not wear your uniform? All the officers back in Meryton are in uniform all the time!"

"But I am off duty," Fitz explained. "It is not right to wear one's uniform when one is off duty."

"But they are so handsome!" The girl blushed as she clamped her hands over her mouth. "Oh, I should not have said that!"

Fitzwilliam bit back a laugh. "I thank you for the compliment, Miss Lucas."

Darcy did something unusual again the next morning. Fitzwilliam was at table, eating his early breakfast, when Darcy came in—not from the passageway that led to the stairs, but from the front hall. The man had been outside, and at such an early hour! Fitzwilliam demanded to know the reason for it, but Darcy remained mute. He took coffee and very little else and requested that they take their leave of the parsonage ere they departed from Kent.

Once there, they learned that Miss Bennet had yet to return from her morning walk. Fitzwilliam was disappointed; he had grown to like the pretty, rather impertinent young lady. But Darcy, who had already shown signs of tension, became downright distracted. He walked up and down the parlor for a moment, then to Fitzwilliam's bewilderment, paid the meanest of farewells to the Collinses and Miss Lucas before making for the door.

Fitzwilliam, of course, had to say something. "Darcy" he hissed in a low voice, "what are you about? This looks very bad."

"Forgive me … please," said his cousin, who to a person that knew him well, appeared distressed. "I must leave."

"Are you well? Have you a headache?"

He would not look at the colonel. "Make my apologies. I must return to Rosings. Do not hurry. We will leave when you are ready."

Fitzwilliam was so astonished at this civility he said nothing as Darcy went away.

"More coffee, Colonel?"

Fitzwilliam waved her off. "No, thank you, Mrs. Collins. I should be off as I am sure my cousin is waiting for me. Allow me to take me leave of you."

Mr. Collins turned from the window, uncharacteristically with a scowl on his face. "Please accept my humble apologies for detaining you, my dear colonel! That you would grace my humble abode for such a length of time is condescension beyond even my noble—"

"Indeed you are correct, Mr. Collins," cut in his good wife, as she extended her hand to the colonel. "We have enjoyed meeting you, Colonel Fitzwilliam."

"It was an honor, ma'am."

"Oh, my dear, dear sir! It is we who are honored by your august presence!"

"Mr. Collins, this is too much—"

"But I do not know where my cousin has gotten to. I should speak to her upon her return."

"Pray do not, my good sir. The woods of Rosings are so delightful that one can hardly tear one's self from them. I do speak from experience."

"True, true—very true! Your most excellent aunt spends a prodigious amount on the care of them, does she not?"

"I cannot say. Good bye, Miss Lucas."

"Colonel," said she, blushing furiously. "I hope we should meet again."

Fitzwilliam felt regret about this. Apparently he had failed to guard his tongue around Mrs. Collins' young and impressionable sister. The lovesick look she bestowed on him made him guilty. He smiled and made his way out of the parsonage as quickly as possible.

* * *

Two hours later, Colonel Fitzwilliam was again with his cousin in the Darcy carriage, this time leaving Kent.

"Darcy, will you stop sitting there like a lump of coal? What the devil is the matter with you?"

"There is nothing the matter with me."

Fitzwilliam shook his head. There was nothing for it—Darcy would either tell him or not. The man was as stubborn as a mule when he wished to be. The colonel settled back and thought of what he could do during his visit to raise the spirits of his dear Georgiana.

He certainly could do naught for Darcy!

Elizabeth Reads Darcy's Letter
by Susan Mason-Milks

April 10, 1812

Elizabeth stood in the grove and watched Mr. Darcy walk away. In spite of how much she disliked him, she could not help but admire his fine figure and the way he carried himself. It was unfortunate that someone with so much to recommend him was also so decidedly unpleasant.

Looking at the letter in her hand, she was in conflict with herself. Even accepting the letter from him – from any man – was highly improper, but it had all transpired so quickly she had been unable to think of a polite way to refuse. Considering her biting words of the day before, perhaps she owed him at least the courtesy of reading whatever explanation he might wish to offer, although nothing he had to say could possibly take away the anger she felt – or the pain of receiving such an offensive marriage proposal.

Mr. Darcy's declaration had taken her completely by surprise yesterday. If only he had stopped after the part about how ardently he admired and loved her, she would have been able to refuse him politely, but he did not. He deemed it necessary to point out to her that he was asking for her hand even though it was against his better judgment to do so! He had continued to raise her ire by reciting a list of the objections against their union. In other words, he asked her to marry him, and then grossly insulted her!

She had been so disturbed by his words at the time that now looking back, she could scarcely remember how she had managed an intelligible response. Through the fog of emotion, she had a vague recollection of accusing him of not behaving in a gentleman-like manner, and then there was something about his being the last man in the world she would ever consider marrying. She could not feel sorry for what she said. He deserved every barb she had shot his way.

Thinking back to when he handed her the letter, she remembered that for just a moment his mask of control seemed to slip, and she thought she saw sadness in his eyes. Was it real? Was she truly so important to him, or was it simply that his pride had been injured by her refusal? She did not imagine there were many times when Mr. Fitzwilliam Darcy did not get what he wanted.

Finally, opening the letter, she reluctantly began to read, and with each line she became more and more agitated. Several times she gasped audibly and was thankful no one was nearby to hear her exclamations. Her immediate response to each part was disbelief. Once she finished the letter – with some parts reviewed several times – she rose with the intention of walking, so she could mull over what she had just learned. After only a few steps, she wavered, her legs too uncertain to hold her up. Immediately, Elizabeth looked for a new place to rest. Then unfolding the pages, she read the letter yet again.

After studying it for some time, she accepted some parts with equanimity, while others reignited her feelings of anger and resentment. At first, she could not actually believe he thought Jane indifferent to Mr. Bingley's attentions, that her sister's heart remained untouched. Then, after reviewing the incidents she remembered, Elizabeth reluctantly allowed Mr. Darcy could have made an honest mistake because he did not know Jane well enough to recognize the indications of her feelings. Ironically, she remembered how Charlotte had warned her Jane should make it more clear to Mr. Bingley how she felt in order secure his affections. It added to the irony that Mr. Darcy had been no better at discerning her sister's feelings for Mr. Bingley than she herself had been at perceiving Darcy's for her.

At the references to her family's improprieties, her anger flared again, but even as she smoldered, she knew, sadly, most of it was true. The boisterous, unbridled behavior of her mother and her younger sisters had been an embarrassment to Elizabeth since childhood. Many times she would see her mother ready to launch into another mortifying speech or action, but she was rarely able to stop it. Mrs. Bennet just did not know how to take a hint. For the most part, Elizabeth took the same attitude as her father by simply ignoring their silliness.

On the other hand, her family was certainly no worse than Lady Catherine, who was controlling, opinionated, and often, simply rude. Because she had an old family name and money, her behavior was tolerated. Elizabeth shifted uncomfortably as she remembered the evening Lady Catherine had offered to allow her to practice on the pianoforte in the room of her daughter's companion, as she would be "in nobody's way" in that part of the house. At the time, Elizabeth thought she had noticed Mr. Darcy cringing at his aunt's tactless statement, but she had not been sure. Now considering what she had learned about his attachment to her, she thought her impression had most likely been correct.

The new information about Wickham enveloped her in confusion and then left her dismayed. Darcy turned everything Wickham had told her on its head. Could it be true Darcy was the party who had been wronged and not the other way around? So much of what Wickham told her was almost the same as the events Darcy had related in his letter, but in each case, it appeared Wickham had twisted the facts just enough to make himself the victim who was deserving of her sympathy.

How could she have been so taken in – she who prided herself on being such a good judge of character? Why had she missed the signs that must have been so clearly before her from the beginning? When she overheard Mr. Darcy call her 'tolerable but not handsome enough to tempt him' on the first night they met, she had been both hurt and amused. Had his rude behavior in general and his insults to her personally made her predisposed to believe the worst of him? Although she liked to think of herself as more impartial than that, if she was completely honest with herself, she had to admit it could be true. Wickham must have sensed this weakness in her and taken advantage of it for his own purposes. Had he singled her out for attention because he sensed Darcy's interest in her and wished to hurt his old enemy in still another way? How could Wickham have detected something that had completely escaped her notice?

As she considered the situation, she chastised herself for missing from the very start the indications of Wickham's duplicity. She had not thought to question the impropriety of his sharing very personal information with her when she was little more to him than a new acquaintance. Over and over she had missed the clues of Wickham's subtle plot to undermine Darcy's credibility and character. For that grievous error, she reproached herself harshly. Most of all, Elizabeth flushed with embarrassment at having been taken in by Wickham's charms. How could she ever have been favorably impressed by him? What had happened to her good judgment?

The most shocking part of the letter dealt with Wickham's near seduction of poor Miss Darcy. Her heart went out to this innocent girl who was just about the same age as her own youngest sister, Lydia. Thankfully, Mr. Darcy had been able to avert disaster and save his sister's reputation before any damaging rumors could begin. The explanation of Miss Darcy's close escape and Wickham's part in it must be true, or Mr. Darcy would not have offered to have his cousin, Colonel Fitzwilliam, verify the story for her.

Could this be part of the sadness she had seen appear on Mr. Darcy's face from time to time when he thought no one was looking? If he was truly the honorable man reflected in this letter, then he must blame himself for his sister's situation. That would be a very heavy burden indeed to bear. It did not escape her notice that Mr. Darcy trusted her enough to tell her about Wickham's deception of his sister.

Elizabeth wandered the lane for almost two hours, reading and rereading the letter, walking as she turned the facts over and over in her mind. The emotion of this effort left her drained of energy, but she could not bring herself to face anyone yet. If she had only known Mr. Darcy would be here visiting his aunt at Easter, she would have arranged her visit for later in the spring. What an insufferable, arrogant, irritating man!

Finally, she realized if she did not return to the parsonage soon, Charlotte might begin to worry. Reluctantly, she prepared for the inevitable challenge of looking calm when there was a storm raging inside her. If her friend knew how upset she was, she might ask questions Elizabeth would rather avoid having to answer.

After apologizing to Charlotte for any concern she might have caused by being away from the house for so long, Elizabeth excused herself to her room. Finally, exhausted, she lay down on the bed and fell asleep, awaking mid-afternoon. This short period of rest went a long way in helping her to regain her good humor. After splashing water on her face, she joined Charlotte in the parlor. Just as she knew it would, the topic eventually turned to Mr. Darcy.

"So what do you think about Mr. Darcy now, Lizzy? I still maintain he has taken a keen interest in you," said Charlotte.

Elizabeth turned red to the tips of her ears. "Oh, no, Charlotte, I cannot believe it. If Mr. Darcy truly had an interest in me, do you not think he would invent some excuse to extend his visit to Rosings?"

Charlotte considered this and then went back to her embroidery. Elizabeth hoped she had diverted her friend enough to allay her suspicions. Several times during the evening, Elizabeth found her thoughts turning to Mr. Darcy again. Whenever this happened, she put her hand in her pocket to touch the letter, as if to ensure it was real.

After staying up late that evening studying the letter, Elizabeth finally went to bed but slept very little in spite of being emotionally and physically exhausted. The next morning as she lay in bed, she heard a carriage pass by the house. Jumping up and running to the window, she saw the coach with the Darcy livery passing by headed in the direction of the main road. Elizabeth realized she felt both relieved and disappointed.

"It is over," she told herself. "I am grateful I will never have to face him again." At that thought, she sat down on the bed and cried.

Lady Catherine's Company
by Diana Birchall

April 21, 1812

"I hope," sniffed Lady Catherine, "that those young ladies were sensible of the favour we bestowed upon them in the warmth of our farewells."

"Why, Lady Catherine, only you in your modesty could have any doubt in the matter!" enthused Mr. Collins. "How could they be anything but all gratitude? Your graciousness! I am sure my esteemed father-in-law would agree that there were few instances of anything like it, even at the Court."

Lady Catherine smiled benevolently. "But there was one thing – I did wonder, Anne, if you were not a little too warm, too over cordial, at the parting. Actually giving your hand to them both!"

Mr. Collins sighed with admiration. "Miss Anne's condescension was particularly well judging," he said. "As is everything she does. A Miss Anne of Rosings can do no wrong when it comes to manners. She is a perfect lesson-book of them. All young ladies can learn from the manners of the great. Do you not think so, my dear?"

Charlotte looked up from her stitching. She often brought a little piece of embroidery with her on their visits to Rosings. Nothing vulgar, like socks; but Lady Catherine did not object if it was something genteel. She sometimes went so far as to praise Charlotte's industry, though seldom without thinking of something else for her to do. A lace baby's-cap was the appropriate thing to embroider at Rosings; not too high, not too humble.

"I am sure Miss Anne did and said all that was polite," she agreed sedately, "and I know my sister and my friend were very grateful for the kind treatment they received here."

"Grateful!" exclaimed her husband. "I should say so! Nothing can be compared to it. The young ladies to be invited, again and again! Treated to the splendours of Rosings. Such dinners! And not least of all, admitted into the company of such fine gentlemen as Mr. Darcy and Colonel Fitzwilliam. It was a veritable coming-out for Maria; as good as being presented to the Queen."

"And Lizzy enjoyed herself," added Charlotte, more moderately, "she told me she had a very good time."

"Enjoyed herself! As who would not, on being admitted to the privilege of visiting at Rosings."

"I confess," admitted Lady Catherine, "that I feel myself a little dull tonight, without the young ladies, and my nephews. They all seemed to get on very well, I thought. I almost suspected, on one evening, that the dear Colonel admired Miss Bennet a little – but of course, I deceived myself. He is far too sensible."

"Oh surely not," bleated Mr. Collins. "Pray, do not let such a thought enter your head, Lady Catherine. "Our young guests know their place. Miss Elizabeth could never aspire to – that is, the Colonel was only treating her with the extreme graciousness that he shows all the world. A truly knightly spirit. Never was a man with such peculiarly warm, open manners!"

"He does form rather a contrast to Darcy, I admit," said Lady Catherine thoughtfully. "Darcy will sometimes sit for half-an-hour, staring at nothing. When Miss Bennet was playing those rather ill chosen Burns songs, he had his eye very firmly fixed upon the pianoforte, I saw."

"Oh no – oh no," Mr. Collins assured her, "do you not recollect, Lady Catherine, that Miss Anne was on the same side of the room as the piano – I am sure that his looking at the instrument was merely a pretext, so that we would not observe how intent he was in fixing his eyes upon *her*."

"I wish I could think so," said her ladyship, "but I was a trifle disappointed in Darcy, to say the truth. It is time he thought of settling down, you know, and Anne is ready, more than ready. I really thought that this time would be the charm."

"Of course he was charmed with her, never anybody more so, Lady Catherine – he could hardly tear his eyes away from her," assured Mrs. Jenkinson, leaning forward and adjusting Miss de Bourgh's pink headpiece with its silk rose. "I distinctly heard him say that pink was his favorite colour, you know, and he had a great air of meaning as he said it, I do assure you."

Charlotte remembered that Elizabeth had worn pink, but she knew much better than to say so.

"Well. I hope you are right," said Lady Catherine. "The colour did not affix him, but best not to speak of that. I do wish you had talked a bit more, Anne."

"I said everything that I could Mama," she protested, brushing aside Mrs. Jenkinson's tender consoling pats impatiently. "Did not you hear me ask Darcy how he liked going down to Ramsgate last summer, and if it was his favorite watering-place?"

"Yes, you did," Lady Catherine conceded, "and I was rejoiced, for that is a very promising topic, and well thought of. Darcy can be difficult to speak to, you know, with his singular reticence, the reticence of a gentleman; and he seems to require a lively – I thought you did very well, my dear. I was in hopes that he would talk of his knowledge of Weymouth and Worthing, but the subject of Ramsgate did not seem to interest him after all. And yet Georgiana was down there all last summer."

"I think he does not care for watering-places," Charlotte ventured to say. "He said as much, did he not? I thought I heard him."

"He did. He said he could not understand why the English people went to so much trouble to be at noisy sand-infested places where they forgot their morals and were parted from a good deal of money," Anne told her.

"No, that does not sound as if he liked watering-place holidays, Anne, does it. I wonder you could venture upon the topic, if you knew it. Perhaps you had better not, another time," said her mother.

"No, Mama, I won't."

Lady Catherine brightened. "And do not forget, we will have another chance to see Darcy, next month, when we go to London."

"I remember you said you have business in London," Mr. Collins observed. "I hope not of any unpleasant sort."

"Oh no, nothing particular. We will be there only a week, so I can see my man of business, and settle my quarterly accounts. And we shall visit the best mantua-makers while we are in town, to see about Anne's fall wardrobe. Oh, we have a great deal to do!"

"Will Mr. Darcy and Colonel Fitzwilliam also be in London?" asked Charlotte. "I do not know if Elizabeth and her sister Jane will be in town then. They sometimes stay with my uncle's family."

"Oh! But of course we are not likely to meet – This is your uncle who lives in Cheap Street, is not he?"

"Cheapside. He is a very gentleman-like man however."

"But in trade, of course. And the Bennet girls visit him often, do they? I do not know if that is wise, as it will assuredly lessen their chances of meeting a better sort of company. Though, to be sure, they cannot aspire to moving in circles such as Darcy's, in London. Here in the country it is quite a different thing. People do not make those same sorts of distinctions in the country."

"True, true. Ten to one Miss Elizabeth and Maria may never have the honour and distinction of being noticed by your nephews again, Lady Catherine," Mr. Collins bowed toward her, "unless, indeed, that event takes place which we all expect, and the future Mrs. Darcy should be so kind as to invite the girls to Pemberley. But that is far too much to presume. I would think it the greatest privilege of my life, to be invited to see such a place myself; and the young ladies have not the advantage of our intimate acquaintance in your family."

"Indeed you may depend upon it, Mr. Collins," said Lady Catherine condescendingly, "that when my daughter is mistress of Pemberley, you and Mrs. Collins will be very welcome to pay a visit there."

"Thank her ladyship for the compliment, Charlotte! Thank her!" he urged in ecstasy, and Charlotte complied, but in a much more quiet and proper fashion.

"I think even when at Pemberley we should rejoice in having company," sighed Lady Catherine. "We certainly do feel its loss at present."

Darcy Cleanses His Palate
by Abigail Reynolds

April 25, 1812

Georgiana held out a leather-bound volume to him. "The bookseller thought I might enjoy this one."

Darcy took the book and turned the spine up. *The Cottagers of Glen Burnie* by Miss Elizabeth Hamilton. *Elizabeth.* He caught his breath as a stab of pain lanced through him. Could he not even put her from his mind for a few minutes while visiting a bookshop with Georgiana? Why did she have to haunt his every thought?

He knew he would forget her eventually, or at least stop remembering her a thousand times a day, but how long would it take? When his father had died, it had been months before he could go an hour without remembering his loss, but surely an acquaintance of a few months could in no way to compare to a beloved father. *Except that Elizabeth is still alive and thinks ill of you,* his conscience reminded him, *and she humiliated you, which your father never did. How many people has she told of your proposal, laughing all the time at your foolishness?* The familiar surge of sick anger was back until he remembered he was being unfair. She had humiliated him, yes, but he had never known her to mock someone when they were not present to defend themselves. How she had teased him during her stay at Netherfield, and how it had delighted him, never imagining there was bitterness behind her arch tones!

"Brother? Fitzwilliam, are you ill?"

He glanced down to see Georgiana's delicate hand balanced on his arm. Georgiana, who had also been taken in by that devil Wickham! How delighted George Wickham would be if he knew his efforts had cost Darcy the woman he loved. Perhaps he already knew. Perhaps Elizabeth had not believed his letter and had confided in that scoundrel once more. Darcy cleared his throat. "I am quite well, dearest, merely lost in thought."

"You do not look well." Now even Georgiana was fretting over him, just like everyone else. His cousin Richard demanding to know what was bothering him. His aunt sweetly asking whether something was troubling him. His fencing instructor shouting at him in his heavy French accent *Non, Monsieur Darcy! What is wrong with you? That is an epee, not a pig-sticker!* Even his damned valet pestered him a dozen times a day whether there was not something else he required.

"Perhaps a little tired, but nothing more. I think Miss Hamilton's book will be an excellent choice for you. She is quite erudite; her *Letters on Education* made an excellent case for reforming the way we view education." Miss *Elizabeth* Hamilton. A woman of intelligence, integrity and decided opinions, just like his Elizabeth. Dear God, how could she have refused him? All those hundreds of times when he had imagined himself heroically overcoming his dangerous attraction to her, and when he finally gave in, she had refused *him*. And refused him cruelly – there had been no polite "thank you for the compliment of your attentions, but my heart is given elsewhere" for Elizabeth. No, she had to tell him he was the last man in the world she could be prevailed upon to marry. And she seemed to think *he* had been unkind to her! How hypocritical to accuse him of cruelty when she could give lessons on the subject!

Georgiana's face cleared. "I am a bit fatigued myself, since we returned home so late from the theatre last night. But what an amazing performance it was!"

Darcy could not have said for certain whether the play had been good or bad, or even if it had been in English. His mind had stopped paying attention when he saw the play's title. *The Hypocrite.* Yes, that was him, counseling Bingley against allying himself with Miss Bennet and then making an offer himself for her younger sister. Perhaps Elizabeth's refusal was his celestial punishment for hypocrisy. But damn it, he had been right to advise Bingley to forget Jane Bennet! The reason he deserved punishment was for forgetting to apply that lesson to himself. But oh, what a cruel punishment it had been! And then, after the play, he had gone home to his empty bed, the one he would never share with Elizabeth. Damn her for being so bewitching and so hard-hearted!

She had been so gentle and caring to her ill sister. Her playing and singing had a warmth that stirred his heart. He had seen her concern for others a dozen times. But to him she suddenly become a virago, calling him proud, conceited, and selfish, when all he wanted was her smiles, her tenderness, her fine eyes shining at him. Elizabeth had not hidden any of her scorn for him. He flinched away from the thought that insisted on intruding, asking *why* she had felt that scorn.

She saw things differently than he did. She had claimed her sister was in love with Bingley; he would have sworn her sister indifferent to his friend. What did she see in *him* to make her decide he was insufferable? His head ached, and he longed for the comfort of his favorite leather chair in the quiet of his study, a glass of brandy beside him. No, that was a lie; what he longed for was Elizabeth, for her arms around him, soothing him, telling him she understood she had been mistaken, that she believed his explanations, that a future between them was still possible.

He realized Georgiana was looking at him oddly. "I will have them wrap this up. Would you like to stop at Gunter's on the way home for an ice?" It was her favorite treat; he needed to know he could at least make Georgiana happy.

She smiled shyly and put her arm through his. "I would like that very much, if you are not too tired."

"An ice is precisely what I need to refresh me," he said firmly. It was not true. Elizabeth was what he needed, but all that was available to him was a frozen sweet that would melt away to nothing in his mouth.

Lydia Bennet Has Something to Say!
by Susan Mason-Milks

May 8, 1812

Lydia Bennet's moods were as changeable as…well…changeable as the spring weather. In the vast experience of her fifteen years, if she had learned one thing, it was the wisdom of never dwelling too long on anything unpleasant. This time, however, she simply could not shake off the despair that came along with the latest gossip from Meryton. Two days ago, Lydia had learned the militia would be removing to Brighton in a few weeks, and she was absolutely convinced her whole world was coming to an end.

Walking along on her way to Meryton, she thought about how the winter months in Hertfordshire had been made exceedingly enjoyable by the presence of all the lively, young militia officers with their dashing red coats. Now they were ruining everything! She kicked a stone in the road to emphasize her disappointment. Who would she flirt with? Who would she tease? All the local young men were as dull as rocks, but the regiment was full of handsome, fun-loving officers like Lt. Denny, Lt. Kendall, Lt. Jameson, and of course, Lt. Wickham. The others were charming, but Wickham was… He was delicious. She grinned as she thought about him.

Ah, George Wickham! Just saying his name gave her a little thrill. When first he arrived last fall, Lydia's sister Elizabeth had caught his eye. Much to Lydia's delight, this spring with Lizzy away visiting Charlotte in Kent, he had turned more of his attentions her way. In her opinion, no one was as handsome or as clever as Wickham. No one was more elegant or lighter on his feet on the dance floor, and no one made her laugh as much as Wickham.

Today, she was on her way to visit with her dear friend Harriet Forster. Since Harriet's husband was the commander of the militia, she would be going to Brighton, too. It did not bear thinking about. In Harriet, Lydia had found a kindred spirit, someone who loved to laugh as much as she did. Lydia tried to find comfort that they would be able to enjoy a few more afternoons of lovely gossip before her friend left forever.

Knocking on the door of the Forsters' house, Lydia was admitted and shown into a small parlor. When Harriet saw her friend, she put aside her sewing. Immediately, they began sharing funny stories, talking about the attractive physical attributes of particular members of the regiment, all the while giggling as they always did when they were together.

"Oh, Lydia, my dear friend," said Harriet, wiping the tears of laughter from her eyes. "I am so pleased you are here. We always have such fun. How dull it is just sitting here and sewing. Truly, I was beginning to go mad with boredom. The most exciting thing I have done all day is choosing colors of thread. Is that not sad?" She held up the handkerchief she was embroidering and waved it in the air.

"Not as sad as the fact that very soon you will be gone, and I will never see you again. Oh, Harriet, I do not know how I will ever survive the loss! When you leave, Meryton will return to being the dreariest place in England." By now her smile had turned to a frown.

"Then I have news which should cheer you. We may not be parted so soon after all."

Lydia looked up hopefully at her friend. "Do not tease me."

"I told the Colonel I could not bear to be all alone in a new place with no friends around me." Harriet reached over and squeezed Lydia's arm. "He has given his permission for me to ask you to accompany us to Brighton for the summer as my special companion. Lydia, say you will come. We shall have such a grand time together!"

Throwing her arms around her friend, Lydia squealed, "Oh, dear Harriet, there is nothing in the whole entire world I would like more."

Then standing up, Lydia pulled Harriet to her feet, and they began to dance around the parlor chanting, "Oh, what joy! What joy! We are off to Brighton!"

Finally, out of breath, they collapsed back on the settee and started making plans. They talked at the same time, finished each other's sentences, and laughed about the grand time they would have together.

"You do think your parents will give their permission for you to come with us?" Harriet asked.

"Oh, la! Of course, they will," said Lydia with a wave of her hand. "My mother will think it a wonderful idea because it may help me catch a husband in a beautiful red coat." She grinned wickedly. "Mama has a partiality for red coats, you know."

"And your father? Will he approve?"

"Oh, do not worry about Papa. If he has any objections, Mama and I will wear him down quick enough. He is never able to resist a little pouting and a few tears."

The two friends spent the remainder of the afternoon dreaming of all the parties and balls they would attend in Brighton, and as they were nearly the same size, they talked of the gowns they would lend each other. Suddenly, there was so much to do – ribbons to buy, hats to decorate, and trunks to be packed.

On the walk back to Longbourn, Lydia's feet scarcely touched the ground. Her head overflowed with thoughts of all the handsome young officers she would flirt with and of one particular officer whom she liked best of all.

"I am going to Brighton! I am going to Brighton!" she chanted as she skipped along. How she would enjoy lording this special invitation over her sisters! Yes, things were looking up indeed.

What Was Wickham Thinking?
by Shannon Winslow

May 21, 1812

He was by no means discouraged. Mary King may have slipped through his fingers, but what did it matter? There were plenty more fish in the sea. And after all, it would have been selling himself pretty cheap to settle for a freckled face with only ten thousand pounds. He could… he would… do better in the end for being rid of her.

In the meantime, it might be entertaining to renew his flirtation with the intriguing Elizabeth Bennet. He'd had the girl fairly eating out of his hand before she went to Kent and, with any luck, absence had made that naïve young heart grow even fonder of him.

Marrying Miss Bennet was still out of the question, of course, but bedding her was not. In fact, it would be just the thing to cheer him. A little flattery, a few of his boyish smiles, charm skillfully and liberally applied, and she would be his. The juicy peach was clearly ripe for the picking, and who was better equipped to do it properly?

Such were George Wickham's contemplations upon learning that Elizabeth Bennet had returned to the neighborhood. But a fortnight later, after having been frequently in company together, precious little headway had he made with her despite all his varied and strenuous exertions.

Mr. Wickham was now to see Elizabeth for perhaps the final time. On the very last day of the regiment's remaining in Meryton, he dined with the others of the officers at Longbourn. Although he had nearly given up on the idea of an actual conquest (the time for that sort of thing running perilously short), he fully intended that

Elizabeth should be excessively sorry to see him go all the same. And once he was away, she would no doubt repine, sorely regretting having kept him at arm's length.

After dinner, Mr. Wickham adeptly drew her aside and launched his closing campaign to win her over. By way of striking on a new topic – one which he hoped would cast him in a favorably light – he remarked, "You have become quite the traveler, Miss Bennet – now bound for the lake country and only just returned from Kent. Did your time pass agreeably in Hunsford?"

"Yes, it was very pleasant indeed to be reunited with my dear friend Charlotte."

"And Mr. Collins too?" He grinned conspiratorially. "I am thinking that, after a few days, the proportions and conversation of the parsonage must have proved... a little confining, shall we say?" Surely, he thought, she could not help but appreciate the contrast with their own lively banter over the course of their acquaintance.

"Not at all, sir, since we were rarely restricted to the parsonage. I am happy to report that we enjoyed a very frequent intercourse with the inhabitants of Rosings Park whilst I was there – a blessing of which very few could boast."

Wickham looked at Elizabeth quizzically. "Forgive me, but I would hardly have expected you to find Lady Catherine's conversation to your taste."

"Oh, but I do not refer to Lady Catherine alone. Did I not tell you that Mr. Darcy and Colonel Fitzwilliam were visiting there as well?"

Momentarily taken aback, Wickham recovered his composure soon enough. "No, I don't believe you mentioned that fact."

"Are you much acquainted with the colonel, Mr. Wickham?" Elizabeth continued with a glint in her eye. "I suppose you must have seen him very often at Pemberley as you were all growing up together."

"Quite true," he admitted, although he did not like the turn the conversation had taken... or the amused look on Miss Bennet's face. Could she possibly know something, he wondered. But then, with a moment's recollection and a returning smile, he replied, "I have not seen much of him in recent years, as you might well imagine. However, I believe him to be a very gentlemanly man. How did you like him?"

"Very much indeed! In fact, I believe I have rarely met with a man that I liked better, or whose sound judgment I could depend upon so completely. I found him to be kind, generous, and entirely trustworthy. He was designated Miss Georgiana Darcy's guardian, you know, and I think there can be no finer testimony to Colonel Fitzwilliam's character than that."

Wickham noticed that the room had suddenly grown overly warm. He could feel sweat beginning to bead on his forehead, and the collar of his military jacket drew curiously tighter and tighter round his throat. Affecting an air of indifference, he asked, "How long did you say that he was at Rosings?"

Her spirited report quite alarmed him. It sounded as if Miss Bennet had spent the better part of three weeks in the man's company, talking in depth about all manner of subjects. How near their conversations might have come to his own private concerns, Wickham could only guess. Elizabeth's way of speaking seemed intentionally designed to torment him with uncertainty, to leave him dangling on tenterhooks. Had she really learned all his secrets? He shuddered at the thought.

When Elizabeth's animated narrative moved on to Mr. Darcy and her improved opinion of him, Wickham's uneasiness only increased. There was a something in her countenance which made him listen with an apprehensive and anxious attention.

How he answered her, Wickham hardly knew. Although deeply shaken, his self-command and polished manners did not desert him. He covered his embarrassment as well as he might and carried on, ending with an undeniably handsome speech:

"You, Miss Bennet, who so well know my feelings towards Mr. Darcy, will readily comprehend how sincerely I must rejoice that he is wise enough to assume even the appearance of what is right. His pride, in that direction, may be of service, if not to himself, to many others, for it must deter him from such foul misconduct as I have suffered by."

He was careful that the last words were accompanied by an appropriately sorrowful bearing and the slightest quavering of his voice. Yet these tried and true tactics proved singularly ineffectual on this occasion. Wickham could see at once that he had failed to excite the lady's sympathies over his longstanding grievances, as he had so effortlessly done in the past.

Clearly, Elizabeth had changed... towards himself anyway, and those she saw at Hunsford had the blame for it. That he should have lost the devotion of this prized pearl was something he could learn to live with. Knowing his defeat had apparently come at the hands of his old nemesis was quite another thing.

Wickham waited, but Elizabeth ignored the invitation to indulge in what had formerly been their favorite topic. Instead, by the curl of her lip and the way she tilted her head to one side, she seemed to be mocking him.

Enough! He refused to demean himself by lingering any longer only to be suspected and ridiculed by this impertinent chit, desirable as she might otherwise be. He excused himself from her presence at once and made no further attempt to distinguish her that night. If there were any justice in the world, the means to even the score would one day come his way. If so, he surely would not pass them by. Until such time, however, he very much hoped never to see Elizabeth Bennet's face again.

Darcy Attempts to Forget Elizabeth Bennet - Part 1 by Regina Jeffers

June 12, 1812

"I am pleased you have come so quickly, Edward," Georgiana said as she served his tea.

"Your note said it was important," he teased with a bemused smirk. The colonel could not remember a time his cousin had ever thought to consult with him on matters concerning her brother's state of mind. His Georgiana had known her own tribulations. George Wickham, a man Edward Fitzwilliam had never liked, had attempted to seduce the innocent Georgiana and to arrange an elopement. Thankfully, Darcy had arrived in time to thwart the scoundrel's plans. However, for many months following that incident, Georgiana had suffered from a lack of confidence, but her demand that he call upon her perhaps signaled a turn for the better.

"I pray I did not interfere with your duties or your personal life," she said contritely, but her countenance spoke of an emotion he could not identify.

Edward sipped the tea. "I am at your disposal, Cousin. Mayhap you should explain your concerns and then permit me to draw my own conclusions."

Georgiana squared her shoulders. She bit her bottom lip in hesitation, but she said, "I likely am making a misstep, but I must know whether the foul mood that has consumed Fitzwilliam of late has something to do with my earlier indiscretion. I could not bear it if my brother had not forgiven me."

Edward's frown crinkled his forehead. "I am certain Darcy would never believe what happened between you and Mr. Wickham to be of your doing." Even saying the miscreant's name left a foul taste in Edward's mouth. "Would you explain what changes you have noted in my cousin's demeanor that brings on your alarm?"

Georgiana sighed heavily. Her voice broke ever so slightly, a poignant, telling little break. "I pray my estimation of Fitzwilliam's melancholy does not prove true. My brother often locks himself into his study, even sleeping on the chaise in the room. During those long hours, he only opens the door to Mr. Norton, who serves Fitzwilliam a decanter of brandy. He ignores estate business, and I cannot remember the last time we spent time together." Warmth burned a path across her cheekbones.

A protective urge swept through him: He caught the pain underscoring her words. "What you describe is most unusual. Darcy is normally most conscientious. I cannot imagine my cousin acting thusly." Edward had his own suspicions. "Has Darcy spoken of problems at Pemberley?"

"No, nothing," she assured. "I have hinted to my brother's steward and to his man of business, and they both assure me Pemberley thrives under Fitzwilliam's hand."

It was Edward's turn to hesitate. "Perhaps I should stay to supper. It would provide me the opportunity to observe my cousin."

Her hold on the teacup relaxed. "Thank you, Edward."

Darcy's haggard looks had shocked Edward, and Darcy's reserve, even with his relatives, spoke chapters. "Fitz," Edward began tentatively. "I thought you might want to know that Miss Elizabeth is in Town." Edward had noted Darcy's animation whenever they encountered the lovely Miss Elizabeth Bennet at Hunsford. He suspected his cousin had formed a *tendre* for the woman.

Edward watched as Darcy's whole being reflected his discomposure. "Miss Elizabeth, you say? Pray tell where you encountered the lady in London."

362

He could easily read his cousin's expression, and Edward could hear the feigned nonchalance in Darcy's voice. His cousin had more interest in the lady than he portrayed. "I did not speak to her directly. She, Miss Lucas, another young lady fair of countenance, and an older couple were in a drapers shop in Pall Mall, near Harding and Howell, Tuesday last. I had just completed another round of training for some new recruits and was not presentable to greet her party properly. I assumed, Cousin, that you would know of Miss Bennet's itinerary."

"I am not one of Miss Elizabeth's intimates," Darcy snapped. They sat in silence for several minutes. Darcy downed a large glass of brandy. "The mercantile district, you say?" His cousin's voice had softened.

"From the window, I observed the lady had chosen a fine lace, even returning to it several times, but Miss Elizabeth did not purchase the item." Edward shared conspiratorially. "I thought you might be interested."

"Miss Elizabeth is of no consequence to me," Darcy announced as he stood. "Edward, I have some estate matters to address. If you will excuse me, I will retire to my study. Please enjoy Georgiana's company. She deserves someone more cordial than I have been of late." With that, his cousin strode from the room.

Pausing long enough for Darcy's footsteps to announce his retreat, Georgiana whispered, "Miss Elizabeth Bennet? The one from Hertfordshire?"

Edward nodded his affirmation. "I believe your brother has a broken heart," he shared privately.

"Oh, my!" Georgiana gasped. "I would never have suspected as such. Fitzwilliam has shunned the advances of so many women among the ton. I never thought he might prefer a country miss."

Edward smiled knowingly, "I doubt Fitz had any knowledge of his own vulnerability." He assisted Georgiana to her feet. They turned their steps toward the drawing room. "The problem lies in the fact Miss Elizabeth does not welcome your brother's attentions."

Georgiana shook her head. "How is that possible? Cannot Miss Elizabeth see that Fitzwilliam is the most honorable of men?"

He considered the problem for a moment. Edward explained, "Darcy's stubborn nature and his heightened need for privacy can often be misinterpreted. Miss Elizabeth's exuberance is a sharp contrast to Darcy's silence. I doubt if the lady realizes your brother could be a counterweight to her impulsivity."

"Are matters of the heart always so convoluted?" she asked innocently. "If so, I may consider a nunnery."

Edward caught her hand and brought it to his lips. "That would be a crime against nature. Someday, you will find the perfect match, and I will toast your happiness."

Several hours later, Edward knocked lightly at Darcy's study door, but no response came from within. He rapped louder the second time before he opened the door to peer in. His eyes fell to the papers resting on the floor; then he spied Darcy slumped over his desk, the remnants of a glass of brandy clutched tightly in his cousin's hand. Edward eased the door closed behind him. "Just as I suspected," he said under his breath. The smell of stale cigar smoke and spilled alcohol filled the space. The colonel had assisted more than one of his military acquaintances in similar situations, but to discover Darcy as such was disconcerting. He could not recall a time when Fitzwilliam Darcy allowed himself to lose control. "Come Cousin." He slid an arm under Darcy's to lift his cousin to his feet. "Permit me to assist you to your chambers."

"Ah, Edward." Darcy swayed as he stood. "My good cousin. Have I ever told you how jealous I am of you?" Darcy slurred his words.

"Why, Darcy?" Edward positioned his cousin's arm around his shoulder. "You have so much more than I."

"You could have had Miss Elizabeth," Darcy declared. Slouching, Darcy's whole composure crumbled. "The lady enjoyed your company so much more than mine."

Edward assisted Darcy to a nearby chair. At Rosings Park, the colonel had witnessed Darcy's vying for Elizabeth Bennet's attentions, but even he remained uncertain as to the extent of Darcy's feelings. Earlier, he had told Georgiana Darcy's heart was engaged; yet, he had said so for Georgiana's sake. In truth, he had wondered if his cousin had simply wished a seduction rather than a commitment. Despite her affability, one part of the colonel thought Darcy deserved better than Miss Elizabeth, a woman with little to offer a man of Darcy's stature. Therefore, he tested Darcy's purpose. "Miss Elizabeth has her charms, but, as you kindly noted, her connections are low. I cannot imagine anyone of our acquaintance aligning himself with the likes of Miss Bennet. The lady possesses no qualities to deem her a suitable match."

Although he was deeply intoxicated, Darcy still had taken the bait. Edward's words incensed his cousin. Darcy pulled himself up straight and spoke with indignation. "Sir, I will beg you not to speak so of Miss Elizabeth. Your censure is most unwelcome."

Edward's smile went unnoticed by Darcy as the man collapsed into the colonel's arms. "I apologize, Cousin," he began. "Permit me to call for some coffee. Then perhaps you can speak of Miss Elizabeth's many allurements."

Clinging to Edward, Darcy lurched forward. Reaching for the chair's arm, he fell heavily into the seat. "Elizabeth Bennet is an incomparable woman, and I am the last man in the world she could be prevailed upon to marry." Thus said, Darcy passed out from the effort. Interest piqued, Edward set himself the task of discovering the depth of Darcy's regard for the woman.

It had taken more coffee and more time than he had anticipated, but Edward managed to bring Darcy around to some semblance of his former self. Darcy sat with his head in his hands and elbows propped upon his knees. It was very late, but Edward pressed on. "Cousin, we should speak earnestly. You have become a shadow of the person you once were; you withdraw from Georgiana and from your acquaintances; your work remains untouched on your desk; and you made a reference to Miss Elizabeth that we should address."

Darcy sat up and looked vaguely about him. "I suppose I owe you some sort of an explanation, but I am uncertain I can speak the words."

"It is Georgiana to whom you owe an explanation. Have you not noticed your sister blames herself for your current misery? She believes she disappoints you."

"How is that so?" his cousin began, but the realization crossed Darcy's countenance. "I have wounded someone I love dearly."

Edward accused, "You have given Elizabeth Bennet your heart?"

Darcy said reluctantly, "Am I that obvious?"

"Fitz, we have been more than cousins. You are more of a brother to me than is Roland." Darcy chuckled, then winced, as he acknowledged Edward's words. "I realized before we journeyed to Rosings that you held an interest in Elizabeth Bennet. When the great Fitzwilliam Darcy mentions a woman twice, I notice. When he mentions her repeatedly, I know something is amiss."

"Miss Elizabeth holds me in contempt; she said as much when I offered her everything I had," Darcy confessed.

"Elizabeth Bennet refused you? This cannot be." He thought to give Darcy hope for a resolution. "You are perfect for each other. The woman makes you laugh, Fitz; no one has ever made you laugh." Darcy smiled easily. His cousin, obviously, enjoyed the image. "Darcy, you must tell me what happened."

"Mr. Wickham poisoned the lady's mind. I am lost to Miss Elizabeth," Darcy moaned. "Plus, in my pomposity, I injured Miss Elizabeth by hurting her sister."

"How could you have offered the elder Miss Bennet an offense?"

"Do you recall my bragging about separating Bingley from an inappropriate connection?"

"Not Miss Elizabeth's sister!"

366

"Unfortunately," Darcy confessed.

The muscles along his jaw twitched. "Darcy, I fear Miss Elizabeth heard of your perfidy from my lips. No wonder the lady suddenly took ill that day in the park."

"Do not concern yourself, Cousin. I realized from whom Miss Elizabeth heard the news before we took our leave of her at Rosings. Elizabeth Bennet would have discovered my deceit sooner or later; she is a clever woman. Miss Elizabeth settled against me before I convinced Bingley to leave Netherfield; I treated her poorly, and then professed my love for her; my duplicity only encouraged her scorn."

"Then I am to assume you actually offered Miss Elizabeth your hand in marriage?"

Darcy hesitated. "I did request Miss Elizabeth's assent, but I fear I did not articulate my intentions well. I planned what I wished to say, but in the lady's presence, my mind could not recall the words I wished her to know."

Edward chuckled, "What, may I ask, did you say?"

"I explained the torment of my decision, my qualms about her lack of connections, and the impropriety shown by her family…"

Edward laughed loudly as he refilled his cousin's cup. "Only you, Cousin, would tell a woman you loved her by telling her how repugnant you found her family. Is it not surprising Miss Elizabeth did not find this endearing?"

A sough escaped Darcy's throat, and he buried his face in his hands. "It appears," he said at last, "I have been a simpleton when it come to Elizabeth Bennet; my folly does not speak well of my intentions, does it?"

"Men, in love, are often foolhardy," Edward added quietly. "Let us finish this tomorrow. Do you think you can make it to your chambers?"

Darcy nodded his compliance. The colonel rang for Henry's assistance, and together they managed to maneuver Darcy safely to his bed. Henry departed to prepare a room for Edward. Thinking

Darcy's labored breathing indicated his cousin had found sleep, Edward moved quietly to the door. However, a muffled call from Darcy stayed Edward's retreat. "Colonel, which shop in the mercantile district did Miss Elizabeth frequent?"

"Concern not yourself," Edward assured as he took several steps in the direction of the bed. "I will send a servant around tomorrow for the lace. Some day you will present it to Miss Elizabeth as a symbol of your regard for her." Darcy's arm waved his acceptance of Edward's suggestion, and the colonel slipped from the room.

Darcy Attempts to Forget Elizabeth Bennet - Part 2
by Regina Jeffers

June 13, 1812

"So, Darcy, where do you go from here?"

The words choked him, but he managed to say, "I know my duty; the Darcy name and Pemberley must survive. I must forget Elizabeth Bennet and find a suitable match. I am a rich man, and I will settle upon an appropriate woman as soon as I am tempted by her charms. I am ready to marry with all speed; I have a heart prepared to accept the attentions of the first pleasing woman to come my way." Excepting Elizabeth Bennet. This was his only secret exception to his declarations. "A woman with a little beauty and some words of flattery will have me as her own, whether she be fifteen or thirty or somewhere in between. I am perfectly prepared to make a foolish match."

"Then you mean to have our cousin Anne?" Edward questioned.

"As much as I respect and admire Anne," Darcy said seriously, "she is not the woman I envision as the mistress of Pemberley. Despite Lady Catherine's wishes, Anne will not be the object of my search. Even with Miss Elizabeth's refusal," he added hastily. "The woman I want will possess a handsome countenance, a lilt figure, and a quickness of mind. I must find a woman who can assist me in the running of Pemberley. Her character must be an adventurous one; she must not be easily intimated. I may choose to settle for something a bit less, but I will not compromise my standards; I have thought on this for a long time."

Later, Darcy found Georgiana in the music room. She was listlessly stroking the keys of the pianoforte. His sister sprang to her feet when he entered the room. Darcy purposely strode toward her, took her hand, and said, "Come with me, Georgiana; we must speak honestly."

Darcy hated how she tentatively followed him across the room to a settee. He despised how his actions of late had affected her. Even after they were well settled, he did not release her hand. Apparently fearing his disappointment, she sat with eyes downcast; yet, he would have none of it. Darcy cupped her chin gently with his fingers and lifted it to where he might look lovingly upon her countenance. "Georgiana, my girl," he said softly. "I have dealt you a disservice, and I beg your forgiveness. You did not deserve the treatment you have received at my hand of late."

Uncontrollably, the tears rolled down his sister's cheeks, and Darcy reached up to gently brush them away; she caught his hand to kiss his palm. "Fitzwilliam, you have never forgiven any fault of your own while you have forgiven many of those around you, especially me." He started to protest, but she shushed him with a touch of her finger to his lips. "Please, allow me to finish. You have always been available when I required your attention. You have accepted my sorrow and made it your own. Edward spoke of your hopes and your loss. It would do me proud to offer you my support in your time of need."

He protested, "I could not impose on your sensibilities. Our father left you in my care."

"No, Fitzwilliam," she contradicted him. "Our father left you as my guardian, but we are to care for each other. How can you know pain without my feeling it?" Darcy could not comprehend his sister's transformation; she was still the shy, innocent girl he had always cherished, but she had developed an emotional strength of which he was not aware before now. He could never think of George Wickham's betrayal without loathing, but his sister had added a new sense of maturity because of the experience. Regrettably, Georgiana had known the rebukes of love. "Our parents were of superior birth," she continued. "We learned to be proud of being a Darcy, but we have not learned to acknowledge the true worth of others. Mrs. Annesley has given me a 'mother's' view of the world. Oh, Fitzwilliam, there are so many who require our generosity; aiding the poor in Derbyshire is persuading me to care more for myself. If we do not love ourselves, my Brother, how may we expect others to love us?"

"When did you become so wise?" he whispered hoarsely and stroked her hair from her countenance.

"You taught me these things, Fitzwilliam. You simply never listened to your own lessons," she giggled.

"Today, you are the instructor and I, the student." He pulled her to him in a tight embrace. "And I welcome more of your teachings."

Attempting to forget Elizabeth Bennet and Hertfordshire, Darcy threw himself into London's society. He became a regular at his gentleman's club; he escorted Georgiana to concerts and the theatre; he dined with old acquaintances and made new ones. Yet, try as he may, it was too soon for him to forget Miss Elizabeth. Darcy acknowledged, if only to himself, that he could truly love none but her. She could not be replaced in his mind as the woman he was meant to love; he would never find her equal. Unconsciously, he vowed to remain constant to Elizabeth Bennet. He had meant to forget her, and he had honestly believed it possible. He had told himself that he held no preference, but, as the days passed, he accepted the fact that she had wounded his pride. That he was only angry. Angry at her for refusing him and at himself for making a cake of the Darcy name. Elizabeth Bennet's character became fixed in his mind as perfection itself; at Hertfordshire, he had learnt to do her justice, and at Hunsford, he had begun to understand himself.

In his attempts, attempts of angry pride, to attach himself to another, he had felt it to be impossible. He could not forget the perfect excellence of Elizabeth Bennet's mind or the way she possessed him. From her, he had learned the steadiness of principle, and Darcy had to admit to admiring the way she had withstood his arguments in her defense of George Wickham.

"Of course, I would prefer the lady had not placed her trust in Mr. Wickham, but I understand if I had opened myself to her prior to when I thought to propose, mayhap, Mr. Wickham's perfidy would not have taken root in Miss Elizabeth's sensibility," he had shared with his image in his dressing room mirror. "I would like to believe a different outcome possible if I had come to this knowledge sooner."

Reluctantly, Darcy admitted to himself that his desire to protect Bingley had not really been for altruistic reasons. "If I had truly cared for Bingley's future, I would not have abandoned my objections to the Bennet family's connections in order to secure my own happiness," he said to the darkness encompassing his chambers. "It is difficult to acknowledge my motives were quite selfish. If I could not attain Miss Elizabeth's affections, I had to make a choice, and I chose to keep Bingley's friendship. In reality, I could never remain Bingley's friend if he married Miss Bennet. Seeing their happiness would remind me too much of what I had lost." It was a sobering realization for a man who prided himself on his earnest regard for Charles Bingley.

"The problem lies in what is my duty to my family line," he grumbled over his solitary breakfast. "If I yield to what most declare to be my duty, and I marry a woman who is indifferent, all risk would be incurred and all duty violated."

Unable to place his heart in the pursuit of a proper companion, Darcy abandoned the farce and prepared for an early retreat to Pemberley. Both he and Georgiana accepted the need for solitude. Darcy would care for his estate and wait for acceptance to come; Georgiana would continue the journey upon which she had recently set her feet. She would find a means to know contentment through selfless acts. Together, they would safeguard each other's love.

A few evenings prior to their departure, Edward returned to assess Darcy's progress. While Georgiana and Mrs. Annesley prepared to entertain them in the music room, Darcy and the colonel lingered in the dining room.

"Am I to understand you have been to Kent?" Darcy asked as he poured them both a brandy.

"Yes, and our aunt was most insistent I relay her anxiousness for your return to Rosings Park," Edward explained.

"I will not be fulfilling our aunt's wishes," Darcy said dismally. "When I marry, our cousin Anne will not be my choice for mistress of Pemberley."

"Lady Catherine will not take your obstinate refusal straightforwardly," Edward said.

"Hopefully, the family will support my decision," Darcy said uneasily. Family meant Edward's father, the Earl of Matlock, and his older cousin, Edward's brother Roland.

"The Earl knows how best to handle our aunt's contentious ways," Edward assured. They sat in companionable silence for several minutes, before the colonel ventured. "I do bring news from Kent, but I dare not speak of Mrs. Collins's friend."

Hoping to belie his interest in the subject, Darcy fixed his countenance. "Edward, you may speak Elizabeth Bennet's name; I cannot avoid the lady forever; my most excellent friend lets an estate in Hertfordshire; her best friend is married to Lady Catherine's cleric; I must harden myself to Miss Elizabeth's memory and to my former feelings." When the colonel continued to delay, Darcy sighed heavily, "Out with it, Man!"

With a shrug of his shoulders, Edward said, "Anne shared some news of Miss Elizabeth that she had learned from her companion, Mrs. Jenkinson. One afternoon, our cousin and I were having our own amusement at Mr. Collins's expense." Darcy rolled his eyes at the mention of Mr. Collins. The man was a complete nincompoop. "Did you know, Fitz, prior to marrying Miss Lucas that Mr. Collins proposed to Miss Elizabeth? Evidently, that was the day after Mr. Bingley's ball at Netherfield." Just the mention of the ball brought exquisite memories; holding Miss Elizabeth's hand and staring into her eyes were some of his fondest memories of the woman. "Miss Elizabeth's mother demanded the lady save the family estate by marrying Collins; Mr. Bennet refused to force his daughter into the marriage. The Bennet estate is entailed upon Mr. Collins. We wondered how Collins had come to marry Miss Lucas. It makes so much sense in hindsight. Can you imagine Miss Elizabeth's vitality in the hands of a superfluous arse such as Collins?"

He attempted to downplay his reaction, but the thought of Collins kissing Elizabeth and taking husbandly privileges with her caused Darcy to redden with abhorrence. A shudder of disdain shook him to his core. He had not taken more than one drink since the night he had confessed everything to his cousin, but he did not think all the brandy in his cellars would deaden the distaste filling his soul. With irony, he said, "It does not make me happy to know the lady places me in company with our aunt's clergyman. She has refused two proposals of marriage. That is quite incomparable."

"One would think Miss Elizabeth's lack of a dowry would have the lady accepting any appropriate offer," Edward reason. "Refusing Mr. Collins is understandable. The man would smother Miss Elizabeth's spirit. But to refuse a man of your standing, Darcy, is not to be reasoned."

Darcy swallowed hard. "The lady wishes a love match," he said softly.

Georgiana's musical interlude was as superb as ever, but all Darcy could see were Elizabeth's eyes and her smile and how the images faded whenever he reached for them.

Lydia Attends a Ball
by Susan Adriani

June 28, 1812

By eight o'clock in the evening the most majestic ballroom in Brighton was heaving with ivory-skirted ladies and red-coated officers. They adorned every corner of the place, lingering and laughing, dining and dancing. In the thick of things was none other than Lydia Bennet, her head thrown back in laughter, Harriet Forster, wife of Colonel Forster and Lydia's particular friend, laughed uproariously at her side.

Never in her fifteen years had Lydia had so much fun. Ever since the Forsters' carriage rolled into Brighton she had done precisely what her mother had instructed her to do: enjoyed herself at every opportunity. And how could she not? There were parties and assemblies held every other night, not to mention officers as far as the eye could see, many of whom, she could not help but notice, appeared to notice her as well.

The orchestra began to play a lively air and Lieutenant Denny stepped forward, an engaging smirk on his face as he addressed her. "Miss Lydia, I do believe you promised this particular dance to me."

With a laugh, Lydia offered him her hand. "Lord, I almost forgot! I cannot recall ever having my dance card so full."

"If you will permit me," Denny replied, tilting his head closer to her own, "you do look particularly lovely tonight, Miss Lydia. It is no wonder you are so much in demand."

Lydia grinned with satisfaction as her partner led her to the center of the room, where countless other couples were taking their places and making their way down the dance. Her fingertips fluttered along the lace trimming her rather daring décolleté. She could not help but notice Denny's eyes followed her movements, lingering appreciatively at the swell of her bosom.

Lydia wanted to laugh. *I daresay Denny is right. I do look lovely this evening, especially since he and half the officers in the room can hardly keep their eyes from me! Why, I must look even lovelier than Jane, for I doubt her bosom would fill this bodice half as well as mine does. Lord, I hope no one notices the lace on my gown is not genuine Belgian lace!*

Dancing with Denny was just as gratifying as dancing with every other officer who partnered her. Each man looked dashing in his regimentals; each claimed her hand most eagerly, full of warm looks and flattering words. At the end of each set, each officer returned her to her smirking friend, offering to fetch refreshments for the ladies, for both must surely be parched after dancing so energetically all evening. Lydia and Harriet watched them go, admiring the set of their shoulders and the pleasant way their muscular legs filled out their breeches, their voices carrying a bit more with each cup of punch they consumed. There was much giggling to be had between the two ladies, and many sly looks exchanged between the officers as they attended them.

In this manner did Lydia enjoy herself for the duration of the evening, but her most gratifying partner, by far, was George Wickham. It was not that he had paid her prettier compliments than the other men she danced with at the ball, but the fact that he had singled her out at all. She had admired him exceedingly in Hertfordshire, for, in her opinion, George Wickham was everything a man ought to be: handsome, tall, and indulgent; but Lydia had grown used to him singling out her sister Elizabeth while they resided in the country, much to her consternation. Oh, Lydia had certainly flirted with him, but, while he was always friendly enough, the engaging Lieutenant more often than not diverted his attention back to Lizzy. It was exceedingly discouraging.

But Lizzy was not in Brighton; Lydia was, and she was determined to make the most of it. She thought it a very good joke if she could make some handsome, young redcoat wild in love with her and return to Longbourn a married woman. It would be all the better if she were to wed the man who had first admired her impertinent sister, and whom she also suspected Lizzy admired as well. What a good joke indeed!

Elizabeth Remembers
by Shannon Winslow

July 1, 1812

Derbyshire. That one word brought it all flooding back to my mind, all that I had so studiously endeavored to put from it. My heart had been set on seeing The Lakes, but my aunt's letter two weeks ago not only put an end to that thrilling expectation, but replaced it with something like apprehension at the thought of diverting to Derbyshire instead. Even now, I am tormented by the idea.

I cannot think of Derbyshire without unhappy associations rising up in my mind. No doubt it is grand country, full of beauties that are not to be missed. But to me it can only ever mean one thing; I will be entering the county wherein resides the owner of Pemberley, a man I had fervently hoped never to meet with again in the whole course of my life. And I know he must feel the same. For proof of it, I have only to refer again to his letter.

Why I have kept it, I cannot rightly say. It is not normally in my nature to dwell on unpleasantness. But in this case, I make an exception. My culpability in the debacle with Mr. Darcy is something I dare not forget entirely, lest I should ever behave so badly again. How despicably I acted! How *dreadfully* I misjudged him! His written words at last taught me to properly know myself, and I have resolved to revisit them occasionally as a sort of penance.

Pulling the letter from its hiding place, I peruse its pages once more. The truth of his explanations concerning the two charges I so vehemently laid at his door, I have long since ceased to question. I need not read those sections again; I know them by heart.

Mr. Darcy's interference with Jane and Mr. Bingley is

something I continue to lament most grievously for my sister's sake, although I can no longer bring myself to hate him for it. There was no malice in the case, only an error in judgment – a failing to which I proved similarly susceptible in the other matter. When I think what he and his sister suffered at the hands of Mr. Wickham, I believe I better understand some portion of his actions in Hertfordshire, some grounds for his distrustful reserve.

Although his careful explanations are most material in exonerating his character, it is always the beginning and the end of Mr. Darcy's letter that cut me to the quick. That is where my conscience seeks to punish me, for that is where the man himself and how I have injured him are most clearly revealed.

> *Be not alarmed, Madam, on receiving this letter, by the apprehension of its containing any repetition of those sentiments, or renewal of those offers, which were last night so disgusting to you. I write without any intention of paining you, or humbling myself, by dwelling on wishes, which, for the happiness of both, cannot be too soon forgotten...*

And then at the end...

> *...If your abhorrence of me should make my assertions valueless, you cannot be prevented by the same cause from confiding in my cousin; and that there may be the possibility of consulting him, I shall endeavour to find some opportunity of putting this letter in your hands in the course of the morning. I will only add, God bless you.*

> *Fitzwilliam Darcy*

Oh, how these words have tortured me! If I still believed him to be a man without feeling, I could laugh at my own blindness well enough. Yet here is evidence that he has a heart after all, one capable of caring deeply... and being just as deeply wounded. Even should he one day find the charity to forgive how I have insulted him, I shall *never* forgive myself. But neither can I be content to wallow forever in self recriminations. I was not formed for unhappiness.

No, the only safe solution is that I never see Mr. Darcy again.

He may get on with his life, well rid of me, and I will get on with mine, a little better for having known him. So there's an end to it. Now, if only I can tour Derbyshire without him crossing my path…

The Gardiners Arrive at Longbourn
Before Their Northern Tour
by Colette Saucier

July 15, 1812

A mixture of relief and gratitude flowed through Mrs. Gardiner as they neared the village of Longbourn. Even with so convenient a distance of twenty-four miles in a well-sprung carriage, the trip from London with four young children had tried her patience. Generally well-behaved, her two sons and two daughters – all under the age of nine – had begun the brief journey in quiet anticipation; but even the best behaved children could only remain enclosed in a carriage for so long before bouncing as much as the horses.

Mrs. Gardiner released a full breath and glanced at her husband, sitting with his typical stoic smile and his eyes fixed on The Times, seemingly impervious to the rambunctious antics of his offspring; but she suspected he used the newspaper as more of a shield than a diversion.

As the coachman brought the carriage to a halt in front of the Bennet household, she peeked out the window. Jane and Elizabeth stood awaiting their arrival, and Mrs. Bennet promptly emerged from the doorway with Mary and Kitty just behind. The moment the carriage door opened, the Gardiner children poured out and ran to Jane's open arms. Sweet Jane. Her attention to the children would allow Mrs. Gardiner's holiday to begin immediately.

Her husband alit from the carriage and offered her his hand, and she braced herself for the onslaught of her sister-in-law's grievances and nervous complaints. Comparing Mrs. Bennet – and Mrs. Philips as well! – to her husband, she often marveled that they could be brother and sister, although on occasion she did wish her husband were not quite so complacent and avuncular.

In the cacophony of greetings that followed, Mrs. Gardiner kissed her nieces in succession then allowed Mrs. Bennet to whisk her into the parlour. Mrs. Bennet took her arm and ushered her to the sofa, where they sat down together. "Hill, Hill," she called out to the housekeeper. "Where are the tea things?"

Mrs. Gardiner turned to find her husband and glimpsed him disappearing with Mr. Bennet towards the library with a nod and a smile in her direction. Yes, they would enjoy a quiet glass of port whilst she succumbed to the tea and hospitality of her sister-in-law. No matter. She knew her sister Bennet would offer a glass of ratafia in short order, which would be a balm to both their nerves.

"Well, sister," said Mrs. Bennet in a confidential accent as their children milled about outside and in the vestibule. "What say you of my Jane? Do you see any change from last you saw her in Town?"

"I… I confess I could not form an opinion in the moments from the carriage to the house, but her face is as healthful and lovely as ever."

"Aye, her beauty has not diminished, but mark my words she still suffers greatly. Who would have thought Mr. Bingley could be so undeserving a young man! And she saw none of him in London?"

"No, but we live in so different a part of town and share no connections, it was very improbable that they would meet."

"I do not suppose there is the least chance in the world of her getting him now. I told Lizzy and my sister Philips I am determined never to speak of it again!"

Mrs. Gardiner could not but doubt the reliability of that assertion, as she had thought they had thoroughly exhausted the topic of Jane's "sad business" when they were together at Christmas.

"I enquired of everyone likely to know," Mrs. Bennet continued, "and there is no talk of his coming to Netherfield this summer, and Lizzy does not believe he will ever live there anymore.

Well, nobody wants him to come. But, however, I shall always say he used my daughter extremely ill. My only comfort is that she will die of a broken heart, and then he will be sorry for what he has done."

Unable to take comfort from such an expectation, Mrs. Gardiner made no answer.

"And when Lizzy stayed with you on her return from Kent, did she speak of how comfortable the Collinses live?"

"She did speak well of them and her delight in Kent but did not say much beyond that."

"Of course she could not say much before Maria Lucas. Oh, sister, that I came so close to having two daughters married! I cannot blame Jane, but Lizzy could even now be at Hunsford instead of Charlotte Lucas. I am sure the Collinses talk often between themselves of having Longbourn one day. I would be ashamed of having an estate not lawfully my own but only entailed on me."

The subject finally came to an end with the arrival of a maid carrying the tea things. Elizabeth and Kitty soon followed, and one poured as the other served.

"Aunt, I suppose you know Lydia is not at home," said Kitty, her tone as peevish as any of the Gardiner children's could be.

"Yes, Lizzy mentioned it in her letter. Lydia is gone to Brighton. Is that right?"

"It is not fair! I am two years older. Mrs. Forster should have invited me as well."

"Oh, quit your grumbling, Kitty," cried her mother. "You know Lydia is Mrs. Forster's particular friend. And if I had had my way, we would all be in Brighton for the summer, but your father has little compassion for my nerves. A little sea-bathing would set me up forever!"

"And you, Lizzy?" Mrs. Gardiner asked her niece. "Would you have preferred Brighton to a tour of the Peak District?"

"Indeed, I had much rather go North with you and Uncle, even if the militia were not encamped at Brighton, but I think we have had our fill of red coats."

Mrs. Bennet knitted her brow and puckered her lips. "Lizzy, what nonsense are you spouting on about? 'Our fill of red coats' indeed!"

"What about Mr. Wickham?" Kitty asked Elizabeth. "Would not you like his company?"

"No, Kitty, not even Mr. Wickham."

"Mr. Wickham?" Mrs. Gardiner's eyes flitted from one niece to the other. "I thought we were soon to hear an announcement of his engagement to Miss King."

Elizabeth dropped her gaze to her teacup as colour rose in her cheeks but said nothing.

"No, there is no danger of Wickham marrying Miss King now," said Kitty. "Her uncle took her to Liverpool two months past, so Wickham is safe."

As the conversation progressed from Mr. Wickham's failed engagement to the contents of Lydia's infrequent letters from Brighton, Mrs. Gardiner turned her attention again to Elizabeth. How odd she found it that her niece had not related this intelligence regarding Mr. Wickham and Mary King in any of her correspondence, particularly as the formation of that attachment had been the subject of much discourse between Elizabeth and herself. Mrs. Gardiner hoped that blush was not due to a renewal of her affection with Mr. Wickham, which she had warned her against; but neither did she want it to be a result of Lizzy being pained by his not renewing his addresses. She resolved to speak to Elizabeth as soon as possible.

That evening after dinner, Mrs. Gardiner sought Elizabeth, who was in her room preparing for their departure early the next day.

"Lizzy, may I help with your packing?"

Elizabeth smiled. "No, I thank you, but I have been instructed on the best method of packing by none other than Lady Catherine de Bourgh herself! There can be only one proper way of placing gowns in a trunk."

Happy to find her niece in good humour, she asked, "How has your time passed here since your return from Kent?"

"Soon after we returned, the impending departure of the militia incited almost universal dread and dejection throughout the neighborhood, and the lamentations of Kitty and Lydia could scarcely compete with those of my mother and her memories of a similar occasion some five and twenty years ago. Then the invitation to join Mrs. Forster in Brighton sent Lydia flying about the house in raptures and threw Kitty into misery and tears. For more than a fortnight after the regiment's departure, Jane and I were forced to listen to the constant repinings of my mother and Kitty, but the gloom and melancholy gave way once some of the families returned from London and summer engagements arose. Now Kitty can once again enter Meryton without tears, I have hope that perhaps by Christmas she might be able to go a full day without mentioning an officer."

Mrs. Gardiner laughed before turning serious again. "And how is Jane? Are her spirits much improved?"

"I fear she is still unhappy, although she represses those feelings to appear as cheerful as possible."

"I am exceedingly sorry to hear it. I had thought it reasonable to believe she might be recovered by now."

"With her disposition," said Elizabeth, "her affection must have greater steadiness than with most first attachments."

"Lizzy, I hope you were not excessively disappointed that your uncle's business requires we curtail our tour."

"At first, perhaps, as I had my heart set on seeing the Lakes; but with all the beauties still to be seen – the rolling hills of the Peak, the river gorge in Dovedale – all was soon right again."

"I think you will find there is enough to be seen in Derbyshire." With the mention of that county, again her niece coloured and occupied herself with her trunk, and Mrs. Gardiner chose to use this as an opening. "Of particular attraction to me, of course, is the town of Lambton where I spent some years growing up. That is in the very part of Derbyshire to which Mr. Wickham belonged. It is not five miles from Pemberley, where he spent much of his youth. He and I discussed it at great length when I met him here at Christmas."

"Yes, I recall you speaking of your acquaintance in common."

"I must own I was surprised to learn from Kitty that Mr. Wickham was no longer attached to Miss King. I wonder you did not mention it in your letters."

Elizabeth answered quickly, as if having anticipated the question. "Yes, I suppose, with the regiment soon to depart Meryton, I thought it of light importance."

Mrs. Gardiner still found the omission curious, especially with so little other news to report. "No doubt you saw him before they departed."

Elizabeth answered by a slight inclination of her head.

"Lizzy, you know I have nothing against him, but I do hope his new circumstance has not renewed an affection between you, which you know to be imprudent."

Elizabeth turned to her aunt with a genuine smile. "No, you have no cause for concern on that account."

"He did not disappoint you in his going?"

"Not at all. You must not fear I have been disappointed in love. He was as amiable as ever, he passed his last evening here at Longbourn with all the appearance of his usual cheerfulness, and we parted with mutual civility."

"I am very glad to hear it. But there was no return of his former partiality to you?"

"I would have discouraged it if there had been. Aunt, pray be well assured that my heart had not been touched by his attentions so much as my vanity."

With this answer, Mrs. Gardiner collected she must be content if not fully satisfied, as she could not help but wonder at Elizabeth's blushes. "I would not wish for you to be carrying any regret on our tour of Derbyshire."

"Indeed I have no reason to repine, and with you and Uncle as companions, I may reasonably hope to have all my expectations of pleasure realized. As I said before: What are men compared to rocks and mountains? I shall enter the county of Derbyshire in pursuit of novelty and amusement with little thought of that gentleman at all."

Jane's Heart
by Susan Mason-Milks

July 23, 1812

The last little face was washed, the bedtime stories told, and the Gardiner children finally all tucked in for the night. Jane closed the door and leaned against it with a sigh. She had forgotten just how exhausting it was to have four small children in the house. Although she had some assistance from Mary and Kitty, the primary responsibility to entertain and care for her nieces and nephews fell on Jane's capable, but weary, shoulders. Jane chuckled to herself reflecting that as usual Mrs. Bennet showed little interest in children who were too young to need her matchmaking advice.

Caring for the Gardiner children this summer was Jane's gift to her beloved sister. She wanted Lizzy to have the pleasure of seeing all the sights as she traveled north with the Gardiners to Derbyshire. Elizabeth always loved discovering new places and meeting new people. Over the years, Jane had realized that she herself was more comfortable at home. While she loved visiting with her aunt and uncle in London, she was perfectly content otherwise to be at Longbourn with her family and friends around her. The other reason she had for wishing to take responsibility for her nieces and nephews this summer was to try out what it would be like to be mother to a small brood of children.

Grabbing her shawl from a hook near the back door, she let herself out of the house, entered the garden, and navigated her way by the bright moonlight to her favorite bench. It was a nearly perfect summer night, the warm daytime weather having cooled into a pleasant, star-filled evening. As the sound of an occasional voice from the house or the clatter of pans from the kitchen drifted her way, she knew the servants were finishing the after dinner clean up and making initial preparations for tomorrow's meals. It was a never-ending cycle, one that usually brought her comfort and reassurance.

Whenever she was alone, her thoughts invariably turned to Charles Bingley, and tonight was no exception. What was he doing at that moment? Was he attending a ball or soiree in London this evening? Was he engaged to someone else? Each time she thought the pain of losing him was completely erased, the tear in her heart fully mended, she would suddenly find herself shaken with a fresh wave of grief. The pain of her loss had less pull than it had six months ago, but when it did rise up from time to time, she was never prepared for the way it nearly knocked her off her feet.

Last winter, when she had been forced to acknowledge that Charles Bingley was forever out of her reach, she had resolved to find a way to let their neighbor, Mr. Wyatt, know she might be receptive to his attentions. Mr. Wyatt was a widower, a good-looking gentleman in his early thirties. Although not as handsome or genial as Mr. Bingley, he was certainly kind and thoughtful. Shortly before the Bingleys had come to Netherfield last fall, Mr. Wyatt had begun venturing out into society again after completing the period of mourning for his wife who had died the previous year giving birth. It was no secret he was looking for a wife, a new mother for his children, but although he had frequently attended assemblies and parties, he seemed to be in no rush to make a choice. Jane had often danced and conversed with the widower, but Charles Bingley's arrival had so completely absorbed her that she had all but forgotten Mr. Wyatt.

One afternoon recently in Meryton with her sister Mary, Jane had encountered Mr. Wyatt in the apothecary shop. It was not too long after she and Lizzy had returned from London. Gathering up her courage, she had made a point of stopping to talk with him and inquire after his children. He, in turn, had asked if she had enjoyed her stay in town. The exchange had been pleasant enough, and he definitely seemed pleased she had made a point of speaking to him.

Jane wondered about the relationship between the Wyatts. Whenever she had seen them together, they had seemed like a loving couple. Appearances could be deceiving, she knew. Was he as he appeared? Could she entrust her future happiness to a man she barely knew? And why was it that she continuously asked herself this question in relation to Mr. Wyatt? She had not known Charles Bingley all that well either but had never thought to ask these questions about him.

Although Mr. Wyatt did not give Jane the same flutters in her heart that she felt when she thought of Mr. Bingley, still the widower was a pleasant man. It was clear that he was interested in her, but was she ready to let go of her former love entirely? Was she truly mourning the loss of Mr. Bingley or was she just chasing the shadow of what might have been? Should she encourage the attentions of someone else? This might be her only chance to marry a decent man, as there were few eligible gentlemen in Hertfordshire.

Although Mr. Wyatt's estate, Willowwood, was about the same size as Longbourn, its owner was a better manager and landlord than her father, and so the income from the land was greater. If she married him, she would have a comfortable, secure life. Was it enough?

Last week, at the church fete, when her nieces and nephews were off playing, she had been presented with another opportunity to observe Mr. Wyatt with his two daughters and was pleased with what she saw. His behavior towards his children was much more like that of her uncle Gardiner than her own father. She admired the way he showed patience with the little girls, and the way his gaze tenderly followed their every move. He could easily have turned them over to their nanny, but he seemed to truly enjoy their company.

As Jane had watched them, it had occurred to her how natural it would be for her to walk past the little group, and casually engage the girls in conversation. Then Mr. Wyatt would undoubtedly ask her to join them for cake, and one thing would lead to another. She could almost hear him asking politely if he might call on her at

Longbourn. Before she knew it, she would be engaged and then married to him. Her life and that of the rest of her family would be secure. Wasn't that what she wanted? What she needed? Then why had her feet stayed rooted to the ground? Why did she hesitate to take those first few steps toward a new future for herself?

Just then, a voice had interrupted her thoughts. "You seem very far away." It was Mary.

Jane gave a sharp intake of breath at being caught out.

"I was just thinking...thinking it is time for me to take my turn tending the refreshment table," she said with a false brightness.

"I do not believe anyone is required at the moment," Mary said looking around. "There is time enough for you to go talk to the Wyatts, if you wish. You may leave the other children to me for a few minutes."

"What makes you think that?" Jane began, looking at her sister in confusion.

"I could see by the look on your face what you were contemplating. Mr. Wyatt is a very nice man, and his daughters are charming little girls," Mary told her.

"Oh, I had no idea I was so transparent," she said, putting a hand on her sister's arm.

Mary smiled. "I know you think Lizzy is the only one who sees into your heart, but I know you, too. I have seen the shadow of pain that plays across your face in those moments when you think no one is looking. I have been worried about you."

Jane took both her sister's hands in hers. "I will be fine, Mary. Just fine." But they both knew that was not exactly true.

So this evening, sitting on the bench alone in the garden contemplating her situation, Jane felt a hard lump of emotion building in her throat and then the wetness on her cheeks. It was in that moment she knew with certainty that she had not forgotten Mr. Bingley. She still loved him even though she had not seen him in many months - even though she sometimes felt he had betrayed her. No matter how hard she had tried to erase him from her life, she had not been successful. There was no rational explanation for it; it was just true. Her head told her she could not grieve for him forever, but her heart would just not allow her to give up.

"Not yet," she whispered to herself. "Not yet."

Lydia and Wickham Attend a Party
by Susan Adriani

July 28, 1812

"Wickham," Mrs. Forster drawled with a teasing smile, "come here."

With a smile of her own, Lydia watched as her friend led the handsome lieutenant away from the band of officers whose countenances, in her opinion, looked far too droll and serious for a party.

"Of course, ma'am," Wickham said as he obliged his colonel's wife. His voice, to Lydia's ears, sounded relieved. "I am at your service."

And why on earth wouldn't he be relieved? the youngest Miss Bennet thought. How could a man as unaffected and gay as Wickham wish to spend the evening sequestered with such dour faces? Surely, whatever conversation the officers had been having must have been positively depressing!

"Miss Bennet," the lieutenant said pleasantly as he approached, offering Lydia a slight bow. "How do you fair this evening?"

"I am very well, thank you." She looked him boldly in the eye. "You are looking well, Mr. Wickham. Tell me, how do you like my gown?"

Wickham laughed, his eyes lowering to take in her appearance. "I must say I like it very much. Did you get it in Meryton, or here in Brighton? I have heard the other ladies talking about a modiste just around the corner on the green who has some lovely patterns."

"Oh, with all the parties and balls we have been to, Harriet and I have hardly had any time to do any shopping, have we, Harriet?"

Mrs. Forster shook her head with a knowing look and a coy smile. "No, I should say not. We have been far more agreeably engaged, have we not, Lydia?"

Lydia laughed. "I daresay we have. I suppose, though, that one really ought to see the shops, and sooner rather than later. After all, there will be more balls and assemblies before we are to leave, and my mother has given me enough pin money to buy an entire trousseau I daresay! I would not dream of wasting it for the world. Perhaps I shall even write home for more, should I manage to go through it."

"Indeed!" Wickham said, his tone most cordial. "That is exceedingly generous of your mother; but, then again, I have always considered dear Mrs. Bennet to be as kind a woman as ever I have met. You are very fortunate to have such a doting parent, Miss Bennet." His expression turned wistful as he dipped his chin. "Alas, it has been many years since I have had the pleasure and comfort of my own parents. I confess I miss them greatly, my father especially. I cannot think of what he would say if he could see me now. I was to have a very different path to follow, as you know."

Lydia, at this point, laid her arm upon his sleeve in sympathy, as did Mrs. Forster. "Of course. You were to have a living, Mr. Wickham, but the loss of it is hardly your fault, now is it? As far as I am concerned, no one is to blame but that odious Mr. Darcy for tossing off his father's wishes so heartlessly. In my opinion, he ought to be punished, even though regimentals are, by far, more becoming than some stiff, bothersome collar." Lydia wrinkled her nose, thinking of Mr. Collins and his simpering formality, before shaking her head and offering Mr. Wickham a demure smile.

"That is true," Wickham conceded with an inclination of his head, his lips quirking upward. "And for such a compliment, I thank you. If it were not for my benefactor's son, I suppose my life would have taken another turn entirely, which would have prevented me from making such wonderful friends as I have in Hertfordshire. For that, at least, I must count my blessings. I would have liked giving sermons, of course," he sighed heavily, but with a quick smile to his colonel's wife, quickly added, "but I am exceedingly gratified to be able to call myself a soldier in His Majesty's Army. It is a hard profession, to be sure, but a noble one. I would not change a thing for the world."

Both ladies beamed at his words, and the flirtatious turn of his lips. The handsome lieutenant cleared his throat. "I am at leisure tomorrow, and would be honored if I could be of service to you ladies in any way."

Mrs. Forster raised her eyes to her friend's with a sly look. "Well, then, perhaps, Wickham, you could escort Lydia and I to the shops? My husband has been too much engaged with his duties of late, and I daresay we have nothing at all appropriate to wear into the machines. We are not so brave as you men, after all, who I hear have no need for clothes when you bathe in the sea, and I am growing absolutely desperate to bathe myself."

Lydia gasped, covering her mouth with her hand to hide her laughter. "Harriet!" she exclaimed. "You are very bold!"

"Besides," Harriet continued, ignoring her friend, "Lydia has funds to spend, and I daresay we are both in need of a man's opinion. What say you, Wickham?"

A slow smile spread over Wickham's face as his gaze fell upon Lydia, who could not have concealed her hopefulness and admiration of him if her life had depended upon it. "I say Amen to that, madam. Amen to that."

Lydia Decides to Leave Brighton
with Wickham
by Susan Adriani

July 31, 1812

Not only did Lydia Bennet and Harriet Forster see the village and visit the shops the next morning on the arm of Mr. Wickham, but the following day Colonel Forster hired a bathing machine for the ladies. While Lydia found the idea of submerging herself in the sea exciting beyond belief, the thought of the act was nothing when compared to the thrill she actually experienced taking part of the exercise.

Despite the sharp instructions and heavy hand of the matron who accompanied them, Lydia stayed in the water for a full half hour, splashing and laughing, much to Mrs. Forster's chagrin. While Lydia had taken to the water with no trouble at all, poor Harriet had not enjoyed her experience in the least. She sputtered and flailed in the waves from the moment she was dipped until the very second she was hauled back into the machine. It was an experience the colonel's young wife would not be repeating, no matter how often and insistently Lydia begged her to reconsider.

After spending the entirety of that afternoon and evening at home (for Mrs. Forster insisted she required rest in order to recover from her encounter with the sea) the colonel invited some of his officers to dine with them. Among them were a few of Lydia's favorites: Denny, Pratt, Chamberlain, and Wickham. The party was a gay one, and when they all sat down to the card tables after supper, Lydia found herself most agreeably engaged with Lieutenant Wickham, who begged a seat beside her with an engaging smile.

"I am sorry that you did not find anything in the shops yesterday to please you, Miss Bennet," he said.

"No one is sorrier than I, I daresay, for I had my heart set on a new gown or two. At least they had ices."

Wickham laid down a card and said, "I understand you went bathing yesterday morning. I have not gone myself. How did you enjoy it? Hopefully, you had a better time of it than poor Mrs. Forster."

"Oh!" cried Lydia, "but you should! I have never enjoyed anything so much, but Harriet flatly refuses to bathe ever again. I do not know what I shall do while I am here, Mr. Wickham, for I had such fun yesterday. Alas, today was nothing like yesterday. Harriet imagines herself ill at every turn, but it is all in her head I daresay. We stayed in all day, you know, and never even ventured out of doors into the garden."

"I am excessively sorry to hear that. Tomorrow, perhaps, you shall find something to better occupy your time. From what I understand Mrs. Forster was feeling under the weather after her turn in the bathing machine, though she appears to be in good enough spirits now."

Lydia scowled. "I certainly hope so, for I fear I cannot bear to be confined to this insufferable house for so much as another day. If we were in London I daresay I would be able to slip away without anyone being the wiser, but here in Brighton Colonel Forster is always about, postulating about what is proper and right. In my opinion, he is being very droll, for he was not half so concerned about any of that when we were in Hertfordshire." She sighed deeply and selected another card. "If only we were in London. I could buy a proper gown and perhaps go to the theatre. Harriet would forget all about sea bathing and being ill. Oh, what fun I could have!"

Wickham only smiled, but his look was warm and Lydia soon found herself unable to keep her attention entirely on the game at hand.

* * *

"Will you take a turn with me about the room, Miss Bennet? I daresay it will be refreshing after sitting in one attitude for so long."

Lydia was surprised indeed by his continued attentiveness, but pleasantly so, and readily agreed. She took Wickham's proffered hand and almost sighed aloud as he tucked hers into the crook of his arm. She could not deny she had a very pleasant evening, despite the fact that her day had been extremely dull; the highlight being the gentleman currently leading her to the opposite side of the drawing room, where they might have some privacy. Lydia could hardly believe her good fortune.

Wickham glanced around the room before tilting his head toward her own and saying in a low voice, "Can you keep a secret, Miss Bennet?"

"Of course, sir," she said, her eyes wide, eager for gossip.

"It is not common knowledge, but I am to be sent to Town tomorrow night on urgent business for the regiment. In fact, not even Denny and Pratt know. No one knows, except Colonel Forster and myself, and now you." He gave her a quick smile, laying his free hand over hers.

Lydia thought she might melt.

"The nature of my business," he continued, "is quite secretive. So secretive, in fact, that Colonel Forster has not even shared it with Mrs. Forster." The corners of Wickham's mouth turned upward ever so slightly. "But I could not bear to deceive you in such a manner. The thought of parting with you, Miss Bennet, without saying a proper adieu after we have grown so close leaves a bad taste in my mouth."

Lydia gasped, thrilled that the handsome Lieutenant would make such an intimation. "I would be very angry with you if you were to go away without saying goodbye, Mr. Wickham; indeed, things will be very dull without you. I do not know how I shall pass the time. How long will your business keep you in Town?"

Wickham sighed heavily, patting her hand. "It will be many

weeks before I may be able to return. By then, I am afraid you may have gone home to Longbourn, and we shall be parted forever."

"How dreadful!" Lydia cried, truly horrified by the prospect of parting with Mr. Wickham for so long a time as forever. "I cannot imagine how I shall bear your absence if we are never to meet again. I have enjoyed your company very much, Mr. Wickham. Tell me, do you truly have to go?"

"It is all arranged. I leave tomorrow after nightfall. I do wish there was some way that we might see one another. I confess I have grown most attached to you, Miss Bennet. If only I had more to offer. If only you would agree to…" Here, he shook his head and looked away. "But, alas, I am but a lowly lieutenant. If I were to ask, your father would never permit me to court you, never mind mar—. But I am afraid I have said too much. Forgive me."

"Do you mean to say that you wish to marry me?" Lydia asked on a breath.

Wickham's eyes held her own. "The idea of never meeting again is one that grieves me. If I could but convince you to wait for me, but even that, I am afraid, would be asking too much. As I mentioned before, I may be gone many weeks. Of course, you would not wish to leave your friends, though traveling to Scotland would not be such a stretch beyond London. But I am a sentimental fool, thinking of such a thing with such a lovely creature as yourself."

Lydia bit her lip. Scotland, to her, sounded wonderful. She would be married—and before any of her sisters, too! She would be Mrs. George Wickham, esquire. Oh! she thought. How well that sounds! "I would not be gone forever. I daresay Harriet would hardly miss me. And I do have more than enough money to buy wedding clothes, and maybe even go to the theatre. Of course, we would have to stop in London first, for I cannot imagine buying wedding clothes anywhere else. Oh!" she cried. "What fun we shall have! I can hardly wait!"

Wickham's answering smile was slow as he quickly flicked his eyes from Lydia's happy countenance to the cluster of officers taking refreshment with Colonel and Mrs. Forster. "That is settled, then," he said.

Denny Learns of Lydia's Elopement
by Jack Caldwell

August 1, 1812

Lieutenant Denny had just finished his breakfast when Lieutenant Chamberlayne walked in. "I say, have you seen Wickham? He seems to be missing."

Denny sat up. "Missing? Are you certain? Sometimes he sleeps in town."

At that moment, an angry Captain Carter walked in, followed by Lieutenant Pratt. "There is no doubt about it," he thundered without preamble. "Wickham has fled!"

"We just came from his tent," added Pratt, "and all his money and valuables are gone. He's lit out, the bastard! He owes me money!"

Chamberlayne paled. "He owes me money, too."

Denny felt a sinking feeling in his stomach. He knew that things were getting tight for George, almost desperate, his gambling debts being pressing, but surely he wouldn't just desert!

"Miss Bennet is missing, as well." Carter eyed Denny. "Colonel Forster wants to talk to you."

Denny just stared in horror at his captain. *George could not have done that! He could not have!*

* * *

Somehow, Denny made it to Colonel Forster's office without losing his breakfast. He stood at attention, watching his commander pace up and down the small space. Never had Denny seen the affable colonel in such a state.

"She's gone, she's gone, and I was responsible for her," he said over and over again. "How can I tell her father? I never should have let Harriet talk me into this foolishness!" He finally addressed Denny. "All right, you are friends with George Wickham. Where the devil is he? Where did he go?"

"Sir, I do not know. Are you saying that Lieutenant Wickham absconded with Miss Bennet?"

"Yes, yes, we are certain of it. She left a note." He tossed a piece of paper in his direction. "Read it, if you like."

Denny picked it up and read.

> *My Dear Harriet, You will laugh when you know where I am gone, and I cannot help laughing myself at your surprise tomorrow morning, as soon as I am missed. I am going to Gretna Green, and if you cannot guess with who, I shall think you a simpleton, for there is but one man in the world I love, and he is an angel. I should never be happy without him, so think it no harm to be off. You need not send them word at Longbourn of my going, if you do not like it, for it will make the surprise the greater, when I write to them, and sign my name 'Lydia Wickham.' What a good joke it will be! I can hardly write for laughing...*

There was more, but Denny had read enough. His disappointment, pain, and horror nearly brought him to his knees. Only his will kept him upright.

"Well?' the colonel demanded. "What do you know about this business?"

Denny's mind swirled with the possibilities. "Sir, I did not know that Wickham was going to desert. I was aware of his debts of honor as well as other financial difficulties, but I did not think him capable of this. Looking back, I suppose I should not be surprised that he left. I am disappointed in him.

"But I had no idea about Miss Bennet! Not a breath of this sort of action was ever hinted between us. I own myself shocked."

The colonel drew close. "You have called on Miss Bennet very regularly at my house, lieutenant. You had no suspicions of her attachment to Wickham?"

"None at all, sir!" Denny cried with more feeling than he intended. "I … I knew that Miss Bennet liked George, but she showed him no especial attention. She was attentive to many of the officers." Including me was Denny's depressing thought.

Colonel Forster seemed to catch the level of Denny's disappointment. The interview became much less an interrogation. "So, you believe that the two are well on their way to Gretna Green?"

This was Denny's nightmare. "I am afraid, Sir, that Wickham had often talked about his plans for the future. He has always held that marriage to an heiress was his goal." At Forster's look, he added, "For example, his courtship of Miss King in Meryton." Denny looked down at the note. "From this I can tell that Miss Lydia—Miss Bennet—believes that she and Wickham are eloping to Scotland. I have had many conversations with Wickham, sir, and I can categorically state that such a thing would be in opposition to all his long-term plans. Miss Bennet is not an heiress."

"Good God, do you know what you are saying?"

Denny came to attention. "Colonel, I do not know where Wickham has gotten to, but he would never willingly go to Gretna Green for anything less than ten thousand pounds."

Forster blanched and cursed. "Get Cater in here—now! I must find that bastard! There is not a moment to lose!" He glared at Denny. "As for you, you and the other officers are confined to quarters until I return! I will get to the bottom of this!"

* * *

Denny's mood darkened as he sat helplessly in his tent. He did not share his space, thanks to his seniority, so he could escape Pratt's grumblings and Chamberlayne's gossip. He had heard enough from the latter when he informed his comrades of their colonel's orders.

"I am surprised Wickham made off with that Bennet girl. I thought sure he had his eye on Mrs. Forster! You have seen how she practically monopolized his attentions. Hah! Perhaps he was playing a double game! Who knows, maybe he had both of them at once!"

How it was Denny did not break Chamberlayne's jaw for that, only the Good Lord knew.

Denny thought over his entire acquaintance with Lydia Bennet. Certainly she was a beautiful, young, spirited girl, but liveliness was no sin. Perhaps she was too young to be out in society. Denny conceded that she was, even though she looked and acted older than her years. However, there was no excuse for any officer to take advantage of a young lady, even one who was naïve and flirtatious. As a gentleman's daughter, Miss Lydia should have been protected from those who would harm her—even protected from her own mistakes. That was the duty of an officer and a gentleman.

I should have done more, Denny realized. *I should have protected her.*

Denny was infatuated with the lovely Lydia Bennet, and had she been older and had he more fortune, he would have offered for her. But marriage had been out of the question. At just fifteen, Miss Lydia was too young to marry, and as a lieutenant in the militia, Denny was too poor. In only two more months, he was to leave the regiment to join the regulars. Then, with three years of hard work and advancement, and the better pay that came with it, he would be fully able to support the daughter of a gentleman, and he intended to travel to Hertfordshire and court the then eighteen-year-old Miss Lydia.

Denny sighed. He thought the lady favored him as much as any man in the regiment. Now he saw that he had been a fool. Of course, she would fall in love with George Wickham—handsome, clever, witty George—not with poor, plain Archie Denny.

He recalled what he knew about Wickham. George was charming and affable—everyone's friend. Yes, sometimes he drank too much, and he certainly gambled too much, but Denny was sure there was not a wicked bone in Wickham's body. Foolish, boastful, and impulsive—yes. But evil? No.

George had suffered much misfortune in his life—losing his mother at a young age and later his father, the son of his godfather stealing George's inheritance, and that same Mr. Darcy interfering with George's courtship of Miss Darcy. George deserved Denny's pity and friendship.

Perhaps this misadventure was not George's idea? Mayhap Miss Lydia had learned of George's plans to desert and invited herself along. Could that be it?

There—that would explain it. Miss Lydia was in love with George and wanted to marry him. The only question that remained was would George marry her? George said he would only marry an heiress, but he said many things and did the opposite. Could this be another example of his unpredictability?

Archibald Denny was a man who strived to live above his station. He wanted one day to be a gentleman, so he taught himself to think and behave like one. Therefore, he tried to look at the world with a rational eye. But he was also a soldier, a good one. He had never been in combat, but he had taken to his training as a duck to water. If the time came to fight for his king, Denny expected that he would do his duty without hesitation.

He was a man of strong passions. Loyalty and trustworthiness were important to him. Wickham had been a good friend to him, so Denny would give him the benefit of the doubt. But Denny had spent time in London and had seen what happened to young girls who had been seduced and abandoned by their lovers. There was no way for them to earn their bread except on their back. It was horrible.

Denny wanted desperately to think well of George Wickham and Lydia Bennet, so he convinced himself that all would end well. Miss Lydia's charms and good humor would prove to be as irresistible to Wickham as they had been to himself, Denny was sure of it. They would marry, Wickham would somehow extract himself from this scrape, and they would settle quietly somewhere. Lydia would be as happy as she deserved.

Denny had to think that, for if George did Lydia wrong, if he abandoned her to the mercy of the streets, Denny knew he would hunt his friend down and kill him.

Midnight Express for Longbourn
by Shannon Winslow

August 2, 1812

The Bennet household had just settled down for the night after a day of industrious occupation. Mrs. Bennet had been to Meryton and argued not only with the butcher about her bill, but also with various ones of her neighbors who seemed to be circulating malicious rumors about that handsome officer she and her girls so much admired: Mr. Wickham. After exhausting herself in this manner, Mrs. Bennet had retired early, saying her head was very ill indeed.

Jane and Kitty had once again spent the entire day entertaining the lively Gardiner children whilst their parents were away to Derbyshire on holiday with Elizabeth Bennet in tow.

Mr. Bennet alone had been able to preserve himself from excessive exertion, and had thus found he was quite able to stay up late, reading once again his favourite of Shakespeare's plays (*Much Ado About Nothing*) and chuckling to himself at the silliness and absurdity he found there. Upon finishing, he thanked his lucky stars that his own household suffered no such dramas, and then he likewise retired to a gentle slumber.

Shortly after twelve, however, such a pounding came at the front door as would surely have awakened the dead. One by one, the Bennets tumbled out of their beds and down the stairs to see what the cause of all this unwelcome commotion was. It was an express, the contents of which turned out to be even more unwelcome.

Mr. Bennet, after paying the man and closing the door again, in silence read the letter, which was addressed to him:

407

My Dear Mr. Bennet,

It is with a heavy heart that I write to you with news that must bring you considerable distress. But I am afraid of alarming you. Be assured that your daughter is well, so far as it is within my power to judge. I am sorry to say that Miss Bennet last night removed herself from my house and from my protection. She has in fact eloped with one of my officers – Lieutenant George Wickham, whom you will remember.

From her own information – a brief letter left for my wife – we do at least know that she departed with him of her own accord and in very high spirits, stating that the couple's intention was to make for Gretna Green and there to wed. I have no real reason for doubting this, only a general uneasiness over the gentleman's character. He at first seemed to me to be as fine a young man as ever one could hope to meet with. On closer acquaintance, however, I have observed in him a worrying trend toward imprudence, this event being yet another evidence of it.

I feel myself in part responsible for what has occurred. You entrusted your daughter to my care, and I have failed to keep her safe from harm. I now pledge myself to do everything within my power to assist you in recovering her. I will closely question the men under my command, especially Wickham's particular friends, to see what is to be learned here. Then I plan to come to you directly at Longbourn, to offer whatever service I may render you. Till then, please extend my humble apology and sincere respects to all your family.

Yours, etc.

Col. Forster

"Oh! What is it, Mr. Bennet?" cried his wife when he let his hand and the letter drop to his side. "Tell me at once. Have you no compassion for my nerves?" Thunderstruck and thoroughly incapable of speech, Mr. Bennet gave the letter to his wife, who in turn passed it on to her eldest daughter. "You read it to me, Jane. I am in too much of a tremble."

But hearing the letter only increased Mrs. Bennet's agitation. She was taken ill with hysterics immediately, and the whole house disintegrated into a state of utter confusion not soon to be recovered from. Moreover, there was nary a servant belonging to the business who did not know the whole of the story before the day was out. Within two more days the whole community knew of the Bennets' troubles. Half their neighbors then had the goodness to pity them their great misfortune, and the other half were only too proud to say they had always predicted such an unfavorable outcome for the family.

Colonel Forster Arrives
at Longbourn
by C. Allyn Pierson

August 3, 1812

Colonel Forster left Brighton at first light, before the sun had actually appeared above the hump of Beachy Head to the east. The day was lovely, with a light mist filtering the sunlight and giving the trees along the highway an ethereal, mysterious beauty. But the colonel was oblivious to the wonders of nature as it awoke, and to the bird songs heralding the end of the dawn chorus; his thoughts were turned inwards to the reason for his ride.

Not two nights before, his wife's guest, Miss Lydia Bennet, had left their house with one of his men...to own the truth, with George Wickham. He could hardly believe it even now that one of his men would behave in such a scaly way towards a guest in his superior officer's house! Miss Bennet, of course, had gone willingly, and she had shown herself during her stay to have very little in the way of dignity or propriety. He had thought she would keep his wife happy while he pursued his duties, and, indeed, she had enjoyed having her friend stay...He shook his head to try to clear it of the tumbling thoughts roiling in it.

The two eldest Miss Bennets were lovely young women who always behaved like ladies. The two youngest girls, however, were the most unrestrained, rambunctious young women he had ever met. It was not long after the regiment moved to Brighton for the summer that he began having serious reservations about the influence Miss Lydia might have on his wife. His wife! He had married her for her good humour and her dowry of one thousand pounds, but she was twenty years younger than he. At first he had enjoyed her light heart and how young she made him feel, but the summer in Brighton with Miss Lydia had opened his eyes to the difference between youth and immaturity. Both girls (he could not call them ladies…they were far too young) enjoyed flirting with the officers and he had often wished that his wife would behave more like a well-bred matron than like a feather-headed girl just out of the schoolroom. Several times he had had to restrain their exuberance for some scheme which threatened to hurt their reputations…and his.

What would he say to Mr. Bennet when he reached Longbourn? At least they would have received his express and he would not have to deal with the hysterics which he was positive had overcome Mrs. Bennet when the express had arrived.

He stopped at midday to bait his horse and to refresh himself with a tankard of ale and a light nuncheon of cold meat and bread before continuing on towards Hertfordshire. When he approached London he began making inquiries at the inns but could not trace the fugitives beyond Clapham. There they had, unfortunately, changed to a hackney coach and continued on the London road…and there the trail petered out. He could find no trace of them on the road they would have taken to Scotland. He finally gave up the search and found a small but comfortable inn along the road for the night (and not a very restful one) and set out very early again the next day. It was very fortunate that his horse was large and strong and that he rode very light, or the poor beast would have been done in by the exertion of the past days.

It was very late in the day when he finally arrived at Longbourn, covered in dirt and sweat from the long ride and wishing only for a glass of Madeira and a comfortable chair. Instead, he found himself in Mr. Bennet's library facing an angry father.

But it was not so bad as he had feared. Mr. Bennet placed the blame for Lydia's folly directly onto his daughter's shoulders and accepted the colonel's apologies…although without any lightening of his expression. He accepted Mr. Bennet's offer of dinner, (and a

411

grim affair it was!) then set out for the return to Brighton, where he had engagements the next evening. As he left Longbourn he shook his head over the follies of youth and was glad his wife would no longer be influenced by Miss Lydia. She was stunned by the elopement of her friend…and shocked she had so misjudged her as to think her flirting was merely pretense, rather than a deep-seated lack of breeding. Perhaps, once this fiasco was over, his wife would start to settle down…certainly when they started a family it would give her something better to think about than parties and routs. The colonel managed a smile over that scenario as he cantered towards Brighton.

Mrs. Reynolds Gives
a Tour of Pemberley
by Susan Mason-Milks

August 4, 1812

To prepare for the arrival of the Darcys, Mrs. Reynolds mobilized the staff with all the efficiency of a military commander. Mr. Darcy would reach Pemberley tomorrow with Mr. Bingley and his family for a stay of at least a fortnight. Although Mrs. Reynolds was not looking forward to trying to please the ever temperamental Miss Bingley, as always, she would put forth her best effort. This was, after all, Pemberley, and there were certain standards to be maintained. It was part of her job to attempt the impossible and try to make each guest's stay a pleasant one.

This morning, Mrs. Reynolds, along with her assistant, Margie, was in the process of checking the linens, when Watkins, Pemberley's ancient and dignified butler, appeared at the door looking anxious. "Mrs. Reynolds, a group of three travelers has applied for a tour of the house. I know you are occupied today with preparations for the master's return. I was tempted to turn them away, but thought I should consult with you first before doing so."

Mrs. Reynolds hesitated, considering the long list of tasks ahead of her. As it was a point of pride for her to never turn visitors away, she would somehow have to make time for them. "No, Mr. Watkins, I will take them around," she said.

"I have shown them to the small visitor's room. Are you able to meet with them now or would you prefer to have them tour the grounds first?"

Mrs. Reynolds sighed and handed the record book to Margie. "I shall attend to them immediately. Margie, please carry on here, and also…well, you know what to do," she said with a reassuring smile to her assistant.

Upon reaching the visitor's room, Mrs. Reynolds found a well-dressed couple, who had the look of people who lived in town. They introduced themselves as Mr. and Mrs. Gardiner. The wide-eyed young lady with dark hair was their niece, Miss Elizabeth Bennet. At first, Mrs. Reynolds thought she might give them the abbreviated tour to save time. In all likelihood they would not be aware she was skipping certain rooms in order to move the group along more quickly. Later, reflecting back, she was glad she had taken time for the full tour.

"We have heard the family is away at this time," said Mr. Gardiner.

"Oh, yes, but we expect him tomorrow with a large party of friends," Mrs. Reynolds replied. At that, she heard the young lady take a quick, nervous breath.

After the tour, Mrs. Reynolds was just resuming her preparations for the arrival of Mr. Darcy's guests, when Margie came at a run to let her know Mr. Darcy had arrived home early and was in a somewhat agitated state. Hearing a commotion in the hallway outside, she arose and was startled to find herself face-to-face with the master himself.

"Mr. Darcy!" Her surprise was not only at seeing him there in her office but also at the condition of his person. He was dusty and disheveled, his face red from exertion, and he was out of breath as if he had run all the way from the stables.

"Welcome home, sir," she said trying to regain her usual calm demeanor. "I am sorry for not greeting you myself, but we did not expect you until tomorrow."

Waving off her apology he said quickly, "Yes, I rode ahead to meet with Mr. Jones on some estate business." He hesitated a moment taking time to wipe some sweat from his brow with his handkerchief.

Mrs. Reynolds waited patiently. She knew him well enough to be certain he had something else to say. "Mrs. Reynolds, I believe you gave a tour of the house to three people who are now viewing the grounds."

"Yes, sir, I did. The Gardiners and Miss Bennet." Sensing something was not right, she added, "I did not think my taking the time would be a problem, as our preparations for your arrival are nearly complete."

Sensing her concern he assured her, "No, no, I was not chastising you at all. In fact, I am well pleased you were able to show them the house. How do you think they liked it?"

Mrs. Reynolds furrowed her brow as she examined his face. This was an unusual question. Mr. Darcy rarely took an interest in people who came to tour the house. In fact, he always avoided them assiduously.

"What did she…what did they have to say? About Pemberley? Did they like it?" he asked looking at her with something more than his usual intensity.

"They seemed very well pleased with the house, but how could they not be?"

"Good. Good," he said nodding his head. "Tell me more about their visit."

Mrs. Reynolds began by recounting the time they had arrived and the rooms they had toured. "I believe they are from London, at least the Gardiners are from town. I was not certain about Miss Bennet."

"Did Miss Bennet mention she and I are acquainted?" he asked hesitantly.

"Why, yes, sir. She did say she knew you slightly."

His dark eyes widened. "How did that come about?"

"I believe it was as we were looking at the miniatures on the mantelpiece. Mrs. Gardiner asked Miss Bennet how she liked the one of George Wickham. I told them he was the son of your father's steward."

"Did Miss Bennet make any comment about Mr. Wickham?"

"No, not a word. When I said he had gone into the army and turned out quite wild, she did not disagree."

"Please continue, Mrs. Reynolds."

"Then I pointed out the miniature of you. I think it was Mrs. Gardiner who said she had heard much about you. She said you had a handsome face and then turned to Miss Bennet to inquire if she thought it was a good likeness of you. That was when I realized Miss Bennet was acquainted with you."

"And?" he said impatiently.

Mrs. Reynolds thought back over the conversation. It was very unusual for him to interrogate her like this about visitors. Clearly, for some reason the opinion of this young lady was very important to him. "I asked her if she did, in fact, know you, and she said she was a little acquainted with you."

At this, Darcy gave a deep exhale as if he thought it might now be safe for him to breathe again.

"And then since she knew you, I asked if she thought you were a handsome gentleman," Mrs. Reynolds added with a smile.

At this, Darcy's eyes grew wide and he made a noise that resembled a stifled groan. "Mrs. Reynolds, I hope this is not something you regularly ask our visitors?"

Now it was Mrs. Reynolds turn to redden. "No, sir. I thought that since she knew you...," she trailed off. "I was simply making pleasant conversation. After all, they were very nice people."

Darcy sighed. "Yes, I am certain they were. Please tell me exactly what Miss Bennet said."

Mrs. Reynolds wrinkled her forehead. "Said about what, sir."

Darcy grimaced. He hesitated and then said very slowly, "What did Miss Bennet say of me?"

Mrs. Reynolds noticed that he was uncomfortably shifting his weight from one foot to the other. It was something he had done as a boy when he was called to account for his actions. Clearly, the mention of Miss Bennet was having the effect of disquieting Mr. Darcy.

"Oh, Miss Bennet agreed that you are," she answered softly. "Handsome, that is, sir."

At that, Mrs. Reynolds saw the corner of Darcy's mouth turn up in a slight smile. Yes, there was definitely more to this than he was willing to admit.

"Is there anything else they said about the house or..." Darcy hesitated putting a fist to his mouth as he cleared his throat. "Or about me?"

"I showed them the portrait of Miss Darcy, the one taken when she was just eight, and they inquired about her."

"What did you say about Georgiana?"

"When they asked me if she was as handsome as her brother, I told them she was the handsomest young lady that ever was and all about how she loves her music, playing all day sometimes. I showed them the new pianoforte you bought for her. I hope that was not wrong of me. Oh, it is so lovely. I know Miss Darcy will be thrilled when she sees it tomorrow."

Mrs. Reynolds blushed as she recalled the way she had praised Mr. Darcy for his kindness and good-temper, as well as his generosity to the people who depended upon him on the estate. Mr. Darcy was a modest man, and if he knew just how freely she had spoken about him, he might be upset.

"I believe you are not revealing all to me, Mrs. Reynolds. Did something else happen during their visit that you are reluctant to share? You may speak freely. I am not unhappy with you."

Now it was Mrs. Reynolds turn to shift uncomfortably. "Mr. Gardiner inquired if you were much at Pemberley during the year, and I told them you spend nearly half the year here, although we always wish it were more. Then Mr. Gardiner suggested that if you were to marry perhaps we might see more of you."

Darcy raised an eyebrow.

"I agreed that was indeed possible, but I also said we had no idea when you would marry."

"Hmm…" He rubbed his chin thoughtfully.

"I think I might also have said I did not know who might be good enough for you," she confessed reluctantly.

Darcy groaned putting his fingers to his temple. "I am almost afraid to ask what Miss Bennet had to say about that."

"Miss Bennet said I was very fortunate to have such a master, and I told her if I were to go through the world, I could not meet a better."

Suddenly, Mrs. Reynolds found herself enveloped in a hug. "I thank you for your kind words, Mrs. Reynolds. You are too generous in your praise."

"I only speak as I see, Mr. Darcy. You are a good man, a very good man. Everyone who knows you says so."

Darcy mumbled something that sounded a bit like, "Not everyone."

"When I showed them the picture gallery, Miss Bennet did spend some time studying your portrait. Quite some time, in fact," said Mrs. Reynolds with a smile.

Suddenly, Darcy seemed to remember he had been in a hurry. "I believe I would like to show our guests around myself, but I must change my traveling clothes first. The road was very dusty. Who is taking them on the grounds tour?" he asked.

"I believe it is Mr. Eldridge, sir."

"Very good. Would you please send someone to speak with him? I would like him to go slowly – very slowly – so I may catch up with their group." Examining his dirty and rumpled shirt, he added, "Would you please send someone up to help me change. My valet is following later today with the baggage. And of course, I shall require some water although you do not need to take time to heat it."

Then before she could respond, he disappeared.

After following his instructions, Mrs. Reynolds took a moment to consider what had just transpired. Something was different about Mr. Darcy. What did this young woman mean to him? How had they met?

Although Mrs. Reynolds prided herself on not interfering in the Darcys' private business, her curiosity to understand the situation was just too much to resist. Unable to concentrate on the pile of papers on her desk, she kept returning to thoughts of the polite young lady with the expressive brown eyes. Finally, she gave up and went to stand at the window overlooking gardens at the back of the house. After a few minutes, she saw Mr. Darcy exit the house and stride off in the direction the visitors had taken, straightening his cravat as he hurried along. Turning back to her desk, she smiled. It did not escape her notice that Mr. Darcy was dressed in what she knew to be one of his favorite coats.

Miss Darcy Meets Elizabeth Bennet
by C. Allyn Pierson

August 5, 1812

Miss Darcy alighted from the dusty carriage carefully; she did not want to soil her gown and embarrass her brother by appearing disheveled in front of his guests. After greeting Mrs. Reynolds, she retired to her room to change out of her traveling gown and freshen up. It was a delight to be alone after the long days of traveling with Mrs. Hurst and Miss Bingley. She knew her brother would not associate with unworthy or ill-bred people, but she had to admit she did not like Mr. Bingley's sisters. How her brother could tolerate Miss Bingley's odious fawning was beyond Georgiana's understanding, and Mrs. Hurst followed wherever Miss Bingley led in the matter of gossip.

Miss Bingley fawned over Georgiana, as well, but she could tell that the attention was all for her brother's ear – Miss Bingley constantly glanced at Mr. Darcy and made sure her affectionate conversation with Georgiana was carried on in his presence.

Before she had proceeded further in her ruminations, Georgiana heard a scratch on her door. Her maid admitted Mr. Darcy and then he sent her off. He pulled a chair up to Georgiana's dressing table, where she was seated, and took her hand.

"Georgiana, my dear, I know that you have just arrived and are probably needing a rest, but I wonder if you could do something for me?"

Georgiana was surprised, but responded immediately, "Of course, brother! What do you want me to do?"

He looked down at her hand as he caressed it soothingly, then, with a look grim fortitude said, "I-I would like you to drive into Lambton with me. I want you to meet someone."

She stared at him in astonishment. "Who is it?"

He fidgeted with his cravat and straightened his cuffs. "It is Miss Elizabeth Bennet and her aunt and uncle. They visited Pemberley yesterday while touring Derbyshire, and I would like to introduce you. They are friends of Bingley's... and mine."

She was still more astonished! Her brother had never behaved so in her entire life! Obviously, this Miss Bennet was special to her brother in some way. She looked at him for a moment, then said, "Could they not come to Pemberley? Surely Mr. Bingley will want to see them also."

He flushed a little. "I do not wish to have you meet them in a crowd of people. I want Miss Bennet to be able to talk to you without being interrupted or without having to carry on several conversations at once." He smiled at his shy little sister. "I do not want you to be able to hide in the corner, my love."

His blush and his words gave her quite a different picture of her brother's motivations in this affair. Could he, perhaps, actually be in love with Miss Bennet? She answered the question in his eyes. "Of course, dear brother! I am ready to go at any time! But how will we leave without revealing our plans to the Bingleys?"

"I have the carriage waiting by the stables...we will leave through the kitchen. We will return before our guests even know we are gone."

They executed this plan, but it did not turn out quite the way they expected. When they came down the back stairs from Georgiana's room they ran into Bingley, who was looking for his man.

Darcy sighed quietly and gave in, explaining their errand to Lambton. Bingley insisted on accompanying them, even offering to wait downstairs until they had sought Miss Bennet's approbation for his visit. Darcy ordered tea for Miss Bingley and the Hursts when they came down, and the three of them sneaked out through the back door.

It did not take long to reach Lambton as it was only four or five miles from Pemberley. Darcy and Bingley kept up a light, effortless conversation during the first part of the drive, but as they approached the inn at Lambton Darcy fell silent. Bingley also seemed wrapped in his own thoughts and Georgiana could see tension in both the men's faces. How very odd!

When they stepped out of the carriage, Darcy and Georgiana went upstairs to the Gardiners' rooms and were announced by the innkeeper. Georgiana hardly heard her brother's introduction…Miss Bennet was lovely and had a beautiful, low-pitched voice. Georgiana curtseyed and spoke with her, while watching her brother out of the corner of her eyes. As Miss Bennet talked he seemed to relax his stiff stance, and he talked calmly with Mr. Gardiner, a genteel, well-dressed older man.

The visit went quickly, and Georgiana was not surprised when, while Bingley was renewing his acquaintance with Miss Bennet, her brother asked her to invite them to dine at Pemberley. She did so, rather awkwardly, but the Gardiner's did not seem to see any flaws in her manner, so she was reassured.

They were all quiet on the ride back to Pemberley. Georgiana did not know what her brother and his friend were thinking, but she was very full of speculation. It seemed her brother had finally fallen in love…not surprising when Miss Bennet was so beautiful and kind. She would watch him carefully while the Gardiners and Miss Bennet dined with them!

Mrs. Gardiner and Elizabeth
Visit Miss Darcy
by C. Allyn Pierson

August 6, 1812

After much thought during a fairly sleepless night, Mrs. Gardiner had come to no conclusions about her niece's relationship to Mr. Darcy. It was clear the handsome landowner had a soft spot in his heart for Lizzy, but his dignified reserve made it difficult to interpret his thoughts. Still, he could not take his eyes off Lizzy, and the extreme embarrassment evident between them was highly suspicious.

And then there was Mr. Darcy's visit with his sister, to introduce her to Lizzy, and coming when she had barely stepped out of her coach at Pemberley! Yes, Mr. Darcy loved Lizzy, but how did Lizzy feel? Her blushing and stammering when Mr. Darcy came upon them suddenly certainly suggested she cared about his opinion, but Mrs. Gardiner could not be sure if she liked him, or if she was merely embarrassed to be in a position where she must be polite to someone she disliked.

Elizabeth said virtually nothing the next morning while they breakfasted, so finally Mrs. Gardiner spoke. "Lizzy? Do you not think we should visit Pemberley this morning? I feel we should do something to return Mr. and Miss Darcy's exceeding politeness in waiting on us yesterday…and so soon after her arrival! Does that meet with your approbation?"

Elizabeth blushed, but answered in a calm voice, "Indeed, yes! I believe you are right. I would hate to seem rude to Miss Darcy. The poor girl is very shy, and I wouldn't want her to feel we did not appreciate her courtesy."

So it came about that they took their carriage to Pemberley to visit Miss Darcy. When they arrived they found Miss Darcy was in the saloon with her companion, Mrs. Annesley while Miss Bingley and her sister sat down the room examining a bracelet Mrs. Hurst was wearing.

When Mrs. Gardiner and Lizzy were announced, Mrs. Annesley and Georgiana stood up to greet them, and Georgiana introduced them to her companion, briefly, then flushed with embarrassment. Mrs. Annesley smoothly took up the dangling conversation and invited the two visitors to sit. Mrs. Gardiner ended up nearest Miss Darcy with Lizzy across from Mrs. Annesley, and they carried on a conversation of little content, but great goodwill. Occasionally, Miss Darcy would whisper a contribution to the topic of conversation, but they were so quiet that her guests could not hear her.

Eventually, Mrs. Annesley, after several significant looks at Miss Darcy, induced her charge to ring for refreshments and the awkward behavior of everyone relaxed while they all selected some fruit and cake. While they were involved with the lovely trays of fruit the door of the saloon opened and Mr. Darcy entered, his eyes immediately going to his sister. It was clear to Mrs. Gardiner that he cared very much for his sister and for her comfort while entertaining the guests, and it seemed to her that he was very much aware of her niece and trying not to focus all his attention on her.

Mr. Darcy began several topics of conversation with his sister and Elizabeth immediately came to his aid and talked to Georgiana about some concerts she had attended while in Town. Things were going well until Miss Bingley suddenly piped up with a sarcastic comment to Elizabeth about the militia leaving Meryton, and how distressing that must be to the Bennets...especially having Mr. Wickham leave.

Elizabeth deflected the ill-natured comment, but Mrs. Gardiner was quite astonished at the reaction of Miss Darcy to it. She flushed to the roots of her hair and then went ghastly white, her lips compressed tightly. Mrs. Gardiner was afraid for a moment that the poor girl was going to swoon! Good heavens! What has come over the girl? Is she ill?

Her brother seems to not feel that she is ill...he is continuing to talk to Lizzy as if nothing is going on, although he gives Miss Bingley a withering look at the end of her little comment.

After a few minutes further conversation, Mrs. Gardiner felt it was time to go as they had already been there for a half hour. On the drive back to Lambton she chatted with her niece about all the non-essentials of Pemberley: the grounds, the fruit, the cake, the décor. What they did not discuss was what Mrs. Gardiner was most interested in: her niece's feelings toward Mr. Darcy, whom she clearly knew much better than her aunt and uncle had realized. She was disappointed, but did not feel she had the right to interrogate her niece over this matter...but still her curiosity was most frustrating!

Fishing at Pemberley
by Colette Saucier

August 6, 1812

That Mr. Gardiner could engage Mr. Hurst in lively conversation was a credit to the manners and breeding of the first gentleman. They spoke animatedly of common diversions in London; and Darcy did not remember another time in their acquaintance when Mr. Hurst had had so much to say, perhaps as the early hour had kept him from the port. When introduced to Miss Bingley and Mrs. Hurst, Mr. Gardiner was amiable without being obsequious and, if he noticed, did not acknowledge that each lady would only see him from the end of her nose.

Darcy, Bingley, Mr. Hurst, and Mr. Gardiner walked down to the trout stream with footmen following with tackle, rods, and bait, as well as refreshment for the anglers. They settled in on the bank in the warmth of the July day and talked genially for a while before falling into a companionable silence more conducive to fishing. Sitting next to Mr. Gardiner, Darcy struggled to remain still, not to prevent scaring the fish but because he feared all that might come pouring forth should he not maintain control.

Some time passed in the quiet of the sounds of nature before Mr. Gardiner, perhaps sensing the younger man's distress, spoke sotto voce to Darcy. "I cannot thank you enough for this invitation, sir. There truly is nothing quite so pleasant as fishing."

"You are most welcome any time."

"Yes, indeed, the ladies do not know what they are missing."

If possible, Darcy sat up straighter than before. "And what were Mrs. Gardiner and your niece planning for today?"

"Actually," he said, casting his line, "they planned to call on your sister."

A tingling sensation permeated Darcy's face as he held his expression in check. "Indeed? When did they plan to wait on her?"

Mr. Gardiner pulled his watch from his pocket. "Oh, I would say they should be there by now."

Darcy did not, dared not react nor even breathe. He stared out onto the stream, holding his rod steady.

Mr. Gardiner allowed several minutes to pass before speaking again. "You know, Mr. Darcy, I appreciate your hospitality, but I would not want to impose on your time. I know what a busy man you are. You must not feel compelled to remain here as host if you have any estate matters that require your attention."

Darcy glanced at his companion's profile and saw the slight turn of his lips as indication that Mr. Gardiner understood more than his words would suggest. "If you are certain, sir, there is an important matter I need to address," Darcy said, rising.

"Go to it, young man. Surely you will have more success in that quarter than you will fishing, seeing as you lost your bait some half hour ago."

Darcy Cancels the Dinner
at Pemberley
by Abigail Reynolds

August 7, 1812

After tearing himself away from Elizabeth at the Lambton Inn, Darcy had given free rein to both his horse and his temper. Galloping over the familiar countryside was the perfect situation for venting his rage at George Wickham, who once more had come between Darcy and his Elizabeth. Darcy wanted Wickham's blood. He would thrash him for ruining Lydia Bennet, then pummel him bloody for making Elizabeth cry. Darcy had never felt more helpless than when he had seen tears running down Elizabeth's lovely cheeks. He had longed to take her into his arms, to tell her that he would fix everything, that all would be well again, but all he could do was to offer her a glass of wine. He would have been happy to rip Wickham limb from limb.

By the time Darcy reached Pemberley, he had dismissed his fury and was once more a civilized man. If he wanted to help Elizabeth, he would have to render courtesy and no doubt a substantial sum of money to Wickham, rather than the beating he deserved. His love for Elizabeth and his responsibility as master of Pemberley left him no other choice.

Inside the house, Georgiana flew down the stairs to meet him, her face alight. "What did she say?" Then, as she took in his sober countenance, her smile vanished. "Oh, no. Did she refuse you? I am so sorry."

For a moment Darcy was taken aback by her question. "I did not ask her," he said shortly. "It was not the right time. She had just received some bad news from home, and will be returning there immediately."

Georgiana hesitated. "I hope it is nothing too serious."

Darcy did not meet her eyes. "Some scandal concerning one of her sisters, nothing more. Hopefully it will come to nothing."

His sister looked puzzled by his vagueness, but did not question him.

Miss Bingley, of course, could not leave well enough alone when he announced that the Gardiners and Miss Bennet had sent their apologies and would not be dining with them that evening. "What a pity!" she cried with patent insincerity. "I had so looked forward to seeing dear Eliza again." Her attempt at civility annoyed Darcy as much as her insulting comments on Elizabeth's appearance had done the previous day.

"I say, Darcy," Bingley said. "Did they give any reason for their sudden departure? I had thought they planned to remain in the area for several more days."

"Just that they were returning home immediately," said Darcy. He had promised Elizabeth that he would hide the truth as long as he could, and with any luck, the whole matter of Lydia Bennet could be resolved before Bingley heard of it.

"No doubt one of the Gardiners' children has some trifling ailment," said Mrs. Hurst. Her tone suggested that such an ailment must have been deliberately planned by the child.

"Children seem to recover so quickly," said Miss Bingley, who apparently could not leave the subject of Elizabeth's family quickly enough. "Do you suppose tomorrow will be as fair a day as today? Perhaps we could take a drive through the grounds. I declare, there is no spot in England that can make the beauty of the park here!"

"I hope the weather will permit it, but you will have to excuse me. Some pressing business has arisen in Town that requires my personal attention, and I will be leaving early tomorrow morning." Darcy braced himself for the storm that was sure to follow his announcement.

It did not materialize, apart from an agonized look from Georgiana. Miss Bingley merely tightened her lips, and all conversation came to a halt until Mrs. Annesley displayed her good breeding by changing the subject.

Darcy let the discussion flow around him as his thoughts turned to his plans for locating George Wickham. He was not so preoccupied, though, that he did not notice Mrs. Hurst speaking urgently in her sister's ear. From their whispered conversation, he suspected that Miss Bingley had not missed the significance of his sudden change of plans immediately following Elizabeth's departure. Perhaps now she would finally stop pestering him with her obsequious attentions.

The image of Elizabeth's reddened eyes rose before him again. Damn George Wickham!

Mrs. Gardiner Receives a Letter
from her Husband
by C. Allyn Pierson

August 11, 1812

The Longbourn family had settled down into a routine, of sorts, after Mr. Gardiner left for London to help his brother-in-law look for Lydia and Wickham. The members of the family went about their usual activities – stitching and walking, discussing fashions and reading, with at least an appearance of calm. If Elizabeth or Jane spent more than their usual time staring at the same page of their book or went up to their rooms for a "rest" more than one would expect, Mary and Kitty did not seem much changed by the tension in the air.

Mrs. Gardiner spent a part of every day with Mrs. Bennet, hoping to bring her gently to a sense of resignation over the loss of her favorite daughter...or at least to the realization that it was a good idea to not pour every wild thought in her head into the ears of the servants. When she at last gave up, she would spend most of the day with her elder nieces, and her four children gave the elder sisters a source of entertainment and distraction which made the day go by more quickly.

After watching for the post avidly every day, the household was finally rewarded with a letter from Mr. Gardiner enumerating his efforts in the search for Lydia. Mrs. Gardiner shared the letter with her two eldest nieces:

My dear wife:

I write to you with a heavy heart. I found my brother Bennet at his hotel and convinced him to remove with me to Cheapside where we could at least be comfortable during our search. Unfortunately, Mr. Bennet's efforts for finding Lydia have been met with complete failure and we have not had a single clue to their whereabouts. He has spent much time since settling in London doing a systematic search of all the hotels that were likely to have sheltered to couple, but has heard nothing to the purpose.

I have heard from Colonel Forster, and it sounds as if he has spent considerable time interviewing Wickham's friends and acquaintances in Brighton, but he has found no one who has any idea where he could be. Apparently, he has said enough to make his fellow officers believe he has neither friends nor family outside the regiment who might be sheltering them. He has, however, left behind in Brighton considerable debts to many of the tradesmen and, worse yet, many debts of honor amongst his fellows. The men who earlier had found him a good fellow and ripe for any spree now curse him as a man who cannot be trusted to play and pay fairly."

Jane burst out at this point, "A gamester! This is wholly unexpected, I had not an idea of it!"

Mrs. Gardiner said soothingly, "I know, my dear, but surely it is all of a piece with his other behavior." She turned back to her letter:

Colonel Forster feels it will take at least one thousand pounds to clear Wickham's debts.

The one piece of good news I have for you is that I have finally convinced Mr. Bennet that he has done all he can for now and that his wife and remaining daughters need him. He will leave town the day after you receive this and will be home before dinner. I fear it will be hopeless, but I will continue the search for the absconding couple without him, and I hope to have

432

some success, but we must face the possibility that Lydia is lost to us forever.

I hope, my love, you will find yourself able to leave Longbourn to the care of Mr. Bennet and Jane and Elizabeth and will come home on the carriage that brings my brother to you. I miss you and the children; the house is empty shell without you, my dear. Share with my nieces and sister what you think appropriate from this letter, and I hope to see you soon.

Your loving, Edward

After Mrs. Gardiner shared the letter, they all sat for a few moments staring blankly at the trees visible through the window. Eventually, Elizabeth rose briskly and said, "Well, we cannot sit here and mope. Nothing has changed from what we believed before. I am going to go up and sit with my mother for a while. I will send Betsy to help you, aunt, as I am sure you will want to pack your portmanteaux and trunks for your journey tomorrow."

The three women embraced, then scattered to various parts of the house.

Darcy Calls on Mr. Gardiner
by Abigail Reynolds

August 15, 1812

Mr. Gardiner felt he deserved the luxury of spending the afternoon reading the book on fishing he had purchased during their visit to Oxford. He had been trying to finish it for days. He had started it in Lambton, but was interrupted by the urgent need to return to London. There had been no time to read on that chaotic journey, especially since all his energies had been devoted to consoling Elizabeth as best he could. When he finally reached London, he had to find Mr. Bennet's hotel; and once he had discovered his brother-in-law and brought him back to Gracechurch Street, there was no peace to be had. Mr. Bennet's disturbance of mind was evident.

He was fond of his brother-in-law, but on occasion Mr. Gardiner found Mr. Bennet's directionless behavior exasperating. By God, he did not intend to allow his own daughters to run wild simply because it was too much trouble to rein them in! For the last few days, Mr. Bennet had required his constant guidance in the search for Lydia. Although he would never have admitted it to anyone, Mr. Gardiner was glad to see Mr. Bennet depart.

He looked forward to seeing his dear wife and children again that evening, but he knew that their arrival would bring a happy chaos with it that would preclude time to himself. That was why he intended to make the most of this quiet time at home.

Mr. Gardiner had not even finished one chapter when he heard a sharp knock at the door. A minute later, his manservant appeared and handed him a calling card. Mr. Gardiner's eyebrows shot up when he read the name on it.

Why in the world would Mr. Darcy be calling on him here? Not only was their acquaintance slight, but Darcy was supposed to be at Pemberley, a full two days journey away. Mr. Gardiner chuckled to himself. Lizzy had been sly indeed! Apparently she and Darcy had far more of an understanding than she had admitted. But that still did not explain Darcy's appearance on his doorstep. Well, most likely he was in search of news of Lizzy, and did not want to interrupt the household at Longbourn during this crisis. That was fair enough. Mr. Gardiner instructed the servant to send Mr. Darcy in.

Mr. Darcy's face was marked with lines of tension, but he shook Mr. Gardiner's hand and exchanged cordial greetings. He did not hesitate in turning immediately to his business. "You have no doubt guessed that I am here to discuss your niece's situation."

"Well, that is good news! It is unfortunate you were not here yesterday, as Lizzy's father was still in town then." So Darcy must be on the verge of making an offer – good news indeed!

The corners of Mr. Darcy's lips turned down and his brows drew together, then his expression cleared with understanding. "My apologies, sir; I should have been more precise. I am here regarding your niece Miss Lydia."

Now it was Mr. Gardiner's turn to be surprised. "I was not aware you had a particular connection to Lydia," he said cautiously.

"I do not. My connection – my unfortunate connection – is to Mr. Wickham. I feel a certain responsibility for failing to prevent the current situation, and having some knowledge of Wickham's confidantes, I felt I was in a good position to discover his present location."

"I will certainly be grateful for any information you can share with me. Our searches have been fruitless to date."

"I can do somewhat better than that, sir. I have already discovered them, and I believe the resolution is near to hand."

Stunned, Mr. Gardiner pushed himself half-way out of his chair. "You have seen them? Is Lydia well?"

Darcy hesitated. "Miss Lydia is in good health, but I am sorry to say that I was unable to persuade her to leave her present situation, even when I offered to assist her in returning her to her friends. She is absolutely resolved on remaining where she is, expecting they will be wed sooner or later. Under the circumstances, I felt my only option was to secure a marriage between them.

"Is Mr. Wickham agreeable to that?"

"He admitted marriage was not his design, but he has some very pressing debts of honor, and was therefore open to negotiation. He wanted more than he could get, of course, but in time we came to an agreement. He is now prepared to marry Miss Lydia, provided that certain conditions are met."

That was fast work indeed! Mr. Gardiner wondered just how expensive those conditions were. "Of course, the question is how to present this matter to her father. He is hardly likely to believe Wickham is marrying Miss Lydia for nothing more than her charms and her slight dowry."

"Indeed." Darcy looked out the window for a moment, as if gathering his courage. "This matter is my responsibility, and as such I will bear the financial burden. However, I would prefer that none of the Bennets be aware of my part in this."

Mr. Gardiner could not quite repress a smile at this. A secret from all the Bennets? Hardly likely; it was obvious that Lizzy must be party to this whole manner, since it was utterly ridiculous to think that Darcy had any responsibility of his own in this matter, regardless of what he might say. Still, if Darcy wished to pretend that it had nothing to do with Lizzy, that was his business. Clearly he would soon enough be a member of the family, and it would no longer matter. He could hardly wait to tell his wife!

But he only said, "Mr. Bennet is not a fool, and he has his pride. You would perhaps do better to allow him to pay some small part of what is required, allowing him to believe it to be the entire amount."

436

The corners of Darcy's mouth turned up in a slight smile. "Then perhaps we should discuss the details."

Darcy Calls on the Gardiners
with News of Lydia and Wickham
by Regina Jeffers

August 16, 1812

Friday brought Darcy a short letter from Georgiana. She and the Bingleys had traveled to Nottingham, and she told Darcy of a few items she purchased from the local merchants. The most important part of the letter was the last paragraph.

> *Now that Miss Bingley no longer examines this letter to comment on how much my handwriting resembles my brother's, I can say what I wanted to tell you. Your sister, my darling Fitzwilliam, praises your efforts to save Miss Elizabeth, especially considering the mortifications you must be suffering at Mr. Wickham's hands. You see, I have no doubt you have found him, and a resolution is at hand. I await your return and news of your success.*
>
> *With love, Georgiana*

Reading the letter a second time, Darcy realized the blessing of having Georgiana as his sister rather than the impetuous Lydia Bennet. He held no doubt Georgiana would gladly have suffered the public humiliation of rumors of her brief encounter with Mr. Wickham in order to save Miss Elizabeth where Lydia Bennet cared not for anyone but herself. The girl had refused his every attempt to save her reputation and that of her sisters. Miss Lydia and George Wickham deserved each other; Wickham would marry an embodiment of Mrs. Bennet; mayhap Darcy would have the final revenge.

In late afternoon, Darcy made a short trip to Cheapside to speak to Mr. Gardiner. "I am sorry, Sir, but the master is within with his brother Bennet. Mr. Gardiner left specific orders he not be disturbed," the Gardiners' manservant explained.

Darcy had no desire to encounter Mr. Bennet; he did not want Elizabeth's father to know to what extremes he had gone to save Elizabeth and her sisters. If he won Miss Elizabeth's heart, he preferred to do so without her feeling a debt in accepting his hand in marriage. "I will return on the morrow, if that is acceptable?" Darcy said as he stepped away from the Gardiners' door.

"The master will be home most of the day, Sir. His brother returns to Hertfordshire. I heard Mr. Gardiner say so, Sir."

When he called on Mr. Gardiner the following day, he received a genuine welcome. "Mr. Darcy, it is with unexpected pleasure to see you again so soon. When Mr. Witmore said I had a visitor yesterday, I had no idea it was you; Mr. Bennet and I would have received you had we known."

"It is of no consequence, Mr. Gardiner," Darcy stated as he accepted the seat Gardiner indicated. "My business is of a delicate nature, and I purposely avoided Mr. Bennet's knowledge of it."

Mr. Gardiner said seriously, "You have my undivided attention, Sir."

"As you are aware, I was with your niece Elizabeth when she received the news from Miss Bennet, which has distressed your family of late."

"Elizabeth has told us of the comfort your presence provided her, but I do not understand how that fact affects you, Sir." The knowledge Elizabeth had spoken kindly of his effort to allay her fears soothed Darcy's bruised ego. He wondered how she would react if Elizabeth ever discovered his secrecy. He prayed she would understand he had to protect her; the tears she shed at the Lambton inn had torn his heart into pieces.

"Mr. Wickham's relationship with my family has been a tenuous one, but my many dealings with the man has provided me intimate knowledge of his habits, which neither you nor your brother would have. My knowledge of George Wickham comes from the late Mr. Wickham being my father's steward. Mr. Wickham and I attended Cambridge together, and I have dealt with him in such nefarious matters as this one on prior occasions. I brought that knowledge to London. I realize I have taken on more than is appropriate, but I pray you will forgive my intrusion into such a private matter when I tell you I have found Mr. Wickham and Miss Lydia and have spoken to them on several occasions regarding their folly."

"You found them!" Mr. Gardiner's relief showed upon his countenance. "I would gladly forgive your intrusion for such happy news. Where are they? Are they married?"

"They are not married," Darcy said with regret, and Gardiner's happiness faded. "But I have presented myself to both Mr. Wickham and to Miss Lydia as being your family's agent in this matter. I concocted a prevarication, which I hope you will also forgive, to achieve an agreement with Mr. Wickham and your family. Yesterday, he applied for an ordinary license with the minister at St. Clements Church. He and Miss Lydia will be married in a little over a fortnight."

Gardiner ran his fingers through his hair. He took a deep breath. "Mr. Darcy, my sister's family will be ever in your debt."

"When I spoke to Miss Lydia," Darcy explained, "no matter what I offered as a logical reason for her leaving, the girl's loyalty remains with Mr. Wickham. She openly expressed wanting nothing to do with 'boring old Longbourn' or with 'sisters who never wanted to do anything that was adventurous.' Miss Lydia believes Mr. Wickham plans to marry her as soon as his "luck" changes. She wants nothing to do with any of her 'so-called' friends. Despite my best arguments for her leaving, Miss Lydia speaks only of Mr. Wickham's goodness."

Although Darcy's news astounded him, his niece's lack of concern for her family, however, did not surprise Mr. Gardiner. "I fear only the two eldest Bennet sisters possess good sense, Mr. Darcy. They are our favorites, as you can well imagine." Darcy could easily imagine Elizabeth; he had done so every day since the assembly at Meryton, but he made no comment. Mr. Gardiner, he was certain, recognized Darcy's affection for Elizabeth. Why else would he have become involved in this most private matter if he did not care about Elizabeth Bennet? He no longer attempted to deny his feelings for her. "I have suggested that Miss Lydia be married from your home. Obviously, she cannot return to Longbourn without bringing shame upon her sisters."

"Of course, Mr. Darcy. That is most prudent. Mrs. Gardiner is to return to Gracechurch Street a bit later today. After services tomorrow, we will make arrangements to retrieve Lydia from her reprehensible employment." Mr. Gardiner said tentatively, "From what Lizzy and my brother Bennet have said of Mr. Wickham's true nature, I suspect the man has demanded a hefty sum to bring about this marriage."

Darcy smiled somewhat stiffly. "As I explained earlier, I held a prior knowledge of Mr. Wickham's weaknesses. I have attempted to use those failings against the man, and I have negotiated in your family's behalf what I believe to be a manageable solution." He paused and searched for the words to explain what he had done in Elizabeth's name. "After three days of negotiations, I have promised Mr. Wickham the following: your future nephew will resign his position in the militia and accept a comparable one in the regulars; my cousin Colonel Fitzwilliam has assisted me in locating a lieutenancy in Newcastle; Mr. Wickham's debts in Brighton and Meryton will be paid; and as a dowry, Mr. Wickham will receive three thousand pounds." He waited for the business savvy Mr. Gardiner to digest the terms.

"Likely close to five thousand pounds in total," Gardiner calculated, and Darcy nodded his agreement. "It will be a strain on the Bennets' finances, but my brother Philips and I will share the expenses of my sister's family."

Darcy cleared his throat in trepidation. "Actually, I would take on the wedding's expenses and Mr. Wickham's placement." He looked curiously at Elizabeth's beloved uncle. Gardiner's shock was evident, but Darcy had more to reveal. "It is my wish that neither Miss Elizabeth nor her father know of my involvement. It would not do to make my deeds known to those most innocent in this matter. I want no false gratitude."

"You would have me wear borrowed feathers?" Mr. Gardiner said in disbelief. "I cannot allow you to assume such a debt, Mr. Darcy!"

"I will hear of no compromise," Darcy insisted. "It is my conviction that if George Wickham's worthlessness had been better known, it would be impossible for him to persuade any young woman of character to make an alliance without proper bonds. I knew of his low character, but my foolish pride would not permit me to make known the extent of his depravity. I once thought myself above his actions. However, I have come to realize if I had acted with honor, none of this would have been possible. I cared only for private affairs, and I did not consider the ramifications of Mr. Wickham's evil on others." Darcy would never speak of his sister's shame, but he gave Mr. Gardiner to know Mr. Wickham had betrayed Darcy's family. He was obstinate about his involvement and would not relent, no matter how much Mr. Gardiner attempted to change his mind.

"Well, Mr. Darcy," Mr. Gardiner offered, "it seems you have Mr. Wickham's life planned."

Darcy laughed conspiratorially. "Mr. Wickham said something similar."

Gardiner sighed and rumpled his hair again. "Will you join me for dinner, Sir?"

Darcy said apologetically, "I cannot, Mr. Gardiner, I have other obligations this evening."

"When Mrs. Gardiner returns, I wish to discuss your proposal with her. Will you join us tomorrow evening as our guest?"

"It would be a pleasure to spend time with you and Mrs. Gardiner again."

The men parted, each with a degree of satisfaction. Mr. Gardiner would see an end to the troubles Lydia had brought on the family; Darcy would preserve Elizabeth's respectability and maintain his slim hopes she would one day change her mind and marry him.

* * *

"I will not change my mind, Mr. Gardiner." Darcy renewed his obstinacy in acting as the sole benefactor in the Wickham matter for Mr. Gardiner had had second thoughts about taking credit for Darcy's triumph.

"I cannot see my way clear to give voice to your scheme," Gardiner insisted.

"Mr. Gardiner, I shall not relent. You must allow me to be of service to your family."

Mrs. Gardiner's hand rested on her husband's arm. "Perhaps, it is best, my Dear," she said encouragingly. "Mr. Darcy appears earnest in his request, and if you feel a need to make things right, I am certain Mr. Darcy will consider his investment in Lydia's future as a loan. You may repay our Derbyshire friend for his kindness."

Darcy had no intention of considering his outlay as a loan, but he would not argue with the lady. It was quite obvious Mrs. Gardiner recognized Darcy's preference for their niece. A preference he hoped one day to make public.

"I must tell you, Mr. Darcy, we will be forever in your debt," Mr. Gardiner began. "We accept your offer reluctantly in hopes by doing so we maintain the respectability of Lydia's more deserving sisters. They should have fulfilling lives despite their youngest sister's folly."

The Gardiners had the pleasure of Darcy's company that evening for supper, and Darcy had the pleasure of listening to them tell stories of Jane and Elizabeth as children and as young ladies growing up in the Bennet household. Those tales of Elizabeth's precociousness most interested him, but he also took delight in learning more of Jane Bennet. He had misjudged her nature, and he knew making amends to Bingley must come soon. "Those two girls!" Mrs. Gardiner laughed so hard at the story she told that tears came to her eyes. "They would look at you and maintain their innocence, which was usually true for Jane, but not so much for Lizzy. Even when one was angry over what they had done, a person could not be upset with either of them. Their goodness would make me love them even when my favorite vase lay in a hundred pieces on the drawing room floor." Darcy knew he could love Elizabeth with all his heart. He ached for her. Darcy had a fleeting remembrance of how his heart had jumped in his chest when he had discovered her at Pemberley.

The Gardiners' own children joined them for part of the evening, and the rambunctious brood showed an interest in Mr. Darcy because he was a "favorite," according to their parents, of both "Cousin Jane" and "Cousin Elizabeth." Having children in the house made Darcy fancy Elizabeth even more than usual. It was a perfect way to end a most pleasurable evening.

On Monday, Darcy finalized the plans for the church, the transfer of funds to Lydia Bennet, and the purchasing of the commission. Calling on the Gardiners one last time, he found they had sent a dispatch to Longbourn with news of the impending marriage. Finally, he thought, Elizabeth will be free of all these provocations: She will be able to laugh again; he dearly missed that laugh. Lydia was coming to Gracechurch Street, and he would return to Pemberley on Wednesday. He would return to London for the actual wedding; Mr. Wickham had no one to stand up with him; plus, Darcy's need for meticulous planning required he be there to assure nothing went awry before the nuptials.

Mrs. Bennet Comes Downstairs
by Mary Simonsen

August 17, 1812

*The scene: Mr. Bennet's return to Longbourn after
Lydia and Wickham's elopement*

"Does your mother still keep to her room?" Mr. Bennet asked Jane. As her father already knew the answer, a weary Jane merely nodded. "Admirable! Truly admirable! If I thought I could get away with it, I should do the same. I would lie in bed in my dressing gown and nightcap and give as much trouble as I pleased."

"Mama no longer spends the day in bed, Papa. She is now in her chair."

"Truly! Mrs. Bennet has moved from bed to chair? Alert the town crier!"

Knowing there was little to be gained by continuing such a conversation, after returning her mother's breakfast tray to the kitchen, Jane went in search of Lizzy and found her in the garden. Since learning of Lydia's flight from Brighton to London with George Wickham, Lizzy had been downcast. She believed if she had succeeded in taking Wickham's true measure during his time in Hertfordshire, the elopement would not have happened.

They were in the garden but a short time when Mrs. Hill came in search of the two eldest Bennet daughters. "A post rider has come with a letter!" the servant announced, and Jane and Lizzy went running to their father's study.'

"What news, Papa?" the pair asked in breathless unison. After pointing to a piece of paper on his desk, Lizzy was the first to reach

445

it.

The paper, a letter from Uncle Gardiner, stated that Lydia and Wickham had been found in Town. After the meat of the letter was digested, it was determined the couple had not married, but would wed upon Mr. Bennet's agreement to settle on Lydia one hundred per year during his life and fifty a year after his death.

Although Jane was elated by the news, Lizzy and her father exchanged glances. How was it possible that Wickham could be induced to marry on so slight a temptation?

"I must tell Mama," Jane said and quickly departed.

Proof of the reception of the news that Lydia was to be wed came with Mrs. Bennet's hosannas seeping through the floorboards and settling, like dust, upon the inhabitants of the study below.

The news of the impending marriage brought about a miracle. After a two-week absence, the lady of the house took her seat at the head of the table. As Mrs. Bennet made plans to rent various houses in the neighborhood for the newlyweds, her husband remained silent. But once the servants had departed, he informed his wife that if she wished to visit with the couple, she would have to make arrangements to do so somewhere other than at Longbourn because it was his intention to never welcome the pair into his home.

To that declaration, he added he would not advance so much as a guinea for wedding clothes. "Lydia may enter into marriage in the same way she came into this world—wearing nothing!"

After supper, Mrs. Bennet asked Lizzy to speak to her father. "It is our Christian duty to welcome the prodigal sheep back into the fold," Mama said, making a hash of the Gospel parables.

Lizzy was of a different mind. How dare Lydia bring scandal into the heart of her family? There was also the matter of Mr. Darcy. She was now heartily sorry to have acquainted that gentleman with her fears for her sister. But Lizzy understood the reality of village life. If her family was seen to have turned their backs on Lydia, everyone else would follow suit.

"What do you want me to say to Papa?" Lizzy asked.

"Oh, you will think of something," Mrs. Bennet said. "You are just like your father—never at a loss for words."

After initially rejecting Lizzy's argument for welcoming Mr. and Mrs. George Wickham into the bosom of the Bennet family, Mr. Bennet saw the wisdom of his daughter's argument.

"I know that tomorrow your mother will be in the village bragging—actually bragging—that she has a daughter married at sixteen," Mr. Bennet said, shaking his head. "The fact that the man is a villain, a pirate, a scoundrel, will not enter into her thinking. But there will be no peace at Longbourn if I do otherwise than what she asks.

"Now that the matter is settled, do you have any words of joy for your father, Lizzy? Please tell me Mr. Bingley is hiding at Netherfield for the purpose of surprising Jane with an offer of marriage. Or that Mr. Collins has a friend who will marry Mary. Or that the apothecary's son has stopped flirting with Kitty and is moving the relationship forward."

"No, Papa. I have no news to cheer you." Nor would she. Lydia had seen to that.

Lydia's Letter
by Shannon Winslow

August 31, 1812

My Dearest Harriet,

What adventures I have had since I saw you! I write to you now from Longbourn, where Wickham and I have just come to visit after our wedding in London. Yes, London! Are you not surprised? Or perhaps you have already heard that our plans changed after I left you in Brighton. My dear husband (for so he now is!) knew I should prefer London to Gretna Green, and I said I did not care where we went so long as we were to be married in the end.

There was a little delay of the wedding itself, and some horrid unpleasantness with my Aunt and Uncle Gardiner, but I will not take the space for such tediousness here. Only I must say that they were very ungenerous in their attentions to me in all respects. They could not be bothered to give one single party in my honor, to show me about the town, or even to see to it that the church was tolerably filled with well-wishers and flowers for the wedding. My aunt only gave me some lilies from her garden to carry, and are not lilies more appropriate for funerals? Then there was some last minute business my uncle said he had to attend to, which vexed me greatly.

But at last we were at St. Clement's and there was Wickham waiting for me at the altar, looking vastly handsome. La! I thought I should have fainted for happiness, and what a good joke that would have been. However, I did not faint (for I have a very sturdy constitution), and my uncle gave me away. Then the rector talked on and on — about what, I have no idea, for I was thinking only of my dear Wickham.

Now I will tell you a great secret, for I would not hide anything from you, my dear, and I know you are quite capable of keeping a confidence. Mr. Darcy was at my wedding! He came to stand up beside Wickham. What do you say to that? I never had any idea before that they were on such friendly terms, but my husband has since explained it, saying that Mr. Darcy has always had the greatest admiration for him. Now that is the kind of friend whom it is very well worth having, for Mr. Darcy is exceedingly rich and no doubt has many favours in his gift.

I could only wish that my sisters had been at St. Clement's to see me married. Since returning to Longbourn, however, I have at least had the satisfaction of observing how they all envy me. They try to hide it, of course, (excepting Kitty who freely admits it), looking grave and self-conscious, but I see that they are really embarrassed for having been outdone by myself, the youngest of them all. Jane had to give up her place to me, you know, since I am now a married woman. And Mary is sure to have noticed how hopeless her own situation is by comparison. But it is Elizabeth who suffers most acutely, I believe, for I daresay she wanted Wickham for herself. I did not mean to be cruel. I was just telling the story of shewing off my ring to a neighbor I chanced to come across, when in fact Lizzy got so upset as to run out of the room!

Do not you think it a certain proof that she envies me? Well, I was as kind as I could be to her after that. But it is no wonder she and all the others are jealous, for my dear Wickham is the greatest catch in the world! He truly is the handsomest man that ever was seen, as well as being the boldest rider. Did not your own husband once say that he had the finest seat in the regiment? And tomorrow, when the shooting starts, I daresay Wickham will kill more birds than anybody else in the county. So I have told my sisters. They would be fortunate to have half my good luck in finding husbands. I have promised to help in that regard by putting them in the way of meeting some very smart officers when they come to visit me in Newcastle.

Poor Mama! She regrets my going so far away more than anybody else, but it cannot be helped. I am wife to a military man now, and I must follow by dear Wickham's side wherever his duty takes him. You understand these things, Harriet, as my other friends cannot.

449

I hope that we may all meet again one day, but I hardly know when that may be — perhaps not these two or three years. In the meantime, you must write to me often. Wickham and I send our love to you and to Colonel Forster, and we shall remember to drink to your health, as I hope you may on occasion drink to ours.

Your most affectionate friend,

Lydia Wickham

Darcy Dines with the Gardiners
by Colette Saucier

September 1, 1812

> *They name thee before me,*
> *A knell to mine ear;*
> *A shudder comes o'er me —*
> *Why wert thou so dear?*
> *They know not I knew thee,*
> *Who knew thee too well: —*
> *Long, long shall I rue thee,*
> *Too deeply to tell.*

— When We Two Parted, Lord George Gordon Byron

Soon after the wedding of Lydia to Wickham, Darcy stood between his solicitor and the Gardiners outside the house at Gracechurch Street watching the newlyweds' coach depart for Longbourn, and the last tenuous thread tying him to Elizabeth snapped. In a few hours, they would be with her, the woman he loved whom he would never see again.

Darcy knew scores of reasons he should decline the Gardiners' invitation to dinner, but he heeded only the one reason he had to accept: he could not yet cede all connection to Elizabeth. To himself he acknowledged that, a mere four months before, he would not have deigned to break bread with a family so far below his social strata; and now he could scarcely conceal his eagerness.

The house near Cheapside had defied his expectations. While certainly the furnishings were not comparable to his own in worth, unharnessed from the weight of generations of wealth, they bespoke a lightness, so fresh and new, which Darcy found appealing. The laughter and chatter of children contributed to the harmony that caused a bittersweet sensation to well within him. Here was a home the likes of which he would never know.

During the first courses, an implied moratorium on discussing the inhabitants of Longbourn hung over the dining room table, perhaps no one wanting the recent unpleasantness to spoil their meal. How Darcy craved, though, any word of Elizabeth – even to hear them pronounce her name. Instead, Darcy and Mrs. Gardiner spoke at length of Lambton and her childhood there and all the places in Derbyshire they knew in common.

Darcy then addressed Mr. Gardiner. "And you grew up in Meryton?" Edging ever so slightly closer to the one of whom he longed to hear.

"Yes, that is quite so, although I have not resided in Hertfordshire in over thirty years."

"How is it you came to London?"

"As you might know, my father was an attorney in Meryton, and he hoped I would join him in that profession; but I had my own idea of making it in the world. My father invested greatly in my education and sent me to Oxford for two years."

"Indeed!"

"Yes, but perhaps he erred in that. During breaks, I found myself coming to Town more often than going home to Hertfordshire until I had no notion of returning to Meryton at all. His clerk Mr. Philips took the position intended for me – and my sister, as well!"

Darcy smiled. "So it was you and two sisters, then, growing up?" Darcy could not reconcile this elegant man of good breeding with those vulgar women.

Mr. Gardiner gazed into his wine glass pensively before taking a sip. "You may have noticed that I am more than ten years older than Mrs. Philips and Mrs. Bennet – much like yourself and Miss Darcy. After I was born, my parents did not have any other children for quite some time, at least none that survived. Then my sisters came along not even a year apart, but my dear mother...well, she was not strong. I believe her passing broke my father's heart."

Mr. Gardiner cleared his throat as if the unpleasant memory had caught in his craw. "After raising a son for ten years, my father had no notion of what daughters were all about. Not having a wife to guide him, he left it to the housekeeper to raise the girls, but that was no parenting to speak of. I stayed busy with my studies and treated them like dolls when I paid them any attention at all. Then I went away to school, and I suppose they were left to their own devices, no guidance or discipline."

Darcy comprehended the intent of Mr. Gardiner's story as an apologia for his sisters, and he could not but be moved to sympathize with those motherless little girls – not so different from Georgiana in that regard, but denied the affection and structure his sister had been privileged to receive. He nodded at Mr. Gardiner in acknowledgment.

Darcy turned to Mrs. Gardiner, his patience nearing the end. "You are quite close to your nieces, yes?"

Mrs. Gardiner gave him a knowing smile. "Yes, particularly with Jane and Elizabeth." Elizabeth. "They lived here in Town with us for almost two years."

"Ah, so that must have been when Miss Bennet became acquainted with a young poet."

Mrs. Gardiner smiled. "Why, yes, in a manner of speaking. How did you know about that?"

"I recall hearing that his verse brought an end to the romance." Darcy had often wondered how the two eldest Bennet sisters could demonstrate a comportment unknown to the youngest, and now he recognized the influence of this refined couple. "How did they come to reside with you here?"

"I understand you have heard Elizabeth play the pianoforte, have you not?"

"Yes, I have had that honour." Now that the conversation had veered to his most desired topic, Darcy struggled to remember he was supposed to be eating.

"Elizabeth has a genius for the instrument and might have been quite the proficient. She came here to study with a master; but she and Jane were so close, so we invited them both to stay with us."

"You say she might have been a proficient. Did she stop working with the master?"

Mr. and Mrs. Gardiner passed a look between them as if silently discussing how much they should reveal. "I fear I am to blame," said Mr. Gardiner. "You see, I took Jane and Elizabeth to the British Museum. Elizabeth was fascinated with the Rosetta Stone, as if it unlocked a whole new world to her. With her avid curiosity, she became absorbed with the Ancient Egyptians. She began reading about them, which led to another subject and then another. She soon turned into such a voracious reader, she lost interest in music for the most part. At least she would not practise to the satisfaction of the master."

Darcy scowled in confusion. "Eli – Miss Bennet once insisted that she was not a great reader."

"Her mother believes she ought not spend so much time with her head in a book," said Mrs. Gardiner, "or at least not own it lest she be thought of as a bluestocking, which Mrs. Bennet considers a sure path to spinsterhood. A woman, especially, if she has the misfortune of knowing anything, should conceal it as well as she can."

Darcy marveled at all he was learning about his beloved and yet how clearly he could see how Elizabeth had become the only woman he could love. He smiled and glanced down and, reminded of the plate before him, pushed his food around. "I had been given to believe Mary Bennet the musician in the family."

"Elizabeth taught Mary how to play. We tried to bring her here to study with a master; but after two months, she declared London 'wicked' and returned to Longbourn."

Darcy smiled with his hosts. He recalled his time at Netherfield when he had joined Bingley's sisters in their ridicule of Elizabeth's relations, denigrating her uncle for being in trade without having ever met the man. Now he found he envied him: his light and happy home, his laughing children, his loving wife, all those things Darcy's wealth and status would never provide. Mostly, though, he envied him Elizabeth, that he would see her smiles and hear her play and enjoy her wit – all lost to Darcy.

His envy and consciousness of his own loss, however, did not dissuade Darcy from his next objective. Indeed, realizing the happiness he would be denied made him determined to undo his unconscionable actions so Bingley might have a chance at the joy that he himself would never know. Darcy hoped it not too late to make amends. Many months had passed – perhaps her heart, if ever it had been touched, had now turned against Bingley. Nevertheless, if Jane Bennet harboured any affection for his friend, Darcy must do all within his power to effect a reunion. If that meant he must face Elizabeth again, so be it.

As the Business with Wickham
Is at an End, Darcy Leaves London
by Regina Jeffers

September 3, 1812

All were happy to welcome his return to Pemberley, with his sister most anxious to seek his company privately; but that would wait; today Darcy served as the "excellent" host. "Mr. Darcy, you were grievously missed on our journey to Nottingham," Caroline called to him.

He answered her politely, "I am sorry to cause you grief, Miss Bingley."

"Has your urgent estate problems been resolved?" Bingley implored.

"Generally so," Darcy lied. "But I will return to London for a day or two at the end of the month. Then everything will be finalized." He emphasized the last words to give Georgiana some peace while she waited to learn the whole story.

"I would have wished to be of service to you, Darcy," Bingley offered. "You do so much for my family."

"Your caring for Georgiana was of service to me, Bingley. I would never have left her in your care if I did not value your friendship. She means more to me than does Pemberley." Georgiana blushed with his words, and her eyes misted with emotions. "In fact," he continued, "I hoped to keep you at Pemberley when your sisters depart for Scarborough. Besides wishing you to care again for Georgiana in my absence, I would wish to spend some time with you in gentlemanly pursuits."

"I would enjoy that, Darcy." Bingley smiled from ear-to-ear.

* * *

Later that evening, Georgiana tapped lightly on his study door. "I wondered when you would make your way here, Dearest One," he teased.

"I wanted to guarantee that our guests had retired for the night." Georgiana seated herself across from his desk. "Please tell me what happened in London. Did you find Mr. Wickham?"

"Are you certain you want to hear all the unsavory details?"

"Besides knowing Miss Elizabeth is going to be well, your story can only confirm how fortunate I am to have you as my brother. Although it would probably upset me to ever see Mr. Wickham again, I do want to know his fate and your advantage."

Darcy summarized the events of the previous ten days, accenting the squalor in which he found both Mrs. Younge and George Wickham, but he assured Georgiana, "Mr. Wickham will marry Lydia Bennet; along with the Gardiners, I will attend the service at St. Clements Church."

"Then you will be able to pursue Miss Elizabeth again," Georgiana encouraged.

"Have you considered the ramifications of that action, Georgiana?" he started. "If I earn Elizabeth's love, it would mean Mr. Wickham would be my brother–our brother."

"Fitzwilliam, we have many relations we rarely see. Mr. and Mrs. Wickham will be in Newcastle; I am certain Miss Elizabeth would understand Mr. Wickham would never be welcomed at Pemberley. You could not have done all these things and then forsake the prize. You must find a way to win Miss Elizabeth; you deserve her, and although she does not know it yet, she needs you."

"Georgiana, the man who earns your heart will be winning a true romantic." He chuckled while she blushed. They finished the evening with his relating some of the more amusing Elizabeth

Bennet stories shared by the Gardiners; they laughed and talked into the late hours.

* * *

As promised, he returned to London to witness the exchange of vows and to finalize the money matters. The wedding had taken place on a Monday at eleven of the clock. A month had passed since Mr. Wickham and Lydia Bennet had left Brighton, and finally to be rid of the chaos gladdened Darcy. In Lydia Bennet, Darcy saw the same effusive, immature girl from Hertfordshire; the results associated with her actions meant nothing to her. Instead, she babbled on about whether Mr. Wickham should wear his blue coat for the ceremony. Mrs. Gardiner attempted to caution the girl, but silence could not be attained. Darcy thanked his stars for giving him a sensible sister rather than having someone like Mrs. Wickham in his family.

Darcy spent time with the Gardiners on Tuesday, but they spoke more of Lydia's insolence rather than of Elizabeth and Jane; he would have preferred to hear about the latter. One of the Gardiner children, Cassandra, presented him a crayon picture of himself, Jane, and Elizabeth walking in a garden and holding hands. Although the likenesses were not accurate, the sentiment touched his heart in a way he had never known. He carried the drawing to Pemberley and placed it in a special spot in his study.

Returning to the security of Pemberley and having both Georgiana's and Bingley's companies brought him comfort. The turmoil of the past few weeks had taken its toll on his usually resilient composure. He required the company of family and friends after his dealings with the nefarious Mr. Wickham. Yet, being with Bingley constantly reminded Darcy he must make amends for his duplicity in separating Bingley from Jane Bennet. One early autumn day, he and Bingley sought time outdoors.

As he accepted the loaded gun from Darcy's servant, Bingley said wistfully, "I believe the last time we partook of the season's shooting was at Netherfield."

458

"I believe you correct, Bingley." Darcy paused as he planted the idea. "That was a pleasant time, was it not?" Although he did not purposely initiate it, a sigh slipped from his lips. If he were to maintain his sanity, he desperately required Elizabeth's company again. "I was wondering Bingley, have you made a decision on Netherfield? It appears a waste of your father's inheritance to let an estate one never uses."

As expected, Bingley readily seized upon Darcy's veiled suggestion. "Not having stayed through the winter, I remain uncertain of the house's soundness. Mayhap I should consider returning to Netherfield and make my decision based on what I find."

"That appears a most prudent means of constructing your verdict."

Bingley asked cautiously, "Would you consider joining me, Darcy? We could shoot, ride, and enjoy my estate. My sisters remain in Scarborough. I would be indebted if you would come with me."

Darcy chuckled with the success of his ploy. "I would enjoy that, Bingley."

"Capital! I will send servants to open the house. We can travel to Hertfordshire next week if you are agreeable."

Darcy's heart leapt. He would see Elizabeth again. Could they continue what they had begun at Pemberley? "I would be happy for the time together." His friend took his words to mean his time with Bingley, but Elizabeth remained foremost in Darcy's mind.

Over supper that evening, Bingley told Georgiana of his plan to return to Netherfield. "Your brother consented to join me," he shared. Georgiana smiled knowingly at Darcy, but she said nothing other than to assure Bingley she and Mrs. Annesley would be quite content to remain at Pemberley. Georgiana knew Darcy well enough to know the uncertainty he felt in returning to Elizabeth's home. Everything could change in the next few weeks.

When he and Bingley set out on the following Monday, Georgiana hugged Darcy a bit longer than usual and reached up to caress his cheek. "I shall say a prayer for your safe and successful journey, Brother. As always, I wish you the greatest of happiness." He smiled weakly at her as he boarded his coach; Darcy could think of nothing but Elizabeth and the tenuous situation of their relationship.

Elizabeth's Letter to Aunt Gardiner
by Marilyn Brant

September 4, 1812

My Dear Aunt Gardiner,

Elizabeth paused in thought and worry. Not that this wasn't an appropriate beginning for a letter, but she was at odds with herself as to what the next line should be. Mentally, she tried out a few possibilities:

> *I have been meaning to ask you about some specifics regarding Lydia's wedding. Aside from you and Uncle Gardiner, the minister and the bride and groom, of course, who else was there?*

No, that made her query too open ended and it was, in fact, not what she desperately wished to know.

> *I'd heard some mention of Mr. Fitzwilliam Darcy being in attendance at my youngest sister's wedding. Could that be true?*

Better, but her aunt could merely confirm or deny his presence. Elizabeth needed to know WHY he was there.

> *Why on earth was Mr. Darcy — of all people! — at my sister Lydia's wedding?!! What possessed you to invite him? Or did he just barge into the ceremony? And for what reason? And for how long? What did he say or do? Tell me everything!*

Ah, that was exactly what Elizabeth wanted to write, but it sounded a bit, well, on the verge of hysterics...even just on paper.

Still, her curiosity on the subject was too powerful to be denied. What was the meaning of Mr. Darcy's attendance at the wedding? Her mind raced for a way to broach her inquiries with tact and delicacy. But ten, twelve, fifteen entire seconds went by and she was no closer to finding the perfect phrasing and, let's face it, Elizabeth knew patience was hardly her strong suit.

She snatched the pen and hastily scribbled:

> *My sister Lydia had let slip that Mr. Darcy was gathered with you all at the wedding, but she likewise revealed that his attendance was not intended to be generally known. You may readily comprehend what my curiosity must be to know how a person unconnected with any of us, and (comparatively speaking) a stranger to our family, should have been amongst you at such a time. Pray write instantly and let me understand it — unless it is, for very cogent reasons, to remain in the secrecy which Lydia seems to think necessary; and then I must endeavour to be satisfied with ignorance.*

"Not that I shall, though," Elizabeth added to herself, as she quickly brought her note to a close. "And my dear aunt," she muttered, "if you do not tell me in an honourable manner, I shall certainly be reduced to tricks and stratagems to find out."

With that, she sealed her letter and called for Hill. She wanted this to be posted at once.

Then she just held her breath…waiting…

Mrs. Gardiner Receives a Surprising Letter
by Abigail Reynolds

September 5, 1812

The morning post brought a letter from Longbourn to Gracechurch Street. Mrs. Gardiner was delighted to recognize Lizzy's handwriting on the outside. Jane's letter reporting the arrival of the newlyweds at Longbourn had satisfied her basic curiosity on the subject, but she knew she could count on Lizzy to provide a more amusing version. She settled herself in her favorite chair to enjoy it.

She was disappointed to see how brief it was, but as she began to peruse it, those thoughts were replaced by astonishment. By the time she reached the last line, she was already on her feet and hurrying to her husband's study, where Mr. Gardiner peered at her over his ledger with an inquiring look.

Mrs. Gardiner waved the letter. "Oh, my dear, I have just received the most startling intelligence from Lizzy! It seems she had no knowledge of Mr. Darcy's involvement in Lydia's marriage, and she writes to me asking for an explanation after Lydia let something slip about his presence at the wedding."

Mr. Gardiner's brows drew together. "She was not aware of it? How can that be? She herself admitted in Lambton that she had told Darcy of their elopement. Of course, he never told me directly that she was aware of his involvement, but I would never have allowed him to act as he did but for the belief of her being a concerned party!"

"I know, my dear. Everything pointed to Lizzy's involvement – his ability to find our house in London, his detailed knowledge of the situation; and of course his admiration of her at Pemberley could not be denied!" She handed him the letter.

He scanned it with a frown. "I assumed that he would be a member of the family very soon. What must he have thought of me, to accept such a sum from a man wholly unconnected to us?"

Mrs. Gardiner laughed. "Do you suppose it would have made any difference, had you refused his assistance? I have never met any gentleman so determined on following his own course. If you had declined his offer, he would simply have gone ahead with it on his own."

"But why has he not made Lizzy an offer? Everything points in that direction."

"Perhaps he wished the matter of Lydia to be resolved before he spoke to her?" Mrs. Gardiner suggested.

"Perhaps so. After all, it would be better to allow this scandal to die down before tying the proud Darcy name to the Bennet family."

"Well, I for one hope he does not wait long! Poor Lizzy must be in such suspense. I will have to send her a reply without delay." She turned to go, then looked back over her shoulder with an arch smile. "Oh, how I will tease her about her great conquest!"

The Wickhams Leave Longbourn
by Susan Adriani

September 10, 1812

"Oh! My dear Lydia," Mrs. Bennet cried, "when shall we meet again?"

"Oh, Lord! I don't know. Not these two or three years perhaps."

"Write to me very often, my dear."

"As often as I can," Lydia replied. "But you know married women have never much time for writing. My sisters may write to me. They will have nothing better to do."

In the wake of such a statement Mr. Bennet cast an appraising look at his second eldest daughter, unsurprised to find her lips pursed as she followed the newly-weds out of the house. Surely, he thought, his Lizzy could not repine the end of her youngest sister's visit as their mother did, and here was his proof. He cleared his throat, anticipating the moment her eyes would meet his so they might share a conspiratorial look, but was soon met with disappointment. Her eyes, much like her somber mood, remained downcast as she stood obediently behind her mother.

Mr. Wickham's adieus were much more affectionate than his wife's. He smiled, looked handsome, and said many pretty things.

It was with a heavy heart that Mrs. Bennet raised her handkerchief to wave at the chaise as the driver urged the horses toward the road. Lydia leaned precariously out of the window to return her mother's gesture, shouting her goodbyes to her sisters, and promising them she shall soon find husbands for them all should they come to her at Christmas.

"Oh, yes!" Mrs. Bennet cried. "We would love that above anything, would we not, girls?"

While Kitty responded with an affirmative, Jane and Elizabeth remained silent on the subject, opting instead to wave to their departing sister. Mary merely turned and went into the house with a huff.

Once the Wickhams were finally on their way and nearly out of sight, Longbourn's master glanced once more at Elizabeth and said, "He is as fine a fellow as ever I saw. He simpers and smirks and makes love to us all. I am prodigiously proud of him. I defy even Sir William Lucas himself to produce a more valuable son-in-law."

Elizabeth offered her father nothing beyond a tight smile, however, before turning to go into the house with the others. Her father followed with a frown, his eyes upon his two eldest daughters as they paused before the staircase. His wife's shrill voice could be heard from within the front parlour, lamenting the fact that her youngest daughter was settling so far from home.

"Lizzy! Jane!" she called. "Where have you girls gotten to? Why are you all so eager to leave me alone with nothing but my nerves?"

Mr. Bennet shrugged with distaste at the same moment Elizabeth's shoulders slumped in resignation. "Coming, Mamma," she replied. With a sigh, she and Jane shared a look between them and quietly proceeded to the parlour.

Mr. Bennet felt for them, truly he did, but not enough to come to their rescue by waiting on his wife and two sillier daughters. Pushing the door to his library open, he went immediately to his bottle of port and his books, eager to immerse himself in their familiarity. Here, would he find quiet. Here, would he find comfort. Here, would he be able to forget the trials of the last ten days.

Darcy and Bingley Call
at Longbourn
by Regina Jeffers

September 19, 1812

"Darcy, we have been at Netherfield for two days," Bingley mused, "and Mr. Bennet has yet to call. Would it be bad manners if we would call on him first?" His friend stared morosely out the library's window. Darcy had taken up residence in one of the overstuffed chairs, but, in reality, his mind was no more on the book he held on his lap than was Bingley's mind on the gardeners he watched. Darcy had found it as frustrating as his friend that Mr. Bennet had ignored Bingley's return. The snub would make it more difficult for Darcy to determine if Miss Bennet would accept a renewal of Bingley's affections, and Darcy still required a legitimate excuse to call upon Miss Elizabeth.

"Let us wait until tomorrow to see if the situation changes. If not, then, we can offer our own civilities," Darcy said evenly. He prayed his hopes did not pepper his words.

"Tomorrow it is then." Bingley continued to stare out the window. "It has been too long since we have enjoyed the Bennets' companies."

Darcy's heart clinched in anticipation. The past two days had played havoc with Darcy's emotions. There were few places at Netherfield where images of Elizabeth did not dance through Darcy's head. He saw her on the staircase, as she was on that last Sunday before she and her sister had returned to Longbourn; he saw her carrying the water through the upper passage to Jane Bennet's sickroom; he saw Elizabeth reaching for a book of poetry in the library. The images haunted his waking, as well as his sleeping hours. Tomorrow, he thought, tomorrow will speak to whether I declare my love to Elizabeth Bennet again.

* * *

Riding beside Bingley as he entered the pathway leading to Longbourn, both gentlemen remained silent, deep in the bewilderment of what the next hour would bring. Darcy held no doubt Bingley wondered if he could renew his relationship with Jane Bennet; meanwhile, Darcy wondered whether Elizabeth would welcome his presence in her home. Of course, this was Longbourn, not Pemberley. The excellent company he had found in Mr. and Mrs. Gardiner would be replaced by the simple-mindedness of Mrs. Bennet, but what Mrs. Bennet said did not interest him. Elizabeth was his only concern. He could tolerate any insensibility on Mrs. Bennet's part for the pleasure of seeing the lady's second daughter smiling genuinely at him. Today, Darcy had a dual purpose for this visit: assess Jane Bennet's feelings for Bingley and Elizabeth Bennet's feelings for him.

"Mr. Darcy and Mr. Bingley," the Longbourn servant announced as the door to the small drawing room opened to the sight of Mrs. Bennet surrounded by four of her daughters.

Darcy's eyes immediately sought Elizabeth. Weeks had passed since he had last seen her; his wish was to determine whether she had recovered from that awful day at the Lambton inn when Elizabeth had wept for the ruination of her youngest sister and for her family. Those tears had driven him to action. Memorizing Elizabeth's every gesture and the full gamut of her emotions, he had observed his Elizabeth for weeks last fall; therefore, he instantly recognized her uneasiness; however, the source of the awkwardness remained in question. Was it his presence at Longbourn? Was it that others might discover what happened at Hunsford and at Pemberley? Was it embarrassment regarding his knowledge of Miss Lydia's folly? I must be patient, he cautioned his foolish heart. Permit me first to see how she reacts to my coming to

Hertfordshire; then I will decide my next step. Regrettably, Elizabeth lowered her eyes before she made both gentlemen a curtsy and then eagerly returned to her needlework.

Mrs. Bennet warmly welcomed Bingley. "Please, Mr. Bingley, you must come sit by me," she insisted. "Allow me to send Mrs. Hill for refreshments." Barely civil, she acknowledged Darcy only by name. "And you are welcome as well, Mr. Darcy. Please have a seat."

Darcy chose a chair where he might observe both Elizabeth and her elder sister. Jane Bennet appeared a bit paler and more sedate than he expected; but she received them with tolerable ease. If Jane Bennet held no resentment, Charles stood a chance to recapture the lady's heart. Darcy wished her sister would show him some preference. As far as he could tell, Elizabeth had ventured only one glance in his direction. He wanted to be alone with her, to hear her voice, to observe her smile; he wanted only the opportunity to profess his continued love. Instead, he swallowed hard and forced himself to say, "Miss Elizabeth, may I inquire about the health of your aunt and uncle?"

"They are...they are well, Sir," she stammered.

"I am pleased to hear it." He smiled easily at her. It was important for her to know she brought him great pleasure.

"They were," she hazarded another quick glance in his direction, but, in reality, she spoke to the floor, "so pleased with Pemberley. My uncle still speaks fondly of enjoying the sport he found there."

Darcy said earnestly, "He will always be most welcome there."

Before the conversation could continue, however, Mrs. Bennet interrupted, "You may not be aware, Mr. Bingley, of changes in the neighborhood. Miss Lucas has married Mr. Bennet's cousin, Mr. Collins, and my youngest daughter has married Mr. Wickham. Although I cannot think it necessary for Mr. Wickham to accept a commission that has sent him to Newcastle, I must tell you, Mr. Bingley, having a daughter well situated is a great relief."

The mention of Wickham's name sent a shiver down Darcy's spine. He could easily recall the immundity in which he had found Mr. Wickham and Miss Lydia. He regretted that the foolish girl would not accept Darcy's warning she must marry quickly if she were to save her own reputation and the reputations of her sisters. He seriously wished he could have placed the youngest Bennet sister in a better situation, but the girl appeared to hold Darcy's former friend in deep affection. He hoped it would be enough to carry them forward for he knew Mr. Wickham loved no one but himself.

Too mortified to look at him, Elizabeth notably stiffened as Mrs. Bennet asked, "Mr. Bingley, did you by some chance see the announcement of our dear Lydia's marriage in the London papers? She married from my brother Gardiner's home, and, of course, he did not put in more than a brief mention of her family." Elizabeth may not meet his gaze, but Darcy could not force his eyes from her.

"I did see it; may I offer my congratulations," Bingley replied. Darcy purposely did not join the conversation for fear his tone would betray his true thoughts of George Wickham's worthiness.

Mrs. Bennet lamented, "With Mr. Wickham being stationed in the North, I have no idea when we might see our dear Lydia again." Personally, Darcy had rejoiced in Mr. Wickham's removal. The commission Darcy had purchased for his former friend was under a very strict comm.

Mrs. Bennet's next remark offered Darcy a purposeful cut. "Thank Heavens, Mr. Wickham has some friends, though perhaps not so many as he deserves!" If Mrs. Bennet only knew what Wickham truly deserves, Darcy thought. Hopefully, the lady would never know of the perfidy that Mr. Wickham regularly practiced.

This time it was Darcy's turn to lower his eyes. He could not say what he wished to tell the Bennets: How much he loved Elizabeth, how he had rushed to Miss Lydia's rescue, and how foolish Mrs. Bennet was to consider Mr. Wickham a proper match for the lady's youngest daughter. Instead, he assumed the characteristically aloof air that had served him well in the past, but which he knew would mark him as a proud, disdainful man in the Bennet family's estimation.

As he cursed under his breath, Darcy heard Elizabeth ask, "Do you plan to stay long in the country, Mr. Bingley?"

Her words reached Darcy as nothing else could; even the simplest phrase added to the image he drew of her. The words she said did not fascinate him; it was the way she responded to each situation–how she knew him–had known he needed her to deflect her mother's attention. She had reacted in a similar manner at Netherfield when Mrs. Bennet had argued against his comment regarding the simplicity of country life. Elizabeth had a way of manipulating her family to protect him, and Darcy loved her for it. Her tenacity added to his portrait of Elizabeth Bennet.

Nervousness echoed in Bingley's response, "I hope to stay several weeks, Miss Elizabeth–for the shooting. Several weeks would be most gratifying." Bingley hesitated as he shot a quick glance at Jane Bennet.

Both Elizabeth and Darcy observed how Bingley's response to Elizabeth's question affected Miss Bennet. Darcy wondered why he had never seen the admiration the lady held for Bingley. Elizabeth glowed as the spark between her sister and Bingley was rekindled. Darcy wished she would look at him with such persuasion. Elizabeth had protected him from her mother, but was that because she feared further embarrassing censure of her family or because she held feelings for him?

When Bingley and Darcy rose to take their leave, Mrs. Bennet issued an invitation to Mr. Bingley for dinner in a few days' time. "You are quite a visit in my debt, Mr. Bingley, for when you departed last winter you had promised to take dinner with us as soon as you returned. I have not forgot, you see." A less civil invitation was also issued to Darcy. "Of course, you may join us too, Mr. Darcy."

"That would be most congenial," Bingley said with a full smile.

The gentlemen were shown to the door. As the Bennet family gathered around, there was no way for Darcy to speak to Elizabeth again. His bow and her curtsy were all they could manage.

Returning to Netherfield, Bingley was obviously ecstatic, his hopes held possibilities. Jane Bennet did not turn from his friend's attentions, as Bingley had successfully engaged her over and over. Miss Bennet smiled at him, laughed lightly at his attempts at humor, and made eye contact with Charles repeatedly.

Darcy, on the other hand, experienced pure misery. Elizabeth had appeared uneasy from the beginning; she had answered his questions, and her voice became stronger with each response, but she barely looked at him, and she had offered him no encouragement. His hopes plummeted as scenes from previous encounters at Netherfield and Hunsford flashed before his eyes. You were the last man in the world whom I could ever be prevailed on to marry.... I hear such different accounts of you as puzzle me exceedingly.... I have every reason to think ill of you.... Had you behaved in a more gentleman-like manner.... All the old insecurities had returned. Would he never succeed in making her love him? He had thought positively when they were alone at Pemberley, but at Longbourn she had been so different. How was he to judge her sentiment? Mayhap, he should leave. The feel of the hand as he had assisted Elizabeth into her uncle's carriage said otherwise; the backward gaze as she and her family departed his home said she cared; her caress of the petals of the boxwood rose said she believed in constancy. Which images? Which images should he believe regarding Elizabeth Bennet? He would wait until after he and Bingley dined at Longbourn before making his decision. Possibly, it was the shock of his being in her home. Possibly, she was embarrassed by her mother's actions. Possibly, she was more concerned with Miss Bennet's welfare. All of these possibilities were characteristic of Elizabeth. "I must remain calm and allow life to take its course," he cautioned his bruised heart. After Mrs. Bennet's invitation is met, he would confirm his resolve. "Only if Miss Elizabeth offers me proper encouragement will I remain in Hertfordshire. In addition, I must assess Jane Bennet's estimation of

Bingley's affections before I confessed my previous deceit." Darcy told himself all these things. Surely, if Elizabeth cared for him as he hoped she did, their hearts would find each other before long.

Darcy and Bingley Dine
at Longbourn
by Regina Jeffers

September 22, 1812

Several of the Bennet sisters welcomed Bingley and Darcy upon their entrance to Longbourn. Elizabeth had accepted their greatcoats and briefly greeted Darcy with a hint of a smile and an obligatory curtsy. When they repaired to the dining room, Darcy had hoped to be seated near Elizabeth, but finding himself seated instead close to Mrs. Bennet dashed those hopes. Bingley located a seat near Jane Bennet; oh, for such pleasure with Elizabeth! Darcy could hear nothing of what she said. Only once did he notice Miss Elizabeth's attentions towards him. It was when Bingley placed himself beside Miss Bennet; Elizabeth gave Darcy a triumphant look, and he bore it with presumed indifference. The meal included venison and a white soup. Darcy attempted to make conversation with Mrs. Bennet, "I extend my compliments on the partridge, Ma'am," he said a bit awkwardly.

"Thank you, Mr. Darcy," the house's mistress said with equal awkwardness. However, Darcy noticed his words had obviously pleased Elizabeth's mother.

She clearly had made a statement with the menu, and his good breeding required he take notice, but he would rather have taken notice of her second daughter's eyes. Generally though, Darcy spoke very little to anyone at the table.

He had hoped for the opportunity of some conversation with Elizabeth as the evening progressed; all he required was a few moments alone. He would ask her to meet him privately, and then he would offer her his hand again. Following the meal, useless and mundane time was spent in the dining room with the gentlemen; he was anxious to return to the ladies. When the gentlemen entered the drawing room, Darcy planned immediately to approach Elizabeth, but she served coffee to the guests and was surrounded by ladies who appeared to be protecting her, for they stood close by. He moved toward her, but one of the girls stepped closer, taking on a conspiratorial stance. Darcy, therefore, took his cup and walked away to another part of the room.

The evening went badly, but, eventually, Darcy returned with his coffee cup. Elizabeth, thankfully, seized the opportunity of saying, "May I inquire of Miss Darcy?" Her gaze met his, and Darcy felt the comfort of her countenance.

"Georgiana is at Pemberley with Mrs. Annesley. She will remain there until the Festive Season."

"Then her friends have gone to Scarborough?"

"They have, Miss Elizabeth." Darcy was barely able to utter the words; her beauty enthralled him.

"I am sorry we could not dine at Pemberley as we had planned." She struggled to express her regrets.

"Georgiana and I both regretted your sudden departure. We hope to see you at Pemberley again." Did she understand the double meaning of his words?

The conversation staled at that point. Searching for something more to say, he stood by her, but what he wished to tell her could not be done so in public. He wanted only a few minutes' conversation with Elizabeth again, and he would be satisfied if only the opportunity occurred. Noting the girl still listened in, Darcy eventually walked away.

That was the last of their conversation for he was relegated to a table of whist at Mrs. Bennet's insistence; Elizabeth sat at a different table. Darcy's mind searched for her rather than paying attention to the game, causing him to play poorly. When the others took their leave, Mrs. Bennet attempted to keep him and Bingley for supper, but their carriage had been ordered, and his friend and Darcy were soon on their way to Netherfield.

Although he guarded his feelings from Darcy, Bingley rejoiced in the progress he made with Miss Bennet. Memories of Darcy's censure of Jane Bennet required Bingley to be cautious. Obviously, his friend wanted to retain Darcy's regard, but Bingley also desired Miss Bennet's affection. Despite his own misery, Darcy knew the time for telling Bingley the truth had arrived, but he could not do so this evening. His own heart was breaking as he wrote a quick passage to his sister.

Darcy Apologizes to Bingley
for his Duplicity
by Regina Jeffers

September 23, 1812

When Bingley entered the morning room, finding Darcy dressed for a journey brought a surprise to his friend's countenance. "Darcy, it appears you plan to leave Netherfield today?"

"I do, Bingley." He had spent a restless night anguishing over what he would say to his best friend.

"Why must you leave so soon? Are you not satisfied at Netherfield? I know country society does not appeal to you, but I had hoped you would find it more pleasurable this time," Bingley reasoned.

"Bingley," Darcy established the tone of what he had would make his confession. "Would you please join me at the table? I have something important to impart."

"Darcy, you sound so deliberate." Bingley walked cautiously to the table and slid onto a chair.

"Bingley, I am not leaving Netherfield because of country society. In fact, I have been served an education; some parts of the country can be very agreeable." The ambiguity of Darcy's speech obviously confused Bingley, but Darcy could not seem to bring himself to leave thoughts of Elizabeth Bennet behind. "I do have business to address in London, but that is not my main reason for leaving. After I say what I have to tell you, you will desire my going."

"Darcy, this speech lacks sensibility; I could never turn away a friend such as you have proved to be."

"I have been a deplorable friend, Bingley. You have trusted me unwisely."

"Darcy . . .?" Bingley began, but Darcy dismissed Bingley's protest with a flick of his wrist.

"Please, Bingley, I must say this while I still possess the nerve. I have given you a disservice." Uncertain where the conversation led, Bingley sat unresponsive. Having to finish this sad business quickly, Darcy swallowed hard before saying, "I conspired with your sisters last fall to separate you from Miss Bennet; I did so because I considered you to be my dearest friend, and I believed, at the time, that Miss Bennet was indifferent and did not desire your affection; however, that is no excuse for what I have done."

"Darcy?" Bingley said incredulously. His friend was immediately on his feet and pacing the room. "Am I to understand you kept me from Miss Bennet with some sort of deceit? How could you? You of all people! You recognized how I felt about the lady? You have consulted your will and made it mine without my permission. You have brought me pain, but what is worse, you have wounded Miss Bennet!"

"Bingley, you are correct to be so upset. I am without reason; my conceit at thinking I knew what was best for you is unforgivable." Darcy, eyes lowered; realizing he had ruined his relationship with Charles Bingley, he sat dejected.

Several minutes passed before Bingley spoke again. "Darcy," Bingley forced evenness into his voice, "I am not certain how I will be able to forgive you, but I must assume some of the blame in this matter. This much I know: My nature is too changeable. What you did, you completed in my name, and I allowed it to happen. I should have returned to Netherfield as I planned; I have known that fact for a long time. I should have been man enough to seize my own happiness."

Realizing how much in his vain glory he had damaged the one true acquaintance that Darcy treasured, Darcy grimaced, but his conscience would not permit him to tell Bingley only half-truths. "Bingley, you are excellent to offer your absolution; yet, I have something else to confess."

Bingley's countenance displayed his vexation. He was seeing Darcy for the first time. Turning his disappointment on Darcy, he said, "Please continue."

Darcy lifted his head to meet his companion's dark, lethal gaze. "Miss Bennet was in London last winter for nearly three months; she stayed with Mr. and Mrs. Gardiner. Miss Bennet sent word to Caroline and even called at the townhouse one day. Caroline, with my permission, gave Miss Bennet a cut by not returning the visit for many weeks. She led Miss Bennet to believe you were interested in Georgiana. I was aware of the lady's presence in London, but I told you not. Again, I had witnessed your falling in and out of love so often I did not judge your affections to be constant. Since the time I realized you and Miss Bennet were meant to be together, I have attempted to turn back the clock."

"Darcy, you have overextended your influence on my life. Is it no wonder Miss Bennet sees me as being a lothario." Bingley's hands fisted at his side, and Darcy did not blame the man. If the situation were reversed, he would have planted his friend a facer. Yet, even in the tension-filled room, Darcy found hope. Bingley, evidently, did not observe the true regard his friend found in Jane Bennet's countenance.

"Bingley," Darcy smiled largely. "Miss Bennet, if I may be allowed one last judgment, loves no one but you."

Bingley protested, "She can not! Miss Bennet must think me a cad–to be indifferent to her!"

"Charles, there are not many things of which I am absolutely certain, but the constancy of Miss Bennet's feelings for you is one of the few things upon which I would venture a gamble. At Hunsford, Miss Elizabeth reprimanded me for my misgivings regarding the lady, and the Gardiners have showed me how thoughtful Miss Bennet can be. I came to Netherfield to observe the lady's reactions to your renewed entreaties; her love still rests in you, Charles, if you are willing to ask her."

"Ask her? Ask her what?" Bingley nearly shouted.

"Ask her to marry you, Bingley," Darcy said confidently. "Miss Bennet will accept you."

Bingley frowned. "How can you be so certain? I am not of the same mind, and it is I to whom you reportedly believe the lady directs her attentions!"

Darcy sucked in a deep breath as the vivid memory of Elizabeth Bennet flared in his mind. "You are too close to observe the look in the lady's eyes when you walk into the room. Most men would give their life for one such glimpse. The lady stirs your soul, Charles; with Miss Bennet you can share your innermost self with respect and dignity. You can wait; you can postpone, but if I were you, I would grab 'happiness' with both hands and ask Miss Bennet to marry me."

A faint smile touched his friend's lips. "The lady will say 'yes;' will she not, Darcy?" Bingley appeared awestruck by the realization of what Darcy shared.

"Miss Bennet will say 'yes,' Charles."

Bingley began to pace, to spin, to stop, and to start all over again. "If Miss Bennet agrees, Darcy, then you will be completely forgiven." Bingley laughed nervously.

"Then I am forgiven," Darcy smiled. "You will send me news of your happiness, but pray write legibly."

"I will send you my fate," Bingley could not control his thoughts; but then he recalled his sisters' parts in his misery.

"I hope you have predicted Miss Bennet's response accurately, Darcy, for it will offer me an opportunity for revenge when I demand Caroline and Louisa give Jane her proper due as my wife. They believe me to be with you at Pemberley. What I would not give to see their faces when they read I am at Netherfield, and I have offered Miss Bennet my hand."

Darcy retrieved his gloves from a nearby table. He shook Bingley's hand and then slapped him on the back. "I must leave you now, Bingley."

"When will you return? If Miss Bennet accepts, you will stand up with me?"

"Although I do not deserve your honest consideration, it would be my honor, Bingley. I will return within a fortnight; your fate should be decided by then."

Darcy claimed his hat and walking stick and headed for the waiting carriage. Bingley followed close behind. At the carriage, Darcy turned, and Bingley extended his hand. "Friend," he said.

Darcy firmly grasped the offered hand. "Friend," came his thankful reply.

* * *

There was little to do in London, but Darcy did not care; his mind could not be happily employed. He had gone to the theatre one evening, for his spirits wanted the solitude and silence, which only numbers could give. A protégé of David Garrick performed magnificently, but the drama *The Chances* reminded Darcy of Elizabeth for like the character's jealousy, Darcy remained jealous of the possibility of anyone else having Elizabeth as his wife.

At Longbourn, they had not spoken beyond common civilities. He had once believed their hearts were intertwined, and that nothing could come between them. Their natures so similar–their understanding so perfect–he could never imagine their not finding each other. It was impossible for him to forget how to love Elizabeth, but the fact was when they last met, she did not appear to want to be near enough for conversation–near enough to him. Darcy convinced himself Elizabeth did not return his regard; he held no choice but to put distance between them. The distance between Pemberley and Longbourn was one kind of distance, but he would also have to build a wall around his heart. Darcy was Bingley's friend; Bingley would marry Miss Bennet; Darcy could not avoid seeing Elizabeth…but he could force himself to be indifferent.

After a week, a dispatch arrived from Bingley. It read

28 September

Darcy,

You are forgiven. Miss Bennet said "yes." My fate is sealed! We await your return to Netherfield. Your most humble servant...

Charles Bingley

In many ways, the letter brought Darcy relief, but he envied Bingley's chance for happiness. Bitterness and lost opportunities had marred his prospects: if he realized how much a refusal to dance at an assembly would have change his life, he would have danced with Elizabeth the first time he met her; if he.... The pain brought him up short. He did not know whether he could live with all his regrets—with this profound ache of love lost.

Much Ado About Nothing
by Shannon Winslow

September 24, 1812

A new craze has overtaken London and the surrounding area – that of daily documenting ones activities and thoughts in writing – spurred on by the rumor that the Prince Regent himself has taken up the hobby. Many of the more staunchly conservative members of society outwardly label the practice a frivolous occupation. But, in private at least, a surprising number of the same judge their own thoughts more worth recording for posterity than the incoherent ramblings of their friends and neighbors. Consequently many a fine lady and gentleman have taking up the pen in secret.

Tuesday

Fitzwilliam Darcy: I humor Georgiana by writing this, for it was her idea that I should begin recording my daily actions. As she pointed out, even the captain of a ship does the same in the ship's log, so perhaps there is some merit in it. At least documenting today's performance cannot be considered an exercise in self-importance, for this evening I was required to abjectly humble myself and beg Bingley's pardon for my role in separating him from Miss Bennet last fall. He was angry, and rightly so. However, I believe I shall be fully forgiven the moment Jane agrees to marry him. I trust that day is near. With my objections withdrawn (and my presence soon to be removed to town for several days), nothing can stand in the way of Bingley's following his original inclinations. I trust they will be a happy couple. Would that my own hopes for Miss Bennet's sister should be settled so soon and so felicitously.

Charles Bingley: I am all astonishment! It turns out my

illustrious friend is fallible after all. He has this day confessed to me that it is largely to him that I owe the one great misery of my life – that of being forced to part ways with Miss Bennet. Darcy has admitted he was wrong to interfere, and that he may also have been wrong about Miss Bennet's being indifferent to me. Dare I hope that sweet Jane would receive a renewal of my addresses favorably, even after so much time has passed? Darcy seems to think she might, and has by his manner indicated he would have no objection to my proceeding as my heart would dictate. I must take courage, therefore, and go to Longbourn again as soon as possible, with one mission in mind: to make Miss Bennet a proper offer of marriage, as I should have done before.

<u>Mrs. Bennet:</u> Bingley came to call again today! Oh, he is the handsomest man who ever was seen, and with five thousand a year too! What a fine thing for Jane, whom I daresay he admires as much as ever. I would think him the most agreeable man in all the world if only he would stop bringing that odious Mr. Darcy with him every time he comes.

<u>Jane Bennet:</u> Mr. Bingley called again today, and I am afraid I still find him the most amiable man I have ever known. But I must take care to remember that we are only indifferent acquaintances now, despite Lizzy's smiles and insinuations.

<u>Elizabeth Bennet:</u> Whether by his design or purely bad luck, I had no opportunity to speak to Mr. Darcy when he called with Mr. Bingley today. I envied every one he spoke to and had scarcely patience enough to be civil to anybody else, proving that I am quite clearly a weak and ridiculous creature. My one consolation is that I may yet see my dearest sister made happy, for I believe Bingley is as much in love with Jane as I have ever seen a man to be.

Wednesday

<u>Mrs. Bennet:</u> Bingley did not come, and as to why, I cannot imagine. Everything passed off so uncommonly well yesterday that I thought sure he would not fail to return to Longbourn today.

<u>Mary Bennet:</u> Blessedly, we had no callers to Longbourn today, so at last I was able to apply myself to my work properly. One

cannot expect to ever become a truly accomplished young lady without constant study and practice, after all.

Thursday

<u>Mr. Bingley:</u> I did not go to Longbourn yesterday, nor today. It is not that I am at all weakening in my resolve to offer for Miss Bennet, but I must not be presumptuous and always imposing myself on the Bennets' kind hospitality. In any case, Darcy leaves for town early tomorrow, and I think perhaps I will have more courage with him out of the way.

<u>Mrs. Bennet:</u> Still Bingley does not come! My head is very ill tonight.

Friday

<u>Mrs. Bennet:</u> Today he came, but he went away again without declaring himself or even taking dinner. What is the man thinking of to keep my dear Jane waiting like this? At least he did not bring with him that odious Mr. Darcy. We are safe from him for the next ten days, thank goodness.

<u>Mr. Bingley:</u> I called at Longbourn again today and was very graciously received. I sat with the ladies for above and hour, my chief object to try and ascertain Miss Bennet's sentiments toward me, in the hope that I might be sufficiently encouraged to proceed – not an easy task since the serenity of her countenance betrayed little in the way of strong feeling. This uncertainty kept me from speaking out, and when Mrs. Bennet invited me to stay to dinner I quickly made the excuse of being engaged elsewhere. Whilst it was perfectly true that I was obligated to go to the Longs, my conscience accused me of cowardice. Consequently, I readily agreed to dine with them tomorrow instead, and I hereby swear that I shall not lose another opportunity. Tomorrow I shall be bold; tomorrow I shall ask Miss Bennet to be my wife.

The writing of personal journals continued with some practitioners far longer than with others. Mr. Darcy was the first to give it up, preferring to keep his thoughts inside his head where he deemed they more correctly belonged. Elizabeth, Jane, and Mr. Bingley carried on a little while longer, persevering sufficiently so as to preserve on paper the monumental events taking place in their lives during this unique period. Then they too set their pens aside in favor of endeavors with more chance of yielding tangible benefits. Only Mrs. Bennet presumed to make writing in her diary a life-long habit. Never did she tire of transcribing the simple fare upon which her mind typically fixated. But, upon revisiting those written sentiments sometime later, even she had to admit they were hardly worth the reading.

Mr. Bingley Proposes
by Susan Mason-Milks

September 27, 1812

Charles Bingley had never experienced such nervous anticipation in his life. Today was the day. No excuses. No delays. Today, he was going to ask Miss Jane Bennet to be his wife. He'd been looking into the mirror rehearsing what to say when James, his valet, interrupted him.

"Are you ready to dress for the day, Mr. Bingley?" the older man inquired politely as he entered the room.

Bingley's heart did a wild dance. Was he ready?

"I would like to look my very best today," he said nervously running a hand through his unruly hair.

James raised an eyebrow. "I do not believe, sir, that I have ever allowed you to leave your dressing room on any day looking anything less than your very best."

That brought a smile to Bingley's lips and some of his nervousness vanished. "Of course, you are completely correct. I trust your good taste implicitly. Now what have you planned for me today?"

When Bingley finally stood before the mirror to examine himself, he was very pleased with what he saw. Then James held out his pocket watch, brushed the back of his coat one more time, and pronounced him ready. Just as Bingley was almost to the door, the valet rushed after him.

"One more thing, sir," James said holding out a fresh handkerchief.

Bingley looked at him quizzically. "I believe you have already provided me with one of these."

"I was just thinking, that on today of all days, you might wish to have another available. In the event that…" James' voice trailed off. He was clearly somewhat embarrassed.

"In the event that what?" Bingley repeated quizzically.

"If Miss Bennet…in case she is so happy that…well, you know women can be rather emotional in circumstances such as this," James explained.

Finally, Bingley understood. "How did you…?"

"Mr. Bingley, many years ago your father commissioned me with helping you learn to look and act like a true gentleman. In the course of the past ten years, I have come to know you, and well, I just had a feeling that today was the day."

Charles Bingley marveled at how James sometimes seemed to know his very thoughts before he himself was even aware of them. Bingley touched the pocket in his waist coat where he had tucked the ring he planned to give Jane when she accepted him.

"Wish me luck then."

"I do not believe luck will be required, sir. And let me add that your father would be very proud of you indeed."

Bingley decided to ride rather than take the carriage. The fresh air and exercise would be good for him. Darcy had returned to town the day before and would be absent for more than a week leaving Bingley very much on his own. The conversation had been tense when Darcy had explained how he had withheld knowledge of Miss Bennet's presence in London last winter. Bingley had been shaken, but as he considered what that confession must have cost his friend in terms of pride, he found it easier to forgive him. The look of relief on Darcy's face had been genuine. For years, Darcy had been like an older brother to him. Finally, Bingley was seeing this complex man in a clearer light. Darcy was not infallible, and he had wisely acknowledged that deciding whom to marry was a choice only Bingley could make.

After just a short time in Hertfordshire, he knew he was more in love with Jane Bennet than ever. Most importantly, this time he was certain it was love and not just infatuation. Last fall, when he had talked to Jane, danced with her, courted her, he had been so in awe of her beauty that he had failed to fully appreciate her other qualities – qualities that in a wife were even more important than her elegant profile, porcelain skin and golden hair.

The long winter months had afforded him an abundance of time to contemplate what he had given up. When he compared Jane Bennet to the other ladies he met and to his own sisters, there was really no one quite like her. What he loved about Jane was how she always believed the best of people – even of him. She had been so quick to forgive him that he wondered daily what he had ever done to deserve her. He also loved how she never shared gossip of any kind. Every time he heard his sisters tittering and giggling, he knew it was at someone else's expense.

After reaching the decision to return to Hertfordshire, he had recognized it was time to assert himself with his sisters. He was, after all, the head of the family, and could no longer afford to have Caroline manipulate him. Bingley smiled as he thought back to that day in London when he had announced he would be traveling to Netherfield for some hunting. The ten-minute-long tirade from Caroline and Louisa about what a mistake he was making had been unpleasant and actually, rather boring. It did not matter to them that he had already heard their extensive list of objections numerous times before. Listening without saying a word, he had bubbled over inside with impatience. Prior to making the announcement, he had decided not to argue with them, as it would just prolong the confrontation. His mind was made up; nothing would change it.

During the entire conversation, Darcy, who happened to be visiting at the time, was curiously silent in spite of Caroline's efforts to solicit his help and take their side. "I expect Bingley knows what he is doing," was all Darcy would say.

When it reached the point at which Bingley thought his head might just pop off his neck and launch itself toward the ceiling, he finally did what he knew he should have done ages ago.

"Caroline! Louisa! Stop!"

Their shock was so profound at hearing their gentle brother raise his voice that they actually ceased speaking for a moment and sat with their mouths open in surprise.

"You are my dear sisters, and I would do almost anything to secure your happiness," he began, "but what I will not do is give up the one person who is so essential to my own happiness that I cannot imagine a life without her. I am going to Netherfield, and if I discern even the smallest sign that Jane Bennet still holds me in high regard, I plan to ask for her hand!"

"Dearest Charles, one would think you do not believe that your well-being is the most pressing and important concern in our lives. Of course, we want everything that is good for you. It is hurtful to think you do not believe we care," said Caroline with a pout and a barely audible sniffle.

Bingley opened his mouth to say what he usually said in these situations when Caroline managed to make him feel guilty, but this time was different. He stopped himself.

Very softly, he said, "And furthermore, I will not tolerate a single disparaging word from either of you about Miss Bennet or any other member of her family. They may soon become our family, and you will treat with them with the utmost respect — even Mrs. Bennet. Am I understood?"

When there was silence, he made his best effort to turn up the intensity of his glare and repeated, "Am I understood?"

Louisa had the good grace to nod and look a bit sheepish, but Caroline simply watched him with an air of studied boredom.

"Caroline? Should I take your silence to mean you wish to go live with Aunt Emmeline in Manchester until next spring?"

Suddenly, Caroline's eyes grew wide. Aunt Emmeline was the one person in the family who would brook no nonsense from her and had the potential to make her life a misery. Manchester in the winter? Cut off from the London season? Caroline would rather dress in burlap sacks!

She sighed heavily for effect before she spoke. "No, Charles, I promise I will do my very best to make the Bennet family feel welcome. May I ask when we leave for Netherfield?" Her voice suddenly turned sweet as honey.

"Darcy and I are leaving tomorrow. You and Louisa are staying in London until I send for you."

"But, Charles, dear, who will…," Caroline began.

Bingley stared at his truculent sister and mouthed one word – "Manchester" – causing Caroline to turn instantly white.

"Is there anything I may do to help you prepare for your journey?" she said brightly. He knew she was only pretending, but at least it was a start.

Once inside the carriage and on their way to dinner at their club, Bingley leaned back in satisfaction stretching out his legs and putting his hands behind his head. "I do not know about you, Darcy, but I am ravenous. I feel as if I could eat an entire cow at one sitting!"

Darcy gave his friend one of his rare smiles. "Standing up for yourself is very hungry work, Bingley. I congratulate you."

Now he was on his way to Longbourn, and despite everything that his family and friends had tried to tell him, he felt confident in the strength of Jane's affections. There was no artifice to Jane. No saying one thing and meaning something else as those coy young ladies he had met in London. Last fall, nearly a year ago now, when his sisters and Darcy had confronted him, his own lack of confidence had caused him to be swayed, and he had nearly lost her. For reasons he did not fully understand, but for which his heart rejoiced, Jane had forgiven him for abandoning her. That was a mistake he would never make again.

Later that evening when it was time for Bingley to retire, he found James waiting up for him in his dressing room. Before the valet could begin his work, Bingley asked him to pour a glass of brandy for each of them from the bottle he had requested be placed there. Darcy was gone, his family still in London, so there was no one else with whom he could share his elation.

"I hope you will drink a toast with me on this special occasion."

Picking up the glass, the valet looked at Bingley expectantly.

"A special occasion, sir?" he asked, although Bingley was certain the news of the engagement had already traveled from Longbourn to Netherfield earlier in the day.

Bingley could not stop himself from grinning. "This morning Miss Jane Bennet made the happiest of men by accepting my hand in marriage."

James looked as pleased as Bingley had hoped he would be. "Congratulations, sir. That is indeed excellent news! If I may be so bold as to say, sir, you have made a wise choice. Miss Bennet is a lovely young lady, and I am certain you will be very happy together."

As they sipped the rich brandy, a strange awkwardness descended. Although a conversation such as this was not so unusual between them, for some reason, tonight, it felt odd. James seemed to sense his master's mood and began to ask about Bingley's activities for the following day so he would be able to plan his wardrobe. When the brandy was gone, the valet deftly took up his work. Once ready for bed, Bingley started toward his bedchamber but hesitated as he reached the door. So many things were running through his head, so many things he would like to say, but he realized that something important had shifted. Soon he would be a married man and head of the family in a way he had not been before. He would have to rely more on himself and on Jane. In the past, he might have said more, but tonight, he did not.

"Good-night and thank you," he said with simple sincerity, and then he waited for James' usual response.

"My pleasure, sir."

Bingley smiled to himself and headed off to bed.

Mr. Collins Shares Gossip
with Lady Catherine
by Mary Simonsen

October 1, 1812

Charlotte Collins scanned the walls of the reception room of Rosings Park looking for something on which to fix her attention, her eyes settling on a magnificent Gobelin's tapestry of very large dogs bringing down a stag. Following hard on the heels of the mastiffs were riders with spears poised in preparation for finishing off the wounded beast. While Charlotte made a study of the grisly scene, her husband, the Reverend William Collins, studied the face of the tapestry's owner for some clue that she wished for him to begin a conversation. When she raised her teacup to her lips and pointed her extended small finger in his direction, he saw it as a sign that he might begin. Instead, the great lady spoke:

"I noted in your garden, Mr. Collins, that your vegetables are of a middling size. If the soil is not properly prepared in the spring, you will never achieve the size or volume of the vegetables produced here at Rosings Park."

"Yes, of course, Your Ladyship. But you may recall my early efforts yielded exceptionally large cucumbers and radishes. If the vegetables had not gone missing, I could have shown you a cucumber as long as…"

"Mr. Collins, you need not mention your cucumber every time you visit. As you are the only one who saw this gourd of mythical size, I am convinced it existed only in your mind."

I have seen it, Charlotte thought, and a slight smile crossed her lips.

Anne de Bourgh, who had been sitting quietly next to her mother, gave her mother a sideways glance. Mama knew very well that the cucumber was no illusion. Not only had she seen it with her own eyes, but she had tasted it the very next day when, at dinner, cucumber sandwiches, garnished with sliced radishes, were served at table at Rosings Park.

"Your Ladyship, I can assure you…"

"Mrs. Collins, have you any news from Hertfordshire," Lady Catherine asked, turning the conversation away from the missing gourd. "Are your parents in good health?"

Charlotte informed Lady Catherine that all was well at Lucas Lodge and that there was no news to report. As Her Ladyship loved "news," Mrs. Collins statement earned a look of displeasure.

"Although there is no news from Lucas Lodge, there is news from the neighborhood," Mr. Collins quickly chimed in.

"Mr. Collins, why on earth would I care to hear stories about people who are not of my acquaintance?"

"Well, this particular bit of news concerns Mr. Charles Bingley, a friend of your nephew, Mr. Darcy."

Lady Catherine chewed on this information for a few minutes before declaring Mr. Collins could share the report concerning her nephew's friend.

"We have had a letter from Charlotte's sister, Maria, who, you will recall, visited us at the parsonage last…"

"The news, Mr. Collins, the news!"

"Mr. Bingley is to be married to my cousin, Miss Jane Bennet of Longbourn Manor," the parson hurriedly said. "She is the sister of Miss Elizabeth Bennet, whom you met last April when she…"

"If this report is true, then Miss Bennet has made a most advantageous marriage," Lady Catherine said, interrupting. "Although Mr. Bingley is a man of inferior rank to my nephew, I understand he is very rich and a gentleman."

Again, Anne looked at her mother sideways. *Is Mama admitting that a man, not to the manor born, could be a gentleman? Is she actually shedding some of her prejudices?*

"Of course, Mr. Bingley must never come to Rosings Park. I do have standards," Lady Catherine added, and Anne sighed.

Encouraged by her responses about Mr. Bingley and Jane Bennet, Mr. Collins added that Maria's letter contained a bit of neighborhood gossip that might be of interest to Her Ladyship. A look of alarm appeared on Charlotte's face. To warn her husband that he should not share that particular item of gossip, she coughed, twitched, and affected a fake sneeze before finally clinking her teacup with a tiny spoon, but all was for naught. Mr. Collins blurted out Maria's news.

"Apparently, during his time here in Kent, your nephew, Mr. Darcy, formed an attachment for my cousin, Miss Elizabeth Bennet. With Mr. Darcy's return to Netherfield Park, Mr. Bingley's home in Hertfordshire, there is speculation that an announcement of an engagement will be forthcoming. It is said…"

In the next minute, Lady Catherine rose up from her chair, and after growing to a prodigious height, she aimed a lightning bolt at Mr. Collins's heart before sentencing the parson to the netherworld where the heat of Hades would purge him of his sin of telling malevolent falsehoods—or at least that is how Anne imagined it. Lady Catherine's actual response was only slightly less dramatic. In a screech that could be heard in the village, Her Ladyship called for her butler so that her carriage might be ordered.

"Your destination, Milady," the butler asked.

"Longbourn Manor, Hertfordshire!"

Darcy Learns of Lady Catherine's Confrontation with Elizabeth by Regina Jeffers

October 3, 1812

On Saturday he returned from an afternoon outing to discover a familiar chaise and four before his townhouse. "Mr. Darcy," on cue, his butler approached privately, "although I told her you were not at home, your aunt, Lady Catherine de Bourgh, insisted on being admitted. She demanded, Sir, to await your return."

He looked beyond Thacker's shoulder to where Lady Catherine likely held court. It was a favorite maneuver of Her Ladyship–one of which Darcy was well aware. "You were correct to admit her, Mr. Thacker. Would you have tea brought to the drawing room?" he said authoritatively.

"Yes, Mr. Darcy."

Darcy did not like uninvited visitors; his aunt knew his distaste for such intrusions upon his privacy. He supposed something could be amiss. Could Anne have suffered further? He certainly hoped not. He strode into the drawing room expecting to find his aunt in tears. Instead, she was agitated; she was angry; she was demanding. "Lady Catherine, what brings you to London? I was unaware of your plans to travel. Please tell me my Cousin Anne has not taken ill again."

His aunt ceased her pacing. "Darcy, you came at last; I am so distressed–such an inconvenient situation!"

No Anne. What supposed crisis could Lady Catherine have conjured for his attention this time? Irritated, Darcy said, "Aunt, I could possibly empathize with you if I knew of what you speak."

"Then you have no knowledge of it? I suspected as not." Her voice rose in volume with each subsequent phrase.

The tea arrived at that precise moment. After the servant placed the tray on the table, Darcy waited until Thacker poured the distraught Lady Catherine a cup and then prepared one for Darcy. He motioned Thacker away and waited for the servants to close the door before he began again, "Let us enjoy our tea, and then allow me the opportunity to ascertain what most disturbs you."

Lady Catherine made to sip the tea, but her discomfort overwhelmed her, and she decidedly placed the saucer on the table to emphasize her agitation. "That girl!" His aunt spit out the words.

Darcy expected another of his aunt's diatribes on Anne's lack of social graces. It had been a constant disappointment to the vibrant Lady Catherine to bear such a mouse of a girl, as was Anne de Bourgh. "What girl, Madam?"

She declared, "Miss Elizabeth Bennet, of course!"

Darcy froze. Had he heard his aunt correctly? "Miss Elizabeth Bennet?" he attempted nonchalance. "What could Miss Elizabeth have to do with our family?" Just the mention of the lady's name sent his heart pounding a staccato.

With disdain, Lady Catherine insisted, "She is an insincere young lady, one not to be given proper address!"

Darcy's mind raced; about what could his aunt be speaking? "I thought Miss Elizabeth had earned your approval, Aunt."

Her Ladyship snapped, "She most certainly has not! Miss Elizabeth spreads scandalous falsehoods, and I came to London to demand you deny her report."

Darcy stood before forcing himself to walk casually to the mantel. "What falsehood has Miss Elizabeth spread to cause you such torment?"

Lady Catherine squeezed her eyes shut and shuddered with revulsion. "That girl," she began again, "let it be known she intends to be united in marriage with you, Nephew."

Darcy's heart leapt at the words. He knew Elizabeth would never spread such a rumor; it was beyond her. "Are you certain, Aunt? This appears uncharacteristic of what I know of Miss Elizabeth. From whom did you hear this rumor?" He attempted to disguise his own turmoil.

"From Mr. Collins, of course," she exclaimed. "He is Miss Bennet's cousin! I have it on my curate's good authority, and I expect you to publicly contradict this braggart."

"No one," he started deliberately, "of any consequence will repeat such stories. The Lucases are a gossipy lot. These are only Collins's assumptions; falsely based, I might add, on Charles Bingley's plans to marry Miss Elizabeth's eldest sister. Mr. Collins exaggerates the situation. There is nothing for me to contradict."

"First the girl will not retract the rumors, and now you refuse to contradict them!" she lamented.

"Lady Catherine, have you spoken to Miss Elizabeth?" He could not believe his aunt confronted Elizabeth with these accusations; Elizabeth must hate him for bringing such censure into her life!

"I have, Sir. I am almost your nearest relative, and I will expunge your reputation even if you will not!" Her haughtiness spoke of her true nature.

Darcy gripped the mantel for support; he must keep his aunt talking to know what happened, but at the moment all he wanted was to drive the woman from his house for attacking Elizabeth. "May I ask what you so kindly told Miss Elizabeth?"

Pulling herself up in a prideful stance, Her Ladyship declared, "I confronted her, demanding she contradict the rumor she started. Of course, Miss Bennet feigned innocence, claiming my coming to Longbourn would only give merit to a rumor if it existed."

Darcy smiled wryly. Miss Elizabeth was not the type to take Lady Catherine's attack as an absolute. "The lady makes a reasonable point, Lady Catherine."

"Nonsense! I asked Miss Elizabeth if she could declare there was no foundation for the rumor, and that impertinent young lady told me I may ask questions which she may choose not to answer! Can you imagine such insolence?"

Imagining Elizabeth Bennet was his existence. Word of her brazen confrontation of his aunt caused Darcy to stifle an ironic laugh. "Go on, Your Ladyship," he encouraged for he had to know whether Elizabeth spoke positively of him or not.

Her expression settled in stubborn lines. "When I told her that as your aunt I had a right to know all your dearest concerns, Miss Bennet claimed I had no right to know hers." She warned, "Her arts and allurements are many; I fear you have succumbed to them, Nephew."

Darcy could not respond; all he could consider was that although Elizabeth did not say she affected him, she refused to say she did not hold him in her regard. "What else happened, Lady Catherine?" He attempted to control the chaos of his mind by steadying his voice and by encouraging his aunt's retelling of the events.

Her countenance flushed as the words tumbled easily from his aunt's lips. "I reminded the lady of your engagement to my daughter and how it was your mother's wish for it to be so; and I told her as a young woman of inferior birth, she had no claim on a man of your standing. I reminded her of propriety and delicacy."

He gritted his teeth and bit the words as he said them, but miraculously, Darcy controlled his ever-building anger. "What was Miss Elizabeth's answer?"

"The response reeked of more insolence! Miss Elizabeth said although she heard of your engagement to Anne, that fact would not keep her from marrying you if neither your honor nor inclination confined you to your cousin." His aunt's eyes narrowed in disapproval. "Miss Elizabeth insisted that if you were to make another choice, and she should be that choice, she had the right to accept the proposal."

Darcy's breath came in short bursts. Elizabeth did not say she would accept his proposal; only she had the right to accept it. Was there still hope for his suit? He had to know more; he schooled his mind and his stance to appear in tune with Lady Catherine's sentiments, but Her Ladyship waited not for his response. "I told Miss Bennet such an alliance would bring her only disgrace; she would never be recognized or accepted by your family and acquaintances. Obstinate headstrong girl! Miss Bennet claimed being your wife would have its own attached happiness, and that happiness would be great enough to keep your lady from feeling any regret in her choice."

Again, Darcy heard Elizabeth thought being married to him could bring a woman happiness. Yet, would she think it possible to bring her happiness? Hope took root. "I assume that was the end of this confrontation," he added as a manipulation of his aunt's ire. Thankfully, she ignored his poorly disguised response.

"It most certainly was not! I reminded her of your noble lineage on your mother's side and that your father was from a respectable, honorable, and ancient, though untitled, family. I told Miss Bennet if she were sensible of her own good, she would not wish to quit the sphere in which she had been brought up."

Darcy cringed from Lady Catherine's lack of prudence and decorum. "Miss Elizabeth probably did not appreciate your bringing this to her attention."

"The lady was livid! She insisted that by marrying you, she would not be quitting her sphere because she is a gentleman's daughter." Lady Catherine's excitement grew. "I had her there, Nephew! I had her there! I explained how I knew of her mother's low connections, but she insisted if you did not object to her connections, it was nothing to me."

Much to his regret, Darcy remembered saying something very similar to his aunt's words at one time to Elizabeth. Now, however, he had come to a new realization: Lady Catherine repeatedly abused

Elizabeth, and Elizabeth had a right to deny any connection to him. If she had, his aunt would have ceased her tirade, but even with all Lady Catherine had said to her, Elizabeth never said she would not marry him. He walked toward the window; he feared if his aunt could see his countenance at the moment, it would betray how happy this conversation had made him.

"I demanded to know if you were engaged." Darcy's back stiffen with anger directed toward Her Ladyship's intimidation of someone lower in standing. "Thankfully, she confirmed you were not engaged, but Miss Bennet refused to promise she would never enter into such an engagement." Elizabeth would not promise to refuse him. "I told her I would never abandon this mission. Being wholly unreasonable, Miss Bennet claimed my application to be ill-judged and my arguments to be frivolous, saying even if she refused your hand, it would not make you turn to Anne."

With conflicted emotions, Darcy frowned. "Madam, do you not think you overstepped your status? This is my life of which you speak."

She declared, "I have not, Sir. Family resentment will follow such a union."

"I doubt our family would dare resent any woman I chose."

"Miss Bennet said something similar. She insisted she would not allow her decision to marry you to be affected by duty, honor, or gratitude. Resentment from your family or indignation from the world would mean nothing to her if you were excited by being married to her; the world, according to Miss Bennet, would have too much sense to join in the scorn!"

"Miss Elizabeth is correct, Madam. If I chose her, your disapproval would mean nothing; I would regret the loss of your affection as my aunt, but it would not alter my decision." He did not turn to face her.

"Darcy, you cannot mean as such. Have you forgotten your mother's wish for you to marry Anne?" she protested.

"My mother never expressed such a desire to me, and I will not allow it to control my heart nor my choice. As much as I respect Anne, she is not the woman for me. I require a mistress for Pemberley and a mother for my children, Pemberley's heirs. Anne and I have spoken; she and we are of a like mind in this matter."

Lady Catherine stood abruptly. "So, you intend to make this girl your wife despite my objections?"

Darcy turned to confront her. "If Elizabeth Bennet will have me, my life would be complete."

"It is her arts and allurements," she said as she headed towards the door, "which make you speak so foolishly. I will give you one week to come to your senses; if not, you will never be welcomed at Rosings again." With that, she walked brusquely away. Darcy watched as she shooed servants from her way.

When the front door closed behind her, Darcy collapsed into the chair she had vacated. Lady Catherine had given him hope; where days before he resolved to put distance between him and Elizabeth, now he thought only of returning to Netherfield and to her.

Darcy most welcomed Edward's arrival at Kensington Place that evening. He required his cousin's advice because his own emotions were far too out of control for him to think sensibly. The gentlemen took dinner leisurely, stopping several times for intense conversation and then returning to the meal to "chew" over the ideas as much as to consume the food. Darcy updated Edward on the pleasure of finding Elizabeth at Pemberley, sharing many of the intimate details and asking for Edward's astute interpretation of what Elizabeth said and did. When Darcy spoke of how Elizabeth thwarted Miss Bingley's attempt at a cut and maintained Georgiana's secret, the news astounded Edward. "I always found Miss Bennet to be most engaging," he said with a smile

Next came the story of George Wickham and Lydia Bennet's "arranged" marriage. "Now you understand why I purchased the commission," Darcy related.

"In some ways I wish Miss Elizabeth realized the depth of your affection, Darcy. Only a man as honorable as you would assist his worst enemy to secretly save the woman he loves. My estimation of you has increased substantially, and it was always of the highest regard."

This brought Edward to the news of Darcy's return to Netherfield. "I went with Bingley when he called on the Bennets the first time. I hoped to be able to speak to Miss Elizabeth, but she barely looked at me. Her needlework was never as beloved as it was that day."

"Darcy, she had not seen you since sharing her sister's shame with you. She must be confused. Why would you come to her home? Miss Elizabeth has to know how you feel by now, but she must wonder how you could renew your affections to her with George Wickham as her brother."

"What you say is so reasonable when you say it but not when I am living it," Darcy chuckled ironically. "But things did not change at the dinner two days later. I spent the meal seated beside Mrs. Bennet; she spent the evening surrounded by other ladies, and we were unable to speak."

"Again, Darcy, was that Miss Elizabeth's doing or Mrs. Bennet's?"

"Why would Mrs. Bennet want to keep me from Miss Elizabeth? If she threw Elizabeth at Mr. Collins, my wealth should earn me a right to court her daughter. The woman may dislike me, but her only goal is to marry off her daughters to well-suited matches. She would not keep me from Elizabeth!"

"Mrs. Bennet does not realizes your interest in her second daughter. If what you say about the woman is true, and she knew how you felt, Elizabeth would be sitting on your lap. Instead, I think Mrs. Bennet was attempting to keep you from Mr. Bingley. By now, the Bennets must know of Miss Bingley's cut in London of Miss Bennet. You and Caroline Bingley are intimates in the Bennets' opinions. Keeping you from interfering with her plans to marry off

Miss Bennet to Mr. Bingley seems a more likely explanation of what happened. Did Miss Elizabeth not say anything?"

"She only asked about whether Georgiana was at Pemberley."

"Cousin, Miss Elizabeth asked about Pemberley because it was the place where you shared something special. If you do not stop second guessing everything, you will lose this woman." Ashamed at how easily Edward saw what he did not, Darcy moaned in frustration. "Now what of this dark conversation between Miss Elizabeth and our indomitable aunt?"

"Her Ladyship heard from her favorite gossipmonger Mr. Collins that Elizabeth started a rumor of our impending marriage, and Lady Catherine demanded it be universally denied. Lady Catherine went to Longbourn to confront Miss Elizabeth."

"That must have been an impressive altercation! I cannot imagine Lady Catherine displaying much civility."

"Our aunt was quite frank about what she said to Elizabeth. I kept myself in check to ascertain the extent of the accusations and the exact discourse, but it was difficult. She reminded Miss Elizabeth of her connections, berated her for her insolence, and demanded Elizabeth honor my pledge to Anne."

Edward pleaded, "Please tell me Miss Elizabeth withstood Lady Catherine's demands. She is the only person who could be so defined."

"Miss Elizabeth refused to say she would not marry me if I asked, but she also never said she would accept my proposal. How do I know she desires my affections? She could have been obstinate and disagreeable because of our aunt's interference in her private affairs. I know the words Miss Elizabeth said, but I still do not know the tone of those words."

"Darcy, she could have simply promised Lady Catherine to never marry you, and her ordeal would have been over. Instead, Miss Elizabeth withstood our formidable aunt's accusations rather than to promise she would not marry you. Darcy, do you not see Miss Elizabeth will accept you this time?"

"I am afraid to think as such; my heart cannot take such disappointment again."

"Then do nothing, but are you not the one who told Bingley his fate would be the same whether he chose to wait or not? You should heed your own advice, Cousin. Miss Elizabeth will be yours if your cautious temperament will allow it."

Between them, they settled how to proceed; Darcy would return to Netherfield on Monday. His fate was in his own hands. As he departed, Edward embraced his cousin and reminded Darcy, "Take the package of lace with you, Cousin. Miss Elizabeth will want it for her wedding attire."

Lady Catherine Leaves
Longbourn in a Dudgeon
by Diana Birchall

October 3, 1812

Lady Catherine de Bourgh sat very straight in her seat in the chaise. Her always formidable mouth was compressed into an angry, thin line, and there were patchy spots of red on her cheeks. The waiting-woman, Mrs. Dawson, a widow forced into service owing to her poverty, shrank back onto the other side of the seat. Since tersely directing the coachman to drive at all speed to Mr. Darcy's London residence, Lady Catherine had not opened her lips; and the speed and energy of the four post-horses she had hired, seemed to promise that they would reach their destination in a very few hours.

It was not until they were quite out of sight of Longbourn, Meryton, and anything connected with the vile Bennet family, and indeed fast approaching the Hertfordshire border as they pounded down the good, smooth turnpike road, that she spoke.

"I am excessively displeased," she said. "My journey has been for nothing."

Mrs. Dawson might have said that her employer's displeasure was evident, but she knew much better, and only murmured a sympathetic sound, inviting her Ladyship to say more.

"That girl. That pert, uncouth creature. I tell you, she intends to marry my nephew!"

"The Colonel, do you mean, my Lady? That will be too bad, won't it?"

"No!" Lady Catherine exploded. "Don't pretend ignorance, Dawson. That is as good as insolence and I shall not brook any such thing. You know very well I mean Darcy, and that Pemberley will be – rooo-hooo-ined!" At this point she gave a great glottal gulp and reached for her lace handkerchief.

If she knew nothing else, Mrs. Dawson knew how to deal with hysterical fits, in employers and their daughters alike; and she brought out a practiced technique in soothing. The smelling salts, the lavender-water bottle, the powder-puffs and the linen were all brought out of her handy well-stocked reticule, and applied over Lady Catherine's broad, red face, to the accompaniment of little mewing sounds and caresses. She straightened her Ladyship's lace head-piece, which resembled the figurehead on a ship's prow, and had slipped sideways with the bounce of the carriage, in a most undignified manner.

"I am very sorry to hear this, my dear Lady Catherine," she said apologetically. "No wonder you are distressed. I thought how it might be, when you did not direct coachman to take us to Lucas Lodge."

"What business had you to think at all, Dawson?" Lady Catherine expostulated. "Naturally I would not remain in the same county with that impertinent young woman for ten minutes longer than necessary. The Lucases do not deserve the honour of a visit from me. I am certain they have promoted this disgraceful match."

"Oh – but surely – they would not dare – "

"Speak only of what you know, Dawson. News of this wretched attachment came to me through their means, as they wrote to rejoice over the connection with their daughter, Mrs. Collins. Her stupid fool of a husband brought the tidings to me at once. They want the privilege of visiting at Pemberley, mark my words, and they completely forgot what they owe me."

"What – what do they owe you?" Mrs. Dawson ventured timidly.

"Loyalty!" Lady Catherine spat out. "And respect! After all the attentions I have bestowed upon them, and the great notice I have paid to their daughter. To promote my nephew's marriage with that girl, from a low, disgraced family, her sister no better than a – " She stopt, and wiped her face.

"Perhaps it is not so bad as you fear," Mrs. Dawson consoled. "They are not actually engaged, are they?" "No," Lady Catherine conceded, "and I will take care of Darcy." She nodded. "Yes, I will remind him of what he owes the family, of the duty he owes to me, who have always loved him so tenderly and been a second mother to him."

"Indeed you have," breathed Mrs.Dawson, over the rattle of the carriage.

"I will represent to him," she continued, "every mutinous, insubordinate phrase that girl used. I remember them all. She pretended not to know what I came for – she dared to deny that she and her family and the Lucases have spread the report of the attachment themselves – and she refused to confess that she has used her arts and allurements to infatuate him!"

"Did she indeed," said Mrs. Dawson, not without a sympathetic pang for Elizabeth, "that was very bad."

"Bad! You may well say that. Even when I explained the nature of the engagement subsisting between Darcy and Anne, she utterly refused to promise not to marry him!"

"Poor Miss de Bourgh will be very sorry," agreed Mrs. Dawson, a little tactlessly. "It will be a great disappointment to her. I know she has always looked forward to being mistress of Pemberley."

Lady Catherine could sit it no longer. She reached out with her heavy, ham-like hand, made no lovelier by the delicate lace half-glove that draped it, and slapped Mrs. Dawson in the face. "Be silent!" she fumed. "It is not your place to say what your superiors think and feel."

"No, ma'am," muttered the poor woman, casting down her eyes to hide tears and rubbing her reddened cheek, where a handprint mark was swiftly forming.

"You are lucky I do not turn you out of this carriage, and dismiss you without a character. But I am ever celebrated for my extreme charity and tenderness of heart."

"To be sure, my Lady," replied Mrs. Dawson, as she knew she must.

"Where are we now. Coachman!" called Lady Catherine. "Can you tell us how many miles from London?"

"Tisn't that far now, your Ladyship," he bawled back, "we just passed the turnpike post sign, and it ain't more than a matter of another twenty mile or so."

Lady Catherine sat back with some satisfaction. "There. We should be with Darcy by dinner time. You may close your eyes if you like, Dawson; I am going to revolve in my mind what it is I will say to my nephew."

"Very good, your Ladyship," said the other woman obediently, and shut her eyes, exhausted. Before she could fall into a fitful doze, however, Lady Catherine spoke again. "I will tell him," she said, "that Miss Bennet is stubbornness itself; she has a nasty little spirit of independence, and obduracy, and contrary-ness, and she has told me herself that she is determined to have him."

"Did she?" asked Mrs. Dawson, opening her eyes.

"She as much as said so. I threatened her with all that would befall her, were she so foolish as to go through with her scheme; she should be shunned, and censured, and disgraced. You may well conceive, however, that she was only thinking of the advantages of being Darcy's wife. She cares for the man not at all, only the place. I pressed her hard, Dawson, very hard; but to all my representations, and importunings, she held to her position with a firmness that is positively uncanny in so young a woman. Mark my words, if Darcy does marry her, he will find himself tied to a termagant."

"I have no doubt," said Mrs. Dawson faintly.

"Yes. And that is what I am going to London to tell Darcy. Of the ambition, the calculation, the headstrong determination of this girl, who is bound to ruin him entirely."

"I daresay he will be very much concerned," said Mrs. Dawson.

"I mean he shall be," said Lady Catherine with some satisfaction. "You wait and see, I will open his eyes and show him what this young woman really is, a scheming creature; and we will have Anne at Pemberley at last, I am perfectly sure of that."

"I hope we will," echoed the waiting woman obediently.

Mr. Bennet Hears from Mr. Collins
by Shannon Winslow

October 4, 1812

Mr. Bennet reposed in his library after breakfast, his feet propped up on a stool and a highly enjoyable book before his nose. With the most troublesome of his daughters permanently gone from the house and the most angelic one advantageously engaged, he had little left to wish for but that the peace of his household might last. He did not expect it to, however. Just as the little tyrant across the channel could not seem to behave himself for long, so too his own wife and at least one of his offspring were bound to soon involve him in another round of hostilities.

But the interruption that particular morning came from an entirely different source, and one not at all unwelcome. It was a letter – a letter from his cousin Mr. Collins.

In the months since the renewal of their acquaintance, Mr. Bennet had come to regard Mr. Collins's correspondence as a priceless source of amusement. He would by no means have given up the association on any grounds less consequential than the impediment that death itself would have constituted. So Mr. Bennet tossed his book aside; the newly arrived missive promised the finer entertainment.

He was not disappointed.

The absurdity of the letter's style – all affected humility and artificially formal language – was just what Mr. Bennet had come to expect. But the content was far beyond anything he had imagined.

It began predictably enough with an extravagant discourse in congratulation of the approaching nuptials of Mr. Bennet's eldest daughter.

…You may be assured, my dear sir, that Mrs. Collins and I send our very sincere felicitations to my cousin Jane and to you, her honored parent. What a triumph for you all – especially after that most regrettable affair with your youngest daughter – that your fortunes are so quickly on the rise again. I must confess that it has astonished me exceedingly. The thing speaks in credit to Mr. Bingley, I suppose, that he is so generous as to overlook what many certainly could not have – that is, your family's fatally tainted circumstances. He must be a gentleman of true worth, as well as being one of greater consequence than my cousin had any cause to hope for. I am sure you are all to be heartily congratulated on forming such a favorable alliance.

From these flattering and solicitous remarks, Mr. Collins moved on to his real purpose for writing, and to what was for Mr. Bennet the truly diverting portion of the letter. It seemed that the pompous clergyman had got it into his head that Mr. Darcy was violently in love with Elizabeth and meant to make her an offer.

"Oh, this is admirable!" Mr. Bennet told himself, laughing aloud after reading this delightful passage. "Mr. Darcy, of all men!"

Had Mr. Collins canvassed the whole world, he could not have hit upon a more ridiculous notion and a less plausible suitor for Mr. Bennet's favorite daughter. That Lizzy should be the romantic object of that proud, disagreeable man stretched the limits of credulity. Lizzy, who had been so outspoken in her pointed dislike of the man! Surely her true sentiments could not have escaped anybody's notice. Regardless of his high opinion of himself, Mr. Darcy could not be such a fool as to contemplate approaching her.

Mr. Bennet chuckled as he pictured the scene that might ensue if the man ever tried. No doubt his high-spirited daughter would make quick work of poor Mr. Darcy. She would probably hiss like an incensed feline at his first avowal of affection, and threaten to scratch his eyes out if he ventured anywhere nearer the question than that. It would certainly be a sight to behold, one Mr. Bennet would give a tidy sum to witness for himself.

The rest of the letter was pure Mr. Collins – his obsequious attentions to Lady Catherine de Bourgh's opinions in the matter (she disapproved, not surprisingly), his not-so-subtle hints of what was due that lady's opinion, and his intended kindness in warning the Bennets against crossing her. Then there was the bit about Charlotte's interesting situation, the expected young "olive-branch," which struck Mr. Bennet as being in poor taste to mention.

Finally Mr. Bennet could no longer keep these overpowering temptations to mirth for himself alone, not when his daughter would likewise appreciate the absurdities involved. Leaving the sanctuary of his library, Mr. Bennet ran straight into the person he sought.

"Lizzy," said he, "I was going to look for you; come into my room…"

Bingley Brings Darcy the (Second) Proposal ~ Elizabeth Confides in Jane by Colette Saucier

October 6, 1812

Mrs. Hill rushed up the path from Meryton to Longbourn, anxious to bring Cook the ducks and spices required for the elaborate dinner Mrs. Bennet had planned for Mr. Bingley that afternoon. If only Mrs. Philips had not detained her, begging that she pass the message to her sister that Miss Bennet's engagement had indeed hushed the gossip surrounding the elopement of Miss Lydia – er – Mrs. Wickham. Honestly! Has the woman not sense enough not to speak of such matters to the housekeeper? Even one who has been with the family four and twenty years. But Mrs. Philips and Mrs. Bennet both readily relied on the assistance of the servants to bring them news.

Mrs. Hill's thoughts were thus occupied when she noticed the approach of two young people. Assuming they to be Miss Bennet and her Mr. Bingley, she took a deep breath and adopted a smile to greet them; but within a few steps, the couple halted, and she realized it was not Mr. Bingley but his friend Mr. Darcy – and in close conversation with Miss Elizabeth!

Her polite smile faded as she stopped walking. They had not yet noticed her, quite seriously engaged and – Good gracious! – Mr. Darcy had taken Miss Elizabeth's hands in his! A genuine grin now spread across Mrs. Hill's face as she quietly slipped off the path into the sparsely wooded grove.

Mrs. Hill scurried towards Lucas Lodge then back on the path to Longbourn and entered the Bennet house through the kitchen where the cook and a housemaid were at work on the meal preparations.

"Thank heavens, Mrs. Hill!" cried Cook. "You are finally come. I hope you have my mace. It seems we are to have another guest at table today."

"Mr. Darcy?" Mrs. Hill responded with a sly smile.

"Aye, which means we must have mutton and veal." Cook stopped chopping the onion before her. "How d'you know?"

"I've just seen him on the path to Meryton – and with Miss Elizabeth."

"Was not Miss Bennet and her beau with 'em?"

Mrs. Hill shook her head. "I expect we shall be hearing of another engagement soon enough."

"D'ya mean it?" asked the maid. "Miss Elizabeth and that tall, handsome Mr. Darcy?"

"Aye, Katie, the very one – master of that grand estate, Pemberley!"

"But he is such a proud, unpleasant kind of man. Not nearly so pleasant as Mr. Wickham or Mr. Bingley. Oh! But he is very rich. Isn't he, Mrs. Hill?"

"Mind your work there, Katie," said Cook. "I suppose now he will be a daily visitor just as Mr. Bingley. The mistress says he has three French cooks!" She rammed the knife blade through an onion. "No rest for the weary, all I can say. We'll need plenty o'butter for the vegetables, Katie. And you got my pepper, Mrs. Hill, and my cloves?"

"Yes, yes, it's all there along with your ducks. Quite a heavy parcel, walking from Meryton," said Mrs. Hill. "I have found Mr. Darcy quite agreeable, if a bit shy. And, Katie, you watch yourself around that Mr. Wickham."

"Does this mean Mr. Collins won't turn us out of Longbourn?"

"No, Katie. The estate is just as entailed as ever, and that odious man is still to inherit, but with two such wealthy sons, my mistress is sure to keep her own household when the master passes and not have need to live at Netherfield, and she will require servants. We will be secure."

"Or mayhap I could be a maid at Netherfield – or Pemberley!"

"I'd not want to be goin' to Pemberley, I's you," said Cook. "Derbyshire is far north, away from everyone you know."

"You's not be goin' to Pemberley anyway, now would you," said Katie, "seeing as Mr. Darcy has three French cooks already."

Cook pulled back on the knife. "You mind your tongue there, Katie, or I might be of a mind to cut it out."

Their attention was soon captured by the sound of the front door closing and voices in the drawing room, and they were arrested in silence.

"Is that Miss Elizabeth come back?" Katie finally asked in a whisper.

They listened a moment before Mrs. Hill went out to the dining-parlour and called to the footman.

"Miz Hill, the mistress is asking after you," he said when he entered the kitchen.

"Who is just come in, Harold?"

"'T's just Miss Bennet with Mr. Bingley." Then looking around at the six eyes gaping at him, he said, "What's all this? Why such a fuss?"

"Mrs. Hill thinks the gentleman from Derbyshire is gonna offer for Miss Elizabeth."

"Hush now, Katie," said Mrs. Hill.

"Do you, now?" Harold pulled out a cheroot. "S'pose then I won't be turned out when the master is kingdom come."

"Harold! You mustn't speak so! And don't you even think of smoking that in the house!"

"Right, Miz Hill. D' you s'pose that's why that gran' duchess called here for Miss Elizabeth?"

The three women gasped in unison.

"I hadn't thought of that," said Mrs. Hill. "Aye. Why else would her ladyship come? That seems the only probable motive for her calling."

"I'd not mind working in Mr. Darcy's household."

"You'd go to Derbyshire, Harold?" asked Katie.

"Pfft. A gentleman such as he is sure to have a house in Town. That's where I'll be. Miz Hill, don't be forgettin' you're wanted upstairs."

Mrs. Hill took the small bundle labeled British East India Company and sighed. "I better go on, then, before the mistress has a fit of nerves."

Mrs. Hill walked up the back stairs to the family wing and scratched at the door to Mrs. Bennet's apartment.

"Hill, Hill, is that you? Come."

Mrs. Hill entered to find Sarah attending to Mrs. Bennet's hair. "Yes, ma'am."

"My dear Hill, where have you been? Bless me, you know I cannot manage without you."

"I've been to Meryton, ma'am. I brung the tea."

"Do put it in the caddy," Mrs. Bennet said and handed her the key. "I cannot be bothered. Good gracious, if that disagreeable Mr. Darcy must always be coming here with our dear Bingley! No compassion for my poor nerves. What can he mean by being so tiresome as to disturb us with his constant company? But, however, he is very welcome if he likes, as he is a friend of Mr. Bingley."

With such a speech as this, Mrs. Hill could depend on her mistress having no intelligence on the understanding between a man of ten thousand a year and her second eldest daughter. "I met Mrs. Philips at the butcher, ma'am, and she sent a message to you. She says all of Meryton has pronounced the Bennets to be the luckiest family in the world." And soon to be thought luckier still!

"Aye, and why would they not, with two daughters well married? I am sure not a soul in all of Meryton would not want to be at Jane's wedding." Mrs. Bennet chose to entertain herself in this manner for some time while Mrs. Hill and Sarah assisted with her toilette.

As Sarah made to leave to help Miss Bennet, Mrs. Hill pulled her aside. "Now, Sarah, as soon as you are done with all the ladies, you make haste and hurry down to the kitchen. You understand?"

The young maid nodded and then left Mrs. Hill alone to listen to her mistress's repetitions of delights.

"Mr. Bingley is the handsomest young man that ever was seen. And with five or six thousand a year! Last year when he first came into Hertfordshire, as soon as I saw him I thought how likely it would be that they should come together. My dear Jane could not be so beautiful for nothing…."

Having heard this speech not less than incessantly for nigh ten days, Mrs. Hill knew when to offer the appropriate response without paying strict attention, allowing her thoughts to return to their previous meditations until such time as she could return to the kitchen.

"They're come back," said Harold when she arrived.

"Did you see Miss Elizabeth?" Katie asked her.

"I've been with Mrs. Bennet all this time. Has Sarah been down?" When they responded in the negative, she continued. "I asked her to come as soon as she has finished with the ladies' hair. She might have news then."

The sound of silver clanking coming from the butler's pantry then drew their notice, and Mrs. Hill called out to him. "Mr. Sloan, might I ask you into the kitchen a moment?"

The butler came to stand in the entryway to the kitchen. "Yes, Mrs. Hill?"

"Has Mr. Darcy requested a private audience with Mr. Bennet?"

"Mrs. Hill, surely you do not propose that I gossip about my master, and here in the kitchen?"

"Aye, that is precisely what I am asking you to do. This affects us all."

"And, pray, how are you entitled to any knowledge of Mr. Bennet's affairs?"

"I think Mr. Darcy intends to ask his consent to marry Miss Elizabeth."

"Indeed?" Mr. Sloan's eyebrows lifted at this. "The gentlemen are in my master's library, but Mr. Bingley is within as well."

"Is the door closed?"

"It was open, last I knew."

"Then go on, bring us a report," she said, urging him with a flap of her hands.

The butler opened his lips to protest but, perhaps anticipating an argument, sighed and withdrew. The others were fixed in wretched suspense, which was rewarded by his prompt return.

"My overhearings succeeded in nothing but lowering my own opinion of myself. They speak of nothing of consequence, merely speculating on the Tsar's response and if it might realign the coalition against Napoleon." His audience's disappointment was quite evident. "And how did you come upon this intelligence, Mrs. Hill, that another wedding is imminent?"

"I saw them walking together on my return from Meryton."

"That by no means equates to matrimony. Mr. Bingley had proposed they all go out when he and Mr. Darcy arrived, and Miss Catherine went as well."

"They may have all gone out together, but they did not return together, now. Did they? When I come upon them, they were quite alone, and they had stopped their walking. Mr. Darcy stood close to Miss Elizabeth and held her hands."

"And from this you make such inferences?"

"And that there duchess came to wait on Miss Elizabeth," offered Harold.

"Duchess?"

"He means Lady de Bourgh," said Mrs. Hill. "Have you not heard nor seen anything yourself?"

Mr. Sloan's countenance turned more solemn, as if considering his next words carefully. "Mr. Darcy, I think, has long admired Miss Elizabeth, as he looks on her a great deal; but his last visit before going away, when I brought in the tea things after dinner, I noticed Miss Elizabeth to be out of spirits, and her eyes never left him as he walked to the other side of the room."

"Lovers' quarrel," said Harold.

"Harold, you appear quite at your leisure. I believe the sideboard is in need of polishing."

"Yes, Mr. Sloan," he said while walking past.

"This may all come to nothing. Now, if we are done with this nasty business, I will go lay the table."

"You must contrive to have Miss Elizabeth sit beside Mr. Darcy at table," said Mrs. Hill.

"How might you propose I do that?"

"Oh, you will think of something."

Mr. Sloane quit the room but not before rolling his eyes and shaking his head. Mrs. Hill scarcely had time to talk over these new developments with Katie and Cook before Sarah arrived.

"You wanted to see me, Miz Hill?"

"Yes, Sarah. Were you just with Miss Bennet and Miss Elizabeth?" She answered in the affirmative. "Well? Did they say anything?"

"I don' take your meanin'. Say anything of what?"

"Miss Elizabeth's walk with Mr. Darcy."

Sarah hesitated, clearly uncomfortable under the scrutiny of the other women awaiting her reply. "When Miss Elizabeth came in, Miss Bennet asked where she'd been walkin' to for so long."

"And what did she say?"

"She said they wandered about until she was lost."

"Psst," said Cook. "Lost in his eyes, more likely. She could find her way across half of Hertfordshire on a moonless night."

"She said nothin' of Mr. Darcy?" asked Katie.

"None at all. Why would she?"

They then related all they knew and their conjectures as to the meaning of it.

"Mr. Durst was in the paddock when the duchess were here," said Sarah, "and he was right there on that side of the lawn when she spoke with Miss Elizabeth."

"Do we still have some plum cake left from breakfast? Katie, go fetch Mr. Durst. Say we have plum cake for him. Go on, make haste!"

Katie returned shortly with Mr. Durst, but Cook stopped him in the doorway.

"You are not bringing dirt all into my kitchen. Take off your shoes before you come in here."

Disinclined to do so, he said, "I don' need to come in. Jus' give me the cake and I'll eat it out here."

Mrs. Hill rushed to his side. "Now, now, don't be daft. Just knock the mud off your boots. That'll do well enough. Then come sit down."

He did as told, and Cook set the plum cake before him, but not in good humour, and the four women sat down around him.

"Now, Mr. Durst," began Mrs. Hill, "do you recall a few days ago when that chaise and four with the fine livery brought Lady de Bourgh."

"Well, 'course I recollect it. Was but three days ago. I'm not some cod's head." He looked up then and froze upon facing the

521

expectant stares, his fork suspended in mid-air. "Right. What's all this about?"

"Were you there when Miss Elizabeth was with her ladyship?"

"I was goin' about my duties, but I happen by there a few times."

"What was her reason for coming? Did she have anything particular to say to Miss Elizabeth?"

His cheeks then overspread with the deepest blush, and he dropped his gaze down to his plate. "I don' think it'd be right for me to talk of it."

"You had better," said Cook, "or that will be the last piece of cake you'll ever have from me!"

He seemed to struggle to push past his discomposure before speaking. "Her ladyship was in high dudgeon. She accuse Miss Elizabeth of trying to lure Mr. Darcy and draw him in to marrying her."

"I knew it! They are engaged!" declared Mrs. Hill.

"Now, jus' a minute. Her ladyship said that she being his closest relation, she would never allow it, and a marriage could never take place because he's engaged to her daughter." This pronouncement elicited a mixture of disappointed gasps and groans.

"So he did not offer for her."

Mr. Durst shook his head. "Her ladyship asked if she were engaged to her nephew, and Miss Elizabeth said no. Then her ladyship demanded a promise that she'd not accept if he asked."

"Hateful, hateful woman!"

"Then she stormed off and well-nigh jumped into her carriage before it bolted off."

The women were all discouraged and sorry. They were then forced to return to their duties without having gained any satisfactory information. Mrs. Hill relinquished any remaining hope when, during dinner, Harold came into the kitchen for the next remove and told her that Miss Elizabeth seemed quite agitated being seated beside Mr. Darcy and hadn't said a word, although the gentleman himself appeared quite at ease. Then Mrs. Hill was left to regret her part in this arrangement, which caused Miss Elizabeth such embarrassment. Nothing more was said on the subject for the remainder of the afternoon.

That night, after seeing to Mrs. Bennet's needs and listening to her relate all the particulars of Mr. Bingley's visit, Mrs. Hill stepped out into the hall and, closing the door behind her, turned to find Sarah with her ear nearly pressed against Miss Bennet's door.

"Sarah," Mrs. Hill cried out in a harsh whisper, but Sarah waved for her to come near. They both leaned in to hear the muffled voices through the door.

"You are joking, Lizzy. This cannot be! Engaged to Mr. Darcy! No, no, you shall not deceive me. I know it to be impossible."

"This is a wretched beginning indeed! My sole dependence was on you; and I am sure nobody else will believe me, if you do not. Yet, indeed, I am in earnest. I speak nothing but the truth. He still loves me, and we are engaged."

At this, Sarah and Mrs. Hill gaped at each other with eyes as wide as their grins.

"Oh, Lizzy! It cannot be. I know how much you dislike him."

"You know nothing of the matter. That is all to be forgot. Perhaps I did not always love him so well as I do now. But in such cases as these, a good memory is unpardonable. This is the last time I shall ever remember it myself."

Mrs. Hill and Sarah quietly stepped back from the door and embraced.

"Mrs. Bennet must yet know nothing of it, or she would be in raptures! So you mustn't say a word to anyone in the family," said Mrs. Hill, to which Sarah readily agreed.

They then hurried away to the kitchen, eager to relate news which would give such pleasure to so many.

Bingley and Jane Take a Walk
by Susan Mason-Milks

October 19, 1812

"Oh, Mr. Bingley," trilled Mrs. Bennet, "What a pleasant surprise! We were not expecting you back from London so soon."

"I hope I have not come at an inconvenient time, Mrs. Bennet," Bingley said politely.

"Oh, no! You are welcome here at any time. Our dear Jane will be so pleased to see you."

Mrs. Bennet took Mr. Bingley's arm and towed him down the hallway toward the sitting room all the while chattering to him about the wedding plans. When the door opened and he stepped inside, Jane looked up and gave him that sweet smile of hers causing his heart to do a little dance. Now that they were engaged, he experienced a particular thrill in knowing her special look was for him alone.

"Mr. Bingley," Jane said, setting aside her sewing, "you have returned early. I hope your business was successfully concluded."

"Doesn't our Jane look lovely today?" asked Mrs. Bennet urging him toward the chair next to Jane's.

All morning he had tried to think of a way to be alone with his angel but had not been able to come up with a better excuse than a walk.

"Miss Bennet, I was hoping we might walk out to take advantage of this fine weather."

"I will go fetch my pelisse and bonnet," she said without hesitation. As she crossed the room, he thought, not for the first time, just how much her grace and beauty never failed to please him.

While waiting for Jane to return, Mrs. Bennet proceeded to carry on about all about her plans for improvements to Netherfield. Trying to put an interested look on his face, he half-listened as she chattered on. Finally, to his relief, Jane reappeared, and they were able to make their escape.

Once they had turned down a nearby lane and were out of sight of the house, Bingley stopped and turned to look into his fiancée's upturned face. Holding both of her hands in his, he said, "Oh, my angel! While I was in London, I could think of nothing but you. I concluded my business as quickly as possible so I could return. I hope you thought of me, too."

Jane smiled sweetly. "Of course I did, Mr. Bingley."

"I thought we had agreed you would use my first name, especially when we are on our own?"

At that, Jane blushed and fixed her eyes on the ground. Putting a crooked finger gently beneath her chin, he lifted her face up. Even one look into her clear, blue eyes was enough to tempt any man. After all, they were engaged now. Perhaps…

"When we are apart, you are never far from my mind, Charles," she admitted shyly.

The sound of his Christian name on her lips was too much. Unable to resist temptation, Bingley pulled her into his arms. Much to his delight, Jane responded by relaxing against him and laying her head gently on his shoulder. Her faintly lavender scent was intoxicating. Bingley could still scarcely believe his luck that after all those months apart she still loved him. He was forgiven for not returning to Netherfield last fall, and in just a short time, she would be his. He wanted nothing more than to kiss her, but discretion won out, and he decided they were too near the public road for any privacy. Still, once she was in his arms, it was difficult to let her go, and he was pleased to discover that she made no attempt to pull away. After enjoying the intimacy of their embrace for a few moments more, he reluctantly pushed back, took her hand, and tucked it safely in the crook of his arm.

"You cannot know how much I wish we could steal a few moments alone. Really alone," he confessed in a low voice.

"And you, sir, might be surprised to know that is exactly what I most wish for, also," she said very softly.

Bingley was so surprised by her comment that he was temporarily unsure if he had heard her correctly. Turning, he discovered she was watching him, and they shared an awkward, nervous laugh. Feeling his self-control slipping away at this revelation, he decided to change the subject to something less volatile.

"Your mother was telling me about her plans for improvements to Netherfield," he said lightly.

"You know you must not take her too seriously. She is always full of plans."

"I was just wondering how much of what she told me is her idea and how much is yours," he asked with some hesitation.

"There has been so much to do! I have not had time to turn my mind to that yet, although I have heard it said that it is best to live in a house for a while before making serious redecorating decisions. Do you also think that is true?"

Bingley breathed a sigh of relief.

As if reading his mind, she said, "Charles, although I have always tried to please my mother, you must know by now that she does not speak for me."

"I know, but I am pleased to hear you reaffirm it." He patted her hand as it rested on his arm. Although the temperature was cool, the sun was warm as they slowly strolled down the lane. He knew he was stalling but how to begin? The subject he really wished to discuss with her was delicate, and he had no experience of how to start such a conversation, but start it he must.

"You know I was able to renew the lease on Netherfield for another year without committing to a purchase."

"Yes, you have mentioned that."

"I have until next summer to decide whether or not we will settle here more...ah... permanently. Since the owner's ultimate goal is the sale of the estate, he has written certain terms into the lease agreement. As a result, I have just one more year in which to decide whether to buy Netherfield or look for a different property."

"Making such a significant purchase is an important decision," Jane said quietly.

"Darcy thinks the property would be an acceptable choice although some major improvements would be necessary if we stay. Netherfield is large enough to bring in a good income but not so large that I will not be able to learn to manage it with the help of my new steward. And of course, with Darcy's counsel, too."

"Yes, Mr. Darcy has been very helpful to you," Jane said.

"I have always thought you would want to live here in Hertfordshire to be near your parents. That started me wondering if I should begin negotiations with the seller now rather than wait for summer."

Jane looked up at him calmly. "As your wife, I will, of course, let you make an important decision such as that. I am certain you know what is best," she demurred.

Blast! Why couldn't this be easier, he thought.

"Yes, but I would like to hear what you think so that I may take that into consideration," he asked boldly.

"Oh, I see," she murmured. They walked on for a few minutes in silence.

"Of course, there are certainly advantages to being near family. When we have children, for example," she said.

Bingley could see that Jane's cheeks had reddened slightly at the mere mention of their children and found that his own face felt a bit warm, too.

"On the other hand, I shall miss Lizzy terribly," she added. "In fact, possibly more than I will miss my mother and father."

Bingley tried his best to puzzle out what she was not saying. Finally, he decided to be more direct.

"Do you mean you would prefer to live near your sister rather than your parents?"

"Lizzy and I have always been very close," she said. "Also, I confess I am not certain how I feel about the thought of my mother being able to drop in at any time she chooses." At this, her sweet smile turned into a slightly impish grin.

Although he had been thinking that very thing, to hear it from Jane was a great relief. It meant she was not as tied to her mother as he had feared. Although he was prepared to make the adjustments necessary to live in such close proximity to the Bennets, he had not exactly been relishing the idea. He only knew that he would do whatever made Jane happy.

"Apparently, your sister has had similar thoughts. Darcy recently offered to keep his eyes open for any possible leases in Derbyshire, but I was uncertain if I should tell him to go ahead."

"I would very much like to visit Derbyshire," Jane said brightly.

Bingley had a difficult time containing his excitement. "Then when we visit Pemberley, we will also make a tour of the area to see if it is to our liking," he said.

Jane squeezed his arm. "That would please me greatly."

They walked on for some time talking about small things. He told her funny stories about his childhood, and in turn, she shared some of her misadventures, although he noted that Elizabeth had generally been the one to instigate these escapades. Late afternoon arrived too quickly and the sun's warmth began to fade signaling time for their return. Reluctantly, they turned back. Not too far from Longbourn, they passed by a small wooded area very near the lane.

"This is a perfect spot for gathering pine cones," she said indicating the nearby stand of trees. "Will you assist me?"

When he gave her a questioning look, she grinned and taking his hand, gently pulled him away from the lane.

"Those woods look rather dense, Jane. We might lose sight of the road or become turned around."

"Oh, Charles, my dear, that was exactly what I was hoping for!" And blushing all over, she firmly led him toward the trees.

Suddenly, Bingley thought that gathering pine cones seemed like the best idea in the world.

Darcy Surprises Elizabeth
by Sharon Lathan

October 29, 1812

For the hundredth time in the past hour, Lizzy glanced away from the dress she was attempting to sew and peered out the window. A tiny stretch of the main road could be seen through the trees and shrubs shielding Longbourn from the passing traffic, that glimpse of gravel the precise spot her eyes zeroed in on each time. The humor in remembering that, until a couple weeks ago, she had never been aware of the fact that the road could be seen if sitting before this window at exactly this angle, normally brought a small smile to her face. Today she only sighed forlornly.

I am sure he has already left for London, she thought, glancing to the mantel clock, which had only inched two-minutes past the ten-o'clock hour when she last glanced at it. Shaking her head with a mixture of disgust and sadness, Lizzy released a second unconscious sigh.

"Do not be sad, Lizzy. We will be in London soon ourselves, and there you will be reunited with Mr. Darcy."

Lizzy turned to smile at Jane. "And then I will have an opportunity to comfort you, dear Jane, while you are separated from the gentleman you love. Of course, you will certainly exhibit better restraint than me. You would never stare out windows in the hope of a flash of your betrothed riding by!"

"Believe that if you must, and I shan't admit to the numerous attempts I have made to peer through the miles and draw Netherfield into greater focus."

Laughing at their joint whimsies instigated by hearts giddy with newfound love, neither noticed the appearance of Mr. Hill until he cleared his throat.

"Pardon me, ladies, but Miss Elizabeth has a visitor."

Lizzy's brows rose, then furrowed. "I do?" She glanced at the clock as she stood, her mind racing over the list of people she knew who would call so early in the day. Charlotte might have, but she was now Mrs. Collins and dwelling in far away Kent. That led her to imagining Lady Catherine – well known for barging in at odd hours of the day – but before she could decide whether that prospect frightened or irritated her, Mr. Hill stepped aside.

"William!"

"Mr. Darcy!" Mrs. Bennet's fawning exclamation drowned Lizzy's started one, the older woman across the room faster than the speed of light. "How absolutely delightful to see you! Oh my! I am all aflutter! We were not yet expecting guests. I am afraid you just missed breakfast, although I am sure Hill can have Cook prepare something in no time at all! We have fresh biscuits with strawberry jam made not a week ago past, and coffee of course, with cream as you like it, or if hot cocoa is preferred?"

"Please, do not trouble yourself, Mrs. Bennet." Darcy quickly jumped in when she finally paused for breath, tearing his eyes away from Lizzy's sparkling gaze. "I dined well this morning, thank you. And I apologize for calling unannounced at this early hour. However, as I drew close to Longbourn on my way to Town, I feared the appearance of rudeness if I did not pay my respects, and latched onto the chance to again express my deep appreciation for your hospitality these past weeks."

"Oh, Mr. Darcy! You are so very kind!" Her voice broke, one hand dabbing a handkerchief at a teary eye. "My Lizzy is the most fortunate of women to have gained the notice of such a great man."

Darcy bowed his head slightly, and then rapidly glanced toward Lizzy. "Thank you, madam, although I judge myself the truly fortunate one. And with that in mind," he rushed on before another word passed Mrs. Bennet's parted lips, "may I be granted a moment alone with Miss Elizabeth?"

"Mama," Jane took her mother's arm, steering toward the door, "I just recalled that Cook needed our opinion on the marzipan for the wedding cake…"

Seconds later they were alone, Jane's voice drifting down the hall through the half-closed door. Darcy wasted no time. Three long strides and he was before Lizzy with both her hands encased within his.

"I had to see you again—"

"I am so surprised—"

They laughed as their words tumbled over each other, Darcy deciding to forego conversation for the preferred pleasure of kissing her soft lips. A mere brush of mouths, tender and brief, although the jolt of electricity piercing their bodies was vocalized with susurrate exhales. Not trusting himself, Darcy stepped back a pace and drew a shaky breath. Smiling, her hands still firmly engulfed between his palms, Darcy led to the nearest sofa.

"I do apologize, Elizabeth, for arriving at this improper hour. I honestly did not plan to, sure that I was content with our affectionate parting last evening, and with the knowledge that I will see you in London three days hence. Yet, even as I mounted Parsifal at Netherfield, I knew I could not ride past your gate, envisioning you sitting here, and not stop. It was simply beyond my capabilities to resist."

"The stalwart Mr. Darcy confesses to a weakness, does he?"

"With you, dearest Elizabeth, I find my strength and control seriously lacking. Daily I pray for time to hurry faster than normal so that November sixteen will arrive sooner. I daresay I may lose my mind before then."

"Well, I certainly would not wish for that to happen! I shall increase my prayers, that are also asking for time to swiftly pass, and perhaps the joint effort, along with Jane and Mr. Bingley, who are undoubtedly appealing to the heavens in a similar vein, will tug at God's ear."

"If nothing else, He may grant the request simply to shut us up."

"Indeed," she said as they laughed. "Of course, I must admit that I am looking forward to an extensive shopping expedition in London. A girl only has one chance to buy a wedding dress and trousseau, after all. It is far too serious a task to be rushed."

"Yes, I suppose that is true." Darcy lifted one hand, fingertips caressing over her cheek. "And there is also the leisurely time I am allotting for your thorough examination of your future home in London. Darcy House on Grosvenor Square is not nearly as vast as Pemberley, but large enough to require time to peruse. And any decorating alterations you wish to make will take time to accomplish."

Lizzy shook her head. "William, If Darcy House is half as lovely as Pemberley then I can't imagine it needing to be redecorated, especially by me, when I know nothing of such matters."

"I trust your instincts, Elizabeth. Certainly you will want to renovate my mother's bedchamber to your taste. That, at least, must be done before we are wed."

The odd inflection to his voice when he spoke the word "bedchamber" was not lost on Lizzy. Nor was the stormy glint in his eyes, especially when they dropped to her breasts and swept over her figure. His fingers glided down her neck and across the delicate edge of her shoulder, the touch as light as a feather yet sending sparks of heat searing under her skin. Shivering, instinctively leaning closer to him, Lizzy nearly whimpered when he pulled his fingers away before traveling any lower.

Roughly clearing his throat, Darcy went on in an almost normal tone, "I also hope we can arrange at least one dinner with my cousin, Colonel Fitzwilliam. Another, sensible reason for stopping this morning was to inform you that a letter from Richard awaited me last evening when I returned to Netherfield. I had not written to him yet, as you know, because I was unsure of his precise whereabouts. Fortunately, he will be returning to London later this week, or early the following week, so I can tell him of my tremendous fortune in person."

"That is excellent news! I enjoyed Colonel Fitzwilliam when we met in Kent, and now that I fully comprehend how dear he is to you, it will be a pleasure to meet him again."

"Try not to 'enjoy' him too much, Elizabeth," Darcy growled, a dark frown creasing his thick brows.

She smiled impishly and cocked her head. "Does this mean I can add jealous and possessive to your list of faults, Mr. Darcy?"

"If you view them as faults, then yes you may. I, however, embrace them as traits any sane man must have when the woman he loves is beautiful, witty, desirable, and near perfection."

Lizzy rubbed a fingertip over the ridges between his brows. "You have nothing to fear," she whispered. "You are the man I want, and no one else, no matter how pleasant, will ever change that."

The clock striking eleven o'clock interrupted the long, penetrating kiss that was showing scant signs of stopping. Darcy withdrew from her lips, cast a baleful glower at the clock, and reluctantly removed the tiny hands tangled in his hair.

"I must be on my way. I have a two o'clock appointment with my solicitor and a four o'clock appointment with my tailor. You are not the only one who wishes for new garments for our wedding."

He kissed the tip of her nose, smiled, and stood, pulling her up with him. They wobbled on weakened knees, laughed nervously, and glanced aside until under partial control of their faculties.

"I will miss you, and be counting the hours." Suddenly serious, he cupped her face and leaned close. "I love you, Elizabeth Bennet. With all my soul. Never forget that."

"I love you, Fitzwilliam Darcy, with all my soul. Don't you forget that either!" And this time she lifted on her toes, initiating the kiss. It was a short one, but fierce, Darcy wrapping his arms around her for a bone crunching squeeze, before releasing and pivoting, his goodbye hastily tossed over his shoulder as he lurched out the door.

Lizzy felt stung and bereft for half a second. Then a triumphant smile spread. It was exhilarating and empowering to cause the taciturn, disciplined Mr. Darcy to lose control! So much so that her mind spun with ideas. Never had she anticipated a trip to London more than this one. And shopping was suddenly far down the list of reasons.

A Most Important Dinner
at Darcy House
by Sharon Lathan

November 1, 1812

Darcy walked slowly through the parlor, crossed the entrance foyer, and entered the dining room. Pausing near his chair at one end of the long table, he swept his scrutinizing gaze over the place settings, candelabras, flowers, chairs, and every other item in the room, just as he had done in the previous chambers. Hosting dinner parties was, without a doubt, his least favorite duty. When the occasion called for it, he rose to the challenge, and in keeping with his character, ensured perfection and protocol down to the tiniest detail. Over time he had hosted gatherings with aristocracy and persons of eminence, managed capably despite his discomfort, and invariably his guests were satisfied.

Considering this, Darcy knew it was illogical to fret over menus and ambience for the small group of people expected tonight. Yet never, in all of his years, had a dinner at Darcy House held greater significance than this one.

"Is all to your specifications and satisfaction, Mr. Darcy?"

"Excellent, Mr. Travers, as always." He read the label on the wine bottle the butler held for his inspection. "Two bottles should suffice, but have two more within easy access."

They were still discussing the list of spirits for the evening when Georgiana glided into the room. She waited until Mr. Travers left, greeting her brother with a kiss and a query.

"How many glasses of that chardonnay am I allowed to have?"

Darcy pursed his lips and frowned sternly. "Perhaps I will allow a half."

"A half! A drank a full glass when dining with Uncle and Aunt last week! I am seventeen, William–"

"I am aware, Georgiana. I was there celebrating your birthday, if you recall. Why this sudden need to imbibe? Could it be you are nervous, my dear?" He tweaked the tip of her nose.

Georgiana blushed, but tilted her head and smiled. "Who was it stalking the rooms since noon, rearranging flowers and straightening pillows? And am I correct that you buffed your nails?" She lifted his hand, twisting until the light shimmered off each shiny fingernail.

Darcy jerked his hand away. "You may have one glass of wine, perhaps two," he growled. "Little imp." Then he chuckled and hugged her tight before grasping her upper arms and stepping backward. "You are a vision, Georgiana. So grown up, especially in this gown and with your hair arranged elaborately. You resemble Mother more every day," he finished in a soft whisper.

"Thank you, Fitzwilliam."

"It is the truth. And as for tonight, you have naught to be nervous about. Mr. Bennet, Miss Bennet, and the Gardiners are honest, pleasant people, and Elizabeth is very fond of you."

"And she loves you, so you," she poked one finger into his chest, "have nothing to be nervous about either!"

The doorbell interrupted further sibling banter. Swiftly they positioned themselves in the foyer, Darcy's tug on his jacket and Georgiana's pat to her hair their last fidgety gestures. Mr. Travers opened the door, two footmen at the ready to take coats and hats, while the Master of Pemberley and Darcy House welcomed his guests and introduced them to his sister. As soon as Darcy was able to draw Elizabeth off to the side, clasp her hand, bestow an earnest kiss to her knuckles, and gaze into the warm, brown depths of her eyes, his nervousness evaporated.

"Miss Elizabeth," he greeted, pitching his resonant voice even lower for her ears only. "It is my supreme joy to welcome you to

Darcy House. Tonight you are my honored guest, and my happiness is immense. Yet greater still shall be my euphoria when you are here as Mrs. Darcy."

He straightened before she could utter a word, slipped her arm under his and pressed firmly on the dainty hand resting on his forearm, and lifted his voice to gain the attention of the others. "Dinner will be served at precisely seven o'clock, which allots me, and Miss Darcy, adequate time to conduct a short tour of the main rooms and terrace. Fresh air is frequently desired after a bountiful meal, and before, so perhaps the terrace and gardens are the best place to begin."

"I don't suppose you have a trout pond here in London?"

"I am afraid not, Mr. Gardiner." Darcy laughed. "There is a large fountain, but it has never occurred to me to utilize it as a home for fish. Somehow I doubt more than four or five trout would deem it a sufficiently ample habitat."

The fountain he spoke of sat in the exact center of the yard, water bubbling and splashing in a musical cadence. Freshly cut grass covered a generous portion of the area, stretching into the shadows beyond reach of the glass-domed torches nearer the house. Two gaslight lamps illuminated the stone patio and revealed the cushioned chairs, small round tables, and potted shrubs and vines spaced evenly along the wall. A few of the varied bushes and trees planted amid the flowering garden could be seen, but if the shapes vaguely discernible were any indication, the rear enclosure was enormous and generously vegetated.

"Mr. Darcy, this is impressive! I never realized any of the houses in Town came with yards this large."

"Not all do, Mrs. Gardiner. My great-great grandfather was a friend of Sir Grosvenor, and married his cousin, in fact. This townhouse was one of the first built, purchased before it was completed and designed specifically. One of the requests was a substantial garden area. There are more torches that can be lit if further investigation is wanted, although I would suggest waiting until the natural light of day for the optimum effect. I do assure that strolling the lawn in the moonlight is safe, as it is level and daily examined for hazards."

Lizzy moved away from Darcy's side to join Jane and Georgiana at the fountain. She felt her betrothed's eyes following her, even as he carried on animated conversation with her father and uncle. Mr. Bennet asked a number of botanical questions, Darcy answering with superb knowledge of the subject. Mr. Gardiner was most curious as to which tradesman supplied the plants and furnishings.

Lizzy did not listen to the words as much as the tone. Rarely had she heard Mr. Darcy speak in such a relaxed manner and with casual humor. She had grown familiar with this side of his personality emerging when they were alone or with close friends, just as she had long ago recognized his silence when surrounded by presses of people. Initially, to her shame, she had misjudged his reticence, attributing it to unseemly pride and disdain for others. Later, she came to accept her error, comprehending the bashfulness and disquietude felt in unfamiliar situations or crowds, his struggle to hide and overcome only making it worse. Many times in these past weeks since he proposed, she witnessed his discomfort during dinners with her own family and the incessant social demands from Hertfordshire friends.

The relief to watch him laugh, joke, and talk with ease was massive. All through dinner, from his place of command at the end of the table, Lizzy sat to his right and delighted in his open demeanor. Conversation flowed freely. Darcy often remained silent or leaned to whisper brief comments with Lizzy, but he was aware of everything, and added to the discourse as appropriate. With each passing minute her amazement increased.

At Pemberley she had caught glimpses of *this* Mr. Darcy, but never would she have imagined him capable of being the gregarious, witty, vibrant man sitting beside her tonight! It wasn't until they rose from the table, her hand on his arm, that she was able to hold him back as the others followed Georgiana into the parlor.

"Mr. Darcy—"

"William," he corrected, smiling "You have successfully separated us from the group, leaving us somewhat alone, and thus you, my love, are obliged to address me by my Christian name."

"William," she repeated softly, caressing the name and momentarily flustered at the wave of emotion that crossed his face when she did. "I wanted to thank you for a fabulous evening, in case I did not have another opportunity. And, I also wanted to comment, and hope I do not offend or distress you, on how pleasurable it is to see you so relaxed and obviously enjoying yourself. I admit it is… startling."

"We still have much to learn of each other, Elizabeth. But know this, never have I felt such giddiness and lightness of spirit. I am content as I have no recollection of ever being, even in my youth." He traced his fingertips down her cheek, pausing under her chin. "The reason is you, Elizabeth. Only you."

He bent closer, and for a breathless moment Lizzy was certain he planned to kiss her. Then he straightened, removed his fingers, and escorted her from the room without another word.

Miss Darcy served as hostess to the women in the parlor while Mr. Darcy led the gentlemen to the billiard room. It was the standard protocol, of course, but clearly one he would have preferred to forego. Sooner than typical, the men rejoined the ladies, and conversation resumed as they sipped tea and nibbled on cakes. A blushing Georgiana was induced to entertain on the pianoforte, Mr. and Mrs. Gardiner lending their voices.

During this musical interlude, Lizzy was surprised to observe Darcy stealthily exit the room. Not quite sure why, she slipped out the door to follow. He stood on the terrace, staring into the sky. Hesitating, unsure whether she should disturb him, she latched onto the moment to silently admire his manly physique elegantly displayed by fine clothing and the stateliness of his pose.

"William?" She finally murmured, unable to resist.

"Elizabeth," he whispered, turning toward her. "I was dreaming about you and here you are, as if conjured."

She laughed softly, taking several steps closer to him. "Not quite that magical, I am afraid. I saw you leave the parlor and wanted to make sure you were well. And," she shrugged, "I wished to share a moment alone with you."

He closed the gap between them, again touched her cheek with his fingertips, speaking in a husky timbre. "Then it is magic, for I wished the same and here you are."

Then he bent, cupped her face, and tenderly brushed his lips over hers. Perhaps it was the moonlight weaving magic. Or perhaps it was simply that chaste kisses and regulated touches were no longer satisfying. In the span of a dozen heartbeats of sweet intimacy, mutual desire flared and took over. Sensation ruled, and it was blissful.

With a gravely groan, Darcy insistently parted her lips, exploring rapturously and hungrily. There was nothing tender about this kiss. It was consuming and heated. Deliriously pleasurable as nothing in her existence had ever been. Fire spread throughout her body, head to toes. Greedily she circled his waist under the open jacket, hands seeking, as she pressed into his hard chest. When he ran one hand down her back, grasped onto her buttocks, and crushed her harshly against his lower body, she should have been shocked, yet the only sensation was a wild urgency for more.

Five minutes of blinding ecstasy passed before they were jerked to reality by Mr. Bennet's voice calling his daughter's name. Darcy released her abruptly, recoiled, and melted into the shadows by the wall. She saw guilt and shame replace the passion in his eyes, but had no time to decipher the meaning. Surprising herself, she answered her father in a semi-normal tone, and rejoined the party.

Darcy returned fifteen minutes later. He was composed, met Lizzy's eyes and flashed a wan smile, and if not quite as animated as before, did carry on as the perfect host.

All too soon it was time to depart, sleep necessary for the busy day of shopping ahead. Taking Lizzy's cloak from the footman, Darcy draped it over her shoulders and fastened each button, taking his time with the procedure and focusing intently, as if the task an extremely difficult one. For several seconds he said nothing, Lizzy waiting for him to break the disagreeable awkwardness that had sprung up between them, since she had no clue what to say.

"Miss Elizabeth, I am—" He pressed his lips together, then shook his head slightly. Lifting his eyes to finally meet hers, he rushed on, "I pray you sleep well and that your expedition tomorrow is fruitful. As it pleases you and accommodates your schedule, I will be awaiting your return for a thorough tour of Darcy House."

"That will be the high point of my day, William." She stressed the familiar address, stared directly into his eyes, and lifted his fingers to her lips for a gentle kiss. "Until tomorrow."

An Enlightening Tour
of Darcy House
by Sharon Lathan

November 2, 1812

The carriage rattled along the cobblestone street passing one stunning townhouse after another. Lizzy's eyes darted between the right and left sides of Oxford Street, much as they had all day while shopping at the finer London establishments her Aunt Gardiner insisted were required for the elevated station her nieces would soon be marrying into. Mr. Bennet had blanched at the amount of money being spent, yet each time Lizzy or Jane opened their mouth to protest, Mrs. Gardiner shook her head and smoothly interrupted. Usually by dangling a pretty piece of merchandise before their eyes!

It had been a gratifying, and exhausting, day thus far, and Lizzy should have been yearning for an afternoon slumber as Jane was enjoying. Instead she was invigorated. And nervous.

Her excess of energy sprung from the excitement at viewing Darcy House in broad daylight. At dusk, with darkness rapidly falling and the artificial illumination from gaslight and smoldering lamps ineffective in dispelling the shadows bathing the grand townhouse, it had still taken her breath away. She could not imagine the impact on a sunny day. Then, of course, there was the vitalizing prospect of wandering through the rooms she had not yet entered, all while attempting to wrap her mind around the fact that in just over two weeks Darcy House would be home.

This unfathomable concept was partially where her anxiety germinated. Predominately her thoughts *had* centered on her love and happiness with Mr. Darcy. The reality of precisely how radically her life would change as his wife, and more importantly, the expectations and duties that would be thrust upon her narrow shoulders, were lightly shoved aside when in his adoring company in modest Hertfordshire. In London these serious actualities crashed over her.

As true as these concerns and their assault to her normally steady emotions, today Lizzy discovered that her trepidation arose principally from what had occurred the night before.

Not the kiss or embrace itself! Indeed she had lost count the number of times her mind, awake or asleep, had relived the delirious joy of those five minutes. She could instantly recall the taste of him on her tongue, feel the pressure of his mouth and insistent hands, hear his ragged respirations, smell the heated aroma of his cologne, and see the glaze of desire flooding his eyes. Daily her innocence receded. The escalating, fiery responses whenever they touched were enlightening, encouraging, and intoxicating. There was much to the art of lovemaking she was ignorant of. Yet there was no shame, or fear, in how William made her feel.

No, what bothered her was his reaction. The guilt and shame on his face, the wall of awkwardness, and worst of all, the apology she was certain he had started to make. What, precisely, did he need to apologize for?

"Lizzy, you have nothing to worry about. You are my clever, capable daughter. The girl who once chastised an angry bull, and who memorized Act 5, Scene 2 of *Love's Labour Lost* just because Lydia dared you, can handle any challenge set before her. Including being Mrs. Darcy."

Mr. Bennet's reassuring voice and humorous grin interrupted her unpleasant musings and lifted her spirits. Just in time. The carriage turned the corner off Duke Street onto Grosvenor Square and there before her eyes was Darcy House. Tiny compared to the vastness of Pemberley, it was still majestic. Constructed of polished white stone that glowed in the sunlight, each of the five bays on the lower level contained tall, multi-paned windows allowing beams of light into the house. Dozens of wide windows cut into the flat surface of the upper floors. Flowers bloomed from boxes underneath each window. Ornately wrought, iron fencing barricaded the passageway to the basement service areas, and curved elegantly up the steps before the gleaming, blue entryway doors.

"It is so beautiful," Lizzy whispered.

"Yes," Mr. Bennet agreed, "but it is still just a house. One with a reputed fine library, I hasten to add."

"I have a suspicion you will enter that room and need to be physically evicted for dinner!" Lizzy teased, then squeezed his hand and kissed his cheek. "Thank you, Papa."

Mr. Darcy greeted them formally, Georgiana at his side, and after a light repast in the parlor, they began the tour on the upper floors. Primarily consisting of uniquely decorated bedchambers and guest quarters, each was comfortable, luxurious, and modern. At the present the only occupied suite was Georgiana's, although one with a masculine quality was revealed as belonging to Colonel Fitzwilliam.

"When in Town he usually dwells at the barracks, in an officer's apartment. If he is forced to, that is," Darcy explained with a short laugh. "Richard much prefers the luxury found here, or at the Matlock townhouse. It depends on who is in London at the given time, but he seems to stay here mostly. Probably due to the superior grade liquor and the dart board."

"He shows up on our doorstep, like a lost puppy," Georgiana added with a dramatic sigh. "Tragic soul. How can we resist?"

Naturally there had to be a billiard room – a necessity in a Darcy household – this one including a host of gaming entertainments, including the aforementioned dart board. Although a fourth the size of Pemberley's, the ballroom was stunning. Dark oak boards thickly varnished contrasted beautifully with the gold and cream walls, the sunlight shimmering on the glossy surfaces dazzling to the eye. How the shine from the three crystal chandeliers and dozen wall sconces would warm the ambience at night was a vision Lizzy longed to behold.

As if reading her thoughts, Darcy said, "Sadly this room has not been used in years. Not to its full purpose, that is. Family members and friends have amused themselves with casual dancing upon occasion, but not a ball since before our mother died."

"Fitzwilliam and Cousin Richard taught me how to dance in this room." Georgiana spoke without the hint of sadness in her brother's tone. "And, my brother has promised that after my debut we can host a ball!"

"It was a promise extracted under duress," he sniffed, then winked at Mr. Bennet – who nodded his head with complete understanding of how pretty young girls connived to get their way. "However, with a new mistress of Darcy House, I suppose parties and balls will become a frequent event, God help me." His smile for Lizzy was warm, but he quickly glanced away.

The dining room and parlor they were familiar with, Darcy bypassing those rooms to head next into the library. Not nearly as large as Pemberley's library – a fact Lizzy teasingly dangled before her father's face, much as bait to a fish – the room was substantial and lined ceiling to floor with shelves of books. As predicted, Mr. Bennet immediately lost himself amongst the titles.

One end of the room served as Darcy's office. An enormous desk with a supple leather wingback chair sat near a window facing the rear garden. Additional wooden cases against the wall behind the chair held some books, but primarily objects of an obvious personal nature to Darcy. Lizzy wanted to examine each one, ask questions so as to learn more about the man she loved and was soon to marry, but unfortunately the tension between them had not disappeared. He hid it well, but Lizzy saw through his strained attempts to interject gaiety.

Upon entering the chamber once occupied by his mother, especially when Georgiana excused herself and left them alone, the situation grew worse. Darcy stood ramrod stiff by a porcelain wash basin, fidgeting and droning on to fill the silent void. Lizzy could not concentrate on a single word. Her sadness, frustration, irritation, and unrelenting desire to kiss him combined to roil inside her chest and fog her senses. She knew it was on the brink of bursting forth.

An unseen curled edge of rug became the catalyst.

In her inattentiveness, Lizzy stumbled on the rug, the fabric wrapping around her ankle making it impossible to correct her balance. A squeak of shock barely passed her lips before being muffled against the hard planes of Darcy's chest. How he had crossed the room so fast defied logic, not that she gave the matter any thought, every thought spiraled out of her brain, in fact! Her only awareness was that of his radiant heat, harsh breathing, wildly beating heart, and firmly muscled arms embracing her. Then he buried his face into her hair, inhaled deeply, and murmured her name.

Unquestionably there was no forethought to the exquisite interval of fierce, penetrating kisses and unrestrained, insatiable caresses that spontaneously followed. It was glorious! Lizzy felt loved and cherished. Desire thrummed through her veins – his for her and hers for him – the mutual need bonding her heart to his. It was as if she were flying, powered by an unstoppable force.

Abruptly the rapturous accord was shattered. Darcy released her, pivoted away, emitted a strangled cry, and lunged to the window. Lizzy swayed, her mind in chaos as she watched him lean onto the sill, hands balled into fists of steel.

"Elizabeth, you need to leave this room now! Please!"

She stepped to the door in hypnotic compliance, and then stopped. Ten minutes of erratic breathing, trembling, and wild emotions passed before Lizzy realized she was furious. She shut the door, walked to where he stood hunched at the window, and snapped, "No, William, I will not leave. Tell me truthfully; am I to conclude that our mutual love and desire are emotions to be disdained and ashamed of? Is this contempt and repugnance to continue after we are wed? Or is it that you honestly reckon you are such an uncontainable beast that you would hurt the woman you love? Or do you have so little faith in my own self-control and decorum that you assume I would willingly allow you to ravage me like a bought woman?"

Darcy was staring at her, open-mouthed, his face pale and utterly shocked. She leaned closer, fists clenched at her waist and her face a mask of monumental rage.

"Answer me!"

"No, Elizabeth,"—he swallowed—"I love you! Please… I have never wanted anything in all my life as I want you. You… are my life… you must know that? Surely…"

Elizabeth interrupted him in a voice more controlled. "Fitzwilliam, I do not believe any of the questions I asked are true of you. However, this is what I do believe: You are afraid of letting go of your emotions. You are wrapped in an inflexible cocoon of discipline and righteousness and are terrified that if you loosen one single cord you will unravel completely. You love me and desire me, yet resist showing me how much because you fear I will be disgusted or disappointed to discover you are not the towering paragon of virtue and excellence you deem yourself."

She paused for a deep breath. His grief stricken countenance suddenly drained her anger, replacing it with a fresh rush of irrepressible love. Placing both hands about his face, she whispered, "My God, William! Do you not yet comprehend how deeply I love you? You can be free with me and I will always love you. I trust you with my life, my virtue, my body, and my heart! You have nothing to fear from me and I fear nothing from you, except this distance between us. I beg you, do not push me away!"

"Elizabeth," he moaned, pulling her into his arms for a tender embrace. "I am so sorry. You are correct, absolutely correct. I have feared… all that you said, and more. Opening my inner being is not easy for me. Surrendering to my passionate nature after so long subduing it has been difficult, the lack of control at odds with the disciplined man I proclaimed to be. Thank you for understanding, but mostly for removing the bounds around my heart."

He kissed her reverently, a soft, closed lip kiss that was strangely as enlivening and precious as the wild one. "I feel liberated already. And happier, and more in love with you than I was before, which is remarkable!"

A few controlled kisses later, they rejoined Mr. Bennet in the library. He had only moved deeper into the room, his duty as chaperone a dismal failure since he was ignorant that they had ever left. Darcy and Lizzy shared a private smile, neither willing to point out Mr. Bennet's error. Instead Lizzy walked directly to the case behind Darcy's desk and pointed to a miniature Austrian chateau.

"What is the story behind this?"

Fripperies and Fineries
by Nina Benneton

November 2, 1812

"Carriage dresses, dinner dresses, evening dresses, full evening dresses, garden dresses, morning dresses, opera dresses, promenade dresses, theater dresses, walking dresses." Mrs. Bennet silently checked the list in her hand, sure she'd forgotten to jot down some important event for which her eldest daughters would need to be properly attired.

The coach swayed then bounced through a pothole, and Mrs. Bennet heard the coachman's muffled curse. She frowned, but then shrugged. At least they would not have to find their footing with care in the foul streets.

"We must thank my Uncle Gardiner's for arranging the carriage." Her eldest daughter, Jane, sat between Mrs. Bennet and Mrs. Gardiner. "It's a beautiful day to go shopping for wedding clothes."

"However did you manage to persuade my father to put off buying the horses for the farm for another year, Maman?" Lizzy asked from her seat directly across from Mrs. Bennet.

"Bah! What are horses to having one's daughters dressed properly?" Mrs. Bennet glanced out the carriage window on her side. Nothing but a pile of cobbles. She turned back to her list and smiled to herself. After some wifely exertion on her part, Mr. Bennet was persuaded to be liberal with his purse.

Shopping for one's daughters' wedding trousseaus—the pinnacle of woman's achievements as a mother—for years, Mrs.

Bennet had feared this day would never come. Her gaze flickered from Jane to Lizzy. Well done, girls.

Jane's beauty and sweet personality catching Mr. Bingley was a certain success, she had no doubt. But what a sly girl Lizzy was. How smart of her to turn down Collins for a bigger fish. Ten thousand pounds a year and he the grandson of an earl, too. Mrs. Bennet straightened. Court dresses. Lizzy would need a court dress. She scribbled the item on her list and folded the paper before putting it in her reticule. If that coxcomb Sir William Lucas could be presented at court, for certain the wife of a grandson of an earl would merit a presentation.

In the midst of Mrs. Bennet's mental planning of the arrangement of the seven ostrich plumes on Lizzy's headdress for her appearance at St. James's, Mary lifted her head from her book and intruded, "Must Kitty and I be subjected to this excursion, Mama?"

"Subjecting yourself?" Mrs. Bennet narrowed her eyes. However did she spawn such a graceless, bookish child? "Why did I not leave you back in Longbourn with your father You consider it a chore to be in town, shopping?"

Barely lifting her pressed face from the window, Kitty said, "Mary may consider herself ill-used, Maman, but she does not speak for me. Wait until I write Lydia and tell her she missed out on shopping for clothes in Mayfair. Are we near Bond street?"

Mrs. Bennet frowned. However did she spawn such a witless child? "Kitty, stop looking out of the window like you are common ware for the gentlemen."

Kitty's hand suddenly flapped. "Look, Lizzy, I believe that's Mr. Darcy next to the iron post there, in front of that shop."

Kitty did not get to finish, for her sister Lizzy had indecorously thrown herself across Mary to sweep aside the window's curtains.

Mrs. Bennet's mouth opened. Jane and Mrs. Gardiner both chuckled at Lizzy's eagerness.

Just when Mrs. Bennet was about to pull her hoyden of a daughter back, Lizzy's face fell. She drew back from the window. "That is not Mr. Darcy."

Kitty said, "Are you sure? He has the same tall, proud look."

Mrs. Gardiner glanced outside the carriage's window before she determinedly drew the curtains closed. "I believe that is Mr. Beau Brummel—a man deemed by the *ton* as the greatest arbiter of fashion, wit, and address—whom Kitty has mistaken for Mr. Darcy."

Mrs. Bennet laughed. "La! What a joke. Such a man and Kitty mistaken him for Mr. Darcy."

"May I remind you, Maman," Lizzy said with an edge in her voice, "that Mr. Darcy had the ultimate good taste to choose one of your daughters, a daughter whose expectations are non-existent, to be Mrs. Darcy?"

Speechless, Mrs. Bennet stared at her second eldest, whose eyes flashed impudently. However did she spawn such a headstrong, obstinate, contrary girl? Surely Lizzy must be aware of everyone's true opinion: that Mr. Darcy, ten-thousand pounds and grandson of an earl or not, cannot hope to match Mr. Bingley, or, Mrs. Bennet's favorite, dear Wickham—in fashion, wit, or address?

"I believe you misheard my mother, Lizzy." Jane's voice was its usual placating tone.

"I believe what Lizzy meant," Mrs. Gardiner said, entering the conversation, "is that Mr. Darcy's interests are of a more steady, serious-minded, and practical nature, which greatly benefit all those—friends, family, tenants—people who are dependent on him. As a responsible landed gentleman, his interests are not frivolous and trifling such as those of Mr. Brummel's, whose chief concern in life is whether his snuff is sniff-worthy and his cravats starched stiff enough, if I may be so impertinent toward a friend of the prince."

"Thank you, Aunt, I had no idea my betrothed has such a champion in you." Amusement briefly replaced the flash of ire in Lizzy's eyes. She then turned and met Mrs. Bennet's eyes. "My apologies, Maman, for my…uh…misunderstanding. It is just that I do not care to hear Mr. Darcy being slighted."

Surprised, Mrs. Bennet leaned against the carriage side and studied her daughter. She knew Mr. Darcy, as strange as it seemed, must have been captivated by her daughter, else why would he have offered marriage, but could Lizzy truly have tender feelings for the dour and solemn Mr. Darcy? Mrs. Bennet's eyes widened. Was her daughter making a love-match with Mr. Darcy, of all people?

Mary lowered her book. "It seems to me a useless business, this dashing about town amassing fripperies to prepare for life as a Missus, when one has already caught the Mister."

Five pairs of eyes fixed on her. Jane exclaimed, "Mary!"

Lizzy laughed. "Ah, but, Mary, you forget that women do not dress for their husbands. We dress for other women. I certainly do not wish for Mr. Darcy's female relations to think me more of a portionless country nobody than I already am."

Though Lizzy's tone was glib, Mrs. Bennet detected a note of nervousness in her normally indomitable daughter. Lizzy would not be nervous meeting anyone unless she cared to make a good impression. It must be a love-match. Much as Mrs. Bennet admitted Lizzy was never her favorite child, as a mother, she did not like to see her strong daughter unconfident.

Mrs. Gardiner teased. "Now, my dear Lizzy, was it not the liveliness of your mind which brought him up to scratch? Or did Kitty's eavesdropping prove wrong?"

While Lizzy blushed and scolded her younger sister, and Jane and Mrs. Gardiner chuckling again, Mrs. Bennet ignored them and took out her list.

How could she forget? A riding habit for Lizzy after the wedding. *La Belle Assemblee, The Lady's Magazine, Le Beau Monde, The Repository*, Mrs. Bennet had been diligently studying the fashion magazines used by the modistes and mantua-makers. Many fashionable brides these days wear riding habits as their traveling dresses on their wedding days. Though Lizzy was no horsewoman, she could use it as a carriage dress or a walking dress during her wedding trip.

Mrs. Bennet tapped the paper against her chin. A carmine or Devonshire brown woolen, styled in the same cut as Mr. Darcy's great coat, would highlight Lizzy's dark tresses, or a Bishop's blue thick muslin, perhaps with a frilled collar on the habit shirt, which would frame the shape of her delicate face quite nicely?

Her daughter's lively mind might have caught Mr. Darcy's interest, but his female relations would not be impressed with a bluestocking young Mrs. Darcy.

A newly married woman adorned, embellished, and clothed in the right style of fripperies and fineries, expensive fripperies and fineries, that's what would impress and silence any cattiness.

Portionless country nobody? Bah! After Mrs. Bennet was done with Lizzy's wedding clothes, her daughter will hold her head high walking into St. James's.

Mr. Darcy Goes Shopping
by Sharon Lathan

November 3, 1812

Darcy paused on the walkway across the street from the massive building with windows spanning the entire front facade, and stared at the gaping portal where a veritable sea of people were entering and exiting. Perhaps that was a slight over-exaggeration, if he was being honest. Yet compared to the individual shops and exclusive merchants he typically patronized, the number of men and women were significantly more than what he was used to. Not unlike the crowds bustling through the walks inside the Royal Exchange, of course, but at the Exchange men were the predominant sex, and business was of a serious financial nature. Judging by the audible laughter and trailing servants laden with colorful boxes and bags, the establishment known as Harding, Howell, & Co. on Pall Mall had scant in common with the Royal Exchange!

All four of the merchants he had spoken with about his particular dilemma had instructed him to come here. He also knew it was Lady Matlock's favorite shopping mall. "Much nicer than the Pantheon Bazaar," she had recently mentioned, "unless you want an exotic product or children's item." That latter tidbit of information Darcy tucked into his brain for future reference. For the present it was his soon-to-be bride – coincidentally the someday-mother of the children he longed to buy merchandise for – that occupied his thoughts and sent him on this excursion.

Get on with it, Darcy, how bad can it possibly be? He took a deep breath, squared his shoulders, and stepped off the curb. Minutes later he didn't want to attempt answering that question. Every sense was deluged and instantly overloaded. Maintaining composure and not allowing his jaw to literally drop was a Herculean feat. Strangely enough, the clamor of hundreds of voices echoing wasn't the biggest assault. It was the profuse array of merchandise lining every last inch of space, wall to ceiling and case upon case. And he was only standing in the entrance foyer! At a reputed one-hundred-fifty feet square, Harding, Howell, & Co was gigantic by anyone's standards. Computing the math on how much could be stuffed into a building that size was beyond his capacity at the moment.

How am I ever going to find the perfect Wedding gift for Elizabeth?

Logically the assumption was that with so many prospects, his quest could easily be fulfilled. That was the opinion of the previous shop owners when he was unsatisfied with their wares. As he scanned the quantity of furs and fans proudly on display close to the main entrance – a drop in the bucket of goods in total – Darcy felt rising panic that he would need weeks searching through the possibilities. Weeks he did not have! Why had he never paid more attention to the unique requirements for a woman? The folly of that oversight was definitely biting him now. Never one to shrink from a challenge or failing to educate himself in record time when necessary, he feared he may have discovered the one area destined to be his defeat.

His gaze fell on an ermine muff, and suddenly the potential opportunity dawned on him. Why limit to only one gift for Elizabeth? She was a treasure priceless compared to jewels, and more beautiful than any dress ever made, yet that did not negate his desire to buy her fine things as an expression of his love and appreciation. And he had it on good authority (his sister) that all women were giddily happy with dresses and pretty accessories.

It was an epiphany! No wonder such businesses existed! Here he could, in one afternoon, acquire an abundance of women's accoutrements, surely one of them ideal as a wedding present, but all of them certain to please her. Nothing was more important than that. Furthermore, with so many women milling about and dozens of knowledgeable salesmen, the odds were in his favor that his educational dilemma would be solved. Quite conveniently, in fact, provided he bravely risked embarrassment and being branded an incompetent fool for asking imbecilic questions!

In order to be a proper husband for Elizabeth, I shall gamble my reputation.

Three hours later these considerations were moot. Darcy still tended to whisper his name when the seller asked where to deliver the purchased items, but no longer hesitated engaging random customers in conversation or asking questions. Naturally the salesmen were thrilled to talk about their wares in fine detail. No shock there. What pleasantly surprised Darcy was how willing the shopping ladies were to chat with him, imparting their unique opinions and expertise to the obviously deficient gentleman. For almost an hour a trio of middle-aged women insisted on "taking him under their wings" and escorting personally to the very best stock in the mall, their three voices an endless flood of information on the "myriad ways to make his beloved happy." Darcy possessed an excellent memory, nevertheless, he fervently wished for a small portable writing implement and parchment pieces so he could jot it all down!

At the milliner and dress department every woman present – customer and sales assistant, young and old – held up gowns and donned hats to model how it would look. Darcy knew his face was red as a beet the entire time, never in his life surrounded by a surfeit of females parading and posing as they invited him to brazenly ogle. Only the humor in the situation deflected his utter humiliation.

The perfect wedding gift was discovered in the third partitioned shop where perfumery and toilette articles were sold. The second Darcy saw it, there was no longer any debate. Deciding on the style out of the twelve options required some deliberation, and for a few minutes he mused on what to have engraved, but that was the extent of it. Already the vision of watching Elizabeth open the present once alone on their wedding night, and better yet when she used it, sent tingles of pleasure flittering through his body. The reality would surely surpass even his vivid imagination where Elizabeth and intimacy were concerned, a thought it was wise to avoid if he wanted to escape the mall with his dignity intact.

Finally satisfied that his mission's goal was accomplished exceeding his wildest expectations, and that each purchase was accounted for and prepped for delivery to Darcy House, a relieved Darcy headed for the exit. He was famished, and never had the prospect of a restoring brandy sounded more appealing. Just as he passed the fur display where the ermine muff now owned by him had been replaced by a mink one, he heard his name being called.

"Mr. Darcy! Is that you? Oh indeed it is! See Lizzy. I told you I thought I saw him when we were in the haberdashery."

He turned, and instantly froze. There was the animated Mrs. Gardiner bearing down on him, with a radiantly smiling Elizabeth and relaxed Jane in tow.

"What a delightful surprise, isn't it girls? In a town the size of London the odds of encountering someone known is unusual, but especially one's betrothed. Quite fortuitous and extraordinary. Would you not agree, Lizzy?"

"Indeed I do, Aunt. How are you, Mr. Darcy?"

"I am quite well, Miss Elizabeth. Thank you." He cleared his suddenly bone dry throat. "I pray you three are equally as well and enjoying your afternoon?"

Mrs. Gardiner and Jane responded in the affirmative, as did Lizzy, after which she added, "And what brings you to Harding, Howell, & Co.? For some reason I never pictured you frequenting this type of establishment."

Her eyes were sparkling, the tease not lost on Darcy. He shrugged as nonchalantly as possible, and attempted to reply in an identical lighthearted tone, "I am full of surprises, Miss Elizabeth. I have discovered the supreme benefits in enlisting the aid of other women when acquiring objects specifically for the fairer sex. Much more efficient, and wise, than trying to judge for myself what is best for a lady."

"I see," she said, after a pause. "So you are very familiar with Harding, Howell & Co. then? Perhaps your knowledge of such merchants in Town will benefit us as well, if you do not mind sharing your accumulated wealth of information on the subject?"

Darcy frowned at the sharp undertone to Elizabeth's question. She was smiling, but not as sincerely, and her sparkling eyes held a glint of something else that took him a full minute to decode.

She is jealous! The revelation staggered him. And, as unattractive as it was to admit, sent his ego soaring. He knew the decent response was to disabuse her of the idea that he was a seasoned expert who often bought trinkets for women, but God help him if it didn't cast a glow upon his heart to see the possessive fire in her lovely eyes and know it was because of her sentiments toward him.

Instead he said, "I am afraid my knowledge is not as vast as I am certain Mrs. Gardiner's is. She brought you here, so clearly knows the best stores to patronize. You are correct, Miss Elizabeth, that I avoid such places unless I am forced to enter them."

"Were you forced this time as well, Mr. Darcy?"

He glanced at Mrs. Gardiner and Jane, who were both trying not to laugh, and leaned closer to Elizabeth, whispering in her ear. "Wedding present, my dear."

"For me?" She breathed, her body visibly relaxing as a flush spread over her cheeks.

"Well, I did think it might be nice to gift Miss Bennet, as the second most beautiful bride-to-be in England," he winked at Jane. *Mental note: Buy a gift for Jane.* "Other than that I shall not utter another word. I suggest you accustom yourself to pleasant surprises, love."

He straightened, slyly captured her hand for a fleeting squeeze, and spoke in a normal voice. "Ladies, if it is appealing to you, and not contrary to your plans, there is a marvelous coffee house not one block south. The food is excellent, and view of Pall Mall and St. James's Palace unobstructed. Care to join me?"

Mrs. Bennet Plans the Wedding
and Breakfast
by C. Allyn Pierson

November 3, 1812

"Oh, my dear sister! I am so delighted that I think I may have a spasm! I finally get to plan Jane and Lizzy's wedding!" Mrs. Bennet fanned herself with the bonnet she had just removed as she plopped down onto the settee in Mrs. Philips' saloon. "I was so afraid Mr. Darcy or Bingley's sisters would insist on St. George's Hanover Square, and, of course, I would have had to let my sister Gardiner assist me. As much as I love her and my brother, I must say they made a mess of Lydia's wedding – no guests, no flowers except a paltry little posy for Lydia to carry. I was ashamed of the niggardly arrangements. They did not even have a wedding breakfast afterwards!"

She breathed a deep sigh and allowed Mrs. Philips to pat her hand and nod consolingly before continuing. "That would not do at all for Jane and Lizzy! They are marrying into the *ton* and must have a wedding that will not embarrass their husbands by being miserly with the biggest event of my daughters' lives! And…I think I will be able to convince Mr. Bennet to go along with my plans – after all, Lizzy is his favourite daughter…surely he will wish to give her a lovely send off! I already have cook working on the menu for the wedding breakfast…I told her we want everything to be prime about it! Of course, I don't know how many guests there will be yet. I am sure Mr. Darcy's sister and Bingley's sisters will be here, but I am not sure about Darcy's cousin, Colonel Fitzwilliam and his parents. Darcy and Fitzwilliam are very good friends, from what

Lizzy has told Jane about her visit in Kent, but his parents' estate is all of one hundred miles away...surely too far to travel for a wedding! Since the wedding is to be at Longbourn Church instead of at St. George's, I am afraid that not many of Mr. Darcy's and Bingley's fashionable friends will come to Hertfordshire...Oh, well, those that do will find Hertfordshire can put on a wedding just as well as London can!"

Mrs. Philips started to speak: "Yes my dear sister, indeed..." when Mrs. Bennet interrupted her. "And oh sister! Jane and Lizzy are in London right now, shopping for their wedding clothes with our sister Gardiner." She compressed her lips for a moment. "I wanted to go with them...after all I am their mother, and I have shopped in London before! But Mr. Bennet said I was needed at Longbourn to plan the wedding...and he is quite right, of course. Jane has such exquisite taste that I have no compunction about letting her help her sister choose what is needed for their clothes...and, of course, Mrs. Gardiner lives in London and so knows all the warehouses. Mr. Bennet suggested to me that perhaps Mr. Gardiner could save some money by arranging for the girls to shop at the warehouses of some of his business acquaintances! It is not the thing to have a brother in trade, but perhaps he will turn his tradesman contacts to good use."

As she sipped her rapidly cooling tea she reviewed the plans she had made for the wedding. Mrs. Philips murmured on in the background of her thoughts, until Mrs. Bennet interrupted her again. "Oh! I will decorate the pews with ribbons and the girls' bouquets will be asters...there is not much selection of flowers this time of year, and we do not have a greenhouse to force flowers all year. Perhaps Mr. Gardiner could find orchids in London...they would be very expensive, but oh so elegant! I must have a new gown made for the wedding, too, as well as gowns for Mary and Kitty!" They must look their best. After all, there may be some wealthy single gentlemen who are friends of Bingley's. Would that not be fine, if Kitty would meet an eligible gentleman at her sisters' wedding! Ah me! It is all so exciting! I must go now...there are a thousand things to do before the 16th of November! It's been lovely talking to you, my dear sister!" She bustled out, her face flushed and her eyes brilliant, leaving Mrs. Philips with her mouth open.

After Church Picnic and Surprise
by Sharon Lathan

November 4, 1812

Sunday morning dawned with a slight chill in the air due to the intermittent breeze, but sunny and blue-skied. For everyone it was a planned day of rest. No shopping, business, or other major undertakings were on the agenda. In every way the fine weather and minimal expectations were advantageous to Mr. Darcy.

While dining at the Gardiner house the night before, Darcy casually mentioned that depending on the weather it might be a lovely afternoon to stroll to Hyde Park, perhaps enjoying a relaxing picnic. Easily accessible from Grosvenor Square, the eastern portions of Hyde Park required only a short walk and were typically less crowded than the popular areas, such as Rotten Row. It was kept tentative, although the two Bennet women were agreeable, and the Gardiner children thought it a capitol idea! Darcy had a special reason for hoping Sunday remained as pleasant as the days previous, but in an effort to maintain the surprise, he acted blasé.

The meager thespian skills he possessed served to divert suspicion as to his Sunday afternoon plotting, but failed utterly when Lizzy asked him if he and Georgiana planned to attend worship services the following day in hopes that she could accompany them.

"We do plan to attend service, yes," he answered, brows lifted as he trained wide eyes on Lizzy. "We typically do unless absolutely unable for some reason. Of course you are welcome to join us, Elizabeth, but would you not prefer to worship at the church you usual do when in Town? With the Gardiners?"

"You are very kind, William," she patted his hand where it lay on his thigh, "but there is no need to spare my sensibilities. You know that we are not regular church goers, as I know you are. Faith is important to you, and I respect this. I cannot promise my beliefs or dedication will immediately align with yours – maybe they never will – but as your wife it will be my duty, and joy, to accompany you as often as you wish to worship."

Never one to easily articulate his innermost feelings, especially when caught unawares as he was in this instance, Darcy simply lifted her hand and bestowed a lingering kiss. "Thank you," he whispered, traveling his lips to fingertips, palm, and inner wrist before being reminded by the gruff clearing of Mr. Bennet's throat that they were not alone!

A carriage was sent for Lizzy and Jane early in the morning, Mr. Bennet badgered into accompanying as an additional chaperone, and together the group of five walked from Darcy House to Grosvenor Chapel, a mere two blocks south on Audley Street. A deeply spiritual man since his youth, primarily the result of his grandfather's intense personal faith, Darcy was overcome with happiness to be escorting his betrothed to the place where the Darcy family had worshipped while in London since the church was built nearly a hundred years prior. The only thought more profoundly stirring to his soul was the vision of standing beside her at Pemberley Chapel. That led to imaginings of their babies being christened there, and their children someday married within the ancient stone walls, at which point he forcefully shoved the thoughts aside or he would never be able to concentrate on the service!

By noon the Gardiners arrived at Darcy House, the children jumping about the foyer in their enthusiasm to enjoy the promised picnic, feed ducks, blow dandelions, catch frogs, and all the other magical delights envisioned at Hyde Park. Darcy smiled at their antics, ensuring the youngsters that while frogs may prove challenging to uncover this close to winter, the ducks were plentiful. That statement was enforced by the appearance of a maid with four bags of bread crumbs specifically to feed the ducks. The shrieks of glee from the children would have rattled the rafters, if Darcy House had rafters. The youngest Gardiner child hugged Darcy's leg, his big hand ruffling the soft hair before the sprite danced back to her siblings.

At that moment he glanced up to see Lizzy observing him with a tender expression and moisture glistening in her eyes. He was baffled at first, and then it dawned on him that she had never seen him interacting with children. Perhaps she assumed, or feared, that he did not care for them or would consider them unruly. Logically he could understand if that were her presumption. He was well aware of the attitude he conveyed by his serious demeanor and rigidly disciplined pose. It was an appearance he struggled to alter, Lizzy's pointed condemnation at his disastrous first proposal still ringing in his ears. Although he knew that she understood him better now, and had seen his lighter side and frivolous nature in smaller portions while with his sister and close friends, he also comprehended that she probably held on to doubts.

Crossing to where she stood by the door, he bent and kissed her cheek. Finally deciding he did not know what to say, especially with people within earshot, Darcy chose to offer his arm, bringing her as close to his body as possible. In time he was confident that his actions would speak louder than words.

Eventually the necessary supplies for a perfect outdoors dining experience were assembled, including an assortment of items required for entertainment and frog capture – if so fortunate – and the group set off. Darcy and Lizzy were the last ones through the door, Darcy pausing on the threshold to hand Mr. Travers a folded and sealed parchment.

"I expect him within the hour. Two at most. Make sure he gets this when he arrives. Instructions are inside."

The butler affirmed the order would be carried out. Lizzy held her curiosity until down the steps, but Darcy's answer was cryptic.

"You shall see in good time, Miss Elizabeth."

In no time at all the blankets were spread and the adults settled comfortable. The children had dashed off to explore, the nanny scurrying about to keep track of them. Mrs. Annesley, Georgiana's companion, laughed and rose to assist the poor woman. The fine food prepared by the kitchen staff was served, wine was poured, and conversation flourished.

Eventually Mr. Gardiner left his relaxed perch to stroll toward the pond, "Just out of curiosity," gesturing for Mr. Bennet to come along. Mrs. Gardiner rolled her eyes. Georgiana shared a conspiratorial glance with her brother, turning then to Jane and Mrs. Gardiner to suggest a walk along the edge of the wooden area to the north. It was unlikely they did not understand Georgiana's true purpose was to allow her brother a solitary interlude with his betrothed.

Lizzy wasn't fooled either, but she calmly gazed at the shimmering blue water and gently waving bulrushes, saying nothing. Nevertheless, she didn't expect more than the luxury of private conversation with the man she loved, so was very surprised when he pulled a box from the bottom of one basket.

He placed it unopened on his lap and took hold of her left hand before speaking. When he did, huskily choked with emotion he tried to hide, Lizzy's heart began to flutter.

"I have something I wish to give you, Elizabeth. Well, two somethings, actually. First I must apologize for the delay in bestowing these. They were safely under lock at Pemberley and required a secure, trusted staff member to deliver them to me. Then I wanted to have them cleaned, polished, properly sized, and inspected for any damage or necessary repairs. After years of wear, and many more years of sitting undisturbed, I was unsure of their condition."

His fingers traveled to the simple diamond ring encircling the third finger of her left hand, twisting it slightly. Looking back at her eyes, he smiled, the power of his love beaming from his eyes and hitting her forcibly. "When I placed this on your finger, what I did not tell you because I wished it to be a surprise, was that, while lovely and now yours, I never intended this to be your betrothal ring."

Darcy slipped it off her finger, placing it into her right hand and curling her fingers around. Opening the box on his lap, he reaching inside and withdrew another ring. "That honor belongs to this ring."

Lizzy gasped. The ring was gold and adorned with a one-carat star sapphire of vivid blue, centered between two half-carat diamonds. It was exquisite.

"My father designed this ring for my mother," Darcy explained as he slid it onto her finger. "We tend to believe it an embellished tale, but the story was that he searched all over England for the most exquisite sapphire he could find. Each time he told the story the search took longer and his travels extended," Darcy laughed softly in remembrance, "but I know the basics are true. He waited four years to marry Mother, until she was old enough according to old Lord Matlock's opinion, and loved her profoundly. Nothing but the very best was ever good enough for her, as far as my father was concerned. I know she would want you to wear this, Elizabeth, not because it is my desire, and of course it is, but because Father told me so."

Lizzy was so overwhelmed that she could not speak. The ring was gorgeous, and fit her perfectly, but it was the emotions and history attached that touched her heart. Darcy rarely spoke of his parents. She knew this was solely due to the rawness of grief that all these years later continued to weigh on his soul. Perhaps it was too soon when she still knew little of his past and deepest thoughts, but she hoped that someday her love and the family they would create together, God willing, would heal the residual wounds.

She had no time to recover and stammer an inadequate thank-you, however, because Darcy was again reaching into the box.

"This gift is yours, as will be all the jewels at Pemberley, and I do not want you to feel obligated to wear this at our wedding if it does not properly accompany your gown. I simply wanted you to have it, since it has always been my favorite of Mother's jewels, and to consider it, if possible."

Lizzy wanted to laugh at his polite entreaty. As if she would dream of refusing! It could be a hideous piece and she would not have the heart to deny him! Fortunately, that was not the case.

The necklace was stunning. A chain of sapphires and diamonds, delicate and masterfully crafted with gold filigree arabesque. He placed it around her neck, not latching since it was far too elaborate to wear at a picnic, but held it there while his fingertips caressed her nape.

"Beautiful," he whispered. "Almost as beautiful as you."

They continued to stare at each other, bodies close but not touching, other than his fingers – which were driving her mad with fiery sensations sweeping down her spine – and the spell may never have been broken if not for a voice intruding.

"Sorry to interrupt, Darcy, but I was hoping you might direct me to where my betrothed disappeared to? Nice to see you, of course, and you as well, Miss Elizabeth, lovely necklace by the way, but my Jane is who I really wanted to see."

The surprise appearance of Mr. Bingley, who was not expected to arrive in London until tomorrow, was greeted with great fanfare. Jane saw him from afar, dashing away from Mrs. Gardiner and Georgiana in an impulsive manner more typical of Lizzy. Naturally Lizzy teased her mercilessly about it, but Jane did not care in the least. She was too delighted to be reunited with her love. Darcy made no attempt to hide his smug satisfaction at pulling off the secret.

It would be hours before Lizzy had a chance to capture Darcy alone. At that point she was abundantly clear how delighted she was to wear the necklace for their wedding, how honored she was by the ring, how much she appreciated him sharing of his parents, how much she had enjoyed the Sunday service, and a long list of other items she was happy about. There were many words spoken during this period of thankful expression. There were also many, many non-verbal communications. Both agreed that the latter got the message across more succinctly, and certainly in a more pleasurable manner.

Georgiana Hosts a Tea Party
by Sharon Lathan

November 5, 1812

"Miss Bennet. Miss Elizabeth. I am so pleased to see you both." Georgiana curtsied before her guests, the fidgety hands and rosy cheeks indicative of her nervousness not affecting the graceful motion. "Thank you for accepting my invitation."

"An invitation to pass the afternoon in your company, Miss Darcy, is one we are happy to accept. Neither Jane, nor I, could fathom a greater delight, could we, Jane?"

Georgiana's blush deepened at Lizzy's sincerely spoken words and Jane's earnest agreement. "That is very kind of you to say. However, I know London boasts many fascinating entertainments, especially shopping!"

Lizzy laughed at the quip, laced her arm companionably through Georgiana's, and gently steered toward the parlor. "Frankly, I am sick to death of shopping. Indeed I am!!" Lizzy emphasized at Georgiana's incredulous expression. "After a while all the fabrics and lace look exactly the same, and I can no longer distinguish between sable or fox. On top of that, I am quite certain my feet shall never be the same after walking miles over rough stones. Tragic, really."

"Now I know you are teasing me, Miss Elizabeth. My brother often mentions your fondness for walking, as well as your delight in teasing. I would be suspect at your claim of sore feet, but the sure evidence is that everyone knows the difference between sable and fox!"

Amid the three-way laughter, they sat on the sofas surrounding the low table already laden with a three-tiered silver plate rack and two porcelain salvers piled with an assortment of edibles. The housekeeper, Mrs. Smyth, entered at that moment and deposited another tray, upon which sat three china cups, a teapot, and the usual additives.

"Shall I serve, Miss Darcy?"

"Thank you, Mrs. Smyth, but I wish to attend to my guests." The housekeeper nodded and silently exited the room. Georgiana began pouring the hot tea into the cups, inquiring as to preferences, and encouraged Lizzy and Jane to help themselves to the snacks.

"May I ask if Mr. Darcy is at home?"

"Not presently, Miss Elizabeth," Georgiana answered without glancing up from her task. "He left early for an appointment with Mr. Daniels, his solicitor. I suspect that currently he is either fencing at Angelo's, or at the track riding his horse. He mentioned needing exercise, and those are his preferred choices to expend energy. I am not sure when he will return. Oh!" She jerked her eyes to Lizzy's, concern etched upon her face. "How terribly inconsiderate of me! Of course you would wish to see my brother! I do apologize for not being clearer in my invitation!"

"Miss Darcy, it is I who should apologize. Your invitation was perfectly clear, and we accepted for the sole purpose and pleasure of your company, alone. I asked of Mr. Darcy merely out of curiosity. In truth, it is a boon that he is elsewhere. Female conversation is far more interesting, to my way of thinking, and having a man about would only disrupt. Isn't that so, Jane?"

"Absolutely. At the first mention of gowns or hair accessories he would run screaming from the room."

"I will take your word for it since my experiences are minimal. Although it is true that William's eyes glaze over whenever I mention garments or the like. He immediately sends me to Mrs. Annesley or Aunt Madeline."

"As I suspected," Lizzy nodded. "Although, to be fair, my mind wanders the second the topic of cigars or firearms is broached." They all laughed at that truism. "See, we are having fun already and have barely begun!"

Jane leaned forward to brush a finger over the teapot. "This is a beautiful tea service, Miss Darcy, and these tarts are exquisite."

"Credit for the food I cannot claim, nor the tea set since it has been around for longer than I remember. But I am gladdened to hear you are satisfied. I confess to being quite nervous." She peeked at her guests through her lashes, a flush emerging across her cheeks as she murmured, "This is the first tea party I have hosted myself."

Jane glanced at Lizzy, the sisters sharing a smile. Jane responded first. "I am stunned to hear this, Miss Darcy. You are an excellent hostess. Like you have been doing so for decades."

"Well, I have attended numerous, small social gatherings," Georgiana offered, her voice firmer. "Frequently I have assisted my aunt, that is, Lady Matlock. She has taught me the proper etiquette, of course, yet the greater benefit is in observation. She is elegant and skilled in the art of casual conversation. Wait until you meet her, Miss Elizabeth, then you will know of what I speak."

"You are fortunate to have a gifted, and willing, relative living near you, Miss Darcy. Her influence shows."

"Indeed Jane is correct," Lizzy agreed. Then she cocked her head, her arch smile and twinkling eyes a warning. "On the other hand, Miss Darcy, think how improved the fortune of your education if you lived closer to Lady Catherine! She is prodigiously knowledgeable on every subject, you know, and, by her own admission, greatly accomplished. Oh! To be frequently exposed to a grand house decorated with imposing sophistication and refined style. Rosings Park, where quality is visible even in the windows and glazings. Just imagine how improved your manners as hostess and stimulating our conversation, Miss Darcy, if she were the aunt fate settled you near."

"Lizzy," Jane softly admonished, glancing at Georgiana who sat with a hand pressed against her mouth.

"Indeed, it is quite all right, Miss Bennet," Georgiana finally squeaked between her lips, silent laughter shaking her shoulders. "Surely William would scold me for unkind thoughts, but I confess my sentiments refuse to behave properly where Lady Catherine is concerned. She has terrified me since I was a child! Father hated Rosings and never visited, my one vague memory of the house as a very small child lingering and unpleasant, and on those few occasions our aunt came to Pemberley he never forced me to interact beyond the basics of hospitality. Her criticism of me was one of the rare times I saw Father angry. Luckily William never asked me to accompany him on his visits."

"So he frequently travels to Rosings?"

Georgiana nodded. "At least twice yearly, sometimes more, especially after Uncle Lewis passed on. My brother is acutely loyal to family and friends, Miss Elizabeth. I am sure you have learned this yourself so I am not revealing anything private?" Lizzy nodded, her smile slightly dreamy and proud. Georgiana went on, "In the case of Rosings, my brother's loyalty was to Sir Lewis – He was a nice man, if you did not know. Very gentle. – Yet, mostly because of Cousin Anne. My brother is very fond of her. Not," she emphasized, "as he is fond of you, Miss Elizabeth. Never was it like that!"

Lizzy laughed gaily. "No need to worry, dear girl. Mr. Darcy has unraveled the misunderstandings on that relationship with extreme clarity. I envy him, and you as well. Jane and I have few cousins our age, and none live close to us."

"Neither do we, in truth. Cousin Richard is the only one, really. But I am much younger then he, and have no female friends my age."

She spoke without sadness or rancor, simply stating the facts as they were. Nevertheless, the abrupt comprehension of how lonely her childhood must have been struck Lizzy and Jane simultaneously. For all the times they may have wished there weren't so many flighty females crammed into Longbourn annoying each other, neither could they imagine their life another way or not recognize how blessed they were to have sisters.

"Very soon that will change, Miss Darcy." Georgiana looked at Jane with puzzled creases marring her brow. Jane smiled and patted Lizzy's hand, speaking tenderly, "You will have a sister."

"Absolutely!" Lizzy fervently concurred. "And one who comes with an army of sisters in tow! Jane you already know is wonderful," – Jane blushed and demurred – "and I am certain you will like Kitty and Mary too." In truth she was certain of no such thing, but there was no advantage at this juncture in not being positive.

Georgiana, however, felt equal parts hopeful and terrified at the prospect. Instead of following up with questions on that unnerving topic, she rapidly changed the subject.

"Has Mr. Bingley taken you to his townhouse in Berkeley Square, Miss Bennet?"

"Not as yet. I am dining with him tonight. He requested the day to ensure the house was ready for visitors." The remembrance of his exact words, *For my angel every detail must be perfect*, and the sweet kiss then placed on her lips, cast a delicate rosiness over her cheeks that she hid by sipping her tea.

"I am sure you will love the house. It has very nice proportions to the rooms, tall windows, a lovely garden, and a parlor on the uppermost floor with an excellent view. And it is very near us."

"How is the decor? Mr. Bingley intimated with a hint of… discomfort that I would probably want to update and purchase new furnishings."

Georgiana glanced away and busied her hands with pouring hot tea into half-empty cups. "The decor is… unique. There are plenty of furnishings, no doubt of that. Whether you will care for them is… questionable."

Lizzy burst out laughing. "Miss Bingley has been in charge of the house, hasn't she?" Georgiana nodded miserably. "Oh, my dear Jane! I foresee endless fun and challenges ahead! Do not distress yourself, Miss Darcy. We are quite familiar with Miss Bingley's peculiar personality."

For over an hour they chatted as only females who are wholly at ease with each other can. Topics ranged widely, both Lizzy and Jane impressed by the intelligence Miss Darcy hid behind her shy exterior. The fondness they already felt toward the young girl on the cusp of womanhood grew rapidly to sincere friendship. Lizzy, especially, no longer doubted that in time she would love Georgiana as dearly as if a blood relative.

Additionally Jane and Lizzy learned more about the men soon to become their husbands. Georgiana's innocent comments about her brother revealed a wealth of information, some of it trivial and some significant. At one point Jane laughed so hard she was gasping for oxygen, her pronounced mirth the result of Georgiana describing Mr. Bingley at nineteen. That was the occasion when Mr. Darcy first brought his new friend to Darcy House for dinner. Georgiana's hitherto unknown wittiness and dramatic skills painted a vivid scene of the gawky young man interacting with the stern, humorless Darcy at twenty-three, sending them into gales of laughter.

It was amid this near hysteria inside the parlor that Mr. Darcy walked in. Attempts to formally welcome the Bennets or join the conversation proved impossible, Darcy escaping the madness for the serenity of his office. Once there, he fell into his chair with a gushing sigh of relief. Then he replayed the scene of his beloved sister carefree and friendly with Elizabeth, and he began to smile.

Charlotte Collins
on Bonfire Night
by Abigail Reynolds

November 5, 1812

Across the clearing, sparks flew as the stuffed guy was engulfed in flames. Flickering yellow and orange tendrils shot up from the bonfire toward the sky. Charlotte remembered how huge and out of control the bonfires on Guy Fawkes Day had seemed to her as a child. She had always feared that the sparks would set a building alight, perhaps the result of all those years of stern cautions from her mother about taking care with candles, and her graphic descriptions of the possible consequences of carelessness. Now, of course, Charlotte did not give a second thought to the risk of the fire spreading. She could see the precautions the men were taking – the circle of stones to contain the fire, the buckets of water standing at regular intervals around the clearing.

It was a different kind of fire that Charlotte associated with Bonfire Night now. Had it only been a year ago that she had allowed Mr. Robinson to lead her off into the dark woods? That night had changed her life so completely, and none of it in the manner which she had expected. She was no longer an aging spinster, her future uncertain and dependent completely on her family, an easy target for a flattering seducer. Now she was Mrs. Collins, with a home of her own and security beyond any she could have expected.

Of course, that home of her own was precious little good at the moment, since she and Mr. Collins had fled the vicinity of Rosings Park. Lady Catherine de Bourgh's wrath over Mr. Darcy's engagement to Elizabeth Bennet, showing no sign of abating a fortnight after receiving the news, had been enough to convince Mr. Collins that absence was his best defense. And so Charlotte, now a married woman, was back at Lucas Lodge on Bonfire Night, which had been when it all began.

Now there was to be another new beginning. Elizabeth would be marrying Mr. Darcy in less than a fortnight. Who would have thought it? Even she, who had seen Mr. Darcy's interest in Elizabeth before anyone else, had not believed it would lead to marriage. It made her wonder now whether Lizzy had been hoping for this all along, despite her early air of dislike for him.

Had that hope been what lay behind her friend's refusal to consider Mr. Collins' offer? Perhaps Charlotte was being too cynical, though. Lizzy had never had a practical thought in her head, so the benefits of marrying Mr. Collins would not have occurred to her – neither the financial benefits, nor the advantages of a husband who could be easily managed. Charlotte could not help smiling at the idea of any woman trying to manage Mr. Darcy! She hoped his attitude would not have too much of a detrimental effect on Lizzy's high spirits. Her friend was accustomed to making her own decisions, since her parents exercised so little authority. Marriage would be quite a change for Lizzy!

There seemed no question, though, that Lizzy loved him, and that he was overflowing with admiration for her. Charlotte did not envy Lizzy the riches and fine clothes she would have as Mrs. Darcy, but she could not help feeling a qualm when she considered that her husband would never look at her with that glow in his eyes. Not that she particularly wanted Mr. Collins to do so, but the idea of a husband who would love her so very much still drew something from her heart – a husband with whom she could share a marital bed without having to pretend he was someone else. Lizzy was fortunate in that regard.

Her husband came over to her then with a banal compliment for the festivities. As usual, she barely listened except to insert the occasional murmur of agreement which was all he expected of her.

But she had no cause to complain. For all that he was not clever, witty, or well-mannered, her husband was a decent man who provided well for her and never beat her. And if he was not clever enough to notice that sometimes she would disappear for hours at a time with no particular excuse... well, all the better for her. Her lips curved as she thought about those secret hours and the man who shared them with her. Indeed, she was very fortunate, even if she would never have thought it a year ago.

Mr. Collins looked at Charlotte with great satisfaction, and congratulated himself on how much his wife had blossomed since he had chosen to marry her. She was indeed a fortunate woman to have attracted his interest last November!

Colonel Fitzwilliam Learns of Darcy's Engagement by Jack Caldwell

November 6, 1812

On a cold November afternoon, Colonel the Honorable Richard Fitzwilliam jauntily ascended the steps of Darcy House in London. His knock on the door was swiftly answered.

"Ah, Thacker, has my cousin returned?"

The butler glanced at the door. The colonel was a constant and welcomed guest at Darcy House, but the knocker was not in evidence, a clear sign that the family was unavailable to visitors.

The colonel laughed. "Oh, do not bother, old man." He moved inside the vestibule. "I will just call on Miss Georgiana." He handed the imperturbable servant his hat and gloves and was removing his coat when a tall gentleman made his appearance.

"I thought I heard your voice, Richard," said a smiling Fitzwilliam Darcy, his hand extended in welcome.

"Darce! You have returned and looking exceedingly well, I might add. Now, where the devil have you been? What have you been up to?"

"Come into my study, Fitz. Your arrival is most timely if you mean to stay for dinner."

"Of course! You would not throw your poor cousin upon the mercy of the kitchens of Horse Guards, would you? The horses eat better!"

Darcy harrumphed. "I seriously doubt that the Crown's food is that deficient, but we will suffer your company. Thacker, be so good as to alert Cook that we have a guest for dinner." The butler nodded as the two gentlemen continued down the hall.

"You have not answered my question," Fitzwilliam pointed out. "You have been gone for a month. Did you return to Pemberley?"

Darcy's response was lost to posterity, for at that instant, a pretty young lady dashed from the music room.

"Richard," cried Georgiana Darcy. "Oh Richard, have you heard the news?" She leapt into an embrace with her cousin and guardian. "Brother is getting married!"

Fitzwilliam was dumbfounded. "Married?" His arms full of Georgiana, he peered over her head at Darcy. "To whom?"

Butter would not melt in Darcy's grinning mouth. "You are acquainted with the lady—Miss Elizabeth Bennet."

* * *

Thirty minutes later, the two gentlemen were comfortably ensconced in Darcy's study with cigars and wine, a roaring fire in the grate, and Georgiana was upstairs changing for dinner.

"Now that you have successfully distracted me with cigars and wine," said Fitzwilliam presently, "shall you tell me how things came to pass? Engaged to Miss Bennet? I am all astonishment!"

"I thought you had some wind of it. You must have seen evidence of my admiration in Kent."

"I thought I saw something, but to this degree? No. You have been very sly."

"Not in the least. I must wonder at your astonishment; surely my aunt spoke to the earl last month."

"I have not heard anything, and I would be surprised if I did. You know Father and Aunt Catherine hate each other. But why would—oh!" Fitzwilliam frowned. "She knew? You told Lady Catherine of your intentions and not me?"

"Peace, Cousin! It was not so much a matter of telling her as her finding out."

Mollified, the colonel sat back. "How did that come about? Anne?"

"No, I did not tell Anne, either." He imparted the story of Lady Catherine's journey to Longbourn, her confrontation with Elizabeth, and her attempt to warn Darcy off. By the time Darcy finished his tale, the colonel was excessively diverted.

"Ho, this is rich! The old bat thought she would have you bend to her will, but in all probability, she drove you right into Miss Bennet's arms! How Father will laugh when he learns of this!"

Darcy sat up. "Must you tell him?"

"Of course! I can keep nothing from him—especially if I wish to stay in his best books. My allowance depends upon it!" At Darcy's dark look, Fitzwilliam sobered and patted his cousin's knee. "It would be all for the best, Darce. You cannot think he will look kindly on your betrothal to a county lady of no note."

Darcy ground his teeth. "Elizabeth is a gentleman's daughter; we are equals."

"Do not be foolish! You know this will disrupt his plans for you. However, I can be of service. As much as he dislikes being thwarted, he enjoys thwarting Auntie Cathy more! The very fact that our aunt disapproves of Miss Bennet will raise her in my father's eyes."

Darcy was hardly mollified. "I will stand no disrespect for Elizabeth."

Fitzwilliam almost laughed at the image Darcy presented—glowering face, arms crossed over his chest. Why, if only he bit his lip, he would be the perfect picture of an angry, stubborn child. "Miss Elizabeth is charming. She will win over Father in no time, and Mother too, I have no doubt."

"And the viscount?"

Fitzwilliam's smile faded. "That will be a harder task. You know how much stock my *dear sister* Eugenie puts in appearances, and Andrew follows wherever she leads." The colonel's and the viscountess' mutual loathing was well-known within the family. "However, Father demands a unified public front in all things. Win his acceptance and the rest of the family will fall in line—including Lady Catherine."

Darcy relaxed. "My uncle is a reasonable man. I am satisfied. I shall write him presently. He is still in Derbyshire, I recall." He took a sip of his wine. "Shall you attend the wedding? If so, I would ask you to escort Georgiana."

Fitzwilliam nodded. "I shall be happy to if I am granted leave. After all, someone must represent the family. It certainly will not be Lady Catherine." He frowned. "I wish Anne could... but that is nonsense. Her health would not allow it, even if by some miracle our aunt gave permission."

The two sat for some time, drinking, the crackling fire the only sound in the room.

"Darcy," Fitzwilliam began again, "are you certain about this? Please understand I am only concerned with your happiness. Miss Bennet is all that is lovely and charming, but—"

Darcy held up a hand. "Fitz, I am certain. I shall not change my mind—I shall marry Elizabeth." He sighed. "It is hard for me to speak of this. In her presence, I feel—calm. Complete. At peace. I find she is as necessary to me as food and drink. I do not think I can now live without her, knowing I have finally won her tender affections."

"Have you?"

"She says I have, and I believe her." He chuckled. "I certainly know my fortune means little to her!"

Fitzwilliam frowned, the source of his misgivings now on the table. "Forgive me, Darce, but how do you know that?"

Darcy laughed out loud. "Because she turned me down at Rosings!"

"*What?*"

Darcy ignored his cousin's inelegant outburst and gave an abbreviated recounting of his misadventure in the parsonage at Easter. "So you see?" he concluded his tale. "If she were mercenary, she would have accepted my boorish proposal, and I never would have been the wiser until it was too late! But she had mercy on me and taught me a hard lesson on what it takes to please a woman worthy of being pleased."

"Apparently, you have learned this lesson."

"I will endeavor to put my better understanding to good use for the remainder of my days."

Normally, Fitzwilliam would have disregarded such a statement as mere hyperbole had it come from any other man. "She has bewitched you, has she not?"

"I am a better man for knowing her."

Fitzwilliam raised his glass and offered a toast. "Then I wish you joy with all my heart."

Darcy's eyes were suspiciously moist. "Thank you, Fitz. Your words mean more to me than I can say." He gathered himself and stood. "Shall we to dinner? Georgiana is surely waiting for us by now."

Fitzwilliam grinned, already relishing whatever arts Darcy's cook was to employ that evening. "Excellent! Lead the way, Cuz." *And if what you say about Miss Elizabeth is true, Darce, I shall love her as if she were my own sister, he thought to himself.*

Colonel Fitzwilliam's News
for Darcy
by Sharon Lathan

November 7, 1812

York's Coffee House, located across from Green Park on Piccadilly Street, was a favorite place for Darcy and his cousin Colonel Richard Fitzwilliam to meet. The address was a rough halfway point between Grosvenor Square and the townhouse of Lord Matlock on St. James's Square, but easy access was not the only reason the two men had chosen York's years ago. For one, the coffee was excellent. All the beverages were, in fact, as was the food. Many coffee houses in London could boast the same, so even this was not the primary reason. It came down to atmosphere, more than anything. Urbane and elegant it was, yet with an air of casual comfort not felt in a pretentious gentlemen's club, such as White's, where both Darcy and Richard were members.

York's spanned the entire ground level and two-thirds of the first level, and unlike the majority of coffee houses, did not cram seating places into every last available inch of space. Instead there was ample room for the tables and booths, with none too close together. The black brick building sat on the corner, the windows on both outer walls providing adequate lighting during the day and a nice view of Green Park. If privacy was desired, that could be arranged – for a price – in the upper room where thick walls separated the booths.

All in all it was the perfect place to relax, drink, and converse freely without fear of eavesdropping or having one's behavior censured.

Richard's note was typical of his cousin. *York's. 1 p.m. Usual table. I have news.*

It didn't leave room for speculation, or for refusal since he had no idea where Colonel Fitzwilliam presently was! Darcy never left the house without his butler, and steward if at Pemberley, knowing his planned agenda. It was a habit, born out of no single situation, and infrequently put to the test since emergencies or vital messages were rare. If Richard had not specifically said to deliver the message immediately, Mr. Travers would have sat it on Darcy's desk. As it was, a footman brought it to Darcy at his tailor's, where he was in the middle of a final fitting for his wedding garments.

Odd, but knowing Richard's penchant for mischief and rattling his serious cousin, Darcy didn't anticipate the "news" being anything of significance. Probably just a way to make Darcy spend a lazy afternoon so that the on-holiday colonel wouldn't feel guilty for doing nothing all day, was Darcy's opinion. Nevertheless, his interest was piqued and, he admitted, hot coffee, friendly male conversation, and lounging sounded appealing.

So he crossed the threshold of York's with a smile on his face, heading directly up the stairs to the booth next to a south-facing window where Richard was already sitting, coffee in hand.

"Scoot over, and remove your dusty boots from my bench."

"I'll scoot," Richard drawled, "but I am terribly comfortable stretched out, so you will have to suffer the boots. I wiped the muck off and a little dust won't kill you."

"If it does, I will return to haunt you." Darcy sat across and motioned to a passing waiter. Once his order was placed, he bobbed his chin Richard's direction. "No uniform today. Did they finally catch on and toss you out of the army?"

"I'm incognito. Actually, I am a notorious spy blending in with the common folk for an ultra-secret mission for the Crown. Quite heroic and dangerous. Are you impressed?"

"Exorbitantly. I always suspected York's a hideout knee-deep in traitors of the King."

"The world is a strange place, Darcy."

"Hmm. So, is this drivel practice for captivating women? Or is your 'news' that you are fully delusional?"

"Neither, although the women angle isn't a bad idea. Thanks, Cousin!"

Darcy laughed and shook his head. The waiter brought his coffee, Richard silently grinning while Darcy prepared the hot beverage to his taste. Once the first gulp was swallowed, the grin faded and the colonel got serious.

"I do have news. Good and bad. What do you want first?"

"I prefer to forego the bad news altogether, thank you very much. I am to be married in less than two weeks to the most marvelous woman in all of England, if not the world, and have discovered I enjoy being giddy with happiness. It is a refreshing change."

"If I wasn't truly delighted for you and Miss Bennet, I would jump on that 'giddy' comment with glee. I shall resist and save the taunting for later. At the present, I believe your positive attitude will serve in this situation. Here it is: Father and Mother are in Town."

"Is that the bad news? I wrote to Lord Matlock not long after Elizabeth accepted my proposal, and I was honest as to her family, station in Society, and modest dowry. I also was abundantly clear that I love her. I wish I could say he was completely understanding and approving, but compared to Lady Catherine's... vociferous disapproval," he growled, face dark with the anger simmering under the surface, "Uncle's reservations were mild."

"Yes, Father told me that. What you don't know, William, is that while you have been blissfully living in giddy happiness, our dear, sweet Aunt Catherine has been busy."

Darcy looked genuinely startled. "How do you mean?"

"You really need to pay more attention to gossip. I have been back in Town for two days and have gotten an earful, while your head is floating in a cloud. Primarily it is the anticipated chatter heard whenever a rich, handsome, eligible bachelor gets taken off the market. And don't let the fancy words go to your head; they aren't mine, God knows."

Darcy smiled grimly. Richard's levity was appreciated, but he sensed he wasn't going to like the rest.

"The talk is juicier, of course," Richard continued, "due to the fact that no one has ever heard of Elizabeth Bennet. Speculation is rife, and that is to be expected, but it was when I detected certain 'facts' added on that I grew suspicious."

"I don't care for the sound of this at all. Explain what you mean by 'facts'?"

Richard shrugged, although his face was nearly as tense as Darcy's. "Details about her appearance, where she lives, her family – that sort of thing. Details that would be difficult to discover unless one searched for them, but even if one did, facts like that are emotionless. I have actually done some spying and collecting of intelligence in my time, so I know." He paused, removing his feet from the bench and leaning forward. "Cousin, some of what I heard was, for lack of a better term, vicious."

Darcy listened as Richard imparted a sampling of the rumors disseminating through the ton. The scandal of Lydia, the crassness of the Bennet parents, Elizabeth's lack of proper connections or money or education, that the Bennet girls used unsavory arts to ensnare the first two wealthy men to ever appear in Meryton, the degradation of close relatives in trade, and so on. Kernels within were truth, although exaggerated and painted bleakly, but most were blatant lies or information no one should know. It was the latter that hit Richard.

"At first," he said, "I suspected Caroline Bingley as the source, and I do think to a degree this may be true. But she has been in Hertfordshire for the most part, and now off in Bath, and despite her general nastiness, she isn't vindictive, or overly creative. It was the story of Lydia Bennet, and your involvement, that captured my attention. Assuming, as I did at first, that it was fabricated, it didn't fit with coming from Miss Bingley. I asked a few careful questions – in my capacity as a spy, you see – and it didn't take long to uncover that it was not only based on truth, how much I do not know nor do you have to enlighten me, but also that the story came directly from Lady Catherine."

Darcy's countenance and entire body exuded cold fury. Anyone other than Richard would have stuttered to a halt in terror. Even he, oldest friend and closer than a brother, hesitated to continue. But Darcy deserved to be aware, and prepared.

"Even then I might have denied it, William. I am no fonder of our aunt then you are, but I would not have believed her capable of this, for no other reason then to preserve family honor and reputation. Then I met with my parents this morning." He took a sip of cold coffee, grimaced, and waved for a fresh pot.

"I might need something stronger then coffee before we are through here. Continue, Richard."

"In a nutshell, Lady Catherine has been writing to Father. I didn't see the letters, but based on what he related from them, it matches a lot of what I was hearing bandied about. Needless to say, he is… upset. Now, let me be clear, Cousin. You know your uncle. He is a fair man, and he loves you. Mother too, probably even more, being a woman and your mother's dear friend. Additionally, Father isn't an innocent regarding his sister. Because of Anne he knows Aunt C has a very good reason to want your relationship with Miss Bennet to end. That is the point of it all, in case you didn't figure that out yourself. Shame you amongst your peers, and pressure you via Lord Matlock to come to your senses and break the engagement. Of course, if she had ever bothered to really know you she wouldn't have wasted her time. Oh don't glare at me! You know very well you are the most stubborn man on the planet. Once you make a decision, it takes a visitation from God to change your mind. Catherine, no matter what she may think, isn't God."

He was pleased to hear a short laugh pass Darcy's lips. "So all that was the bad news. Yes, Father wants to talk with you, and meet the mystery woman causing all the uproar. The summons… I mean, invitation," — Darcy again laughed — "to dinner tomorrow night is probably already on your desk. But remember, William, that while

587

Father can be stern and take the whole "I am an earl" stuff quite seriously, he does know you, very well, and he truly does love you. James was his dearest friend, and he would never impose his will over that reality. Personally I am of the opinion he would have been far more upset if you had succumbed to Catherine's demands about Anne. No offense, as I love Anne as much as you, but the two of you together would be a disaster. Family inheritances are important to him, but not at the expense of your happiness. Mother is even worse when it comes to sentimental, romantic rot." He shuddered dramatically.

Darcy had relaxed, somewhat, and refreshed his cold coffee. "Once they meet Elizabeth, their concerns will be gone."

"That is what I told him! You can thank me later, maybe let me win at billiards just once or buy me something special," Richard grinned, "but I sang Miss Bennet's praises. Not that it isn't easy to do. She is a good match for you, William. I suspected it at Rosings this past spring. I am very happy for you, truly I am. I am confident my parents will agree."

They sipped in silence for a time. Darcy stared into his cup, absorbing all that Richard had revealed. Finally he glanced upward. "So, tomorrow night for dinner. I think that can be arranged."

"Excellent! Oh, and I'll be there too, so can guarantee the evening will be entertaining!"

Lord & Lady Matlock
Pass Judgement
by Sharon Lathan

November 8, 1812

For the remaining hours passed at York's Coffee House, Darcy and Richard reverted to their standard male discussion topics. Darcy unabashedly spoke of Elizabeth with words of gushing praise so laced with romantic sentiment that eventually even Richard ran out of ways to harass him! Little else was said about Lady Catherine, the rumors circulating, or the impact of Lord and Lady Matlock's opinion of his choosing Elizabeth Bennet as his wife. They spent an enjoyable afternoon, and parted with expressed anticipation of the following night's dinner engagement.

Once back at the townhouse, Darcy retired to his office with orders not to disturb him. He read the missive from Lord Matlock, which said nothing of Lady Catherine or his concerns. It was a straightforward invitation to a family dinner for the purpose of acquainting with his future wife. Darcy knew his uncle wasn't being duplicitous by not mentioning the serious issues behind the invitation. There was no need to expound upon it in a letter, for one, because his lordship knew damned well that Richard would report to his cousin. No surprise or disapproval in that reality since the cousins a mere three years apart had supported each other from their days as rowdy boys in the nursery! Furthermore, even if by a fluke Richard didn't enlighten Darcy, Lord Matlock trusted in his nephew's extreme intelligence to figure out there was more than a casual meal at stake.

Darcy sat in his chair, staring sightlessly out the window and fiddling with a glass ball on his desk, while he methodically sorted through the information. The situation with Lady Catherine infuriated him. In order to rationally proceed, that, he decided coldly, must be pushed aside and dealt with another time. And make no mistake, he would confront her in due course.

As for the rumors circulating through the high-and-mighty of London, it disturbed him only for the sake of protecting Elizabeth. Nothing could be done to halt gossip. This he knew, it being one of many reasons he despised Society, and, he fully comprehended, one of the reasons he loved Elizabeth. In every way she was a breath of fresh air into the stifled world he had been raised in, her artless honesty unique and invigorating. A fool he most certainly was not, and the consequences of his choice in wife, in relation to his future in Society, were a fact that must also be faced… later. So he wasted minimal time on that point.

Thus, the relevant subject of Lord and Lady Matlock's opinion is what occupied his mind. Truthfully, he did believe they would adore Elizabeth. All that Richard had said, of their love for him and desire for his happiness, Darcy doubted not for a second. Nevertheless, the earl was the patriarch of a noble, ancient family. Tradition, duty, and honor to one's name, country, and ancestry were codes embedded into his cells. Strangely enough, the same codes had caused Darcy to leave Elizabeth last year, and then bungle his first proposal. Those tenets were embedded into his cells and every bit as strong still today, the difference being that finally, after months of heartbreak, Darcy had learned that the foundation supporting all of it was love. Perhaps his Uncle Malcolm had learned that truth along the course of his life. Perhaps Darcy could convince that, for him, everything fell apart and was moot without Elizabeth. He wished for their strong familial ties to remain intact, but if not, so be it. Nothing would ever change his mind about marrying Elizabeth. In that, Richard was one hundred percent correct. Darcy was the most stubborn man on the planet!

He concluded there was no advantage to talking with his uncle before the dinner. Darcy understood Lord Matlock's stance, especially in light of the fabrications by Lady Catherine, and appreciated his objective in ascertaining the truth for himself. Additionally, Darcy respected his lordship's position within their family, and while nothing could possibly be said to deter his path to the altar, it was proper to grant Lord and Lady Matlock an opportunity to judge and courteously say their peace.

To Elizabeth, Darcy said nothing other than that his uncle and aunt were in Town, and had invited them for dinner. She was thrilled to meet more of his family and reacquaint with Colonel Fitzwilliam. Once again Darcy was in awe at her ease with unknown people and utter lack of diffidence. He honestly wondered if coming face-to-face with the Prince Regent would intimidate her!

The intimate family party at the townhouse on St. James's Square included Georgiana and Richard, as well as the heir to the Matlock earldom, Richard's older brother Jonathan, with his wife Priscilla. Mr. Bennet escorted his daughter, shocking everyone, including Lizzy, by wearing a new suit in the latest style, made specifically for the wedding. Lizzy gushed on at how dashing and young he looked, Mr. Bennet preening under the praise, and Darcy had to vocally agree that he presented a handsome picture. Maybe the suit helped, Darcy would never know, but to his astonishment, Mr. Bennet and Lord Matlock instantly took a liking to each other, the two frequently in deep conversation. Mr. Bennet was the archetypical country gentleman: Intelligent and proper when he exerted the effort – as he did this night – yet with a vague irreverence and wry humor. Lord Matlock, for all his elevated rank, was the master of a country estate and appreciated men such as Mr. Bennet for their unpretentious mannerisms.

Not remotely to Darcy's surprise, Elizabeth dazzled everyone. Including him! He was simply unable to look away from her sunny face as she spoke with gay animation, charming everyone, including his cousin Jonathan, who was rarely charmed or impressed by anyone. The beauty was that Elizabeth didn't try. The same natural wit and liveliness that had captivated him – quite against his will initially – captivated Lord and Lady Matlock.

What Darcy did not realize, was that Elizabeth Bennet's enchanting personality and confident demeanor had subtly altered in the past month. Mr. Bennet saw the differences, as did Colonel Fitzwilliam even from their short acquaintance while at Kent. The Matlocks and Fitzwilliams did not have this reference, but reached a similar conclusion by observing Darcy, and noting the silent, expressive interplay between the two. The love they held for each other was a palpable entity practically taking corporeal form with every shared glance, spoken exchange, and furtive touch.

One example of this occurred after dinner while in the parlor. Georgiana and Priscilla Fitzwilliam entertained on the pianoforte. The others sat or stood in relaxed companionship, sipping tea or brandy. Lady Matlock began to speak of Derbyshire and Pemberley, reminiscing to Lizzy of her own days as a new bride relocating to an unfamiliar land.

"You have been to Pemberley, I understand?" Lizzy affirmed Lady Matlock's inquiry. "It may seem imposing, Miss Bennet, but the Darcys have made it a home. Fitzwilliam is the soul of patience and kindness. I assure you will be most happy there."

"Thank you, Your Ladyship. I have no doubt Mr. Darcy will lead me gently."

She smiled at her betrothed, who stood nearby with Richard at his side. He smiled in return, eyes sparkling.

Richard nodded, his eyes mischievous as he glanced at his cousin. "Indeed, Mr. Darcy is patience personified, as all can attest. Even his horses declare it so!"

"Sadly a lesson I could never impart to you, Richard. Your horses habitually choose to throw you rather than listen to instruction."

"That happened one time, I was fifteen, and the horse refused to jump that creek!" Richard turned to Lizzy with a chuckle and pointed toward Darcy. "He, braggart, was twelve with a horse larger than mine, and cleared the creek without hesitation. Very well, I concede. He is the superior horseman. I, on the other hand, excel at dancing and witty conversation."

"You are now witness, Miss Bennet, to what shall henceforth pervade your existence whenever these two are in the same room together." Lady Matlock interjected with a long-suffering sigh. "They delight in baiting the other, have since they were children, and likely will be doing so in their senility."

"Miss Bennet knows it to be true, having confessed to me the dreadfulness of William's dancing and conversation in Hertfordshire."

"Colonel! You tease as well as color the truth," she laughingly accused. "I said that Mr. Darcy refused to dance, not that he danced poorly. He proved his skill at the Netherfield Ball, dancing with the grace of a gazelle."

"Grace of a gazelle? High praise indeed. Is this true, Fitzwilliam?" Lord Matlock grinned at his nephew's discomfiture.

Darcy coughed, color high, but face alit with humor as he gazed upon his impish love. "Miss Bennet is being generous, as always. I managed to avoid stepping on her feet or making a total fool of myself. In my particular case it remains fortunate that dancing proficiency and engaging repartee are not the only inducements to affection."

"Quite so," Jonathan Fitzwilliam agreed. "I abhor dancing and socializing more than you, Darcy, and that is saying something, yet my wife tolerates me. One's beguilements and personality can be well hidden secrets for only select individuals to divine."

"I concur, Mr. Fitzwilliam," Lizzy nodded. "Rather like a fine bottle of aged red wine. The cork must be removed; the wine poured and allowed to breathe. One must wait patiently for the aroma to rise in the air to captivate those who wish to partake of its delights. The wine warms in the glass, as the flavor softens and mellows, exposing its true essence." She paused in her mesmerizing speech. Her gaze had locked on Darcy's startled eyes, the lovers focusing on each other to the exclusion of everyone in the room.

"Some people are structured so and are abundantly worth the wait," she finished in a soft whisper.

For a very long minute the occupants in the room were caught in the spell. Even the pianoforte was silent, Georgiana and Priscilla misty-eyed.

"Well spoken, Miss Bennet," Lady Matlock murmured. She cast a pointed look toward her husband, who nodded once.

As they were preparing to leave, Lord Matlock drew Darcy aside. Peering intently at his nephew, Lord Matlock began, "I won't insult your intelligence, William, by denying the main purpose of why we traveled to London and arranged this dinner. I like her, my boy, enormously. There is absolutely no doubt she loves you, and that you are wildly in love with her. Her father is a gentleman and their manners are impeccable, as far as I can tell."

"Thank you, Uncle Malcolm. Your opinion, and Aunt Madeline's, means a great deal to me."

"I appreciate the sentiment. However, liking her and recognizing your mutual love is one thing. What if I still do not approve of the marriage? She is not quite in your class, manners notwithstanding. What if I agree with your Aunt Catherine?"

Darcy returned his uncle's indecipherable gaze with the same intensity. "Sir, I would be grieved, as I am with Lady Catherine's attitude. However, my choices are just that … mine. Elizabeth is my life. I am nothing without her."

Lord Matlock nodded, still watching his nephew's face. "And Pemberley?"

Darcy was silent for a moment, mulling over his response. "I understand what you are asking, sir. All my adult life I have placed Pemberley's needs before my own. I believe I have been a worthy Master of Pemberley and that I carry the Darcy name proudly. Years have I searched for a woman of quality, someone strong and brave, intelligent and wise, empathetic and giving. All the characteristics the Mistress of Pemberley must have. I am not a fool, Uncle. Elizabeth possesses these attributes, every one, and much more. I have fallen in love with a woman my equal, if not superior. Yet this is inconsequential compared to the fact that she loves me and I her. Her paramount value to me, and to Pemberley, is in this truth."

Lord Matlock nodded seriously, and then smiled. Clasping a hand onto Darcy's shoulder, he spoke his final word on the subject. "Your father would be very proud of you, Fitzwilliam, as would your mother. James and Anne loved each other, as you know. It is an emotion uncommon in our society, sadly. They were better human beings because of it, and Pemberley thrived. I do approve of your Miss Bennet, wholeheartedly. You have my blessing... for what it is worth," he ended with a wink.

Anne de Bourgh Sends Regrets
by Marilyn Brant

November 9, 1812

To Mr. Fitzwilliam Darcy of Pemberley
Sent on Behalf of Anne de Bourgh of Rosings by Mrs. Jenkinson

My Dear Cousin,

I have but a moment alone whilst my mother is attending to a number of decorative details at the parsonage — you know how keenly she wishes to be of service to Mr. and Mrs. Collins — so I must endeavor to keep this note brief.

This morning, I happened upon my mother's letter to you in response to your kind wedding invitation. Indeed, she shared with me several passages from it and seemed, at times, rather feverish as she read it aloud. Although she may have presented to you my opinion on your upcoming nuptials in a somewhat different manner from what I, in fact, stated to her in private, I did want to assure you personally that I wish you and your bride the very best as you begin your life together.

Having had the pleasure of Miss Eliza Bennet's lively company at multiple dinners during her visits to Rosings, I could see clearly the attention the two of you paid to one another. Certainly, it was apparent to me (and, I daresay, even to my mother) that your interest in her was of a deep and - lasting nature. I was pleased to learn that Miss Bennet shared your affections. My only regret now is that I will not be able to make the journey to watch your exchange of vows from the nearest pew.

May the two of you pass many wonderful years together at Pemberley. I dearly hope to be able to congratulate you both in person before too long.

Fondly,

Anne de Bourgh

Lady Catherine Sends Regrets
by Marilyn Brant

November 9, 1812

My Very Own Nephew…

What have you done? I have no words.

The shades of Pemberley are darkening as I write this, and my speechlessness at your pointed betrayal of our family is equaled only by my shock. And after our recent conversation, too! We discussed this in London, Darcy!! You were standing but two feet in front of me. I know you heard my well-informed opinion of Miss Elizabeth Bennet and my report of her alarming behavior in Hertfordshire. I relayed it to you at length! You were neither asleep nor in some lamentable comatose state, which might have at least justified slightly your having not comprehended the full meaning of our discourse. But there is no excuse. You heard every sentence.

So, what could possibly have induced you to make an offer of marriage to that woman?!! I cannot account for such a frightening lapse in judgment.

I can only conclude that you must have been drugged at the time, perhaps by one of her many relatives. She seems to have an unlimited supply of sisters. Or you were otherwise induced by bribery or by the dark arts. Were some gypsies casting spells while you were dallying about in the wilderness? I am quite certain I saw a clan of them skittering along the side of the road when I visited that little place where she lives. Long…something. Out in the middle of nowhere fashionable. Not a high-class lady or gentleman to be found. Oh, Nephew, I am most seriously displeased.

Such stupidity in a marital choice might not be nearly as damaging to your young friend Bingley, as I have heard reports of his family's origins and, well, his reputation and place in society are not the equal of yours. But your foolishness in this matter is not to be borne!

Even if I were to overlook the grave insult in your having chosen a wife from amongst the ranks of virtual commoners, how could I possibly look the other way at your insensitive disregard for the dearest wishes of your mother, your cousin Anne and myself? My poor daughter is inconsolable. I know not how to express to you the pain you have willingly caused your nearest relations in the world. And for whom? For an upstart young woman of inferior birth, paltry connections and questionable taste?

It is unfathomable, Darcy.

I daresay, neither Anne nor I will attend such an event as your impending nuptials. I only pray you will have the good sense to call off such a scandalous engagement before it is too late.

Your Aunt,

Lady Catherine de Bourgh

A Sisterly Talk before the Wedding
by Maria Grace

November 10, 1812

The evening turned cold quickly and they all retreated upstairs somewhat earlier than usual. Elizabeth and Jane withdrew to Jane's room. They sat together on the bed heaped high with pillows. Elizabeth brushed Jane's hair in the crackling firelight. Her hair was so beautiful, shining like molten gold under the brush and always so well-behaved, submitting the plait and pins as serenely as Jane herself walked through life, not like her own unruly locks.

She ran her fingers through Jane's hair. They did this so often; she would comb Jane's hair and Jane hers. How many more such moments would they share? Precious few. Life as Mrs. Darcy promised so much, but this she would miss.

"Have you become contemplative again, Lizzy?" Jane turned over her shoulder and caught her eyes. "You have. I can see it in the melancholy turn of your lips." Jane clasped Lizzy's hands. "How can you be sad when so much joy awaits us? We have already made Mama so very happy."

"So she has said, countless times and to countless souls." Elizabeth laughed and slowly plaited Jane's hair, savoring the moment.

The door behind them squeaked and they both turned. Mary and Kitty, in their dressing gowns, peeked through the doorway. They and Lydia had done than when they were small, sneaking out of their beds to join their big sisters in clandestine sisterly gatherings.

"Come in come in." Jane beckoned them in and slid toward the head of the bed.

Elizabeth patted the counterpane beside her. Mary and Kitty rushed in and piled on the feather bed, tucking their feet up underneath them.

"Do you remember how we used to do this after Mama would say good night?" Kitty giggled. "She would get so cross when she heard us laughing. She used to call us her 'little titter mice'"

Jane wrapped her arms around her knees. "But she did not send us back to bed. I think maybe she and Aunt Philips did the same thing." She pulled her shoulders up around her ears and laughed softly.

Mary pulled her shoulders into a funny hunch and looked up like an old woman craning her neck. Her voice turned thin and brittle. "Remember how Lizzy would read us stories and do all the voices for the characters."

Elizabeth guffawed. "I had not thought of that in years." That would be another thing she missed. What would Mr. Darcy think of her?

"You must promise to do that for your children—" Mary said.

"And mine," Jane added, eyes sparkling.

Kitty clapped her hands softly. "You shall have the most delightful children."

Elizabeth rolled her eyes, not if any of Mama's predictions were correct. "Hardly, they will be all mischief and nonsense to be sure. Jane's, though, shall be angels, like her."

Jane's cheeks glowed. "Not if they resemble their father." She looked away.

What? Jane had never mentioned—

"Indeed?" Kitty scooted closer to Jane and pressed her chin on Jane's shoulder. "You must tell us, genteel Mr. Bingley is not as he seems? What secrets have you discovered about your betrothed?"

"Oh, Kitty, no." Mary's hand flew to her mouth.

Jane laughed and turned back to her sisters. "No, no, nothing so outrageous as that. But he was a most high-spirited lad, or se he tells me."

"Nothing like your staid Mr. Darcy, I am sure." Kitty blinked with the same feigned innocence she used on Mama so often.

Elizabeth smiled, brows lifted, and cocked her head. There were those stories Colonel Fitzwilliam had told her in Kent.

"Oh, Lizzy." Kitty gasped.

"What have you not told us?" Mary pressed her shoulder against Elizabeth's.

"How are his kisses Lizzy? You seemed to like them very much." Kitty sing-songed.

Elizabeth gasped and traded looks with Jane. If her face burned any hotter, it would have burst into flame.

"That is not appropriate, Kitty." Mary said softly.

"But I saw—" Kitty leaned back on her heels and pouted.

Elizabeth swallowed hard. "What do you think Charlotte's children will be like?"

Jane choked back laughter and hid her face in her knees. Mary and Kitty's jaws dropped.

"I am sure Lady Catherine will have to approve the child before he is born." Elizabeth peered down her nose. "Really, Mr. Collins, you must be certain to tell Mrs. Collins that the most proper time to be born is between three and four in the afternoon so as to allow the household to settle and have a proper dinner that evening." She pressed her fist to her mouth to contain her giggles.

Jane picked her head up and looked at Elizabeth, tears streaming down her cheeks. She fell onto her knees in helpless peals of laughter. Mary and Kitty dropped on each other's shoulders in breathless giggles. Elizabeth rocked back and forth, smiling broadly.

Mary wiped her eyes on her sleeve. Kitty pulled up the sheet and dragged it over her cheeks.

Only Jane had a handkerchief tucked up her sleeve. She blotted her eyes. "I shall dearly miss these times."

"I will too." Elizabeth's mirth faded away. How odd. Until now she had never contemplated her coming marriage and considered loneliness might accompany her move to Derbyshire. But perhaps it would.

Kitty sniffled. "I cannot imagine what it will be like without both of you here."

"I have never imagined Longbourn without you." Mary blinked rapidly, her eyes bright.

Elizabeth patted Mary's arm and blinked back the burning in her eyes. "Well, never fear, unlike Lydia, I am quite certain I shall write so often you will quite tire of paying the post."

"You must, Lizzy—truly you must." Mary bit her lip. "Might we come to visit you?"

"Absolutely."

Jane clutched her breast exactly as Mama did. "After all, she might put you in the path of other rich men."

A fresh wave of laughter nearly choked them all. Few knew what a talented mimic Jane was, the most proficient of all of them. Did Mr. Bingley know yet? Doubtless, he would soon.

Elizabeth sighed. "I will need some time to settle into my role as mistress of Pemberley, but perhaps we might apply to Papa for you to visit during the summer."

"Really? You think Papa might agree?" Kitty clasped her hands below her chin.

"I do." The corners of Elizabeth's lips turned up. Pemberley would certainly not be like a trip to Brighton.

The glitter in Jane's eye confirmed their shared thought.

"You and Mr. Bingley too, if you would be free to come then."

"I am sure Mr. Bingley would appreciate the invitation. He speaks most fondly of Pemberley."

"Might we do this whilst at Pemberley?" Kitty asked in a very small voice.

"I am sure it can be arranged. It would not be a proper visit without an assembly of Mama's titer-mice."

Georgiana Arrives in Hertfordshire
for the Wedding
by Monica Fairview

November 10, 1812

They changed horses at the Hart and Hounds Inn, their last stop before arriving at Netherfield.

"Almost there, now, Miss Darcy. It won't be long," said Mrs. Annesley, smiling as the carriage began its familiar sway and buck over the cobblestones leading out of the inn.

Everything suddenly became all too real. The thought of reaching her destination now filled Georgiana with apprehension. She shivered and drew her tippet closer around her.

Until this moment, it had all seemed like a fairy tale. She was so happy for her brother. Fitzwilliam was in love. There was a glow to him she'd never seen before, and that careworn look on his face that had been stamped there ever since their father had died was gone. His every footstep had a spring to it. There was such an eagerness to his face, such a sense of purpose and energy that it made her want to laugh and sing and play the piano as loudly as possible, which was really shocking because she'd always prided herself on the evenness of her playing.

Yes, she was very happy, not just for her brother, but for herself as well.

Her brother was to marry, and she was to have a sister. She had dreamed of having a sister for so long, someone to keep her company during the long days at Pemberley when Darcy was busy doing accounts or attending to the estate. Someone with whom she could sit and embroider. Someone who would look over fashion plates with her and discuss menus. Someone who would share with her all the female occupations which escaped her brother's interest. Then perhaps, too, if Darcy was married, he would spend more time at Pemberley, and she would not have to deal with long weeks of isolation in which she saw hardly anyone except for the five young ladies from neighboring families who occasionally came to call on her.

There were a thousand reasons to be happy, and none at all not to be. But still, there was that clenching feeling inside her, as if someone had tightened her stays too much. It made it hard for her to breathe. She felt guilty for feeling that way, but now that it had become rooted there was no getting rid of the anxiety.

She couldn't help being shy around strangers. It wasn't that she didn't meet enough people when she went down to London, but she wasn't always in London, and she was left to her own devices too often. The thing was, she had spent such a large part of her life alone. Her mother had died, then later her father, and Fitzwilliam – well Fitzwilliam was a young man and a young man with means and time at his disposal who wanted to see the world. It was only natural that he would spend large amounts of time away from Pemberley – weeks at a time, even.

And then there was all that business with Wickham. Georgiana had made a terrible mistake. She had trusted Mrs. Younge, her governess, to keep her out of harm's way, never dreaming that there had been an agreement between Mrs. Younge and Wickham. She never could have imagined that Wickham was using her. Well, perhaps she had imagined it, just a little, because why else had she felt compelled to tell her brother about their secret plan to elope?

"Do you think Lady Catherine will be attending?" said Mrs. Annesley.

Oh, Lord. She hadn't thought at all of Lady Catherine. As if it wasn't enough to be meeting all those people without Lady Catherine there watching her like a hawk and telling her every minute to lift her chin and keep her back straight and stop simpering like a fool. She did not need constant reminders of how she needed to live up to the Darcy family name.

She sighed.

"I hope not, Mrs. Annesley," she said. "It will all be so much easier if she did not come."

"Don't you worry about her, Miss Darcy," said Betsy, Georgiana's maid, rousing out of her sleep. "She won't have much cause to chide you if the Master's there. You know how Mr. Darcy always puts a stop to it."

But Darcy would not always be there to protect her, especially when the ladies withdrew and left the men to their port. She would be alone in a room full of complete strangers and Lady Catherine would make her play the piano then issue instructions while she was playing and embarrass her in front of everybody.

She tried to reassure herself that there was nothing to worry about. After all, she already knew quite a few of those who would be there. She had met Elizabeth and the Gardiners in Pemberley, and she had seen them a few times when they came down to London, and of course she had known the Bingleys for years. Still, there was the whole Bennet family to meet as well as their friends.

Cousin Robert would be there. She had already met him in London. He was kind, and he had paid her some attention and told her stories about America, but she hardly knew him at all.

She would be an outsider.

Her only consolation was that all eyes would be on the wedding couples, and she would be left to her own devices.

"I do believe we've arrived," said Mrs. Annesley, as the carriage turned off the main road into a lane and through a large wrought-iron gate.

"I can hardly wait, Miss Darcy," said Betsy, her eyes shining. "You must be so excited."

Georgiana felt her throat go so dry she was afraid she wouldn't be able to say a word. It would be awful, not to be able to say anything at all.

Then the carriage stopped and a footman in red livery opened the door and helped her down the step.

There was the scent of lavender water, then Georgiana was gripped in a fierce hug. Elizabeth's laughing eyes met hers.

"There you are, Georgiana!" said Elizabeth. "What took you so long? We have been expecting you the last two hours, and your brother has been having dreadful thoughts of your carriage having overturned on some forsaken country lane."

Fitzwilliam was there behind Elizabeth, laughing too.

Happiness soared inside Georgiana and she started to laugh with them. It was going to be alright. Darcy and Elizabeth would take care of her.

"Welcome to Netherfield, little sister," said Darcy.

It was all going to be all right.

The Musings of Mr. Collins Regarding His Cousin's Wedding
by Maria Grace

November 12, 1812

Breakfast should have been a quiet affair, but it seemed few meals at Lucas Lodge were. Mr. Collins squeezed his temples. So much banal chatter soured his stomach and ruined his appetite.

His wife's brothers brought reports on new arrivals at Netherfield Park while her younger sister was brimming over with talk of lace and dresses. Collins could not bring himself to care about the brides' gowns and even less what the other ladies of their party would wear. How could Charlotte listen so patiently to all that blather? He was embarrassed that her parents failed to curb the exuberance of the young people at their table.

Thank heavens his wife did not bring such manners with her into his home. Though she patiently listened and politely smiled thought the entire disgraceful display, he was certain his wife would agree with his sentiment. She shared all his opinions, as a proper wife did. Without a doubt, young people should keep their trivial interests and conversations to themselves during meals. His children, when they came, would be taught properly.

Collins excused himself as quickly as could be, claiming a need for fresh air. Charlotte smiled and encouraged him to go, noting that he must miss the time spent he usually spent in his garden and that a walk seemed necessary to his constitution.

A blast of chill wind buffeted his face as he stepped out. Though it burned the tips of his ears, he welcomed the discomfort to distract him from his own rising agitations. He pulled his hat down more snugly and tightened his scarf.

While Hertfordshire was pleasant enough and Lucas lodge offered many comforts, it was nothing to his parsonage in Kent, the place he was currently unwelcome because of the thoughtless, headstrong actions of his dear cousin Elizabeth. His shoulders twitched at the thought.

How he despised Lady Catherine's wrath. On his own count, he never felt it, but now that his unruly and unrepentant cousin had crossed her ladyship, he felt its full fury. The hair on the back of his neck prickled. He rubbed it though his muffler though it did little to ease his discomfort.

Lady Catherine sounded just like his mother when in high dudgeon, and her temper was much like his father's. How vexed her ladyship would be if she knew she were compared to such common folk. He chuckled, nonetheless. Certainly she would never hear that from him. Since both his parents had passed there was no chance Lady Catherine would ever notice the similarities.

His brisk steps crunched in the dry leaves underfoot. The sharp wind whipped dust around his feet and slapped small branches against his face. Bother! The gardener responsible for such unkempt paths should be fired, immediately. He grumbled under his breath and rubbed his chin. Bah. His razor was going dull again. What other vexations were going to plague him now?

In the distance, he saw the tips of Longbourn's chimneys. Providence smiled on him the day Cousin Elizabeth had so cruelly refused his offer of marriage. His bruised ego had not yet forgiven her, but her visit to Kent demonstrated her total lack of suitability. Collins winced. What a disaster it would have been to have brought her home to the parsonage. Cousin Elizabeth would never have treated Lady Catherine with the proper deference and respect like his dear Charlotte, with a bit of gentle coaching, did.

How was it that even now that hoyden of a cousin still continued to plague him? How could she have such audacity as to marry Mr. Darcy? Did she not understand what she was doing to

609

her father's heir? Even though she would not marry him, she owed him respect. Cold and unfeeling girl. It was her fault he was here in Hertfordshire, instead of enjoying the comforts, and quiet, of his own home in Kent.

There had to be some way to soothe Lady Catherine's ire and return to her good graces. He never failed to find a way to appease his volatile parents. He would find a way to mollify his patroness.

He kicked a small rock out of his way. Letter after letter of apology had been sent but to no avail. More of the same would accomplish nothing. He needed a different tack.

How much easier his life would be now if not for his impudent, ill-mannered, ill-bred… There was a thought. The corners of his lips lifted. Yes, yes, there was nothing that soothed his father faster than to be agreed with. He rubbed his hands together.

He could quite look forward to writing his next letter—no letters. Ah, the pages and pages he could fill dedicated to the wrongs of his dear cousin. The critiques he could arrange for the pleasure of her ladyship would be most satisfying to write. What a gratifying change from finding another way to apologize for wrongs he never committed.

Surely he would be back in favor and on his way back to his own home soon. He ticked off the days in his mind. A fortnight should do it, perhaps a few days more. He turned back toward Lucas Lodge, his feet so light he nearly ran. He had letters to write.

The Gardiners Arrive for the Wedding Festivities
by C. Allyn Pierson

November 12, 1812

It was much more comfortable in the carriage with just the two of them, reflected Mrs. Gardiner, but it was still a rather long journey from London to Longbourn, and she already missed their four children, bless their little hearts! Still, neither she nor Mr. Gardiner would consider missing the wedding of his two favourite nieces…and to two very worthy and rich young men! It pleased her that their trip into Derbyshire the previous summer had been the turning point of Elizabeth's relationship with Mr. Darcy. What an excellent young man he was! They would be as happy as dear Jane and Bingley.

The carriage turned off the turnpike and onto the road to Longbourn; she recognized the house that stood at the crossroads, unchanged in the fifteen years she had been married to Mr. Gardiner. She glanced over at him and met his eye.

"Yes, my dear, they will be very happy together." He twinkled at her, able to read her thoughts after all these years. She took his hand and held it until they pulled onto the gravel sweep and stopped in front of the entrance of Longbourn manor.

Mrs. Bennet swept out of the house, her ribbons flying and a lace handkerchief in her hand, ready to dab at her tears over the loss of her current favorite daughters. Mrs. Gardiner sighed. Her sister-in-law had not changed with the engagements of her two eldest daughters.

"Oh my dears! I am so happy you made it safely! I have been worried to death these two hours, thinking your carriage had lost a wheel, or that highwaymen had robbed you!"

"Now, now, sister," Mr. Gardiner said soothingly, "you know we were to arrive at 4 of the clock...and it is not yet half three!"

"But you are always early, Edward!" she snapped, the whites of her eyes showing. "You know very well that I am very ill...I don't know how I have managed to finish the wedding preparations with my spasms so often forcing me to my bed when I am most needed to advise Jane and Lizzy!"

The two eldest Bennet girls came out of the house to greet their aunt and uncle, Lizzy rolling her eyes at her aunt and whispering in her ear, "Everything is ready for the wedding, my dear aunt! Please try to calm our mother down, I beg of you!"

Mrs. Gardiner gave her a secret smile. "Of course I will, my dear Lizzy. I will distract her in some way, you may be sure."

Lizzy sighed with relief, as did Jane, and they linked arms with Aunt Gardiner and went slowly into the house.

Elizabeth Reflects on Questionable Marital Advice
by Shannon Winslow

November 12, 1812

I know that many brides go to the altar in complete ignorance – and consequently in great trepidation – of what will follow afterward. Neither Jane nor I shall suffer such an unfortunate fate, however. No, with our double wedding only a few days off, I expect we will both be supplied sufficient information on the topic in time. We shall have enough in quantity, at least. Considering the available sources, it is the quality of the information that is in doubt.

Months ago, Charlotte gave me the advantage of her wedded wisdom – painfully acquired, I fear – in the expectation that it would one day be of material benefit to me. I still remember what she told me then, and I have not withheld her penetrating insights from my dear sister Jane.

"The secret to connubial contentment," Charlotte had said, "is to organize one's life in such a way as to spend as little time as possible in one's husband's company. By day, any number of clever contrivances can be called into use. But at night, there is nothing so universally helpful in avoiding unwanted intimacy as a quarrel, and preferably separate bedchambers to go to afterward."

Amused, I responded with, "Dear Charlotte, you cannot possibly divine some fresh argument every night!"

"It is true that occasionally my resources fail me. I find, however, that being married to Mr. Collins is usually sufficient cause to put me in a very disagreeable humour by the end of the day."

This I could well believe. But such a philosophy will never do for me. I passionately long to spend more time, not less, with Mr. Darcy. And I secretly hope to find that the marriage bed is something mutually satisfying, not something to be avoided. Although Jane is too modest to speak of it, I suspect she feels the same. Perhaps, then, we should heed Lydia's candid opinion on the subject, as expressed in a recent letter addressed to us both:

"Oh, what a surprise you will each have on your wedding night!" she began. "I laugh to think of it. I daresay you will faint dead away, Jane, when your husband first approaches you. But Lizzy, I expect you to have a little more backbone. And you know there really is nothing to fear. Furthermore, I do not see why it should be only men who are allowed to admit taking pleasure in the physical act of love. In truth, it is often the only thing my dear Wickham and I can agree upon. So I find that, along with its other benefits, the conjugal act provides a very useful way of settling arguments."

Jane gasped when I read this part out to her in the privacy of her chamber. "Oh, my! What are we to think, Lizzy?" she asked, blushing furiously.

"A puzzling case, indeed. One friend says we are to use a quarrel to avoid the marriage bed, and another says the opposite – that we are instead to settle all our differences there."

"'Tis not sound, this advice!"

"I am quite of your opinion, Jane. If I love my husband, I must believe that his company will always – or at least almost always – be desirable. And temporary distraction is no way to settle disputes. No, we must hope to find more competent counsel elsewhere."

But where is this sage advice to come from? From our mother? Earlier today she dropped a hint that she wishes to have "a serious-minded discussion" with her two eldest daughters after dinner. She said this with a significant look that conveyed considerable embarrassment, leaving little doubt in my mind as to the intended topic of conversation. And alas, the time is now at hand.

"Lizzy, Jane, come with me," says Mama.

We rise and dutifully follow her from the dining room, leaving Papa and our two younger sisters behind. Papa gives me a pitying look, but I see that he is really amused.

Once in the sitting room, Mama closes the door. "We will not be disturbed here," says she with a wink. "Let us get comfortable by the fire, and then we can begin our little… our little chat. The wedding is almost here, girls, and it is my duty as your mother to prepare you in some measure for what comes afterward. You cannot, either one of you, have much idea of what goes on between a husband and wife behind closed doors, I suppose."

Jane and I look to each other for help, but neither one of us attempts an answer.

"Goodness!" continues Mama in some exasperation. "I never imagined this would be so very difficult. But it must be done, so I will speak as plainly as I can. You must surely know that there is a certain duty every wife owes to her marriage by way of procreation. If you are lucky, your husband may be patient and allow you a day or two to get used to the idea first. Sooner or later, however, he will insist on coming to your bed and having his way. I am afraid there is no avoiding it, my dears! You simply must each make up your mind to be brave about it."

Mama lets that somber tiding take its effect before continuing. "You have a right to know the truth, but I will give you a word of encouragement as well. Unpleasant as the business may seem in the beginning, it is part of the natural order of things and one tends to get used to it. Some women actually learn to enjoy it in time… or so I am told." Now it is Mama's turn to blush.

So what am I to conclude from the testimony of these three witnesses? I find little of their information to credit and even less to emulate. I believe I must take none of their advice too much to heart. Instead I resolve to keep an open mind. I trust Mr. Darcy and I will make our own way. And perhaps my own investigations into this matter will come to a much more gratifying conclusion. I fervently hope that shall be the case.

The Bennet Women Prepare for a Major Change at Longbourn
by Sharon Lathan

November 13, 1812

Over the past weeks, when not otherwise engaged entertaining their handsome future husbands, Jane and Lizzy had gradually sorted through their possessions in preparation for relocating to their new homes. Headway had been made in packing what they wished to take, and discarding what was no longer appropriate, yet not as extensive as one might presume. The sisters were very excited to be married, their minds barely able to think of much else, in fact. Perhaps a portion of their laxity was a result of being preoccupied and pleasantly distracted. The greater reason, they each privately understood, was an odd mixture of nostalgia and childish hesitation to relinquish their familiar life until they absolutely must. With the wedding less than a week away, procrastination was no longer an option.

Thus it was that today the Longbourn bedroom shared by Jane and Lizzy Bennet for longer than either could recollect, looked as if a dozen wardrobes and bureaus had violently regurgitated their contents. Gowns, undergarments, stockings, hats, gloves, shawls, coats, shoes, hair accessories, and more were strewn across every available surface in a flood of lace and fabrics. Those items purchased in London on their recent shopping spree joined those already owned, Jane's property piled haphazardly with Lizzy's. Somewhere underneath were boxes filled with books, treasured objects, wall hangings, needle crafts, and so on.

Initially the eldest Bennet daughters had arranged their respective belongings in an organized manner. If left alone, the necessary packing would have flawlessly concluded. That possibility perished hours ago when Kitty, Mary, and Mrs. Bennet arrived to "help." While annoying at first, Lizzy and Jane soon recognized that their sisters and mother were secretly struggling with their own emotions at the prospect of life radically changing in the gulf created by their absence. None of these deeper thoughts were verbalized, the five women opting to enjoy the camaraderie.

"Lizzy, you and Jane should put on your wedding dresses so we can see how they look."

"It is bad luck to wear your wedding dress before the day itself, Kitty." Lizzy snatched her gown out of Kitty's hand, winking at Jane as she turned to hang it carefully in the wardrobe.

"That is nonsense!" Kitty snorted. "You of all people would never believe that!"

"Normally I do not believe in superstitions, but when it comes to marriage and my future I am not tempting the Fates. Additionally, I can't risk mussing it, as I inevitably do ten minutes after donning any garment, and I wish to maintain the surprise."

Kitty rolled her eyes, and then cast a pleading look toward Jane. Before she could say a word, Jane shook her head. "I am afraid not, dear Kitty. Customs are to be respected, even silly ones, nor do I want to chance a stain or tear."

"Ha!" This time it was Lizzy who exclaimed and rolled her eyes. "When have you ever done that to any of your clothing?"

"I have… a few times… I am sure of it…" Jane stammered to a halt, rosiness highlighting her cheeks as four pairs of dubious eyes swiveled her way. "If you didn't run across dirt fields and help feed the barn animals, you would keep your clothes cleaner and in better repair too, Lizzy."

Laughing at the hint of asperity in Jane's voice, Lizzy sang, "Oh, indeed that is a charge I cannot deny! I suppose I shall soon need to learn how to properly comport myself as a lady," – she dropped a purposefully awkward curtsey – "and forego digging in the dirt or wallowing with the pigs. I suspect the Pemberley gardeners and groomsmen would frown at their mistress treading in their designated zones."

"I cannot speak with knowledge on the staff of a grand manor, Lizzy, but I do know Mr. Darcy enjoys your outside activities. He stares at you with the most intense, animated expression when your cheeks are flushed from the brisk air and tendrils of hair have escaped your bonnet."

"Kitty!" Jane admonished.

"Well, he does! An imbecile would know what he is thinking! Isn't that so, Mary?"

Mary did not reply, her lips primly pressed together as she continued to fold Jane's shawls into precise square piles. Lizzy had again turned toward the wardrobe, busying herself at nothing so as to hide her dreamy face. Kitty's teasing observation ignited a host of sensations threatening to overwhelm her regulation. None of them did she attempt to contradict or plan to restrain once finally alone with her husband. She yearned for it, in fact. Nevertheless, even skirting the edge of the subject was the last thing she wanted at the moment, as it would certainly instigate another diatribe from her mother on the "discomforts of the marriage bed" or how to avoid "a man's urges."

Unfortunately, avoiding the topic wasn't within her control.

"Why do all of your new shifts, stays, and other undergarments have these lace and ribbon accents?" Mrs. Bennet held up an example, the shift one of Lizzy's constructed of a semi-sheer cotton with pale blue ribbons weaving across and under the bodice in a pretty pattern.

"And did you see their new nightclothes, Mama?" Kitty lifted a particularly flimsy nightdress off the bed and directed the question to Mrs. Bennet, but her taunting eyes and smirk were directed toward Jane and Lizzy.

Internally Lizzy shrugged. No point in postponing the inevitable, she thought. Widening her eyes in as innocent an expression as possible, she met her mother's gaze.

"Our Aunt Gardiner was of the opinion that garments of this type were essential for a new bride. She spoke at length, and in eloquent details, on the positive developments to be attained in the wearing of them, most especially in regards to our duty as obedient wives to please our husbands, although she was adamant that we too would reap the benefits in a most pleasurable manner."

Jane was open-mouthed, her face a remarkable shade of red Lizzy was sure she had never seen before! Kitty had collapsed into a chair, shaking with suppressed laughter. Even stuffy Mary was smiling, her eyes tender and thoughtful as she smoothed a palm over a silky creation nearly transparent. The biggest surprise, however, was Mrs. Bennet. Rather than blanching, launching into a contradictory lecture, or suffering an abrupt attack of her nerves as Lizzy expected, she had a completely different reaction.

Mrs. Bennet frowned for a moment, as if puzzling through a complex mathematics equation, and then began to smile in an odd way. Her eyes were unfocused, and one hand briefly pressed against the skin under which her heart beat before lifting to feather her fingertips across a rosy cheek.

"Well… yes," she murmured, still gazing at the shift, "my sister is a wise woman."

Lizzy glanced at Jane, both their brows rising. Not quite sure what to make of their mother's unusual demeanor – and not wanting to analyze too deeply, to be honest – and trusting that the spell would soon be broken, Lizzy jumped in with a new topic.

"By the way, Mama, I forgot to mention in the excitement, but there are to be three more guests at the wedding. Nothing you need fret over," she hastened to console at the instant tinge of panic popping into Mrs. Bennet's eyes. "They are relatives of Mr. Darcy, so will stay at Netherfield, and they will not arrive until the afternoon before the wedding and leave after breakfast."

"Oh my! We must adjust the amount of food!"

"It will be quite sufficient, Mama," Jane placated. "We have an abundance of food purchased. We will be eating off the remains for a week, so three additional mouths will not be a burden."

"Indeed," Lizzy nodded, squeezing her mother's hand. "It is nothing to concern yourself with. Mr. Darcy was unsure of their attendance until a few days ago, and I only inform you so as to prepare." She glanced at Jane, who nodded for her to go on. "It is Mr. Darcy's aunt,—"

"Lady Catherine de Bourgh! Oh, goodness gracious! I never imagined that woman… oh dear, oh dear—"

"No, Mama. It isn't Lady Catherine. I can assure you that she will not be at our wedding. It is Mr. Darcy's other aunt and uncle, the Earl and Countess of Matlock, and their son, Mr. Darcy's cousin, Colonel Fitzwilliam."

"A colonel? A colonel is coming to the wedding?" Mrs. Bennet threw the shift onto the bed, her eyes jerking to Kitty. "How marvelous! A colonel, you say? And, would this officer and son of an earl be a bachelor, by chance?"

Lizzy nodded, and then groaned. *How in the world did I not see this coming?* All the discussion she and Jane had had over how to break the news of an earl and countess attending the wedding, sure that would send Mrs. Bennet into hysterics, and not once did they think of the possibilities of raptures over Colonel Fitzwilliam!

Marital beds and diaphanous undergarments were forgotten in the thrill of a flesh and blood army officer.

Poor Colonel Fitzwilliam! He has no idea what he is in for. Oddly the thought was more humorous than sympathetic. Lizzy and Jane shared an amused, non-verbal exchange. This was definitely a wedding ceremony and reception that promised to be fun!

Lizzy Steps toward her New Life
By Sharon Lathan

November 14, 1812

"These are the last two, Mr. Hill." Lizzy pointed at the boxes stacked by the door. "Be careful as they each have books inside and are heavy."

"I can manage, Miss Elizabeth, but thank 'e for the warning."

Lizzy hid her smile, and did not embarrass the determined butler by watching him struggle to lift the weighty pieces. Instead she turned away and finished the task of stowing her belongings into the luggage bags to be carried with her day after tomorrow. Ignoring the grunts and muttered curses as Mr. Hill carried the boxes to the waiting wagon; Lizzy latched the portmanteau and sat it beside her wardrobe, it now empty except for her wedding dress and a couple other garments. For probably the twentieth time that morning and most certainly not for the last time that day or the next to come, her eyes scanned over the room. Slowly she walked from corner to corner, traversing the modest space of the bedchamber that she would sleep in for only two more nights. Her fingertips brushed the worn furniture surfaces, hands opened drawers and doors to make sure she had forgotten nothing important, and eyes traveled along the walls and floor edges just in case a vital object had been overlooked or fallen to the ground and hidden.

Jane's boxes were neatly stacked by the window. She hadn't needed to be as thorough as Lizzy due to the close proximity of Longbourn to Netherfield. Lizzy was suddenly very thankful of this fact. Having a portion of Jane's possessions lying about cast an illusion of normalcy – if one didn't stare too hard. The contrast between the once cozy, lived-in chamber and the gutted room to be a week or so hence, wasn't as jarring to the senses as long as some clothing, cosmetics, and trinkets were present.

Nevertheless, the typically unsentimental Elizabeth Bennet was far too frequently feeling overcome with waves of emotion and stinging tears.

A pair of slender arms slipped around her waist, squeezing tight as a dulcet voice near her ear whispered, "No shame in shedding tears, my Lizzy. I have shed a few, and I will be able to gradually distance myself from Longbourn. For you the pain will be stronger, even with Mr. Darcy to comfort, as I am certain he will."

Lizzy brushed a tear off her cheek and attempted to laugh at her childishness. It came out as a choked squeak. "I vacillate between feeling an utter fool, and telling me it is normal to be a bit sad. Oh Jane! I want to marry William with all of my soul, can think of little else, and know deep inside my bones that he is the man for me and that Pemberley will grow to become my home. Yet I cannot relinquish the melancholy either. How does that make sense?"

Jane squeezed tighter, her husky chuckle oddly comforting. "It doesn't make sense, and that is to be expected! I could try to quote words of philosophy, or from the Bible or a poet, but in the end I judge we are normal soon-to-be-brides dealing with nervousness as all brides have since the dawn of time. Somehow they survived, most at least, so I am sure we will too."

Lizzy turned, smiled and kissed her beloved sister on the cheek. "As always, dearest Jane, your serene soul soothes me. What will I ever do without you to tame my tumultuousness?"

Jane laughed aloud. "Once I might have submitted that Mr. Darcy is the epitome of calm, disciplined logic. I suppose he is, to a degree far more than you, Lizzy. However now, thanks to your vivid enlightenment, I am aware of his wild, passionate side. Thus, I can extend no hope for you in that area!"

"Then I am doomed," Lizzy sighed dramatically.

"That I seriously doubt. Now, I came not with the intent to cheer you, or depress further as it were, but to alert you to the fact that Mr. Darcy has arrived. He expressed his desire to personally oversee the loading of your personal possessions before they headed to Pemberley."

Tears were replaced by the ridiculous grin and sparkling eyes that spontaneously emerged whenever Mr. Darcy was near. Or whenever his name was mentioned, for that matter. Maintaining a casual pace descending the stairs and weaving toward the front of the house required diligent attention, it seeming to take a horribly long time until the sisters entered the main parlor on the way to the foyer. They were halted, however, by Kitty.

"Lizzy, come here!" Kitty motioned vigorously from her stance to the side of the half opened window. Curiosity won over the yearning to touch her betrothed, Lizzy, with Jane in tow, steering around the sofas to see what Kitty was grinning about. One peek out the window and Lizzy clamped a hand over her mouth to arrest the giddy giggle.

Mr. Darcy, dressed in his usual full attire with every button and loop of cravat perfect and pristine, was circling the loaded wagon, tugging on the tied ropes, adjusting the thick canvas tarp, and testing the packed boxes and objects for security. All the while, one of the drivers followed in his wake, performing the same actions, but chattering in a carefree manner. Most remarkable of all was that Mr. Darcy was smiling, laughing, and chattering in the same jaunty way!

"A moment ago," Kitty whispered, "they were talking about a fight in London. I gathered it was a sporting event of some sort. Mr. Darcy remarked on losing his bet on someone named Clubber Clyde. The man there," Kitty indicated the lanky fellow trailing alongside Darcy, "his name is Mr. Hocking, or Tims, according to the other driver, who is Scotty, or Mr. Scott," she pointed at a short man checking the hitches and horses, "was telling Mr. Darcy that he should never bet against Gentleman Joe. I have no idea what any of that means, but you should have seen the way Mr. Hocking was taunting Mr. Darcy!"

Lizzy was watching her beloved and the driver Tims, her smile widening. She could only hear snippets of their conversation through the cracked window, but clearly they were relating on a level plain, the current topic involving the laxity of police patrol at the docks. This reference brought to mind the whole reason why Mr. Darcy was able to converse in a familiar way with the rough men.

When the business of transporting Lizzy's possessions to Pemberley was broached, Mr. Darcy insisted on utilizing the company he employed to carry cargo from the cotton mill he was part owner of in Derby. This news had come as a shock to Mr. Bennet. To Lizzy it wasn't a surprise, her betrothed having gradually acquainted her with the various business enterprises he engaged in, including Pemberley. This same company, while not owned or exclusively contracted to Mr. Darcy and his partners, was also paid – and paid very well – to convey the assortment of goods brought from foreign ports into London via the ships owned by the Pemberley Estate. Mr. Darcy had shared this information humbly with a stunned Mr. Bennet, not out of embarrassment for having wise interests in numerous financial enterprises, but merely because he did not want Mr. Bennet to be offended by his insistence on paying for the transit. The fact was, Mr. Darcy trusted the company, and the men employed, and, as he said to Lizzy's father, "this way my mind will be at ease, knowing Miss Elizabeth's prized possessions will reach Pemberley safely." Mr. Bennet could not argue that logic, the reality being that Mr. Darcy could pay more than he was capable, yet until that moment, even with the extremely generous settlement given his favored daughter, Mr. Bennet hadn't fully realized the scope of wealth Mr. Darcy possessed.

Musing on this, Lizzy noted that the conversation around the wagon had changed.

"This chest is not cushioned enough for my taste. Hand me one of those blankets, Mr. Scott, and let's move this between the boxes of books. That will add stability."

Mr. Darcy had lifted a corner of the canvas, revealing a small curio chest that Lizzy had received for Christmas years ago. She almost hadn't chosen to send it, deciding in the end that although cracked along the bottom edge it was perfect for her collection of miniature tea cups, and held too many memories to leave behind. Observing the personal care he was giving the item, surely worth less than a single china plate at Pemberley, touched her heart to an exquisitely painful degree.

Pivoting from the window, she dashed out of the room, took the steps in one leap, and was beside Mr. Darcy in a matter of seconds. The suddenness startled him, especially with his attention focused on looping another rope around the chest and tightly tying it to the hooks on the wagon's sides.

"Miss Elizabeth! Lovely to see you," he smiled gaily. "As you can see, we are securing your belongings. Mr. Scott and Mr. Hocking are the most capable drivers I know, ensuring with their lives that every last hair clip and handkerchief will reach Pemberley intact. Isn't that right, gentlemen?"

"This is very kind of you, William," Lizzy spoke softly, her hand clasping onto his to gain full attention. "You are very dear to extend yourself, and I hope you realize how tremendously I appreciate it. But, nothing here is worth enough to warrant you taking time away from something more pleasant on this lovely day. You do not need to trouble yourself with tying knots and spreading canvas. Frankly, I cannot imagine most of my things even fitting into the splendor of Pemberley!"

"Walk with me, please, Elizabeth?" He offered his arm, and after a quick order to finish the task directed at the waggoneers, he led a confused Lizzy to the small garden.

Once secluded, he stopped and turned to face her. He was frowning severely. Then he grasped her shoulders in a somewhat painful grip, speaking in a grave tone, "Elizabeth, you must understand that my home will be yours. Every chamber, from my personal bedchamber to yours, even to the smallest parlor or closet, will be under your jurisdiction. Foremost of all, you absolutely must be comfortable within your private rooms. Strip them bare, turn them into replicas of the room you now share with Miss Bennet, or decorate in French or Egyptian motifs, it makes no difference to me as long as you are happy dwelling within them. You are precious to me, do you understand? By extension, all that you own is precious to me, in that it adds to your happiness and is a part of who you are. In all honesty, I would be heartbroken if you left anything special behind at Longbourn since I am excited for the opportunity to sit with you and examine every bit of it so as to learn more of your past and your heart. I apologize if this reveals me as a maudlin sentimentalist, but there you have it! Hopefully our wedding is too far advanced in the planning stages for this to frighten you away."

Lizzy shook her head, words failing her. So, as they were increasingly discovering to be a far better way to express their emotions toward each, she leapt into his waiting arms, showing him the depth of her pleasure and appreciation through kisses and caresses. Not too surprisingly, Mr. Darcy received the message loud and clear.

Mrs. Gardiner's Wedding Night Advice
by C. Allyn Pierson

November 14, 1812

Finally, after a busy and nerve-wracking day of wedding preparations, Jane and Elizabeth found themselves, limp and exhausted, in their shared bedroom preparing for bed. Elizabeth was just finishing tying her nightcap on, fluffing up a perky bow below her left ear and wondering what her wedding night would be like two nights hence. Her mother's "advice" to both girls, given earlier in the week in a private conference, had not relieved her nervousness over that important beginning to her marriage... no, not at all.

Jane was obviously thinking about the same subject, as she hesitantly said, "Um, Lizzy?"

"Yes, my dear?"

"Are you nervous about tomorrow?"

Lizzy pretended to misunderstand her, not quite sure how to answer. "Oh no, the wedding is all planned... nothing can go too terribly wrong... unless Lady Catherine decides to attend." Her attempt to soothe and reassure Jane elicited a weak smile from her beautiful sister.

"No, I am not nervous about the wedding itself... it is... it is the wedding night. All the advice we have received has my mind whirling... in fact, I feel... ill... quite ill." He voice dropped on the last two words so that Lizzy barely heard them. Before Lizzy could respond to her sister's fearful words and her ghastly white face, they heard a gentle tap on the door. Lizzy opened the door to her Aunt Gardiner.

"I hope I do not disturb you, my dear nieces, but I thought I would have a few words with you before bedtime." She paused and her face flushed. "I-I wanted to make sure that your mother talked to both of you about the wedding night."

Lizzy gave her a tremulous smile. "We were just talking about that subject... Mama's dissertation was not terribly... reassuring... nor was it... well, very informative. Poor Jane is feeling quite unwell, in fact."

Mrs. Gardiner sat on the edge of the bed between them and took their hands. "This is, of course, a rather embarrassing subject but I do not want either of you to marry without some idea of what to expect"

Lizzy gave a harsh laugh. "The problem is that we have been given far too much idea about what to expect... and all of it contradictory!"

Her aunt smiled slightly. "I am not really surprised, my dears. Conjugal relations with your husband is a subject about which women have varying opinions. I believe that some of these variations are because of the common practice of marrying for family reasons, security, or wealth. If your husband regards you as a source of wealth, increased social status... or for passing your breeding onto his heirs, it is not surprising that he may not take care of either your heart or your body. I thank God you are both marrying for love... I am sure a marriage of convenience would be so much more difficult when it comes to physical intimacy. Well, to move on to the facts... the wedding night is a little frightening to a young girl, but it can be the beginning of a loving and fulfilling relationship with your husbands. Ummm... the first time you are... with your husbands on your wedding night... you will, of course feel awkward... but you must realize this is the fulfillment of the relationship between a man and a woman who love each other."

She cleared her throat and continued, glancing at her nieces' pink faces. "God has designed men and women to fit perfectly together, but the first time is a little... difficult. Over time you will change and it will be easier, and you will find that you look forward to the private time you spend together."

Lizzy hemmed, then asked, "Do you have any advice for us, my dear aunt?"

"Try to relax and remember that this is the person you trust to care for you for the rest of your life. I am sure your husbands will be gentle and show you what to do.... I would suggest having a glass of wine together to relax and get comfortable with each other and then, go slowly. Although a gentleman would never discussed his previous experience in this area, I hope they have some... it makes things much easier if one of you is experienced, and you, naturally must depend on your husband for that knowledge, as you do not have it yourselves." She blushed even more, but had a determined look on her face as she dug in the pocket of her dressing gown. "My mother gave me this salve to use... down there... it can help ease things and also make you more comfortable the next day." She handed them each a small glass jar. "I guess my advice comes down to trusting your husband and trying to relax."

"Thank you, my dearest aunt." Both Bennet girls embraced their aunt before she left the room, then bustled around putting their clothes away, each tucking their little jar into the bottom of her going-away bag, before jumping into bed. Jane sighed and whispered in Lizzy's ear, "I hope she is right."

The Reflections of
Thomas Bennet
by Maria Grace

November 14, 1812

Thomas Bennet was not by his nature a reflective man. Reflection tended to bring on discomfort and discontent, neither of which he favored. But his house—and his life—were in disarray on the cusp of his daughters' weddings and a little reflection could hardly make his discomfiture worse.

He picked his way around the trunks and boxes piled in the hall way. It was only a matter of time before Mrs. Bennet began demanding they be removed somewhere else lest the guests for the wedding breakfast see them. Thankfully, Mr. Bingley had offered space at Netherfield for his daughters' things.

He slipped into the study and fell into his favorite chair. All the lumps and bumps in the seat matched his own. At least some things in his life would not change. He had had this old chair for decades and resisted all Mrs. Bennet's insistence that it be replaced.

But it seemed like everything else around him was changing and he was certain he did not like it. Change brought disorder and discomfort. Change took away…

A lump rose in his throat. He pushed up from his chair and locked the door. A visit to the brandy decanter, then he returned to his chair.

Lizzy told him Lady Catherine said a daughter was never of much consequence to a father, but the great lady was very, very wrong. He sipped his brandy and leaned his head back. Society told him he should want fine strapping sons—ah heir and a spare to inherit his estate and carry on his name. But he did not.

Oh, he had intended to father a son, to be sure, but his heart had not been in it. Perhaps that was why Fanny only conceived daughters. That was what his father argued when he scolded his eldest son for not producing the required heir. As if a father's will could influence the choices of Providence. He shook his head and closed his eyes.

Though he would never say it aloud, it was best this way. After living with his father and a brother who was just like his sire, Bennet did not trust himself with sons. He could not shake the lingering fear that a son might be like his grandfather or like Collins's father. He shuddered. No, far better to have daughters.

Upon daughters, a man could dote. He could delight in them rather than try to shape them into the image of himself. He laced his fingers and rubbed his thumbs together. He was satisfied with his girls, except for one thing, they were about to leave him.

True, he hardly missed Lydia, but she was her mother's daughter. Jane, and especially Lizzy were more his girls. Jane would sit and read to him. She had the most delightful reading voice. Lizzy was his chess partner and the one with whom he could discuss his interests. How he would miss them. Only yesterday he had bounced them on his knees, taught them to love the classics and to reason. Those days had flown so quickly. If only there were some way to recapture them.

He pulled his top lip down over his teeth. What we would give to turn back time and be with his little girls again. But that could never be. Perhaps the emptiness that kept threatening his consciousness would become a permanent fixture in his life. He stroked his chin.

On the other hand, he could tolerate Bingley's company with some equanimity and, though he would not admit it aloud, Darcy's presence grew more and more tolerable as well. If he could keep Fanny from alienating Jane with constant intrusions, they might remain welcome at Netherfield and even Pemberley. If, no when, there were children, his grandchildren, he could be the grandfather his girls never had. Surely one among them would have Jane's disposition and another Lizzy's. He might be able to recapture those days after all.

He smiled, eyes a little moist. Sometimes a little reflection was indeed good for the soul.

Darcy and Bingley Have a Last Glass Together
by C. Allyn Pierson

November 15, 1812

Darcy was relieved when Georgiana finally went up to bed. His little sister was excited about the wedding and eager to show her enthusiasm by discussing it endlessly, but Darcy felt too jittery to be patient with her. He could not settle down, so he paced, his hands clasped behind his back, to the window and back, wishing he was in his book room at Pemberley instead of the tiny library at Netherfield, where he could barely take three steps before he must turn back. He had paced the same path four times before Bingley came in looking for him.

"There you are Darcy! Did Miss Darcy go upstairs?"

Darcy nodded briefly. "Yes... she must be up early tomorrow, so she wanted to get a good night's sleep. We should probably do the same."

Bingley smiled. "I suppose so... but somehow I don't feel that I shall sleep much."

Darcy ran his hand over the bristles on his chin, embarrassed to be so... what? Nervous? Frightened? Terrified?

His face must have conveyed something of these emotions to Bingley, for his friend quietly went to the decanter and pulled the stopper out of the brandy. "Brandy, Darcy? We must drink to the future."

Darcy took his glass and held it up. "To the future, then, Bingley!" He managed a slight smile. "You seem very calm about getting married, Bingley."

"Calm?" Bingley considered. "No, I do not believe that is the correct word… Excited to wed my beautiful Jane… yes. Exultant to be able to spend the rest of my days and nights with the most beautiful woman in England?…yes… Nervous about finally being alone with my wife-to-be? Definitely."

Darcy, in spite of himself, laughed. "Bingley, you are a delightful breath of fresh air."

"Don't tell me, Darcy, that you have doubts about marrying Miss Elizabeth! Surely not!"

"No… not doubts… not really." He took another sip of his brandy and gazed up at the ceiling for a moment, before saying, "Elizabeth has entrusted me with her heart forever. I find that a sobering responsibility… I would not feel this way if I were marrying my cousin, as my aunt and my mother wished. It would be a business arrangement made by our families. I just hope I am able to make her happy." He shrugged, trying to appear relaxed as he swirled the brandy in his glass.

Bingley thought about these words as he rolled the fine brandy over his tongue. "I do not feel that way, Darcy. I guess I trust Jane enough to have made the right choice accepting me. I know she is the one woman I will ever love. I trust that it will be enough to get us through any difficulties in life."

Darcy stared at him for several beats, then set his almost empty brandy glass on the table next to him. "You know what, Bingley? Sometimes you are not such a puddinghead as you appear!" He grinned and clapped his friend on the shoulder, then went upstairs to bed.

A Conversation between Jane and Lizzy on the Eve of their Weddings
by Jane Odiwe

November 15, 1812

Elizabeth watched Jane take the pins from her hair as she sat before the looking glass on the dressing table. She noted, as if for the first time, Jane's nimble fingers following the nightly ritual Lizzy had witnessed for years. With swift strokes, Jane brushed her hair back from the crown and the sides before inclining her head to reach underneath the tresses at her nape. Lustrous curls tumbled about her shoulders and cascaded down the back of her nightgown. In candlelight, her sister thought she'd never looked more beautiful.

Jane sat up to meet Elizabeth's eyes in the mirror.

'Oh, Lizzy, do you realise this is the last night we shall spend together? I've been so caught up in wedding preparations that I'm not certain I have fully comprehended the fact until now.'

'Do you mean to tell me that you have only just understood our mother's timely advice that we shall be expected to share our husband's beds?' quipped Lizzy. 'Or, that you've not fully grasped that implicit in her motherly counsel was a pearl of a reminder that in future we should be "slaves to our masters in order to warrant connubial felicity for all eternity!"'

Jane laughed, delighting in her sister's humour. 'I have never been so embarrassed in all my life. From Aunt Gardiner such advice is so well-meaning, so tactfully done, but our mother could not have made a more uncomfortable speech.'

'Lizzy! Don't snigger!' mimicked Elizabeth in imitation of her mama, 'How do you think your father and I have enjoyed such a happy marriage for so long? It isn't by the efficacy of separate sleeping arrangements such as the Longs and the Lucas's have adopted except, I daresay, if I'd produced an heir I might have befallen such a fate myself. Though, truth to tell, Mr. Bennet has never made a secret of the fact that he still finds me irresistible and if you can still say the same after twenty four years of marriage, you will be doing well!'

'Please stop, Lizzy, my sides are aching with laughter.'

'Oh, Jane, I shall miss our evening conversations.' Elizabeth sat down nudging her sister further along the seat.

'And all our confidences,' said her sister. 'How shall I do without you? Mr. Darcy is to have all your good humour and share all your secrets besides the attention of your 'fine eyes', which look as pretty tonight as I ever saw them.'

'You'll do very well, I am sure, when you're lying in the arms of Mr. Bingley. I never saw a couple so well suited, so made to have confidences in one another. There are few people who become a superior entity together than are able to work as two halves but I sincerely believe that you and Charles are the exception. You were made for one another. Besides, you will not have time to think about me. As mistress of Netherfield, you will be a very busy lady.'

'But, will I be mistress of Netherfield, Lizzy? I am sure Caroline Bingley will have very firm ideas about who is in charge and I cannot think she will take kindly to me attempting to step into her shoes.'

'If anyone can deal with Miss Bingley, it is you, sweet Jane, and I believe you will achieve your ends with grace and charm. In any case, I am certain that Charles will make it clear from the start that you have precedence. He may be the most obliging, complying gentleman that ever lived but he loves you with all his heart. Your happiness will be his own and if that means he has to speak sternly to his sister, I am certain he will be your champion.'

'As I am sure Mr. Darcy will be, too, when it comes to his aunt, Lizzy.'

'Goodness, Lady Catherine, I hadn't given her a thought! Well, I doubt we shall ever see her. After all, from tomorrow the shades of Pemberley will be thoroughly polluted!'

'I wouldn't be so sure, dearest Elizabeth. Curiosity may well get the better of her. She may be planning a visit as we speak.'

'Now, you are teasing, Jane. At least we are spared her glowering presence at the wedding.'

'The wedding – Lizzy, can you believe it? We are getting married tomorrow.'

Elizabeth took her sister's hands in her own. 'My love, I can believe it and I know we shall both be very happy. And, even if we shall be apart for a while, as we have never been before, I know our husbands will not let us suffer.'

'No, it will be difficult enough for both of them to be apart; they have become so like brothers!'

'You and Charles shall come to Pemberley as soon as Christmas if you would like it and I shall persuade you both to look at houses whilst you are there. I have one in mind that Mr. Darcy tells me is very suitable and only just over the border in the next county. If I have my way, we will not be separated for long.'

Jane threw her arms around her sister hugging her tightly. 'You will write to me, won't you?'

'Every day, I promise.'

Though not sentimental by nature, Elizabeth felt the tears prick at her eyelids. In her heart she knew life would never be quite the same and that tomorrow they would face new lives, not as the young girls they'd been at Longbourn House but as married women with all the excitement and challenges that would bring.

'Oh look, Jane,' she said turning her face to the window to hide her emotions, 'it's snowing!'

Whirling through the night sky snowflakes plummeted, settling like swan feathers against the casement window. A robin flashing his scarlet breast flew into the tree whose branches tapped at the glass. Beyond, the fields formed a patchwork across the Hertfordshire countryside. Familiar scenes and sounds, and a lifetime of reminiscences were wrapped around the sisters in that moment like the arms that clasped them so tightly.

Mr. Bennet, Mr. Darcy, Mr. Gardiner, and Mr. Bingley Share a Brandy
by Vera Nazarian

November 15, 1812

After the splendid meal was over, the gentlemen retired to Mr. Bennet's library for some soothing peace and after-dinner brandy, leaving the ladies to laugh and exclaim and fuss over tomorrow's double nuptials.

Mr. Bennet, who under normal circumstances hardly ever allowed anyone to breach the comfort of his personal retreat and literary sanctuary, welcomed his two future sons-in-law and Mr. Gardiner with a pleasure unprecedented—even if he only revealed the extent of it by the appearance of a wily and infinitesimal smile when no one was looking directly at him. Mr. Bennet simply could not help himself.

Mr. Darcy and Mr. Bingley availed themselves of additional comfortable chairs that had to be brought into the room, since the small chaise longue was permanently covered with casual piles of opened books. Meanwhile, Mr. Bennet gave up his own favorite reading chair to accommodate Mr. Gardiner. He himself remained standing before the window, refusing a seat and decidedly too excited to stay in one spot. He soon occupied himself by choosing his finest decanter and glasses and personally pouring brandy for everyone.

"You have a handsome library indeed, Mr. Bennet," said Darcy, receiving his glass. "It is apparent where your two eldest daughters have acquired their love of erudition."

"I always recall Pemberley's magnificent library," said Bingley with a happy glance at his friend. "I agree, this little room houses an extraordinary number of books. My dearest Miss Bennet must come here often."

"That she does indeed, when I allow it," replied Mr. Bennet. "And so does Lizzy, who admittedly must be turned out by force whenever I need a bit of my usual reading time. Smart girl, that one! I do say, Darcy, you've gotten yourself a sharp mind in a wife; a rather remarkable one, I must say. To be sure she will outwit your wittiest and outthink your most thoughtful; indeed, with time I believe you will come to appreciate it even more. For unlike beauty, which fades rather quickly from the onslaught of foolishness, a truly fine female mind is much like a fine vintage. You shall be sipping well unto old age."

Darcy smiled. "Oh, I am very well aware of it, and more than appreciative."

"Elizabeth is a delightful and clever child," remarked Mr. Gardiner pleasantly, partaking of his brandy, "and so is our lovely Jane, who may not be as outspoken, but feels and thinks just as well, as deeply, I note; and Mrs. Gardiner tells me constantly. You have raised several remarkable daughters, Mr. Bennet."

"I do believe much of the credit for it goes to this library," the proud father replied. "Now, if only the two youngest ones spent a bit more time here, and the middle one spent a bit less, and the mother actually entered this chamber-of-learning's wondrous confines and picked up but a single tome now and then—then our family would have nothing but brilliance to show for itself."

"Bah!" said Mr. Gardiner, and shook his head in kind amusement.

"What? You think I jest, gentlemen?" said Mr. Bennet with an entirely too straight a countenance. And after general hearty chuckles were shared, Mr. Bennet proposed a toast.

"To the library! To daughters, and to my new sons!" said Mr. Bennet. "In wit, intelligence, wholesomeness, and rational family connections, I am suddenly the most extravagantly wealthy man I know. Tomorrow you all wed, and I gain!"

The gentlemen raised their glasses; much joyful clinking was heard, and then they drank.

Darcy and Elizabeth Take a Walk
by Sharon Lathan

November 15, 1812

The unseasonably pleasant weather for November in Hertfordshire was perfect for a walk. That was one of the voiced reasons daily given to the Bennets for what had swiftly evolved into a habitual activity for the betrothed couples. Mr. Darcy and Mr. Bingley offered the benefits of exercise and fresh air for one's health, as well as the selfless wish to provide a period of peaceful quiet to reign at the increasingly chaotic Longbourn, as additional logic for spiriting the eldest Bennet daughters away from their watchful parents.

Mrs. Bennet typically waved them off without a glance, her attention engaged with some wedding detail. Mr. Bennet pretended to consider the matter, extended the obligatory warnings to stay together and not stray too far – knowing full well his orders would be disregarded – and pierced each gentleman with as stern a glare as he could muster, before granting permission.

On this day, the afternoon before the scheduled nuptials, the ruse was all but ignored, with only the stickler-for-propriety Mr. Darcy making the slightest attempt to act interested in Mr. Bennet's opinion.

While in eyesight of the house, the foursome walked in a close knot as they set out on the frequently trod trail leading between Longbourn and Netherfield. As they strolled along, conversation was light and companionable, laughter and banter flowing easily. In every way it was a highly enjoyable activity equally appreciated by all, which is one reason why the inevitable conclusion to their joint exercise was surprising.

Never was it precisely planned. Never could either couple recall exactly when the four-way discourse ended or when the gap widened or who diverted onto a side trail first. It simply…. happened. Yet, surprising as it may be in one respect, not a soul considered retracing steps to find the others! To put it bluntly, as the day when controlling their passions would no longer be an issue loomed closer, both ardent young man unconsciously decided to toss caution into the wind. Clearly the ladies were of the same opinion.

"Georgiana insisted I reiterate her pleasure in spending yesterday shopping with you in Meryton," Darcy said. "If I had forgotten to relay her message she would be devastated beyond repair."

Lizzy laughed at his dramatic tones. "I would never wish for Miss Darcy to be devastated, however she adequately expressed her appreciation yesterday with enthusiastic praise. I am quite certain that never has a living soul been so utterly delighted by the charms of Meryton. If I had not seen Lambton myself, I might presume it no more than a crude village with mud huts and pigs wandering freely in the streets, based on Miss Darcy's response to our humble town."

"In her desire to please she can be overly dramatic at times."

Lizzy glanced upward into his calm, serious face. "Indeed. I have noticed this propensity within certain Darcys. It begs the question as to where this trait originated. One of your parents? Or better yet is it a familial connection with a famed stage actor? How scandalous and exciting would that be!"

Darcy met her impish expression with a teasing grin. "I deem it best to wait until after our wedding before revealing the skeletons hidden in our closets, my dear. Allow me another day of being perfection in your sight."

Lizzy rolled her eyes, harrumphing and jabbing her elbow into his side. "Arrogant man! Must I again chronicle your numerous faults?"

"There is no need. I now have them memorized." He leaned to kiss her cheek, chuckling and drawing her closer to his side. "In truth, neither of my parents was particularly gifted in dramatics. They possessed excellent humors, loving to laugh and jest much as you do, but displayed minimal acting skills. The tendency runs deepest with my Uncle George, and my Aunt Beryl as well. I long for the day when you can meet them both."

"As do I."

"Soon we shall be at Pemberley, together as a family. There you can acquaint yourself with my ancestry and feel the strength of our relations."

"Our relations," she repeated in a whisper, pausing on the trail to stare into his tender eyes. An affectionate, slow smile spread. "I like the sound of that."

Darcy matched her wide smile with one equally as brilliant and filled with love. And, a generous allotment of raw passion that sent a pleasant shiver racing up Lizzy's spine. The wild flutters attacking her insides were simultaneously exhilarating and flustering. The latter emotion provided the strength necessary to break the mesmerizing pull of his gaze, Lizzy's eyes darting across the landscape surrounding and noting, for the first time in nearly an hour, exactly where they were.

They shared a mischievous grin, nodded once, and without speaking a word broke into a chase toward the copse of willow trees located on a small rise near the fenced boundary of Netherfield Park. It was a preferred destination during their walks, the secluded spot a childhood favorite Lizzy had shown to her betrothed weeks ago.

Lizzy reached the trees first, although the long-legged Darcy obviously forfeited. Her shout of triumph morphed into a squeal when he grabbed her about the waist, lifted her off her feet, and twirled twice in a circle before halting their laughter with a firmly planted kiss. As was becoming more and more common, the playful, caste kiss rapidly spiraled into a serious breach of all propriety.

Within seconds their bodies were fused along every plane, hands roaming freely as the kiss accelerated.

Abruptly they pulled apart, and retreated to lean onto opposite trees. Staring at each other with passion-drugged eyes, a full five minutes of silence passed – not counting the heavy panting and pounding heartbeats – before speech was remotely possible. And then it was Lizzy blurting the only coherent thought ringing in her brain.

"I love kissing you!" She felt the blush flooding her cheeks, released a nervous laugh and stammered while peering at the ground, "I imagine that is obvious."

"Yes." Darcy choked the word, clearing his throat before continuing, "as I am certain it is obvious I love kissing you, Elizabeth. Ardently so, in fact, which is why it best I remain over here for at least a few more minutes."

Lizzy lifted her gaze. Darcy was standing with hands flattened harshly against his thighs. He wore a dreamy smile, the shadows of the shaded alcove unable to hide his darkly glittering eyes.

"Fortunately, by this time tomorrow I will no longer be required to halt the joyous delight of kissing you. You shall then be Mrs. Darcy, my wife," he whispered the word reverently, "and kissing you will only be the beginning to all the ways I intent to express my love for you."

He paused, inhaled deeply, and visibly shook himself. Flashing a grin almost normal and speaking in a lightly jesting tone, he went on, "The timing of our wedding is fortuitous, since I do believe my prized forbearance has been exhausted. One more day and you would have another fault to add to your list."

"Considering the pleasure I receive in teasing you about your faults, Mr. Darcy, perhaps adding another would be a kindness."

"Ah! Do not tempt me, Elizabeth! Trust me when I say that the pleasure I intend to bestow upon you tomorrow night will be far greater than a mere tease will grant."

Lizzy flushed scarlet at his implication, but she did not look away from his lusty gaze. Rather, she met it with as much intensity as possible considering her general lack of experience in such matters. Silence again inundated the dimly lit willow grove, broken this time by Darcy as he crossed to where she stood.

"Now, Miss Bennet, I must return you to Longbourn. I somehow doubt the fact that we will be husband and wife in less than twenty-four hours shall prevent your father from skinning me alive if darkness has fallen before you are safely inside." Cupping her face between his broad hands, he bent until a breath away from her upturned and parted lips. "Not, however, before I thoroughly kiss you one last time so your dreams tonight will be of me, our love, and the promise of pleasure soon to come."

Later Lizzy would inform him that his final kiss as her betrothed accomplished the task remarkably well.

Preparing the Wedding Breakfast
by Nina Benneton

November 15, 1812

"What do you mean we have to make another Bride Cake by tomorrow?" The cook all but shouted at Mrs. Hill. "What's wrong with the two cakes we have made?"

Mrs. Hill cringed. She didn't blame the cook for being upset. "Mrs. Bennet has learned Mr. Darcy detests orange, lemon or citrons, and Mrs. Bennet now directs the kitchen to make a new bride cake."

"Mr. Darcy! Mr. Darcy!" Cook waved a wooden spoon wildly about, narrowly missing a game hanging from the rafter. "I'm heartily sick of that gentleman. He has caused me no ends of trouble. Everything must be done for his highness's particulars tastes, says the Missus. The ham must not be so salty, the lobster must be fresh, the white soup must be…"

"I'll get the eggs." Leaving the cook to rant, Mrs. Hill escaped. She doubted the solemn Mr. Darcy cared about the cake or the ham or much of anything except sitting and staring at Miss Elizabeth, but that was not something one could tell Mrs. Bennet, especially when the mistress's nerves were quite frazzled already on the eve of her daughters' wedding.

Within yards of the hen house, Mrs. Hill heard, somewhere behind the coop, a woman's soft voice giggling, followed by the man's rumbled laughter. Undoubtedly that kitchen maid she'd hired to help with the wedding preparations was now carrying on with one of the stable boys. Mouth pressed tight, Mrs. Hill rounded the bush, prepared to harshly discipline the servants. She stopped short at the sight of the couple in front of her.

"Mrs. Hill, whatever is the matter?" Miss Elizabeth, wearing a straw poke bonnet and a pistache-colored pelisse, was standing perhaps too close to her fiancé than was proper, but forgivable considering in less than twenty-four hours, she would be Mrs. Darcy.

Mr. Darcy, imperturbable as always, merely inclined his head in greeting. Tap tap, his walking stick impatiently made muffled noise against a low stump at his feet.

"Beg pardon, Sir, Miss Bennet." Flustered, Mrs. Hill curtsied. From the heightened color on Miss Elizabeth's cheeks, and the anticipatory gleam in Mr. Darcy's eyes, the pair was setting out for a walk, likely to the secluded grove of willows near Netherfield. "I was on my way to the hen's house for some eggs."

"Should you not get a kitchen maid to do it?" Miss Elizabeth stepped closer. "Poor Hill, you looked peaked. Has my mother been unbearable with the wedding breakfast preparation?"

"Not at all," Mrs. Hill protested. Mrs. Bennet was no more unbearable than usual, but she would not dream of uttering that.

"Come, Hilly," Elizabeth said. "I shall not have you run to the ground on my last day at home. What is the latest calamity that has sent my normally unflappable Hilly to the hen house to escape? What impossible feat has my mother directed the kitchen staff to undertake now?"

Perhaps it was the way Miss Elizabeth said 'Hilly,' or perhaps it was the realization that the young woman standing in front of her would be leaving Longbourn for the wilds of the north country, and thus Mrs. Hill would be bereft of her favorite Bennet daughter, the housekeeper found herself embolden with frankness. Before she knew it, she told about the mistress's latest order, ending with, "'Tis not that it's impossible to bake another bride cake, but that means a very late night tonight for the kitchen staff. I would not be surprised if cook gives notice before the wedding breakfast tomorrow, and we all will be at sixes and sevens."

"There, now, Hill, no need to make yourself overwrought," Miss Elizabeth soothed. She turned to her fiancé. "Sir, how shall we fix this?"

"Not have a wedding breakfast tomorrow?" Mr. Darcy said placidly, his walking stick never stopped its tap tap. "Bingley and Miss Bennet may have our share of the Bride Cake and we leave for our wedding trip immediately after the service."

Miss Elizabeth crossed her arms and lifted an eyebrow at her fiancé.

"No?" Mr. Darcy quirked an eyebrow back at her. "Pity."

"You did tell my mother earlier you detest the sharp taste of oranges, lemons, and citron, if I remember correctly," Miss Elizabeth said.

"She repeatedly enquired about my particular gustatory delights; I was simply humoring her." Mr. Darcy stilled his walking stick and straightened. "Very well. I shall go to the kitchen and talk to the staff."

Mr. Darcy in the kitchen? Mrs. Hill nearly fainted at the thought. "Please, no need, sir."

Miss Elizabeth's eyes were lively, though her voice was calm. "Thank you, Mr. Darcy. Shall I hold your walking stick for you?"

"No, this shan't take long." Mr. Darcy swung the walking stick in a jaunty arc and headed toward the kitchen.

Gracious heavens! He was serious. Mrs. Hill rushed to follow him.

Miss Elizabeth's hands pulled on Mrs. Hill's arm, stopping her. "Let him handle it, Hill."

Mr. Darcy was now near the kitchen's entrance. Mrs. Hill shook off Miss Elizabeth's hand and hurried to catch up to the long-legged gentleman. "But, sir, whatever will you say to the kitchen staff?"

"I shall remind them when the Bride Cake is served tomorrow, I will already, God's willing, be a married man." Mr. Darcy paused at the entrance and threw his fiancée a mischievous smile. "As such, it would not be too early for me to become used to the tart taste of things."

Taking no offense at all at being called a tart taste, the soon-to-be Mrs. Darcy laughed gleefully and clapped her hands as Mr. Darcy disappeared into the kitchen. "See, Hill, there is no need at all to make a new Bride Cake."

Mrs. Hill slumped against the door frame and fanned herself. Smelling salts. She needed smelling salts. Mr. Darcy was now in the kitchen!

Mr. & Mrs. Bennet Share a Moment before the Wedding
by Vera Nazarian

November 16, 1812

With the moment of the wedding approaching, and the two eldest Bennet daughters getting ready upstairs, the household was in a joyful uproar. Mrs. Bennet spent her time wringing her hands, rushing up and down the stairs, pointing out bits of lace, jewelry, and attire to the maids who assisted the brides, and directing Mrs. Hill and the other servants to "make haste, make haste!" in setting the table for the wedding breakfast that was to take place soon afterwards. She then stood fussing over every tiny detail, commenting on the servants' performance, the condition of the plates and cutlery, and the setting out of fine spotless glasses—until Mr. Bennet gently took her aside, and they sat down together "to catch a breath" in the nearby parlor.

"Oh, Mr. Bennet! I am expiring! I am departed! How I shall be driven to distraction! And they are not even wed yet!" his wife exclaimed, collapsing on the sofa, but continuing to fidget with nervous energy. She was worrying her handkerchief, the same one that she had managed to carry with her everywhere these past few days—not unlike a small pug, it occurred to Mr. Bennet with amusement—and it was apparent the bit of muslin was soon to be in tatters.

"Now, now, my dear; no need to be driven to anything, at least not yet—not until a quarter of an hour. At that point the wedding carriages will be doing the driving, and you will be spared that odious duty normally given to horses or conveyances."

"Oh! You make jest now, Mr. Bennet, how can you! Our two eldest are about to be married to the finest gentlemen in the realm! How can you sit so calmly now?"

"My dear, if you prefer, I shall stand or march in place. But I do not believe it will make any difference for my own peace of mind."

"Stand, sit, gallop—do whatever you like, Mr. Bennet! Our daughters are getting married to ten and five thousand a year!"

"Well, yes, and so they are; and a fine union they shall have, currency and young girls. Their offspring shall be shillings and pence."

Mrs. Bennet's countenance immediately filled with thunder, and she swatted her spouse with her handkerchief, exclaiming, "Mr. Bennet, I am not capable of amusement right now, I am so distracted; my poor nerves are on the verge of breaking, and I shall have none of it from you! They are getting dressed, just think, RIGHT NOW! In minutes, they shall come down, and then we shall all go to church, and the guests will be there and—and—"

Mr. Bennet spoke not a word. For the first time in a long time, he simply smiled and pulled his wife into his arms.

She squealed, then gave in to his embrace fitfully and started to laugh, or maybe cry, her face pressed against his chest.

"There, there, my love..." he whispered, momentarily forgetting all jest, all her foolishness, all the compounding of the years, for he was remembering their own wedding day.

"Mr. Bennet...," she spoke tentatively, swallowing a sob. "Will they be—"

"They will," he replied, knowing exactly what she was asking.

They remained quiet for one long moment of unexpected wonder, both savoring the memory of their own past, a gift.

In the hallway the clock struck the hour.

Mrs. Bennet started and the moment was gone. "Oh, Mr. Bennet! Gracious me! I must go and help them dress! And surely you need to go do something or other! Dearest Jane and Lizzy!

Dearest Mr. Darcy and Mr. Bingley! The guests! The church! Oh, dear heavens, the rack of lamb! We must make haste! Make haste!" she cried, rising, and her husband signed; then he stood up likewise.

From somewhere upstairs, they could hear the joyful clamor that was the servants and their two eldest daughters getting ready for their weddings.

"Well, my dear," said Mr. Bennet to his wife, or possibly just to himself, "I do believe I am entirely content."

Longbourn Ladies Dress
for the Wedding
by Susan Mason-Milks

November 16, 1812

Elizabeth stood behind Jane carefully pinning her hair up and patiently winding ribbons though the curls.

"This is the last time we will do this, you know," said Lizzy. "From now on your maid Molly will be fixing your hair."

"Lizzy, don't be a goose. We can do this again when we visit," Jane replied trying to cheer her sister.

"But it will not be the same." Lizzy and Jane's eyes met in the mirror and they shared a knowing look.

Just then, Kitty and Mary swept in, giggling as they gathered around.

"What do you think of our new dresses?" asked Kitty, twirling in a circle to display her new pink gown to its fullest advantage. "Mary, show them the beautiful lace on yours."

Mary was usually the last one to be looked at or admired, and so when her sisters turned to look at her dress, the attention made her blush. Then they realized that something was different about her.

"Mary, you look lovely!" Jane exclaimed. And in fact, she did. Her hair was done more softly around her face making her look less severe. Lavender-colored ribbons, the same color as the flowers on her muslin dress, were wound artfully into her hair.

"I fixed her hair," cried Kitty. "Did I not do a splendid job of it? For once she did not insist that I pull it back so tightly. I think it does wonders for her face. Why…"

"Please stop talking about me as if I were not here," Mary said, clearly embarrassed at the compliments she was receiving.

"But, Mary, you look wonderful. In fact, I have never seen you look better." Impulsively, Elizabeth pulled her blushing sister into a hug.

"I think entirely too much is made of how young ladies look. It is our more substantive qualities and accomplishments that are most important," Mary pronounced.

"Yes, however, it does not hurt if the outside is just as lovely, too," Jane said, putting a reassuring hand on Mary's arm.

"We should be talking about you and Lizzy today. After all, it is your wedding day," said Mary, clearly trying to deflect the conversation away from herself.

"What do you think of what I have done with Jane's hair?" Elizabeth asked, returning to the subject at hand.

"I think you should add more ribbons," Kitty suggested.

"And I think it is perfect as it is," said Mary with a rare smile. "She does not need more ribbons to enhance her natural beauty."

"Thank you, Mary, dear. Now enough fussing about me; it is your turn, Lizzy." Jane stood up and offered the seat to her sister.

"Yes, we should all help with Lizzy's hair!" At that, Kitty nudged her sister into the chair and picked up the brush.

As Kitty worked diligently over Elizabeth's dark locks, her sisters giggled with excitement, sometimes all talking at the same time.

"Are you anxious about tonight?" Kitty asked nonchalantly. They all looked at her with wide eyes. "Well, it is what we are all thinking about, is it not?"

The response was more nervous giggles and blushes all around.

"You know that is not a proper topic of discussion for unmarried ladies," Mary scolded.

"Oh, do not be such a bore, Mary. When Lydia was here after her wedding, she told me all about it — how terrifying the marital bed is and all the indelicate things a husband…well, expects," Kitty said with a gulp.

Jane and Elizabeth looked at each other with their eyebrows raised.

"Although I am certain that Mr. Darcy and Mr. Bingley would never behave in such a manner," she quickly added.

There was another awkward silence.

"Oh, heavens, Kitty! You surely did not believe everything she told you," Elizabeth exclaimed.

"Why not? She is now a married woman and knows all about the conjugal mysteries we are not even allowed to think about," Kitty told them.

After a moment of silence, Lizzy spoke. "I cannot go into details, but Jane and I had a letter from Lydia sharing her 'married woman' wisdom. I am certain what she said had at least some elements of truth to it, but it was certainly nothing at all like what Aunt Gardiner has told us to expect. The words 'terrifying' and 'indelicate' were never mentioned at all."

Another moment of complete silence followed during which all of the Bennet girls considered the situation. First, Lizzy started to laugh, then Jane and Mary and finally, Kitty. They laughed until tears rolled down their cheeks, and they were holding their sides. Mary and Kitty leaned on each other for support just to stand. Mary pulled out her handkerchief and patted her eyes.

When at last they were able to be coherent again, Mary said, "You know Lydia is in Newcastle right this moment laughing even harder than we are at the little joke she thinks she has played on you, Kitty."

"I was under the distinct impression you believed her, too, Mary," Kitty replied a little indignantly.

Mary frowned. "I did not."

"Oh, at moment like this, I do wish Lydia was here with us," said Jane wiping away the last of her tears with the back of her hand.

"Yes, so I could get my hands around her little neck," said Kitty, stifling another giggle. "In spite of everything, I do miss her sometimes though."

"Do you also miss chasing men in red coats or running wild at parties so that we are all mortified with shame?" Mary asked.

Kitty turned serious. "No, Mary, my eyes are wide open now. It has become very clear to me that I was following the wrong sister. I only hope Lizzy and Jane will allow me to spend more time with them. I would prefer to learn to be a lady – just as they are." Her eyes began to twinkle with mischief. "Then, perhaps, I will catch a rich husband, too."

Jane was the first to put an arm around Kitty, and then Elizabeth joined them. After Mary was waved over, she finally came and put her arms around her sisters.

"This is more like it – true sisterly affection. I love all of you very much, and you will always be welcome at Pemberley," said Elizabeth. Then she added with a note of humor in her voice, "That is, as soon as I actually manage to learn my way around my new home. It is so large that I know I shall be in constant terror of becoming lost. Why, the house has so many hallways and stairways that I might need to use a ball of thread like Theseus in the Minotaur's Labyrinth. It would be too embarrassing if Mr. Darcy had to send out the footmen or maids looking for me."

"It might be much more fun if Mr. Darcy went looking for you himself," Kitty said with a giggle.

"Kitty! Where do you get these ideas? " Elizabeth cried as she broke into laughter again and her sisters joined her.

"Oh, look at the time! We must hurry! We have only a few minutes before we leave for the church, and there is still so much to do!" Jane told them.

Suddenly, tears formed in Mary's eyes.

"What is it, my dear Mary? This is not like you. Are you unwell?" asked Jane moving quickly to put an arm around her sister.

Mary tried looking at the floor to hide the tears and shook her head. Jane put a gentle finger under Mary's chin and lifted it. The watery pools that were forming seemed to magnify and distort her golden brown eyes. Instead of pulling away, as she normally did in a situation such as this, Mary smiled through the tears as Jane used a linen handkerchief to blot her sister's eyes.

"I am so very happy for you, but after today, you will belong more to your husbands than to us. It will all be so different," Mary told them between sniffles.

"We have talked about this before. We are sisters — forever and always. That is something that no wedding can change."

"I know that."

"Then what is it?" Elizabeth asked. "Are you afraid that you will never fall in love and get married?"

"Oh, romance is for other people, not for me," Mary said, trying to sound serious.

"That does not have to be true, sweetheart, but for love to have a chance, you must open your heart and see the possibilities. If I had not taken the time to get to know Mr. Darcy, I might never have discovered all of his fine qualities. He would have passed out of my life as an enigmatic figure, a puzzle never to be solved, and I would be the poorer for it," Elizabeth told her.

Mary managed a smile. "I shall remember your advice."

"Come here, Mary, let me fix your face so those tears do not show. We cannot have all of Meryton saying that the brides' sisters were crying even before the wedding. They might think you are not happy for us."

"I am happy for you. Truly." Mary hugged Jane.

Then in the distance, they heard their mother's shrill voice calling, "Girls, girls! The carriages are here. You must come at once!"

Scrambling, they picked up bonnets, gloves and other little accoutrements. Jane, Kitty, and Mary rushed off leaving Elizabeth as the last one out. After a brief look around the room, she smiled and closed the door on this part of her life.

Mrs. Bennet's
Wedding Reflections
by Jane Odiwe

November 16, 1812

Happy for all her maternal feelings was the day on which Mrs. Bennet got rid of her two most deserving daughters. With what delighted pride she reflected on the day's events as she and Mr. Bennet sat amongst the detritus left from the celebrations in the dining-parlour.

'Mr. Bennet, did you ever attend such a wedding? What a remarkable day! I think it all passed off exceptionally well. I am excessively pleased with everything. Everyone behaved prettily and I never saw so many onlookers gawping at the church gate. Mrs. Long's nieces seemed enraptured, in particular. Of course, those poor girls will probably never see a wedding of their own. They cannot help being so very plain but I like them well enough for it. Plainer even than Charlotte Lucas – not that I think her exceptionally so, but then she is such a cherished friend. Next to Jane, anyone would be at a disadvantage. I said to Lady Lucas and Mrs. Long, "Did you ever see a more radiant bride?" and, of course, they concurred.'

'How could they do anything else, my dear?'

'And I know you are not fond of discussing lace, Mr. Bennet, but our girls' lace marked them out with distinction. Elizabeth's veil has been in the Darcy family since the time of good old Henry, I believe. I daresay Anne Boleyn herself saw it grace some noble head.'

'More than likely. And before she lost her own, I presume.'

'Mr. Bennet! Nothing you say will vex me today.'

'I am glad to hear it!'

Smiles decked the face of Mrs. Bennet. 'And dear Bingley is so good-looking and everything a gentleman should be even if he has not quite the consequence of dear Darcy.'

'Dear Darcy, is it?' Mr. Bennet smirked and picked up a newspaper before settling himself in a chair by the fire.

'I have always thought so. Dear, dear, Darcy! Did he not look a picture in his black coat? I cannot even think that a red one could improve him, you know, despite my partiality for a uniform. Such a tall and handsome man! Always obliging! So charming! And, so rich!

'He is generous too, for which we are exceedingly grateful – for more weddings than this one,' added Mr. Bennet (under his breath) from behind the paper.

'Well, who else should have done it? Mr. Darcy would not notice if he settled an amount on twenty weddings! The money is a pin-prick on my best gown, a mere drop in the ocean, a single star in the heavens! Though I have to say despite Darcy's generosity, my Lydia did not have the best of it. Her nuptials were a poor affair but I have lately forgiven my son-in-law for he is helping dear Wickham rise in his profession.'

'I am certain Darcy would be delighted if only he knew how magnanimous you are towards him, Mrs. Bennet.'

'To him I could not be anything else. I only hope that Lizzy has a true appreciation of his worth and does not go letting her tongue run away with her, as she is wont to do. I cannot help thinking that Jane with all her sweet ways might not have been a better match for him, but then Lizzy could never have suited Bingley. Yet, I should have thought she might be more capable of keeping Miss Caroline Bingley in her place. What a delight to see my Jane take precedence over her. Did you see her countenance as they left the church?'

'Whose countenance?' Mr. Bennet's own peered around the edge of the newspaper.

'Why, Miss Bingley, of course! She will have to give way to Jane on everything now. I do not suppose Miss High and Mighty will relish playing second fiddle. If only we could get her married off and then she would have to leave Netherfield. Colonel Fitzwilliam might do if he did not seem so keen to marry Miss Georgiana, or Mr. Hurst's brother, if he were perhaps taller. But, then Miss Bingley would be too close to Netherfield and I feel sure she would be better placed far away.'

'I daresay, Jane and Miss Bingley will get along until such time as a suitor comes to call.'

'Well, if anyone can make that sly cat purr, it will be my Jane. And talking of purring cats, it brings to mind the bowls of golden cream served at our wonderful wedding breakfast!'

'Yes, it was a very satisfactory meal, my dear.'

'Satisfactory! Hill outdid herself, I'm sure Mr. Darcy's three French cooks could not have done more! Such sweet ham! The tongue so pink, the cake such a confection! And all a hundred times better than what we endured at Charlotte Lucas's wedding. I never saw a more paltry lack of victuals in my life – stale bread rolls, the cream curdled and a piece of pound cake I wouldn't give to a beggar. Lady Lucas keeps a very poor table, and I keep an excellent one if I say so myself. But, I do not trust my own partiality, it is what everybody says.'

'I'm sure they do, my dear, Mrs. Bennet.'

'Anyway, it is all over and now all I've got left to think on is that three of my dear girls have left me, though it is a comfort for me to know that Jane is so near when my dearest Lydia is so very far away. It is no surprise that Lizzy is gone off to the Peaks – nothing she might do would be a revelation! No doubt, Kitty and Mary will move to Scotland and have done with it! Jane will follow when she wants a home close to her sister and I shall be left, a poor widow all on my own at the mercy of Mr. Collins and his wife!'

'I am glad to see you have plans for me at any rate, Mrs. Bennet. But, I hope you will not put me into too early a grave and deny me the pleasure of knowing my grandchildren.'

'Oh, Mr. Bennet, what a happy thought! Lord bless me! Good gracious! After today, I daresay we shall not have to wait too long for such an announcement!'

Mr. Bennet shook his head and disappeared once more behind the news of the day.

Caroline's Wedding Reflections
by Shannon Winslow

November 16, 1812

"How thrilling!" a woman in the pew behind said in hushed excitement. "A double wedding!"

Caroline Bingley rolled her eyes heavenward and leant closer to her sister. "Double disaster, more like," she whispered. Although she had no choice but to attend this farce, she did not have to make believe she liked it.

Her brother's choice of bride was truly a disaster. He might have married a girl from one of the best families, someone who would have enhanced the prestige of the Bingley name... and perhaps added to the family's fortune as well. What had they all been working for, after all, if not to raise themselves to where nobody would ever remember their humble origins again? Louisa had done her part, at great person sacrifice. But Charles! He was this minute throwing his one chance away on a nobody, and there was nothing she could do about it.

Caroline could not bear to watch her brother disgracing himself, but she did hazard a glance in Mr. Darcy's direction... and a sigh. Were there any justice in the world, she would have been the one standing up beside him now, the one he was regarding so tenderly, the one to whom he plighted his highly covetable troth. It was unaccountable – and patently unfair – that after all her efforts, all her attentiveness, he should also prefer a Miss Bennet! It was not to be borne!

Had Darcy determined to marry Miss de Bourgh over herself, she might have understood, for then she would have been beaten by the undeniable claims of a noble bloodline and a superior fortune. But what did Miss Eliza Bennet have to boast of… except for those notorious "fine eyes"?

It was indeed a harsh blow, and one that was not to be recovered from anytime soon.

Charlotte's Wedding Reflections
by Abigail Reynolds

November 16, 1812

For at least the third time, Charlotte Collins felt an elbow poke itself into her ribs. Her sister Maria was beside herself with excitement at attending Lizzy and Jane's wedding. Her parents were puffed up with pride as well, and her mother was no doubt taking note of every detail so that she could report on it later to her friends. Most of their neighbors were green with jealousy since only family members had been invited to the ceremony. Charlotte felt a distinct sense of satisfaction at knowing her family's invitation was owing to her connection to the Bennets, not because of her father's position.

It had been a revelation for her to return to Meryton as the future mistress of Longbourn. People who had little time for her in the past made an effort to ask her opinion on various matters. After years of being viewed as nothing more than the plain spinster daughter of the former mayor, now she had a position of her own in society and an enviable future. She had never realized before the extent to which she had been disregarded by many people. This was a definite improvement.

Of course, if the change in her status had been a shock to her, it was nothing to what Lizzy must be experiencing. In a few short minutes, she would be Mrs. Darcy of Pemberley. No longer would she be Mrs. Bennet's least favorite daughter, the one whose liveliness had more than once caused people to whisper behind their hands that no man would ever take up with the likes of Lizzy Bennet. Now she would be the one they would go to, hat in hand, to beg a favor, that she put a word in the right ear, that she use her influence for this or for that. It was fortunate that Lizzy was not the gloating sort.

No, Lizzy was the generous sort, and so apparently was her husband to be. A few days ago Lizzy had taken Charlotte aside and told her that Mr. Darcy hoped she would contact them if there were to be any serious difficulties between her husband and Lady Catherine as a result of their marriage. Since Charlotte's great worry these days was that Lady Catherine might make life in Hunsford intolerable for them, she was greatly relieved by her friend's words. It would hopefully be many years before Mr. Bennet departed the earth, leaving Longbourn to Mr. Collins, and in the meantime, they needed a place to live. Charlotte had no desire to leave Hunsford; she was fond of her home and had made friends in the area, but it was good to know they would not be homeless if Lady Catherine continued in her fit of pique.

And there was Lizzy now, being escorted in by her father, with Jane on his other arm. Lizzy's gown of white silk gleamed in the morning light that shone in through the windows, set off with fine lace and a gold sash. The necklace of sapphires around her neck, a gift from Mr. Darcy, marked her future status even more clearly than her elegant dress. Charlotte would never own a dress so lovely, nor jewelry a tenth as expensive, but that was just as well. Lizzy in her finery looked like a rose in bloom; Charlotte would have merely looked overdressed and gaudy. She would not have enjoyed some of the duties Lizzy would face, either. Charlotte was just as glad not to be part of the *ton*, however often her father might speak of his presentation at the court of St. James.

As Lizzy reached Mr. Darcy's side, Charlotte sent her silent best wishes to her dearest friend that her marriage would bring her all the joy she deserved.

I Plight Thee My Troth, or,
The Wedding
by Sharon Lathan

November 16, 1812

The church in Meryton was ancient. Constructed of grey stones, darkly painted oak pillars and ceiling beams, and arched stained-glass windows depicting scenes from the Bible, it was modestly outfitted with the necessary Anglican implements, and simplistic in design. Nevertheless, it was a lovely chapel with plenty of room for the assembled witnesses. The adornment of autumn flowers, ribbons draped over the pews, and lit candles enhanced the natural beauty of the sanctuary, as well as proclaiming the unique purpose of this day's agenda.

A wedding was to occur!

The two eldest Bennet daughters were to be married to the two most eligible bachelors ever to grace Hertfordshire society. The double ceremony was a noteworthy rarity, but the fervour surrounding the wealthy gentlemen who were the grooms increased the excitement. Tiny Meryton had never seen such an extraordinary happening, everyone discussing the topic whether they were invited to the nuptials or not.

Charles Bingley and Fitzwilliam Darcy were blissfully unaware of the scuttlebutt. Like every groom since the dawn of time, they nervously stood on the dais beside the rector, waiting in anticipation while struggling to hide their nerves and present a calm, dignified appearance before the gathering crowd. Dressed in new, impeccably tailored black suits, freshly shaven, hair trimmed and styled precisely, they were the epitome of high style and elegance. The refined exteriors impressed the guests, and served to remind each young man to maintain composure as they waited. Nodding and smiling at friends and family as seats were taken aided in distracting from fears of fumbling their vows or tripping on the steps. To a degree, that is.

Neither man cared a whit about the decorations, barely noticed them in fact, their concentration focused on the door where the women they loved would emerge. After what honestly felt like a million hours, the main chapel door closed and a woman took her place at the organ.

"Breathe, Darcy," Bingley whispered.

"Same to you, Charles."

And then the chords of the wedding march rang out and they both forgot to heed the whispered advice.

Jane entered first. She wore a gown of pale blue with a cobalt sash and matching ribbons laced through the twists of her golden hair. A bouquet of blue geraniums tied with white ribbons was clasped in her hands. Bingley sucked in a tremulous breath, the vision of his bride overwhelming and weakening his knees. Only the serene gaze of vivid blue eyes lovingly locking onto his kept him upright.

Darcy did not glance in Jane's direction. Later he would apologize for his inability to acknowledge her entrance – not that Jane would have been aware if he had, with her attention wholly upon Charles – but it was physically impossible for him to tear his gaze away from the portal where Elizabeth would soon –*God, please soon!*– appear.

Once she did, Darcy ceased to hear or see anything but her. What little breath remaining in his lungs was wrest away! How he managed to stay standing in one place was a mystery. Unless it was the paralyzing awe and stunned wonder at his incredible fortune.

Elizabeth wore a wispy gown of white silk, lace along the edges and a sash of gold. Her thick, chocolate hair was styled elaborately in a design of curls and braids, thin gold ribbons and buds of baby's breath and lavender intertwined. Her bouquet was of the same flowers and ribbons, the strands of gold falling in a cascade to the floor. Adorning her slender neck was the strand of sapphires he had gifted to her while in Hyde Park. Her cheeks were rosy, dark eyes sparkling, and the special smile worn only for him accented her lush lips. It was a picture imprinted upon his mind that would remain there flawlessly rendered for all of his life.

Finally she reached the dais, Darcy descending to claim his bride. Elizabeth clasped onto his hands firmly and eagerly as they turned slightly toward the reverend while staring at each other with transparent love and adoration. Jane and Charles were equally as transfixed. So much so that all four of them jerked when the rector lifted his voice.

"Dearly beloved," he recited from the *Book of Common Prayer* held in his hands, "we are gathered together here in the sight of God, and in the face of this congregation, to join together these two men and these two women in Holy Matrimony; which is an honorable estate, instituted of God in the time of man's innocence, signifying unto us the mystical union that is betwixt Christ and His Church; which holy estate Christ adorned and beautified with His presence and first miracle that He wrought in Cana of Galilee, and is commended of Saint Paul to be honorable among all men. Therefore, it is not by any to be embarked on unadvisedly, lightly, or wantonly to satisfy men's carnal lusts and appetites, like brute beasts that have no understanding; but reverently, discreetly, advisedly, soberly, and in the fear of God; duly considering the causes for which Matrimony was ordained."

Pausing to inhale deeply, the rector then continued. "First, marriage was ordained for the procreation of children, to be brought up in the fear and nurture of the Lord, and to the praise of his holy Name. Secondly, marriage was ordained for a remedy against sin and to avoid fornication; that such persons as have not the gift of abstinence might marry and keep themselves undefiled members of Christ's body. Thirdly, marriage was ordained for the mutual society, help, and comfort that the one ought to have of the other, both in prosperity and adversity. Into which holy estate these four persons present come now to be joined. Therefore, if any man can show any just cause why either of these two couples may not lawfully be joined, let him now speak or hereafter hold his peace."

This pause was longer, as per custom, but the chamber remained silent. Except for the occasional sniffle from a sentimental witness, that is. Darcy squeezed Elizabeth's hands and crooked one brow, the gestures widening her smile. All during the vows recited by Bingley and Jane, Darcy and Elizabeth exchanged subtle, non-verbal communications. The solemn ceremony was taken seriously by both of them; however, the need to defuse the tension to a small degree was necessary because Darcy was convinced he was on the cusp of either collapsing or kissing her senseless! Thankfully the reverend soon turned their direction.

"Fitzwilliam Darcy, wilt thou have this woman to thy wedded wife, to live together after God's ordinance in the Holy estate of Matrimony? Wilt thou love her, comfort her, honor her, and keep her in sickness and in health; and, forsaking all others, keep thee only unto her, so long as you both shall live?"

Darcy's smile was faint, merely a tiny lift to the corners of his mouth, his face awash with serene intensity as he responded clearly, "I will."

Again Darcy squeezed her hands, and so mesmerized was she by the emotion flooding his face that she nearly missed the reverend's next words.

"Elizabeth Bennet, wilt thou have this man to thy wedded husband, to live together after God's ordinance in the Holy estate of Matrimony? Wilt thou obey him, and serve him, love him, honor him, and keep him in sickness and in health; and, forsaking all others, keep thee only unto him, so long as you both shall live?"

The urge to shout her promise was enormous. Therefore, she was surprised when her, "I will," caught in a thick throat. It was heard by the people most important, that being Darcy and the rector, the former grinning from ear to ear, as the latter received permission from Mr. Bennet to give his daughters away.

Once again waiting for Bingley to recite his final vow and place the wedding band upon Jane's finger, Darcy stepped closer to Elizabeth and laid their clasped hands over his heart. Moments later it was his turn.

"I, Fitzwilliam, take thee Elizabeth to my wedded wife, to have and to hold, for better for worse, for richer for poorer, in sickness and in health, to love and to cherish, 'til death us do part, according to God's holy ordinance; and thereto I plight thee my troth."

Looking away only to retrieve the slim, jeweled gold band from the minister's hand, Darcy stared intently into her eyes as he slipped the band onto the third finger of her left hand, nestling it alongside the sapphire and diamond engagement ring that had been his mother's, speaking clearly as he did, "With this ring I thee wed, with my body I thee worship, and with all my worldly goods I thee endow. In the Name of the Father, and of the Son, and of the Holy Ghost. Amen."

Lizzy returned his brilliant smile, lifted her chin, and declared, "I, Elizabeth, take thee Fitzwilliam to my wedded husband, to have and to hold, for better for worse, for richer for poorer, in sickness and in health, to love, cherish, and to obey, 'til death us do part, according to God's holy ordinance; and thereto I plight thee my troth. With my body I thee worship, and all that I possess I share with thee: In the Name of the Father, and of the Son, and of the Holy Ghost. Amen."

The reverend prayed, after which he placed his hands atop each couple's clasped ones, intoning in a ringing voice, "Those whom God hath joined together let no man put asunder! Forasmuch as Charles and Jane, and Fitzwilliam and Elizabeth, have consented together in holy wedlock, and have witnessed the same before God and this company, and thereto have given and pledged their troth either to the other, and have declared the same by giving and receiving of rings, and by joining of hands, I pronounce that they be Man and Wife together, In the Name of the Father, and of the Son, and of the Holy Ghost. Amen."

The urgency to kiss his wife was painful in intensity, but Darcy resisted. Instead he turned toward the witnesses as expected, and managed with the greatest of efforts not to immediately whisk Elizabeth out of the building where he might be able to steal a kiss before they were engulfed with well wishers. In the end it was worth the agonizing delay to hear the reverend say, "May I present, to my honor, Mr. and Mrs. Charles Bingley, and Mr. and Mrs. Fitzwilliam Darcy!"

Organ music swelled and applause echoed from the rafters. Darcy and Bingley both accepted the clamor as a signal to escort their wives down the aisle as rapidly as decorum allowed, launching through the doors as if a pack of wolves were on their heels. Neither wasted a single precious second before encircling their new wife with strong arms, and bending for a heavenly kiss.

Caroline Bingley Acknowledges the New Mrs. Darcy
by Regina Jeffers

November 16, 1812

Never comfortable in large gatherings, Darcy accepted the congratulations of each guest with as much civility as anyone recalled his doing previously. Being always no more than an arm's length from Elizabeth throughout the gathering calmed his heart. His arm often slipped around her waist to keep her close to him, and she rewarded Darcy with enticing smiles. A squeeze of his hand reminded him in a few minutes more they would be alone on the road to London. Each time she did so increased the intensity of Darcy's gaze directed exclusively toward Elizabeth.

They were standing close together, whispering endearments, when the Bingley sisters approached. "Miss Eliza," Caroline Bingley said falsely, "you look lovely today."

"Thank you, Miss Bingley. Being the recipient of Mr. Darcy's regard makes it easy for one to appear lovely." Elizabeth smiled prettily, but Darcy noted the slight smirk in her tone.

"Congratulations, Mr. Darcy." Disappointment laced Caroline's tone. Darcy felt a twinge of guilt. Although he never encouraged Miss Bingley's affection, he had not fully discouraged it either.

"Thank you, Miss Bingley," he said sincerely, but when Darcy noted the lady's grimace, he could not avoid a pointed reply. "I agree with you: Mrs. Darcy is beautiful. Of course, I always thought her eyes as fine. They pierced my soul." Darcy's smile encouraged Elizabeth's response. It spoke of their close connection.

Caroline bit her words. "Yes, I recall your saying as such on several occasions."

Elizabeth turned to her new husband with feigned innocence. "Did you, Fitzwilliam?"

Darcy looked upon his new wife's lovely countenance. Her lush lips were inviting, and Darcy considered drinking of their sweetness. As if they had invaded the Darcys' privacy, Caroline and Louisa retreated a half step. "I believe, Mrs. Darcy, I have thought of no one but you since the Meryton assembly." He pulled Elizabeth closer.

"Miss Eliza," Caroline fought for Darcy's attention in the only means available, by speaking to the man's wife. "Is your necklace a family heirloom?"

"In fact, it is, Miss Bingley." Darcy recognized the slight shift in Elizabeth's tone. His wife meant to bait the Bingley sisters, and poor Caroline had not the why or the wherefore to prevent it.

"Really!" Caroline gasped.

Elizabeth's eyes sparkled with mischief. She laughed easily. "Oh, Miss Bingley," she said with sugar. "I did not mean to mislead you. You, obviously, thought I meant the necklace was a Bennet family heirloom. In truth, Mr. Darcy made me the presentation for I am a Darcy now."

"Actually, it is a gift from my mother and meant for my wife," Darcy added quickly. His eyes met Elizabeth's in loving partnership. "The diamond and emeralds are almost as superb as is Elizabeth. Do you not agree, Miss Bingley?"

Caroline eyed the necklace with obvious regret. She could barely disguise her disgust. With nothing more than a nod of agreement and a quick curtsy, the ladies made their exit.

"Fitzwilliam Darcy," Elizabeth teased, "you are almost as evil as my father. You enjoyed Miss Bingley's humiliation."

"And you did not, Mrs. Darcy?"

"I fear I am my father's daughter. I truly enjoyed Caroline's misery. You have married a shallow woman, Mr. Darcy, and now you know the truth of the matter, I shall remind you the opportunity for an annulment remains. If I offend you, that is…" Elizabeth caressed his arm in a familiar way, and Darcy felt the heat of the moment.

"Do you expect me to consider an annulment when you tease me with your nearness?" Darcy was lost to her alone.

"Then you must suffer forever, Sir. It is my intention of always teasing you with my closeness." Elizabeth's fingertips traced his lips.

"May we leave soon, Elizabeth?" he growled. Darcy's voice was shaky with anticipation.

"I do believe we should say our farewells, Fitzwilliam." Her voice betrayed her true affection for him. "We have a lengthy drive to London. Come, Love, let us make ourselves congenial before we must depart." Taking Darcy's hand, Elizabeth led him from one cluster of neighbors and friends to another. Farewells would come easily on this day for their future awaited.

The Wedding Night of
Charles and Jane Bingley
by Susan Mason-Milks

November 16, 1812

The decision where to spend their wedding night had not been an easy one for the Bingleys. Clearly, staying at Netherfield would have been more familiar and comfortable for Jane, but after a few hints from Mrs. Bennet that she might need to "check" on her darling daughter, the bride-to-be decided that London seemed infinitely more attractive.

Although moving to Bingleys' home in town meant traveling on the day of the wedding, they would have more privacy and the potential for both spending time alone and enjoying the delights of London. Caroline and the Hursts would have to choose between staying at Netherfield and moving to Hursts' family townhouse. This option also had the distinct advantage of installing Caroline, who had so far been maintaining a thin civility toward her future relatives, in another household. Bingley secretly hoped it might set a precedent. Perhaps, she would continue to spend more of her time with the Hursts and less with her brother and his new wife although he knew in all probability that was a futile hope.

The Bingleys arrived at the townhouse early in the evening on the day of the wedding. During the long carriage ride, the groom had refrained from ravishing his bride more from sheer exhaustion than any sense of propriety, although a sleeping Jane snuggled against him had proven to be more than a small temptation. Once at the townhouse, he used up what was left of his self-control to prevent himself from seizing her and rushing up the stairs to their rooms. Although he was always concerned he might alarm Jane with his ardor, he was delighted to find she seemed equally as eager as he to be alone.

Once they had settled in, a light meal was served, but neither the bride nor the groom had much appetite for food. Bingley fed small bites to Jane urging her to keep up her strength, but both were too anxious to even taste the fine fare prepared especially for them. Finally, although slightly embarrassed at the early hour, they decided to retire for the evening and let the servants think what they will.

In Bingley's dressing room, his valet, James, helped him untie his cravat and ease off his coat. After giving his master a quick shave, the valet assisted Bingley into a dark blue velvet dressing gown over his breeches and an open-necked linen shirt. Then James disappeared to check on Mrs. Bingley's progress.

"Molly tells me Mrs. Bingley has completed her bath and will be ready to receive you in her bed chamber in about a quarter hour," James reported upon his return. "Perhaps you would like another glass of brandy or some other refreshment while you wait?"

"No, but you did arrange for the champagne to be put in Mrs. Bingley's room?"

"Oh, yes, sir, just as you requested."

"Hmm...very good," Bingley answered distractedly, his thoughts already wandering into the next room.

Tugging anxiously at the belt of his dressing gown, he checked his appearance in the mirror for at least the tenth time. "How long do you think it has been?" he asked.

James gravely consulted the clock. "I believe approximately four minutes have passed since I returned, sir. Is there anything else I may do for you this evening before you retire?" the valet inquired patiently.

Bingley's groan was almost audible. If he had not been so busy being mortified, he would have noticed James stifling a smile. Then Bingley smiled and thought, what man would not be impatient to be with the most wonderful woman in the world who by some miracle had just become his wife?

"Perhaps I will have a small brandy after all," he replied, fidgeting yet again with his Molly helped the new Mrs. Bingley into a gossamer, blue silk nightdress and matching dressing gown. Seated at the dressing table, Jane glanced in the mirror, nervously checking to make sure the neckline of the new garment revealed just the right amount of pale, delicate skin. It is rather low, she thought wondering what her husband would think. One corner of her mouth turned up as she realized he would probably be delighted. Fingering the fabric, she reveled in the soft feel of it and marveled again at how well the color of the gown set off the warm blue of her eyes. Although everyone, especially her mother, always told her how beautiful she was, she was not, in truth, overly vain or obsessed with her looks. To her, it was only important that Charles thought she was beautiful.

"Would you like me to plait your hair, Mrs. Bingley?" Molly asked politely.

"I think not this evening," Jane replied as she combed through her long hair with her fingers.

Jane's new ladies' maid was a sweet, highly competent young woman whom she had selected after a half dozen interviews conducted during their recent trip to London. At first, Jane had resisted Charles's suggestions that she engage a maid for herself. Practical country girl that she was, she thought it seemed wasteful to have someone who was wholly devoted to taking care of the needs of just one individual. After all, she had shared a maid with her sisters all her life. Neither was she comfortable with the idea of always having someone fluttering around her. Finally, Charles had persuaded her she needed someone to attend her, not because it was the done thing for proper ladies, but for more practical reasons.

"You do not have your sisters to help you anymore, and while I plan to be an attentive husband, I cannot be there for you at all times." He grinned. "Who will do up those tiny buttons at the back of your dress if I am not around?"

Jane looked down to hide the fact that she was blushing and said, "Very well, I suppose I will adjust to the idea."

"Caroline has graciously offered to help you conduct the interviews," she heard him reply.

For an instant, Jane's heart sank. Then glancing up, she realized Charles was looking at her with the most impish grin on his face. Playfully, she pushed at his shoulder.

"I am sorry, sweetheart, but you are so easy to tease that I cannot resist sometimes. Would you prefer it if I…," he began, but she stopped him with a quick kiss.

Pulling back to read his face, she was delighted to see she had taken him completely by surprise.

"If you think a kiss is going to discourage me from teasing you, then you are quite mistaken. In fact, I can assure you it will have the opposite effect."

Jane had only smiled and reached out to him again.

After dismissing Molly for the evening, she was alone and a little anxious as she waited for her husband to come to her room. Glancing at herself in the mirror yet again, she decided that something was missing. After opening the flat velvet jewelry box on her dressing table, she lovingly examined the double-strand pearl necklace Charles had given her the day before their wedding. The clasp was simply decorated with a sparkling cluster of sapphires shaped like a small, delicate flower. "Sapphires to match your eyes," he had told her. After fastening the strands around her neck again, she rechecked her appearance in the mirror and decided the effect was perfect. The lustrous pearls lay gracefully along her collarbones setting off the creamy white of her skin.

Fingering the beads, she thought about how much finer they were than anything she had ever owned. In fact, they might just be the most beautiful thing she had ever seen. Along with the necklace, he had also given her a matching bracelet, as well as pearl combs for her hair. Other women might desire flashier jewelry, but this gift was simply perfect. His choice showed just how well he knew her.

Jane picked up her brush and began to move it slowly through her hair, just as she had done hundreds of times before. Only this was different. In a few minutes, Charles — her husband — would come to her room, and they would begin their life together as man and wife. She was not scared, just a bit uncertain, if truth be told. With all the advice she had received from her family, she had some idea of what was ahead of her, but even armed with all that information, she could still feel her stomach doing a country-dance.

She only knew that every time Charles took her in his arms, her heart beat so loudly she was positive everyone could hear it in the next county. And when he kissed her — well, when he kissed her, she was never certain her legs would continue to hold her up. If that day in the little woods when she had feigned interest in gathering pinecones was a sample of the physical pleasures that were to come as husband and wife, then all would be well tonight. It had certainly been an enlightening experience to realize she could be so wholly taken over by passions she had not even known she possessed. "Trust your husband," her aunt Gardiner had told her, and she planned to do just that.

In spite of expecting his arrival, when she heard his knock at the open door to her dressing room, she almost jumped.

"Come in." Jane hoped she sounded more confident than she actually was.

Charles came and stood behind her putting his hands gently on her shoulders. Her heartbeat quickened as she felt the heat of his hands warming her skin.

"I know I should have waited in your bed chamber rather than come to your dressing room, but I was anxious to see you," he told her.

When their eyes met in the mirror, she saw the kindness and love that was there — kindness and love, but also a deep well of emotion. Yes, she was right to have waited all those months for him. She was as certain as she had ever been of anything in her life that they were meant to be together.

"You are still wearing your pearls."

Her fingers brushed the strands again. "I love them so much that I wanted to wear them for just a little longer."

He smiled. "Every time I looked at you today, it was all I could do to keep myself from doing this," he said giving a demonstration.

She shivered as his finger moved lightly along the pearls against her skin. Closing her eyes, she relished the new sensations. "I know it was just a silly whim of mine to put them on again. You may unclasp them now for me, and I will put them away," she said, reaching for the velvet box.

"Leave them on."

"You want me to...?" She gave him a puzzled look.

"Yes, leave them on."

Will I soon be wearing nothing but my necklace, she wondered. Just the anticipation of what that might be like caused her to turn a rosy pink from the top of her dressing gown to the roots of her hair. She certainly hoped he could not read her mind.

"May I do that?" he asked, indicating the brush still in her hand. Moving tentatively at first, he gained confidence with each stroke. "Your hair is like a beautiful shining halo."

"No wonder you mistook me for an angel when we first met," said Jane with a twinkle in her eyes.

Charles smiled, but then turned more serious. Laying the brush aside, he set his hands gently on her shoulders again.

"It was not a mistake. You are an angel." He kissed the top of her head and inhaled the scent of fresh lemons with a hint of lavender layered in.

"I am not so perfect as you might think," Jane said softly.

Pushing her hair to one side, he exposed the delicate skin of her neck and kissed the hollow just behind her ear. Jane sighed at the touch of his lips.

"To me, you are perfect," he whispered. The feel of his breath against her ear sent a shudder rippling through her body. Then as if overwhelmed by the intensity of the moment, he suddenly changed the subject. "Shall we have some champagne? I thought it might help us both to relax."

Charles poured a glass and handed it to her. After her first sip of champagne, Jane giggled as the bubbles tickled her nose. Flashing her eyes at her husband over the top of the glass, she was thrilled at the reaction she evoked in him.

"I am the most fortunate man in the world. And to think I nearly lost you through my own foolishness. Sometimes, I still cannot believe you have forgiven me," he told her.

"There was nothing to forgive," she said, meaning every word.

"You are too good. Why is it you only ever see the best in me?"

"I am not too good," she said, "and I see what is really important in you – your kindness, your gentleness. I know I can entrust myself to you completely, and you will always take care of me."

Taking the glass from her hand, he set it aside.

"I can hardly believe you are mine." Raising her to her feet, he pulled her into his arms. Jane reached around his waist and pressed her forehead against his chest.

"You are not afraid, are you?" he whispered in her ear.

Jane shook her head and mumbled against the fabric of his dressing gown. "Only a little."

"Someone in your family told you what to expect tonight?"

She nodded.

"You can trust me, you know," he said.

"Always."

Leading her by the hand, Charles walked slowly into the bedchamber. Upon reaching the bed, he sat on the edge and pulled her close until she stood with his legs bracketing either side of her body. Taking her face in his hands, he placed soft kisses on her forehead, her cheeks, her eyes, her nose. Each kiss brought a tiny shiver that only encouraged him more.

"You remember how it was a few weeks ago when we were gathering pinecones?" he said.

"Oh, yes, I do. I confess I have thought of little else of late." She reached up to run her fingers though his curly locks.

Charles groaned softly, and taking her face in his hands again, he kissed her lips. After dreaming of this moment for so long and wondering if he would somehow be disappointed when holding and kissing her this way finally became a reality, he realized he need not have worried. Although he knew Jane to be an innocent, she seemed to know instinctively how to respond. Some of his married friends at the club had warned him wives could be merely passive and submissive on their wedding nights, but that was certainly not the case with his Jane.

"Oh, my dearest angel," he whispered. "How I love you!"

First, he lightly traced along the pearl necklace again and moving down, let his fingers follow the lacy outline at the top of her dressing gown.

Looking into the depths of her husband's blue-green eyes, Jane imagined she was standing on a cliff, his eyes a swelling ocean that she was in danger of drowning in. When she felt Charles impatiently pulling her mouth to his again, she let herself fall.

What followed was beyond heavenly — more exploration, soft touches, and intense kisses along with much fumbling with buttons and ribbons. Finally, both her new dressing gown and nightdress were reduced to a puddle at her feet. With almost no self-consciousness at all, and just as she had imagined, Jane went to her marriage bed wearing nothing more than the golden halo of her hair and her double strand of pearls.

Wedding Night on the Road
to Pemberley
by Sharon Lathan

November 16, 1812

For their first night together as a married couple, Darcy secured lodging at the White Stag Inn near Bedford. Located a few miles off the main thoroughfare to London from Derbyshire, it was the perfect resting point for the two-day carriage ride from Pemberley. That trek was one he had completed more times than he could remember, the White Stag discovered years ago and so frequently stayed at that the owners, Mr. and Mrs. Hamilton, knew him well. They were ecstatic at the idea of hosting him and his new bride.

Arrangements had been made in advance, Darcy thorough in his planning. He secured the largest suite of rooms, those situated on the topmost floor of the sturdy red-brick building and toward the rear with a stunning view of the small lake and park. Aside from comfort and aesthetics, these rooms offered the most privacy. With travelers lighter this time of year, the inn and public rooms would see fewer customers, but Darcy was taking no chances. Everything must be perfect for this night he had awaited with breathless anticipation for a seeming eternity. Never in his life had any evening been so tremendously and lovingly contemplated.

Elizabeth slept during the carriage ride from Netherfield. This bothered Darcy not at all. The joy of holding her in his arms and gazing upon her sleeping face was greater than he ever would have imagined. And after the chaotic activities of the past days, he definitely appreciated the advantage of his new wife regaining her strength before they arrived at the inn! Besides, waking her with gentle kisses was a highly pleasurable experience.

They were greeted enthusiastically by the Hamiltons, and ushered quickly into the welcoming warmth of a private parlor overlooking the moonlit meadow outside the paned windows. A small table near the fire was set for dining, and before either could catch a breath the first course was served.

"Are you pleased, dearest?" Darcy asked, scooting his chair nearer until their knees were touching.

"Oh yes, William, it is wonderful." She reached over and took his hand, squeezing it gently. "You have gone to so much trouble for me, and I do so appreciate it."

"It was no trouble at all, and I must confess I was not only thinking of you," he replied with a laugh, kissing her fingers. "As we have established, I am a rather selfish man and I want you all to myself, far away from Bennets and Bingleys or anyone else!"

"Well, now you have me, for better or worse. I hope I do not disappoint," she said with a sly look from under her lashes and a firm squeeze to his knee.

Suddenly Darcy had difficulty taking a breath. "Oh no, Elizabeth. I am positive that it would be impossible for you to disappoint me in any situation, most especially on this night."

The meal was excellent, but neither were very hungry. Anxiousness, underlying passion, and hints of nervousness dissolved any appetite. As soon as the last, barely eaten course was taken away, Elizabeth announced that she would retire to her dressing room to change. Darcy nearly choked on his wine, but managed to maintain a calm demeanor as she rose from the table and leaned over to give him a brief kiss of passionate promise.

"Will it suit you if I am ready in half an hour?" she asked softly, to which he could only nod. After a tender caress to his cheek, she left the room

Never had thirty minutes lasted so long! Darcy truly thought he would lose his mind. He wandered into the small library and pulled a book off a shelf at random. Any attempt to actually read it was ludicrous in the extreme, but he made a show of it, employing all his well-perfected composure. After twenty minutes he could stand it no longer and briskly strode to his dressing room where the inn's manservant assisted Darcy with his toilette. Darcy again found himself calling upon every ounce of his strength of will not to rush through the agonizingly slow procedures.

Eventually all was done and he nervously entered the bedchamber, only to find it empty. He wandered around the room, pleased with the décor and the attention to detail. There were several vases of flowers about the room, a bottle of chilled champagne, a platter of fruits and sweets and breads, a sofa, and an enormous bearskin rug with several cushions before the blazing fire. The spacious four-poster bed was turned down invitingly. Darcy judged it best to ignore the bed for the present, instead standing by the window and breathing deeply to calm his nerves and halt his trembling.

✳ ✳ ✳

Elizabeth finished her preparations and dismissed her maid. Brushing her hair absently, she relished the silence and reflected on the past weeks. No longer was she afraid of the intimacy to take place this night. In fact, she was excited, as scandalous as her mother would judge that attitude! From the first tender kisses and touches of her betrothed, the sensation engendered made it impossible for her to ignore the realities of marital relations. As the weeks progressed, her emotions vacillated among anticipation, shyness, fear, happiness, anxiety, and many others. Yet, overriding them all was desire. Deep, passionate desire that frequently left her breathless. The conclusion she reached was simple: With such intense love and yearning mutually shared, how could their consummation, and every night thereafter, be less than beautiful and satisfying?

Sitting the brush onto the vanity, Elizabeth took one last look in the mirror, and then entered the bedchamber with a happy smile. The room was lit only by the fire, two oil lamps, the filtered moonlight, and a wall sconce on either side of the bed. For a moment she thought the room empty, but then she noticed her husband standing by a window with his back to her. He was wearing a long maroon robe with a black sash, and every detail of his physique was evident.

Her heart began to race crazily. "William," she whispered.

He turned quickly at her voice and his carefully regulated control slipped instantaneously. Several more deep breaths were necessary to maintain his equilibrium. For a long moment they stood paralyzed, drinking in each other with their eyes. Darcy was the first to break the spell as he moved to meet her in the middle of the room. He longed to grab her and enfold her in his arms, yet at the same time, he wished to study her beauty, memorizing every line and curve of the vision before him.

He stopped a short distance from her and took her outstretched hands, halting her forward movement. "Elizabeth," he said huskily, "may I simply adore you for a moment?"

She smiled and matched his boldness. "Only, sir, if I may do the same!"

She wore a nightgown of sheer satin, pale yellow with tiny bows down the bodice, narrow strap sleeves, a deeply scooped neckline, and pleated gathers just under her bosom. Her hair was loose down her back and shoulders in a chestnut veil of soft curls. Darcy had seen her hair down on a couple of occasions, but never in such an intimate setting, and the sight rendered him breathless and weak in the knees.

Her face was flushed, eyes bright and merry and completely full of love. The gown was thin but not totally transparent, offering tantalizing glimpses of her flawless form underneath. The satin flowed over her hips in gentle folds and over barely visible legs until just touching the tops of delicate feet, leaving tiny toes exposed. The entire vision was delectable and so moving to Darcy's soul. Everything about her was perfection and beauty.

Elizabeth, not completely unaware of the effect she was having on her husband, was nonetheless experiencing her own breathlessness as she carefully examined him for the first time not in full attire and in an intimate setting. While yet fully in charge of her senses, she intended to take note of every detail possible.

He looked so young with his face relaxed; all the tension and careful regulation that usually strained his noble features were gone. His eyes blazed a vivid indigo in the half light of the room, shining and intense with bridled passion and deep love. His robe enclosed his broad shoulders and strong arms completely, yet somehow accented the shape underneath to great advantage. His neck was bare and she could see his pulse beating rapidly in the hollow of his throat. The robe was pulled tight across his muscular chest and belted securely at his lower abdomen. She could only see a triangle of his chest to roughly mid-sternum, dark hairs visible, and her fingers itched to touch his skin. His robe covered the rest of his body, hugging his slender waist, falling to his ankles, leaving his feet bare.

Elizabeth finished her inspection, letting out an involuntary sigh and sound of surprise. Darcy broke from his reverie and looked quickly to her face.

"Elizabeth, are you well?"

"Pardon?"

"You seem startled. Are you displeased in some way?" he asked nervously.

She blushed furiously and looked away, stammering, "Oh, no, I am fine. It is just that …" she trailed off lamely.

"It is just, what?" He did not know whether to be alarmed or to laugh at her sudden discomfiture. He lifted her chin gently until she reluctantly met his eyes. "We promised to be completely honest with each other, remember? Please tell me what you are thinking."

"I … well, I was just noticing … that …," she swallowed and looked at him boldly, "you have nice feet!"

He could not speak for a moment, then burst out laughing. He gathered her into his arms and held her tightly. "My darling Lizzy! You are so very delightful." He pulled back slightly so he could see her face, his grin wide. "Thank you, my love. I can safely assert that no one, with the possible exception of my dear mother, has ever commented on my feet!"

"You are teasing me," she accused, with a playful slap to his chest.

"Of course I am! How could I not? Only you can make me laugh so." He kissed her lips quickly, then proceeded to plant tiny kisses along her jaw until he reached her ear. He inhaled her scent and whispered softly, "Do only my feet delight you, or did you manage to discover other equally pleasing attributes during your inspection?"

Speaking, in fact, coherent thought of any kind, seemed next to impossible with the flutters elicited by his kisses racing through her body. Even so, she answered, "Perfectly adequate, Mr. Darcy, I daresay. Unfortunately, so much remains covered that I cannot in truth render a full accounting. Perhaps we can remedy this oversight on your part posthaste so I can answer your query with total knowledge."

Darcy had ceased his ministrations to her neck and was watching her as she spoke, a happy smile on his lips. *Oh how I love her! How I want her!* But he had promised himself that he would control his desires and take this night slowly. He wanted to enjoy every moment with her, every word, every touch, every sound, and every smell. He was determined that she find pleasure and complete joy in being with him, in becoming his wife in every sense of the word.

"All in due time, Mrs. Darcy. First, I have a wedding present for you." He took her by the hand and seated her on the sofa. He went to the armoire and pulled out a square box wrapped with blue paper and tied with a thick blue ribbon. He returned to her and placed it into her lap, kneeling before her. "For you, my wife, always to remember this day, the happiest day of my life."

Elizabeth shook her head and tears filled her eyes. "William, you should not have. You have given me so many wonderful gifts already! All I need to remember and mark this day is you... only you."

Darcy smiled, "Thank you, dearest. You shall always have me. Now you shall also have this meager token as well. Open it."

Elizabeth untied the bow and pulled the wrapping away. Inside the box, lying on a bed of dark blue velvet, was a vanity set – brush, comb and mirror – made of mother-of-pearl with Elizabeth Darcy engraved on each handle. The craftsmanship was exquisite.

"William, I do not know what to say. They are beautiful! I have never owned anything equal. Thank you so very much!" She leaned over and kissed him soundly.

Darcy beamed at her obvious pleasure. "You would have enjoyed the spectacle, my dear. I have come to realize how lacking my education is in the area of feminine requirements. I have, in fact, studiously avoided the subject in the past. Recently, I have discovered myself extremely fascinated by all the mysteries related to the fairer sex, or more specifically related to you. I scoured my extensive library and found not a single book that could answer the questions I had. I surmised that the only sure avenue open to me was to enter the shops in London that cater to the needs of women."

Elizabeth could picture it clearly and the vision did make her smile. He went on, "I was most relieved to find that I was not the only gentlemen present in the establishments, but I certainly was the most ignorant! Fortunately the proprietors were remarkably sympathetic, and the female customers extremely helpful, all willing to further my education. That is the day you encountered me at Harding, Howell, and Co. It is a story I shall recount in detail later, and will amuse you, I am sure. By the end of my labors, I learned numerous incidentals, which I am certain will aid me in being an understanding husband. As for this particular gift, considering how ardently I admire your beauty and especially your lovely hair, it seemed fitting."

"William, you are too good to me. I truly do not deserve you."

"Nonsense," he replied gruffly, "I love you and enjoy giving you gifts." As he spoke, he absentmindedly reached up under her gown and began running his hand along her right calf.

Time stopped and instantaneously their mutual desires were awakened. Thoughts were immediately riveted by an overpowering need for each other. The ache to touch intimately, feel their heated bodies pressed together, and cross the final barrier into truly becoming one was nearly painful in its intensity.

Gazing into her eyes, Darcy took the box off Elizabeth's lap, laid it on the floor, and then rose onto his knees. He slowly ran his hands along the tops of her thighs and around her bottom, pulling her to the edge of the sofa. Her knees parted and he moved closer, his hands leisurely caressed their way up her back, eventually entwining in her hair as he brought her lips to his for a passionate kiss.

Elizabeth ran her hands up his chest and then under his robe, placing her fingers gently on his shoulders. With slow deliberation she peeled the garment off his shoulders, exposing his upper body as she lovingly ran her palms down his back. Darcy released her long enough to remove his sleeves, baring his arms to her tender caress, and then encircled her again, never once leaving her sweet lips.

Then she boldly reached down and untied his sash, the robe falling to the ground. Darcy moaned and in one swift, graceful motion rose from his kneeling position, gathered Elizabeth into powerful arms, and carrying her to the bed.

* * *

Quite some time later, blissfully satiated, they lay on the mussed bed with limbs entangled. They were awake but drowsy, talking softly of silly things for the pleasure of hearing the other's voice, and simply enjoying being together in sweet harmony. Darcy played with her hair where it cascaded over his arm, while Elizabeth traced lazy circles over his chest and stomach.

The final acts of love had been far superior to any imaginings either of them had entertained. Darcy, never a great admirer of romantic poetry, finally understood. Each day, each moment with Elizabeth had transcended the one before. Tonight they had reached dizzying heights, and it honestly seemed impossible to love her more. Now he knew that she owned him, lived inside of him, kept his heart beating, and gave him purpose. If it had not felt so very right, it might have terrified him.

Contentment flowed through Elizabeth. She was tired, yet exhilarated at the same time. Happiness was a palpable entity that surrounded her and permeated her very soul. *How is it possible to love someone this much? Is it normal? Probably not, but i would not wish it any other way.*

Real life intruded when Darcy's stomach growled, as if in response to Elizabeth's fingers playfully examining his navel. "Hungry, darling?" she asked. "Have your recent exertions increased your appetite?"

"I have eaten sparsely today. Nerves, I suppose." He rolled onto his side and began kissing her bare shoulder. "I was much more interested in satisfying other hungers so that I ignored my more basic needs. What is food compared to your love?"

"Very pretty. However, I am beginning to experience pangs of my own. The Hamiltons have supplied us with an abundance of food and it would be rude to ignore it."

They donned robes – the process delayed by numerous kisses and caresses – and moved to sit on the rugs near the hearth. Neither was shy in attacking the superb provisions and chilled champagne. They fed each other, frequently pausing for sweet kisses, eventually satisfying their hunger and reclining comfortably before the fire.

Darcy was drifting into sleep when he felt Elizabeth untie and open his robe. "Elizabeth?" he whispered curiously.

"I made a promise, sir, to give you a full accounting of all your attributes that are pleasing to my eyes. Never let it be uttered that I do not keep my promises. Now, relax."

"That may be a challenging order to follow, my beloved, if you continue in this manner." He captured one of her tresses and twined it around his fingers. For long moments they gazed at each other, enraptured by the love they felt. Thoughts of sleep vanished. Darcy started to rise up, intent on taking her into his arms, but she stayed him with her hands.

"I am not finished, sir," she murmured and lowered her face to his neck as she stretched fully onto him. It was her turn to bestow feather kisses to all his sensitive places and to discover the secrets of how to please him. This she did with an intensity and directness that left him beyond breathless … and completely satisfied.

Their wedding night was not over yet…

A New Day Dawns for the Darcys
by Sharon Lathan

November 17, 1812

Fitzwilliam Darcy was having the most extraordinary dream of his entire life. Elizabeth was there, although that fact was not unusual since she had graced the vast majority of his dreams for months now. This dream, however, was exceedingly more detailed than the previous ones! Darcy was enjoying this dream enormously, and it was with tremendous dismay that he felt the beginning tendrils of consciousness return. He valiantly fought against waking, but the tingles in his right arm persisted no matter how many times his subconscious self tried to move the offending appendage.

The cold blast of wakefulness was like a knife to his heart. So acute was his disappointment at the dream fading, that one can imagine the soaring heights instantaneously reached when he realized that the object of his dream was in his arms. In fact, it was her head, which had at some point during her sleep crept from his chest to the inner aspect of his elbow, that was causing his arm to burn. The irony of it did not escape him and he chuckled softly.

Memories of the fine dream and their first night together, coupled with the vision of her beauty, were temporarily enough to drive away the ever-increasing discomfort to his poor extremity. For some moments he manfully bore the pain and watched her sleep. It was an enchanting sight with her lush lips slightly parted, her thick lashes resting on her rosy cheeks, her mane of hair scattered haphazardly, and her creamy neck and shoulders visible. Darcy could quite contentedly have stared at her all day, but now his fingers had lost all feeling.

Resolving this issue was suddenly one of the most problematical calamities of his life! He did not want to wake her, nor did he want to remove his arm completely. He thought maybe he could roll her gently back towards his body – a pleasurable prospect – but his arm had lost all sensation and refused to comply with his brain's request. There seemed to be no other option but to use his functional left arm to move her, probably waking her in the process. Fortunately she suddenly sighed deeply, stretched and nestled closer to his side, her head once again on his chest.

Darcy sent silent thanks to whichever guardian angel takes care of these sticky situations.

His relief was short lived, sadly, due to the sudden rush of blood that ignited a blaze of fresh pain in his unfortunate arm. He gritted his teeth, and his whole body tensed and shuddered in his effort not to cry out and wake his peacefully sleeping wife. Eventually the torture subsided and he was able to move his arm again, using it to hug Elizabeth against his side.

Well, that was interesting. Certainly a drawback to sleeping with someone that has never occurred to me! He lifted his head to view the clock. A quarter to nine! When was the last time I slept so late?

He couldn't remember, but then neither could he remember the last time he slept so deeply and contentedly. He felt amazingly refreshed, and blissful. As pleasant as his dream had been, the reality of his wedding night was vastly superior. Darcy never claimed to be a particularly creative man, but after the joy experienced several times, and in varied ways and sites, his mind drifted to all sorts of promising possibilities! He was a trifle embarrassed, nevertheless he recognized that Pemberley had any number of secluded areas, both inside and out, that would work nicely. Good God, man! Listen to yourself! The self-chastisement was ignored, and when Elizabeth woke minutes later, the question of whether she might feel differently or be shocked by the nature of his musing was answered definitively in the negative.

* * *

It was ten o'clock before they arose from their tousled bed. They were famished, so Darcy rang for breakfast before following Elizabeth's example and retiring to his dressing room. Quickly shaving and freshening his cologne, he pulled on a shirt and breeches at random, returning to their bedchamber just as the breakfast tray arrived. Elizabeth entered wearing a lovely burgundy gown, her face pink from washing, and hair hastily tied with a ribbon to hang as a tail down her back.

Darcy was struck anew by how beautiful she was, and how marvelous to be married so he could view her in casual attire. Not surprisingly, Elizabeth was thinking much the same, adoring how handsome her husband looked with his shirt loosely tucked and open at his neck. This was a picture of him that only she would be privy to.

Elizabeth curled up in the chair, tucking her feet under her, and commenced pouring coffee for Darcy and tea for herself. The simple task of serving her husband sent a surge of happiness through her heart. For his part, Darcy could not cease staring at her. After all that had transpired yesterday and last night and this morning, it still seemed a dream to have finally arrived at this place when, for so long, he had despaired of ever being with her.

"You are staring, Mr. Darcy. Do I have a distracting blemish on my face?" she teased.

"Sorry, my dear. No, you do not have any blemishes. I am entranced by your beauty, that is all."

"Quite the flatterer you have become, sir. So charming. Who would believe it of you?"

"Well, as I intend to save my best flattery for when we are alone, no one would believe you even if you were to inform them."

"So, am I to infer that you will be devising and practicing said flattery beforehand? If so, you must remember to give as unstudied an air as possible."

Darcy grinned at her reference. "Perhaps I shall occasionally plan my flattery; however, as you are well aware of how uncreative I am, my dear, I would imagine that the pleasing compliments will usually proceed from the impulse of the moment."

They both laughed and she threw a grape at him. "Ridiculous man! Read your newspaper and let me eat in peace!"

He did his best to comply with her request, discovering that it was quite challenging to focus on world events with her across the table. Neither of them knew it at the time, but they were innocently setting the stage for what was to become a morning ritual for the rest of their lives. Except for those occasions when guests were present or business separated them, they would breakfast together quietly each day in their joint sitting room. Darcy would read the newspaper and Elizabeth would read a book. They would discuss their daily plans or estate business or items from the news. The staff would be instructed not to interrupt, their morning solitude a favorite and necessary part of their day.

"What are we to do with ourselves today?" she asked at one point. "Have you made any specific plans?"

Darcy put the newspaper down. "Nothing specific," he replied, and then grinned. "We could always stay here all day. I am sure we could dream up something to occupy our time." She quirked one brow, Darcy laughing. "Or if you would rather, the village is quite close so we could ramble through it. There is a gig available, and the weather appears fine enough for a drive. Too bad it is winter, as a picnic would be an agreeable pastime."

"Oh? Did a law pass of which I am unaware that we can only enjoy our meals outdoors in the spring or summer?"

"I did not mean to imply that such activities are unlawful in the winter, Mrs. Darcy! I am solicitous regarding your comfort, however. It is late November and quite cold outside."

Lizzy laughed. "Honestly, William, I thought you knew me better than that! When has the weather ever hindered me?"

"As you wish, my love. A picnic it shall be."

They spent a lovely day together, this first day of the rest of their lives.

A luncheon hamper was prepared and loaded into the carriage, along with several thick blankets. To begin with, they drove into the village. It was not a large town, about the size of Meryton, but there were numerous quaint shops to browse through. Lizzy quickly realized that she had to be cautious in exhibiting interest in even the smallest trinket because Darcy would insist on buying it for her. In spite of her guardedness, Darcy's arms were encumbered with packages by the end of two hours, and he was forced to rearrange the blankets and hamper to make room in the gig.

It was a beautiful day, crisp and cool, but the sun was warming and the sky cloud free. They leisurely drove along the edge of the river toward the small lake, Lizzy sitting as close to his side as she could possibly manage. They periodically stopped to marvel at the landscape, using the opportunity to steal a few kisses. A level spot close to the lake's edge proved perfect for their luncheon.

They chatted as they ate, the topics ranging from childhood memories to current events to family matters to literature to future plans and various points in between. Once they had eaten their fill, Darcy laid his head in her lap and read out loud from a book of Shakespeare's sonnets. Elizabeth played with his hair, deliriously content merely to stare at his face and listen to his resonant voice.

After a bit they decided to stroll, holding hands as they meandered. They encountered not a soul. It was as if they were the only two people in the world. When passing a large oak tree, Darcy halted, leaned against the trunk, and gathered Elizabeth into his arms. For some time he merely held her pressed tight to his chest. She experienced a profound sense of peace and protection. His warmth radiated out of him, arms strong about her body, and his cheek resting on the top of her head. In due course his soft lips traveled through her hair to her ear and then her neck, raining gentle kisses and sweet endearments along the way. How wonderful to be married and freely allow their emotions to wash over them! Naturally there was a limit, the edge of their endurance reached with mutual agreement that it was time to return to the inn.

They packed up in haste and drove as speedily as safety permitted. Darcy bordered on curtness in instructing the servant that they would be dining at seven o'clock and not to disturb them for the rest of the afternoon. He failed to notice the servant's smile of understanding, nor would he have cared. The door to their room was barely latched before they were in each other's arms. Clothing was removed as fast as humanly possible, and with a multitude of fumbles and humorous moments. It was a novel experience and tremendously enjoyable. The end result of their playful exertions was as one would expect.

* * *

With colossal effort, they left their bed with barely enough time to make themselves presentable for dinner. The food was delicious, and the room empty most of the time so, between bites, they shared a few kisses.

Darcy was mesmerized by his wife, every movement generating ripples of delight through his body. His need to touch her overwhelmed him. Breaking pieces of bread and fruit, he fed her, lingering on her lips and losing all awareness in her sparkling eyes.

"William, your food is growing cold," she teased, kissing his finger.

He smiled, leaning to nuzzle behind her ear. "I care not. Famished I may be, but touching you is preferable. For once your parents are not present to preclude me fulfilling the fantasy of displaying how even the simple act of eating enhances my desire for you."

"Oh, William! The vision! I wish you had acted on your impulses then so I could see Mama's face, if nothing else!"

Darcy laughed, resuming his seat and picking up his fork. "As entertaining as that may have been, Elizabeth, your father would likely have strangled me. Curbing my inclinations was not always easy, but wise. Thankfully I no longer need to do so. Well, within reason, of course."

After dinner they took a stroll in the silent garden and talked about Pemberley. The plan was to depart early in the morning since the journey home would take most of the day. Darcy was in a state of uncontrollable bliss that Elizabeth would finally be with him in his home …their home. It was a dream he had harbored in his aching heart for so many months. The reality was incredible.

Before long they returned to their room, wishing to thoroughly enjoy the last night at this place which would forever be special to them. They made love again, slowly and reverently, before falling into a deep, peace-filled sleep with limbs entwined and warm bodies cuddled close.

Caroline Explains it All...
by C. Allyn Pierson

November 17, 1812

Caroline Bingley awoke in time to hear the dawn chorus, should she have gone out into the early morning mists. But she did not hear it, nor did she hear anything else as she stared up at the canopy over her head. Mr. Darcy was gone... he was now married to that simpering little milkmaid, Elizabeth Bennet. God, what a fool he was! They would be miserable within a month.

She pulled her coverlet up over her shoulders, trying to stop the shivering that had shaken her all night. She could not believe that he had actually gone through with it. Elizabeth Bennet had nothing... NOTHING to offer him in the way of breeding, education, or beauty that she did not have. Not to mention her dowry, an area where the Bennet's were clearly inferior.

At eight o'clock her maid brought in her chocolate and bread and butter, but her mouth felt like a cold, week-old fireplace, the taste of ashes choking her.

Bad enough that her brother had married the prissy Jane Bennet! But her brother was sometimes a fool... if he did not have a pleasing personality no one in London would have anything to do with him... and then where would Louisa and she have been?

Might as well get up... Louisa and Mr. Hurst would be coming down for breakfast soon.

When she came down in her morning dress, hair as impeccable as always, the Hursts had already sat down with their plates.

"Well, good morning, Caroline!" Louisa chirped, looking disgustingly fresh for the early hour.

"Good morning, sister," Caroline responded dully.

"You look like you celebrated too much after the wedding yesterday." Louisa simpered at her.

"I beg your pardon?" Caroline responded, a touch of acid in her voice.

"You heard me, sister. Now Darcy is gone, bedded down with that pasty-faced wench, and does not even remember you exist. It is time you faced facts." Louisa sent calmly on with her tea and toast.

"How dare you? I do not care this much for Mr. Darcy." She snapped her fingers at her sister. "I do not need your vulgar tongue to make me 'face facts', as you call it. No man who would prefer Elizabeth Bennet to me is even worth knowing."

"Except for his contacts in the *ton.*"

"I suppose. Georgiana is worth knowing, however, no matter how naive and guileless she is."

"What did you think of the wedding, sister?" Louisa's face sneered at her sister's unconcealed distress. Caroline pulled herself together and shrugged.

"Charles looked well. I like that coat he wore. The Miss Bennets gowns were nothing special... probably made by the local seamstress in Longbourn village." She managed to snicker and Louisa laughed with her.

"And the mother! Have you ever seen so many ribbons and so much lace! I am surprised she could walk!"

They both went back to their breakfast, and Caroline's thoughts turned back to Darcy, his face ardent and intense as he undressed his bride on their wedding night. She felt her gorge rise and rose abruptly.

"I do not feel well this morning, Louisa. I believe I have a megrim coming on. Please excuse me...I am going up to lie down."

"Of course, Caroline. I hope you feel better soon."

Caroline gave her a ghastly smile and climbed the stairs, trying to block out the vision of the Darcys' wedding night.

Lady Catherine, Alone at Rosings
by Diana Birchall

November 17, 1812

Rosings! Poor, poor Rosings. No longer allied with Pemberley, no longer a shining crown in the Darcy panoply of great houses, Rosings now stood alone and forlorn. There would be no more visits from the young men with whom Lady Catherine had been so proud to be connected. Mr. Darcy would never come to Rosings now, and Colonel Fitzwilliam, shamefully loyal to his cousin rather than to his aunt, would not pay his respects to her there either. The new Mrs. Darcy, and the deluded Miss Darcy alike, would be henceforth dead to the mistress of Rosings. For Lady Catherine de Bourgh had cut them all off at one stroke: her abusive letter regarding Darcy's disgraceful marriage had been decisive.

Not that Lady Catherine would admit to administering anything more than a mere corrective, though admittedly it was rather like whipping a horse's empty stall, after the beast itself had jumped its traces and escaped. Never mind; she had given her opinion, and stated what she felt to be right, no matter how unpleasant the consequences might be to her personally. But that was her character, for which she was so justly famed. She would brook no compromise. It would be the young men who were the losers, no longer having the entree to the superior society of Rosings.

At Rosings, then, Lady Catherine sat alone in splendid solitude, with nothing but the satisfaction that she had been right: as she always was. No, not quite alone; for there was Anne, to be sure, and her companion Mrs. Jenkinson. Even to a mother's eye, disposed to be prejudiced until inevitable disappointment set in, it was plain that Anne was not the sort of company to satisfy a woman of the world, with education, fortune, and wisdom such as Lady Catherine's. A lifetime of maternal homilies had been directed toward making Anne such another as herself, and by extension, the perfect wife for Mr. Darcy of Pemberley. What was her chagrin, then, to have a daughter who would hardly ever speak, and silently put sickliness up as a wall between herself and everything her mother required her to do.

Lady Catherine occasionally had an uncomfortable inkling that it was her own incessant decrees that had rendered Anne silent; but no, that was impossible. It had all had been done with the best intentions; who could have been a better mother than herself? No one could say where she had failed. Lady Catherine could hardly suppose such a thing. Had not her instructions always been calculated to bring Anne out, to develop her powers of attention, of conversation? No, it was Anne's ill health, unquestionably, that prevented her from attaining the character, the reputation, of the great lady she should not have failed to be. And now she would be an old maid, unless another man like her father, Sir Lewis de Bourgh, could be found for her. Lady Catherine shuddered. She knew that there was not another Mr. Darcy.

At Rosings, apart from Anne, who was there? Jenkinson was an inferior, a distant connection, a widow fallen on destitute times; and most praiseworthy it had been of Lady Catherine to take her in and give her occupation. However, in accepting her condescending charity, the woman had become no more than a servant, and a lady of Lady Catherine's degree could not treat such a one as an equal.

There were other families of fortune in the neighborhood, but none of a lineage to compare with Lady Catherine's own, and what with long standing feuds, and insulting instances of patronage, and intolerable neglect, and bitter enmities that never could be wiped away, there were few families of quality who had anything to do with her any more. All the blame was on the side of these upstart families, of course, for Lady Catherine chose to connect herself only with the best, and there was precious little of that in this sad part of Kent.

It was not surprising, then, that she had placed such great importance on the sort of clergyman who should come to Hunsford. As he would necessarily become an important intimate of her household, he must be someone she could at least endure, if not respect. Mr. Collins had been recommended to her by chance; and when summoned for the all-important interview, he had shewn himself most properly respectful of all her benefits. So, she smiled graciously upon this gentleman, and in due course, accepted his wife. Mrs. Collins was a very proper, sensible, submissive sort of body, and not unladylike; good enough for him, and already well instructed in what her position in the parish must be.

But where were these tame Collinses now? Gone; and most humiliatingly, they had followed her own aristocratic relations. That is human nature, she thought vengefully. The Collinses – how had she ever thought them biddable? They had seemed to know their station so well! Yet it was they who had promoted the marriage between Mrs. Collins's pretty friend and her own nephew, and baser betrayal had never been seen and could not be borne. A pity one could not sack a clergyman, thought Lady Catherine, grinding her teeth; just as one might a thieving bailiff.

Anne had retired to bed, and Mrs. Jenkinson had scuttled off somewhere to hide. Lady Catherine was left alone, in the principal parlour at Rosings, as the sparkling December day outside, pale sun shining on crisp snow, began early to darken into twilight. She irritably removed to the long dining-table to eat her roasted beef and vegetable ragout in silence, before calling for a fire. No venison, no plump little birds shot and killed by the young men, and kept for a winter's evening to be enjoyed, she thought bitterly; her meat now was bought at the butcher's.

The evening sky outside was a velvety indigo, with a sweeping of little twinkling white stars in such profusion as had never been seen in the heavens before; but Lady Catherine would not look out a window to see such vulgar omens. She knew very well, with astronomical exactitude, what tonight was. It was the wedding night of Darcy and Elizabeth. And she was spending it alone.

Resolutely, she picked up the nearest book, but it was Fordyce's Sermons, and she felt she required something more entertaining. No comfortable game of cassino for her, however, no light diverting novel left by an animated young visitor. It came to her, of a sudden, that she was unhappy, and a strange sound emerged from her corseted, iron midsection, that a listener might have thought was almost a wrenching sob. But there were no listeners.

Then, from some remote place long dead within her, arose a memory, of what she had endured from Sir Lewis de Bourgh, so many years ago now. She had not thought of it – oh, almost since it happened. She had firmly suppressed the memory, as one must press down such unsuitable things.

It had been a very proper, approved match, for the de Bourghs were both a rich and ancient family, and Lady Catherine had retained all the rights to be her own mistress, as a strong minded heiress, rising thirty. She intended from the beginning to rule the roost; and Sir Lewis, timid in temperament and frail in health as his only surviving daughter would be, was not the man to gainsay her. Still, there had once been a wedding night, and for what reasons she could not say, with her back to the dark window, gazing at a low glowing fire, Lady Catherine thought of it now. Images rose up in her mind, unbidden.

Sir Lewis had emerged from the closet, his knees knobbly in his nightshirt, and he clambered onto the cold satin sheets. Lady Catherine lay stolidly in the center of the bed and did not move. "My dear, will you make room for me?" he bleated timorously. "Certainly not," she answered. "That is not the proper method of proceeding, at all. Do not you know that a gentleman never approaches his lady on the wedding night, or indeed, ever, until and unless he is invited? And I do not recollect giving you the invitation."

Sir Lewis had meekly gone into another bedchamber, his white shirt pale in the darkness like a ghost. And that was that, until, several years later, her own brother, then Viscount Fitzwilliam, came to visit at Rosings, bringing his lady and their little boys. He had expressed himself surprised at his sister's childlessness, and a few shrewd questions to his brother-in-law had ascertained the state of affairs. A walk in the shrubbery; a hint to Lady Catherine that if Sir Lewis died with the marriage incomplete, unknown heirs might appear to challenge her widow's possession of Rosings.

So she had reluctantly, and with infinite distaste, allowed Sir Lewis to have his fumbling way; the puling sickly Anne had been the result; and the father had faded away soon after, like a gentleman spider eaten by his lady, and not regretted by her in the slightest.

As a full, majestic, bright jubilant winter moon rose at midnight over Pemberley, it rose over Rosings too; but it only gleamed in on a widow in her own majestically caparisoned bed, which reflected white in the moonshine, like a galleon. Lying awake, Lady Catherine allowed her thoughts to drift to her benighted nephew and his bride. Would the new Mrs. Darcy be likely to know how a lady managed her husband on the wedding night? Humph! she thought. That coarse girl, how could a knowledge of proper behavior be expected from her? Why, they were probably behaving like barnyard animals at this very moment…

No. She would not think about such things. Resolutely she turned over, away from the window, and closed her eyes, to sleep the dreamless and undisturbed sleep of the just.

My Mind Was More Agreeably Engaged by Regina Jeffers

November 18, 1812

By the time Darcy had come upon the open doorway of the drawing room, Elizabeth and Georgiana had spent a pleasant three quarters hour together. They spoke of family, of music, and of Darcy. An outside observer might have thought them sisters forever; a natural respect existed between the two. Their laughter drifted from the room, and Darcy found himself reluctant to enter the space and interfere with their kinship.

"Georgiana, may I ask the favor of a response?" Elizabeth said tentatively.

"Anything, Elizabeth."

"Something has dwelled heavy on my mind for some time. When I first met your cousin, Colonel Fitzwilliam, he already knew so much about me. When I asked his source, he said you had told him; yet, we had never met."

"That is simple, Elizabeth. My brother had often spoken of you."

"Really?" She said in true surprise. "What could he have said? Something devious, I am certain."

Georgiana confessed, "Fitzwilliam had never mentioned a woman in his letters prior to meeting you. My brother related many of your conversations at Netherfield. I could not believe anyone spoke so to him. It piqued my interest. When I thought he was most distracted, I would ask about you."

Uncomfortable for having asked her question, Elizabeth attempted to turn the compliments. "My manners were abhorrent. Fitzwilliam's stories must have portrayed me as less than civilized."

Darcy nearly laughed aloud, but he stifled it because he wanted to hear more.

"Oh, no, Elizabeth. Fitzwilliam always said wonderful things about you. I wanted to have your acquaintance, and I had hoped we could be friends." Elizabeth automatically reached for Georgiana's hand. The girl would require a gentle hand to build her confidence. "I was upset Mr. Bingley had quit Netherfield. I had wished to travel to Hertfordshire to take your acquaintance; Fitzwilliam said he wished that for me also." Elizabeth blushed to think how well her dear husband had loved her.

"There is something…something more I believe of which we should speak." Elizabeth hesitated, and Darcy wondered what could be so odious that the "brave" woman of his dreams would shun. Finally, she said, "Georgiana, now that we are sisters, may we revisit our conversation from the previous day?"

The girl's composure slipped, and she mumbled, "What do you mean, Elizabeth?"

Elizabeth sucked in a steadying breath before saying, "With Mr. Wickham, did you believe yourself to feel regard, affection, or love?" Darcy's back stiffened. What in the world was Elizabeth doing? He did not know whether to interrupt or trust her. Reluctantly, Darcy chose the latter.

"I am not certain I understand. I felt all three, of course." The turn of this conversation made Darcy uncomfortable, but he had committed himself to Elizabeth's sensibilities.

"I am not an expert on love, Georgiana, but you are mistaken. If you had held Mr. Wickham in regard, you would have felt foolish at your loss, but the romance would have soon dissipated. If you had felt affection for the man, you would again be foolish, but time would have resolved your loss. If I am correct, you felt one of these emotions rather than love. Is that not true?"

Unwillingly, Georgiana confessed, "I see one of these definitions fitting my situation, but then what is love?"

"Real love, Georgiana, changes your life; your own needs no longer exist. If rejected, you never forget the person; as Fitzwilliam did, you retreat into yourself—you attempt to find solace someplace else, but it cannot be. You might even choose another with whom to spend your life, but there is no love for it died and was replaced with regard or affection. I could not think of loving anyone but your brother; can you say the same of Mr. Wickham?"

"I cannot, Elizabeth. I feel nothing for the man. I only feel my own shame."

"Then may we move forward? You are not the person you were at fifteen. The Darcys must learn self-chastisement is a hard master. Your brother has attended to that lesson; can you not also?"

"Elizabeth, you explained things so logically and so simply. I am pleased to share my life with you. Mayhap if we had been prior confidants, your counsel would have served me well. I acted the role of a fool."

"Georgiana, we all assume the comic role at one time or another. Your brother and I are perfect examples, but we will share a special bond. I may not always have the answers, but we will find our way together, and I will never turn from you."

Darcy could not believe how easily the two spoke of intimate details; at last, Georgiana finally had a female to whom to turn for advice. He started to step into the room, but held for just a moment when Elizabeth stammered one final question.

"Do you...do you believe Lady Catherine will ever forgive your brother for not choosing Anne? Family is so important to me; I despise being the cause of a family rift."

"My aunt is stubborn, but she has neglected the fact that Fitzwilliam is the head of the Darcy family. Those over whom Lady Catherine holds sway will soon be forgotten." Georgiana continued, "If Fitzwilliam had married Anne, our aunt could stay at Rosings because Fitzwilliam is wealthy enough not to require Anne's fortune."

"I feel as if I have destroyed your family, Georgiana."

"That is nonsense, Elizabeth. My brother loves you."

Darcy could bear no more; he stepped into the room. "My sister is correct, Madam, you have bewitched me." He stopped only a few steps within the doorway. Both ladies jumped to their feet as if having been caught misbehaving; Darcy and Elizabeth locked eyes. She blushed deeply.

"You, Sir," she began haltingly, "should...should not be eavesdropping."

His eyes flashed with humor. "How else may I know when the two women I cherish most are conspiring against me?"

Elizabeth raised her chin as if to challenge him, but her bottom lip quivered indicating her words about women always conspiring against men had nothing to do with what she was really thinking.

"You do not intend on rejecting me again do you, Elizabeth? I am afraid my heart could not withstand the pain another time," he taunted her.

Tears filled her eyes as she said, "My loving you has hurt you; I do not want you to ever regret marrying me."

"Elizabeth, I will not give you up again," he said adamantly. "No matter how often I am asked to make the decision, I would choose you. Despite all rumors of my stoic character, I would carry you off to make you my wife over all the world's objections."

She knew he teased, but she rushed into his arms, burying her tears into his chest. Soothing her head, Darcy said, "Shush, Elizabeth, we will have no more tears over Lady Catherine's disapproval. Do you not think I have suffered enough at your hand?" As he said this, he brought her palm to his lips and kissed it gently. "Georgiana," he briefly diverted his eyes to his sister, "why do you not retrieve the gift you brought from London for Elizabeth?" Georgiana curtsied and quickly departed.

Elizabeth raised her chin. "These hands, Sir," she said at last, "will never give you pain again." As she spoke, she stroked his chin line and moved in closer.

He rested his hands on her waistline, pulling Elizabeth even nearer. Darcy's gaze encompassed her features and settled upon her lips. The familiar lavender wafted over him. "Madam, in a few moments, I may forget I am a gentleman, and you are a gentleman's daughter."

Elizabeth's giggle became a purr, silently revealing her undying love. "Ungentlemanly like behavior," she teased, "will have to wait until later, but I would not object to a kiss to seal our promise to each other."

His breath was ragged with anticipation; Darcy kissed her long and hard. "You see, my Dear, our love will go down in history," he whispered.

"Will it now?" she whispered back, her lips only inches from his.

"Great loves are always remembered. We will be Fitzwilliam and Elizabeth."

"Ooh, that is way too long. It does not roll easily off the tongue–Darcy and Elizabeth has more lilt to it." She nibbled on his lower lip.

"So, it is agreed; our love will be of what makes great legend." He turned his head burying it in her hair. "We will be as Romeo and Juliet or Othello and Desdemona."

She rose on tiptoes for another brief kiss. "I hope we do not have to die for our love. May we not be more in the manner of Petruchio and Katherine or Benedick and Beatrice?"

Darcy laughed softly. Even in the middle of an embrace, she would challenge him. Life with Elizabeth Bennet would be anything but boring. "So, the lady prefers comedy to tragedy?" He kissed her lightly, brushing his lips over hers.

"Our relationship has been a comedy of errors at times." She returned his kiss, as her fingers caressed the hair along the back of his neck. Her nearness captured Darcy; he bowed his head to hers once more and kissed her warmly.

Not wishing to disturb them, Georgiana watched this scene from the doorway. She whispered, "This is the type of love I want. It should be obvious to the world when a woman is in love; it should not be hidden. Thank God my brother kept me from making an odious mistake. How could I have been deceived into thinking what Mr. Wickham offered was love? What Fitzwilliam has with Elizabeth is real love." She cleared her voice to announce her presence; the lovers ceased the kiss, but they did not jump apart as one might expect upon being found in such an intimate embrace. They parted naturally, not ashamed of the affection they had shared.

Antony Fitzwilliam Visits
the Bride and Groom
by Mary Simonsen

November 20, 1812

Arm-in-arm, Mr. and Mrs. Fitzwilliam Darcy walked the gardens on their first full day at Pemberley. The previous day, they had arrived at the manor house just as the sun was dipping below the horizon. Nearly exhausted from the wedding breakfast and their travels, the two had dined on a light supper before retiring for the night. After making love, they were quickly asleep in each other's arms.

Since Elizabeth's first visit to Pemberley in August, the gardens had been completely transformed, with vivid yellows, oranges, and reds replacing the softer pastels of a warmer season. There was also another difference. When Lizzy had first admired the gardens, she did so as Elizabeth Bennet, a woman who was contemplating the very real prospect of spinsterhood, having rejected the marriage proposal of Fitzwilliam Darcy at the Hunsford parsonage. Instead, she had returned—triumphantly—as the Mistress of Pemberley.

As they walked the pebbled paths, Elizabeth's role as the mistress of such a great estate was very much on her mind. Her husband was attempting to reassure her that she was more than equal to the task of lady of the manor when they heard the sound of a carriage coming down the drive. From the noise it was making, they knew the conveyance was substantial, and Lizzy wondered aloud who their visitor might be.

"Good grief!" Darcy said as he caught site of the carriage with its two matched pairs of white stallions. With that exasperated exclamation, Lizzy knew who their visitor was: William's cousin,

Antony Fitzwilliam, Earl of _____, the black sheep of the Fitzwilliam clan, an unrepentant reprobate and willing fodder for London's scandal sheets.

Through gritted teeth, Darcy declared he was not ready to return to the house. "Antony can amuse himself. It is so easily done."

Pulling Elizabeth by her hand, he turned in a direction away from the manor.

"William, I know you are unhappy with your cousin's unexpected arrival, but, really, it is our responsibility to make him welcome," Lizzy said, trying to keep up with her husband.

"But he is NOT welcome. He has come for one of two reasons: to make sport at my expense because I am newly married or to find relief from his creditors by hiding out in Derbyshire. In the first instance, he shall fail because I am happy to be married. As for the second reason, he knows better than to ask me for money."

There was a third possibility. His wife, a woman he referred to as the Evil Eleanor, had prevailed—again—in one of their epic rows, and he had to run for his life.

"William, is it not possible he has come to wish us joy?"

"If that was his purpose, then he should have attended the wedding breakfast. Although I did not invite him, you did!"

In the whole of England, there were few who could get a rise out of Fitzwilliam Darcy, but one of those people was now moving his considerable luggage into a guest bedchamber at Pemberley.

* * *

"You can stay the night, but that is it," Darcy said by way of greeting his cousin.

"I am very happy to see you, too, my dearest Fitzwilliam," Antony said, chuckling. After taking Elizabeth's hand, he pressed it against his lips and allowed them to linger.

716

"If you were so keen to see us, why did you not go to the wedding breakfast?" Darcy barked. "And please remove your lips from my wife's hand."

"The reason I did not attend the wedding was because it is the height of rudeness to outshine the bride," Antony said in a serious voice. "Or so I was told by my wife on our wedding day."

In an age of men's fashion dictated by the immaculate Beau Brummel, Antony Fitzwilliam, wearing an embroidered coat, hose, and high-heeled shoes with jeweled buckles, much preferred the more ornate dress of his father's generation. For the earl, "fitting in" was never a desired outcome.

"William, Milord, shall we continue this conversation in a room where there are chairs?" Lizzy asked, leading the men from the foyer to the drawing room.

"Elizabeth, if you don't mind, I would like to speak to my cousin in private," Darcy said.

"Well, I mind," Antony immediately answered. "If you leave, my dear, I shall be subjected to one of William's sermon, and I get preached to on Sunday."

"Nonsense!" William answered, his voice nearly a shout." The last time you were in a church, it was struck by lightning." It also happened to be Antony's wedding day.

"I shall see to the refreshments," Lizzy said, backing out of the room, leaving the two bulls to lock horns.

"Antony, you cannot stay here. I have no intention of beginning my married life with you causing mischief at every opportunity."

"William, William, William. I am not moving in. I am merely paying a call to wish you and your delightful bride connubial bliss."

"I would be more likely to believe you if you did not travel with enough baggage to furnish the court at Windsor," Darcy harrumphed. "And the length of this visit will be...?"

"That depends on you."

"All right. How much do I need to pay to make you go away?" When Antony told him the amount required to satisfy his most pressing creditors, Darcy agreed to advance him the sum. "When do you leave?"

"Another twenty pounds, and I shall be gone by first light."

"Done."

A Princess for a Mistress
by Nina Benneton

November 21, 1812

"Monday we sort and soak soiled linens, Tuesday we wash and boil any that needed boiling, Wednesday we dry and fold, Thursday we mangle, Friday we iron, and Saturday we…" Martha paused.

The wee thing standing in front of her appeared overwhelmed.

Martha glanced around the washroom before lowering her voice, "Have you done any laundering work before?"

"No, Cousin Martha, but I'm very willing to learn. Mr. Martindale has my mum send his wash out every week." The girl's voice was as timid as a poor curate's church mouse. "Please, I can work very hard."

"Don't fret," Martha soothed. "It takes a while to learn how things are done at a grand place like Pemberley."

The poor lass's mum, a distant relative and Mr. Martindale's maid, had begged Martha to find a suitable position for her young daughter, to be out of the way of that reprobate Martindale's too-interested-in-young-girls eyes. Fortunately, little Meg's unexpected arrival a few days ago was on the same day that the newly married master brought the mistress home, and the happy but distracted Mrs. Reynolds had reluctantly agreed to hire the girl as Martha's helper.

Spending fifteen hours a day in the hot, wet and smelly washroom was not the kind of work Martha would wish for an eleven-year-old, but at least the poor girl's virtue was safe from an old man's roving hands.

Behind them, two maids sorted through the dirty clothes and

719

linens. Annie, one of the chambermaids sent down to help with the laundry this week, spoke in her usual too-loud voice. "Now that there's a mistress at Pemberley, Mrs. Reynolds expects the washings will take up the whole week."

Sarah, the other laundry maid who worked with Martha, giggled. "From the look of it, the daily soiled bedclothes from the mistress's apartment alone will keep us busy in the washroom for a while."

Martha reminded them, "There are young ears here."

"A married gentry woman must earn her keeps." Annie's voice retained its loud volume. "If I could learn the mistress's secret of catching a husband, I'd catch me a squire."

Martha rounded on the maids. "You two need to mind your tongues, talking about your new mistress in such a way."

Sarah had the grace to look embarrassed, but Annie coolly threw Martha a dismissive glance.

Martha flushed, not missing the chambermaid's message. A lowly laundress like Martha had no right to correct a chambermaid. Annie had thought it beneath her being assigned to help out in the washroom a few hours a day. Martha snorted, as if carrying the Darcys' refuse down the backstairs each morning was a more honorable chore than washing their soiled unmentionables.

"Cousin Martha, I saw a princess," Meg whispered.

"We're done here for now," Annie said and pulled Sarah to the drying room. Annie's voice could be heard whispering, "Fifty pounds a year as a dowry! That's hardly enough to pay for Mrs. Reynolds' annual wage. I can talk about the mistress any way I wish to the likes of Martha."

Martha decided to ignore them and turned to show Meg how to loosely fold the soiled bed linens in the buck to prepare them to soak in lye. Pointing to a small spigot at the base of the wooden tub, she instructed, "Keep drawing and pouring the lye over the linens until the lye come through clean. Looks like this batch won't need more than a few rinses before it goes on the drying rack in the next room."

Little Meg was right, Martha thought thirty minutes later. The child showed she was a quick learner and a hard worker, performing her chore efficiently and never needing an instruction repeated twice. Still, Martha worried about laundry work being too tiring for the innocent babe. A child her age should be out in sunshine. "What's this about a princess?"

"When the cart stopped at the Bakewell inn, a pretty princess stepped from a fancy coach and passed by me," the child answered. "I asked her why she was smiling, and she told me she'd just married the prince and they were on their way to his castle. Saturday we rest?"

"What?" It took a moment for Martha to realize the child had jumped to a new topic with that last question. "No, Saturday we scrub and clean the washroom, the drying room, and then Sunday—"

Sounds of footsteps approaching the washroom interrupted. Mrs. Reynolds entered, followed by Mrs. Darcy.

"These next three rooms are for the washing of the whole of Pemberley, Mrs. Darcy," the housekeeper was speaking. She smiled at Martha, then catching sight of little Meg, the housekeeper's eyes widened and the smile slipped from her face.

Oh dear. Martha bit her lip. Mrs. Reynolds had forgotten about the child's presence in the laundry. Eyes bulging, the child stared at the mistress. Martha curtsied to Mrs. Darcy and motioned for Meg to copy her.

Head bent, eyes downcast, little Meg finally dipped.

In a hurried manner, one arm pointing to the door where they'd just entered through, Mrs. Reynolds said to Mrs. Darcy, "Let me show you the stables. I believe Mr. Darcy is there making sure the horses are being readied for your riding lesson."

An alert look on her face, Mrs. Darcy said, "My apologies for interrupting your working. Martha, is it?"

"Yes, Ma'm." Martha said, surprised at the new mistress

remembering her name. As all the other lower servants such as the scullery maid and the dairy maid and such, she had only met Mrs. Darcy up close once, when the steward had all the servants lined up to greet their new mistress on her arrival.

Mrs. Darcy turned and studied little Meg for a moment then swept her gaze around the washroom. "Where is the mangle machine kept?"

"In the room beyond the drying room," Mrs. Reynolds answered, glancing in Martha's direction.

Martha met the housekeeper's puzzled eyes. How odd for the young mistress to ask about the mangle at such a moment. Martha hesitantly addressed the mistress, "Would you like to see it, Mrs. Darcy?"

"Not at the moment, thank you," Mrs. Darcy replied in an easy manner. She stepped close to little Meg. "Are you good with chickens?"

Once again Martha's eyes met Mrs. Reynolds's puzzled ones. Their new mistress was definitely uncommon, asking such random, odd questions.

Little Meg's face lit up. "Yes, Ma'am. I helped my mum with the hens at home. That was my job."

"Wonderful." Mrs. Darcy turned to her housekeeper. "I worry about the child with the mangle. The hens in the poultry yard could use a little mistress. Do you not think so?"

Mrs. Reynolds smiled a broad smile. "I do believe you're right, Mrs. Darcy. I shall arrange it."

Speechless, Martha blinked. Praise heavens! Little Meg would be out in sunshine and fresh air. "Thank you, Ma'am."

As regal as any heiress with a dowry of fifty-thousand pounds, Mrs. Darcy inclined her head. "I do believe two laundry maids may not be adequate in here though. Perhaps one of the chambermaids? The one who normally attends to Mr. Darcy's rooms. I noticed earlier today that his bed wasn't aired."

Mrs. Reynolds's eyes narrowed. Martha tipped her head toward the drying room. After a quick glance, the housekeeper turned to the mistress. "I shall take care of it, Mrs. Darcy."

"Thank you, Mrs. Reynolds. Now, please lead me to the stables and help me think of an excuse to tell Mr. Darcy I am too delicate a creature to be sitting atop some beastly moving animal," Mrs. Darcy headed toward the door, followed by a smiling Mrs. Reynolds.

Martha signaled Meg. The child was quick to comprehend. She hurried toward the mistress. "Please, Ma'am, thank you."

Eyes twinkling, Mrs. Darcy paused. "I cannot have anyone, much less little children, in my castle crushed by the mangle, can I?"

The new mistress barely disappeared from the door when a torrent of excited words rushed from little Meg. "Could you help me find someone to write to my mum and tell her I met a princess on the way here to you, and though I wasn't supposed to talk to strangers or my betters, I told the princess I was being sent to work in Cousin Martha's washroom and how fearful I was of being crushed by the mangle…and now I'm to be minding the hens in the poultry yard of the castle…"

Mr. and Mrs. Darcy Enjoy
Pemberley's Myriad Charms
by Sharon Lathan

November 22, 1812

Most days during their first weeks together they rose late and casually strolled around Pemberley. Slowly Lizzy began to acquaint herself with the manor's layout. Darcy was correct in stating that it really was not that confusing. The hallways were set up in a linear fashion and the rooms universally square or rectangular. Perhaps not overly imaginative, but it was easy to navigate. By the end of her first week as Mistress, she was confident enough to wander on her own around the main floor, which she did on those few occasions when Darcy was occupied with a business matter. Nonetheless, she was constantly amazed and, frankly, significantly intimidated by the vastness of the house and by the plethora of art, furnishings, history, wealth, and beauty that Pemberley housed. The more she saw, the more she was awed by the responsibilities her husband carried on his broad shoulders.

The staff was mysteriously everywhere and yet unobtrusive at the same time. Lizzy never once actually witnessed a maid cleaning, yet the manor was spotless. A footman materialized magically when Darcy needed one, then vanished as speedily. Darcy greatly impressed Lizzy by knowing the names of each of them, always making eye contact, and unfailingly inserting "please" and "thank you" into each command. The staff's devotion to their master and Pemberley was apparent in their manner and in the pristine condition of the house.

Lizzy had learned much about the estate's interests during her engagement. Darcy's pride and pleasure regarding Pemberley were unmistakable. Unwittingly, conversations about his home, both then and now, had given Lizzy tremendous insight into the business affairs that her husband managed. She knew that his income stemmed not only from Pemberley itself, but also from investments, trade, and industrial and commercial enterprises in England and abroad. Nonetheless, the bulk of the estate's income came from agriculture, livestock, cotton milling, and horse breeding. The farmlands were extensive and offered varying produce, including fruit orchards and grains. Two mills used the power of the River Derwent and modern technology to process the grains and shorn wool. Livestock consisted primarily of sheep with a few goats and wandering fowl. The wild game was generally left unmolested except for the occasional hunting parties Darcy allowed and, of course, for their own table.

Her husband handled all of these aspects of Pemberley's business efficiently and dutifully. However, Lizzy had rapidly established that his heart lay with his horses. Darcy was a horseman through and through. He confessed to her that, if it were possible, he would happily consign all his responsibilities to someone else and immerse his energies into breeding and training the fine horses of Pemberley.

Thus it was that on this day, Darcy enthusiastically escorted her to the stables.

The complex that accommodated the horses, carriages, and equipment, and the massive staff necessary to maintain it all, was two storeys high and a marvel of exquisite architecture and craftsmanship. A high arch facing south opened onto an enormous courtyard amid the complex where the animals were groomed and cared for. The thoroughbreds were separated from the working horses, each with their own handlers and grooms.

The weather had taken an abrupt turn for the worse. Ominous clouds hovered on the horizon, and Darcy assured Lizzy that it would snow by that evening. Despite the cold, the grooms went about their duties. They acknowledged Darcy's presence and, as always, Darcy addressed each of them by name. Lizzy was not a horse expert, yet it was immediately apparent, even to her uneducated eyes, that the thoroughbreds of Pemberley were magnificent. Darcy seemed intimately acquainted with each one of them. Parsifal, naturally, had the best stall and was visited by his master first. Treats were given and he was again introduced to Lizzy, who overcame her fear enough to stroke his soft nose.

Darcy knew of Lizzy's apprehension around horses, so he thought it best to take her to the new colt first. Who could not fall in love with a baby? They arrived just as one of the grooms was about to feed the young animal. Darcy assumed the task and encouraged Lizzy to assist him. One look into the playful, sweet face of the foal and she was captured. Before long she was kneeling in the straw, Darcy beside her, holding onto the makeshift milk bladder and nipple while the colt suckled. It was a fantastic experience. Despite all expectations to the contrary, Lizzy bonded with the foal and named him Wolfram, after Wolfram von Eschenbach, the poet who wrote *Parzival* from which Darcy had taken Parsifal's name. This brought a huge grin to Darcy's lips and filled his heart with joy.

Next he took her outside to the training pen where a staggeringly feisty stallion was actively being broken. Heedless of what anyone might think, Darcy pulled Elizabeth against his chest, wrapping her with his thick greatcoat. Holding her tight to keep her warm in the gathering gloom, he explained the process unfolding in the corral. Elizabeth was both fascinated and horrified.

"It looks to be rather dangerous," she said.

"Yes, it can be. The stallions are incredibly strong and unpredictable. One must attain the perfect balance between harboring that strength and controlling it. The mares tend to be slightly more docile, but not by far."

"And you do this, William? You get in there with these perilous animals?"

"When I can. Unfortunately my duties do not allow me the freedom I would wish to be consistently hands on."

"Well, I am glad for that! It terrifies me to think of you in there. Have you ever been hurt?"

"No more than an occasional bruise or the wind knocked out of me. Once I had a mild concussion after being thrown, and there was the time I injured my thigh." He outlined his wounds with the same concern as if mentioning a paper cut.

Lizzy shuddered. She wished she could forbid him doing something she considered so reckless, but she had no right. One look at the intense emotion on his face as he watched the trainer at work, and she knew she would never wish him deprived of an occupation he so enthusiastically enjoyed. For his sake, she would exhibit interest in the stables and the world contained therein, but it would never be easy for her.

As Darcy predicted, the rain and then snow hit that afternoon. The inclement weather made exploring the extensive grounds beyond the immediate surrounds impossible for the present. Instead, Darcy took her to a random chamber on the top floor and pointed to features visible from the windows. The panoramic vista was breathtaking.

Pemberley Manor rested on a gentle hill so, from the third storey elevation, the countryside appeared to stretch for endless miles to the hazy horizon. She saw the pastures, orchards, and forest laid out like a patchwork quilt. She had a bird's eye view of the incredible and varied gardens, the Maze, the ponds and streams, the trout lake with fountains, and the cascading waterfall with Greek Temple barely discernible above. In September she had strolled through a couple of the gardens closest to the house, but her emotions had been so taut and her sensibilities so acutely affected by the man next to her that she scarcely recollected any of it.

Today they stood before a tall window, Lizzy enfolded in Darcy's strong arms, and enjoyed watching the snow gently blanket the earth and vegetation far below. Darcy's lips were near her ear, intermittently planting soft kisses as he spoke.

"Up above the Greek Temple is a secluded grotto," he told her. "There is a tiny pool sheltered by tall pines, elder, and willows. The pool is fed from underground so it is perpetually tranquil, acting as a mirror. The trees and bushes are so thick that when you enter, it is as if you have been transported to another world. When I was a child I would escape there with a book or my journal or nothing, just wanting to be alone. I would pretend I had magically left Earth for Mars or Jupiter. I even attempted to write a story once, relaying my adventures as the conqueror of this other planet." He laughed and Lizzy smiled at the vision of Darcy as a young boy. "I do not know what ever happened to that story, although I would surely be mortified if it was unearthed!"

He tightened his grip around his wife and continued, "I had not visited the grotto for years until this past June. After Rosings, and then attempting to drown my sorrow in London and too much brandy, I returned to Pemberley. The first place I thought of was the grotto, which surprised me after so many years, but I went again and again as if compelled. I did my best self-examination there. As you know, beloved, I did not expect ever to have you in my life, to be given this chance to prove my love to you. I only wished to become a better man, to learn from my mistakes. The peace that pervades the place soothed me beyond words. I remember musing once, fleetingly so as not to hope where no hope seemed forthcoming, that if ever I was so blessed as to earn your love, I would take you there. It would become our special place. I only wish the weather allowed me to do so now, but I must content myself with fantasies until the spring."

He smiled down at her. She brought her hand up to caress his face, meeting his loving and intense gaze. She grasped his neck and pulled his head to her, meeting his lips with a hungry kiss. She turned in his arms and encircled his waist, pressing her body to his, and whispered, "So, describe these grotto fantasies. Or better yet, employ this gift for pretending you appear to possess and show me."

Darcy did not hesitate. In quick long strides he crossed the room, locked the door, and returned to her arms. Between kisses and increasingly indulgent and fervent caresses, he painted a picture of hanging branches with dappled sunlight leaking through, gentle breezes, soft grass carpet, and the heady aroma of earth and pine and wild honeysuckle.

If the room was cold, neither of them felt it. The heat they generated was abundantly adequate and the pleasant diversion dissolved any thoughts of snowy landscapes.

An Anniversary
by Sharon Lathan

November 24, 1812

Lizzy was awoken by the sensation of something velvety with a lovely aroma brushing across her face. She opened her eyes to see her husband's handsome face hovering over her. His jubilantly dimpled smile, sparkling blue eyes, and disheveled hair were enough to instantly set her heart racing. It took her a moment to realize that he held a pink rose in his hands and it was this with which he was gently tickling her face.

"Happy anniversary, my precious wife," he declared in his rich, musical voice. "Elizabeth my love ... my light ... my heart ...." He unceasingly grazed her face, neck, and shoulders with the rose, sprinkling kisses between his endearments. "One week ago today, you made me the happiest of men, Mrs. Darcy, my beloved wife." He kissed her deeply then, pulling her body onto his, caressing her back with his hand and the flower.

"My husband, I note you are wearing your trousers. Under the present circumstances, is this not a ludicrous encumbrance?" she tantalized, planting nibbles to his neck.

"Nothing that cannot be easily rectified, my love." He laughed. "I did not think it wise of me to traipse to the conservatory unclothed. The staff has been shocked enough lately at my lack of modesty and propriety."

"You went to the conservatory this morning?" she asked with slight alarm.

"I needed to pick this for you," he touched her adorable nose with the rose, "and those as well." He waved his hand about the room and the five vases of varied flowers scattered about the chamber.

Lizzy sat up in bed, unconscious of the heavenly sight she presented to her husband, and smiled radiantly at the array of blooms. She turned her smile onto Darcy, devastating him further with love and desire, and teased, "You are doing it again, Mr. Darcy. Being entirely too fabulous, spoiling me beyond endurance, and setting the standard so high that you may exhaust yourself in an effort to reach higher than the previous pinnacle!"

He rose and kissed her quickly on the cheek. "Let me worry about that," he responded, and then left the bed before her beguiling charms drove further thought away. He returned from his dressing room swiftly with an enormous box, which he placed on the bed in front of her.

"William, you must cease buying me gifts! I do not require such gestures."

"Whether you require them or not is irrelevant, Mrs. Darcy. I will shower you with presents because I am entirely egocentric and I extract pleasure from admiring your happy face! Humor me, if nothing else."

She pretended to scowl, but could not maintain it for long. She opened the box and gasped in shock. She pulled out an ankle-length pelisse of russet wool, lined and edged with sable. It was by far the most exquisite garment she had ever owned. With a squeal of glee, she robustly hugged her husband and then stood up on the bed, wrapping herself in the lush softness of the coat. The luxuriant contact of the fur on her bare skin was positively vivifying. She pranced seductively about the bed, making Darcy smile and laugh aloud.

"You see," he gushed, "the pleasure is wholly mine. I am selfishly overcome with joy." He clutched her legs and drew her onto his lap. "Now let me see what other self-serving indulgences I can secure."

* * *

Just prior to noon, Lizzy sat in Darcy's study while he worked at his desk. She pretended to read a book, but was more fascinated with inspecting her husband. A small crease sat between his brows as he concentrated. He rolled the quill in his fingers and rubbed his chin when ruminating. Occasionally his lips would silently mouth the words on the document before him. Frequently he would sigh or harrumph or aah or curse or grumble, without being aware he did so. Lizzy adored simply observing him, learning more about him in these unconscious mannerisms.

A knock at the door led to the entrance of Mr. Keith, who requested a moment of Mr. Darcy's time. With alacrity, and a thankful nod to Mr. Keith, Lizzy rose and left the two gentlemen alone. Mrs. Reynolds stood outside the door. "Is everything ready?" Lizzy asked.

"As you requested, Mrs. Darcy."

"Thank you!" and with a brief squeeze to Mrs. Reynolds' hands, Lizzy flew up to her dressing room where Marguerite was waiting.

About forty-five minutes later, Mr. Darcy emerged from his study, asked a footman where Mrs. Darcy could be found, and was told that she was in the conservatory. Darcy walked speedily, already lamenting the absence of his wife. He called to her when he entered, and her voice came from the far side of the room. He made his way around the profusion of potted plants and trees. The tableau before him stopped him dead in his tracks.

A clearing had been made and a luncheon was arranged as if outdoors, hamper and all. Elizabeth stood, wearing her lightest muslin summer gown with only a thin chemise underneath and satin lawn slippers. Her hair was down, with the side strands twisted into an elaborate braid in back. The warmth of the conservatory, the aroma of the blooms, the sunlight shining through the ceiling and walls of glass, along with the blanket on the floor, created the perfect summer scenario.

"Happy anniversary, Fitzwilliam!" Lizzy approached her stunned husband and without preamble began unbuttoning his coat.

"I know it is a poor substitute for your grotto, so we must pretend." She laid his coat aside and then kissed him. "I could not forget the day you made me the happiest woman in the world, my love. One whole week you have tolerated me! You have earned a medal, but instead you will get only lunch. Now sit. I shall serve our food."

Lizzy also had a gift for her husband. "It is rather silly," she blushingly remarked when she handed him the small box. "I did not have the foresight to buy a real gift for you. Instead I recalled an inane French novel I read when I was a girl, a poorly written romantic piece of tripe. There was this one thing I thought sweet, in my girlish idea of romance."

Darcy opened the box and saw a small satin pouch with a drawstring closure. "Look inside," Lizzy said, biting her lip in nervousness. He pulled out a long slender tress of her silky hair that had been braided and tied on each end with fine thread. "You see," she explained, "now you will permanently have a small part of me with you even if I am not there."

He stared at her in disbelief. "You thought this was silly? This is … astounding! Elizabeth, I do not have the words!" He kissed her tenderly and held her chin with his fingers. "My love, I resort to buying gifts because it is what I am accustomed to. You look inward to your heart and give far more generously than I. I will cherish this and bear it with me for all my life. I so love you, Elizabeth."

It was a lovely afternoon. There is something mysterious about picnics—even indoor ones—that immediately causes one to feel mellow and whimsical. One week of wedded bliss, and they both already had scores of memories to record into their journals, not that either of them would ever forget the passion and joy of these first days.

Mr. and Mrs. Darcy at Home at Pemberley by Susan Mason-Milks

November 25, 1812

Elizabeth awoke slightly disoriented but then quickly remembered where she was—the big bed in Darcy's room. The past few days—and nights—had been perfection. Their first night together, their afternoon nap, dinner by candlelight, and then more nights of new experiences and revelations—this kind of intimacy in a relationship was so much more than she had ever dreamed of. At last, she was truly his wife and although her face reddened at the thought of what transpired between them, her body tingled and her heart rejoiced.

As she lay quietly taking time to enjoy becoming more fully awake, she sensed she was alone in the big bed. It seemed strange to her that Darcy could have arisen without waking her, and she began to wonder how late she had slept. The clock told her it was only eight in the morning, not so late as she had first thought. Reaching her arms above her head, she stretched out fully and thought about her plans for the day.

Just as she started to sit up, she realized she was missing something very important—her nightdress. In the rush to be together last night, Darcy had pulled it off and tossed it into the air. It must have landed somewhere on the floor near the bed. Scanning the room, she saw it was now neatly draped across a chair along with her dressing gown. She groaned. Two things came to her mind—how did it get there and more importantly, how was she going to retrieve it.

It was a long way from the big bed to the chair. Reclaiming her nightclothes would necessitate walking eight to ten feet across the room completely unclothed. She would die of embarrassment if one of the servants should choose that exact moment to come into the room! Or what if Darcy returned? It was one thing to be with him under the covers, but it would be something different altogether to be caught out in the open. Just thinking about it made her face warm.

Finally, acknowledging she might be forced to wait for a long time if she did not brave the walk, she took a deep breath and made a dash for the chair. She had just slipped the gown over her head and was starting to reach for the robe when there was a knock on the door. Startled into action, she dashed back to the bed and leaped in pulling the covers up around her.

The door swung open, and Darcy entered carrying a tray with coffee and scones. "I have brought your breakfast, Mrs. Darcy. Ah, I see you have been up already," he said, nodding toward the chair.

"Did you...," she trailed off, waving her hand anxiously in that direction.

"No, your things were there when I awoke."

"So someone came in while we were asleep and..." her voice trailed off again. Elizabeth groaned and pulled the covers over her head. Darcy laughed as he set the tray down on the bed. Gently, he uncovered her face and kissed her forehead.

"Most likely, it was your maid Margaret since your dressing gown was on the chair as well," he said as he began pouring coffee into the delicate china cups.

"I do not think I shall ever become accustomed to having servants around me all the time. Does it never disturb you? Sometimes, I feel as if I am never alone."

Darcy shrugged. "I do not think about it. Their presence is just a fact of life. Of course, there are times when I wish to be alone. Everyone knows not to come into my study without knocking, and usually no one enters my bedchamber in the morning until I ring. Perhaps, you might tell your maid the same."

"I am not sure if I shall ever be completely comfortable. They must know everything we do."

He raised an eyebrow. "Well, not everything." Darcy added milk and sugar to the cup before handing it to her. Reaching up, he fingered a stray lock of her hair and watched her intently. She blushed under his gaze.

"My love, if you are going to turn red every time I look at you...," he began as he stroked her cheek with his thumb. She leaned her head against his hand.

"I cannot control it. It just happens," she told him.

He gave a short laugh. "Strange, isn't it that this is the one sort of situation in which you are the one who is shy and instead of me."

"Do not tease." She set her coffee aside. "Now I feel very much in need of hearing again that you love me."

At that, he smiled. "Lizzy, sweetheart, you must know you are my whole world. I do not think I truly lived until I met you." Starting just below her ear and working his way down to her shoulder, he placed light kisses on her sensitive skin.

She shivered. Tipping her head back slightly, she closed her eyes, lost in the sensations.

When he reached the obstacle of the strap of her nightdress, he gently slid it off her shoulder. "Lizzy?"

"Hmm?" Dreamily she opened her eyes and found him watching her.

"I love you," he said softly.

Putting her arms around his neck, she pulled him down to her. Slowly, taking his time, he made sure his lips communicated exactly the extent of his regard.

A Wife's Power
by Nina Benneton

November 30, 1812

Power. Sturdy half-boots secured on a raised mound, Elizabeth Darcy stood at the tradesman's entrance and surveyed the backside of her new home. Behind two crescent-shaped outbuildings, Pemberley's sixty-six household offices loomed. In those rooms, a regiment of servants, almost all Derbyshire bred, considered Pemberley their home and Fitzwilliam Darcy their beloved master.

Not for anything in the world would she admit to anyone, much less her new husband, how the word 'power' discomposed, if not outright intimidated, her.

"For centuries, ownership of land and estate, and all its attendant responsibility, has been the main and only sure basis of power for any respectable Englishman," Fitzwilliam had once lectured Charles Bingley during a walk to Oakham Mount, just days before the wedding.

"I readily own I possess no little trepidation about taking on the responsibility of a landowner, Darcy," Mr. Bingley had replied. "In my defense, I must remind you that I have neither the temperament nor inclination for it. I was not born and bred, as you have been, to expect the possession of such daunting power as my birthright."

Softly, Elizabeth chuckled. Mr. Bingley was correct in all his points. Fitzwilliam, a tender and attentive a husband as any bride could wish for, was first and foremost the Master of Pemberley. The mantle of power cloaked about his shoulders with an enviable ease that mere mortals, she included, could only marvel at.

Yet, she could not escape the ugly thought which troubled her. In marrying her, a portionless woman who brought him, beyond a lively mind and impertinent wit, no land or fortune, no connection, no discernible advantage, Fitzwilliam's power as a landowner had decreased.

A flock of doves flew overhead. Elizabeth followed them with her eyes. The birds landed on the lantern of a small, octagonal shaped dovecote next to the poultry yard and the duck pond. Curious about the construction of the building, Elizabeth headed toward it, ruminating as she walked.

Mrs. Reynolds was an experienced and efficient housekeeper, ever so helpful and respectful, but Elizabeth had no doubt the success of her own tenure as mistress of Pemberley was dependent on her earning the respect and, if she was fortunate, affection of the rest of the staff.

Elizabeth sighed. How was she to rise to the responsibility as Mistress of Pemberley when she felt so ill-equipped? Pemberley's annual income may be only five times that of Longbourn's, but infinitely more bewilderingly complex. Her new home has a postman's room, a lamp room, a knife room... A room for every imaginable chore there was that she, in her previous life as Miss Elizabeth Bennet, had never even given a thought to, much less took an interest in.

She could blame her mother for ill-preparing her, but it was her own laziness, preferring to spend her hours scampering about the wild paths of Hertfordshire, hiding in her father's library, and losing herself in the fictive world of books, instead of shadowing her mother. Being a responsible mistress of a large household meant more than knowing how to give orders to servants.

"If you were thinking of entering, I wouldn't advise it, Mrs. Darcy," a voice said somewhere to her left. "It's damp and dark in there."

Startled, she stopped and looked around. She had reached dovecote.

An old man, hatless and coatless, the buttons of his waistcoat misaligned, his forehead knotted in a half-fearsome, half-comical frown, stood three feet away.

She glanced down. He was also shoeless. His feet, brown and bare, were caked with a dark green mud. "You have the advantage of me, Mister…?"

"Diggory Field." He raised his hand and gave her a mock doffing of his invisible hat and dipped his knees as if performing a country dance. "I do odd jobs for the farrier and sometimes the gamekeeper."

She deliberated admonishing him for his insolence, but the anticipatory gleam in his eyes told her he was expecting just that reaction. Instead, she glanced back at the building and kept her voice casual. "How many birds does the dovecote hold?"

"Over a thousand, but gamekeeper culled them a few years ago. Building's empty."

"I saw a few birds fly in," she said, curious now why he did not want her to explore the building. Longbourn had a dovecote, half-timbered and smaller, but it held as many birds. In addition to using pigeons' droppings as a fertilizer on the farm, her father's bailiff sold them to the tanner for softening leather.

"Probably no more than ten or so straggling pairs nest in there. The steward thought he might use the building for something else." His bare feet treaded in place on the cold ground. "The Darcys have never been keen on squeakers at the table."

"Squeakers?"

"Squabs, nestlings, you probably call them." He walked toward the pond. "Going to be cold soon, next day or so. That pond is shallow enough for the ice house to be filled if it gets cold enough to freeze. Come, Ma'am."

Elizabeth had taken a few steps before she stopped. Chagrined, she had followed his commanding voice.

He did not pause. "I'll show you the ice house. You'd more than likely trip over it otherwise."

Irritated, she squared her shoulders. "In a moment, Mr. Field. I wish to peek inside of the dovecote first."

He stopped then and favored her with a glare. "You wouldn't look too pretty to the Master with pigeons' slop on you."

"I am familiar with the inside of a dovecote. I shall watch my footing," Elizabeth returned icily, ignoring his mention of her husband. If it weren't for her concern over the servant's shoeless state, she would have him dismissed for his insolence.

A low door, about four feet, on the southeast wall opened with a surprising well-oiled smoothness that startled her momentarily. Immediately, the pungent odor of pigeons' excrement swooped down over her. She grimaced, held her breath, and fought not to gag. Before she stepped inside, she directed the ill-mannered servant to wait outside. Ignoring his protests, she closed the door on him.

She stood still and waited for her eyes to adjust to the dimly lit interior. Faint shafts of light, beaming from the dormer windows, allowed her to see rows and rows of nesting boxes circling the inner walls. Gentle cooing mingled with the soft noises of feathers rustling, intermittently interrupted by the occasional shrill squawks of the nestlings.

From the sounds the birds made, there were definitely more than ten pairs here. Mindful of a central pole with braced horizontal beams where ladders could be hung to access the nesting boxes, she gingerly made her way to the center. As she was about to climb a ladder, the unmistakable sound of person breathing heavily checked her.

Heart leaping to her throat, Elizabeth spun and pressed her back against the wall. "Who is there?"

No answer other than the noises from the birds, then a faint sound of someone trying to muffle their own breathing but failing.

Holding her own breath, her eyes straining to peer into the shadow, Elizabeth inched sideways toward the door.

The door opened. Diggory Field's voice sounded too loud in the dark. "Come on out, Tetty. It's only the young mistress, newly married and as obstinate as you."

A dark, clump of a shadow unfolded upright from a low corner. "Ma'am, are there any men out there, besides him, that is?"

Elizabeth released a breath slowly and willed her heart to settle down to her chest. She shook her head then realized Tetty, whoever she was, may not see her clearly. "No. Is he harming you?"

"No, Ma'am," Tetty said. "But I'm not coming out until there are other men out there."

Despite her words, Tetty did not sound frightened, which reassured Elizabeth. "May I enquire why you are hiding in here?"

Mr. Field said, "Has it occurred to both of you daft women that if I'd a fancy, I could shut this door, lock it, and trap you both in?"

Tetty's shadow scrambled to the door. With what she hoped was a more dignified pace, Elizabeth followed. Once outside, she blinked until her eyes adjusted to the brightness, then turned to examine the other woman.

Wearing a dress that looked as if it hadn't been washed since the last Michaelmas, Tetty appeared to be the same age as Elizabeth herself, though nature had been more generous with her feminine attributes. She, at least, had shoes on her feet and a cap on her head, even if both were tattered and mud-colored. Most curiously, above her right elbow, she wore a horse halter as an arm bracelet.

Elizabeth glanced around. There was no horse within sight.

"Now you've done it, Tetty." Mr. Field settled himself down on a large rock. "You pricked the mistress's curiosity, and she doesn't seem like the type to leave things well enough alone."

Tetty bobbed a curtsy. "Didn't mean to scare you in there, Ma'am. Would you happen to know when's the next market day at Bakewell?"

"I am afraid I do not." Elizabeth wondered at the couple's odd behavior. "I am Mrs. Darcy. May I help you, uh...Tetty, is it?"

"If it pleases you. That's what he calls me now, Ma'am," Tetty tipped her head toward Mr. Field, who was now picking the dry mud off his feet with a twig. "He didn't like calling me by my Christian name, Elizabeth."

"I'd figured if 'Tetty' was good enough for Dr. Johnson's Elizabeth, it's good enough for my missus," Mr. Field paused in his mud scraping and cast Tetty a sardonic glance, "however temporary."

Surprised this shoeless servant was educated enough to know about Dr. Samuel Johnson, Elizabeth stared at him for a moment before she turned toward the woman. Was this young woman truly married to the old man? Had Elizabeth stumbled into a marital spat of this odd, mismatched couple? "Are you Mrs. Field?"

Tetty nodded. "Only until the next market day, Ma'am, if he'll be reasonable."

"If I weren't a reasonable man, I'd still have my hat, my coat and my shoes." Her husband switched to scraping his other foot. "You've caused me trouble with the new Mistress. She's thinking of having the master dismiss me, very likely, all because I tried to stop her from going into your hiding place."

"I wouldn't have had to hide if you'd taken me to the Bakewell fair as you promised," Tetty countered.

He shrugged. "I had to promise you something, else the cart driver giving us a ride would have gladly unloaded us into the ditch, the way you wouldn't stop bawling."

"I was supposed to go home with the baker," Tetty wailed.

"Instead of giving you that fancy name Elizabeth, your parents would have been better to give you some sense to recognize when a man's—" he broke off, rose, and stalked off a short distance away, again muddying his feet.

His young wife promptly burst into tears. "What will become of me!"

Elizabeth approached her. Though the old husband was out of hearing distance, she kept her voice quiet, "I promise that nothing bad will happen to you."

Tetty continued crying for a few moments longer before she raised a tear-stained face and shook her head. "Thank you, Ma'am. But you can't do nothing. If he won't sell me as he promised at the

Bakewell fair, I'm stuck with him."

"What?" Elizabeth shook her head, hoping she had not heard correctly. "You want him to sell you?"

Tetty wiped her face with a dirty sleeve. "You'd want to be sold if you were married to him, wouldn't you?"

"But, but…" Elizabeth had to admit, the other woman had a point. She eyed the halter on Tetty's arm. She had heard of the deplorable practice of wife selling at an auction during some market fairs indulged by the lower order, but she'd never known anyone who'd been a party to such evil deed in Hertfordshire. "How long have you been married to him?"

"Since day before yesterday," Tetty answered. "After he bought me at the Buxton's fair, he told me there's plenty of kind gentlemen who'd be appreciative of a young wife to help with the baking at Bakewell. But as soon as we arrived here, I found he'd lied."

Rage filled Elizabeth. She left Tetty and charged toward the old man, now scraping the mud off one foot against the trunk of a tree. "Mr. Field—"

"You'd be wanting to box for my ears for what Tetty's been telling you, I suppose?" He interrupted without pausing his scraping.

"Is it true?" She forced herself to speak in a calm voice. "You bought her at the Buxton fair?

He examined his scraped foot and made a face. "Guilty as charged."

Her hands balled into fists. "And now you're planning to sell her at Bakewell?"

"That's what she wants." He lowered one foot and raised the other to the trunk. "Ran and hid in the dovecote when I said I have no shoes to take her there."

For the first time in her life, Elizabeth wished to inflict physical harm on another person. "How dare you, buying and selling a woman as if she was a piece—"

"No, not horseflesh, Ma'am." His eyes fierce, both feet on the ground, he faced her. "She's worth less than horseflesh."

She was now Mrs. Darcy of Pemberley, not Miss Elizabeth Bennet of Longbourn, she reminded herself and pressed her balled fists against her sides. Not trusting herself to speak, she clenched her teeth and glared at him.

"There are men who value their horsefleshes more than their wives," his voice harsh, he continued, advancing closer. "Her previous husband, a gin-soused brute, had arranged with her lover, the baker, the sale of Tetty at the public auction in exchange for the baker's mare."

Unclenching her fists, she exhaled a slow breath and took a step back. His ire was not directed at her or Tetty, but at the two men, she realized. She, as was her wont, had jumped to conclusion and misjudged a man without understanding the whole backstory. "I am sorry I have mistaken the situation."

He turned and stared unblinkingly at the dovecote, where a flock of birds was now exiting through the lantern. "You know what the most shameful part of it all is, Mrs. Darcy?"

She glanced at Tetty, who was now worrying the halter with her fingers and staring at them. Though Elizabeth could hazard a guess to his question, she faced him and answered simply, "No."

"That the foolish girl accepted the transaction. She wore that halter around her neck without shame, thinking and accepting she had neither choice nor power to refuse." He stopped and rubbed his hatless head in a weary gesture. "In a foolish fit of chivalry, I impulsively decided to give her some power."

"You stepped in and bought her."

His eyes bleak, he gave her a wry smile. "My hat, my coat, and my shoes were a better bargain than the sick, old nag of the baker's."

Her gaze dropped to her half-boots. Tetty may not have allowed herself to feel humiliation at her circumstance. She had no choice but to submit. A man's wife was his property. According to the laws, a woman ceased to her own person, her own legal entity, the moment she was married.

"At least I talked her into wearing the halter around her arm instead of her neck. She refused to take off the halter 'cause she's fearful I mean to keep her and not sell her," he continued, his voice a mixture of sadness and disgust. "Even if I wanted to—and, trust me, I do not—I cannot keep a wife, much less one young enough to be my granddaughter."

The grimace in his face revealed more of his abhorrence to the idea than his last words did. She again glanced at Tetty, now sitting on a rock and waiting patiently. "What will you do with her?"

He sighed. "I'd give her to the next decent man I'd see for nothing, but that would mean her value is…"

"Less than what you paid for her," she finished when he stopped, looking as if he was embarrassed about his sentimentality.

"It's a rare man who'd value a woman who brought him nothing materially."

Not so rare. She thought of her husband. Reminded of her dear Fitzwilliam and his struggle to win her portionless hand, she smiled at Mr. Field.

He blinked and quickly backed away. "Is this how the young Master was bewitched? You flashed that bright smile at him, and with your pair of fine eyes—"

"Never mind about that," she impatiently interrupted. "I believe I may have a way to relieve you of your current difficulty."

He crossed his arms and shook his head. "Wouldn't work, Mrs. Darcy."

She scowled. "You have not heard of my idea."

"You offering her a position at Pemberley's bakehouse wouldn't work. She wants to be married with her own establishment, preferably to a baker so she can eat all the tarts she wants, she told me on the cart ride."

Not surprised the wily old man guessed her intention, Elizabeth instructed him, "Wait here."

"The young master's aware you're dictatorial as well as obstinate?"

She ignored him and hurried back to Tetty. It took her but a few short minutes of conversation before Tetty handed her the halter and, with nary a glance toward Mr. Field, ran off in the direction of the two outbuildings. Holding the halter in one hand, Elizabeth headed back toward Mr. Field.

He again doffed his imaginary hat and bowed to her. "Happy to see I was wrong about what Tetty wanted, Mrs. Darcy."

"You were not wrong," she corrected. "She does want to be married to a man with an establishment."

His face bore the wretched expression of a man faced with a distasteful task. His shoulders slumped, he said, "I best be seeing about borrowing a pair of shoes for the walk to Bakewell."

"However, I persuaded her to wait until she has earned enough to save for an adequate dowry. With an adequate dowry, she would make an attractive partner to a baker or even an innkeeper. She can choose her own man."

He straightened and exhaled a breath, his relief palpable.

She continued, "Until then, she will be employed at the bakehouse. I shall talk to Mrs. Reynolds."

He gave her a sly smile. "Perhaps I could persuade me wife to slip me a tart or two each day."

"You may have five tarts a day from Pemberley's bakehouse if you wish, but she is no longer your wife." Despite being informed that her 'wedding' and therefore her 'marriage' was not legal, Tetty was insistent she was married until Elizabeth came up with a creative solution. She held up the halter to Mr. Field. "I told her I had bought her from you."

His smile turned broad. "And what was my payment, Mrs. Darcy?"

"A hat, a coat, and a pair of shoes." She walked away. "And the added position of cleaner of the dovecote."

His voice indignant, he followed her. "For all my trouble, I now have to clean pigeons' slop?"

Lightly swinging the halter, she threw him her own sly smile.

"As your perquisite, you may sell it all to the tanner for extra income."

"That's mighty generous of you, Mrs. Darcy." He started to dance but checked himself. "You're certain the gamekeeper and the master are going to agree to my having the slop?"

She stopped and favored him with a glare worthy of her husband's imperious aunt. "I do not know nor care if the gamekeeper agrees. As to my husband, rest assured he supports whatever decision I make as Mistress."

He studied her for a long moment, then a gleam of respect appeared in his eyes. His bow this time was low. And sincere. "Mrs. Darcy, you may be young, but you know your own power."

She inclined her head and left him to his celebratory dance.

Heading towards the tradesman's entrance, she retraced her steps. Once she talked to the gamekeeper and Mrs. Reynolds about Tetty and Fields, she would inspect and learn the function of every one of the sixty-six household offices of her home, however long that took. After she mastered the inside, she would next turn her attention to learning about the dairy, the hoggery, the stew ponds and so forth.

She may not be the daughter of an earl as the late Lady Anne Darcy was, she may not be heiress to a large estate as Fitzwilliam's cousin Anne de Bourgh was, she may not be in possession of twenty-thousand pounds dowry as Miss Bingley was, but, Elizabeth paused on a mound, a small smile tugged at her lips as she surveyed her home, not many women would have turned down a marriage proposal from the Master of Pemberley.

Yes, she, Elizabeth Darcy, knew her own power. Fitzwilliam knew she had accepted his second proposal because she'd come to love him for himself, not for his power as Master of Pemberley.

Her power came from knowing she had given him that gift.

Lizzy at Pemberley
by Monica Fairview

December 10, 1812

"Farewell, my dear Mrs. Darcy."

A shiver of pleasure passed through Lizzy at the sound of her new name. She kissed the tips of her fingers and waved the kiss in his direction. Darcy responded with a half-smile but he didn't send her a kiss back. It was probably an improper thing to do.

She sighed. It was probably not quite proper to be leaning out of her bedroom window either, even if she was fully dressed. She was only too aware of the two liveried footmen standing at the carriage door, staring fixedly ahead as if blind and deaf. Then Darcy stepped into the carriage and one of the footmen, a youngster with blue eyes and an eager attitude, closed the door behind him. As the carriage drew away, she thought the footman glanced towards her window, but she couldn't be sure. It was probably her imagination. Being the mistress of a house like Pemberley was all so new, it wasn't surprising she didn't quite feel comfortable about it.

If she had learned anything from her stay at Netherfield when Jane was ill, it was that the servants watched every move she made and reported everything downstairs. She had discovered this to her chagrin when she had gone down to the kitchen to get some warm milk for Jane, only to discover to her embarrassment that they were talking about her.

"I had to clean her shoes, I should know," said a man's voice. "They were caked with at least two inches of mud. Shocking behavior. Walking across the field like a vagabond, I ask you. That's no lady fit to associate with the likes of Mr. Bingley and Mr. Darcy."

Lizzy shrank into herself and backed away from the doorway. She didn't want the servants to spot her. What would they think of her when they realized she had come downstairs herself to fetch the milk instead of ringing for it?

Well, let them think what they would. She wasn't going to let them intimidate her. If they already thought she wasn't a lady, well, then it didn't matter. They were the ones who were going to be embarrassed, at being caught gossiping.

She raised her head high, hoping her face wouldn't betray her, and swept boldly forward, stepping hard on the stone floor to warn them of her arrival.

The moment they spotted her they sprang to their feet. Lizzy noted a few red faces. Good.

"Miss Bennet? Can we help you?"

A tall thin woman addressed her, the housekeeper, to judge from the large collection of keys at her waist. Was that a sneer on the woman's face? Lizzy had never even met her before, yet already the housekeeper had passed judgement and decided she was not worthy of respect.

"I am here to fetch milk for Miss Bennet," said Lizzy, looking the housekeeper straight in the eye.

The housekeeper looked away.

"You oughtn't to have come down, Miss Elizabeth," said the maid who had done up her hair that morning, moving quickly to the doorway as if to block her way. "You could have rung for milk."

Lizzy looked at rows of faces turned towards her. There were at least twenty servants there. She had never seen so many servants assembled in the same room before.

"I could have," she said, with a small smile, "but I chose to come down. I needed the exercise. It is so very tiresome to be cooped up in a sickroom all day, even when it is my sister I'm caring for. Now if one of you will stop gawking like country bumpkins and give me the milk, I would like to return to Miss Bennet."

She had known as she walked away that they would all whisper about her. They were no different than Miss Bingley, who had made it abundantly clear she considered Lizzy unacceptable as a companion. After all, Miss Bingley had invited Jane but pointedly excluded Lizzy from the invitation. Jane's natural modesty and quiet manners were good enough to pass muster. Lizzy's knew well enough that her behavior was too unconventional for propriety, for most people.

Except for Mr. Darcy.

A heady warmth spread through her and she smiled. Dear Fitzwilliam. Fortunately, he did not think her too unconventional. Or at any rate, he was too madly in love with her to care if she was.

Still, she wasn't such a giddy young bride as to believe that his tolerance would last forever. Her mother had harped on this, and even though Lizzy could discard most of her words, there was one thing her mother said that had stuck in her mind.

"Now remember, Lizzy. Mr. Darcy may be a good catch, but it's much easier to catch a man than to keep him. You tickled his fancy, but we all know those things don't last forever. He is an important gentleman, with a great deal of pride. His uncle is an earl. Think of that! An earl in the family! I never thought I would live to see the day! You had better make sure you don't embarrass him in front of his family and friends. There is nothing more certain to turn a husband away than that. You'll have to learn how to behave in a manner appropriate to your station in life."

To think that she was supposed to take lessons in deportment and manners from her mother, when her mother's behavior had been so very bad. Lizzy still shuddered whenever she thought of it. But for once she had to admit her mother was right.

Lizzy had a difficult task ahead of her. Fitzwilliam had taken a risk, marrying her despite his family's disapproval. She didn't want him to wake up one day and find himself regretting it. She didn't want him to wish he had married someone more worthy of his high social position.

Lizzy watched the carriage until it disappeared behind the line of ancient oaks that bordered the long drive to the gate. She wished she could have gone with him. It was too soon for them to part. She felt a pang of loss, as though a part of her had gone with him. Fitzwilliam would be in London for almost a week. It seemed an unbearably long time.

Long enough, she hoped, for her to start preparing herself for the descent of guests upon Pemberley for Christmas.

Perhaps it was just as well that Darcy was leaving her alone for a while. She had many things to accomplish and very little time in which to do them, and more importantly, do them right.

Lizzy grinned and headed towards the breakfast room in search of Georgiana. She needed all the help she could get and more. Fortunately, she wasn't too proud to ask.

It was going to be hard work, but Lizzy liked a challenge. Almost as much as she liked Fitzwilliam.

Lady Catherine Condescends
to Inspect the
Happiness at Pemberley
by Diana Birchall

December 16, 1812

The approach to Pemberley was on a giant scale – the wide valley, the great house, the vast garden before and forested land rising behind. The inmates of the house, the owner and his family and servants alike, could see from very far off, across the valley, when carriages approached; and they had their choice of windows to watch from, as Pemberley numbered them in the hundreds.

Darcy and Elizabeth both paused for a moment in their busy lives to gaze out the long windows of the library at the bridge that crossed the river. A carriage and six were crossing at a rapid clip, and Darcy was able to identify the arms even from that distance.

"Yes, it's Aunt Catherine." He did not sigh, and his small philosophical shrug was barely noticeable.

Elizabeth peered out apprehensively. "You can't possibly see the de Bourgh arms from this distance, without the eyes of an eagle," she argued. "I do see that the coach is painted purple. I thought only royalty could have carriages that colour."

Mary, who was on a visit and always spent all her time at Pemberley in the library, shut her book. "That is true," she said, "Lady Catherine is breaking with protocol if she has painted her carriage purple. A magistrate for her county ought to know better."

Darcy did not appear to hear her, and took out his watch. "From where she is, it will take just under ten minutes until she is

752

handed out of her carriage. If we know what is good for us, we had better not fail to be standing in the portico to welcome her."

"Yes, indeed," said Elizabeth, following him swiftly out of the room. "And we had better give the signal to Mrs. Reynolds."

"She already knows," Mr. Darcy said with a slight smile, "don't you suppose the intelligence has traveled to her offices as swiftly as to us?"

"Oh, yes. And the whole kitchen staff has been working so hard these two days. The pies are like nothing ever seen outside of France before, I am told. Is it not a pity that the menu is likely to be judged a failure, and myself to blame?"

"My dear," he protested, "you would invite her! It was you who over-persuaded me. I should not, on my own judgment, have ever invited Aunt Catherine here again, after the things she said about you."

"Never mind," she said hastily, putting her hand gently on his lips. "I mean to make a fresh start with her, and forgive the past – if she will allow me."

"Always generous Elizabeth," he murmured, taking her hand and kissing it.

The carriage was drawn up, the appropriate servants opened and shut the doors, and Lady Catherine herself was standing in the hall. She looked from Darcy to his wife with sharp, disapproving eyes, and gave her head a small sententious shake, which made her high feathers quiver, bird like. Darcy bowed, and Elizabeth made a respectful curtsey.

"Welcome, Aunt," he said politely. "My wife and I are glad to see you at Pemberley again."

"Your wife! Sheat least has never seen me at Pemberley before," said Lady Catherine scornfully, turning a cold face toward Elizabeth. "But sometimes we live to see things that we never expected to countenance."

"You must be tired, Lady Catherine," said Elizabeth civilly. "Your room has been made ready, perhaps you may like to rest."

"Rest!" Lady Catherine thumped her silver-topped stick. "I have only driven from Bakewell this morning, and I am not so old for such a drive to completely overset me. I will take some tea. In Lady Anne's green Empress Catherine service, if you please. Our father – the Earl you know," she enunciated for Elizabeth's benefit, "brought it home from his Russian trip."

She turned back to Darcy. "I am glad to see at least, that the drive has not been altered, nor the beeches cut down."

Darcy's eyebrows lifted. "Cut down? Who would cut down such a noble line of trees? What could give you such an idea, Aunt?"

"I have heard of a great many shocking alterations," she said sourly. "It is common talk all over the countryside."

Darcy and Elizabeth wisely ignored this, as they walked through the grand saloon at a pace that accommodated Lady Catherine, who stopped every few steps to peer sharply at some object or inspect some vista.

"There! This is not the original Turkey carpet, I know. And the crystals on your mother's fine French chandeliers – they look peculiarly dark and muddy. It breaks my heart to see them so." She cast an accusing eye at Elizabeth. "I knew the new – wife would not be able to manage a large staff properly," she declared contemptuously. "How could it be expected, coming from such a family? She has not been brought up to it."

"I had the Turkish carpet moved into my room, when making some improvements before our wedding," Darcy informed her coolly. "I feared too many pairs of feet trod over it here. A good many visitors come to tour round Pemberley during the year, you know, Aunt."

She was only partly mollified. "Certainly, you have the right, as Master of Pemberley. But I am not sure the dear old house is properly cleaned." She ran a finger over the pink Italian marble fireplace at the head of the saloon. "I suppose your wife has sacked half the staff, and brought in her own favorites. Flibbertigibbets not trained properly in the art of dusting, no doubt. For it is an art, you know," she nodded significantly.

The staff is exactly as it was before our marriage," Darcy told her calmly, "not one change, except a new lady's maid for my wife." He and Elizabeth smiled into each other's eyes.

"And I know Reynolds has the chandelier crystals dipped in lemon water quite regularly," Elizabeth spoke up, "she told me so."

"Silence! No true lady speaks of her housekeeping. And if you have hired only one new lady's maid, then who, may I ask, will be attending me?"

"Did you not bring your maid?" asked Darcy, surprised. "I was sure I saw someone with you in the carriage."

"And we were hoping to see Miss de Bourgh," added Elizabeth, "and Mrs. Jenkinson."

"You speak of my daughter? You, who have taken her appointed, nay sacred, place – I do not know how you can dare – "

"Aunt Catherine," said Darcy firmly, with a look in his eye that succeeded in quelling her, "this is not the way to speak to Mrs. Darcy. Is Anne unwell, that she could not come?"

"Yes," answered Lady Catherine ungraciously, "she did not want – that is, she has a weak throat, and I fear quinsy, so I left her at home with her companion. I am here with Akers only. Where is she? Where is that fool woman? I want her to take my tippet. You keep it stiflingly hot in here. What is the use of a great fire in this hall, in April too, if we are not to sit here? I hope this does not mean there is a new regime of extravagance abroad at Pemberley."

"Mrs. Akers has been brought to the servant's hall for a hot drink and some victuals," explained Elizabeth. "I will pull the draw, and one of our maids will attend to you. And I thought we might take our tea upstairs in Georgiana's sitting-room, it is more comfortable than these great state-rooms."

"Humph! I can see the whole ordering of the place is in complete disarray," said Lady Catherine with disgust. Before she had finished speaking, a maid had entered, and was quietly helping her off with her ermine-tipped outer coat.

They mounted the stairs, about which Lady Catherine had much to say about proper care of hardwoods, the need to air marble, and the ill advisement of ever permitting a cat to enter a house. The lobby above merited only a brief catalogue of complaints about the placing of its portraits, which had not been changed, though Lady Catherine was sure that they had; but at last they reached Georgiana's pretty sitting-room. The young lady rose to greet her aunt and be kissed by her.

All were soon seated by the fire, and tea was bringing in, as Lady Catherine surveyed Georgiana's appearance. "You look well enough," she said grudgingly, "I hope that the sad demotion from your proper place as mistress of Pemberley has not made you ill."

Georgiana was shy, unwilling to speak at the best of times, and more frightened of her aunt than of most people, but she could not let this pass. "Oh, no, Aunt! I am so happy with my new sister – I do love Elizabeth dearly, and there could be no better mistress of Pemberley."

"You put a good face on it," said Lady Catherine dryly, "but I suppose you must, or risk her temper. There may be no end to the petty ways in which such a termagant will torment you when I am gone."

Georgiana continued to earnestly protest her love for her sister, and Elizabeth did not lift up her eyes, as she wanted to do, but only went on composedly pouring tea.

Mr. Darcy instructed the butler to invite their other guests to join them, if they desired, and in a few minutes Mr. and Mrs. Gardiner entered. With a true ladylike air, Mrs. Gardiner seated herself by Lady Catherine and helped Elizabeth and Georgiana to play hostess, as Elizabeth was uncharacteristically quiet and Georgiana made no more attempt to speak at all.

Lady Catherine seemed not displeased to meet the new lady, who was fashionably dressed and well spoken, and she unbent enough to give her, unasked, all the details of her journey, the dirtiness of the roads between Kent and Derbyshire, the discomforts of the inns, and her apprehension that the fabled luxuries of Pemberley might have diminished, through having a mistress who did not know its ways. "I was quite prepared for it having fallen to the condition of a veritable forlorn old ruin," she lamented.

"Oh, no," Mrs. Gardiner assured her with a smile. "We have been staying here some weeks, and I can tell you we have never been more comfortable in our lives. The beds you know are excellent – such fine old linen, all laid up in lavender – and the dinners deserve their wide fame. Why, John, tell Lady Catherine about the fine haunch of venison that was presented last night. I never saw such a one."

"The finest I have ever seen," her husband beamed, "shot by Darcy and Fitzwilliam, and cooked to such a turn! No French chef, I think, could."

"It will be on the sideboard tonight," said Elizabeth, "and there is a fresh turkey, as well as some astonishing pies."

Lady Catherine drew her heavy eyebrows together and tapped her cane. "Talking of your bill of fare. No lady does that. You will disgrace yourself before these elegant people. I knew how it would be," she sighed. "A constant series of shame."

Elizabeth's eyes sparkled. "I am endeavoring to learn the ways of the great," she said solemnly.

Darcy turned to his aunt and said earnestly, "Aunt Catherine, I believe your prejudices will be gradually removed, as you observe that not only is Pemberley quite unharmed, but the heart of its owner has been made completely happy by marriage – much in the way of my friends the Gardiners, I believe." He bowed to them in his friendliest manner.

"Hey? What is the name? I did not catch it."

"These are Mr. and Mrs. Gardiner – my wife's aunt and uncle."

Lady Catherine flushed a deep red. "Oh, indeed! Not the Cheapside people! Impossible!"

"Yes, our home is there, near my husband's business you know," said Mrs. Gardiner briskly, "we are most comfortably settled."

"Bless me! I had no idea any gentlefolk lived in such a place," exclaimed Lady Catherine, lifting her lace-mitted hands in alarm, "no wonder that – You must be very pleased with Pemberley, as I do not know who is not."

Darcy looked ashamed of his aunt's rudeness, but Mrs. Gardiner responded cheerfully. "The country is always a great refreshment to those who live in the city, indeed Lady Catherine," she said, "the contrast is what is delightful."

"Well, you do seem to have lived among your betters," Lady Catherine observed. "How large a house have you? How many children?"

Mrs. Gardiner submitted to answering a series of impertinent questions quietly, and Darcy looked impatient. But Lady Catherine's conclusions were, on the whole, of a positive nature.

"I see, Mr. Gardiner, that despite your connections in trade, you have married a lady. Your wife is a treasure. I was in fear that my nephew might have involved himself in a complete mesalliance, and those, you know, always turn out badly. Still, it may be that your wife's teachings will make up for the deficiencies of the bride's own mother. I hope so."

"We may hope for a good dinner at least," said Mr. Gardiner jovially, trying to turn the subject.

"Yes; and it is time to go in." Darcy rose and gave his arm to his aunt rather unwillingly, while Elizabeth walked behind with Georgiana, into the dining-salon, lit by hundreds of wax tapers that made the glass glitter. The finest victuals were laid out, in all their appointments, from the pigeon pies to the turkey, and all the removes were accompanied by such very fine wines, that Lady Catherine gradually unbent.

"I must say, this turkey is cooked to a turn," she conceded, "I never had a better dinner at Pemberley, even in the old days. And we have nothing like this wine at Rosings. Darcy's cellar was always famous."

Elizabeth exchanged relieved glances with Darcy.

"Speaking of Kent, we have not asked after Mr. and Mrs. Collins," Elizabeth ventured.

"I hardly ever see them, I assure you. Mrs. Collins is far too busy with her new baby to wait upon me and consider my needs," was the displeased reply. "Her selfishness is now thoroughly manifest. And that odious Mr. Collins – "

"Why, I thought you approved of him," exclaimed Elizabeth.

"Approve of a gossiping clergyman, and his endorsement of infamy!"

"Surely you don't mean our marriage?" asked Mr. Darcy. "Aunt Catherine, that is really the last time you can be allowed to speak disparagingly of our union. That is, if you wish – "

He said no more, but Lady Catherine knew he was referring to visiting rights, and she capitulated. "Very well. I can say that you seem to be happy. And Pemberley has not materially suffered."

"Damned good of her," Mr. Gardiner could not resist murmuring softly to his wife.

"But now tell me, truthfully now, Darcy, for I shall know if you dissemble. How has the county received you? Is Mrs. Darcy welcome in all the great houses? Surely you have had no invitation from Rowlands – or from Tilden Court. Only the very highest quality are admitted as visitors there."

"We made wedding-visits to all the houses round," he answered quietly, "including those you mention; and were kindly received everywhere. Now that I am not a single man, I daresay I am less sought after, but these days I am happiest at home, you see."

"And it is so much pleasanter for me, Aunt Catherine, to have my sister here," spoke up Georgiana diffidently. "We have such good times walking and reading together."

"Oh, indeed? And what do you to read?" asked Lady Catherine incredulously. "A book of manners would be useful," she said pointedly, with a look at Elizabeth.

"We have been reading The Wanderer, and some of the modern poets."

"Not that dreadful Byron," she said with a sniff. "Stuff and nonsense!"

"No; Scott's Marmion, aunt," said Georgiana.

"I do wish they would read Dr. Johnson," put in Mary fretfully.

"Hm! And who is this young lady to give her opinion? Is she one of her sisters?"

"She is. My next sister, Mary," Elizabeth answered concisely.

"And better educated than most of you, I collect."

Mr. Darcy looked askance but Elizabeth hastened to answer, "Mary has always been a very great reader, ma'am."

"But not as good-looking as you and your eldest sister. Well, she looks sensible, at any rate, and if you like her to return to Rosings with me, she may pay us a visit, and make herself useful. Perhaps we will find somebody – Mr. Collins may have an acceptable friend, I suppose."

Elizabeth could barely restrain a shudder, but Mary looked interested, and so Elizabeth civilly accepted of the invitation for her, as she saw she wanted her to do.

It was settled, with Lady Catherine stating her purpose to make her usual tour of the house and grounds, and then in two or three days to return to Rosings, bringing Mary with her. If Darcy said "two birds with one stone," it was not in any one's direct hearing, and Elizabeth ignored what she guessed of it.

The dinner, to the relief of many, was at an end. But as the ladies prepared to withdraw, Lady Catherine remained seated. "I wish," she announced, "to have a private word with my nephew."

Mr. Gardiner was plainly relieved to follow his wife and the other ladies, and aunt and nephew were left to themselves.

"It is time," she told Darcy, "that you explain what made you so forget yourself as to contract this marriage. Oh, do not agitate yourself; I say nothing more against the lady. What's done is done. She is pretty, and she is clever, and does not seem entirely without some acceptable connections. I confess I am relieved to see Pemberley still being run as it ought. More or less," she amended.

"Then I hope you are beginning to discover what my Elizabeth really is," Darcy replied.

She shrugged. "You must know that my astonishment and dismay were not roused by the lady individually, Darcy. No, it is that you, descended from noblemen on your mother's side, and from an ancient, respectable family on your father's, should so forget what you owe to your family, and to their shades. To think that you should so forget your pride!"

"Ah, my pride," said Darcy, leaning back in his throne-like dinner chair. "Yes. You have judged rightly, Aunt Catherine. It is to my great benefit, that I have loosened the bonds of my pride. This, I acknowledge, I owe entirely to Elizabeth."

A smile overspread his face, making it really handsome. "I fail to see," said Lady Catherine indignantly, "what there is to smile about in such a situation. Your dear, late mother, I know, would be grieved to the heart."

"Not so, aunt," he said earnestly. "I loved my dear mother, and she and my father were all that was good; but you know, they lived in another age, and ideas have changed with the times."

"Heaven and earth! I hope not so," exclaimed Lady Catherine, falling back in her seat, and indicating with gestures that she wanted more brandy.

Darcy duly poured, and then leaned forward to explain. "Yes. In their day, and earlier, it was considered as truth that some sets of people were better than others; that noble folk, in particular, were intrinsically superior to others."

"What kind of Revolutionary talk is this?" demanded Lady Catherine. "Have you been corrupted by emissaries from France?

761

Have you become a Leveler? Good God, Darcy, whatever would become of England, if everybody thought like you!"

"But England is what I am thinking of, aunt," he said seriously. "God knows I love and will defend my house, my village, my country, with all my heart and strength and might. But England is not perfect. You must know this to be true – only look, yourself, at all you try to do to improve her."

Lady Catherine was silent, not wanting to contradict that she did a great deal.

"Yes. Even in your parish, there are many poor, who would work if they could; and some people live in great palaces while others are out in the cold."

"True. But that is the way of the world. 'The rich man in his castle, the poor man at his gate,' you know, Darcy. That is how things are ordered. If not so, there would be chaos."

"But we who have feeling hearts, and comfortable lives, have a duty to try to make the world better, Aunt Catherine."

"This is not telling me why you married that girl," she said ironically.

"It does. By Elizabeth I was taught that there are not such differences between people; and it is wicked to perceive yourself as something superior, when we are all God's children."

"Not superior? But, naturally we are superior, Darcy. What can you mean? We are the masters, made to rule, and lead, and others are made to follow and serve."

"Well, I do not wish to debate philosophy with you," he said, with a tone of finality in his voice, "only to make you see that, being brought up to think as you do, had the tendency to make me highly arrogant and indeed obnoxious; and it took a very superior woman to teach me my real place in the world – and hers."

"I see," Lady Catherine sneered, "you will be wound round your wife's apron-strings. She has you right where she intended you to be, from the start."

"Oh, Aunt Catherine – if you only knew! Elizabeth did not even wish to marry me, I assure you, she refused me at first, so strenuously. I can hardly be glad enough that I was able to win her in the end."

His aunt looked skeptical, and sipped at her brandy. "Really, there are no limits to what a scheming woman can make a man believe," she observed, "and she is one of the cleverest women in the world, to make you think what you do. If you could only have seen her, when I had my interview with her; she was positively obstinate in her insistence on having you. Clever, indeed."

"If you wish to think so, aunt, there is no use trying to convince you otherwise. But I believe that if you were able to watch us for the long lifetime we hope will be ours, you would see a couple who bid fair to be the happiest pair in the world."

He rose, and she followed. "Stay," she said, laying her hand on his arm. "You must know, Darcy, that I love you tenderly, and indeed I do wish you every happiness."

He smiled down at her, and his eyes sparkled. "I hoped you could feel so, dear aunt."

They joined the others in the sitting-room again, and Lady Catherine went over to Elizabeth, who looked alarmed.

"Mrs. Darcy," said Lady Catherine, addressing her so for the first time, "I am not a fool, and can accept facts as I see them. My natural discernment was always remarkable; and while many people of my age refuse to acknowledge change, my mind has a singular penetration. I am ready to believe that you may become a good wife to my nephew, and fit chatelaine of Pemberley, on one condition."

"And what is that?" asked Elizabeth, with more curiosity than trepidation.

"Have the patience to let me explain myself. You know that I was own sister to Darcy's mother, and I suffered bitterly when she died. I loved the lad as my own; and all that I have said and done since he was drawn in by your allurements, was only for his own good."

"Yes, I can understand that," said Elizabeth quietly.

"I must and shall continue to have an interest in all his concerns, and I will grant you that he at least looks well and happy – at present."

"That is very good of you."

"Silence, if you please! Impertinence is uncalled-for, when I am conceding so much as this. You know that my brother, the Earl, is provided for in his line. The de Bourgh line continues in another branch, and I still have hopes that my Anne may marry, though if she does her husband must take her name." She fell into reverie.

Elizabeth, and the rest of the company, waited patiently for her to resume.

"The Darcy line is not my own by blood, yet I have respect for it, honouring my beloved sister's marriage as I do. So I would give a great deal to see the succession of Darcy's house ensured." She paused, with a meaningful look.

"Aunt Catherine, that is none of your business," Darcy exploded, really annoyed at last. "You are not entitled to know such personal concerns of ours! We have not been married a six-month."

Elizabeth looked at him fondly. "My dear – may I speak?"

He looked surprised. "Why – if you will. It is your own choice."

Immediately, though with some natural shyness, and hesitancy of manner, she gave his aunt, and all the party, to understand that there was reason to expect that the coming autumn would bring a new small shade to Pemberley.

To say that Lady Catherine was pleased, is only to speak the truth, for she was very eager that all connected with her should prosper grandly, and for Darcy to have a son and heir would tend to the well being of his house. If she nursed a hope that the young mother might not survive the process, and a second wife of a better class of society be required, she at least brought herself to a tolerable enough state of politeness enough not to say so.

Georgiana, and the Gardiners, were truly and unfeignedly delighted, and the rest of the evening was not enough for all their expressions of happiness.

As they mounted the stairs at night, after seeing their guests off to their respective bedrooms, Mr. and Mrs. Darcy were much relieved, and well content.

"The old Gorgon, she was positively civil at last," Darcy said with relief.

"I thought she might be, when she heard all."

"Did you? I confess, I feared she might go into one of her rages, and I could not tolerate your being exposed to such unpleasantness."

Elizabeth smiled a secret smile. "You need not have worried. I have been matched with Lady Catherine before, and you see I did not lose the battle."

Darcy looked amused. "Very true. Though I don't like thinking of myself as the prize in spoils of war. You are the prize, my Elizabeth, and our little one to be."

"And you are mine. Ours," she declared, placing her candle by the bedside, and loosening her dark tresses so they fell down along her white nightgown and the satin counterpane. "Though some might say that the prize is Pemberley."

Table of Contents

Websites of the Austen Authors

Austen Authors
www.austenauthors.net

Susan Adriani
www.thetruthaboutmrdarcy.weebly.com

Nina Benneton
www.ninabenneton.com

Diana Birchall
www.lightbrightandsparkling.blogspot.com

Marilyn Brant
www.marilynbrant.com

Jack Caldwell
www.cajuncheesehead.com

J. Marie Croft
www.prideand.com

Karen Doornebos
www.karendoornebos.com

Monica Fairview
www.monicafairview.com

Maria Grace
www.authormariagrace.com

Regina Jeffers
www.rjeffers.com

Sharon Lathan
www.sharonlathanauthor.com

Kara Louise
www.karalouise.net

Susan Mason-Milks
www.austen-whatif-stories.com

Vera Nazarian
www.veranazarian.com

Jane Odiwe
www.janeaustensequels.blogspot.com

C. Allyn Pierson
www.callynpierson.wordpress.com

Abigail Reynolds
www.pemberleyvariations.com

Caitlin Rubino-Bradway
www.janetility.com

Colette Saucier
www.colettesaucier.com

Mary Simonsen
www.marysimonsenfanfiction.blogspot.com

Shannon Winslow
www.shannonwinslow.com

Made in the USA
Lexington, KY
31 January 2014